FINNEGANS WAKE

FINNEGANS WAKE

James Joyce

With an Introduction by
LEN PLATT

WORDSWORTH CLASSICS

For my husband
ANTHONY JOHN RANSON
with love from your wife, the publisher.
Eternally grateful for your unconditional love.

Readers who are interested in other titles from
Wordsworth Editions are invited to visit our website at
www.wordsworth-editions.com

First published in 2012 by Wordsworth Editions Limited
8B East Street, Ware, Hertfordshire SG12 9HJ

ISBN 978 1 84022 661 4

Text © Wordsworth Editions Limited 2012
Introduction and notes © Len Platt 2012

Wordsworth® is a registered trade mark of
Wordsworth Editions Limited

Wordsworth Editions
is the company founded in 1987 by
MICHAEL TRAYLER

Typeset in Great Britain by Antony Gray
Printed and bound by Clays Ltd, Elcograf S.p.A.

GENERAL INTRODUCTION

Wordsworth Classics are inexpensive editions designed to appeal to the general reader and students. We commission teachers and specialists to write wide ranging, jargon-free introductions and in some cases to provide notes that will assist the understanding of our readers rather than interpret the stories for them. In the case of *Finnegans Wake*, however, a work which takes allusion to new and still unsurpassed extremes, the inclusion of explicatory notes has not been practicable. There is a long tradition of annotative literature in relation to the *Wake* to which the interested reader can turn. It includes such classics as James S. Atherton, *The Books at the 'Wake': A Study of Literary Allusions in James Joyce's 'Finnegans Wake'* (1959); Louis O. Mink, *A 'Finnegans Wake' Gazetteer* (1978); Adaline Glasheen, *Third Census of 'Finnegans Wake': An Index of the Characters and Their Roles* (third edition, 1977); and *A 'Wake' Newslitter*, the journal which ran from 1962 to 1984. The standard synthesis of these extraordinary efforts to unpick the *Wake* is Roland McHugh's *Annotations to 'Finnegans Wake'* (revised edition, 1991). In order to allow readers to use this literature easily and find their way around the *Wake* more generally, the Wordsworth edition gives line numbers on each page and also includes book and episode numbers on each page. It is thus the first and only edition that can be conveniently used in tandem with the referencing system used by both critical and annotative traditions. These reference page number followed by line number, for example: 25.12 for page twenty-five, line twelve.

As Len Platt's introduction makes clear, however, it is the text of the *Wake* itself, as it stands, rather than the referencing of its allusiveness that is the first fascination of Joyce's last great work. In the same spirit, because the pleasures of reading are inseparable from the surprises, secrets and revelations that all narratives contain, we suggest you encounter this book before turning to the introduction.

General Adviser: KEITH CARABINE
Rutherford College, University of Kent at Canterbury

INTRODUCTION

Finnegans Wake (1939) was Joyce's last important work and remains his most challenging by a very long way. Its great strangeness alienated many of Joyce's earlier readers to the extent that even his most loyal supporters, his brother Stanislaus, for example, and his benefactress Harriet Shaw Weaver, had great difficulty in accommodating it. Indeed to some it seemed that with this extraordinary production Joyce had finally lost his wits, a view that he may have partly encouraged. As his daughter's mental illness worsened alongside the composition of the book, Joyce tried to console himself with the idea that Lucia's increasingly alarming condition was somehow aligned to the creative faculties she clearly possessed. The fact that many saw *Work in Progress*, Joyce's working title for the developing text, as a 'book of the night' – a fantastic reproduction of 'dreamwork' and psychodynamic processes – no doubt fuelled that fantasy.

Whether dream, madness or not, the *Wake* has no discernible singular narrative. It does seem to revolve around dozens of tiny stories repeated over and over, but reading across the *Wake* from I.1 to IV.1, it is impossible to recover one reliable narrative framework – although many critics have tried.[1] The ending famously joins up with the beginning, which implies that it is possible to enter the *Wake* at any stage with no loss to understanding, or misunderstanding. There are characters of a kind – notably Here Comes Everybody (HCE), his wife Anna Livia Plurabelle (ALP) and their children: the rival twin brothers, Shem and Shaun, and their sister Issy. But these archetypal figures merge into each other and multiply out into hundreds of parallel identities. Such disconcerting departures from conventions of the novel extend to and are embodied in the language of the *Wake*. This is much more than

---

1 *Finnegans Wake* is in four parts. Book I has eight sections, Books II and III have four each and the final book just one. Versions of narrative reconstruction preoccupied the early Joyce critics. See Joseph Campbell and Henry Morton Robinson, *A Skeleton Key to 'Finnegans Wake'* (London: Faber and Faber, 1947); William York Tindall, *A Reader's Guide to James Joyce* pp. 237–96 (London: Thames and Hudson, 1959), and Adaline Glasheen, *Third Census of Finnegans Wake: An Index of Characters and Their Roles*, pp. xxiii–lxxi (Berkeley: University of California Press, 1977). For a later narrative overview see Finn Fordham, *Lots of Fun at 'Finnegans Wake': Unravelling Universals* (Oxford: Oxford University Press, 2007), pp. 11–15.

simply 'difficult'. For most readers it is virtually unreadable, not because
it has no meaning but, on the contrary, because it allows for such
potentiality of meaning – to the extent that some readers have claimed
it can mean anything and everything. (This is patently untrue,
incidentally. You can be as inventive as you like in interpreting *Finnegans
Wake*, but you cannot turn it into, for example, the story of a great
white whale). Even more than *Ulysses*, the book seems to imply, as Joyce
well understood, a new kind of devotee, one with endless time at his or
her disposal and a willingness not just to read this text but somehow to
study and research it for all its seemingly endless possibilities. Unlike
Ulysses, the *Wake* is comprised not of many styles but, rather, of
one extremely dense, tongue-twisting *Wake* style based on English
vocabulary and syntax, but at the same time self-consciously designed
as a 'machine' that systematically appears to resist any singularity of
meaning. The *Wake* announces a new 'revolution of the word' – a
powerfully resonant cultural practice involving not exactly a new
language, but a new *kind* of language, one that works not to stabilize the
world, but, rather, to unfix it in a wild diversity of possible or potential
significance. Unsurprisingly, the question of how this extraordinarily
original text was put together has become central to Joyce studies,
especially over the last decade when 'genetic' criticism – the study of
how a text develops – has moved so much to the forefront.

Writing *Finnegans Wake*

The finished version of *Finnegans Wake* is six-hundred and twentyeight pages long, but more than twenty-five thousand pages of its textual
record have survived. These include some fourteen thousand pages of
notes currently housed in the Poetry Collection at the University of
Buffalo, State University of New York – which comprise the forty-
eight Buffalo Notebooks – and the approximately nine thousand pages
of manuscripts, typescripts and proofs that Joyce deposited with his
benefactress Harriet Shaw Weaver. Weaver, the first Joyce archivist,
donated her collection to the British Library in 1951 where it was
worked on by David Hayman who produced *A First-Draft Version of
Finnegans Wake* in 1963 and then by Danis Rose with the assistance of
John O'Hanlon, who used it for the *James Joyce Archive* (1978–9).
Even this large archive, supplemented by the discovery of new *Wake*
manuscripts in 2006, is incomplete – there are absences in the early
manuscript history in particular. Some notebooks have been lost and
others are yet to be fully transcribed and annotated. Despite the gaps,
the *Wake* archive together with the sequence of letters that Joyce sent

to Weaver throughout the composition of the *Wake* from 1923 to 1939 has produced what appears to be a broad consensus among genetic critics about how the text was 'engineered'.[2] The story is fascinating in its own right, and in its more familiar contemporary incarnation supports the idea that the 'decentred' *Wake* was built into the *Wake*'s design virtually from the beginning when *Work-in Progress* existed as a series of distinct sites or sketches.

For most purposes that story begins in the early 1920s. In March 1923, Weaver received two pages from Joyce, 'the first', he claimed, 'I have written since the final *Yes* of *Ulysses*' (*Letters* I, 202).[3] This was the sketch of King Roderick O'Connor which was to resurface much later in the *Wake* as part of II.3. A series of further sketches followed, including the hagiographic pieces involving St Patrick and Bishop George Berkeley, St Dympna and St Kevin; a Tristan and Isolde sketch; the piece on the four old men, or Mamalujo, and an early HCE sketch which of all the pieces had most in the way of legs and was to form the basis for Book I. Later that year Weaver received 'the revered letter', analysed in I.5 and eventually appearing as a full text in Book IV of the *Wake*. The 'Anna Livia (ALP) piece' was 'finished' in March 1924 and several Shaun sketches, the 'watches' of Shaun, began to arrive around the same time (see *Letters* I, pp. 212–13). These latter were to form the basis of Book III.

Whereas *Ulysses* developed in a linear way, built from such elements as Homeric correspondence, very specific chronology, the imperative

2 The idea of writing the *Wake* being analogous to 'engineering', now commonplace, was apparently first suggested by Weaver herself. 'I am glad you liked my punctuality as an engine driver', Joyce replied to her in April 1927. 'I have taken this up because I am really one of the greatest engineers, if not the greatest, in the world besides being a musicmaker, philosophist and heaps of other things. All the engines I know are wrong. Simplicity. I am making an engine with only one wheel. No spokes of course. The wheel is a perfect square. You see what I am driving at, don't you?' *Letters of James Joyce*, edited by Richard Ellmann, vol. 2, p. 251 (London: Faber and Faber, 1966). Hereafter cited in the text as *Letters 1*.

3 As Danis Rose and John O'Hanlon have shown, VI.B.10, dated late October 1922, contains notes used for the earliest drafts and is thus the earliest surviving record of the *Wake*. See Danis Rose and John O'Hanlon, 'A Nice Beginning: On the *Ulysses/Finnegans Wake* Interface' in Geert Lernout (ed.), *'Finnegans Wake': Fifty Years*, pp. 165–73 (Amsterdam: Rodopi, 1990). (In the referencing system used for this and other editions of Joyce's notebooks, 'VI.B' refers to the notebook series. Numbers following refer to volume and page number; letters signify line number.)

to represent Dublin and to incorporate other systems – colours, parts of the body and so on – the *Wake*'s growth appears to have been generated differently, developing outwards from the sequence of sketches described above. These produced what David Hayman has called a framework of 'nodality'.[4] The sketches became passages which not only expanded almost beyond recognition but also produced the 'intratextual echoes' eventually so important to holding the writing together. In this way genetic criticism has confirmed the *Wake*'s innovation as a text designed with the sketches as its multiple points of origin. A forwardly developing narrative is dispensed with in favour of circularity, repetition and an 'intratexuality' that becomes operative in unique ways. Genetic criticism also helps position the *Wake* in terms of wider critical tradition where, far from representing reality and embodying epistemologies, the text performs its own nature and the processes of its own making. As the metaphor of the machine suggests, this is a text unique in its capacity for engaging with the idea of meaning – all this confirming Samuel Beckett's famous insight that the *Wake* is 'not about something; it is that something itself.'[5]

What were eventually to figure as Books I and III of the *Wake* comprised the early structure of the *Wake*, if structure is the right term – by November 1926 Joyce was clear that his new book, for all its complex planning, 'really has no beginning or end . . . It ends in the middle of a sentence and begins in the middle of the same sentence' (*Letters* 1, 246). At the same time, Joyce was equally certain that he was working on two distinct large units, suggesting framework if not necessarily linearity. The question of how to join these sections together, the first circulating around the father and mother figures, HCE and ALP, and the third, turning on Shaun's rise and eventual fall, was not settled until 1926 when Joyce began work on 'three or four other episodes, the children's game, night studies, a scene in the "public", and a "lights out in the village" ' (*Letters* I, 241).[6] Development of these episodes, beginning with II.2, was delayed while Joyce worked on I.1 and further sections of Books I and III – indeed Book II was not complete until 1938.

---

4 See David Hayman, *The 'Wake' in Transit* (Ithaca: Cornell UP, 1961).

5 Samuel Beckett's 'Dante . . . Bruno. Vico . . . Joyce' in Samuel Beckett and others, *Our Exagmination Round his Factification for Incamination of 'Work in Progress'*, p. 14 (1929; London: Faber and Faber, 1961).

6 'Public' here refers to the public bar, earthier than the lounge or the saloon and usually reserved for men only in Joyce's day.

As early as June 1926, however, some thirteen years before the *Wake*'s full publication, Joyce was claiming to have 'the book now fairly well planned out in my head' (*Letters* 1, 241). By the same time Joyce also had versions of the *Wake* sigla worked out, the shorthand that not only stood for the individuals in the Earwicker family but also indicated dynamic relationships, like conflict, and which were sometimes combined, often to indicate complementary.[7] He was also proficient in Wakese, which meant that first drafts from this point on were much more complex than the earlier first drafts which had been more standard in their English. Between 1926 and 1935 only three entirely new chapters were produced (I.6, II.1 and II.2), which gives some indication of just how much of the *Wake*'s compositional history was taken up with the extraordinary process of expansion that now characterised Joyce's writing technique.[8]

A particular strand of genetic criticism provides that history of text composition, so implying the self-generating dimensions of the *Wake*. Other strands work more closely with the idea of the *Wake*'s inter-textuality, its dependency on material outside of itself – one key source here being other books by James Joyce. It is sometimes said, with some justification, that *Finnegans Wake* grew out of *Ulysses* and 'Scribble-dehobble', the 'big' notebook containing some of the earliest *Wake* material, does indeed imply that Joyce's new work was conceived 'as an extension not only of *Ulysses* but of all his previous works'.[9] That 'big' notebook is divided into forty-seven parts, each one corresponding to previous works, including the eighteen chapters of *Ulysses*, which would appear to support Richard Ellmann's description of the *Wake* as 'in many ways a sequel to *Ulysses*'.[10]

7 The sigla changed over time and were used with great inventiveness by Joyce. The essential designations, however, are:

E	HCE	X	Mamalujo (the four old men)
Δ	ALP	P	Patrick
Γ	Shem	K	Kevin or Kate
Λ	Shaun	O	the Twelve (jurors)
I	Issy	○	the Maggies (dancing or rainbow girls)
T	Tristram	□	the Book

8 For an engaging account of the development of the text through the various stages of composition see Fordham, *Lots of Fun at 'Finnegans Wake'*.

9 James Joyce's *Scribbledehobble: The Ur-Workbook for 'Finnegans Wake'* edited with notes and an introduction by T. E. Connolly (Evanston: Northwestern University Press, 1961), ix.

10 Richard Ellmann, *James Joyce*, new and revised edition (Oxford: Oxford University Press, 1982.), 545.

But the *Wake* also grew from thousands of pages of notes indicative of everything else – from biographies, histories, novels to newspapers, fanzines, encyclopaedias and so on. The notes were sometimes taken randomly from whatever came to hand, but there was frequently design to the sequences that Joyce took, groups of notes from books on anthropology, magic, sociology, history as well as copious notes taken from the *Catholic Encyclopaedia* and, especially, the *Encyclopaedia Britannica*.

For genetic critics these notes form the foundation of the *Wake*. They are often seen as building blocks, the earliest stages of composition, 'harvested' (or not) for use in drafts and manuscripts where they become part of the extensive expansion of text characteristic of the *Wake*'s development. At the same time, however, the notebooks refer the *Wake* back to the wider culture in which it operates. The Brepols edition, a work in progress which has been under the editorship of Vincent Deane, Daniel Ferrer and Geert Lernout, indicates how important notebook research can be in this respect.[11] Already our notions about what the *Wake* is comprised of, formerly substantially derived from James Atherton's pioneering study *The Books at the Wake* (1959), have been radically challenged. We now know, for example, that as well as working with a huge number of literary works from the canon; with Vico and *New Science* and what Atherton calls 'the sacred books' – the Bible, the Book of the Dead, the Koran and so on – Joyce was also reading a huge range of other materials, so much so that Atherton's idea that there are books of 'structural' importance to the *Wake* can on longer be seriously maintained.

Among those other materials were newspapers, including the *Connaught Tribune*, the *Freeman's Journal*, the *Irish Statesman*, the *Irish Independent* and the *Leader*, as well as the *Daily Mail*, the *Daily Sketch*, the *Daily Express*, the *Evening Standard* and *The Times*. Joyce worked from guide books, biographies – notably the hagiological, but also from much less elevated material, S. M. Ellis's *The Life and Times of Michael Kelly: Musician, Actor and Bon Viveur* (1930) for instance. He used histories. Gibbons's *The Decline and Fall of the Roman Empire* was incorporated into *Wake* notes, as was Stephen Gywnn's *History of Ireland* (1923) and Benedict Fitzpatrick's *Ireland and the Making of Great Britain* (1922). There was a broad engagement with some of the central trends and controversies in European intellectual life – Jules Crepieux-Jamin's

11 Published by Brepols, volumes have now appeared for notebooks 1, 3, 5, 6, 10, 14, 16, 25, 29, 32, 33 and 47.

Les élements de l'écriture de canailles (1923) (*The Features of the Handwriting of Scoundrels*); W. J. Perry's *The Origin of Magic and Religion* (1923) and J. B. S. Haldane's, *Daedalus or the Science of the Future* (1924) seem suggestive here, each for distinct reasons.

Haldane, for example, was a radical scientist whose work strongly influenced Aldous Huxley's dystopia, *Brave New World* (1932) – with Haldane himself attacking the kind of naked social Darwinism that Huxley saw as being operated by the state of the future. Far from recommending eugenics, Haldane protested against those who 'having discovered the existence of biology . . . attempted to apply it in its then very crude condition to the production of a race of supermen . . . They [eugenicists] certainly succeeded in producing the most violent opposition and hatred amongst the classes whom they somewhat gratuitously regarded as undesirable parents'.[12] His comment that 'It took man 250,000 years to transcend the hunting pack. It will not take him so long to transcend the nation'[13] was duly noted by Joyce at VI.B.1, 061 (c) as '250,000 to transcend/hunting pack/ – nation.'

Also significant in this respect was Leon Metchnikoff's *La Civilisation et les Grandes Fleuvres Historique* (1899). Metchnikoff was a radical social scientist, associated with anarchism and important to Joyce because of his work on I.8, the ALP and 'rivers' episode of the *Wake*. *Les Grandes Fleuvres*, which Joyce was reading in 1924, was a work that examined rivers in terms of their social and cultural influence, but Metchnikoff was also a vociferous opponent of scientific racism. His book included a chapter entitled 'Race' (chapter 4) which demolished 'all possible arguments for racist theories by showing the inadequacies of classifications based on skin colour, on the form of the skull, or on language.'[14] Some of the passages that interested Joyce were as follows. The first was noted at VI.B.1, 075 (a) as 'races – hair/skull /hue/':

Since the previous century, frequent attempts have been made to separate the human species into distinct and categorically defined groups. Some of these attempts were grounded on skin-colour and yet no-one would dream of determining which race a dog or horse belonged to on the basis of their fur-coat. Other classed men according

12 J. B. S. Haldane, *Daedalus, or the Science of the Future* (London, Kegan Paul, 1924), 57–8. For an account of Joyce's usage of this text in the notebooks see Geert Lernout (ed), *The Finnegans Wake Notebooks at Buffalo* (Turnout, Belgium: Brepols, 2001), VI.B.1, 5–6.

13 Haldane, *Daedalus*, 84-5.

14 Geert Lernout's introduction to *Notebooks at Buffalo*, VI.B.1, 7.

to the cut of their hair . . . yet others according to the shape of their skull.[15]

This second was noted at VI.B.1, 075 (b) as 'change language/ – marry'.

races were divided, dispersed, mixed and crossed in all proportions, in all directions, for thousands of centuries. Most of them abandoned their language for that of their conquerors only then to abandon that one for a third, if not a fourth.[16]

Notebook evidence is notoriously difficult to interpret, for many reasons. Not least, the nature of Joyce's notes, usually taken without any comment or contextual information, makes it difficult to know whether approval, disapproval, or some entirely different mechanism is at work. At the very least, however, the notebooks confirm the importance of placing the *Wake* in a diversity of historical culture and, partly because of the many contemporary and European sources, greatly improve and problematise our sense of the cultural environment in which the *Wake* was written and which it addresses. The interest of the notebooks is only partly, then, that they help complete the picture of how the *Wake* was constructed. They also help us to position Joyce the intellectual and to develop responses to difficult matters, like the question of Joyce's politics and their development in the1920s and 30s, for example. Indeed, in the end they help us understand what the *Wake* actually is, what it comes out of but also what it writes to.

Reading the *Wake*

In many ways the *Wake* sounds very like a novel. Traditional storytelling is evoked from the first/last sentence. Scheherazade, teller of tales in *1001 Arabian Nights*, Hans Christian Anderson, Jacob and Wilheim Grimm are amongst those present in the storyteller identities that lie behind much of the *Wake*'s framing. There is an obvious ambition, from whatever beginning one turns to, to set the scene, fix the time, establish the characters and tell the story – and there are a great many stories. One chapter, for example, I.3, is structured almost entirely around a sequence concerning the fates of the citizens who eventually turn on HCE, including – A'Hara, Paul Horan, Sordid Sam, Langley, Father San Browne and Phislin Phil, the latter at one stage being 'asked

---

15 See Lernout, *Notebooks at Buffalo*, VI.B.1, 075 (a). The translations in this and the following extract are Lernout's.
16 See *Notebooks at Buffalo*, VI.B.1, 075 (a)

by free boardschool shirkers in drenched overcoats overawall, Will, Conn and Otto, to tell them overagait, Vol, Pov and Dev, that fishabed ghoatstory of the haardly creditable edventyres of the Haberdasher, the two Curchies and the three Enkelchums in their Bearskin ghoats!' (51.11–15).[17] Stories within stories are part of the familiar condition of the *Wake*, especially stories which attempt to arrive at origins. The first man, the first woman, the first copulation, building, city, flood and language – all are important reference points in the *Wake*, albeit points never reached.

Over and over the *Wake* invokes the conventions of storytelling, as in the opening to the story of Jarl van Hoother and the Prankquean – 'It was of a night, late, lang time agone, in an auldstane eld, when Adam was delvin and his madameen spinning watersilts' (21.5–6). The frame that introduces one of many versions of HCE's crime in the park begins similarly: 'They tell the story (an amalgam as absorbing as calzium chloereydes and hydrophobe sponges could make it) how one happygogusty Ides-of-April morning . . . he [HCE] met a cad with a pipe' (35.1–11).[18] Resting points, end pieces, evoke the same traditions. These echo the sounds and rhythms of the conventional narratives that might be found in fairy tales, children's stories or other forms of popular narrative – the joke for instance. This, for example, concludes the story of 'Herr Betreffender' (69.32), also known as 'Bully Acre' (73.23), who at the end of I.4 threatens HCE outside his pub 'from eleven thirty to two in the afternoon without even a luncheonette interval' (70.33–4): 'And thus, with this rochelly exetur of Bully Acre, came to close that last stage in the siegings round our archicitadel which we would like to recall, if old Nestpor Alexis would wink the worth for us, as Bar-le Duc and Dog-an-Doras and Bangen-op-Zoom' (73.23–7).[19]

The *Wake*, 'this scherzarade of one's thousand one nightinesses' (51.4–5), also incorporates many stories outside its own through thousands of traces. Stories from the Bible, the Koran and the Book of

---

17 The names of these supplicants suggest the verbs 'will', 'can' and 'ought' in English and French. See Roland McHugh, *Annotations*, revised edition (Baltimore and London: Johns Hopkins University Press, 1991) 51. Hereafter cited in the text as *Annotations*.

18 Calcium chloride absorbs moisture; whether 'hydrophobe sponges' do is a moot point. See *Annotations*, 35.

19 This passage concerns sieges. It alludes to Balfe's opera, *The Siege of Rochelle*; Bar-le-Duc, the town in France that was the staging post for the siege of Verdun in 1916, and Bergen-op-Zoom, the town in south west Holland that was frequently besieged. See *Annotations*, 73.

the Dead, for example, are everywhere in the *Wake*. Narratives like Tristan and Isolde, Lewis Carroll's *Alice in Wonderland* (1865), Mark Twain's *Huckleberry Finn* (1884) or Sheridan Le Fanu's *The House by the Churchyard* (1863) are returned to repeatedly. Others, Walter Scott's *Rob Roy* (1817) or the Gertrude Page story *Paddy the Next Best Thing* (1916), have a more fleeting appearance.

Given all this activity around narrative, it is perhaps not surprising that readers have been tempted towards a summary of the *Wake*'s story, just as they would be for any other novel, except that here, in face of the *Wake*'s astonishing linguistics, the imperative to establish signposts of narrative stability is particularly pressing. Many such summaries have been produced in the critical tradition – indeed in the early years of *Wake* criticism, synthesising the narrative was high on the critical agenda, whole studies being devoted to not much more than reconstructing a single story from the pages of the *Wake*. Nevertheless, all summaries, however sophisticated they may have seemed, were hugely reductive. They were greatly simplifying in terms of detail and all missed the sheer extent of the slipperiness of things – the amalgamation of identities, for example, so that the story of HCE is somehow mixed up with the stories of Finn MacCool, Howth Head, Noah, Adam Kadmon, St Patrick, John Jameson, Arthur Guinness, St Peter, John Joyce, James Joyce, Roderick O'Connor, Henry VIII, Cromwell, Lewis Carroll, Mark of Cornwall, the Russian General, William I, William Gladstone, Prospero and so on – just as the story of ALP forms itself around such identities as Grace O'Malley, the Prankquean, Elizabeth I, Penelope, Molly Bloom, Nora Joyce, the river Liffey (and many other rivers), Eve and Mrs Noah.

Similar conflations are organised around space and time. The *Wake* is a place where a single paragraph can produce an 'amalgamation' of the Tudor court; nineteenth-century Fenians; vikings; 'Idahore shopgirls' (504.22), along with old soldiers – 'killmaimthem pensioners' – retired from service in the British empire (see pp. 504–5). Or it can conflate Middle Eastern Islam with Western Christianity; a twentieth-century luxury car (the Rolls Royce); Celtic monuments (at Carnac, Brittany); the modern press and legal institutions in classical Greece (see 4.14–36). None of which helps with the idea of narrative summary, indeed it is an obvious condition of the *Wake* that it is specifically designed as a comic intervention that thoroughly undermines the very traditions of story-telling evoked at every opportunity.

For all the awareness that the *Wake* is circular, narrative summaries also imagine a story retaining the dimensions of an unfolding and 'developing' narrative. In fact, the *Wake* is comprised of endless twists and turns which make development let alone completion an impossible ambition. It is 'a meanderthalltale to unfurl' (19.25–6) where 'every busy eerie whig' is just as likely to be 'a bit of a torytale to tell' (20.23). The 'central' tale itself, the narrative of the Earwicker family – HCE, ALP, Shem/Shaun and Issy – is massively overdetermined. Any 'truth' it might involve is indistinguishable from the gossip, told over and over again, by members of the family, friends and enemies, and also by folklorists and other experts – people who knew and people who didn't. It evokes fear, hilarity, respect and disdain and at the same time is itself the subject of endless rumour. It generates multiple variations and is scrutinised in minute detail. Subjected to analysis (in I.5 for example), challenge, rectification and challenge again, it is minutely dissected and also celebrated and turned into song (see I.2). It is also returned to endlessly throughout the *Wake*. One of the last chapters, III.3 for example, is essentially an interrogation of the stories of HCE and ALP and the fall of Finnegan in what turns out to be nowhere near the final attempt to get to the bottom of things.

Joyce fictionalises not just this family tale and many others (including the tales of the meeting of Mutt and Jute; the Mookse and the Gripes; Buckley and the Russian General; the Norwegian sailor and the tailor and the fable of the Ant and the Grasshopper), but also the tale in terms of the cultural contexts that surround it, including the critical processes that annotate and explicate. One result is that the text appears to anticipate the Joyce industry in some ways, containing within itself echoes of the critical traditions that in reality would follow in the wake of the *Wake*. Far from being indifferent to story, as the earlier fictions appear to have been, the *Wake* is exhaustive in this respect. From producing epiphanies; the short stories of *Dubliners* where little seems to happen in the way of 'go ahead plot'; impressionistic images of the artist at different stages of development in *A Portrait of the Artist as a Young Man* and in *Ulysses* a huge one-day novel where story gives way to immediacy, Joyce in the *Wake* moves into a new and unique version of modernism. Here narrative functions at overdrive, every possible dimension of story-telling being activated – except completion of any kind. If at one level 'the tale rambles along' (41.36–42.1), it is just as typically unyielding to any forward motion. The 'Eyrawyggla saga . . . of poor Osti-Fosti' may be 'readable to int from and ind' (44.16–19), but it is also astonishingly recalcitrant to what we normally understand as 'story', not least because its language 'is nat language in any sinse of the world' (83.12). Indeed it may be that 'from tubb to buttom', the

Wake is 'all falsetissues, antilibellous and nonactionable and this applies to its whole wholume' (48.17–20).

The idea of a key *Wake* narrative, then, may be functional for *Wake* readers but in constructing a singular structure all such accounts must be forced into resisting the way the *Wake* fundamentally works. However useful in mapping terms a synoptical account may be, it constitutes only a very partial initial opening up of the *Wake*, one that simplifies and operates at a cost in terms of resistance to how the *Wake* was designed and how it functions.

The idea of meaning in the *Wake* is similarly built around fundamental contradictions. On the one hand the *Wake* makes an astonishing investment in cultures of rationality and processes of reasoning. It treats meaning very much as it does narrative. Just as it seems devoted to narrative procedures at every point, so critical examination, argument, controversy, apologetics and so on are central to the *Wake* and often linked to the idea of meeting, with meeting places and crossroads becoming crucially important sites. There are many such 'encounters' in the *Wake* – quite apart from HCE's fateful meeting with the cad and the collision of the Mookse with the Gripes. The book is framed by the meeting of Mutt and Jute (figuring as a native/outsider; pagan/Christian and St Patrick/Bishop Berkeley) at pages 16–18, for example, which is revisited as a meeting of Muta and Java on pages 609–10. Each of these meetings, while being characterised by hilarious failures of understanding, nevertheless implies the dispersal of knowledge and subsequent processes of interpretation and interrogation.

It is partly against this context that the question seems so characteristic of the *Wake*, a narrative that often implies philosophical procedures, as in 'But in the pragma what formal cause made a smile of *that* to think?' (56.31–2) and 'Isn't that effect?' (322.26), and is frequently concerned with verification, authenticity – with getting the facts right. Here, for example, the question concerns the facts of HCE's name ('nomen gentile' is latin for 'clan name') and thus his true place in 'anthropomorphic' ('andrewpaulmurphyc') chronologies:

> Comes the question are these the facts of his nominigentilisation as recorded and accolated in both or either of the collateral andrewpaulmurphyc narratives. Are those their fata which we read in sibylline between the *fas* and its *nefas*? No dung on the road? And shall Nohomiah be our place like? Yea, Mulachy our kingable khan? We shall perhaps not so soon see.' [20]   (31.33–32.2)

20 See *Annotations*, 31–2 for further explanation of this passage.

There are many occasions when the narrative announces uncertainties – Herwho?' (84.27); 'Why?' (118.17); 'So?' (126.1); 'Who?' (198.10); 'Which was said by whem to whom?' (418.16) – but it appears to retain a fundamental epistemological faith to the extent that asking continues throughout and, indeed, drives the *Wake* at fundamental levels, even if answers are never stable.

Some questions seem to move the narrative forward, as in the first question raised in the *Wake*, concerned with the causes of Finnegan's fall from his ladder – 'What then agentlike brought about that tragoady thundersday this municipal sin business? (5.13–14). Others reflect back on the authorship of the *Wake* ('So why, pray, sign anything as long as every word, letter, penstroke, paperspace is a perfect signature of its own? – 115.6–8) and the condition of its textuality. As Shaun is asked in III.3, 'Are we speachin d'anglas landadge or are you sprakin sea Djoytsch?' (485.12–13) or, indeed, some other language, Hindi perhaps ('Cha kai rotty kai makkar, sahib?' – 54.12–13); Swedish ('Huru more Nee, minny frckans?' – 54.10–11) or Danish ('Hwoorledes har Dee det?' – 54.11).[21] Such questions often turn outwards as well as inwards, where the address is specifically to the reader attempting to make sense of the *Wake* world. 'So This Is Dyoublong?' (13.4), the narrator asks at an early stage. 'Can you rede . . . its world ? It is the same tale told of all. Many. Miscegenations on miscegenations' (18.18–20); 'You is feeling like you was lost in the bush, boy?' (112.3); 'So what are you going to do about it?' (117.8–9).

Typically in Joyce criticism it is the *Wake*'s strangeness that is seen as raising questions, but the *Wake* also literally asks a lot of questions. To put it another way, it has a questioning nature and, for all its chaos, carries a comically insistent and comprehensive drive for epistemological order. It is no accident that so much of this book is built around sites of knowledge acquisition, preservation and performance. I.1, for example, has a generally pedagogic frame. It attempts to articulate a history of events and includes a chronology (see *FW* pages 13–14). At one point it is positioned from within a 'museyroom' (a museum and a place for musing) with the narrator becoming a tour guide. I.4, centred around a courtroom scene, involves forensic questioning, expert testimony and the maintenance of a demeanour appropriate to the serious business of truth building – thus the 'eye, ear, nose and throat

21 See *Annotations*, 54 for glosses on these questions. The first roughly translates as an offer of tea with bread and butter. The second suggests the phrases 'how are you, my young ladies?' and the third 'how are you?'

witness' is 'sullenly cautioned against yawning while being grilled' (86.32–87.1). I.5 similarly concerns an expert examination of evidence, the letter which the 'hardily curiosing entomophilust' believes would once have been mistaken for the work of 'a purely deliquescent recidivist, possibly ambidextrous, snubnosed probably' (107.10–13). I.6 works like an examination or quiz-game, and the responses seem to have encyclopaedic culture at their disposal, albeit in a strangely conflated form. Answering the first question, the respondent describes HCE, 'a Colussus among cabbages', as 'Olaph the Oxman, Thorker the Tourable; you feel he is Vespasian, yet you think of him as Aurelius; whugamore , tradertroy, socianist, commoniser . . . Boomaport, Walleslee, Ubermeerschall, Blowcher and Supercharger, Monsieur Ducrow, Mister Mudson, master gardiner' (132.17–133.23).[22]

This kind of framing continues into Book II and III, shaping the conflict between Shem and Shaun and also the travels of Mamalujo which, however voyeuristic they become in II.4, are ostensibly epistemological and linked to the *Annals of the Four Masters*, the medieval chronicle which narrates Irish history from the flood to AD 1616. II.1 is structured around an extended game of riddling, with Shaun struggling to find the correct answer which takes the form of a colour. Here his guess is that the colour to be divined is yellow: '–Haps thee jaoneofergs? –Nao./ –Haps thee mayjaunties?/ – Naohao./ Haps thee per causes nunsibellies?/–Naohaohao (233.21–26).[23] 2.2, the classroom episode, invokes pedagogic procedure and schoolboy engagement with the classroom – 'Problem ye ferst, construct ann aquilittoral dryankle Probe loom! . . . Can you nei do her, numb? asks Dolph, suspecting the answer know. Oikkont, ken you ninny? asks Kev, expecting the answer guess' (286.19–28). III.2 performs like a homily, sermon or instruction book for manners and behaviour ('Sister dearest, Jaun delivered himself with express cordiality, marked by clearance of diction and general delivery' – 431.21–2). And III.3 is an extended interrogation, sometimes conducted with dark energy where Yawn is put under considerable duress to explain things clearly. His questioners are the 'four claymen'

22 Among the figures alluded to here are Vespasian and Marcus Aurelius (both Roman Emperors); Napoleon Bonaparte; the Duke of Wellington (Wellesley); General Blucher (a Prussian general who fought at Waterloo) and Andrew Ducrow. The latter was a horseman who performed at the Theatre Royal, Dublin as 'The Napoleon of Equestrians'. See *Annotations*, 132–3.

23 The French word for yellow, 'jaune', is implied here, and jaundice – and the season Spring, which might be thought of in yellow terms. See also *Annotations*, 233.

who 'clomb together to hold their sworn starchamber quiry on him. For he was ever their quarrel' (475.18–19). This reference to a judiciary (the Star Chamber) that, especially under the reigns of James I and Charles II, became a byword for injustice and persecution, establishes a keynote to the interrogative nature of the episode.

Above all throughout the *Wake* there is a fascination with particular essential and essentialist questions, thus the obsession with genealogy and lineage, which derives from the fundamental concern with origins to produce a thoroughgoing and hilarious subversion of the family tree, the 'book of breedings' (410.1–2) that the *Wake* struggles to be – a radical cultural position to take in the context of the race politics of Europe at the end of the 1930s. At the beginning of I.2, for example, a broadly ethnographic discourse tries unsuccessfully to trace the origins of HCE's name 'in the presurnames prodromarith period' and insists that there will be a 'discarding once for all those theories from older sources which would link him back with such pivotal ancestors as the Glues, the Gravys, the Northeasts, the Ankers and the Earwickers' (30.3–7). There is a closely associated frame of reference around race identity and classification and the attempt to sort out the ethnographical confusions of such bizarre designations as 'Hispano-Cathayan-Euxine, Castilian-Emeratic-Hebridian, Espanol-Cymric-Helleniky' (263.13–15). That particular conundrum revolves around questions of race dispersal, formulated in part by the many references to Noah and his sons and the patriarchal genealogy of Judaeo-Christian myths. With HCE being associated with Noah, Shaun is strongly linked to Japhet, by tradition the forefather of white Europe. Shem is a composite of both Shem and Ham (see 'Mr Himmyshimmy' at 173.27). The latter figure, subject of a curse, typically featured as the progenitor of the 'black race'. In the *Wake* 'Sham' is aligned with a range of outcast racial configurations (including Irish ones), most aggressively so in I.7 where 'this disinterestingly low human type' (179.12–13) is racialised by his 'white' brother as 'a nogger amongst the blankards of this dastard century' (188.13–14).

At the same time, Western challenges to this tradition, fundamentally shaped by Aryanism, are also incorporated into the *Wake* with allusions to Childeric, for example – reputed to have started the Germanic diasporas; Magog, the mythical son of Japhet and involved in so many European origin myths, including British ones; Olaf, founder of Dublin; Horsa and Hengest, legendary founders of the Anglo-Saxon race in England; 'Hebear and Hairyman' (Heber and Heremon, mythical fathers of the Irish race – 14.35–6) and so on. Firmly fixed 'Inn the

Byggning' (17.22), at the first pub, 'here where race began' (80.16)[24] in
the 'garden of Erin' (203.1) the *Wake* and its people are drawn to such
ancestral schemas and driven by the search for origins.

The great range of potential ur-stories means that no single version
has any more, or less, reliability than any other; indeed the *Wake* is an
astonishing example of the entanglement of histories, again often
racialised as in the composite – a 'celtelleneteutoslavzendlatinsound-
script' (219.17) Nevertheless Shaun, as Yawn in III.3, appears to be
asked to throw light on the question of origins.

> – Remounting aliftle towards the ouragan of spaces. Just how grand
> in cardinal rounders is this preeminent giant, sir Arber? Your bard's
> highview, avis on valley! I would like to hear you burble to us in strict
> conclave, purpurando, and without too much italiote interfairance,
> what you know *in petto* about our sovereign beingstalk, Tonans
> Tomazeus. *O dite*!   (504.14–19)

Except, of course, that the question is actually far from exact. Behind
the phrase 'ouragan of spaces' is the shadow of Darwin and the *Origin of
the Species*, but it is the occlusion, not our 'translation', that is on the
page. What is invested in the 'disguise'? And why, if a scientific order is
being invoked here, does that system of meaning become mixed with
the world of myth and fairy tale suggested by the reference to the Jack
and beanstalk story ('our sovereign beingstalk') and the mythological
(Zeus the Thunderer lies behind 'Tonans Tomazeus')? The religious
frame of reference only confuses things further. Along with references
to science, myth and fairytale, the question invokes the scrutiny of
conservative religious authority, implied initially in the references to
the Vatican and the conclave of cardinals – in *Annotations* Roland
McHugh gives for 'purpurando' 'purpurandus', Vatican slang for 'one
fit to be purpled, i.e. made a cardinal'. The question, then, is obscure, as
most questions are in the *Wake*, and the motives of the questioner
impossible to unpick. Is he inviting confidence, speaking to an equal or
seeking to trip up? For all the apparent desire to know, incompatible
systems of thinking about the world jostle together in an astonishing
clatter in the very framing of this enquiry, as they do throughout this
extraordinary text from its doubtful beginning to its dubious end.

24 This version of the start of things is accompanied by a string of Sanskrit
   words and other Hindu references and is for that reason particularly
   evocative of the Aryan myth.

As the *Wake* is a book obsessed by story telling, so it is a book that desperately tries to establish meaning. But just as its narrative is subject to the most severe disruptions and dislocations, so with its drive towards truth telling and knowledge. As virtually any phrase, sentence, paragraph or page will show, the capacity of the *Wake* for communication is constantly under siege, at every level from the single word, to the sentence, passage, page, episode, and, indeed, the book. It is not that the *Wake* has no meaning, or that it produces from its bizarre amalgamations some version of superior meaning. The typical condition of the *Wake* is rather that it has over-meaning, too many competing possibilities which run entirely counter to expectations raised by the will to knowledge, equally so characteristic of the *Wake*

For many years, traditions of *Wake* criticism have devoted great energy to unpicking the *Wake*, restoring it to the order that Joyce spent years slicing up and disposing of in such hilarious ways. That kind of critical work has produced important insights into the *Wake*, but the practices it promotes goes well beyond any generally acceptable notion of 'reading' as it applies to that familiar but problematic abstraction – the 'ordinary' reader. The annotated *Wake*, however useful it might be, works against everyday ideas of the reader, just it does so against the real *Wake* text. It refuses to accept that the *Wake* is what it is – not a representation of dreaming or 'dreamwork', as was once widely held, but an astonishing interference in our cultures of reading and understanding.[25] That rude interruption remains the great challenge of the *Wake*. It is 'difficult' and challenging not as a result of some secret ambition to achieve some greater truth beyond but, rather, in the sense that its bizarre mix ups and entanglements so much undermine the drive for order and stability in the world.

The first question to ask of the *Wake*, then, is not what does it mean

25 That view was decisively challenged by Derek Attridge writing in 1982 who argued that the *Wake* might indeed see itself on occasion as a dream, although with nothing like the consistency that some critics maintained. But why, he asked, should that one reference point be privileged over all the over possibilities available? The *Wake* also sees itself in terms of 'the letter, the manifesto, the midden, the illuminated page, the photograph, the ballad, the children's game, the television programme, the riddle, the radio broadcast, the bedtime story, the geometrical theorem, the anecdote, the quiz show, the lecture, the homily, the mailbag [...] the list could go on as long as the longest list in *Finnegans Wake*' and would include the idea of the *Wake* as novel. See Attridge, Derek, 'Finnegans Awake: The Dream of Interpretation', *James Joyce Quarterly*, vol. 27 no. 1 (1989), 11–29 (17, 26).

but, rather, why does it *not* mean? What does its refutation of stability, order, clarity and singularity amount to? Why does it both exemplify and yet so ridicule our desires for authenticity and certainty, pedigree and purity? Here the *Wake*, which remains very strange in its delivery, returns us ironically enough to very familiar territory. It becomes a hilarious embodiment of a Western culture struggling to retain epistemological faith and confidence in its own stories and myth-making – against all the odds. This is where Joyce's last great book of punning takes on its proper dimensions, not, as critics once argued, as a poeticised apology for the West a 'dreamlike saga of guilt-stained, evolving humanity' and 'a mighty allegory of the fall and resurrection of mankind'[26] but, rather, as a much sharper, satirical and politically engaged work.

As I have argued elsewhere, this is an agenda that has specific relation to the extremities of politics of Europe in the 1920s and 30s. The point becomes instantly brought to life when the uncertainties of *Wake* speak, with its comic conflations of race, language, territories, gender and so on, are positioned against fascist ideology.[27] The *Wake* registers many references to National Socialism, almost all of them insulting – like 'erst curst Hun' at 76.32; 'Achdung' at 100.5; the reference to 'Finn MacCool' being 'evacuated at the mere appearance of three germhuns' (127.12–13), and the splendid mockery of the Nazi slogan ('Heil Hitler! Ein volk, ein Reich, ein Führer') at 191.7–8 – 'heal helper! one gob, one gap, one gulp and gorger of all'. The Nazi salute is darkly mocked in 'Seek hells' (228.6); the Nazi leader cult diminished and made childish to the rhythm of 'Ten Men Went to Mow' in 'hun men wend to raze a leader' (278.21). Storm troopers, jackboots worn by Tim Finnegan, the Gestapo, the Strength Through Joy movement, Hitler's road building programme and so on, are all meted out a similar treatment. If the *Wake*'s participation in the political was restricted to these lively insults, however, it would be of limited interest. In fact such engagements penetrate much further. The *Wake* locates ideas of race origin and language classification in terms of the Western intellectual tradition and interrupts these with a subversion that is astonishingly original in its form. Notions of pure identities, for example, so much at the heart of scientific racism, are thoroughly disposed of in unique ways. Hilarious

26 Joseph Campbell and Henry Morton Robinson, *A Skeleton Key to 'Finnegans Wake'* (London: Faber and Faber, 1954), 13.
27 See Len Platt, *Joyce Race and 'Finnegans Wake'* (Cambridge: Cambridge University Press, 2007.

versions of origins, race dispersal and race meeting, become parodic assaults on a European academy that for over two hundred years had tried to establish culture as an essential condition of civilisation; to classify, scientifically, racial difference and similarity and to chart history in national and nationalistic terms. In this kind of context the politics of the *Wake* cannot be limited to its 'allusiveness' to National Socialism. On the contrary it goes to the very heart of the *Wake* and the kind of radical cultural practice in which it engages. Its merging of characters and historical periods, for instance, becomes a hugely comic version of cultures merging, a 'confusioning of human races' (35.5), which has the effect of utterly destroying any notion of cultural purity and singularity of race origin. Language functions similarly. Joyce's bizarre version of 'babeling' (164.11) completely undermines any idea of sorting out a confusion of tongues into a scientific order that can be linked to identity let alone any version of destiny.

As well as being conditioned in such ways by the past, however, this extraordinary book has a profound capacity to speak loudly today. Indeed, since the 1960s to the present day, from structuralism through deconstruction and post-structuralism, the *Wake* has been positioned at the forefront of highly controversial ideas about language and culture. Some of the key figures here – Gilles Deleuze, Jacques Lacan, Jacques Derrida, Julia Kristeva, Heléne Cixous – have addressed themselves directly to the *Wake*, understanding it not as a particular reply to 1930s fascism or the specifics of other colonial empires, but rather as a more comprehensive assault on the very idea of the universal, a radical subversion of 'the most cherished preconceptions of Western culture'.[28] Against such ways of thinking through a postmodern world, the *Wake* has become something of a masterwork for contemporary globalising cultures – for realities which as imagined by someone like Zygmunt Bauman are characterised less by material solidities that by the ambiguities of liquidity.[29] This is one of the most surprising things about a continually surprising book, that some seventy years after its full publication it should mean more rather than less to contemporary culture.

LEN PLATT

By kind permission of Continuum, this introduction has been adapted from Len Platt, *James Joyce: Texts and Contexts* (Continuum, London, 2011).

28 Margot Norris, *The Decentred Universe of Finnegans Wake: A Structuralist Analysis* (Baltimore: Johns Hopkins University Press, 1976), 5.
29 See Zygmunt Baumann, *Liquid Modernity* (Cambridge: Polity Press, 2000)

FURTHER READING

Samuel Beckett and others. *Our Exagmination Round his Factification for Incamination*. London: Faber, 1929.

Joseph Campbell and Henry Morton. *A Skeleton Key to Finnegans Wake*. London: Faber and Faber, 1947

A. Walton Litz. *The Art of James Joyce: Method and Design in 'Ulysses' and 'Finnegans Wake'*. London: Oxford University Press, 1961.

Clive Hart. *Structure and Motif in 'Finnegans Wake'*. London: Faber and Faber, 1962.

Jack P. Dalton and Clive Hart (eds.). *Twelve and a Tilly*. London: Faber and Faber, 1966.

William York Tyndall. *A Reader's Guide to 'Finnegans Wake'*. London: Thames and Hudson, 1969.

Margot Norris. *The Decentred Universe of 'Finnegans Wake'*. Baltimore: Johns Hopkins University Press, 1974.

Roland McHugh. *The Sigla of 'Finnegans Wake'*. London: Edward Arnold, 1976.

Danis Rose and John O'Hanlon. *Understanding 'Finnegans Wake': A Guide to the Narrative of James Joyce's Masterpiece*. New York: Garland, 1982.

John Bishop. *Joyce's Book of the Dark: 'Finnegans Wake'*. Madison: University of Wisconsin Press, 1986.

Thomas C. Hofheinz, *Joyce and the Invention of Irish History*. Cambridge: Cambridge University Press, 1995.

Luca Crispi and Sam Slote (eds.). *How Joyce Wrote 'Finnegans Wake'*. Madison: University of Wisconsin Press, 2004.

Finn Fordham. *Lots of Fun at 'Finnegans Wake': Unravelling Universals*. Oxford: Oxford University Press, 2007.

Len Platt. *Joyce, Race and 'Finnegans Wake'*. Cambridge: Cambridge University Press, 2007.

FINNEGANS WAKE

I

riverrun, past Eve and Adam's, from swerve of shore to bend
of bay, brings us by a commodius vicus of recirculation back to
Howth Castle and Environs.

Sir Tristram, violer d'amores, fr'over the short sea, had passen-
core rearrived from North Armorica on this side the scraggy
isthmus of Europe Minor to wielderfight his penisolate war: nor
had topsawyer's rocks by the stream Oconee exaggerated themselse
to Laurens County's gorgios while they went doublin their mumper
all the time: nor avoice from afire bellowsed mishe mishe to
tauftauf thuartpeatrick: not yet, though venissoon after, had a
kidscad buttended a bland old isaac: not yet, though all's fair in
vanessy, were sosie sesthers wroth with twone nathandjoe. Rot a
peck of pa's malt had Jhem or Shen brewed by arclight and rory
end to the regginbrow was to be seen ringsome on the aquaface.

The fall (bababadalgharaghtakamminarronnkonnbronntonner-
ronntuonnthunntrovarrhounawnskawntoohoohoordenenthur-
nuk!) of a once wallstrait oldparr is retaled early in bed and later
on life down through all christian minstrelsy. The great fall of the
offwall entailed at such short notice the pftjschute of Finnegan,
erse solid man, that the humptyhillhead of humself prumptly sends
an unquiring one well to the west in quest of his tumptytumtoes:
and their upturnpikepointandplace is at the knock out in the park
where oranges have been laid to rust upon the green since dev-
linsfirst loved livvy.

What clashes here of wills gen wonts, oystrygods gaggin fishy-
gods! Brékkek Kékkek Kékkek Kékkek! Kóax Kóax Kóax! Ualu
Ualu Ualu! Quáouauh! Where the Baddelaries partisans are still
out to mathmaster Malachus Micgranes and the Verdons cata-
pelting the camibalistics out of the Whoyteboyce of Hoodie
Head. Assiegates and boomeringstroms. Sod's brood, be me fear!
Sanglorians, save! Arms apeal with larms, appalling. Killykill-
killy: a toll, a toll. What chance cuddleys, what cashels aired
and ventilated! What bidimetoloves sinduced by what tegotetab-
solvers! What true feeling for their's hayair with what strawng
voice of false jiccup! O here here how hoth sprowled met the
duskt the father of fornicationists but, (O my shining stars and
body!) how hath fanespanned most high heaven the skysign of
soft advertisement! But waz iz! Iseut! Ere were sewers! The oaks
of ald now they lie in peat yet elms leap where askes lay. Phall if
you but will, rise you must: and none so soon either shall the
pharce for the nunce come to a setdown secular phoenish.

Bygmester Finnegan, of the Stuttering Hand, freemen's mau-
rer, lived in the broadest way immarginable in his rushlit toofar-
back for messuages before joshuan judges had given us numbers
or Helviticus committed deuteronomy (one yeastyday he sternely
struxk his tete in a tub for to watsch the future of his fates but ere
he swiftly stook it out again, by the might of moses, the very water was eviparated and all the guenneses had met their exodus so
that ought to show you what a pentschanjeuchy chap he was!)
and during mighty odd years this man of hod, cement and edi-
fices in Toper's Thorp piled buildung supra buildung pon the
banks for the livers by the Soangso. He addle liddle phifie Annie
ugged the little craythur. Wither hayre in honds tuck up your part
inher. Oftwhile balbulous, mithre ahead, with goodly trowel in
grasp and ivoroiled overalls which he habitacularly fondseed, like
Haroun Childeric Eggeberth he would caligulate by multiplicab-
les the alltitude and malltitude until he seesaw by neatlight of the
liquor wheretwin 'twas born, his roundhead staple of other days
to rise in undress maisonry upstanded (joygrantit!), a waalworth
of a skyerscape of most eyeful hoyth entowerly, erigenating from

next to nothing and celescalating the himals and all, hierarchitec-
titiptitoploftical, with a burning bush abob off its baubletop and
with larrons o'toolers clittering up and tombles a'buckets clottering down.

Of the first was he to bare arms and a name: Wassaily Boos-
laeugh of Riesengeborg. His crest of huroldry, in vert with
ancillars, troublant, argent, a hegoak, poursuivant, horrid, horned.
His scutschum fessed, with archers strung, helio, of the second.
Hootch is for husbandman handling his hoe. Hohohoho, Mister
Finn, you're going to be Mister Finnagain! Comeday morm and,
O, you're vine! Sendday's eve and, ah, you're vinegar! Hahahaha,
Mister Funn, you're going to be fined again!

What then agentlike brought about that tragoady thundersday
this municipal sin business? Our cubehouse still rocks as earwitness
to the thunder of his arafatas but we hear also through successive
ages that shebby choruysh of unkalified muzzlenimiissilehims that
would blackguardise the whitestone ever hurtleturtled out of
heaven. Stay us wherefore in our search for tighteousness, O Sus-
tainer, what time we rise and when we take up to toothmick and
before we lump down upown our leatherbed and in the night and
at the fading of the stars! For a nod to the nabir is better than wink
to the wabsanti. Otherways wesways like that provost scoffing
bedoneen the jebel and the jpysian sea. Cropherb the crunch-
bracken shall decide. Then we'll know it the feast is a flyday. She
has a gift of seek on site and she allcasually ansars helpers, the
dreamydeary. Heed! Heed. It may half been a missfired brick, as
some say, or it mought have been due to a collupsus of his back
promises, as others looked at it. (There extand by now one thousand and one stories, all told, of the same). But so sore did abe
ite ivvy's holired abbles, (what with the wallhall's horrors of rolls-
rights, carhacks, stonengens, kisstvanes, tramtrees, fargobawlers,
autokinotons, hippohobbilies, streetfleets, tournintaxes, mega-
phoggs, circuses and wardsmoats and basilikerks and aeropagods
and the hoyse and the jollybrool and the peeler in the coat and
the mecklenburk bitch bite at his ear and the merlinburrow bur-
rocks and his fore old porecourts, the bore the more, and his

blightblack workingstacks at twelvepins a dozen and the noobi-
busses sleighding along Safetyfirst Street and the derryjellybies
snooping around Tell-No-Tailors' Corner and the fumes and the
hopes and the strupithump of his ville's indigenous romekeepers,
homesweepers, domecreepers thurum and thurum in fancymud
murumd and all the uproor from all the aufroos, a roof for may
and a reef for hugh butt under his bridge suits tony) wan warning Phill filt tippling full. His howd feeled heavy, his hoddit did
shake. (There was a wall of course in erection) Dimb! He stot-
tered from the latter. Damb! he was dud. Dumb! Mastabatoom,
mastabadtomm, when a mon merries his lute is all long. For
whole the world to see.

Shize? I should shee! Macool, Macool, orra whyi deed ye diie?
of a trying thirstay mournin? Sobs they sighdid at Fillagain's
chrissormiss wake, all the hoolivans of the nation, prostrated in
their consternation, and their duodisimally profusive plethora of
ululation. There was plumbs and grumes and cheriffs and citherers
and raiders and cinemen too. And the all gianed in with the shout-
most shoviality. Agog and magog and the round of them agrog.
To the continuation of that celebration until Hanandhunigan's
extermination! Some in kinkin corass, more, kankan keening,
Belling him up and filling him down. He's stiff but he's steady is
Priam Olim! 'Twas he was the dacent gaylabouring youth. Sharpen
his pillowscone, tap up his bier! E'erawhere in this whorl would ye
hear sich a din again? With their deepbrow fundigs and the dusty
fidelios. They laid him brawdawn alanglast bed. With a bockalips
of finisky fore his feet. And a barrowload of guenesis hoer his head.
Tee the tootal of the fluid hang the twoddle of the fuddled, O!

Hurrah, thereis but young gleve for the owl globe wheels in
view which is tautaulogically the same thing. Well, Him a being
so on the flounder of his bulk like an overgrown babeling, let wee
peep, see, at Hom, well, see peegee ought he ought, platterplate. ⋈
Hum! From Shopalist to Bailywick or from ashtun to baronoath
or from Buythebanks to Roundthehead or from the foot of the
bill to ireglint's eye he calmly extensolies. And all the way (a
horn!) from fjord to fjell his baywinds' oboboes shall wail him

rockbound (hoahoahoah!) in swimswamswum and all the livvy-
long night, the delldale dalppling night, the night of bluerybells,
her flittaflute in tricky trochees (O carina! O carina!) wake him.
With her issavan essavans and her patterjackmartins about all
them inns and ouses. Tilling a teel of a tum, telling a toll of a tea-
ry turty Taubling. Grace before Glutton. For what we are, gifs
à gross if we are, about to believe. So pool the begg and pass the
kish for crawsake. Omen. So sigh us. Grampupus is fallen down
but grinny sprids the boord. Whase on the joint of a desh? Fin-
foefom the Fush. Whase be his baken head? A loaf of Singpan-
try's Kennedy bread. And whase hitched to the hop in his tayle?
A glass of Danu U'Dunnell's foamous olde Dobbelin ayle. But,
lo, as you would quaffoff his fraudstuff and sink teeth through
that pyth of a flowerwhite bodey behold of him as behemoth for
he is noewhemoe. Finiche! Only a fadograph of a yestern scene.
Almost rubicund Salmosalar, ancient fromout the ages of the Ag-
apemonides, he is smolten in our mist, woebecanned and packt
away. So that meal's dead off for summan, schlook, schlice and
goodridhirring.

Yet may we not see still the brontoichthyan form outlined a-
slumbered, even in our own nighttime by the sedge of the trout-
ling stream that Bronto loved and Brunto has a lean on. *Hic cubat
edilis. Apud libertinam parvulam.* Whatif she be in flags or flitters,
reekierags or sundyechosies, with a mint of mines or beggar a
pinnyweight. Arrah, sure, we all love little Anny Ruiny, or, we
mean to say, lovelittle Anna Rayiny, when unda her brella, mid
piddle med puddle she ninnygoes nannygoes nancing by. Yoh!
Brontolone slaaps yoh snoores. Upon Benn Heather, in Seeple
Isout too. The cranic head on him, caster of his reasons, peer yu-
thner in yondmist. Whooth? His clay feet, swarded in verdigrass,
stick up starck where he last fellonem, by the mund of the magazine wall, where our maggy seen all, with her sisterin shawl.
While over against this belles' alliance beyond Ill Sixty, ollol-
lowed ill! bagsides of the fort, bom, tarabom, tarabom, lurk the
ombushes, the site of the lyffing-in-wait of the upjock and hock-
ums. Hence when the clouds roll by, jamey, a proudseye view is

enjoyable of our mounding's mass, now Wallinstone national
museum, with, in some greenish distance, the charmful water-
loose country and the two quitewhite villagettes who hear show
of themselves so gigglesomes minxt the follyages, the prettilees!
Penetrators are permitted into the museomound free. Welsh and
the Paddy Patkinses, one shelenk! Redismembers invalids of old
guard find poussepousse pousseypram to sate the sort of their butt.
For her passkey supply to the janitrix, the mistress Kathe. Tip.

This the way to the museyroom. Mind your hats goan in!
Now yiz are in the Willingdone Museyroom. This is a Prooshious gunn. This is a ffrinch. Tip. This is the flag of the Prooshious, the Cap and Soracer. This is the bullet that byng the flag of
the Prooshious. This is the ffrinch that fire on the Bull that bang
the flag of the Prooshious. Saloos the Crossgunn! Up with your
pike and fork! Tip. (Bullsfoot! Fine!) This is the triplewon hat of
Lipoleum. Tip. Lipoleumhat. This is the Willingdone on his
same white harse, the Cokenhape. This is the big Sraughter Willingdone, grand and magentic in his goldtin spurs and his ironed
dux and his quarterbrass woodyshoes and his magnate's gharters
and his bangkok's best and goliar's goloshes and his pullupon-
easyan wartrews. This is his big wide harse. Tip. This is the three
lipoleum boyne grouching down in the living detch. This is an
inimyskilling inglis, this is a scotcher grey, this is a davy, stoop-
ing. This is the bog lipoleum mordering the lipoleum beg. A
Gallawghurs argaumunt, This is the petty lipoleum boy that
was nayther bag nor bug. Assaye, assaye! Touchole Fitz Tuo-
mush. Dirty Mac Dyke. And Hairy O' Hurry. All of them
arminus-varminus. This is Delian alps. This is Mont Tivel,
this is Mont Tipsey, this is the Grand Mons Injun. This is the
crimealine of the alps hooping to sheltershock the three lipoleums.
This is the jinnies with their legahorns feinting to read in their
handmade's book of stralegy while making their war undisides
the Willingdone. The jinnies is a cooin her hand and the jinnies is
a ravin her hair and the Willingdone git the band up. This is big
Willingdone mormorial tallowscoop Wounderworker obscides
on the flanks of the jinnies. Sexcaliber hrosspower. Tip. This

is me Belchum sneaking his phillippy out of his most Awful
Grimmest Sunshat Cromwelly. Looted. This is the jinnies' hastings dispatch for to irrigate the Willingdone. Dispatch in thin
red lines cross the shortfront of me Belchum. Yaw, yaw, yaw!
Leaper Orthor. Fear siecken! Fieldgaze thy tiny frow. Hugact-
ing. Nap. That was the tictacs of the jinnies for to fontannoy the
Willingdone. Shee, shee, shee! The jinnies is jillous agincourting
all the lipoleums. And the lipoleums is gonn boycottoncrezy onto
the one Willingdone. And the Willingdone git the band up. This
is bode Belchum, bonnet to busby, breaking his secred word with a
ball up his ear to the Willingdone. This is the Willingdone's hur-
old dispitchback. Dispitch desployed on the regions rare of me
Belchum. Salamangra! Ayi, ayi, ayi! Cherry jinnies. Figtreeyou!
Damn fairy ann, Voutre. Willingdone. That was the first joke of
Willingdone, tic for tac. Hee, hee, hee! This is me Belchum in
his twelve-mile cowchooks, weet, tweet and stampforth foremost,
footing the camp for the jinnies. Drink a sip, drankasup, for he's
as sooner buy a guinness than he'd stale store stout. This is Roo-
shious balls. This is a ttrinch. This is mistletropes. This is Canon
Futter with the popynose. After his hundred days' indulgence.
This is the blessed. Tarra's widdars! This is jinnies in the bonny
bawn blooches. This is lipoleums in the rowdy howses. This is the
Willingdone, by the splinters of Cork, order fire. Tonnerre!
(Bullsear! Play!) This is camelry, this is floodens, this is the
solphereens in action, this is their mobbily, this is panickburns.
Almeidagad! Arthiz too loose! This is Willingdone cry. Brum!
Brum! Cumbrum! This is jinnies cry. Underwetter! Goat
strip Finnlambs! This is jinnies rinning away to their onster-
lists dowan a bunkersheels. With a nip nippy nip and a trip trip-
py trip so airy. For their heart's right there. Tip. This is me Belchum's tinkyou tankyou silvoor plate for citchin the crapes in
the cool of his canister. Poor the pay! This is the bissmark of the
marathon merry of the jinnies they left behind them. This is the
Willingdone branlish his same marmorial tallowscoop Sophy-
Key-Po for his royal divorsion on the rinnaway jinnies. Gam-
bariste della porca! Dalaveras fimmieras! This is the pettiest

of the lipoleums. Toffeethief, that spy on the Willingdone from
his big white harse, the Capeinhope. Stonewall Willingdone
is an old maxy montrumeny. Lipoleums is nice hung bushel-
lors. This is hiena hinnessy laughing alout at the Willingdone. This is lipsyg dooley krieging the funk from the hinnessy.
This is the hinndoo Shimar Shin between the dooley boy and the
hinnessy. Tip. This is the wixy old Willingdone picket up the
half of the threefoiled hat of lipoleums fromoud of the bluddle
filth. This is the hinndoo waxing ranjymad for a bombshoob.
This is the Willingdone hanking the half of the hat of lipoleums
up the tail on the buckside of his big white harse. Tip. That was
the last joke of Willingdone. Hit, hit, hit! This is the same white
harse of the Willingdone. Culpenhelp, waggling his tailoscrupp
with the half of a hat of lipoleums to insoult on the hinndoo seeboy. Hney, hney, hney! (Bullsrag! Foul!) This is the seeboy,
madrashattaras, upjump and pumpim, cry to the Willingdone:
Ap Pukkaru! Pukka Yurap! This is the Willingdone, bornstable
ghentleman, tinders his maxbotch to the cursigan Shimar Shin.
Basucker youstead! This is the dooforhim seeboy blow the whole
of the half of the hat of lipoleums off of the top of the tail on the
back of his big wide harse. Tip (Bullseye! Game!) How Copen-
hagen ended. This way the museyroom. Mind your boots goan
out.
    Phew!
    What a warm time we were in there but how keling is here the
airabouts! We nowhere she lives but you mussna tell annaone for
the lamp of Jig-a-Lanthern! It's a candlelittle houthse of a month
and one windies. Downadown, High Downadown. And num-
mered quaintlymine. And such reasonable weather too! The wa-
grant wind's awalt'zaround the piltdowns and on every blasted
knollyrock (if you can spot fifty I spy four more) there's that
gnarlybird ygathering, a runalittle, doalittle, preealittle, pouralittle,
wipealittle, kicksalittle, severalittle, eatalittle, whinealittle, kenalittle,
helfalittle, pelfalittle gnarlybird. A verytableland of bleakbardfields!
Under his seven wrothschields lies one, Lumproar. His glav toside
him. Skud ontorsed. Our pigeons pair are flewn for northcliffs.

The three of crows have flapped it southenly, kraaking of de baccle to the kvarters of that sky whence triboos answer; Wail, 'tis well! She niver comes out when Thon's on shower or when Thon's flash with his Nixy girls or when Thon's blowing toom-cracks down the gaels of Thon. No nubo no! Neblas on you liv! Her would be too moochy afreet. Of Burymeleg and Bindme-rollingeyes and all the deed in the woe. Fe fo fom! She jist does hopes till byes will be byes. Here, and it goes on to appear now, she comes, a peacefugle, a parody's bird, a peri potmother, a pringlpik in the ilandiskippy, with peewee, and powwows in beggybaggy, on her bickybacky, and a flick flask fleckflinging its pixylighting pacts' huemeramybows, picking here, pecking there, pussypussy plunderpussy. But it's the armitides toonigh, militopucos, and toomourn we wish for a muddy kissmans to the minutia workers and there's to be a gorgeups trucefor happinest childher everwere. Come nebo me and suso sing the day we sallybright. She's burrowed the coacher's headlight the better to pry (who goes cute goes siocur and shoos aroun) and all spoiled goods go into her nabsack: curtrages and rattlin buttins, nappy spattees and flasks of all nations, clavicures and scampulars, maps, keys and woodpiles of haypennies and moonled brooches with bloodstaned breeks in em, boaston nightgarters and masses of shoesets and nickelly nacks and foder allmicheal and a lugly parson of cates and howitzer muchears and midgers and maggets, ills and ells with loffs of toffs and pleures of bells and the last sigh that come fro the hart (bucklied!) and the fairest sin the sunsaw (that's cearc!). With Kiss. Kiss Criss. Cross Criss. Kiss Cross. Undo lives 'end. Slain.

How bootifull and how truetowife of her, when strengly fore-bidden, to steal our historic presents from the past postprophetti-cals so as to will make us all lordy heirs and ladymaidesses of a pretty nice kettle of fruit. She is livving in our midst of debt and laffing through all plores for us (her birth is uncontrollable), with a naperon for her mask and her sabboes kickin arias (so sair! so solly!) if yous ask me and I saack you. Hou! Hou! Gricks may rise and Troysirs fall (there being two sights for ever a picture) for in the byways of high improvidence that's what makes life-work leaving and the world's a cell for citters to cit in. Let young wimman run away with the story and let young min talk smooth behind the butteler's back. She knows her knight's duty while Luntum sleeps. Did ye save any tin? says he. Did I what? with a grin says she. And we all like a marriedann because she is mercenary. Though the length of the land lies under liquidation (floote!) and there's nare a hairbrow nor an eyebush on this glaubrous phace of Herrschuft Whatarwelter she'll loan a vesta and hire some peat and sarch the shores her cockles to heat and she'll do all a turfwoman can to piff the business on. Paff. To puff the blaziness on. Poffpoff. And even if Humpty shell fall frumpty times as awkward again in the beardsboosoloom of all our grand remonstrancers there'll be iggs for the brekkers come to mournhim, sunny side up with care. So true is it that therewhere's a turnover the tay is wet too and when you think you ketch sight of a hind make sure but you're cocked by a hin.

Then as she is on her behaviourite job of quainance bandy, fruting for firstlings and taking her tithe, we may take our review of the two mounds to see nothing of the himples here as at elsewhere, by sixes and sevens, like so many heegills and collines, sitton aroont, scentbreeched and somepotreek, in their swishawish satins and their taffetaffe tights, playing Wharton's Folly, at a treepurty on the planko in the purk. Stand up, mickos! Make strake for minnas! By order, Nicholas Proud. We may see and hear nothing if we choose of the shortlegged bergins off Corkhill or the bergamoors of Arbourhill or the bergagambols of Summerhill or the bergincellies of Miseryhill or the countrybossed bergones of Constitutionhill though every crowd has its several tones and every trade has its clever mechanics and each harmonical has a point of its own, Olaf's on the rise and Ivor's on the lift and Sitric's place's between them. But all they are all there scraping along to sneeze out a likelihood that will solve and salve life's robulous rebus, hopping round his middle like kippers on a griddle, O, as he lays dormont from the macroborg of Holdhard to the microbirg of Pied de Poudre. Behove this sound of Irish sense. Really? Here English might be seen. Royally? One sovereign punned to petery pence. Regally? The silence speaks the scene. Fake!

So This Is Dyoublong?

Hush! Caution! Echoland!

How charmingly exquisite! It reminds you of the outwashed engravure that we used to be blurring on the blotchwall of his innkempt house. Used they? (I am sure that tiring chabelshoveller with the mujikal chocolat box, Miry Mitchel, is listening) I say, the remains of the outworn gravemure where used to be blurried the Ptollmens of the Incabus. Used we? (He is only pretendant to be stugging at the jubalee harp from a second existed lishener, Fiery Farrelly.) It is well known. Lokk for himself and see the old butte new. Dbln. W. K. O. O. Hear? By the mausolime wall. Fimfim fimfim. With a grand funferall. Fumfum fumfum. 'Tis optophone which ontophanes. List! Wheatstone's magic lyer. They will be tuggling foriver. They will be lichening for allof. They will be pretumbling forover. The harpsdischord shall be theirs for ollaves.

Four things therefore, saith our herodotary Mammon Lujius in his grand old historiorum, wrote near Boriorum, bluest book in baile's annals, f.t. in Dyffinarsky ne'er sall fail til heathersmoke and cloudweed Eire's ile sall pall. And here now they are the fear of um. T. Totities! *Unum.* (Adar.) A bulbenboss surmounted upon an alderman. Ay, ay! *Duum.* (Nizam.) A shoe on a puir old wobban. Ah, ho! *Triom.* (Tamuz.) An auburn mayde, o'brine a'bride, to be desarted. Adear, adear! *Quodlibus.* (Marchessvan.) A penn no weightier nor a polepost. And so. And all. (Succoth.)

So, how idlers' wind turning pages on pages, as innocens with anaclete play popeye antipop, the leaves of the living in the boke of the deeds, annals of themselves timing the cycles of events grand and national, bring fassilwise to pass how.

1132 A.D. Men like to ants or emmets wondern upon a groot hwide Whallfisk which lay in a Runnel. Blubby wares upat Ublanium.

566 A.D. On Baalfire's night of this year after deluge a crone that

hadde a wickered Kish for to hale dead turves from the bog look-
it under the blay of her Kish as she ran for to sothisfeige her cow-
rieosity and be me sawl but she found hersell sackvulle of swart
goody quickenshoon and small illigant brogues, so rich in sweat.
Blurry works at Hurdlesford.

(Silent.)

566 A.D. At this time it fell out that a brazenlockt damsel grieved
(*sobralasolas!*) because that Puppette her minion was ravisht of her
by the ogre Puropeus Pious. Bloody wars in Ballyaughacleeagh-
bally.

1132. A.D. Two sons at an hour were born until a goodman
and his hag. These sons called themselves Caddy and Primas.
Primas was a santryman and drilled all decent people. Caddy
went to Winehouse and wrote o peace a farce. Blotty words for
Dublin.

Somewhere, parently, in the ginnandgo gap between antedilu-
vious and annadominant the copyist must have fled with his
scroll. The billy flood rose or an elk charged him or the sultrup
worldwright from the excelsissimost empyrean (bolt, in sum)
earthspake or the Dannamen gallous banged pan the bliddy du-
ran. A scribicide then and there is led off under old's code with
some fine covered by six marks or ninepins in metalmen for the
sake of his labour's dross while it will be only now and again in
our rear of o'er era, as an upshoot of military and civil engagements, that a gynecure was let on to the scuffold for taking that
same fine sum covertly by meddlement with the drawers of his
neighbour's safe.

Now after all that tarfatch'd and peragrine or dingnant or clere
lift we our ears, eyes of the darkness, from the tome of *Liber Li-
vidus* and, (toh!), how paisibly eirenical, all dimmering dunes
and gloamering glades, selfstretches afore us our fredeland's plain!
Lean neath stone pine the pastor lies with his crook; young pricket by pricket's sister nibbleth on returned viridities; amaid her
rocking grasses the herb trinity shams lowliness; skyup is of ever-
grey. Thus, too, for donkey's years. Since the bouts of Hebear
and Hairyman the cornflowers have been staying at Ballymun,

the duskrose has choosed out Goatstown's hedges, twolips have
pressed togatherthem by sweet Rush, townland of twinedlights,
the whitethorn and the redthorn have fairygeyed the mayvalleys
of Knockmaroon, and, though for rings round them, during a
chiliad of perihelygangs, the Formoreans have brittled the too-
ath of the Danes and the Oxman has been pestered by the Firebugs and the Joynts have thrown up jerrybuilding to the Kevan-
ses and Little on the Green is childsfather to the City (Year!
Year! And laughtears!), these paxsealing buttonholes have quad-
rilled across the centuries and whiff now whafft to us, fresh and
made-of-all-smiles as on the eve of Killallwho.

The babbelers with their thangas vain have been (confusium
hold them!) they were and went; thigging thugs were and hou-
hnhymn songtoms were and comely norgels were and pollyfool
fiansees. Menn have thawed, clerks have surssurhummed , the
blond has sought of the brune: Elsekiss thou may, mean Kerry
piggy?: and the duncledames have countered with the hellish fellows: Who ails tongue coddeau, aspace of dumbillsilly? And they
fell upong one another: and themselves they have fallen. And
still nowanights and by nights of yore do all bold floras of the
field to their shyfaun lovers say only: Cull me ere I wilt to thee!:
and, but a little later: Pluck me whilst I blush! Well may they
wilt, marry, and profusedly blush, be troth! For that saying is as
old as the howitts. Lave a whale a while in a whillbarrow (isn't
it the truath I'm tallin ye?) to have fins and flippers that shimmy
and shake. Tim Timmycan timped hir, tampting Tam. Fleppety!
Flippety! Fleapow!

Hop!

In the name of Anem this carl on the kopje in pelted thongs a
parth a lone who the joebiggar be he? Forshapen his pigmaid
hoagshead, shroonk his plodsfoot. He hath locktoes, this short-
shins, and, Obeold that's pectoral, his mammamuscles most
mousterious. It is slaking nuncheon out of some thing's brain
pan. Me seemeth a dragon man He is almonthst on the kiep
fief by here, is Comestipple Sacksoun, be it junipery or febre-
wery, marracks or alebrill or the ramping riots of pouriose and

froriose. What a quhare soort of a mahan. It is evident the mich-
indaddy. Lets we overstep his fire defences and these kraals of
slitsucked marrogbones. (Cave!) He can prapsposterus the pil-
lory way to Hirculos pillar. Come on, fool porterfull, hosiered
women blown monk sewer? Scuse us, chorley guy! You toller-
day donsk? N. You tolkatiff scowegian? Nn. You spigotty an-
glease? Nnn. You phonio saxo? Nnnn. Clear all so! 'Tis a Jute.
Let us swop hats and excheck a few strong verbs weak oach ea-
ther yapyazzard abast the blooty creeks.

Jute. — Yutah!

Mutt. — Mukk's pleasurad.

Jute. — Are you jeff?

Mutt. — Somehards.

Jute. — But you are not jeffmute?

Mutt. — Noho. Only an utterer.

Jute. — Whoa? Whoat is the mutter with you?

Mutt. — I became a stun a stummer.

Jute. — What a hauhauhauhaudibble thing, to be cause! How,
         Mutt?

Mutt. — Aput the buttle, surd.

Jute. — Whose poddle? Wherein?

Mutt. — The Inns of Dungtarf where Used awe to be he.

Jute. — You that side your voise are almost inedible to me.
         Become a bitskin more wiseable, as if I were
         you.

Mutt. — Has? Has af? Hasatency? Urp, Boohooru! Booru
         Usurp! I trumple from rath in mine mines when I
         rimimirim!

Jute. — One eyegonblack. Bisons is bisons. Let me fore all
         your hasitancy cross your qualm with trink gilt. Here
         have sylvan coyne, a piece of oak. Ghinees hies good
         for you.

Mutt. — Louee, louee! How wooden I not know it, the intel-
         lible greytcloak of Cedric Silkyshag! Cead mealy
         faulty rices for one dabblin bar. Old grilsy growlsy!
         He was poached on in that eggtentical spot. Here

where the liveries, Monomark. There where the mis-
sers moony, Minnikin passe.

Jute. — Simply because as Taciturn pretells, our wrongstory-
shortener, he dumptied the wholeborrow of rubbages on to soil here.

Mutt. — Just how a puddinstone inat the brookcells by a
riverpool.

Jute. — Load Allmarshy! Wid wad for a norse like?

Mutt. — Somular with a bull on a clompturf. Rooks roarum
rex roome! I could snore to him of the spumy horn,
with his woolseley side in, by the neck I am sutton
on, did Brian d' of Linn.

Jute. — Boildoyle and rawhoney on me when I can beuraly
forsstand a weird from sturk to finnic in such a pat-
what as your rutterdamrotter. Onheard of and um-
scene! Gut aftermeal! See you doomed.

Mutt. — Quite agreem. Bussave a sec. Walk a dun blink
roundward this albutisle and you skull see how olde
ye plaine of my Elters, hunfree and ours, where wone
to wail whimbrel to peewee o'er the saltings, where
wilby citie by law of isthmon, where by a droit of
signory, icefloe was from his Inn the Byggning to
whose Finishthere Punct. Let erehim ruhmuhrmuhr.
Mearmerge two races, swete and brack. Morthering
rue. Hither, craching eastuards, they are in surgence:
hence, cool at ebb, they requiesce. Countlessness of
livestories have netherfallen by this plage, flick as
flowflakes, litters from aloft, like a waast wizzard all of
whirlworlds. Now are all tombed to the mound, isges
to isges, erde from erde. Pride, O pride, thy prize!

Jute. — 'Stench!

Mutt. — Fiatfuit! Hereinunder lyethey. Llarge by the smal an'
everynight life olso th'estrange, babylone the great-
grandhotelled with tit tit tittlehouse, alp on earwig,
drukn on ild, likeas equal to anequal in this sound
seemetery which iz leebez luv.

Jute. — 'Zmorde!

Mutt. — Meldundleize! By the fearse wave behoughted. Despond's sung. And thanacestross mound have swollup them all. This ourth of years is not save brickdust and being humus the same roturns. He who runes may rede it on all fours. O'c'stle, n'wc'stle, tr'c'stle, crumbling! Sell me sooth the fare for Humblin! Humblady Fair. But speak it allsosiftly, moulder! Be in your whisht!

Jute. — Whysht?

Mutt. — The gyant Forficules with Amni the fay.

Jute. — Howe?

Mutt. — Here is viceking's graab.

Jute. — Hwaad !

Mutt. — Ore you astoneaged, jute you?

Jute. — Oye am thonthorstrok, thing mud.

(Stoop) if you are abcedminded, to this claybook, what curios of signs (please stoop), in this allaphbed! Can you rede (since We and Thou had it out already) its world? It is the same told of all. Many. Miscegenations on miscegenations. Tieckle. They lived und laughed ant loved end left. Forsin. Thy thingdome is given to the Meades and Porsons. The meandertale, aloss and again, of our old Heidenburgh in the days when Head-in-Clouds walked the earth. In the ignorance that implies impression that knits knowledge that finds the nameform that whets the wits that convey contacts that sweeten sensation that drives desire that adheres to attachment that dogs death that bitches birth that entails the ensuance of existentiality. But with a rush out of his navel reaching the reredos of Ramasbatham. A terricolous vively-onview this; queer and it continues to be quaky. A hatch, a celt, an earshare the pourquose of which was to cassay the earthcrust at all of hours, furrowards, bagawards, like yoxen at the turnpaht. Here say figurines billycoose arming and mounting. Mounting and arming bellicose figurines see here. Futhorc, this liffle effingee is for a firefing called a flintforfall. Face at the eased! O I fay! Face at the waist! Ho, you fie! Upwap and dump em, ꓤace to ꓥace! When a part so ptee does duty for the holos we soon grow to use of an allforabit. Here (please to stoop) are selveran cued peteet peas of quite a pecuniar interest inaslittle as they are the pellets that make the tomtummy's pay roll. Right rank ragnar rocks and with these rox orangotangos rangled rough and rightgorong. Wisha, wisha, whydidtha? Thik is for thorn that's thuck in its thoil like thumfool's thraitor thrust for vengeance. What a mnice old mness it all mnakes! A middenhide hoard of objects! Olives, beets, kimmells, dollies, alfrids, beatties, cormacks and daltons. Owlets' eegs (O stoop to please!) are here, creakish from age and all now quite epsilene, and oldwolldy wobblewers, haudworth a wipe o grass. Sss! See the snake wurrums everyside! Our durlbin is sworming in sneaks. They came to our island from triangular Toucheaterre beyond the wet prairie rared up in the midst of the cargon of prohibitive pomefructs but along landed Paddy Wippingham and the his garbagecans cotched the creeps of them pricker than our whosethere outofman could quick up her whatsthats. Somedivide and sumthelot but the tally turns round the same balifuson. Racketeers and bottloggers.

Axe on thwacks on thracks, axenwise. One by one place one be three dittoh and one before. Two nursus one make a plausible free and idim behind. Starting off with a big boaboa and threelegged calvers and ivargraine jadesses with a message in their mouths. And a hundreadfilled unleavenweight of liberorumqueue to con an we can till allhorrors eve. What a meanderthalltale to unfurl and with what an end in view of squattor and anntisquattor and postproneauntisquattor! To say too us to be every tim, nick and larry of us, sons of the sod, sons, littlesons, yea and lealittlesons, when usses not to be, every sue, siss and sally of us, dugters of Nan! Accusative ahnsire! Damadam to infinities!

True there was in nillohs dieybos as yet no lumpend papeer in the waste and mightmountain Penn still groaned for the micies to let flee. All was of ancientry. You gave me a boot (signs on it!) and I ate the wind. I quizzed you a quid (with for what?) and you went to the quod. But the world, mind, is, was and will be writing its own wrunes for ever, man, on all matters that fall

under the ban of our infrarational senses fore the last milch-
camel, the heartvein throbbing between his eyebrowns, has still to
moor before the tomb of his cousin charmian where his date is
tethered by the palm that's hers. But the horn, the drinking, the
day of dread are not now. A bone, a pebble, a ramskin; chip them,
chap them, cut them up allways; leave them to terracook in the
muttheringpot: and Gutenmorg with his cromagnom charter,
tintingfast and great primer must once for omniboss step rub-
rickredd out of the wordpress else is there no virtue more in al-
cohoran. For that (the rapt one warns) is what papyr is meed
of, made of, hides and hints and misses in prints. Till ye finally
(though not yet endlike) meet with the acquaintance of Mister
Typus, Mistress Tope and all the little typtopies. Fillstup. So you
need hardly spell me how every word will be bound over to carry
three score and ten toptypsical reading throughout the book of
Doublends Jined (may his forehead be darkened with mud who
would sunder!) till Daleth, mahomahouma, who oped it closeth
thereof the. Dor.

Cry not yet! There's many a smile to Nondum, with sytty
maids per man, sir, and the park's so dark by kindlelight. But
look what you have in your handself! The movibles are scrawl-
ing in motions, marching, all of them ago, in pitpat and zingzang
for every busy eerie whig's a bit of a torytale to tell. One's upon
a thyme and two's behind their lettice leap and three's among the
strubbely beds. And the chicks picked their teeths and the domb-
key he begay began. You can ask your ass if he believes it. And
so cuddy me only wallops have heels. That one of a wife with
folty barnets. For then was the age when hoops ran high. Of a
noarch and a chopwife; of a pomme full grave and a fammy of
levity; or of golden youths that wanted gelding; or of what the
mischievmiss made a man do. Malmarriedad he was reverso-
gassed by the frisque of her frasques and her prytty pyrrhique.
Maye faye, she's la gaye this snaky woman! From that trippiery
toe expectungpelick! Veil, volantine, valentine eyes. She's the
very besch Winnie blows Nay on good. Flou inn, flow ann.
Hohore! So it's sure it was her not we! But lay it easy, gentle

mien, we are in rearing of a norewhig. So weenybeeny-
veenyteeny. Comsy see! Het wis if ee newt. Lissom! lissom!
I am doing it. Hark, the corne entreats! And the larpnotes
prittle.

It was of a night, late, lang time agone, in an auldstane eld,
when Adam was delvin and his madameen spinning watersilts,
when mulk mountynotty man was everybully and the first leal
ribberrobber that ever had her ainway everybuddy to his love-
saking eyes and everybilly lived alove with everybiddy else, and
Jarl van Hoother had his burnt head high up in his lamphouse,
laying cold hands on himself. And his two little jiminies, cousins
of ourn, Tristopher and Hilary, were kickaheeling their dummy
on the oil cloth flure of his homerigh, castle and earthenhouse.
And, be dermot, who come to the keep of his inn only the niece-
of-his-in-law, the prankquean. And the prankquean pulled a rosy
one and made her wit foreninst the dour. And she lit up and fire-
land was ablaze. And spoke she to the dour in her petty perusi-
enne: Mark the Wans, why do I am alook alike a poss of porterpease? And that was how the skirtmisshes began. But the dour
handworded her grace in dootch nossow: Shut! So her grace
o'malice kidsnapped up the jiminy Tristopher and into the shandy westerness she rain, rain, rain. And Jarl van Hoother war-
lessed after her with soft dovesgall: Stop deef stop come back to
my earin stop. But she swaradid to him: Unlikelihud. And there
was a brannewail that same sabbaoth night of falling angles somewhere in Erio. And the prankquean went for her forty years'
walk in Tourlemonde and she washed the blessings of the love-
spots off the jiminy with soap sulliver suddles and she had her
four owlers masters for to tauch him his tickles and she convor-
ted him to the onesure allgood and he became a luderman. So then
she started to rain and to rain and, be redtom, she was back again
at Jarl van Hoother's in a brace of samers and the jiminy with
her in her pinafrond, lace at night, at another time. And where
did she come but to the bar of his bristolry. And Jarl von Hoother had his baretholobruised heels drowned in his cellarmalt,
shaking warm hands with himself and the jimminy hilary and

the dummy in their first infancy were below on the tearsheet, wringing and coughing, like brodar and histher. And the prankquean nipped a paly one and lit up again and redcocks flew flackering from the hillcombs. And she made her witter before the wicked, saying: Mark the Twy, why do I am alook alike two poss of porterpease? And: Shut! says the wicked, handwording her madesty. So her madesty a 'forethought set down a jiminy and took up a jiminy and all the lilipath ways to Woeman's Land she rain, rain, rain. And Jarl von Hoother bleethered atter her with a loud finegale: Stop domb stop come back with my earring stop. But the prankquean swaradid: Am liking it. And there was a wild old grannewwail that laurency night of starshootings somewhere in Erio. And the prankquean went for her forty years' walk in Turnlemeem and she punched the curses of cromcruwell with the nail of a top into the jiminy and she had her four larksical monitrix to touch him his tears and she provorted him to the onecertain allsecure and he became a tristian. So then she started raining, raining, and in a pair of changers, be dom ter, she was back again at Jarl von Hoother's and the Larryhill with her under her abromette. And why would she halt at all if not by the ward of his mansionhome of another nice lace for the third charm? And Jarl von Hoother had his hurricane hips up to his pantrybox, ruminating in his holdfour stomachs (Dare! O dare!), and the jiminy Toughertrees and the dummy were belove on the watercloth, kissing and spitting, and roguing and poghuing, like knavepaltry and naivebride and in their second infancy. And the prankquean picked a blank and lit out and the valleys lay twinkling. And she made her wittest in front of the arkway of trihump, asking: Mark the Tris, why do I am alook alike three poss of porter pease? But that was how the skirmishes endupped. For like the campbells acoming with a fork lance of lightning, Jarl von Hoother Boanerges himself, the old terror of the dames, came hip hop handihap out through the pikeopened arkway of his three shuttoned castles, in his broadginger hat and his civic chollar and his allabuff hemmed and his bullbraggin soxangloves and his ladbroke breeks and his cattegut bandolair and his fur-

framed panuncular cumbottes like a rudd yellan gruebleen or-
angeman in his violet indignonation, to the whole longth of the
strongth of his bowman's bill. And he clopped his rude hand to
his eacy hitch and he ordurd and his thick spch spck for her to
shut up shop, dappy. And the duppy shot the shutter clup (Per-
kodhuskurunbarggruauyagokgorlayorgromgremmitghundhurth-
rumathunaradidillifaititillibumullunukkunun!) And they all drank
free. For one man in his armour was a fat match always for any
girls under shurts. And that was the first peace of illiteratise
porthery in all the flamend floody flatuous world. How kirssy the
titler made a sweet unclose to the Narwhealian captol. Saw fore
shalt thou sea. Betoun ye and be. The prankquean was to hold
her dummyship and the jimminies was to keep the peacewave
and van Hoother was to git the wind up. Thus the hearsomeness
of the burger felicitates the whole of the polis.

O foenix culprit! Ex nickylow malo comes mickelmassed bonum. Hill, rill, ones in company, billeted, less be proud of. Breast
high and bestride! Only for that these will not breathe upon
Norrônesen or Irenean the secrest of their soorcelossness. Quarry silex, Homfrie Noanswa! Undy gentian festyknees, Livia Noanswa? Wolkencap is on him, frowned; audiurient, he would
evesdrip, were it mous at hand, were it dinn of bottles in the far
ear. Murk, his vales are darkling. With lipth she lithpeth to him
all to time of thuch on thuch and thow on thow. She he she ho
she ha to la. Hairfluke, if he could bad twig her! Impalpabunt,
he abhears. The soundwaves are his buffeteers; they trompe him
with their trompes; the wave of roary and the wave of hooshed
and the wave of hawhawhawrd and the wave of neverheedthem-
horseluggarsandlistletomine. Landloughed by his neaghboormis-
tress and perpetrified in his offsprung, sabes and suckers, the
moaning pipers could tell him to his faceback, the louthly one
whose loab we are devorers of, how butt for his hold halibutt, or
her to her pudor puff, the lipalip one whose libe we drink at, how
biff for her tiddywink of a windfall, our breed and washer givers,
there would not be a holey spier on the town nor a vestal flout-
ing in the dock, nay to make plein avowels, nor a yew nor an eye

to play cash cash in Novo Nilbud by swamplight nor a' toole o'
tall o' toll and noddy hint to the convaynience.

He dug in and dug out by the skill of his tilth for himself and
all belonging to him and he sweated his crew beneath his auspice
for the living and he urned his dread, that dragon volant, and he
made louse for us and delivered us to boll weevils amain, that
mighty liberator, Unfru-Chikda-Uru-Wukru and begad he did,
our ancestor most worshipful, till he thought of a better one in
his windower's house with that blushmantle upon him from earsend to earsend. And would again could whispring grassies wake
him and may again when the fiery bird disembers. And will
again if so be sooth by elder to his youngers shall be said. Have
you whines for my wedding, did you bring bride and bedding,
will you whoop for my deading is a? Wake? *Usqueadbaugham!*

Anam muck an dhoul! Did ye drink me doornail?

Now be aisy, good Mr Finnimore, sir. And take your laysure
like a god on pension and don't be walking abroad. Sure you'd
only lose yourself in Healiopolis now the way your roads in
Kapelavaster are that winding there after the calvary, the North
Umbrian and the Fivs Barrow and Waddlings Raid and the
Bower Moore and wet your feet maybe with the foggy dew's
abroad. Meeting some sick old bankrupt or the Cottericks' donkey
with his shoe hanging, clankatachankata, or a slut snoring with an
impure infant on a bench. 'Twould turn you against life, so
'twould. And the weather's that mean too. To part from Devlin
is hard as Nugent knew, to leave the clean tanglesome one lushier
than its neighbour enfranchisable fields but let your ghost have
no grievance. You're better off, sir, where you are, primesigned
in the full of your dress, bloodeagle waistcoat and all, remembering your shapes and sizes on the pillow of your babycurls under
your sycamore by the keld water where the Tory's clay will scare
the varmints and have all you want, pouch, gloves, flask, bricket,
kerchief, ring and amberulla, the whole treasure of the pyre, in the
land of souls with Homin and Broin Baroke and pole ole Lonan
and Nobucketnozzler and the Guinnghis Khan. And we'll be
coming here, the ombre players, to rake your gravel and bringing

you presents, won't we, fenians? And it isn't our spittle we'll stint you of, is it, druids? Not shabbty little imagettes, pennydirts and dodgemyeyes you buy in the soottee stores. But offerings of the field. Mieliodories, that Doctor Faherty, the madison man, taught to gooden you. Poppypap's a passport out. And honey is the holiest thing ever was, hive, comb and earwax, the food for glory, (mind you keep the pot or your nectar cup may yield too light!) and some goat's milk, sir, like the maid used to bring you. Your fame is spreading like Basilico's ointment since the Fintan Lalors piped you overborder and there's whole households beyond the Bothnians and they calling names after you. The menhere's always talking of you sitting around on the pig's cheeks under the sacred rooftree, over the bowls of memory where every hollow holds a hallow, with a pledge till the drengs, in the Salmon House. And admiring to our supershillelagh where the palmsweat on high is the mark of your manument. All the toethpicks ever Eirenesians chewed on are chips chepped from that battery block. If you were bowed and soild and letdown itself from the oner of the load it was that paddyplanters might pack up plenty and when you were undone in every point fore the laps of goddesses you showed our labourlasses how to free was easy. The game old Gunne, they do be saying, (skull!) that was a planter for you, a spicer of them all. Begog but he was, the G.O.G! He's duddandgunne now and we're apter finding the sores of his sedeq but peace to his great limbs, the buddhoch, with the last league long rest of him, while the millioncandled eye of Tuskar sweeps the Moylean Main! There was never a warlord in Great Erinnes and Brettland, no, nor in all Pike County like you, they say. No, nor a king nor an ardking, bung king, sung king or hung king. That you could fell an elmstree twelve urchins couldn't ring round and hoist high the stone that Liam failed. Who but a Maccullaghmore the reise of our fortunes and the faunayman at the funeral to compass our cause? If you was hogglebully itself and most frifty like you was taken waters still what all where was your like to lay the cable or who was the batter could better Your Grace? Mick Mac Magnus MacCawley can take you off to the pure perfection and Leatherbags Reynolds tries your shuffle and cut. But as Hopkins and Hopkins puts it, you were the pale eggynaggy and a kis to tilly up. We calls him the journeyall Buggaloffs since he went Jerusalemfaring in Arssia Manor. You had a gamier cock than Pete, Jake or Martin and your archgoose of geese stubbled for All Angels' Day. So may the priest of seven worms and scalding tayboil, Papa Vestray, come never anear you as your hair grows wheater beside the Liffey that's in Heaven! Hep, hep, hurrah there! Hero! Seven times thereto we salute you! The whole bag of kits, falconplumes and jackboots incloted, is where you flung them that time. Your heart is in the system of the Shewolf and your crested head is in the tropic of Copricapron. Your feet are in the cloister of Virgo. Your olala is in the region of sahuls. And that's ashore as you were born. Your shuck tick's swell. And that there texas is tow linen. The loamsome roam to Laffayette is ended. Drop in your tracks, babe! Be not unrested! The headboddylwatcher of the chempel of Isid, Totumcalmum, saith: I know thee, metherjar, I know thee, salvation boat. For we have performed upon thee, thou abramanation, who comest ever without being invoked, whose coming is unknown, all the things which the company of the precentors and of the grammarians of Christpatrick's ordered concerning thee in the matter of the work of thy tombing. Howe of the shipmen, steep wall!

Everything's going on the same or so it appeals to all of us, in the old holmsted here. Coughings all over the sanctuary, bad scrant to me aunt Florenza. The horn for breakfast, one o'gong for lunch and dinnerchime. As popular as when Belly the First was keng and his members met in the Diet of Man. The same shop slop in the window. Jacob's lettercrackers and Dr. Tipple's Vi-Cocoa and the Eswuards' desippated soup beside Mother Seagull's syrup. Meat took a drop when Reilly-Parsons failed. Coal's short but we've plenty of bog in the yard. And barley's up again, begrained to it. The lads is attending school nessans regular, sir, spelling beesknees with hathatansy and turning out tables by mudapplication. Allfor the books and never pegging smashers after Tom Bowe Glassarse or Timmy the Tosser. 'Tisraely the truth! No isn't it, roman pathoricks? You were the doublejoynted janitor the morning they were delivered and you'll be a grandfer yet entirely when the ritehand seizes what the lovearm knows. Kevin's just a doat with his cherub cheek, chalking oghres on walls, and his little lamp and schoolbelt and bag of knicks, playing postman's knock round the diggings and if the seep were milk you could lieve his olde by his ide but, laus sake, the devil does be in that knirps of a Jerry sometimes, the tarandtan plaidboy, making encostive inkum out of the last of his lavings and writing a blue streak over his bourseday shirt. Hetty Jane's a child of Mary. She'll be coming (for they're sure to choose her) in her white of gold with a tourch of ivy to rekindle the flame on Felix Day. But Essie Shanahan has let down her skirts. You remember Essie in our Luna's Convent? They called her Holly Merry her lips were so ruddyberry and Pia de Purebelle when the redminers riots was on about her. Were I a clerk designate to the Williams-woodsmenufactors I'd poster those pouters on every jamb in the town. She's making her rep at Lanner's twicenightly. With the tabarine tamtammers of the whirligigmagees. Beats that cachucha flat. 'Twould dilate your heart to go.

Aisy now, you decent man, with your knees and lie quiet and repose your honour's lordship! Hold him here, Ezekiel Irons, and may God strengthen you! It's our warm spirits, boys, he's spooring. Dimitrius O'Flagonan, cork that cure for the Clancartys! You swamped enough since Portobello to float the Pomeroy. Fetch neahere, Pat Koy! And fetch nouyou, Pam Yates! Be nayther angst of Wramawitch! Here's lumbos. Where misties swaddlum, where misches lodge none, where mystries pour kind on, O sleepy! So be yet!

I've an eye on queer Behan and old Kate and the butter, trust me. She'll do no jugglywuggly with her war souvenir postcards to help to build me murial, tippers! I'll trip your traps! Assure a sure there! And we put on your clock again, sir, for you. Did or didn't we, sharestutterers? So you won't be up a stump entirely. Nor shed your remnants. The sternwheel's crawling strong. I

seen your missus in the hall. Like the queenoveire. Arrah, it's
herself that's fine, too, don't be talking! Shirksends? You storyan
Harry chap longa me Harry chap storyan grass woman plethy
good trout. Shakeshands. Dibble a hayfork's wrong with her only
her lex's salig. Boald Tib does be yawning and smirking cat's
hours on the Pollockses' woolly round tabouretcushion watching her sewing a dream together, the tailor's daughter, stitch to
her last. Or while waiting for winter to fire the enchantement,
decoying more nesters to fall down the flue. It's an allavalonche that
blows nopussy food. If you only were there to explain the meaning, best of men, and talk to her nice of guldenselver. The lips
would moisten once again. As when you drove with her to Fin-
drinny Fair. What with reins here and ribbons there all your
hands were employed so she never knew was she on land or at
sea or swooped through the blue like Airwinger's bride. She
was flirtsome then and she's fluttersome yet. She can second a
song and adores a scandal when the last post's gone by. Fond of
a concertina and pairs passing when she's had her forty winks
for supper after kanekannan and abbely dimpling and is in her
merlin chair assotted, reading her Evening World. To see is
it smarts, full lengths or swaggers. News, news, all the news.
Death, a leopard, kills fellah in Fez. Angry scenes at Stormount.
Stilla Star with her lucky in goingaways. Opportunity fair with
the China floods and we hear these rosy rumours. Ding Tams he
noise about all same Harry chap. She's seeking her way, a chickle
a chuckle, in and out of their serial story, *Les Loves of Selskar
et Pervenche*, freely adapted to *The Novvergin's Viv*. There'll
be bluebells blowing in salty sepulchres the night she signs her
final tear. Zee End. But that's a world of ways away. Till track
laws time. No silver ash or switches for that one! While flattering
candles flare. Anna Stacey's how are you! Worther waist in the
noblest, says Adams and Sons, the wouldpay actionneers. Her
hair's as brown as ever it was. And wivvy and wavy. Repose you
now! Finn no more!

For, be that samesake sibsubstitute of a hooky salmon, there's
already a big rody ram lad at random on the premises of his

haunt of the hungred bordles, as it is told me. Shop Illicit,
flourishing like a lord-major or a buaboabaybohm, litting flop
a deadlop (aloose!) to lee but lifting a bennbranch a yardalong
(ivoeh!) on the breezy side (for showm!), the height of Brewster's chimpney and as broad below as Phineas Barnum; humph-
ing his share of the showthers is senken on him he's such a
grandfallar, with a pocked wife in pickle that's a flyfire and three
lice nittle clinkers, two twilling bugs and one midgit pucelle.
And aither he cursed and recursed and was everseen doing what
your fourfootlers saw or he was never done seeing what you cool-
pigeons know, weep the clouds aboon for smiledown witnesses,
and that'll do now about the fairyhees and the frailyshees.
Though Eset fibble it to the zephiroth and Artsa zoom it round
her heavens for ever. Creator he has created for his creatured
ones a creation. White monothoid? Red theatrocrat? And all the
pinkprophets cohalething? Very much so! But however 'twas
'tis sure for one thing, what sherif Toragh voucherfors and
mapqiq makes put out, that the man, Humme the Cheapner,
Esc, overseen as we thought him, yet a worthy of the naym,
came at this timecoloured place where we live in our paroqial
fermament one tide on another, with a bumrush in a hull of a
wherry, the twin turbane dhow, *The Bey for Dybbling*, this
archipelago's first visiting schooner, with a wicklowpattern
waxenwench at her prow for a figurehead, the deadsea dugong
updipdripping from his depths, and has been repreaching himself like a fishmummer these siktyten years ever since, his shebi
by his shide, adi and aid, growing hoarish under his turban and
changing cane sugar into sethulose starch (Tuttut's cess to him!)
as also that, batin the bulkihood he bloats about when innebbi-
ated, our old offender was humile, commune and ensectuous
from his nature, which you may gauge after the bynames was
put under him, in lashons of languages, (honnein suit and
praisers be!) and, totalisating him, even hamissim of himashim
that he, sober serious, he is ee and no counter he who will be
ultimendly respunchable for the hubbub caused in Eden-
borough.

[2]

Now (to forebare for ever solitte of Iris Trees and Lili O'Rangans), concerning the genesis of Harold or Humphrey Chimpden's occupational agnomen (we are back in the presurnames prodromarith period, of course just when enos chalked halltraps) and discarding once for all those theories from older sources which would link him back with such pivotal ancestors as the Glues, the Gravys, the Northeasts, the Ankers and the Earwickers of Sidlesham in the Hundred of Manhood or proclaim him offsprout of vikings who had founded wapentake and seddled hem in Herrick or Eric, the best authenticated version, the Dumlat, read the Reading of Hofed-ben-Edar, has it that it was this way. We are told how in the beginning it came to pass that like cabbaging Cincinnatus the grand old gardener was saving daylight under his redwoodtree one sultry sabbath afternoon, Hag Chivychas Eve, in prefall paradise peace by following his plough for rootles in the rere garden of mobhouse, ye olde marine hotel when royalty was announced by runner to have been pleased to have halted itself on the highroad along which a leisureloving dogfox had cast followed, also at walking pace, by a lady pack of cocker spaniels. Forgetful of all save his vassal's plain fealty to the ethnarch Humphrey or Harold stayed not to yoke or saddle but stumbled out hotface as he was (his sweatful bandanna loose from his pocketcoat) hasting to the forecourts of his public in topee, surcingle, solascarf and plaid, plus fours, puttees and bulldog boots ruddled cinnibar with

flagrant marl, jingling his turnpike keys and bearing aloft amid
the fixed pikes of the hunting party a high perch atop of which a
flowerpot was fixed earthside hoist with care. On his majesty, who
was, or often feigned to be, noticeably longsighted from green
youth and had been meaning to inquire what, in effect, had caused
yon causeway to be thus potholed, asking substitutionally to be
put wise as to whether paternoster and silver doctors were not
now more fancied bait for lobstertrapping honest blunt Harom-
phreyld answered in no uncertain tones very similarly with a fear-
less forehead: Naw, yer maggers, aw war jist a cotchin on thon
bluggy earwuggers. Our sailor king, who was draining a gugglet
of obvious adamale, gift both and gorban, upon this, ceasing to
swallow, smiled most heartily beneath his walrus moustaches and
indulging that none too genial humour which William the Conk
on the spindle side had inherited with the hereditary whitelock
and some shortfingeredness from his greataunt Sophy, turned towards two of his retinue of gallowglasses, Michael, etheling lord
of Leix and Offaly and the jubilee mayor of Drogheda, Elcock,
(the two scatterguns being Michael M. Manning, protosyndic of
Waterford and an Italian excellency named Giubilei according to
a later version cited by the learned scholarch Canavan of Can-
makenoise), in either case a triptychal religious family symbolising
puritas of doctrina, business per usuals and the purchypatch of
hamlock where the paddish preties grow and remarked dilsydul-
sily: Holybones of Saint Hubert how our red brother of Pour-
ingrainia would audibly fume did he know that we have for sur-
trusty bailiwick a turnpiker who is by turns a pikebailer no sel-
domer than an earwigger! For he kinned Jom Pill with his court
so gray and his haunts in his house in the mourning. (One still
hears that pebble crusted laughta, japijap cheerycherrily, among
the roadside tree the lady Holmpatrick planted and still one feels
the amossive silence of the cladstone allegibelling: Ive mies outs
ide Bourn.) Comes the question are these the facts of his nom-
inigentilisation as recorded and accolated in both or either of the
collateral andrewpaulmurphyc narratives. Are those their fata
which we read in sibylline between the *fas* and its *nefas*? No dung

on the road. And shall Nohomiah be our place like? Yea, Mulachy
our Kingable khan? We shall perhaps not so soon see. Pinck
poncks that bail for seeks alicence where cumsceptres with scen-
taurs stay. Bear in mind, son of Hokmah, if so be you have me-
theg in your midness, this man is mountain and unto changeth
doth one ascend. Heave we aside the fallacy, as punical as finikin,
that it was not the king kingself but his inseparable sisters, uncontrollable nighttalkers, Skertsiraizde with Donyahzade, who
afterwards, when the robberers shot up the socialights came down
into the world as amusers and were staged by Madame Sudlow
as Rosa and Lily Miskinguette in the pantalime that two pitts
paythronosed, Miliodorus and Galathee. The great fact emerges
that after that historic date all holographs so far exhumed initialled by Haromphrey bear the sigla H.C.E. and while he was
only and long and always good Dook Umphrey for the hunger-
lean spalpeens of Lucalizod and Chimbers to his cronies it was
equally certainly a pleasant turn of the populace which gave him
as sense of those normative letters the nickname Here Comes
Everybody. An imposing everybody he always indeed looked,
constantly the same as and equal to himself and magnificently well
worthy of any and all such universalisation, every time he continually surveyed, amid vociferatings from in front of *Accept these
few nutties!* and *Take off that white hat!*, relieved with *Stop his Grog*
and *Put It in the Log* and *Loots in his* (bassvoco) *Boots*, from good
start to happy finish the truly catholic assemblage gathered together
in that king's treat house of satin alustrelike above floats and footlights from their assbawlveldts and oxgangs unanimously to clap-
plaud (the inspiration of his lifetime and the hits of their careers)
Mr. Wallenstein Washington Semperkelly's immergreen tourers
in a command performance by special request with the courteous
permission for pious purposes the homedromed and enliventh
performance of problem passion play of the millentury, running
strong since creation, *A Royal Divorce*, then near the approach
towards the summit of its climax, with ambitious interval band
selections from *The Bo' Girl* and *The Lily* on all horserie show
command nights from his viceregal booth (his bossaloner is ceil-

inged there a cuckoospit less eminent than the redritualhoods of Maccabe and Cullen) where, a veritable Napoleon the Nth, our worldstage's practical jokepiece and retired cecelticocommediant in his own wise this folksforefather all of the time sat having the entirety of his house about him, with the invariable broadstretched kerchief cooling his whole neck, nape and shoulderblades and in a wardrobe panelled tuxedo completely thrown back from a shirt well entitled a swallowall, on every point far outstarching the laundered clawhammers and marbletopped highboys of the pit stalls and early amphitheatre. The piece was this: look at the lamps. The cast was thus: see under the clock. Ladies circle: cloaks may be left. Pit, prommer and parterre, standing room only. Habituels conspicuously emergent.

A baser meaning has been read into these characters the literal sense of which decency can safely scarcely hint. It has been blurtingly bruited by certain wisecrackers (the stinks of Mohorat are in the nightplots of the morning), that he suffered from a vile disease. Athma, unmanner them! To such a suggestion the one selfrespecting answer is to affirm that there are certain statements which ought not to be, and one should like to hope to be able to add, ought not to be allowed to be made. Nor have his detractors, who, an imperfectly warmblooded race, apparently conceive him as a great white caterpillar capable of any and every enormity in the calendar recorded to the discredit of the Juke and Kellikek families, mended their case by insinuating that, alternately, he lay at one time under the ludicrous imputation of annoying Welsh fusiliers in the people's park. Hay, hay, hay! Hoq, hoq, hoq! Faun and Flora on the lea love that little old joq. To anyone who knew and loved the christlikeness of the big cleanminded giant H. C. Earwicker throughout his excellency long vicefreegal existence the mere suggestion of him as a lustsleuth nosing for trouble in a boobytrap rings particularly preposterous. Truth, beard on prophet, compels one to add that there is said to have been quondam (pfuit! pfuit!) some case of the kind implicating, it is interdum believed, a quidam (if he did not exist it would be necessary quoniam to invent him) abhout that time stambuling ha-

round Dumbaling in leaky sneakers with his tarrk record who
has remained topantically anonymos but (let us hue him Abdul-
lah Gamellaxarksky) was, it is stated, posted at Mallon's at the
instance of watch warriors of the vigilance committee and years
afterwards, cries one even greater, Ibid, a commender of the
frightful, seemingly, unto such as were sulhan sated, tropped head
(pfiat! pfiat!) waiting his first of the month froods turn for
thatt chopp pah kabbakks alicubi on the old house for the charge-
hard, Roche Haddocks off Hawkins Street. Lowe, you blondy
liar, Gob scene you in the narked place and she what's edith ar
home defileth these boyles! There's a cabful of bash indeed in
the homeur of that meal. Slander, let it lie its flattest, has never
been able to convict our good and great and no ordinary Southron
Earwicker, that homogenius man, as pious author called him, of
any graver impropriety than that, advanced by some woodwards
or regarders, who did not dare deny, the shomers, that they had,
chin Ted, chin Tam, chinchin Taffyd, that day consumed their
soul of the corn, of having behaved with ongentilmensky im-
modus opposite a pair of dainty maidservants in the swoolth of
the rushy hollow whither, or so the two gown and pinners pleaded, dame nature in all innocency had spontaneously and about the
same hour of the eventide sent them both but whose published
combinations of silkinlaine testimonies are, where not dubiously
pure, visibly divergent, as wapt from wept, on minor points touching the intimate nature of this, a first offence in vert or venison
posture with such attenuating circumstances (garthen gaddeth green
hwere sokeman brideth girling) as an abnormal Saint Swithin's
summer and, (Jesses Rosasharon!) a ripe occasion to provoke it.
which was admittedly an incautious but, at its wildest, a partial ex-
   We can't do without them. Wives, rush to the restyours! Of-
man will toman while led is the lol. Zessid's our kadem, villa-
pleach, vollapluck. Fikup, for flesh nelly, el mundo nov, zole flen!
If she's a lilyth, pull early! Pauline, allow! And malers abushed,
keep black, keep black! Guiltless of much laid to him he was
clearly for once at least he clearly expressed himself as being with
still a trace of his erstwhile burr and hence it has been received of

us that it is true. They tell the story (an amalgam as absorbing as calzium chloereydes and hydrophobe sponges could make it) how one happygogusty ides-of-April morning (the anniversary as it fell out of his first assumption of his mirthday suit and rights in appurtenance to the confusioning of human races) ages and ages after the alleged misdemeanour when the tried friend of all creation, tigerwood roadstaff to his stay, was billowing across the wide expanse of our greatest park in his caoutchouc kepi and great belt and hideinsacks and his blaufunx fustian and ironsides jackboots and Bhagafat gaiters and his rubberised inverness, he met a cad with a pipe. The latter, the luciferant not the oriuolate (who, the odds are, is still berting dagabout in the same straw bamer, carryin his overgoat under his schulder, sheepside out, so as to look more like a coumfry gentleman and signing the pledge as gaily as you please) hardily accosted him with: Guinness thaw tool in jew me dinner ouzel fin? (a nice how-do-you-do in Poolblack at the time as some of our olddaisers may still tremblingly recall) to ask could he tell him how much a clock it was that the clock struck had he any idea by cock's luck as his watch was bradys. Hesitency was clearly to be evitated. Execration as cleverly to be honnisoid. The Earwicker of that spurring instant, realising on fundamental liberal principles the supreme importance, nexally and noxally, of physical life (the nearest help relay being pingping K. O. Sempatrick's Day and the fenian rising) and unwishful as he felt of being hurled into eternity right then, plugged by a soft-nosed bullet from the sap, halted, quick on the draw, and replyin that he was feelin tipstaff, cue, prodooced from his gunpocket his Jurgensen's shrapnel waterbury, ours by communionism, his by usucapture, but, on the same stroke, hearing above the skirling of harsh Mother East old Fox Goodman, the bellmaster, over the wastes to south, at work upon the ten ton tonuant thunderous tenor toller in the speckled church (Couhounin's call!) told the inquiring kidder, by Jehova, it was twelve of em sidereal and tankard time, adding, buttall, as he bended deeply with smoked sardinish breath to give more pondus to the copperstick he presented, (though this seems in some cumfusium with the chap-

stuck ginger which, as being of sours, acids, salts, sweets and
bitters compompounded, we know him to have used as chaw-
chaw for bone, muscle, blood, flesh and vimvital,) that whereas the hakusay accusation againstm had been made, what was
known in high quarters as was stood stated in Morganspost, by
a creature in youman form who was quite beneath parr and several degrees lower than yore triplehydrad snake. In greater support of his word (it, quaint anticipation of a famous phrase, has
been reconstricted out of oral style into the verbal for all time
with ritual rhythmics, in quiritary quietude, and toosammen-
stucked from successive accounts by Noah Webster in the re-
daction known as the Sayings Attributive of H. C. Earwicker,
prize on schillings, postlots free), the flaxen Gygas tapped his
chronometrum drumdrum and, now standing full erect, above
the ambijacent floodplain, scene of its happening, with one Ber-
lin gauntlet chopstuck in the hough of his ellboge (by ancientest
signlore his gesture meaning: ⅁!) pointed at an angle of thirtytwo degrees towards his *duc de Fer's* overgrown milestone as
fellow to his gage and after a rendypresent pause averred with
solemn emotion's fire: Shsh shake, co-comeraid! Me only, them
five ones, he is equal combat. I have won straight. Hence my
nonation wide hotel and creamery establishments which for the
honours of our mewmew mutual daughters, credit me, I am woowoo willing to take my stand, sir, upon the monument, that sign
of our ruru redemption, any hygienic day to this hour and to
make my hoath to my sinnfinners, even if I get life for it, upon
the Open Bible and before the Great Taskmaster's (I lift my hat!)
and in the presence of the Deity Itself andwell of Bishop and
Mrs. Michan of High Church of England as of all such of said
my immediate withdwellers and of every living sohole in every
corner wheresoever of this globe in general which useth of my
British to my backbone tongue and commutative justice that
there is not one tittle of truth, allow me to tell you, in that purest
of fibfib fabrications.

Gaping Gill, swift to mate errthors, stern to checkself, (diag-
nosing through eustacetube that it was to make with a markedly

postpuberal hypertituitary type of Heidelberg mannleich cavern
ethics) lufted his slopingforward, bad Sweatagore good murrough and dublnotch on to it as he was greedly obliged, and
like a sensible ham, with infinite tact in the delicate situation seen
the touchy nature of its perilous theme, thanked um for guilders
received and time of day (not a little token abock allthe same that
that was owl the God's clock it was) and, upon humble duty to
greet his Tyskminister and he shall gildthegap Gaper and thee
his a mouldy voids, went about his business, whoever it was,
saluting corpses, as a metter of corse (one could hound him out
had one hart to for the monticules of scalp and dandruff droppings blaze his trail) accompanied by his trusty snorler and his
permanent reflection verbigracious; I have met with you, bird,
too late, or if not, too worm and early: and with tag for ildiot
in his secondmouth language as many of the bigtimer's verbaten
words which he could balbly call to memory that same kveldeve,
ere the hour of the twattering of bards in the twitterlitter between
Druidia and the Deepsleep Sea, when suppertide and souvenir to
Charlatan Mall jointly kem gently and along the quiet darkenings
of Grand and Royal, ff, flitmansfluh, and, kk, 't crept i' hedge
whenas to many a softongue's pawkytalk mude unswer u sufter
poghyogh, Arvanda always aquiassent, while, studying castelles
in the blowne and studding cowshots over the noran, he spat in
careful convertedness a musaic dispensation about his *hearthstone*,
if you please, (Irish saliva, *mawshe dho hole*, but would a respectable prominently connected fellow of Iro-European ascendances
with welldressed ideas who knew the correct thing such as Mr.
Shallwesigh or Mr. Shallwelaugh expectorate after such a callous
fashion, no thank yous! when he had his belcher *spuckertuck* in his
pucket, pthuck?) musefed with his thockits after having supped
of the dish sot and pottage which he snobbishly dabbed Peach
Bombay (it is rawly only Lukanpukan pilzenpie which she knows
which senaffed and pibered him), a supreme of excelling peas,
balled under minnshogue's milk into whitemalt winesour, a pro-
viant the littlebilker hoarsely relished, chaff it, in the snevel season,
being as fain o't as your rat wi'fennel; and on this celebrating

occasion of the happy escape, for a crowning of pot valiance, this regional platter, benjamin of bouillis, with a spolish olive to middlepoint its zaynith, was marrying itself (porkograso!) erebusqued very deluxiously with a bottle of Phenice-Bruerie '98, followed for second nuptials by a Piessporter, Grand Cur, of both of which cherished tablelights (though humble the bounquet 'tis a leaman's farewell) he obdurately sniffed the cobwebcrusted corks.

Our cad's bit of strife (knee Bareniece Maxwelton) with a quick ear for spittoons (as the aftertale hath it) glaned up as usual with dumbestic husbandry (no persicks and armelians for thee, Pomeranzia!) but, slipping the clav in her claw, broke of the matter among a hundred and eleven others in her usual curtsey (how faint these first vhespers womanly are, a secret pispigliando, amad the lavurdy den of their manfolker!) the next night nudge one as was Hegesippus over a hup a ' chee, her eys dry and small and speech thicklish because he appeared a funny colour like he couldn't stood they old hens no longer, to her particular reverend, the director, whom she had been meaning in her mind primarily to speak with (hosch, intra! jist a timblespoon!) trusting, between cuppled lips and annie lawrie promises (mighshe never have Esnekerry pudden come Hunanov for her pecklapitschens!) that the gossiple so delivered in his epistolear, buried teatoastally in their Irish stew would go no further than his jesuit's cloth, yet (in vinars venitas! volatiles valetotum!) it was this overspoiled priest Mr. Browne, disguised as a vincentian, who, when seized of the facts, was overheard, in his secondary personality as a Nolan and underreared, poul soul, by accident—if, that is, the incident it was an accident for here the ruah of Ecclectiastes of Hippo outpuffs the writress of Havvah-ban-Annah—to pianissime a slightly varied version of Crookedribs confidentials, (what Mère Aloyse said but for Jesuphine's sake!) hands between hahands, in fealty sworn (my bravor best! my fraur!) and, to the strains of *The Secret of Her Birth,* hushly pierce the rubiend aurellum of one Philly Thurnston, a layteacher of rural science and orthophonethics of a nearstout figure and about the middle

of his forties during a priestly flutter for safe and sane bets at the
hippic runfields of breezy Baldoyle on a date (W. W. goes
through the card) easily capable of rememberance by all pickers-
up of events national and Dublin details, the doubles of Perkin
and Paullock, peer and prole, when the classic Encourage Hackney
Plate was captured by two noses in a stablecloth finish ek and nek,
some and none, evelo nevelo, from the cream colt Bold Boy
Cromwell after a clever getaway by Captain Chaplain Blount's
roe hinny Saint Dalough, Drummer Coxon, nondepict third, at
breakneck odds, thanks to you great little, bonny little, portey
little, Winny Widger! you're all their nappies! who in his never-
rip mud and purpular cap was surely leagues unlike any other
phantomweight that ever toppitt our timber maggies.

  'Twas two pisononse Timcoves (the wetter is pest, the renns are
overt and come and the voax of the turfur is hurled on our lande)
of the name of Treacle Tom as was just out of pop following the
theft of a leg of Kehoe, Donnelly and Packenham's Finnish pork
and his own blood and milk brother Frisky Shorty, (he was, to be
exquisitely punctilious about them, both shorty and frisky) a tip-
ster, come off the hulks, both of them awful poor, what was out
on the bumaround for an oofbird game for a jimmy o'goblin or
a small thick un as chanced, while the Seaforths was making the
colleenbawl, to ear the passon in the motor clobber make use of
his law language (Edzo, Edzo on), touchin the case of Mr. Adams
what was in all the sundays about it which he was rubbing noses
with and having a gurgle off his own along of the butty bloke in
the specs.

  This Treacle Tom to whom reference has been made had
been absent from his usual wild and woolly haunts in the land
of counties capalleens for some time previous to that (he was, in
fact, in the habit of frequenting common lodginghouses where
he slept in a nude state, hailfellow with meth, in strange men's
cots) but on racenight, blotto after divers tots of hell fire, red
biddy, bull dog, blue ruin and creeping jenny, Eglandine's choicest herbage, supplied by the Duck and Doggies, the Galop-
ping Primrose, Brigid Brewster's, the Cock, the Postboy's Horn,

the Little Old Man's and All Swell That Aimswell, the Cup and
the Stirrup, he sought his wellwarmed leababobed in a hous-
ingroom Abide With Oneanother at Block W.W., (why didn't
he back it?) Pump Court, The Liberties, and, what with
moltapuke on voltapuke, resnored alcoh alcoho alcoherently to
the burden of *I come, my horse delayed,* nom num, the substance of the tale of the evangelical bussybozzy and the rusinur-
bean (the 'girls' he would keep calling them for the collarette
and skirt, the sunbonnet and carnation) in parts (it seemed he
was before the eyots of martas or otherwales the thirds of fossil-
years, he having beham with katya when lavinias had her mens
lease to sea in a psumpship doodly show whereat he was looking
for fight niggers with whilde roarses) oft in the chilly night (the
metagonistic! the epickthalamorous!) during uneasy slumber in
their hearings of a small and stonybroke cashdraper's executive,
Peter Cloran (discharged), O'Mara, an exprivate secretary of no
fixed abode (locally known as Mildew Lisa), who had passed
several nights, funnish enough, in a doorway under the blankets
of homelessness on the bunk of iceland, pillowed upon the stone
of destiny colder than man's knee or woman's breast, and
Hosty, (no slouch of a name), an illstarred beachbusker, who,
sans rootie and sans scrapie, suspicioning as how he was setting
on a twoodstool on the verge of selfabyss, most starved, with
melancholia over everything in general, (night birman, you served
him with natigal's nano!) had been towhead tossing on his shake-
down, devising ways and manners of means, of what he loved
to ifidalicence somehow or other in the nation getting a hold of
some chap's parabellum in the hope of taking a wing sociable
and lighting upon a sidewheel dive somewhere off the Dullkey
Downlairy and Bleakrooky tramline where he could throw true
and go and blow the sibicidal napper off himself for two bits to
boldywell baltitude in the peace and quitybus of a one sure shot
bottle, he after having being trying all he knew with the lady's
help of Madam Gristle for upwards of eighteen calanders to get
out of Sir Patrick Dun's, through Sir Humphrey Jervis's and
into the Saint Kevin's bed in the Adelaide's hosspittles (from

these incurable welleslays among those uncarable wellasdays
through Sant Iago by his cocklehat, good Lazar, deliver us!)
without after having been able to jerrywangle it anysides. Lisa
O'Deavis and Roche Mongan (who had so much incommon,
epipsychidically; if the phrase be permitted *hostis et odor insuper
petroperfractus*) as an understood thing slept their sleep of the
swimborne in the one sweet undulant mother of tumblerbunks
with Hosry just how the shavers in the shaw the yokels in the
yoats or, well, the wasters in the wilde, and the bustling tweeny-
dawn-of-all-works (meed of anthems here we pant!) had not been
many jiffies furbishing potlids, doorbrasses, scholars' applecheeks
and linkboy's metals when, ashhopperminded like no fella he go
make bakenbeggfuss longa white man, the rejuvenated busker (for
after a goodnight's rave and rumble and a shinkhams topmorning
with his coexes he was not the same man) and his broadawake
bedroom suite (our boys, as our Byron called them) were up
and ashuffle from the hogshome they lovenamed The Barrel, cross
Ebblinn's chilled hamlet (thrie routes and restings on their then
superficies curiously correspondantwith those linea and puncta
where our tubenny habenny metro maniplumbs below the ober-
flake underrails and stations at this time of riding) to the thrum-
mings of a crewth fiddle which, cremoaning and cronauning, levey
grevey, witty and wevey, appy, leppy and playable, caressed the
ears of the subjects of King Saint Finnerty the Festive who, in
brick homes of their own and in their flavory fraiseberry beds,
heeding hardly cry of honeyman, soed lavender or foyneboyne
salmon alive, with their priggish mouths all open for the larger
appraisiation of this longawaited Messiagh of roaratorios, were
only halfpast atsweeeep and after a brisk pause at a pawnbroking
establishment for the prothetic purpose of redeeming the songster's truly admirable false teeth and a prolonged visit to a house
of call at Cujas Place, fizz, the Old Sots' Hole in the parish of
Saint Cecily within the liberty of Ceolmore not a thousand or one
national leagues, that was, by Griffith's valuation, from the site
of the statue of Primewer Glasstone setting a match to the march
of a maker (last of the stewards peut-être), where, the tale rambles

along, the trio of whackfolthediddlers was joined by a further—
intentions—apply—tomorrow casual and a decent sort of the
hadbeen variety who had just been touching the weekly insult,
phewit, and all figblabbers (who saith of noun?) had stimulants
in the shape of gee and gees stood by the damn decent sort after
which stag luncheon and a few ones more just to celebrate yesterday, flushed with their firestufffortered friendship, the rascals came
out of the licensed premises, (Browne's first, the small p.s. ex-ex-
executive capahand in their sad rear like a lady's postscript: I want
money. Pleasend), wiping their laughleaking lipes on their sleeves,
how the bouckaleens shout their roscan generally (seinn fion,
seinn fion's araun.) and the rhymers' world was with reason the
richer for a wouldbe ballad, to the balledder of which the world
of cumannity singing owes a tribute for having placed on the
planet's melomap his lay of the vilest bogeyer but most attrac-
tionable avatar the world has ever had to explain for.

This, more krectly lubeen or fellow — me — lieder was first
poured forth where Riau Liviau riots and col de Houdo humps,
under the shadow of the monument of the shouldhavebeen legis-
lator (Eleutheriodendron! Spare, woodmann, spare!) to an overflow meeting of all the nations in Lenster fullyfilling the visional
area and, as a singleminded supercrowd, easily representative,
what with masks, whet with faces, of all sections and cross sections
(wineshop and cocoahouse poured out to brim up the broaching)
of our liffeyside people (to omit to mention of the mainland mino-
rity and such as had wayfared *via* Watling, Ernin, Icknild and
Stane, in chief a halted cockney car with its quotal of Hardmuth's
hacks, a northern tory, a southern whig, an eastanglian chroni-
cler and a landwester guardian) ranging from slips of young
dublinos from Cutpurse Row having nothing better to do than
walk about with their hands in their kneepants, sucking air-
whackers, weedulicet, jumbobricks, side by side with truant
officers, three woollen balls and poplin in search of a croust of
pawn to busy professional gentlemen, a brace of palesmen with
dundrearies, nooning toward Daly's, fresh from snipehitting and
mallardmissing on Rutland heath, exchanging cold sneers, mass-

going ladies from Hume Street in their chairs, the bearers baited, some wandering hamalags out of the adjacent cloverfields of Mosse's Gardens, an oblate father from Skinner's Alley, brick-layers, a fleming, in tabinet fumant, with spouse and dog, an aged hammersmith who had some chisellers by the hand, a bout of cudgel players, not a few sheep with the braxy, two bluecoat scholars, four broke gents out of Simpson's on the Rocks, a portly and a pert still tassing Turkey Coffee and orange shrub in tickeyes door, Peter Pim and Paul Fry and then Elliot and, O, Atkinson, suffering hell's delights from the blains of their annui-tants' acorns not forgetting a deuce of dianas ridy for the hunt, a particularist prebendary pondering on the roman easter, the ton-sure question and greek uniates, plunk em, a lace lappet head or two or three or four from a window, and so on down to a few good old souls, who as they were juiced after taking their pledge over at the uncle's place, were evidently under the spell of liquor, from the wake of Tarry the Tailor a fair girl, a jolly postoboy thinking off three flagons and one, a plumodrole, a half sir from the weaver's almshouse who clings and clings and chatchatchat clings to her, a wholedam's cloudhued pittycoat, as child, as curiolater, as Caoch O'Leary. The wararrow went round, so it did, (a nation wants a gaze) and the ballad, in the felibrine trancoped metre affectioned by Taiocebo in his *Casudas de Poulichinello Artahut*, stump-stampaded on to a slip of blancovide and headed by an excessively rough and red woodcut, privately printed at the rimepress of Delville, soon fluttered its secret on white highway and brown byway to the rose of the winds and the blew of the gaels, from archway to lattice and from black hand to pink ear, village crying to village, through the five pussyfours green of the united states of Scotia Picta—and he who denays it, may his hairs be rubbed in dirt! To the added strains (so peacifold) of his majesty the flute, that onecrooned king of inscrewments, Piggott's purest, *ciello alsoliuto*, which Mr. Delaney (Mr. Delacey?), horn, anticipating a perfect downpour of plaudits among the rapsods, piped out of his decentsoort hat, looking still more like his purseyful namesake as men of Gaul noted, but before of to sputabout, the

snowycrested curl amoist the leader's wild and moulting hair,
'Ductor' Hitchcock hoisted his fezzy fuzz at bludgeon's height
signum to his companions of the chalice for the Loud Fellow,
boys' and *silentium in curia!* (our maypole once more where he rose
of old) and the canto was chantied there chorussed and christened
where by the old tollgate, Saint Annona's Street and Church.

And around the lawn the rann it rann and this is the rann that
Hosty made. Spoken. Boyles and Cahills, Skerretts and Pritchards,
viersified and piersified may the treeth we tale of live in stoney.
Here line the refrains of. Some vote him Vike, some mote him
Mike, some dub him Llyn and Phin while others hail him Lug
Bug Dan Lop, Lex, Lax, Gunne or Guinn. Some apt him Arth,
some bapt him Barth, Coll, Noll, Soll, Will, Weel, Wall but I
parse him Persse O'Reilly else he's called no name at all. Together. Arrah, leave it to Hosty, frosty Hosty, leave it to Hosty
for he's the mann to rhyme the rann, the rann, the rann, the king
of all ranns. Have you here? (Some ha) Have we where? (Some
hant) Have you hered? (Others do) Have we whered? (Others dont)
It's cumming, it's brumming! The clip, the clop! (All cla) Glass
crash. The (klikkaklakkaklaskaklopatzklatschabattacreppycrotty-
graddaghsemmihsammihnouithappluddyappladdypkonpkot!).

$$\begin{cases} \textit{Ardite, arditi!} \\ \text{Music cue.} \end{cases}$$

"The Ballad of Persse O'Reilly."

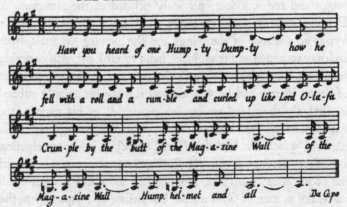

Have you heard of one Hump-ty Dump-ty how he

fell with a roll and a rum-ble and curled up like Lord O-la-fa

Crum-ple by the butt of the Mag-a-zine Wall of the

Mag-a-zine Wall Hump. hel-met and all Da Capo

Have you heard of one Humpty Dumpty
How he fell with a roll and a rumble
And curled up like Lord Olofa Crumple
By the butt of the Magazine Wall,
     (Chorus) Of the Magazine Wall,
              Hump, helmet and all?

He was one time our King of the Castle
Now he's kicked about like a rotten old parsnip.
And from Green street he'll be sent by order of His Worship
To the penal jail of Mountjoy
     (Chorus) To the jail of Mountjoy!
              Jail him and joy.

He was fafafather of all schemes for to bother us
Slow coaches and immaculate contraceptives for the populace,
Mare's milk for the sick, seven dry Sundays a week,
Openair love and religion's reform,
     (Chorus) And religious reform,
              Hideous in form.

Arrah, why, says you, couldn't he manage it?
I'll go bail, my fine dairyman darling,
Like the bumping bull of the Cassidys
All your butter is in your horns.
     (Chorus) His butter is in his horns.
              Butter his horns!

(Repeat) Hurrah there, Hosty, frosty Hosty, change that shirt
                                       [on ye,
Rhyme the rann, the king of all ranns!

                 Balbaccio, balbuccio!
We had chaw chaw chops, chairs, chewing gum, the chicken-
                                 [pox and china chambers
Universally provided by this soffsoaping salesman.

Small wonder He'll Cheat E'erawan our local lads nicknamed him
When Chimpden first took the floor
> (Chorus) With his bucketshop store
> > Down Bargainweg, Lower.

So snug he was in his hotel premises sumptuous
But soon we'll bonfire all his trash, tricks and trumpery
And'tis short till sheriff Clancy'll be winding up his unlimited
[company
With the bailiff's bom at the door,
> (Chorus) Bimbam at the door.
> > Then he'll bum no more.

Sweet bad luck on the waves washed to our island
The hooker of that hammerfast viking
And Gall's curse on the day when Eblana bay
Saw his black and tan man-o'-war.
> (Chorus) Saw his man-o'-war.
> > On the harbour bar.

Where from? roars Poolbeg. Cookingha'pence, he bawls Donnez-
[moi scampitle, wick an wipin'fampiny
Fingal Mac Oscar Onesine Bargearse Boniface
Thok's min gammelhole Norveegickers moniker
Og as ay are at gammelhore Norveegickers cod.
> (Chorus) A Norwegian camel old cod.
> > He is, begod.

Lift it, Hosty, lift it, ye devil ye! up with the rann, the rhyming
[rann!

It was during some fresh water garden pumping
Or, according to the *Nursing Mirror*, while admiring the mon-
[keys
That our heavyweight heathen Humpharey
Made bold a maid to woo
> (Chorus) Woohoo, what'll she doo!
> > The general lost her maidenloo!

He ought to blush for himself, the old hayheaded philosopher
For to go and shove himself that way on top of her
Begob, he's the crux of the catalogue
Of our antediluvial zoo,
    (Chorus) Messrs. Billing and Coo.
           Noah's larks, good as noo.

He was joulting by Wellinton's monument
Our rotorious hippopopotamuns
When some bugger let down the backtrap of the omnibus
And he caught his death of fusiliers,
    (Chorus) With his rent in his rears.
           Give him six years.

'Tis sore pity for his innocent poor children
But look out for his missus legitimate!
When that frew gets a grip of old Earwicker
Won't there be earwigs on the green?
    (Chorus) Big earwigs on the green,
           The largest ever you seen.

    Suffoclose! Shikespower! Seudodanto! Anonymoses!

Then we'll have a free trade Gaels' band and mass meeting
For to sod the brave son of Scandiknavery.
And we'll bury him down in Oxmanstown
Along with the devil and Danes,
    (Chorus) With the deaf and dumb Danes,
           And all their remains.

And not all the king's men nor his horses
Will resurrect his corpus
For there's no true spell in Connacht or hell
    (bis) That's able to raise a Cain.

Chest Cee! 'Sdense! Corpo di barragio! you spoof of visibility in a freakfog, of mixed sex cases among goats, hill cat and plain mousey, Bigamy Bob and his old Shanvocht! The Blackfriars treacle plaster outrage be liddled! Therewith was released in that kingsrick of Ḥumidia a poisoning volume of cloud barrage indeed. Yet all they who heard or redelivered are now with that family of bards and Vergobretas himself and the crowd of Caraculacticors as much no more as be they not yet now or had they then not-ever been. Canbe in some future we shall presently here amid those zouave players of Inkermann the mime mumming the mick and his nick miming their maggies, Hilton St Just (Mr. Frank Smith), Ivanne Ste Austelle (Mr. J. F. Jones), Coleman of Lucan taking four parts, a choir of the O'Daley O'Doyles doublesixing the chorus in *Fenn Mac Call and the Serven Feeries of Loch Neach*, *Galloper Troppler and Hurleyquinn* the zitherer of the past with his merrymen all, zimzim, zimzim. Of the persins sin this Eyrawygg-gla saga (which, thorough readable to int from and, is from tubb to buttom all falsetissues, antilibellous and nonactionable and this applies to its whole wholume) of poor Osti-Fosti described as quite a musical genius in a small way and the owner of an exceedingly niced ear, with tenorist voice to match, not alone, but a very major poet of the poorly meritary order (he began Tuonisonian but worked his passage up as far as the we-all-hang-together Animandovites) no one end is known. If they

whistled him before he had curtains up they are whistling him
still after his curtain's doom's doom. *Ei fui* His husband, poor old
A'Hara (Okaroff?) crestfallen by things and down at heels at the
time, they squeak, accepted the (Zassnoch!) ardree's shilling at
the conclusion of the Crimean war and, having flown his wild
geese, alohned in crowds to warnder on like Shuley Luney,
enlisted in Tyrone's horse, the Irish whites, and soldiered a bit
with Wolsey under the assumed name of Blanco Fusilovna Buck-
lovitch (spurious) after which the cawer and the marble halls
of Pump Court Columbarium, the home of the old seakings,
looked upon each other and queth their haven evermore for it
transpires that on the other side of the water it came about that on
the field of Vasileff's Cornix inauspiciously with his unit he
perished, suying, this papal leafless to old chap give, rawl chaw-
clates for mouther-in-louth. *Booil*. Poor old dear Paul Horan,
to satisfy his literary as well as his criminal aspirations, at the
suggestion thrown out by the doomster in loquacity lunacy, so
says the Dublin Intelligence, was thrown into a Ridley's for
inmates in the northern counties. Under the name of Orani he
may have been the utility man of the troupe capable of sustain-
ing long parts at short notice. He was. Sordid Sam, a dour decent
deblancer, the unwashed, haunted always by his ham, the unwished,
at a word from Israfel the Summoner, passed away painlessly
after life's upsomdowns one hallowe'en night, ebbrous and in
the state of nature, propelled from Behind into the great Beyond
by footblows coulinclouted upon his oyster and atlas on behanged
and behooved and behicked and behulked of his last fishandblood
bedscrappers, a Northwegian and his mate of the Sheawolving
class. Though the last straw glimt his baring this stage thunkhard
is said (the pitfallen gagged him as 'Promptboxer') to have
solemnly said — as had the brief thot but fell in till his head like
a bass dropt neck fust in till a bung crate (cogged!): Me drames,
O'Loughlins, has come through! Now let the centuple celves of
my egourge as Micholas de Cusack calls them, — of all of whose
I in my hereinafter of course by recourse demission me — by
the coincidance of their contraries reamalgamerge in that indentity

of undiscernibles where the Baxters and the Fleshmans may they cease to bidivil uns and (but at this poingt though the iron thrust of his cockspurt start might have prepared us we are well-nigh stinkpotthered by the mustardpunge in the tailend) this outandin brown candlestock melt Nolan's into peese! *Han var.* Disliken as he was to druriodrama, her wife Langley, the prophet, and the decentest dozendest short of a frusker whoever stuck his spickle through his spoke, disappeared, (in which toodooing he has taken all the French leaves unveilable out of Calomne-quiller's Pravities) from the sourface of this earth, that austral plain he had transmaried himself to, so entirely spoorlessly (the mother of the book with a dustwhisk tabularasing his obliteration done upon her involucrum) as to tickle the speculative to all but opine (since the Levey who might have been Langley may have really been a redivivus of paganinism or a volunteer Vousden) that the hobo (who possessed a large amount of the humoresque) had transtuled his funster's latitat to its finsterest interrimost. *Bhi she.* Again, if Father San Browne, tea and toaster to that quaint-esttest of yarnspinners is Padre Don Bruno, tren and troster to the queen of Iar-Spain, was the reverend, the sodality director, that eupeptic viceflayer, a barefaced carmelite to whose palpi-tating pulpit (which of us but remembers the rarevalent and hornerable Fratomistor Nawlanmore and Brawne.) sinning society sirens (see the [Roman Catholic] presspassim) fortunately became so enthusiastically attached and was an objectionable ass who very occasionally cockaded a raffles ticket on his hat which he wore all to one side like the hangle of his pan (if Her Elegance saw him she'd have the canary!) and was semiprivately convicted of mal-practices with his hotwashed tableknife (glossing over the cark in his pocket) that same snob of the dunhill, fully several year-schaums riper, encountered by the General on that redletter morning or maynoon jovesday and were they? *Fuitfuit.*

When Phishlin Phil wants throws his lip 'tis pholly to be fortune flonting and whoever's gone to mix Hotel by the salt say water there's nix to nothing we can do for he's never again to sea. It is nebuless an autodidact fact of the commonest that the shape of the average human cloudyphiz, whereas sallow has long daze faded, frequently altered its ego with the possing of the showers (Not original!). Whence it is a slopperish matter, given the wet and low visibility (since in this scherzarade of one's thousand one nightinesses that sword of certainty which would indentifide the body never falls) to idendifine the individuone in scratch wig, squarecuts, stock lavaleer, regattable oxeter, baggy pants and shufflers (he is often alluded to as Slypatrick, the llad in the llane) with already an incipience (lust!) in the direction of area baldness (one is continually firstmeeting with odd sorts of others at all sorts of ages!) who was asked by free boardschool shirkers in drenched coats overawall, Will, Conn and Otto, to tell them overagait, Vol, Pov and Dev, that fishabed ghoatstory of the haardly creditable edventyres of the Haberdasher, the two Curchies and the three Enkelchums in their Bearskin ghoats! Girles and jongers but he has changed alok syne Thorkill's time! Ya, da, tra, gathery, pimp, shesses, shossafat, okodeboko, nine! Those many warts, those slummy patches, halfsinster wrinkles, (what has come over the face on wholebroader E?), and (shrine of Mount Mu save us!) the large fungopark he has grown! Drink!

Sport's a common thing. It was the Lord's own day for damp (to wait for a postponed regatta's eventualising is not of Battlecock Shettledore - Juxta - Mare only) and the request for a fully armed explanation was put (in Loo of Pat) to the porty (a native of the sisterisle — Meathman or Meccan? — by his brogue, exrace eyes, lokil calour and lucal odour which are said to have been average clownturkish (though the capelist's voiced nasal liquids and the way he sneezed at zees haul us back to the craogs and bryns of the Silurian Ordovices) who, the lesser pilgrimage accomplished, had made, pats' and pigs' older inselt, the southeast bluffs of the stranger stepshore, a *regifugium persecutorum*, hence hindquarters) as he paused at evenchime for some or so minutes (hit the pipe, dannyboy! Time to won, barmon. I'll take ten to win.) amid the devil's one duldrum (Apple by her blossom window and Charlotte at her toss panomancy his sole admirers, his only tearts in store) for a fragrend culubosh during his week-

end pastime of executing with Anny Oakley deadliness (the con-
summatory pairs of provocatives, of which remained provokingly
but two, the ones he fell for, Lili and Tutu, cork em!) empties
which had not very long before contained Reid's family (you ruad
that before, soaky, but all the bottles in sodemd histry will not
soften your bloodathirst!) stout. Having reprimed his repeater
and resiteroomed his timespiece His Revenances, with still a life
or two to spare for the space of his occupancy of a world at a time,
rose to his feet and there, far from Tolkaheim, in a quiet English
garden (commonplace!), since known as Whiddington Wild, his
simple intensive curolent vocality, my dearbraithers, my most
dearbrathairs, as he, so is a supper as is a sipper, spake of the
One and told of the Compassionate, called up before the triad of
precoxious scaremakers (scoretaking: Spegulo ne helpas al mal-
bellulo, Mi Kredas ke vi estas prava, Via dote la vizago rispondas
fraulino) the now to ushere mythical habiliments of Our Farfar
and Arthor of our doyne.

Television kills telephony in brothers' broil. Our eyes demand their turn. Let them be seen! And wolfbone balefires blaze
the trailmost if only that Mary Nothing may burst her bibby
buckshee. When they set fire then she's got to glow so we may
stand some chances of warming to what every soorkabatcha,
tum or hum, would like to know. The first Humphrey's latitu-
dinous baver with puggaree behind, (calaboose belong bigboss
belong Kang the Toll) his fourinhand bow, his elbaroom surtout,
the refaced unmansionables of gingerine hue, the state slate
umbrella, his gruff woolselywellesly with the finndrinn knopfs
and the gauntlet upon the hand which in an hour not for him
solely evil had struck down the might he mighthavebeen d'Est-
erre of whom his nation seemed almost already to be about to
have need. Then, stealing his thunder, but in the befitting le-
gomena of the smaller country, (probable words, possibly said, of
field family gleaming) a bit duskish and flavoured with a smile,
seein as ow his thoughts consisted chiefly of the cheerio, he áptly
sketched for our soontobe second parents (sukand see whybe!)
the touching seene. The solence of that stilling! Here one might

a fin fell. Boomster rombombonant! It scenes like a landescape from Wildu Picturescu or some seem on some dimb Arras, dumb as Mum's mutyness, this mimage of the seventyseventh kusin of kristansen is odable to os across the wineless Ere no œdor nor mere eerie nor liss potent of suggestion than in the tales of the tingmount. (Prigged!)

And there oftafter, jauntyjogging, on an Irish visavis, insteadily with shoulder to shoulder Jehu will tell to Christianier, saint to sage, the humphriad of that fall and rise while daisy winks at her pinker sister among the tussocks and the copoll between the shafts mocks the couple on the car. And as your who may look like how on the owther side of his big belttry your tyrs and cloes your noes and paradigm maymay rererise in eren. Follow we up his whip vindicative. Thurston's! Lo bebold! *La arboro, lo petrusu.* The augustan peacebetothem oaks, the monolith rising stark from the moonlit pinebarren. In all fortitudinous ajaxious rowdinoisy tenuacity. The angelus hour with ditchers bent upon their farm usetensiles, the soft belling of the fallow deers (*doerehmoose genuane!*) advertising their milky approach as midnight was striking the hours (*letate!*), and how brightly the great tribune outed the sharkskin smokewallet (imitation!) from his frock, kippers, and by Joshua, he tips un a topping swank cheroot, none of your swellish soide, quoit the reverse, and how manfally he says, pluk to pluk and lekan for lukan, he was to just pluggy well suck that brown boyo, my son, and spend a whole half hour in Havana. Sorer of the kreeksmen, would not thore be old high gothsprogue! Wherefore he met Master, he mean to say, he do, sire, bester of redpublicans, at Eagle Cock Hostel on Lorenzo Tooley street and how he wished his Honour the bannocks of Gort and Morya and Bri Head and Puddyrick, yore Loudship, and a starchboxsitting in the pit of his St Tomach's, — a strange wish for you, my friend, and it would poleaxe your sonsons grandson utterly though your own old sweatandswear floruerunts heaved it hoch many as the times, when they were turrified by the hitz.

Chee chee cheers for Upkingbilly and crow cru cramwells

Downaboo! Hup, boys, and hat him! See! Oilbeam they're lost
we've found rerembrandtsers, their hours to date link these heirs
to here but wowhere are those yours of Yesterdays? Farseeinge-
therich and Poolaulwoman Charachthercuss and his Ann van
Vogt. D.e.e.d! Edned, ended or sleeping soundlessly? Favour
with your tongues! *Intendite!*

Any dog's life you list you may still hear them at it, like sixes
and seventies as eversure as Halley's comet, ulemamen, sobran-
jewomen, storthingboys and dumagirls, as they pass its bleak and
bronze portal of your Casaconcordia: Huru more Nee, minny
frickans? Hwoorledes har Dee det? Losdoor onleft mladies, cue.
Millecientotrigintadue scudi. Tippoty, kyrie, tippoty. Cha kai
rotty kai makkar, sahib? Despenseme Usted, senhor, en son suc-
co, sabez. O thaw bron orm, A'Cothraige, thinkinthou gaily?
Lick-Pa-flai-hai-pa-Pa-li-si-lang-lang. Epi alo, ecou, Batiste, tu-
vavnr dans Lptit boing going. Ismeme de bumbac e meias de por-
tocallie. O.O. Os pipos mios es demasiada gruarso por O pic-
colo pocchino. Wee fee? Ung duro. Kocshis, szabad? Mercy, and
you? Gomagh, thak.

And, Cod, says he with mugger's tears: Would you care to
know the prise of a liard? Maggis, nick your nightynovel! Mass
Travener's at the mike again! And that bag belly is the buck
to goat it! Meggeg, m'gay chapjappy fellow, I call our univalse
to witness, as sicker as moyliffey eggs is known by our good
househalters from yorehunderts of mamooth to be which they
commercially are in ahoy high British quarters (conventional!)
my guesthouse and cowhaendel credits will immediately stand
ohoh open as straight as that neighbouring monument's fabrica-
tion before the hygienic gllll (this was where the reverent sab-
both and bottlebreaker with firbalk forthstretched touched upon
his tricoloured boater, which he uplifted by its pickledhoopy (he
gave Stetson one and a penny for it) whileas oleaginosity of an-
cestralolosis sgocciolated down the both pendencies of his mut-
sohito liptails (Sencapetulo, a more modestuous conciliabulite
never curled a torn pocketmouth), cordially inwiting the adul-
lescence who he was wising up to do in like manner what all did

so as he was able to add) lobe before the Great Schoolmaster's.
(I tell you no story.) Smile!

The house of Atreox is fallen indeedust (Ilyam, Ilyum! Mae-
romor Mournomates!) averging on blight like the mundibanks of
Fennyana, but deeds bounds going arise again. Life, he himself
said once, (his biografiend, in fact, kills him verysoon, if yet not,
after) is a wake, livit or krikit, and on the bunk of our bread-
winning lies the cropse of our seedfather, a phrase which the
establisher of the world by law might pretinately write across
the chestfront of all manorwombanborn. The scene, refreshed,
reroused, was never to be forgotten, the hen and crusader ever-
intermutuomergent, for later in the century one of that puisne
band of factferreters, (then an excivily (out of the custom huts)
(retired), (hurt), under the sixtyfives act in a dressy black modern
style and wewere shiny tan burlingtons, (tam, homd and dicky,
quopriquos and peajagd) rehearsed it, pippa pointing, with a
dignified (copied) bow to a namecousin of the late archdeacon
F. X. Preserved Coppinger (a hot fellow in his night, may the
mouther of guard have mastic on him!) in a pullwoman of our
first transhibernian with one still sadder circumstance which is a
dirkandurk heartskewerer if ever to bring bouncing brimmers
from marbled eyes. Cycloptically through the windowdisks and
with eddying awes the round eyes of the rundeisers, back to back,
buck to bucker, on their airish chaunting car, beheld with in-
touristing anterestedness the clad pursue the bare, the bare the
green, the green the frore, the frore the cladagain, as their convoy
wheeled encirculingly abound the gigantig's lifetree, our fire-
leaved loverlucky blomsterbohm, phoenix in our woodlessness,
haughty, cacuminal, erubescent (repetition!) whose roots they be
asches with lustres of peins. For as often as the Archicadenus,
pleacing aside his *Irish Field* and craving their auriculars to re-
cepticle particulars before they got the bump at Castlebar (mat
and far!) spoke of it by request all, hearing in this new reading
of the part whereby, because of Dyas in his machina, the new
garrickson's grimacing grimaldism hypostasised by substintua-
tion the axiomatic orerotundity of that once grand old elrington

bawl, the copycus's description of that fellowcommuter's play
upon countenants, could simply imagine themselves in their bosom's inmost core, as *pro tem locums* timesported acorss the yawning (abyss), as once they were seasiders, listening to the cockshy-
shooter's evensong evocation of the doomed but always ventri-
loquent Agitator, (nonot more plangorpound the billows o'er
Thounawahallya Reef!) silkhouatted, a whallrhosmightiadd, a-
ginsst the dusk of skumring, (would that fane be Saint Muezzin's
calling — holy places! — and this fez brimless as brow of faithful
toucher of the ground, did wish it were — blessed be the bones!
— the ghazi, power of his sword.) his manslayer's gunwielder
protended towards that overgrown leadpencil which was soon,
monumentally at least, to rise as Molyvdokondylon to, to be, to
be his mausoleum (O'dan stod tillsteyne at meisies aye skould
show pon) while olover his exculpatory features, as Roland rung,
a wee dropeen of grief about to sillonise his jouejous, the ghost
of resignation diffused a spectral appealingness, as a young man's
drown o'er the fate of his waters may gloat, similar in origin and
akkurat in effective to a beam of sunshine upon a coffin plate.

  Not olderwise Inn the days of the Bygning would our Traveller remote, unfriended, from van Demon's Land, some lazy
skald or maundering pote, lift wearywilly his slowcut snobsic
eyes to the semisigns of his zooteac and lengthily lingering along
flaskneck, cracket cup, downtrodden brogue, turfsod, wild-
broom, cabbageblad, stockfisch, longingly learn that there at the
Angel were herberged for him poteen and tea and praties and
baccy and wine width woman wordth warbling: and informally
quasi-begin to presquesm'ile to queasithin' (Nonsense! There
was not very much windy Nous blowing at the given moment
through the hat of Mr. Melancholy Slow!)

  But in the pragma what formal cause made a smile of *that* to-
think? Who was he to whom? (O'Breen's not his name nor the
brown one his maid.) Whose are the placewheres? Kiwasti, kis-
ker, kither, kitnabudja? Tal the tem of the tumulum. Giv the gav
of the grube. Be it cudgelplayers' country orfishfellows' town or
leeklickers' land or panbpanungopovengreskey. What regnans

raised the rains have levelled but we hear the pointers and can gauge their compass for the melos yields the mode and the mode the manners plicyman, plansiman, plousiman, plab. Tsin tsin tsin tsin! The forefarther folkers for a prize of two peaches with Ming, Ching and Shunny on the lie low lea. We'll sit down on the hope of the ghouly ghost for the titheman troubleth but his hantitat hies not here. They answer from their Zoans; Hear the four of them! Hark torroar of them! I, says Armagh, and a'm proud o'it. I, says Clonakilty, God help us! I, says Deansgrange, and say nothing. I, says Barna, and whatabout it? Hee-haw! Before he fell hill he filled heaven: a stream, alplapping streamlet, coyly coiled um, cool of her curls: We were but thermites then, wee, wee. Our antheap we sensed as a Hill of Allen, the Barrow for an People, one Jotnursfjaell: and it was a grummelung amung the porktroop that wonderstruck us as a thunder, yunder.

Thus the unfacts, did we possess them, are too imprecisely few to warrant our certitude, the evidencegivers by legpoll too untrustworthily irreperible where his adjugers are semmingly freak threes but his judicandees plainly minus twos. Nevertheless Madam's Toshowus waxes largely more lifeliked (entrance, one kudos; exits, free) and our notional gullery is now completely complacent, an exegious monument, aerily perennious. Oblige with your blackthorns; gamps, degrace! And there many have paused before that exposure of him by old Tom Quad, a flashback in which he sits sated, gowndabout, in clericalease habit, watching bland sol slithe dodgsomely into the nethermore, a globule of maugdleness about to corrugitate his mild dewed cheek and the tata of a tiny victorienne, Alys, pressed by his limper looser.

Yet certes one is. Eher the following winter had overed the pages of nature's book and till Ceadurbar-atta-Cleath became Dablena Tertia, the shadow of the huge outlander, maladik, multvult, magnoperous, had bulked at the bar of a rota of tribunals in manor hall as in thieves' kitchen, mid pillow talk and chithouse chat, on Marlborough Green as through Molesworth Fields, here sentenced pro tried with Jedburgh justice, there acquitted con-

testimony with benefit of clergy. His Thing Mod have undone
him: and his madthing has done him man. His beneficiaries are
legion in the part he created: they number up his years. Greatwheel
Dunlop was the name was on him: behung, all we are his bisaacles.
As hollyday in his house so was he priest and king to that: ulvy
came, envy saw, ivy conquered. Lou! Lou! They have waved his
green boughs o'er him as they have torn him limb from lamb.
For his muertification and uxpiration and dumnation and annu-
hulation. With schreis and grida, deprofound souspirs. Steady,
sullivans! Mannequins pause! Longtong's breach is fallen down
but Graunya's spreed's abroad. Ahdostay, feedailyones, and feel
the Flucher's bawls for the total of your flouts is not fit to fan his
fettle, o! Have a ring and sing wohl! Chin, chin! Chin, chin!
And of course all chimed din width the eatmost boviality. Swiping rums and beaunes and sherries and ciders and negus and cit-
ronnades too. The strongers. Oho, oho, Mester Begge, you're
about to be bagged in the bog again. Bugge. But softsies seuf-
sighed: Eheu, for gassies! But, lo! lo! by the threnning gods,
human, erring and condonable, what the statues of our kuo, who
is the messchef be our kuang, ashu ashure there, the unforgettable
treeshade looms up behind the jostling judgements of those, as
all should owe, malrecapturable days.

　　Tap and pat and tapatagain, (fire firstshot, Missiers the Refusel-
eers! Peingpeong! For saxonlootie!) three tommix, soldiers free,
cockaleak and cappapee, of the Coldstream. Guards were walking,
in (*pardonnez-leur, je vous en prie, eh?*) Montgomery Street. One
voiced an opinion in which on either wide (*pardonnez!*), nodding, all the Finner Camps concurred (*je vous en prie, eh?*). It
was the first woman, they said, souped him, that fatal wellesday,
Lili Coninghams, by suggesting him they go in a field. Wroth
mod eldfar, ruth redd stilstand, wrath wrackt wroth, confessed
private Pat Marchison *retro*. (Terse!) Thus contenters with san-
toys play. One of our coming Vauxhall ontheboards who is
resting for the moment (she has been callit by a noted stagey ele-
cutioner a wastepacket Sittons) was interfeud in a waistend pewty
parlour. Looking perhaps even more pewtyflushed in her cherry-

derry padouasoys, girdle and braces by the Halfmoon and Seven
Stars, russets from the Blackamoor's Head, amongst the climbing
boys at his Eagle and Child and over the corn and hay emptors
at their Black and All Black, Mrs. F . . . A . . . saidaside, half in
stage of whisper to her confidante glass, while recoopering her
cartwheel chapot (ahat! — and we now know what thimbles a
baquets on lallance a talls mean), she hoped Sid Arthar would
git a Chrissman's portrout of orange and lemonsized orchids with
hollegs and ether, from the feeatre of the Innocident, as the
worryld had been uncained. Then, while it is odrous comparison-
ing to the sprangflowers of his burstday which was a virid-
able goddinpotty for the reinworms and the charlattinas and all
branches of climatitis, it has been such a wanderful noyth untirely,
added she, with many regards to Maha's pranjapansies. (Tart!)
Prehistoric, obitered to his dictaphone an entychologist: his pro-
penomen is a properismenon. A dustman nocknamed Seven-
churches in the employ of Messrs Achburn, Soulpetre and
Ashreborn, prairmakers, Glintalook, was asked by the sisterhood
the vexed question during his midday collation of leaver and
buckrom alternatively with stenk and kitteney phie in a hash-
housh and, thankeaven, responded impulsively: We have just been
propogandering his nullity suit andwhat they took out of his ear
among my own crush. All our fellows at O'Dea's sages with
Aratar Calaman he is a cemented brick, buck it all! A more nor
usually sober cardriver, who was jauntingly hosing his runabout,
Ginger Jane, took a strong view. Lorry hosed her as he talked
and this is what he told rewritemen: Irewaker is just a plain pink
joint reformee in private life but folks all have it by brehemons
laws he has parliamentary honours. Eiskaffier said (Louigi's, you
know that man's, brillant Savourain): *Mon foie*, you wish to ave
some homelette, yes, lady! Good mein leber! Your hegg he must
break himself. See I crack, so, he sit in the poele, umbedimbt!
A perspirer (over sixty) who was keeping up his tennises panted
he kne ho har twa to clect infamatios but a diffpair flannels climb
wall and trespassing on doorbell. After fullblown Braddon hear
this fresky troterella! A railways barmaid's view (they call her

Spilltears Rue) was thus expressed: to sympathisers of the Dole
Line, Death Avenue anent those objects of her pity-prompted
ministrance, to wet, man and his syphon. Ehim! It is ever too
late to whissle when Phyllis floods her stable. It would be skar-
lot shame to jailahim in lockup, as was proposed to him by the
Seddoms creature what matter what merrytricks went off with
his revulverher in connections with ehim being a norphan and
enjoining such wicked illth, ehim! Well done, Drumcollakill!
Kitty Tyrrel is proud of you, was the reply of a B.O.T. official
(O blame gnot the board!) while the Daughters Benkletter murmured in uniswoon: Golforgilhisjurylegs! Brian Lynsky, the cub
curser, was questioned at his shouting box, Bawlonabraggat, and
gave a snappy comeback, when saying: Paw! Once more I'll
hellbowl! I am for caveman chase and sahara sex, burk you! Them
two bitches ought to be leashed, canem! Up hog and hoar hunt!
Paw! A wouldbe martyr, who is attending on sanit Asitas where
he is being taught to wear bracelets, when grilled on the point,
revealed the undoubted fact that the consequence would be that
so long as Sankya Moondy played his mango tricks under the
mysttetry, with shady apsaras sheltering in his leaves' licence and
his shadowers torrifried by the potent bolts of indradiction, there
would be fights all over Cuxhaven. (Tosh!) Missioner Ida Wombwell, the seventeenyearold revivalist, said concerning the coinci-
dent of interfizzing with grenadines and other respectable and
disgusted peersons using the park: That perpendicular person is
a brut! But a magnificent brut! 'Caligula' (Mr. Danl Magrath,
bookmaker, wellknown to Eastrailian poorusers of the Sydney
Parade Ballotin) was, as usual, antipodal with his: striving todie,
hopening tomellow, Ware Splash. Cobbler. We have meat two
hourly, sang out El Caplan Buycout, with the famous padre's
turridur's capecast, meet too ourly, matadear! Dan Meiklejohn,
precentor, of S.S. Smack and Olley's was probiverbal with his
upsiduxit: *mutatus mutandis*. Dauran's lord ('Sniffpox') and Moir-
gan's lady ('Flatterfun') took sides and crossed and bowed to
each other's views and recrossed themselves. The dirty dubs upin
their flies, went too free, echoed the dainly drabs downin their

scenities, una mona. Sylvia Silence, the girl detective (*Meminerva*, but by now one hears turtlings all over Doveland!) when supplied with informations as to the several facets of the case in her cozy-dozy bachelure's flat, quite overlooking John a'Dream's mews, leaned back in her really truly easy chair to query restfully through her vowelthreaded syllabelles: Have you evew thought, wepowtew, that sheew gweatness was his twadgedy? Nevewtheless accowding to my considewed attitudes fow this act he should pay the full penalty, pending puwsuance, as pew Subsec. 32, section 11, of the C. L. A. act 1885, anything in this act to the contwawy notwithstanding. Jarley Jilke began to silke for he couldn't get home to Jelsey but ended with: He's got the sack that helped him moult instench of his gladsome rags. Meagher, a naval rating, seated on one of the granite cromlech setts of our new fish-shambles for the usual aireating after the ever popular act, with whom were Questa and Puella, piquante and quoite, (this had a cold in her brain while that felt a sink in her summock, wit's wat, wot's wet) was encouraged, although nearvanashed himself, by one of his co-affianced to get your breath, Walt, and gobbit and when ther chidden by her fastra sastra to saddle up your pance, Naville, thus cor replied to her other's thankskissing: I lay my two fingerbuttons, fiancee Meagher, (he speaks!) he was to blame about your two velvetthighs up Horniman's Hill — as hook and eye blame him or any other piscman? — but I also think, Puellywally, by the siege of his trousers there was someone else behind it — you bet your boughtem blarneys — about their three drummers down Keysars Lane. (Trite!).

Be these meer marchant taylor's fablings of a race referend with oddman rex? Is now all seenheard then forgotten? Can it was, one is fain in this leaden age of letters now to wit, that so diversified outrages (they have still to come!) were planned and partly carried out against so staunch a covenanter if it be true than any of those recorded ever took place for many, we trow, beyessed to and denayed of, are given to us by some who use the truth but sparingly and we, on this side ought to sorrow for their pricking pens on that account. The seventh city, Urovivla,

his citadear of refuge, whither (would we believe the laimen and
their counts), beyond the outraved gales of Atreeatic, changing
clues with a baggermalster, the hejirite had fled, silentioussue-
meant under night's altosonority, shipalone, a raven of the wave,
(be mercy, Mara! A he whence Rahoulas!) from the ostmen's
dirtby on the old vic, to forget in expiating manslaughter and,
reberthing in remarriment out of dead seekness to devine previdence, (if you are looking for the bilder deep your ear on the
movietone!) to league his lot, palm and patte, with a papishee.
For mine qvinne I thee giftake and bind my hosenband I thee
halter. The wastobe land, a lottuse land, a luctuous land, Emerald-
illuim, the peasant pastured, in which by the fourth commandment
with promise his days apostolic were to be long by the abundant
mercy of Him Which Thundereth From On High, murmured,
would rise against him with all which in them were, franchisab-
les and inhabitands, astea as agora, helotsphilots, do him hurt,
poor jink, ghostly following bodily, as were he made a curse for
them, the corruptible lay quick, all saints of incorruption of an
holy nation, the common or ere-in-garden castaway, in red resurrection to condemn so they might convince him, first pharoah, Humpheres Cheops Exarchas, of their proper sins. Business bred to speak with a stiff upper lip to all men and most occasions the Man we wot of took little short of fighting chances but
for all that he or his or his care were subjected to the horrors of
the premier terror of Errorland. (perorhaps!)

We seem to us (the real Us!) to be reading our Amenti in the
sixth sealed chapter of the going forth by black. It was after the
show at Wednesbury that one tall man, humping a suspicious
parcel, when returning late amid a dense particular on his home
way from the second house of the Boore and Burgess Christy
Menestrels by the old spot, Roy's Corner, had a barkiss revolver
placed to his faced with the words: you're shot, major, by an un-
knowable assailant (masked) against whom he had been jealous
over Lotta Crabtree or Pomona Evlyn? More than that Whenn
the Waylayer (not a Lucalizod diocesan or even of the Glendalough see, but hailing fro' the prow of Little Britain), mention-

ing in a bytheway that he, the crawsopper, had, in edition to
Reade's cutless centiblade, a loaded Hobson's which left only twin
alternatives as, viceversa, either he would surely shoot her, the
aunt, by pistol, (she could be okaysure of that!) or, failing of such,
bash in Patch's blank face beyond recognition, pointedly asked
with gaeilish gall wodkar blizzard's business Thornton had with
that Kane's fender only to be answered by the aggravated
assaulted that that that was the snaps for him, Midweeks, to sultry
well go and find out if he was showery well able. But how trans-
paringly nontrue, gentlewriter! His feet one is not a tall man, not
at all man. No such parson. No such fender. No such lumber. No
such race. Was it supposedly in connection with a girls, Myramy
Huey or Colores Archer, under Flaggy Bridge (for ann there is
but one liv and hir newbridge is her old) or to explode his
twelvechamber and force a shrievalty entrance that the heavybuilt
Abelbody in a butcherblue blouse from One Life One Suit (a
men's wear store), with a most decisive bottle of single in his
possession, seized after dark by the town guard at Haveyou-
caught-emerod's temperance gateway was there in a gate's way.

Fifthly, how parasoliloquisingly truetoned on his first time of
hearing the wretch's statement that, muttering Irish, he had had
had o'gloriously a'lot too much hanguest or hoshoe fine to
drink in the House of Blazes, the Parrot in Hell, the Orange Tree,
the Glibt, the Sun, the Holy Lamb and, lapse not leashed, in
Ramitdown's ship hotel since the morning moment he could
dixtinguish a white thread from a black till the engine of the
laws declosed unto Murray and was only falling fillthefluthered
up against the gatestone pier which, with the cow's bonnet
a'top o'it, he falsetook for a cattlepillar with purest peaceablest
intentions. Yet how lamely hobbles the hoy of his then pseudo-
jocax axplanation how, according to his own story, he was a
process server and was merely trying to open zozimus a bottlop
stoub by mortially hammering his *magnum bonum* (the curter the
club the sorer the savage) against the bludgey gate for the boots
about the swan Maurice Behan, who hastily into his shoes with
nothing his hald barra tinnteack and came down with homp,

shtemp and jumphet to the tiltyard from the wastes a'sleep in his
obi ohny overclothes or choker, attracted by the norse of guns
playing Delandy is cartager on the raglar rock to Dulyn, said
war' prised safe in bed as he dreamed that he'd wealthes in mormon halls when wokenp by a a fourth loud snore out of his land
of byelo while hickstrey's maws was grazing in the moonlight
by hearing hammering on the pandywhank scale emanating from
the blind pig and anything like (oonagh! oonagh!) it in the
whole history of the Mullingcan Inn he never. This battering
babel allower the door and sideposts, he always said, was not in
the very remotest like the belzey babble of a bottle of boose
which would not rouse him out o' slumber deep but reminded
him loads more of the martiallawsey marses of foreign musi-
kants' instrumongs or the overthrewer to the third last days of
Pompery, if anything. And that after this most nooningless
knockturn the young reine came down desperate and the old
liffopotamus started ploring all over the plains, as mud as she
cud be, ruinating all the bouchers' schurts and the backers'
wischandtugs so that be the chandeleure of the Rejaneyjailey
they were all night wasching the walters of, the weltering walters
off. Whyte.

Just one moment. A pinch in time of the ideal, musketeers!
Alphos, Burkos and Caramis, leave Astrelea for the astrollajerries
and for the love of the saunces and the honour of Keavens pike
puddywhackback to Pamintul. And roll away the reel world, the
reel world, the reel world! And call all your smokeblushes,
Snowwhite and Rosered, if you will have the real cream! Now for
a strawberry frolic! Filons, filoosh! *Cherchons la flamme!* Fammfamm! Fammfamm!

Come on, ordinary man with that large big nonobli head, and
that blanko berbecked fischial ekksprezzion Machinsky Scapolo-
polos, Duzinascu or other. Your machelar's mutton leg's getting
musclebound from being too pulled. Noah Beery weighed stone
thousand one when Hazel was a hen. Now her fat's falling fast.
Therefore, chatbags, why not yours? There are 29 sweet reasons
why blossomtime's the best. Elders fall for green almonds when

they're raised on bruised stone root ginger though it winters on
their heads as if auctumned round their waistbands. If you'd had
pains in your hairs you wouldn't look so orgibald. You'd have
Colley Macaires on your lump of lead. Now listen, Mr. Leer!
And stow that sweatyfunnyadams Simper! Take an old geeser
who calls on his skirt. Note his sleek hair, so elegant, *tableau
vivant*. He vows her to be his own honeylamb, swears they will
be pápa pals, by Sam, and share good times way down west in a
guaranteed happy lovenest when May moon she shines and they
twit twinkle all the night, combing the comet's tail up right and
shooting popguns at the stars. Creampuffs all to dime! Every
nice, missymackenzies! For dear old grumpapar, he's gone on
the razzledar, through gazing and crazing and blazing at the stars.
Compree! She wants her wardrobe to hear from above by return
with cash so as she can buy her Peter Robinson trousseau and cut
a dash with Arty, Bert or possibly Charley Chance (who knows?)
so tolloll Mr Hunker you're too dada for me to dance (so off she
goes!) and that's how half the gels in town has got their bottom
drars while grumpapar he's trying to hitch his braces on to his
trars. But old grum he's not so clean dippy between sweet you
and yum (not on your life, boy! not in those trousers! not by a
large jugful!) for someplace on the sly where Furphy he isn't by
old grum has his gel number two (bravevow, our Grum!) and he
would like to canoodle her too some part of the time for he is
downright fond of his number one but O he's fair mashed on
peaches number two so that if he could only canoodle the two,
chivee chivoo, all three would feel genuinely happy, it's as simple
as A. B. C., the two mixers, we mean, with their cherrybum
chappy (for he is simply shamming dippy) if they all were afloat
in a dreamlifeboat, hugging two by two in his zoo-doo-you-doo,
a tofftoff for thee, missymissy for me and howcameyou-e'enso for
Farber, in his tippy, upindown dippy, tiptoptippy canoodle, can
you? Finny.

Ack, ack, ack. With which clap, trap and soddenment, three to
a loaf, our mutual friends the fender and the bottle at the gate seem
to be implicitly in the same bateau, so to singen, bearing also

several of the earmarks of design, for there is in fact no use in
putting a tooth in a snipery of that sort and the amount of all
those sort of things which has been going on onceaday in and
twiceaday out every other nachtistag among all kinds of pro-
miscious individuals at all ages in private homes and reeboos
publikiss and allover all and elsewhere throughout secular
sequence the country over and overabroad has been particularly
stupendous. To be continued. Federals' Uniteds' Transports'
Unions' for Exultations' of Triumphants' Ecstasies.

But resuming inquiries. Will it ever be next morning the postal
unionist's (officially called carrier's, Letters Scotch, Limited)
strange fate (Fierceendgiddyex he's hight, d.e., the losel that
hucks around missivemaids' gummibacks) to hand in a huge
chain envelope, written in seven divers stages of ink, from blanch-
essance to lavandaiette, every pothook and pancrook bespaking
the wisherwife, superscribed and subpencilled by yours A Laugh-
able Party, with afterwite, S.A.G., to Hyde and Cheek, Eden-
berry, Dubblenn, WC? Will whatever will be written in lappish
language with inbursts of Maggyer always seem semposed, black
looking white and white guarding black, in that siamixed twoa-
talk used twist stern swift and jolly roger? Will it bright upon us,
nightle, and we plunging to our plight? Well, it might now, mircle,
so it light. Always and ever till Cox's wife, twice Mrs. Hahn, pokes
her beak into the matter with Owen K. after her, to see whawa
smutter after, will this kiribis pouch filled with litterish fragments lurk dormant in the paunch of that halpbrother of a herm,
a pillarbox? The coffin, a triumph of the illusionist's art, at first
blench naturally taken for a handharp (it is handwarp to tristin-
guish jubabe from jabule or either from tubote when all three
have just been invened) had been removed from the hardware
premises of Oetzmann and Nephew, a noted house of the gone-
most west, which in the natural course of all things continues to
supply funeral requisites of every needed description. Why needed, though? Indeed needed (wouldn't you feel like rattanfowl
if you hadn't the oscar!) because the flash brides or bride in
their lily boleros one games with at the Nivynubies' finery ball

and your upright grooms that always come right up with you
(and by jingo when they do!) what else in this mortal world,
now ours, when meet there night, mid their nackt, me there naket, made their nought the hour strikes, would bring them right-
came back in the flesh, thumbs down, to their orses and their
hashes.

To proceed. We might leave that nitrience of oxagiants to take
its free of the air and just analectralyse that very chymerical com-
bination, the gasbag where the warderworks. And try to pour
somour heiterscene up thealmostfere. In the bottled heliose case
continuing, Long Lally Tobkids, the special, sporting a fine breast
of medals, and a conscientious scripturereader to boot in the brick
and tin choorch round the coroner, swore like a Norewheezian
tailliur on the stand before the proper functionary that he was up
against a right querrshnorrt of a mand in the butcher of the blues
who, he guntinued, on last epening after delivering some carcasses mattonchepps and meatjutes on behalf of Messrs. Otto
Sands and Eastman, Limericked, Victuallers, went and, with his
unmitigated astonissment, hickicked at the dun and dorass against
all the runes and, when challenged about the pretended hick (it
was kickup and down with him) on his solemn by the imputant
imputed, said simply: I appop pie oath, Phillyps Captain. You
did, as I sostressed before. You are deepknee in error, sir, Madam
Tomkins, let me then tell you, replied with a gentlewomanly
salaam MackPartland, (the meatman's family, and the oldest in
the world except nick, name.) And Phelps was flayful with his
peeler. But his phizz fell.

Now to the obverse. From velveteens to dimities is barely a
fivefinger span and hence these camelback excesses are thought
to have been instigated by one or either of the causing causes of
all, those rushy hollow heroines in their skirtsleeves, be she ma-
gretta be she the posque. Oh! Oh! Because it is a horrible thing
to have to say to say to day but one dilalah, Lupita Lorette, shortly after in a fit of the unexpectednesses drank carbolic with all
her dear placid life before her and paled off while the other
soiled dove that's her sister-in-love, Luperca Latouche, finding

one day while dodging chores that she stripped teasily for binocular man and that her jambs were jimpjoyed to see each other, the
nautchy girly soon found her fruitful hat too small for her and
rapidly taking time look she rapidly took to necking, partying
and selling her spare favours in the haymow or in lumber closets
or in the greenawn *ad huck* (there are certain intimacies in all
ladies' lavastories we just lease to imagination) or in the sweet
churchyard close itself for a bit of soft coal or an array of thin
trunks, serving whom in fine that same hot coney *a la Zingara*
which our own little Graunya of the chilired cheeks dished up
to the greatsire of Oscar, that son of a Coole. Houri of the coast
of emerald, arrah of the lacessive poghue, Aslim-all-Muslim, the
resigned to her surrender, did not she, come leinster's even, true
dotter of a dearmud, (her pitch was Forty Steps and his perch old
Cromwell's Quarters) with so valkirry a licence as sent many a
poor pucker packing to perdition, again and again, ay, and again
sfidare him, tease fido, eh tease fido, eh eh tease fido, toos top-
ples topple, stop, dug of a dog of a dgiaour, ye! Angealousmei!
And did not he, like Arcoforty, farfar off Bissavolo, missbrand
her behaveyous with iridescent huecry of down right mean false
sop lap sick dope? Tawfulsdreck! A reine of the shee, a shebeen
quean, a queen of pranks. A kingly man, of royal mien, regally
robed, exalted be his glory! So gave so take: Now not, not now!
He would just a min. Suffering trumpet! He thought he want.
Whath? Hear, O hear, living of the land! Hungreb, dead era,
hark! He hea, eyes ravenous on her lippling lills. He hear her voi
of day gon by. He hears! Zay, zay, zay! But, by the beer of his
profit, he cannot answer. Upterputty till rise and shine! Nor needs
none shaft ne stele from Phenicia or Little Asia to obelise on
the spout, neither pobalclock neither folksstone, nor sunkenness
in Tomar's Wood to bewray how erpressgangs score off the rued.
The mouth that tells not will ever attract the unthinking tongue
and so long as the obseen draws theirs which hear not so long
till allearth's dumbnation shall the blind lead the deaf. Tatcho,
tawney yeeklings! The column of lumps lends the pattrin of the
leaves behind us. If violence to life, limb and chattels, often as

not, has been the expression, direct or through an agent male, of womanhid offended, (ah! ah!), has not levy of black mail from the times the fairies were in it, and fain for wilde erthe blothoms followed an impressive private reputation for whispered sins?

Now by memory inspired, turn wheel again to the whole of the wall. Where Gyant Blyant fronts Peannlueamoore There was once upon a wall and a hooghoog wall a was and such a wall-hole did exist. Ere ore or ire in Aaarlund. Or you Dair's Hair or you Diggin Mosses or your horde of orts and oriorts to garble a garthen of Odin and the lost paladays when all the eddams ended with aves. Armen? The doun is theirs and still to see for menags if he strikes a lousaforitch and we'll come to those baregazed shoeshines if you just shoodov a second. And let oggs be good old gaggles and Isther Estarr play Yesther Asterr. In the drema of Sorestost Areas, Diseased. A stonehinged gate then was for another thing while the suroptimist had bought and enlarged that shack under fair rental of one yearlyng sheep, (prime) value of sixpence, and one small yearlyng goat (cadet) value of eight-pence, to grow old and happy (hogg it and kidd him) for the re-minants of his years; and when everything was got up for the purpose he put an applegate on the place by no means as some pretext a bedstead in loo thereof to keep out donkeys (the pig-dirt hanging from the jags to this hour makes that clear) and just thenabouts the iron gape, by old custom left open to prevent the cats from getting at the gout, was triplepatlockt on him on purpose by his faithful poorters to keep him inside probably and possibly enaunter he felt like sticking out his chest too far and tempting gracious providence by a stroll on the peoplade's egg-day, unused as he was yet to being freely clodded.

O, by the by, lets wee brag of praties, it ought to be always remembered in connection with what has gone before that there was a northroomer, Herr Betreffender, out for his zimmer hole-digs, digging in number 32 at the Rum and Puncheon (Branch of Dirty Dick's free house) in Laxlip (where the Sockeye Sammons were stopping at the time orange fasting) prior to that, a Kom-merzial (Gorbotipacco, he was wreaking like Zentral Oylrubber)

from Osterich, the U.S.E. paying (Gaul save the mark!) 11/- in
the week (Gosh, these wholly romads!) of conscience money in
the first deal of Yuly wheil he was, swishing beesnest with bles-
sure, and swobbing broguen eeriesh myth brockendootsch, making his reporterage on Der Fall Adams for the Frankofurto Siding,
a Fastland payrodicule, and er, consstated that one had on him
the Lynn O'Brien, a meltoned lammswolle, disturbed, and wider
he might the same zurichschicken other he would, with tosend
and obertosend tonnowatters, one monkey's damages become.
Now you must know, franksman, to make a heart of glass, that
the game of gaze and bandstand butchery was merely a Patsy
O'Strap tissue of threats and obuses such as roebucks raugh at
pinnacle's peak and after this sort. Humphrey's unsolicited visitor,
Davy or Titus, on a burgley's clan march from the middle west,
a hikely excellent crude man about road who knew his Bullfoost
Mountains like a starling bierd, after doing a long dance untidled
to Cloudy Green, deposend his bockstump on the waityoumay-
wantme, after having blew some quaker's (for you! Oates!) in
through the houseking's keyhole to attract attention, bleated
through the gale outside which the tairor of his clothes was hog-
callering, first, be the hirsuiter, that he would break his bulshey-
wigger's head for him, next, be the heeltapper, that he would
break the gage over his lankyduckling head the same way he
would crack a nut with a monkeywrench and, last of all, be the
stirabouter, that he would give him his (or theumperom's or any-
bloody else's) thickerthanwater to drink and his bleday steppe-
brodhar's into the bucket. He demanded more wood alcohol to
pitch in with, alleging that his granfather's was all taxis and that
it was only after ten o'connell, and this his isbar was a public
oven for the sake of irsk irskusky, and then, not easily dis-
couraged, opened the wrathfloods of his atillarery and went on at
a wicked rate, weathering against him in mooxed metaphores
from eleven thirty to two in the afternoon without even a luncheonette interval for House, son of Clod, to come out, you jew-
beggar, to be Executed Amen. Earwicker, that patternmind, that
paradigmatic ear, receptoretentive as his if Dionysius, longsuffer-

ing although whitening under restraint in the sititout corner of
his conservatory, behind faminebuilt walls, his thermos flask and
ripidian flabel by his side and a walrus whiskerbristle for a tusk-
pick, compiled, while he mourned the flight of his wild guineese,
a long list (now feared in part lost) to be kept on file of all abusive
names he was called (we have been compelled for the rejoicement
of foinne loidies ind the humours of Milltown etcetera by Josephine Brewster in the collision known as Contrastations with Inkermann and so on and sononward, lacies in loo water, flee, celestials,
one clean turv): *Firstnighter, Informer, Old Fruit, Yellow Whigger,
Wheatears, Goldy Geit, Bogside Beauty, Yass We've Had His
Badannas, York's Porker, Funnyface, At Baggotty's Bend He
Bumped, Grease with the Butter, Opendoor Ospices, Cainandabler,
Ireland's Eighth Wonderful Wonder, Beat My Price, Godsoilman,
Moonface the Murderer, Hoary Hairy Hoax, Midnight Sunburst,
Remove that Bible, Hebdromadary Publocation, Tummer the Lame
the Tyrannous, Blau Clay, Tight before Teatime, Read Your
Pantojoke, Acoustic Disturbance, Thinks He's Gobblasst the Good
Dook of Ourguile, W.D.'s Grace, Gibbering Bayamouth of Dublin,
His Farther was a Mundzucker and She had him in a Growler,
Burnham and Bailey, Artist, Unworthy of the Homely Protestant
Religion, Terry Cotter, You're Welcome to Waterfood, signed the
Ribbonmen, Lobsterpot Lardling, All for Arthur of this Town,
Hooshed the Cat from the Bacon, Leathertogs Donald, The Ace
and Deuce of Paupering. O'Reilly's, Delights to Kiss the Man
behind the Barrel, Magogagog, Swad Puddlefoot, Gouty Ghibeline,
Loose Luther, Hatches Cocks' Eggs, Muddle the Plan, Luck before
Wedlock, I Divorce Thee Husband, Tanner and a Make, Go to
Hellena or Come to Connies, Piobald Puffpuff His Bride, Purged
out of Burke's, He's None of Me Causin, Barebarean, Peculiar
Person, Grunt Owl's Facktotem, Twelve Months Aristocrat,
Lycanthrope, Flunkey Beadle Vamps the Tune Letting on He's
Loney, Thunder and Turf Married into Clandorf, Left Boot Sent
on Approval, Cumberer of Lord's Holy Ground, Stodge Arschmann,
Awnt Yuke, Tommy Furlong's Pet Plagues, Archdukon Cabbanger,
Last Past the Post, Kennealey Won't Tell Thee off Nancy's Gown,*

*Scuttle to Cover, Salary Grab, Andy Mac Noon in Annie's Room,
Awl Out, Twitchbratschballs, Bombard Street Bester, Sublime
Porter, A Ban for Le King of the Burgaans and a Bom for Ye Sur
of all the Ruttledges, O'Phelim's Cutprice, And at Number Wan
Wan Wan, What He Done to Castlecostello, Sleeps with Feathers
end Ropes, It is Known who Sold Horace the Rattler, Enclosed
find the Sons of Fingal, Swayed in his Falling, Wants a Wife and
Forty of Them, Let Him Do the Fair, Apeegeequanee Chimmuck,
Plowp Goes his Whastle, Ruin of the Small Trader, He ——
Milkinghoneybeaverbrooker, Vee was a Vindner, Sower Rapes,
Armenian Atrocity, Sickfish Bellyup, Edomite, — 'Man Devoyd of
the Commoner Characteristics of an Irish Nature, Bad Humborg,
Hraabhraab, Coocoohandler, Dirt, Miching Daddy, Born Burst Feet
Foremost, Woolworth's Worst, Easyathic Phallusaphist, Guiltey-
pig's Bastard, Fast in the Barrel, Boose in the Bed, Mister Fatmate,
In Custody of the Polis, Boawwll's alocutionist, deposed,* but anar-
chistically respectsful of the liberties of the noninvasive individual,
did not respond a solitary wedgeword beyond such sedentarity,
though it was as easy as kissanywhere for the passive resistant in
the booth he was in to reach for the hello gripes and ring up Kimmage Outer 17.67, because, as the fundamentalist explained, when
at last shocked into speech, touchin his woundid feelins in the
fuchsiar the dominican mission for the sowsealist potty was on at
the time and he thought the rowmish devowtion known as the
howly rowsary might reeform ihm, Gonn. That more than
considerably unpleasant bullocky before he rang off drunkishly
pegged a few glatt stones, all of a size, by way of final mocks
for his grapes, at the wicket in support of his words that he was
not guilphy but, after he had so slaunga vollayed, reconnoi-
tring through his semisubconscious the seriousness of what he
might have done had he really polished off his terrible intentions
finally caused him to change the bawling and leave downg the
whole grumus of brookpebbles pangpung and, having sobered
up a bit, paces his groundould diablen lionndub, the flay the
flegm, the floedy fleshener, (purse, purse, pursyfurse, I'll splish
the splume of them all!) this backblocks boor bruskly put out

his langwedge and quite quit the paleologic scene, telling how
by his selfdenying ordnance he had left Hyland on the dissenting
table, after exhorting Earwicker or, in slightly modified phrase-
ology, Messrs or Missrs Earwicker, Seir, his feminisible name of
multitude, to cocoa come outside to Mockerloo out of that for
the honour of Crumlin, with his broody old flishguds, Gog's
curse to thim, so as he could brianslog and burst him all dizzy,
you go bail, like Potts Fracture did with Keddle Flatnose and
nobodyatall with Wholyphamous and build rocks over him, or
if he didn't, for two and thirty straws, be Cacao Campbell he
didn't know what he wouldn't do for him nor nobody else nomore nor him after which, batell martell, a brisha a milla a stroka
a boola, so the rage of Malbruk, playing on the least change of
his manjester's voice, the first heroic couplet from the fuguall
tropical, Opus Elf, Thortytoe: *My schemes into obeyance for This
time has had to fall:* they bit goodbyte to their thumb and, his
bandol eer his solgier, dripdropdrap on pool or poldier, wishing
the loff a falladelfian in the morning, proceeded with a Hubble-
forth slouch in his slips backwords (*Et Cur Heli!*) in the directions
of the duff and demb institutions about ten or eleven hundred
years lurch away in the moonshiny gorge of Patself on the Bach.
Adyoe!

     And thus, with this rochelly exetur of Bully Acre, came to
close that last stage in the siegings round our archicitadel which
we would like to recall, if old Nestor Alexis would wink the
worth for us, as Bar-le-Duc and Dog-an-Doras and Bangen-op-
Zoom.

     Yed he med leave to many a door beside of Oxmanswold for
so witness his chambered cairns a cloudletlitter silent that are at
browse up hill and down coombe and on eolithostroton, at
Howth or at Coolock or even at Enniskerry, a theory none too
rectiline of the evoluation of human society and a testament of
the rocks from all the dead unto some the living. Olivers lambs
we do call them, skatterlings of a stone, and they shall be gathered unto him, their herd and paladin, as nubilettes to cumule,
in that day hwen, same the lightning lancer of Azava Arthur-

honoured (some Finn, some Finn avant!), he skall wake from
earthsleep, haught crested elmer, in his valle of briers of Green-
man's Rise O, (lost leaders live! the heroes return!) and o'er dun
and dale the Wulverulverlord (protect us!) his mighty horn skall
roll, orland, roll.

For in those deyes his Deyus shall ask of Allprohome and call
to himm: Allprohome! And he make answer: Add some. Nor
wink nor wunk. Animadiabolum, mene credidisti mortuum?
Silence was in thy faustive halls, O Truiga, when thy green
woods went dry but there will be sounds of manymirth on the
night's ear ringing when our pantriarch of Comestowntonobble
gets the pullover on his boots.

Liverpoor? Sot a bit of it! His braynes coolt parritch, his pelt
nassy, his heart's adrone, his bluidstreams acrawl, his puff but a
piff, his extremeties extremely so: Fengless, Pawmbroke, Chil-
blaimend and Baldowl. Humph is in his doge. Words weigh no
no more to him than raindrips to Rethfernhim. Which we all
like. Rain. When we sleep. Drops. But wait until our sleeping.
Drain. Sdops.

As the lion in our teargarten remembers the nenuphars of his
Nile (shall Ariuz forget Arioun or Boghas the baregams of the
Marmarazalles from Marmeniere?) it may be, tots wearsense full
a naggin in twentyg have sigilposted what in our brievingbust,
the besieged bedreamt him stil and solely of those lililiths un-
deveiled which had undone him, gone for age, and knew not
the watchful treachers at his wake, and theirs to stay. Fooi, fooi,
chamermissies! Zeepyzoepy, larcenlads! Zijnzijn Zijnzijn! It may
be, we moest ons hasten selves te declareer it, that he reglimmed?.
presaw? the fields of heat and yields of wheat where corngold
Ysit? shamed and shone. It may be, we habben to upseek a bitty
door our good township's courants want we knew't, that with
his deepseeing insight (had not wishing oftebeen but good time
wasted), within his patriarchal shamanah, broadsteyne 'bove citie
(Twillby! Twillby!) he conscious of enemies, a kingbilly white-
horsed in a Finglas mill, prayed, as he sat on anxious seat, (kunt
ye neat gift mey toe bout a peer saft eyballds!) during that three
and a hellof hours' agony of silence, *ex profundis malorum*, and
bred with unfeigned charity that his wordwounder (an engles to
the teeth who nomened Nash of Girahash would go anyold where
in the weeping world on his mottled belly (the rab, the kreepons-
kneed!) for milk, music or married missusses) might mercy to
providential benevolence's who hates prudencies astuteness un-
fold into the first of a distinguished dynasty of his posteriors,

blackfaced connemaras not of the fold but elder children of his household, his most besetting of ideas (*pace* his twolve predamanant passions) being the formation, as in more favoured climes, where the Meadow of Honey is guestfriendly and the Mountain of Joy receives, of a truly criminal stratum, Ham's cribcracking yeggs, thereby at last eliminating from all classes and masses with directly derivative decasualisation: *sigarius* (sic!) *vindicat urbes terrorum* (sicker!): and so, to mark a bank taal she arter, the obedience of the citizens elp the ealth of the ole.

Now gode. Let us leave theories there and return to here's here. Now hear. 'Tis gode again. The teak coffin, Pughglasspanelfitted, feets to the east, was to turn in later, and pitly patly near the porpus, materially effecting the cause. And this, liever, is the thinghowe. Any number of conservative public bodies, through a number of select and other committees having power to add to their number, before voting themselves and himself, town, port and garrison, by a fit and proper resolution, following a koorts order of the groundwet, once for all out of plotty existence, as a forescut, so you maateskippey might to you cuttinrunner on a neuw pack of klerds, made him, while his body still persisted, their present of a protem grave in Moyelta of the best Lough Neagh pattern, then as much in demand among misonesans as the Isle of Man today among limniphobes. Wacht even! It was in a fairly fishy kettlekerry, after the Fianna's foreman had taken his handful, enriched with ancient woods and dear dutchy deeplinns mid which were an old knoll and a troutbeck, vainyvain of her osiery and a chatty sally with any Wilt or Walt who would ongle her as Izaak did to the tickle of his rod and watch her waters of her sillying waters of and there now brown peater arripple (may their quilt gild lightly over his somnolulutent form!) Whoforyou lies his last, by the wrath of Bog, like the erst curst Hun in the bed of his treubleu Donawhu.

Best. This wastohavebeen underground heaven, or mole's paradise which was probably also an inversion of a phallopharos, intended to foster wheat crops and to ginder up tourist trade (its architecht, Mgr Peurelachasse, having been obcaecated lest

he should petrifake suchanevver while the contractors Messrs.
T. A. Birkett and L. O. Tuohalls were made invulnerably venerable) first in the west, our misterbilder, Castlevillainous, openly
damned and blasted by means of a hydromine, system Sowan and
Belting, exploded from a reinvented T.N.T. bombingpost up
ahoy of eleven and thirty wingrests (*circiter*) to sternbooard out
of his aerial thorpeto, Auton Dynamon, contacted with the ex-
pectant minefield by tins of improved ammonia lashed to her
shieldplated gunwale, and fused into tripupcables, slipping
through tholse and playing down from the conning tower into
the ground battery fuseboxes, all differing as clocks from keys
since nobody appeared to have the same time of beard, some
saying by their Oorlog it was Sygstryggs to nine, more holding
with the Ryan vogt it was Dane to pfife. He afterwards whaan-
ever his blaetther began to fail off him and his rough bark was
wholly husky and, stoop by stoop, he neared it (wouldmanspare!)
carefully lined the ferroconcrete result with rotproof bricks and
mortat, fassed to fossed, and retired beneath the heptarchy of
his towerettes, the beauchamp, byward, bull and lion, the white,
the wardrobe and bloodied, so encouraging (insteppen, alls als
hats beliefd!) additional useful councils public with hoofd off-
dealings which were welholden of ladykants te huur out such as the
Breeders' Union, the Guild of Merchants of the Staple *et*, a.u.c. to
present unto him with funebral pomp, over and above that a stone
slab with the usual Mac Pelah address of velediction, a very fair-
worded instance of falsemeaning adamelegy: We have done ours
gohellt with you, Heer Herewhippit, overgiven it, skidoo!

But t'house and allaboardshoops! Show coffins, winding sheets,
goodbuy bierchepes, cinerary urns, liealoud blasses, snuffchests,
poteentubbs, lacrimal vases, hoodendoses, reekwaterbeckers,
breakmiddles, zootzaks for eatlust, including upyourhealthing
rookworst and meathewersoftened forkenpootsies and for that
matter, javel also, any kind of inhumationary bric au brac for
the adornment of his glasstone honophreum, would, met these
trein of konditiens, naturally follow, halas, in the ordinary course,
enabling that roundtheworlder wandelingswight, did suches pass

him, to live all safeathomely the presenile days of his life of
opulence, ancient ere decrepitude, late lents last lenience, till
stuffering stage, whaling away the whole of the while (hypnos
chilia eonion!) lethelulled between explosion and reexplosion
(Donnaurwatteur! Hunderthunder!) from grosskopp to megapod,
embalmed, of grand age, rich in death anticipated.

But abide Zeit's sumonserving, rise afterfall. Blueblitzbolted
from there, knowing the hingeworms of the hallmirks of habita-
tionlesness, buried burrowing in Gehinnon, to proliferate through
all his Unterwealth, seam by seam, sheol om sheol, and revisit
our Uppercrust Sideria of Utilitarios, the divine one, the hoar-
der hidden propaguting his plutorpopular progeniem of pots and
pans and pokers and puns from biddenland to boughtenland, the
spearway fore the spoorway.

The other spring offensive on the heights of Abraham may
have come about all quite by accidence, Foughtarundser (for
Breedabrooda had at length presuaded him to have himself to be
as septuply buried as the murdered Cian in Finntown), had not
been three monads in his watery grave (what vigilantes and ridings
then and spuitwyne pledges with aardappel frittling!) when
portrifaction, dreyfussed as ever, began to ramp, ramp, ramp, the
boys are parching. A hoodenwinkle gave the signal and a blessing paper freed the flood. Why did the patrizien make him scares
with his gruntens? Because the druiven were muskating at the
door. From both Celtiberian camps (granting at the onset for the
sake of argument that men on the two sides in New South Ireland and Vetera Uladh, bluemin and pillfaces, during the ferment
With the Pope or On the Pope, had, moors or letts, grant ideas,
grunted) all conditions, poor cons and dives mor, each, of course,
on the purely doffensive since the eternals were owlwise on their
side every time, were drawn toowards their Bellona's Black
Bottom, once Woolwhite's Waltz (Ohiboh, how becrimed,
becursekissed and bedumbtoit!) some for want of proper feeding
in youth, others already caught in the honourable act of slicing
careers for family and carvers in conjunction; and if emaciated
nough, the person garrotted may have suggested to whomever he

took the ham of, the plain being involved in darkness, low cirque
waggery, nay, even the first old wugger of himself in the flesh,
whiggissimus incarnadined, when falsesighted by the ifsuchhewas
bully on the hill for there had circulated freely fairly among his
opposition the feeling that in so hibernating Massa Ewacka, who,
previous to that demidetached life, had been known of barmi-
cidal days, cook said, between soups and savours, to get outside
his own length of rainbow trout and taerts atta tarn as no man
of woman born, nay could, like the great crested brebe, devour
his threescoreten of roach per lifeday, ay, and as many minnow a
minute (the big mix, may Gibbet choke him!) was, like the salmon
of his ladderleap all this time of totality secretly and by suckage
feeing on his own misplaced fat.

Ladies did not disdain those pagan ironed times of the first
city (called after the ugliest Danadune) when a frond was a friend
inneed to carry, as earwigs do their dead, their soil to the earth-
ball where indeeth we shall calm decline, our legacy unknown.
Venuses were gigglibly temptatrix, vulcans guffawably eruptious
and the whole wives' world frockful of fickles. Fact, any human
inyon you liked any erenoon or efter would take her bare godkin
out, or an even pair of hem, (lugod! lugodoo!) and prettily pray
with him (or with em even) everyhe to her taste, long for luck,
tapette and tape petter and take pettest of all. (Tip!) Wells she'd
woo and wills she's win but how the deer knowed where she'd
marry! Arbour, bucketroom, caravan, ditch? Coach, carriage,
wheelbarrow, dungcart?

Kate Strong, a widow (Tiptip!) — she pulls a lane picture for
us, in a dreariodreama setting, glowing and very vidual, of old
dumplan as she nosed it, a homelike cottage of elvanstone with
droppings of biddies, stinkend pusshies, moggies' duggies, rotten
witchawubbles, festering rubbages and beggars' bullets, if not
worse, sending salmofarious germs in gleefully through the
smithereen panes — Widow Strong, then, as her weaker had
turned him to the wall (Tiptiptip!), did most all the scavenging
from good King Hamlaugh's gulden dayne though her lean
besom cleaned but sparingly and her bare statement reads that,

there being no macadamised Sidetracks on those old nekropolitan
nights in, barring a footbatter, Bryant's Causeway, bordered
with speedwell, white clover and sorrel a wood knows, which
left off, being beaten, where the plaintiff was struck, she
left down, as scavengers, who will be scavengers must, her
filthdump near the Serpentine in Phornix Park (at her time called
Finewell's Keepsacre, but later tautaubapptossed Pat's Purge),
that dangerfield circling butcherswood where fireworker oh
flaherty engaged a nutter of castlemallards and ah for archer
stunned's turk, all over which fossil footprints, bootmarks,
fingersigns, elbowdints, breechbowls, a. s. o. were all succes-
sively traced of a most envolving description. What subtler
timeplace of the weald than such wolfsbelly castrament to will
hide a leabhar from Thursmen's brandihands or a loveletter,
lostfully hers, that would be lust on Ma, than then when ructions
ended, than here where race began: and by four hands of forethought the first babe of reconcilement is laid in its last cradle
of hume sweet hume. Give over it! And no more of it! So pass
the pick for child sake! O men!

For hear Allhighest sprack for krischnians as for propagana
fidies and his nuptial eagles sharped their beaks of prey: and
every morphyl man of us, pome by pome, falls back into this
terrine: as it was let it be, says he! And it is as though where
Agni araflammed and Mithra monished and Shiva slew as maya-
mutras the obluvial waters of our noarchic memory withdrew,
windingly goharksome, to some hastyswasty timberman torch-
priest, flamenfan, the ward of the wind that lightened the fire that
lay in the wood that Jove bolt, at his rude word. Posidonius
O'Fluctuary! Lave that bloody stone as it is! What are you
doing your dirty minx and his big treeblock way up your path?
Slip around, you, by the rare of the ministers'! And, you, take
that barrel back where you got it, Mac Shane's, and go the way
your old one went, Hatchettsbury Road! And gish! how they
gushed away, the pennyfares, a whole school for scamper, with
their sashes flying sish behind them, all the little pirlypettes!
Issy-la-Chapelle! Any lucans, please?

Yes, the viability of vicinals if invisible is invincible. And we
are not trespassing on his corns either. Look at all the plotsch!
Fluminian! If this was Hannibal's walk it was Hercules' work.
And a hungried thousand of the unemancipated slaved the way.
The mausoleum lies behind us (O Adgigasta, *multipopulipater!*)
and there are milestones in their cheadmilias faultering along
the tramestrack by Brahm and Anton Hermes! Per omnibus
secular seekalarum. Amain. But the past has made us this present
of a rhedarhoad. So more boher O'Connell! Though rainy-
hidden, you're rhinohide. And if he's not a Romeo you may
scallop your hat. Wereupunder in the fane of Saint Fiacre! Halte!

It was hard by the howe's there, plainly on this disoluded and a
buchan cold spot, rupestric then, resurfaced that now is, that
Luttrell sold if Lautrill bought, in the saddle of the Brennan's
(now Malpasplace?) pass, versts and versts from true civilisation,
not where his dreams top their traums halt (Beneathere! Bena-
there!) but where livland yontide meared with the wilde, saltlea
with flood, that the attackler, a cropatkin, though under medium
and between colours with truly native pluck, engaged the Adver-
sary who had more in his eye than was less to his leg but whom for
plunder sake, he mistook in the heavy rain to be Oglethorpe or
some other ginkus, Parr aparrently, to whom the headandheel-
less chickenestegg bore some Michelangiolesque resemblance,
making use of sacrilegious languages to the defect that he would
challenge their hemosphores to exterminate them but he would
cannonise the b — y b — r's life out of him and lay him out
contritely as smart as the b — r had his b — y nightprayers
said, three patrecknocksters and a couplet of hellmuirries (*tout
est sacré pour un sacreur, femme à barbe ou homme-nourrice*) at the
same time, so as to plugg well let the blubbywail ghoats out of
him, catching holst of an oblong bar he had and with which he
usually broke furnitures he rose the stick at him. The boarder
incident prerepeated itself. The pair (whethertheywere Nippo-
luono engaging Wei-Ling-Taou or de Razzkias trying to recon-
noistre the general Boukeleff, man may not say), struggled
apairently for some considerable time, (the cradle rocking equally

to one and oppositely from the other on its law of capture and
recapture), under the All In rules around the booksafe, fighting
like purple top and tipperuhry Swede, (Secremented Servious of
the Divine Zeal!) and in the course of their tussle the toller man,
who had opened his bully bowl to beg, said to the miner who
was carrying the worm (a handy term for the portable distillery
which consisted of three vats, two jars and several bottles though
we purposely say nothing of the stiff, both parties having an
interest in the spirits): Let me go, Pautheen! I hardly knew ye.
Later on, after the solstitial pause for refleshmeant, the same
man (or a different and younger him of the same ham) asked in
the vermicular with a very oggly chew-chin-grin: Was six vic-
tolios fifteen pigeon takee offa you, tell he me, stlongfella, by
picky-pocky ten to foul months behindaside? There were some
further collidabantèr and severe tries to convert for the best part
of an hour and now a woden affair in the shape of a webley (we
at once recognise our old friend Ned of so many illortemporate
letters) fell from the intruser who, as stuck as that cat to that
mouse in that tube of that christchurch organ, (did the imnage of
Girl Cloud Pensive flout above them light young charm, in
ribbons and pigtail?) whereupon became friendly and, saying not
to tear his shirt, wanted to know, laying all joking and knob-
kerries aside, if his change companion who stuck still to the invention of his strongbox, with a tenacity corrobberating their
mutual tenitorial rights, happened to have the loots change of
a tenpound crickler about him at the moment, addling that hap
so, he would pay him back the six vics odd, do you see, out of
that for what was taken on the man of samples last Yuni or Yuly,
do you follow me, Capn? To this the other, Billi with the Boule,
who had mummed and mauled up to that (for he was hesitency
carried to excelcism) rather amusedly replied: Woowoo would
you be grossly surprised, Hill, to learn that, as it so happens, I
honestly have not such a thing as the loo, as the least chance of
a tinpanned crackler anywhere about me at the present moho-
moment but I believe I can see my way, as you suggest, it
being Yuletide or Yuddanfest and as it's mad nuts, son, for you

when it's hatter's hares, mon, for me, to advance you something
like four and sevenpence between hopping and trapping which
you might just as well have, boy baches, to buy J. J. and S. with.
There was a minute silence before memory's fire's rekindling and
then. Heart alive! Which at very first wind of gay gay and whisk-
wigs wick's ears pricked up, the starving gunman, strike him
pink, became strangely calm and forthright sware by all his lards
porsenal that the thorntree of sheol might ramify up his Sheo-
fon to the lux apointlex but he would go good to him suntime
marx my word fort, for a chip off the old Flint, (in the Nichtian
glossery which purveys aprioric roots for aposteriorious tongues
this is nat language at any sinse of the world and one might as
fairly go and kish his sprogues as fail to certify whether the
wartrophy eluded at some lives earlier was that somethink like a
jug, to what, a coctable) and remarxing in languidoily, seemingly
much more highly pleased than tongue could tell at this opening
of a lifetime and the foretaste of the Dun Bank pearlmothers
and the boy to wash down which he would feed to himself in
the Ruadh Cow at Tallaght and then into the Good Woman at
Ringsend and after her inat Conway's Inn at Blackrock and, first
to fall, cursed be all, where appetite would keenest be, atte,
funeral fare or fun fain real, Adam and Eve's in Quantity Street
by the grace of gamy queen Tailte, her will and testament: You
stunning little southdowner! I'd know you anywhere, Declaney,
let me truthfully tell you in or out of the lexinction of life and
who the hell else, be your blanche patch! on the boney part!
Goalball I've struck this daylit dielate night of nights, by golly!
My hat, you have some bully German grit, sundowner! He
spud in his faust (axin); he toped the raw best (pardun); he
poked his pick (a tip is a tap): and he tucked his friend's leave. And
with French hen or the portlifowlium of hastes and leisures, about
to continue that the queer mixture exchanged the pax in embrace
or poghue puxy as practised between brothers of the same breast,
hillelulia, killelulia, allenalaw, and, having ratified before the
god of the day their torgantruce which belittlers have schmall-
kalled the treatyng to cognac, turning his fez menialstrait in the

direction of Moscas, he first got rid of a few mitsmillers and
hurooshoos and levanted off with tubular jurbulance at a bull's
run over the assback bridge spitting his teeths on rooths with the
seven and four in danegeld and their humoral hurlbat or other
uncertain weapon of *lignum vitae*, but so evermore rhumanasant of
a toboggan poop, picked up to keep some crowplucking appointment with some rival rialtos anywheres between Pearidge
and the Littlehorn while this poor delaney, who they left along
with the confederate fender behind and who albeit ballsbluffed,
bore up wonderfully wunder all of it with a whole number of
plumsized contusiums, plus alasalah bruised coccyx, all over him,
reported the occurance in the best way he could, to the flabber-
gaze of the whole lab giving the Paddybanners the military
salute as for his exilicy's the O'Daffy, in justifiable hope that,
in nobiloroman review of the hugely sitisfactuary conclusium
of their negotiations and the jugglemonkysh agripment dein-
derivative, some lotion or fomentation of poppyheads would be
jennerously exhibited to the parts, at the nearest watchhouse in
Vicar Lane, the white ground of his face all covered with digon-
ally redcrossed nonfatal mammalian blood as proofpositive of the
seriousness of his character and that he was bleeding in self
defience (stanch it!) from the nostrils, lips, pavilion and palate,
while some of his hitter's hairs had been pulled off his knut's
head by Colt though otherwise his allround health appeared to
be middling along as it proved most fortunate that not one of
the two hundred and six bones and five hundred and one muscles
in his corso was a whit the whorse for her whacking. Herwho?

Nowthen, leaving clashing ash, brawn and muscle and brass-
made to oust earthernborn and rockcrystal to wreck isinglass but
wurming along gradually for our savings backtowards mother-
waters so many miles from bank and Dublin stone (olympiading
even till the eleventh dynasty to reach that thuddysickend Hamlaugh) and to the question of boney's unlawfully obtaining a
pierced paraflamme and claptrap fireguard there crops out the
still more salient point of the politish leanings and town pursuits
of our forebeer, El Don De Dunelli, (may his ship thicked stick

in the bottol of the river and all his crewsers stock locked in the
burral of the seas!) who, when within the black of your toenail,
sir, of being mistakenly ambushed by one of the uddahveddahs,
and as close as made no matter, mam, to being kayoed offhard
when the hyougono heckler with the Peter the Painter wanted
to hole him, was consistently practising the first of the primary
and imprescriptible liberties of the pacific subject by circulating
(be British, boys to your bellybone and chuck a chum a chance!)
alongst one of our umphrohibited semitary thrufahrts, open to
buggy and bike, to walk, Wellington Park road, with the curb
or quaker's quacknostrum under his auxter and his alpenstuck in
his redhand, a highly commendable exercise, or, number two of
our *acta legitima plebeia*, on the brink (beware to baulk a man at
his will!) of taking place upon a public seat, to what, bare by
Butt's, most easterly (but all goes west!) of blackpool bridges, as
a public protest and naturlikevice, without intent to annoy either,
being praisegood thankfully for the wrathbereaved ringdove and
the fearstung boaconstrictor and all the more right jollywell
pleased, which he was, at having other people's weather.

But to return to the atlantic and Phenitia Proper. As if that
were not to be enough for anyone but little headway, if any, was
made in solving the wasnottobe crime cunundrum when a child
of Maam, Festy King, of a family long and honourably associated with the tar and feather industries, who gave an address in
old plomansch Mayo of the Saxons in the heart of a foulfamed
potheen district, was subsequently haled up at the Old Bailey
on the calends of Mars, under an incompatibly framed indictment
of both the counts (from each equinoxious points of view, the one
fellow's fetch being the other follow's person) that is to see, flying
cushats out of his ouveralls and making fesses immodst his forces
on the field. Oyeh! Oyeh! When the prisoner, soaked in methylated, appeared in dry dock, appatently ambrosiaurealised, like
Kersse's Korduroy Karikature, wearing, besides stains, rents and
patches, his fight shirt, straw braces, souwester and a policeman's
corkscrew trowsers, all out of the true (as he had purposely torn
up all his cymtrymanx bespokes in the mamertime), deposing for

his exution with all the fluors of sparse in the royal Irish vocabulary
how the whole padderjagmartin tripiezite suet and all the sulfeit
of copperas had fallen off him quatz unaccountably like the
chrystalisations of Alum on Even while he was trying for to stick
fire to himcell, (in feacht he was dripping as he found upon stripping for a pipkin ofmalt as he feared the coold raine) it was
attempted by the crown (P.C. Robort) to show that King, *elois*
Crowbar, once known as Meleky, impersonating a climbing boy,
rubbed some pixes of any luvial peatsmoor o'er his face, plucks
and pussas, with a clanetourf as the best means of disguising himself and was to the middlewhite fair in Mudford of a Thoorsday,
feishts of Peeler and Polee, under the illassumed names of
Tykingfest and Rabworc picked by him and Anthony out of a
tellafun book, ellegedly with a pedigree pig (unlicensed) and a
hyacinth. They were on that sea by the plain of Ir nine hundred
and ninetynine years and they never cried crack or ceased from
regular paddlewicking till that they landed their two and a
trifling selves, amadst camel and ass, greybeard and suckling,
priest and pauper, matrmatron and merrymeg, into the meddle
of the mudstorm. The gathering, convened by the Irish Angri-
cultural and Prepostoral Ouraganisations, to help the Irish muck
to look his brother dane in the face and attended thanks to
Larry by large numbers, of christies and jew's totems, tospite of
the deluge, was distinctly of a scattery kind when the bally-
bricken he could get no good of, after cockofthewalking through
a few fancyfought mains ate some of the doorweg, the pikey
later selling the gentleman ratepayer because she, Francie's sister,
that is to say ate a whole side of his (the animal's) sty, on a
struggle Street, *Qui Sta Troia*, in order to pay off, hiss or lick,
six doubloons fifteen arrears of his, the villain's not the rumbler's
rent.

Remarkable evidence was given, anon, by an eye, ear, nose
and throat witness, whom Wesleyan chapelgoers suspected of
being a plain clothes priest W.P., situate at Nullnull, Medical
Square, who, upon letting down his rice and peacegreen cover-
disk and having been sullenly cautioned against yawning while

being grilled, smiled (he had had a onebumper at parting from
Mrs Molroe in the morning) and stated to his eliciter under his
morse mustaccents (gobbless!) that he slept with a bonafides and
that he would be there to remember the filth of November,
hatinaring, rowdy O, which, with the jiboulees of Juno and the
dates of ould lanxiety, was going, please the Rainmaker, to
decembs within the ephemerides of profane history, all one with
Tournay, Yetstoslay and Temorah, and one thing which would
pigstickularly strike a person of such sorely tried observational
powers as Sam, him and Moffat, though theirs not to reason why,
the striking thing about it was that he was patrified to see, hear,
taste and smell, as his time of night, how Hyacinth O'Donnell,
B.A., described in the calendar as a mixer and wordpainter, with
part of a sivispacem (Gaeltact for dungfork) on the fair green
at the hour of twenty-four o'clock sought (the bullycassidy of
the friedhoffer!) to sack, sock, stab and slaughter singlehanded
another two of the old kings, Gush Mac Gale and Roaring
O'Crian, Jr., both changelings, unlucalised, of no address and
in noncommunicables, between him and whom, ever since wallops before the Mise of Lewes, bad blood existed on the ground
of the boer's trespass on the bull or because he firstparted his
polarbeeber hair in twoways, or because they were creepfoxed
andt grousuppers over a nippy in a noveletta, or because they
could not say meace, (mute and daft) meathe. The litigants, he
said, local congsmen and donalds, kings of the arans and the dalk-
eys, kings of mud and tory, even the goat king of Killorglin,
were egged on by their supporters in the shape of betterwomen
with bowstrung hair of Carrothagenuine ruddiness, waving crimson petties and screaming from Isod's towertop. There were
cries from the thicksets in court and from the macdublins on the
bohernabreen of: Mind the bank from Banagher, Mick, sir! Pro-
dooce O'Donner. Ay! Exhibit his relics! Bu! Use the tongue
mor! Give lip less! But it oozed out in Deadman's Dark Scenery
Court through crossexanimation of the casehardened testis that
when and where that knife of knifes the treepartied ambush was
laid (roughly spouting around half hours 'twixt dusk in dawn,

by Waterhose's Meddle Europeic Time, near Stop and Think,
high chief evervirens and only abfalltree in auld the land) there
was not as much light from the widowed moon as would dim a
child's altar. The mixer, accordingly, was bluntly broached, and
in the best basel to boot, as to whether he was one of those
lucky cocks for whom the audible-visible-gnosible-edible world
existed. That he was only too cognitively conatively cogitabun-
dantly sure of it because, living, loving, breathing and sleeping
morphomelosophopancreates, as he most significantly did, whenever he thought he heard he saw he felt he made a bell clipper-
clipperclipperclipper. Whether he was practically sure too of his
lugs and truies names in this king and blouseman buisness? That
he was pediculously so. Certified? As cad could be. Be lying! Be
the lonee I will. It was Morbus O' Somebody? A'Quite. Szer-
day's Son? A satyr in weddens. And how did the greeneyed
mister arrive at the B.A.? That it was like his poll. A cross-
grained trapper with murty odd oogs, awflorated ares, inquiline
nase and a twithcherous mouph? He would be. Who could bit
you att to a tenyerdfuul when aastalled? Ballera jobbera. Some
majar bore too? Iguines. And with tumblerous legs, redipnomi-
nated Helmingham Erchenwyne Rutter Egbert Crumwall Odin
Maximus Esme Saxon Esa Vercingetorix Ethelwulf Rupprecht
Ydwalla Bentley Osmund Dysart Yggdrasselmann? Holy Saint
Eiffel, the very phoenix! It was Chudley Magnall once more
between the deffodates and the dumb scene? The two childspies
waapreesing him auza de Vologue but the renting of his rock
was from the three wicked Vuncouverers Forests bent down
awhits, arthou sure? Yubeti, Cumbilum comes! One of the ox-
men's thingabossers, hvad? And had he been refresqued by the
founts of bounty playing there — is — a — pain — aleland in
Long's gourgling barral? A loss of Lordedward and a lack of sir-
philip a surgeonet showeradown could suck more gargling
bubbles out of the five lamps in Portterand's praise. Wirrgeling
and maries? As whose wouldn't, laving his leaftime in Blackpool. But, of course, he could call himself Tem, too, if he had
time to? You butt he could anytom. When he pleased? Win and

place. A stoker temptated by evesdripping aginst the driver who
was a witness as well? Sacred avatar, how the devil did they
guess it! Two dreamyums in one dromium? Yes and no error.
And both as like as a duel of lentils? Peacisely. So he was pelted
out of the coram populo, was he? Be the powers that be he was.
The prince in principel should not expose his person? Mac-
chevuole! Rooskayman kamerad? Sooner Gallwegian he would
say. Not unintoxicated, fair witness? Drunk as a fishup. Askt to
whether she minded whither he smuked? Not if he barkst into
phlegms. Anent his ajaciulations to his Crosscann Lorne, cossa?
It was corso in cursu on coarser again. The gracious miss was
we not doubt sensible how yellowatty on the forx was altered?
That she esually was, O'Dowd me not! As to his religion, if
any? It was the see-you-Sunday sort. Exactly what he meant by
a pederast prig? Bejacob's, just a gent who prayed his lent. And
if middleclassed portavorous was a usual beast? Bynight as useful
as a vomit to a shorn man. If he had rognarised dtheir gcourts
marsheyls? Dthat nday in ndays he had. Lindendelly, coke or
skilllies spell me gart without a gate? Harlyadrope. The grazing
rights (Mrs. Magistra Martinetta) expired with the expiry of the
goat's sire, if they were not mistaken? That he exactly could not
tell the worshipfuls but his mother-in-waders had the recipis for
the price of the coffin and that he was there to tell them that
herself was the velocipede that could tell them kitcat. A maundarin tongue in a pounderin jowl? Father ourder about the
mathers of prenanciation. Distributary endings? And we recom-
mends. *Quare hircum?* No answer. *Unde gentium fe . . . ?* No ah.
Are you not danzzling on the age of a vulcano? Siar, I am deed.
And how olld of him? He was intendant to study pulu. Which
was meant in a shirt of two shifts macoghamade or up Finn,
threehatted ladder? That a head in thighs under a bush at the
sunface would bait a serpent to a millrace through the heather.
Arm bird colour defdum ethnic fort perharps? Sure and glomsk
handy jotalpheson as well. Hokey jasons, then, in a pigeegeeses?
On a pontiff's order as ture as there's an ital on atac. As a gololy
bit to joss? Leally and tululy. But, why this hankowchaff and

whence this second tone, son-yet-sun! He had the cowtaw in his
buxers flay of face. So this that Solasistras, setting odds evens at
defiance, took the laud from Labouriter? What displaced Tob,
Dilke and Halley, not been greatly in love with the game. And,
changing the venders, from the king's head to the republican's
arms, as to the pugnaxities evinxed from flagfall to antepost
during the effrays round fatherthyme's beckside and the regents
in the plantsown raining, with the skiddystars and the morkern-
windup, how they appealed to him then? That it was wildfires
night on all the bettygallaghers. Mickmichael's soords shrieking
shrecks through the wilkinses and neckanicholas' toastingforks
pricking prongs up the tunnybladders. Let there be fight? And
there was. Foght. On the site of the Angel's, you said? Guinney's
Gap, he said, between what they said and the pussykitties. In the
middle of the garth, then? That they mushn't toucht it. The devoted couple was or were only two disappainted solicitresses on
the job of the unfortunate class on Saturn's mountain fort? That
was about it, jah! And Camellus then said to Gemellus: I should
know you? Parfaitly. And Gemellus then said to Camellus: Yes,
your brother? Obsolutely. And if it was all about that, egregious
sir? About that and the other. If he was not alluding to the whole
in the wall? That he was when he was not eluding from the whole
of the woman. Briefly, how such beginall finally struck him now?
Like the crack that bruck the bank in Multifarnham. Whether he
fell in with what they meant? Cursed that he suppoxed he did.
Thos Thoris, Thomar's Thom? The rudacist rotter in Roebuck-
dom. Surtopical? And subhuman. If it was, in yappanoise language, ach bad clap? Oo! Ah! Augs and ohrs with Rhian O'-
kehley to put it tertianly, we wrong? Shocking! Such as turly
pearced our really's that he might, that he might never, that he
might never that night. Triely and rurally. Bladyughfoulmoeck-
lenburgwhurawhorascortastrumpapornanennykocksapastippata-
ppatupperstrippuckputtanach, eh? You have it alright.

Meirdreach an Oincuish! But a new complexion was put upon
the matter when to the perplexedly uncondemnatory bench
(whereon punic judgeship strove with penal law) the senior

king of all, Pegger Festy, as soon as the outer layer of stuccko-
muck had been removed at the request of a few live jurors,
declared in a loudburst of poesy, through his Brythonic interpreter on his oath, mhuith peisth mhuise as fearra bheura muirre
hriosmas, whereas take notice be the relics of the bones of the
story bouchal that was ate be Cliopatrick (the sow) princess
of parked porkers, afore God and all their honours and king's
commons that, what he would swear to the Tierney of Dundal-
gan or any other Tierney, yif live thurkells folloged him about
sure that was no steal and that, nevertheless, what was deposited
from that eyebold earbig noseknaving gutthroat, he did not fire
a stone either before or after he was born down and up to that
time. And, incidentalising that they might talk about Markarthy
or they might walk to Baalastartey or they might join the nabour
party and come on to Porterfeud this the sockdologer had the
neck to endorse with the head bowed on him over his outturned
noreaster by protesting to his lipreaders with a justbeencleaned
barefacedness, abeam of moonlight's hope, in the same trelawney
what he would impart, pleas bench, to the Llwyd Josus and the
gentlemen in Jury's and the four of Masterers who had been all
those yarns yearning for that good one about why he left
Dublin, that, amreeta beaker coddling doom, as an Inishman was
as good as any cantonnatal, if he was to parish by the market steak
before the dorming of the mawn, he skuld never ask to see sight or
light of this world or the other world or any either world, of Tyre-
nan-Og, as true as he was there in that jackabox that minute, or
wield or wind (no thanks t'yous!) the inexousthausthible wassail-
horn tot of iskybaush the hailth up the wailth of the endknown ab-
god of the fire of the moving way of the hawks with his heroes in
Warhorror if ever in all his exchequered career he up or lave a
chancery hand to take or throw the sign of a mortal stick or stone
at man, yoelamb or salvation army either before or after being
puptised down to that most holy and every blessed hour. Here,
upon the halfkneed castleknocker's attempting kithoguishly to
lilt his holymess the paws and make the sign of the Roman God-
helic faix, (Xaroshie, zdrst! — in his excitement the laddo had

broken exthro Castilian into which the whole audience perse-
guired and pursuited him *olla podrida*) outbroke much yellach-
ters from owners in the heall (Ha!) in which, under the mollifi-
cation of methaglin, the testifighter reluctingly, but with ever so
ladylike indecorum, joined. (Ha! Ha!)

The hilariohoot of Pegger's Windup cumjustled as neatly
with the trititone of the Wet Pinter's as were they *isce et ille*
equals of opposites, evolved by a onesame power of nature or of
spirit, *iste*, as the sole condition and means of its himundher
manifestation and polarised for reunion by the symphysis of
their antipathies. Distinctly different were their duasdestinies.
Whereas the maidies of the bar, (a pairless trentene, a lunarised
score) when the eranthus myrrmyrred: Show'm the Posed:
fluttered and flattered around the willingly pressed, nominating
him for the swiney prize, complimenting him, the captivating
youth, on his having all his senses about him, stincking thyacinths
through his curls (O feen! O deur!) and bringing busses to his
cheeks, their masculine Oirisher Rose (his neece cleur!), and
legando round his nice new neck for him and pizzicagnoling his
woolywags, with their dindy dandy sugar de candy mechree me
postheen flowns courier to belive them of all his untiring young
dames and send treats in their times. Ymen. But it was not un-
observed of those presents, their worships, how, of one among
all, her deputised to defeme him by the Lunar Sisters' Celibacy
Club, a lovelooking leapgirl, all all alonely, Gentia Gemma of the
Makegiddyculling Reeks, he, wan and pale in his unmixed admiration, seemed blindly, mutely, tastelessly, tactlessly, innamorate
with heruponhim in shining aminglement, the shaym of his hisu
shifting into the shimmering of her hers, (youthsy, beautsy, hee's
her chap and shey'll tell memmas when she gays whom) till the
wild wishwish of her sheeshea melted most musically mid the
dark deepdeep of his shayshaun.

And whereas distracted (for was not just this in effect which
had just caused that the effect of that which it had caused to occur?) the four justicers laid their wigs together, Untius, Mun-
cius, Punchus and Pylax but could do no worse than promulgate

their standing verdict of Nolans Brumans whereoneafter King, having murdered all the English he knew, picked out his pockets and left the tribunal scotfree, trailing his Tommeylommey's tunic in his hurry, thereinunder proudly showing off the blink patch to his britgits to prove himself (an't plase yous!) a rael genteel. To the Switz bobbyguard's curial but courtlike: Commodore valley O hairy, Arthre jennyrosy?: the firewaterloover returted with such a vinesmelling fortytudor ages rawdownhams tanyouhide as would the latten stomach even of a tumass equinous (we were prepared for the chap's clap cap, the accent, but, took us as, by, surprise and now we're geshing it like gush gash from a burner!) so that all the twofromthirty advocatesses within echo, pulling up their briefs at the krigkry: Shun the Punman!: safely and soundly soccered that fenemine Parish Poser, (how dare he!) umprumptu right-oway hames, much to his thanks, gratiasagam, to all the wrong donatrices, biss Drinkbattle's Dingy Dwellings where (for like your true venuson Esau he was dovetimid as the dears at Bottome) he shat in (zoo), like the muddy goalbind who he was (dun), the chassetitties belles conclaiming: You and your gift of your gaft of your garbage abaht our Farvver! and gaingridando: Hon! Verg! Nau! Putor! Skam! Schams! Shames!

And so it all ended. Artha kama dharma moksa. Ask Kavya for the kay. And so everybody heard their plaint and all listened to their plause. The letter! The litter! And the soother the bitther! Of eyebrow pencilled, by lipstipple penned. Borrowing a word and begging the question and stealing tinder and slipping like soap. From dark Rasa Lane a sigh and a weep, from Lesbia Looshe the beam in her eye, from lone Coogan Barry his arrow of song, from Sean Kelly's anagrim a blush at the name, from I am the Sullivan that trumpeting tramp, from Suffering Dufferin the Sit of her Style, from Kathleen May Vernon her Mebbe fair efforts, from Fillthepot Curran his scotchlove machree-ther, from hymn Op. 2 Phil Adolphos the weary O, the leery, O, from Samyouwill Leaver or Damyouwell Lover thatjolly old molly bit or that bored saunter by, from Timm Finn again's weak tribes, loss of strenghth to his sowheel, from the wedding

on the greene, agirlies, the gretnass of joyboys, from Pat Mullen,
Tom Mallon, Dan Meldon, Don Maldon a slickstick picnic made
in Moate by Muldoons. The solid man saved by his sillied woman.
Crackajolking away like a hearse on fire. The elm that whimpers
at the top told the stone that moans when stricken. Wind broke
it. Wave bore it. Reed wrote of it. Syce ran with it. Hand tore
it and wild went war. Hen trieved it and plight pledged peace.
It was folded with cunning, sealed with crime, uptied by a harlot,
undone by a child. It was life but was it fair? It was free but was
it art? The old hunks on the hill read it to perlection. It made
ma make merry and sissy so shy and rubbed some shine off Shem
and put some shame into Shaun. Yet Una and Ita spill famine
with drought and Agrippa, the propastored, spells tripulations
in his threne. Ah, furchte fruchte, timid Danaides! Ena milo melo-
mon, frai is frau and swee is too, swee is two when swoo is free,
ana mala woe is we! A pair of sycopanties with amygdaleine
eyes, one old obster lumpky pumpkin and three meddlars on
their slies. And that was how framm Sin fromm Son, acity arose,
finfin funfun, a sitting arrows. Now tell me, tell me, tell me then!
What was it?

A . . . . !
? . . . . O!

So there you are now there they were, when all was over
again, the four with them, setting around upin their judges'
chambers, in the muniment room, of their marshalsea, under the
suspices of Lally, around their old traditional tables of the law
like Somany Solans to talk it over rallthesameagain. Well and
druly dry. Suffering law the dring. Accourting to king's evelyns.
So help her goat and kiss the bouc. Festives and highajinks and
jintyaun and her beetyrossy bettydoaty and not to forget now
a'duna o'darnel. The four of them and thank court now there
were no more of them. So pass the push for port sake. Be it soon.
Ah ho! And do you remember, Singabob, the badfather, the
same, the great Howdoyoucallem, and his old nickname, Dirty
Daddy Pantaloons, in his monopoleums, behind the war of the
two roses, with Michael Victory, the sheemen's preester, before

he caught his paper dispillsation from the poke, old Minace and
Minster York? Do I mind? I mind the gush off the mon like Bal-
lybock manure works on a tradewinds day. And the O'Moyly
gracies and the O'Briny rossies chaffing him bluchface and playing him pranks. How do you do, todo, North Mister? Get into
my way! Ah dearome forsailoshe! Gone over the bays! When
ginabawdy meadabawdy! Yerra, why would he heed that old
gasometer with his hooping coppin and his dyinboosycough and
all the birds of the southside after her, Minxy Cunningham, their
dear divorcee darling, jimmies and jonnies to be her jo? Hold
hard. There's three other corners to our isle's cork float. Sure, 'tis
well I can telesmell him $H_2 C E_3$ that would take a township's
breath away! Gob and I nose him too well as I do meself, heaving up the Kay Wall by the 32 to 11 with his limelooking horse-
bags full of sesameseed, the Whiteside Kaffir, and his sayman's
effluvium and his scentpainted voice, puffing out his thundering
big brown cabbage! Pa! Thawt I'm glad a gull for his pawsdeen
fiunn! Goborro, sez he, Lankyshied! Gobugga ye, sez I! O
breezes! I sniffed that lad long before anyone. It was when I was
in my farfather out at the west and she and myself, the redheaded
girl, firstnighting down Sycomore Lane. Fine feelplay we had
of it mid the kissabetts frisking in the kool kurkle dusk of the
lushiness. My perfume of the pampas, says she (meaning me)
putting out her netherlights, and I'd sooner one precious sip at
your pure mountain dew than enrich my acquaintance with that
big brewer's belch.

And so they went on, the fourbottle men, the analists, ungu-
am and nunguam and lunguam again, their anschluss about her
whosebefore and his whereafters and how she was lost away
away in the fern and how he was founded deap on deep in anear,
and the rustlings and the twitterings and the raspings and the
snappings and the sighings and the paintings and the ukukuings
and the (hist!) the springapartings and the (hast!) the bybyscutt-
lings and all the scandalmunkers and the pure craigs that used to
be (up) that time living and lying and rating and riding round
Nunsbelly Square. And all the buds in the bush. And the laugh-

ing jackass. Harik! Harik! Harik! The rose is white in the darik!
And Sunfella's nose has got rhinoceritis from haunting the roes
in the parik! So all rogues lean to rhyme. And contradrinking
themselves about Lillytrilly law pon hilly and Mrs. Niall of the
Nine Corsages and the old markiss their besterfar, and, arrah,
sure there was never a marcus at all at all among the manlies and
dear Sir armoury, queer sir rumoury, and the old house by the
churpelizod, and all the goings on so very wrong long before
when they were going on retreat, in the old gammeldags, the
four of them, in Milton's Park under lovely Father Whisperer
and making her love with his stuffstuff in the languish of flowers
and feeling to find was she mushymushy, and wasn't that very
both of them, the saucicissters, *a drahereen o machree*!, and (peep!)
meeting waters most improper (peepette!) ballround the garden,
trickle trickle trickle triss, please, miman, may I go flirting?
farmers gone with a groom and how they used her, mused her,
licksed her and cuddled. I differ with ye! Are you sure of yourself now? You're a liar, excuse me! I will not and you're another! And Lully holding their breach of peace for them. Pool
loll Lolly! To give and to take! And to forego the pasht! And
all will be forgotten! Ah ho! It was too too bad to be falling
out about her kindness pet and the shape of OOOOOOOO
Ourang's time. Well, all right, Lelly. And shakeahand. And
schenkusmore. For Craig sake. Be it suck.

Well?

Well, even should not the framing up of such figments in the
evidential order bring the true truth to light as fortuitously as
a dim seer's setting of a starchart might (heaven helping it!) un-
cover the nakedness of an unknown body in the fields of blue
or as forehearingly as the sibspeeches of all mankind have foliated (earth seizing them!) from the root of some funner's stotter
all the soundest sense to be found immense our special mentalists
now holds (*securus iudicat orbis terrarum*) that by such playing
possum our hagious curious encestor bestly saved his brush with
his posterity, you, charming coparcenors, us, heirs of his tailsie.
Gundogs of all breeds were beagling with renounced urbiandor-

bic bugles, hot to run him, given law, on a scent breasthigh,
keen for the worry. View! From his holt outratted across the
Juletide's genial corsslands of Humfries Chase from Mullinahob
and Peacockstown, then bearing right upon Tankardstown, the
outlier, a white noelan which Mr. Lœwensteil Fitz Urse's basset
beaters had first misbadgered for a bruin of some swart, led
bayers the run, then through Raystown and Horlockstown and,
louping the loup, to Tankardstown again. Ear canny hare for
doubling through Cheeverstown they raced him, through
Loughlinstown and Nutstown to wind him by the Boolies. But
from the good turn when he last was lost, check, upon Ye Hill
of Rut in full winter coat with ticker pads, pointing for his room-
ing house his old nordest in his rolltoproyal hessians a deaf fuchser's volponism hid him close in covert, miraculously ravenfed
and buoyed up, in rumer, reticule, onasum and abomasum, upon
(may Allbrewham have his mead!) the creamclotted sherriness of
cinnamon syllabub, Mikkelraved, Nikkelsaved. Hence hounds
hied home. Preservative perseverance in the reeducation of his
intestines was the rebuttal by whilk he sort of git the big bulge
on the whole bunch of spasoakers, dieting against glues and gra-
vies, in that sometime prestreet protown. Vainly violence, viru-
lence and vituperation sought wellnigh utterly to attax and a-
bridge, to derail and depontify, to enrate and inroad, to ongoad
and unhume the great shipping mogul and underlinen overlord.

But the spoil of hesitants, the spell of hesitency. His atake is
it ashe, tittery taw tatterytail, hasitense humponadimply, heyhey-
heyhey a winceywencky.

Assembly men murmured. Reynard is slow!

One feared for his days. Did there yawn? 'Twas his stom-
mick. Eruct? The libber. A gush? From his visuals. Pung? De-
livver him, orelode! He had laid violent hands on himself, it was
brought in Fugger's Newsletter, lain down, all in fagged out,
with equally melancholy death. For the triduum of Saturnalia
his goatservant had paraded hiz willingsons in the Forum while
the jenny infanted the lass to be greeted raucously (the Yardstat-
ed) with houx and spheus and measured with missiles too from

a hundred of manhood and a wimmering of weibes. Big went
the bang: then wildewide was quiet: a report: silence: last Fama
put it under ether. The noase or the loal had dreven him blem,
blem, stun blem. Sparks flew. He had fled again (open shun-
shema!) this country of exile, sloughed off sidleshomed *via* the
subterranean shored with bedboards, stowed away and ankered
in a dutch bottom tunk the Arsa, *hod* S.S. Finlandia, and was
even now occupying, under an islamitic newhame in his seventh
generation, a physical body Cornelius Magrath's (badoldkarak-
ter, commonorrong canbung) in Asia Major, where as Turk of
the theater (first house all flatty: the king, eleven sharps) he had
bepiastered the buikdanseuses from the opulence of his omni-
box while as arab at the streetcoor he bepestered the bumbashaws
for the alms of a para's pence. Wires hummed. Peacefully general
astonishment assisted by regrettitude had put a term till his existence: he saw the family saggarth, resigned, put off his remain-
ders, was recalled and scrapheaped by the Maker. Chirpings
crossed. An infamous private ailment (vulgovarioveneral) had
claimed endright, closed his vicious circle, snap. Jams jarred.
He had walked towards the middle of an ornamental lilypond
when innebriated up to the point where braced shirts meet knic-
kerbockers, as wangfish daring the buoyant waters, when rod-
men's firstaiding hands had rescued un from very possibly several
feel of demifrish water. Mush spread. On Umbrella Street where
he did drinks from a pumps a kind workman, Mr. Whitlock,
gave him a piece of wood. What words of power were made fas
between them, ekenames and auchnomes, *acnomina ecnumina?*
That, O that, did Hansard tell us, would gar ganz Dub's ear
wag in every pub of all the citta! Batty believes a baton while
Hogan hears a hod yet heer prefers a punsil shapner and Cope
and Bull go cup and ball. And the Cassidy — Craddock rome
and reme round e'er a wiege ne'er a waage is still immer and
immor awagering over it a cradle with a care in it or a casket
with a kick behind. Toties testies quoties questies. The war is
in words and the wood is the world. Maply me, willowy we,
hickory he and yew yourselves. Howforhim chirrupeth evereach-

bird! From golddawn glory to glowworm gleam. We were
lowquacks did we not tacit turn. Elsewere there here no concern of the Guinnesses. But only the ruining of the rain has
heard. *Estout pourporteral!* Cracklings cricked. A human pest
cycling (pist!) and recycling (past!) about the sledgy streets, here
he was (pust!) again! Morse nuisance noised. He was loose at
large and (Oh baby!) might be anywhere when a disguised ex-
nun, of huge standbuild and masculine manners in her fairly fat
forties, Carpulenta Gygasta, hattracted hattention by harbitrary
conduct with a homnibus. Aerials buzzed to coastal listeners of
an oertax bror collector's budget, fullybigs, sporran, tie, tuft,
tabard and bloody antichill cloak, its tailor's (Baernfather's) tab
reading V.P.H., found nigh Scaldbrothar's Hole, and divers
shivered to think what kaind of beast, wolves, croppis's or fourpenny friars, had devoured him. C. W. cast wide. Hvidfinns lyk,
drohneth svertgleam, Valkir lockt. On his pinksir's postern, the
boys had it, at Whitweekend had been nailed an inkedup name
and title, inscribed in the national cursives, accelerated, regres-
sive, filiform, turreted and envenomoloped in piggotry: Move
up. Mumpty! Mike room for Rumpty! By order, Nickekellous
Plugg; and this go, no pentecostal jest about it, how gregarious
his race soever or skilful learned wise cunning knowledgable
clear profound his saying fortitudo fraught or prudentiaproven,
were he chief, count, general, fieldmarshal, prince, king or Myles
the Slasher in his person, with a moliamordhar mansion in the
Breffnian empire and a place of inauguration on the hill of Tully-
mongan, there had been real murder, of the rayheallach royghal
raxacraxian variety, the MacMahon chaps, it was, that had done
him in. On the fidd of Verdor the rampart combatants had left
him lion with his dexter handcoup wresterected in a pureede
paumee bloody proper. Indeed not a few thick and thin wellwishers, mostly of the clontarfminded class, (Colonel John Bawle
O'Roarke, fervxamplus), even ventured so far as to loan or beg
copies of D. Blayncy's trilingual triweekly, Scatterbrains' Aften-
ing Posht so as to make certain sure onetime and be satisfied of
their quasicontribusodalitarian's having become genuinely quite

beetly dead whether by land whither by water. Transocean atalaclamoured him; The latter! The latter! Shall their hope then be silent or Macfarlane lack of lamentation? He lay under leagues of it in deep Bartholoman's Deep.

Achdung! Pozor! Attenshune! Vikeroy Besights Smucky Yung Pigeschoolies. Tri Paisdinernes Eventyr Med Lochlanner Fathach I Fiounnisgehaven. Bannalanna Bangs Ballyhooly Out Of Her Buddaree Of A Bullavogue.

But, their bright little contemporaries notwithstanding, on the morrowing morn of the suicidal murder of the unrescued expatriate, aslike as asnake comes sliduant down that oaktree onto the duke of beavers, (you may have seen some liquidamber exude exotic from a balsam poplar at Parteen-a-lax Limestone. Road and cried Abies Magnifica! not, noble fir?) a quarter of nine, imploring his resipiency, saw the infallible spike of smoke's jutstiff punctual from the seventh gable of our Quintus Centimachus' porphyroid buttertower and then thirsty p.m. with oaths upon his lastingness (*En caecos harauspices! Annos longos patimur!*) the lamps of maintenance, beaconsfarafield innerhalf the zuggurat, all brevetnamed, the wasting wyvern, the tawny of his mane, the swinglowswaying bluepaw, the outstanding man, the lolllike lady, being litten for the long (O land, how long!) lifesnight, with suffusion of fineglass transom and leadlight panes.

Wherefore let it hardly by any being thinking be said either or thought that the prisoner of that sacred edifice, were he an Ivor the Boneless or an Olaf the Hide, was at his best a onestone parable, a rude breathing on the void of to be, a venter hearing his own bauchspeech in backwords, or, more strictly, but tristurned initials, the cluekey to a worldroom beyond the roomwhorld, for scarce one, or pathetically few of his dode canal sammenlivers cared seriously or for long to doubt with Kurt Iuld van Dijke (the gravitational pull perceived by certain fixed residents and the capture of uncertain comets chancedrifting through our system suggesting an authenticitatem of his aliquitudinis) the canonicity of his existence as a tesseract. Be still, O quick! Speak him dumb! Hush ye fronds of Ulma!

Dispersal women wondered. Was she fast?

Do tell us all about. As we want to hear allabout. So tellus tel-las allabouter. The why or whether she looked alottylike like ussies and whether he had his wimdop like themses shut? Notes and queries, tipbids and answers, the laugh and the shout, the ards and downs. Now listed to one aneither and liss them down and smoothen out your leaves of rose. The war is o'er. Wimwim wimwim! Was it Unity Moore or Estella Swifte or Varina Fay or Quarta Quaedam? Toemaas, mark oom for yor ounckel! Pigeys, hold op med yer leg! Who, but who (for second time of asking) was then the scourge of the parts about folkrich Luca-lizod it was wont to be asked, as, in ages behind of the Homo Capite Erectus, what price Peabody's money, or, to put it bluntly, whence is the herringtons' white cravat, as, in epochs more cainozoic, who struck Buckley though nowadays as then-times every schoolfilly of sevenscore moons or more who know her intimologies and every colleen bawl aroof and every red-flammelwaving warwife and widowpeace upon Dublin Wall for ever knows as yayas is yayas how it was Buckleyself (we need no blooding paper to tell it neither) who struck and the Russian generals, da! da!, instead of Buckley who was caddishly struck by him when be herselves. What fullpried paulpoison in the spy of three castles or which hatefilled smileyseller? And that such a vetriol of venom, that queen's head affranchisant, a quiet stink-ingplaster zeal could cover, prepostered or postpaid! The lounge-lizards of the pumproom had their nine days' jeer, and pratsch-kats at their platschpails too and holenpolendom beside, Szpasz-pas Szpissmas, the zhanyzhonies, when, still believing in her owenglass, when izarres were twinklins, that the upper reaches of her mouthless face and her impermanent waves were the better half of her, one nearer him, dearer than all, first warming creature of his early morn, bondwoman of the man of the house, and murrmurr of all the mackavicks, she who had given his eye for her bed and a tooth for a child till one one and one ten and one hundred again, O me and O ye! cadet and prim, the hungray and anngreen (and if she is older now than her teeth she has hair that

is younger than thighne, my dear!) she who shuttered him after
his fall and waked him widowt sparing and gave him keen and
made him able and held adazillahs to each arche of his noes, she
who will not rast her from her running to seek him till, with the
help of the okeamic, some such time that she shall have been after
hiding the crumbends of his enormousness in the areyou looking-
for Pearlfar sea, (ur, uri, uria!) stood forth, burnzburn the gorg-
gony old danworld, in gogor's name, for gagar's sake, dragging
the countryside in her train, finickin here and funickin there,
with her louisequean's brogues and her culunder buzzle and her
little bolero boa and all and two times twenty curlicornies for her
headdress, specks on her eyeux, and spudds on horeilles and a
circusfix riding her Parisienne's cockneze, a vaunt her straddle
from Equerry Egon, when Tinktink in the churchclose clinked
Steploajazzyma Sunday, *Sola*, with pawns, prelates and pookas
pelotting in her piecebag, for Handiman the Chomp, Esquoro,
biskbask, to crush the slander's head.

Wery weeny wight, plead for Morandmor! *Notre Dame de la
Ville*, mercy of thy balmheartzyheat! Ogrowdnyk's beyond her-
bata tay, wort of the drogist. Bulk him no bulkis. And let him
rest, thou wayfarre, and take no gravespoil from him! Neither
mar his mound! The bane of Tut is on it. Ware! But there's a
little lady waiting and her name is A.L.P. And you'll agree. She
must be she. For her holden heirheaps hanging down her back.
He spenth his strenth amok haremscarems. Poppy Narancy, Gial-
lia, Chlora, Marinka, Anileen, Parme. And ilk a those dames had
her rainbow huemoures yet for whilko her whims but he coined a
cure. Tifftiff today, kissykissy tonay and agelong pine tomauran-
na. Then who but Crippled-with-Children would speak up for
Dropping-with-Sweat?

> *Sold him her lease of ninenineninetee,*
> *Tresses undresses so dyedyedaintee,*
> *Goo, the groot gudgeon, gulped it all.*
> *Hoo was the C. O. D.?*
>   Bum!

> *At Island Bridge she met her tide.*
> *Attabom, attabom, attabombomboom!*
> *The Fin had a flux and his Ebba a ride.*
> *Attabom, attabom, attabombomboom!*
> *We're all up to the years in hues and cribies.*
> *That's what she's done for wee!*
> > Woe!

Nomad may roam with Nabuch but let naaman laugh at Jordan! For we, we have taken our sheet upon her stones where we have hanged our hearts in her trees; and we list, as she bibs us, by the waters of babalong.

In the name of Annah the Allmaziful, the Everliving, the Bringer of Pluralabilities, haloed be her eve, her singtime sung, her rill be run, unhemmed as it is uneven!

Her untitled mamafesta memorialising the Mosthighest has gone by many names at disjointed times. Thus we hear of, *The Augusta Angustissimost for Old Seabeastius' Salvation, Rockabill Booby in the Wave Trough, Here's to the Relicts of All Decencies, Anna Stessa's Rise to Notice, Knickle Down Duddy Gunne and Arishe Sir Cannon, My Golden One and My Selver Wedding, Amoury Treestam and Icy Siseule, Saith a Sawyer til a Strame, Ik dik dopedope et tu mihimihi, Buy Birthplate for a Bite, Which of your Hesterdays Mean Ye to Morra? Hoebegunne the Hebrewer Hit Waterman the Brayned, Arcs in His Ceiling Flee Chinx on the Flur, Rebus de Hibernicis, The Crazier Letters, Groans of a Briton-ess, Peter Peopler Picked a Plot to Pitch his Poppolin, An Apology for a Big* (some such nonoun *as Husband* or *husboat* or *hose-bound* is probably understood for we have also the plutherple-thoric *My Hoonsbood Hansbaad's a Journey to Porthergill gone and He Never Has the Hour*), *Ought We To Visit Him? For Ark see Zoo, Cleopater's Nedlework Ficturing Aldborougham on the Sahara with the Coombing of the Cammmels and the Parlourmaids of Aegypt, Cock in the Pot for Father, Placeat Vestrae, A New Cure for an Old Clap, Where Portentos they'd Grow Gonder how I'd Wish I Woose a Geese; Gettle Nettie, Thrust him not, When the*

*Myrtles of Venice Played to Bloccus's Line, To Plenge Me High
He Waives Chiltern on Friends, Oremunds Queue Visits Amen
Mart, E'en Tho' I Granny a-be He would Fain Me Cuddle, Twenty
of Chambers, Weighty Ten Beds and a Wan Ceteroom, I Led the
Life, Through the Boxer Coxer Rising in the House with the Golden
Stairs, The Following Fork, He's my O'Jerusalem and I'm his
Po, The Best in the West, By the Stream of Zemzem under Zig-
zag Hill, The Man That Made His Mother in the Marlborry
Train. Try Our Taal on a Taub, The Log of Anny to the Base
All, Nopper Tipped a Nappiwenk to his Notylytl Dantsigirls, Prszss
Orel Orel the King of Orlbrdsz, Intimier Minnelisp of an Extor-
reor Monolothe, Drink to Him, My Juckey and Dhoult Bemine
Thy Winnowing Sheet, I Ask You to Believe I was his Mistress,
He Can Explain, From Victrolia Nuancee to Allbart Noahnsy,
Da's a Daisy so Guimea your Handsel too, What Barbaras Done
to a Barrel Organ Before the Rank, Tank and Bonnbtail, Huskvy
Admortal, What Jumbo made to Jalice and what Anisette to Him,
Ophelia's Culpreints, Hear Hubty Hublin, My Old Dansh, I am
Older northe Rogues among Whisht I Slips and He Calls Me his
Dual of Ayessha, Suppotes a Ventriliquorst Merries a Corpse,
Lapps for Finns This Funnycoon's Week, How the Buckling Shut
at Rush in January, Look to the Lady, From the Rise of the
Dudge Pupublick to the Fall of the Potstille, Of the Two Ways
of Opening the Mouth, I have not Stopped Water Where It Should
Flow and I Know the Twentynine Names of Attraente, The Tortor
of Tory Island Traits Galasia like his Milchcow, From Abbeygate
to Crowalley Through a Lift in the Lude, Smocks for Their Graces
and Me Aunt for Them Clodshoppers, How to Pull a Good Horus-
coup even when Oldsire is Dead to the World, Inn the Gleam of
Waherlow, Fathe He's Sukceded to My Esperations, Thee Steps
Forward, Two Stops Back, My Skin Appeals to Three Senses and
My Curly Lips Demand Columbkisses; Gage Street on a Crany's
Savings, Them Lads made a Trion of Battlewatschers and They
Totties a Doeit of Deers, In My Lord's Bed by One Whore Went
Through It, Mum It is All Over, Cowpoyride by Twelve Acre Ter-
riss in the Unique Estates of Amessican, He Gave me a Thou so I*

serve Him with Thee, Of all the Wide Torsos in all the Wild Glen,
O'Donogh, White Donogh, He's Hue to Me Cry, I'm the Stitch
in his Baskside You'd be Nought Without Mom, To Keep the
Huskies off the Hustings and Picture Pets from Lifting Shops, Nor-
sker Torsker Find the Poddle, He Perssed Me Here with the Ardour
of a Tonnoburkes, A Boob Was Weeping This Mower was Reaping,
O'Loughlin, Up from the Pit of my Stomach I Swish you the White
of the Mourning, Inglo-Andean Medoleys from Tommany Moohr,
The Great Polynesional Entertrainer Exhibits Ballantine Braut-
chers with the Link of Natures, The Mimic of Meg Neg and
the Mackeys, Entered as the Lastest Pigtarial and My Pooridiocal
at Stitchioner's Hall, Siegfield Follies and or a Gentlehomme's Faut
Pas, See the First Book of Jealesies Pessim, The Suspended Sen-
tence, A Pretty Brick Story for Childsize Heroes, As Lo Our Sleep,
I Knew I'd Got it in Me so Thit settles That, Thonderbalt Captain
Smeth and La Belle Sauvage Pocahonteuse, Way for Wet Week
Welikin's Douchka Marianne, The Last of the Fingallians, It Was
Me Egged Him on to the Stork Exchange and Lent my Dutiful
Face to His Customs, Chee Chee Cheels on their China Miction,
Pickedmeup Peters, Lumptytumtumpty had a Big Fall, Pimpimp
Pimpimp, Measly Ventures of Two Lice and the Fall of Fruit,
The Fokes Family Interior, If my Spreadeagles Wasn't so Tight
I'd Loosen my Cursits on that Bunch of Maggiestraps, Allolosha
Popofetts and Howke Cotchme Eye, Seen Aples and Thin Dyed,
i big U to Beleaves from Love and Mother, Fine's Fault was no
Felon, Exat Delvin Renter Life The Flash that Flies from Vuggy's
Eyes has Set Me Hair On Fire, His is the House that Malt Made,
Divine Views from Back to the Front, Abe to Sare Stood Icyk
Neuter till Brahm Taulked Him Common Sex, A Nibble at Eve
Will That Bowal Relieve, Allfor Guineas, Sounds and Compliments
Libidous, Seven Wives Awake Aweek, Airy Ann and Berber Blut,
Amy Licks Porter While Huffy Chops Eads, Abbrace of Umbellas
or a Tripple of Caines, Buttbutterbust, From the Manorlord Hoved
to the Misses O'Mollies and from the Dames to their Sames, Many-
festoons for the Colleagues on the Green, An Outstanding Back and
an Excellent Halfcentre if Called on, As Tree is Quick and Stone is

*White So is My Washing Done by Night, First and Last Only
True Account all about the Honorary Mirsu Earwicker, L.S.D.,
and the Snake (Nuggets!) by a Woman of the World who only can
Tell Naked Truths about a Dear Man and all his Conspirators how
they all Tried to Fall him Putting it all around Lucalizod about
Privates Earwicker and a Pair of Sloppy Sluts plainly Showing all
the Unmentionability falsely Accusing about the Raincoats.*

The proteiform graph itself is a polyhedron of scripture.
There was a time when naif alphabetters would have written it
down the tracing of a purely deliquescent recidivist, possibly
ambidextrous, snubnosed probably and presenting a strangely
profound rainbowl in his (or her) occiput. To the hardily curiosing entomophilust then it has shown a very sexmosaic of nym-
phosis in which the eternal chimerahunter Oriolopos, now frond
of sugars, then lief of saults, the sensory crowd in his belly
coupled with an eye for the goods trooth bewilderblissed by
their night effluvia with guns like drums and fondlers like forceps
persequestellates his vanessas from flore to flore. Somehows this
sounds like the purest kidooleyoon wherein our madernacerution
of lour lore is rich. All's so herou from us him in a kitchernott
darkness, by hasard and worn rolls arered, we must grope on till
Zerogh hour like pou owl giaours as we are would we salve aught
of moments for our aysore today. Amousin though not but. Closer
inspection of the *bordereau* would reveal a multiplicity of personalities inflicted on the documents or document and some prevision
of virtual crime or crimes might be made by anyone unwary
enough before any suitable occasion for it or them had so far
managed to happen along. In fact, under the closed eyes of the in-
spectors the traits featuring the *chiaroscuro* coalesce, their con-
trarieties eliminated, in one stable somebody similarly as by the
providential warring of heartshaker with housebreaker and of
dramdrinker against freethinker our social something bowls along
bumpily, experiencing a jolting series of prearranged disappoint-
ments, down the long lane of (it's as semper as oxhousehumper!)
generations, more generations and still more generations.

Say, baroun lousadoor, who in hallhagal wrote the durn thing

anyhow? Erect, beseated, mountback, against a partywall, below
freezigrade, by the use of quill or style, with turbid or pellucid
mind, accompanied or the reverse by mastication, interrupted
by visit of seer to scribe or of scribe to site, atwixt two showers
or atosst of a trike, rained upon or blown around, by a right-
down regular racer from the soil or by a too pained whittlewit
laden with the loot of learning?

Now, patience; and remember patience is the great thing, and
above all things else we must avoid anything like being or becoming out of patience. A good plan used by worried business
folk who may not have had many momentums to mastes Kung's
doctrine of the meang or the propriety codestruces of Carpri-
mustimus is just to think of all the sinking fund of patience possessed in their conjoint names by both brothers Bruce with whom
are incorporated their Scotch spider and Elberfeld's Calculating
Horses. If after years upon years of delving in ditches dark one
tubthumper more than others, Kinihoun or Kahanan, giardarner
or mear measenmanonger, has got up for the darnall same purpose of reassuring us with all the barbar of the Carrageehouse
that our great ascendant was properly speaking three syllables
less than his own surname (yes, yes, less!), that the ear of Fionn
Earwicker aforetime was the trademark of a broadcaster with
wicker local jargot for an ace's patent (Hear! Calls! Everywhair!)
then as to this radiooscillating epiepistle to which, cotton, silk or
samite, kohol, gall or brickdust, we must ceaselessly return, whereabouts exactly at present in Siam, Hell or Tophet under that
glorisol which plays touraloup with us in this Aludin's Cove of
our cagacity is that bright soandsuch to slip us the dinkum oil?

Naysayers we know. To conclude purely negatively from the
positive absence of political odia and monetary requests that its
page cannot ever have been a penproduct of a man or woman of
that period or those parts is only one more unlookedfor conclusion leaped at, being tantamount to inferring from the nonpre-
sence of inverted commas (sometimes called quotation marks)
on any page that its author was always constitutionally incapable
of misappropriating the spoken words of others.

Luckily there is another cant to the questy. Has any fellow, of the dime a dozen type, it might with some profit some dull evening quietly be hinted — has any usual sort of ornery josser, flatchested fortyish, faintly flatulent and given to ratiocination by syncopation in the elucidation of complications of his greatest Fung Yang dynasdescendance, only the son of another, in fact, ever looked sufficiently longly at a quite everydaylooking stamped addressed envelope? Admittedly it is an outer husk: its face, in all its featureful perfection of imperfection, is its fortune: it exhibits only the civil or military clothing of whatever passionpallid nudity or plaguepurple nakedness may happen to tuck itself under its flap. Yet to concentrate solely on the literal sense or even the psychological content of any document to the sore neglect of the enveloping facts themselves circumstantiating it is just as hurtful to sound sense (and let it be added to the truest taste) as were some fellow in the act of perhaps getting an intro from another fellow turning out to be a friend in need of his, say, to a lady of the latter's acquaintance, engaged in performing the elaborative antecistral ceremony of upstheres, straightaway to run off and vision her plump and plain in her natural altogether, preferring to close his blinkhard's eyes to the ethiquethical fact that she was, after all, wearing for the space of the time being some definite articles of evolutionary clothing, inharmonious creations, a captious critic might describe them as, or not strictly necessary or a trifle irritating here and there, but for all that suddenly full of local colour and personal perfume and suggestive, too, of so very much more and capable of being stretched, filled out, if need or wish were, of having their surprisingly like coincidental parts separated don't they now, for better survey by the deft hand of an expert, don't you know. Who in his heart doubts either that the facts of feminine clothiering are there all the time or that the feminine fiction, stranger than the facts, is there also at the same time, only a little to the rere? Or that one may be separated from the other? Or that both may then be contemplated simultaneously? Or that each may be taken up and considered in turn apart from the other?

Here let a few artifacts fend in their own favour. The river felt she wanted salt. That was just where Brien came in. The country asked for bearspaw for dindin! And boundin aboundin it got it surly. We who live under heaven, we of the clovery kingdom, we middlesins people have often watched the sky overreaching the land. We suddenly have. Our isle is Sainge. The place. That stern chuckler Mayhappy Mayhapnot, once said to repeation in that lutran conservatory way of his that Isitachapel-Asitalukin was the one place, *ult aut nult*, in this madh vaal of tares (whose verdhure's yellowed therever Phaiton parks his car while its tamelised tay is the drame of Drainophilias) where the possible was the improbable and the improbable the inevitable. If the proverbial bishop of our holy and undivided with this me ken or no me ken Zot is the Quiztune havvermashed had his twoe nails on the head we are in for a sequentiality of improbable possibles though possibly nobody after having grubbed up a lock of cwold cworn aboove his subject probably in Harrystotalies or the vivle will go out of his way to applaud him on the onboiassed back of his remark for utterly impossible as are all these events they are probably as like those which may have taken place as any others which never took person at all are ever likely to be. Ahahn!

About that original hen. Midwinter (fruur or kuur?) was in the offing and Premver a promise of a pril when, as kischabrigies sang life's old sahatsong, an iceclad shiverer, merest of bantlings observed a cold fowl behaviourising strangely on that fatal midden or chip factory or comicalbottomed copsjute (dump for short) afterwards changed into the orangery when in the course of deeper demolition unexpectedly one bushman's holiday its limon threw up a few spontaneous fragments of orangepeel, the last remains of an outdoor meal by some unknown sunseeker or placehider *illico* way back in his mistridden past. What child of a strandlooper but keepy little Kevin in the despondful surrounding of such sneezing cold would ever have trouved up on a strate that was called strete a motive for future saintity by euchring the finding of the Ardagh chalice by another heily innocent and beachwalker whilst trying with pious clamour to wheedle Tip-

peraw raw raw reeraw puteters out of Now Sealand in spignt
of the patchpurple of the massacre, a dual a duel to die to
day, goddam and biggod, sticks and stanks, of most of the
Jacobiters.

The bird in the case was Belinda of the Dorans a more than
quinquegintarian (Terziis prize with Serni medal, Cheepalizzy's
Hane Exposition) and what she was scratching at the hour of
klokking twelve looked for all this zogzag world like a goodish-
sized sheet of letterpaper originating by transhipt from Boston
(Mass.) of the last of the first to Dear whom it proceded to
mention Maggy well & allathome's health well only the hate
turned the mild on *the van* Houtens and the general's elections
with a *lovely* face of some born gentleman with a beautiful present
of wedding cakes for dear thankyou Chriesty and with grand
funferall of poor Father Michael don't forget unto life's & Muggy
well how are you Maggy & hopes soon to hear well & must now
close it with fondest to the twoinns with four crosskisses for holy
paul holey corner holipoli whollyisland pee ess from (locust may
eat all but this sign shall they never) affectionate largelooking
tache of tch. The stain, and that a teastain (the overcautelousness
of the masterbilker here, as usual, signing the page away), marked
it off on the spout of the moment as a genuine relique of ancient
Irish pleasant pottery of that lydialike languishing class known as
a hurry-me-o'er-the-hazy.

Why then how?

Well, almost any photoist worth his chemicots will tip anyone
asking him the teaser that if a negative of a horse happens to melt
enough while drying, well, what you do get is, well, a positively
grotesquely distorted macromass of all sorts of horsehappy values
and masses of meltwhile horse. Tip. Well, this freely is what
must have occurred to our missive (there's a sod of a turb for
you! please wisp off the grass!) unfilthed from the boucher by
the sagacity of a lookmelittle likemelong hen. Heated residence
in the heart of the orangeflavoured mudmound had partly ob-
literated the negative to start with, causing some features palpably nearer your pecker to be swollen up most grossly while

the farther back we manage to wiggle the more we need the loan
of a lens to see as much as the hen saw. Tip.

You is feeling like you was lost in the bush, boy? You says:
It is a puling sample jungle of woods. You most shouts out:
Bethicket me for a stump of a beech if I have the poultriest notions what the farest he all means. Gee up, girly! The quad gos-
pellers may own the targum but any of the Zingari shoolerim
may pick a peck of kindlings yet from the sack of auld hensyne.

Lead, kindly fowl! They always did: ask the ages. What bird
has done yesterday man may do next year, be it fly, be it moult,
be it hatch, be it agreement in the nest. For her socioscientific
sense is sound as a bell, sir, her volucrine automutativeness right
on normalcy: she knows, she just feels she was kind of born to
lay and love eggs (trust her to propagate the species and hoosh
her fluffballs safe through din and danger!); lastly but mostly, in
her genesic field it is all game and no gammon, she is ladylike in
everything she does and plays the gentleman's part every time.
Let us auspice it! Yes, before all this has time to end the golden
age must return with its vengeance. Man will become dirigible,
Ague will be rejuvenated, woman with her ridiculous white burden will reach by one step sublime incubation, the manewanting
human lioness with her dishorned discipular manram will lie
down together publicly flank upon fleece. No, assuredly, they are
not justified, those gloompourers who grouse that letters have
never been quite their old selves again since that weird weekday
in bleak Janiveer (yet how palmy date in a waste's oasis!) when
to the shock of both, Biddy Doran looked ad literature.

And. She may be a mere marcella, this midget madgetcy,
Misthress of Arths. But. It is not a hear or say of some anomo-
rous letter, signed Toga Girilis, (teasy dear). We have a cop of
her fist right against our nosibos. We note the paper with her
jotty young watermark: *Notre Dame du Bon Marché*. And she
has a heart of Arin! What lumililts as she fols with her falli-
mineers and her nadianods. As a strow will shaw she does the
wind blague, recting to show the rudess of a robur curling and
shewing the fansaties of a frizette. But how many of her readers

realise that she is not out to dizzledazzle with a graith uncouthre-
ment of postmantuam glasseries from the lapins and the grigs.
Nuttings on her wilelife! Grabar gooden grandy for old almea-
nium adamologists like Dariaumaurius and Zovotrimaserov-
meravmerouvian; (dmzn!); she feel plain plate one flat fact thing
and if, lastways firdstwise, a man alones sine anyon anyons
utharas has no rates to done a kik at with anyon anakars about
tutus milking fores and the rereres on the outerrand asikin the
tutus to be forrarder. Thingcrooklyexineverypasturesixdix-
likencehimaroundhersthemaggerbykinkinkankanwithdownmind-
lookingated. Mesdaims, Marmouselles, Mescerfs! Silvapais! All
schwants (schwrites) ischt tell the cock's trootabout him. Ka-
pak kapuk. No minzies matter. He had to see life foully the
plak and the smut, (schwrites). There were three men in him
(schwrites). Dancings (schwrites) was his only ttoo feebles.
With apple harlottes. And a little mollvogels. Spissially (schwrites)
when they peaches. Honeys wore camelia paints. Yours very
truthful. Add dapple inn. Yet is it but an old story, the tale of
a Treestone with one Ysold, of a Mons held by tentpegs and his
pal whatholoosed on the run, what Cadman could but Badman
wouldn't, any Genoaman against any Venis, and why Kate takes
charge of the waxworks.

    Let us now, weather, health, dangers, public orders and other
circumstances permitting, of perfectly convenient, if you police,
after you, policepolice, pardoning mein, ich beam so fresch, bey?
drop this jiggerypokery and talk straight turkey meet to mate, for
while the ears, be we mikealls or nicholists, may sometimes be inclined to believe others the eyes, whether browned or nolensed,
find it devilish hard now and again even to believe itself. *Habes
aures et num videbis? Habes oculos ac mannepalpabuat?* Tip! Drawing nearer to take our slant at it (since after all it has met with
misfortune while all underground), let us see all there may remain
to be seen.

    I am a worker, a tombstone mason, anxious to pleace avery-
buries and jully glad when Christmas comes his once ayear. You
are a poorjoist, unctuous to polise nopebobbies and tunnibelly

soully when 'tis thime took o'er home, gin. We cannot say aye
to aye. We cannot smile noes from noes. Still. One cannot help
noticing that rather more than half of the lines run north-south
in the Nemzes and Bukarahast directions while the others go
west-east in search from Maliziies with Bulgarad for tiny tot
though it looks when schtschupnistling alongside other incuna-
bula it has its cardinal points for all that. These ruled barriers
along which the traced words, run, march, halt, walk, stumble
at doubtful points, stumble up again in comparative safety seem
to have been drawn first of all in a pretty checker with lamp-
black and blackthorn. Such crossing is antechristian of course,
but the use of the homeborn shillelagh as an aid to calligraphy
shows a distinct advance from savagery to barbarism. It is
seriously believed by some that the intention may have been
geodetic, or, in the view of the cannier, domestic economical.
But by writing thithaways end to end and turning, turning and
end to end hithaways writing and with lines of litters slittering
up and louds of latters slettering down, the old semetomyplace
and jupetbackagain from tham Let Rise till Hum Lit. Sleep,
where in the waste is the wisdom?

Another point, in addition to the original sand, pounce powder, drunkard paper or soft rag used (any vet or inhanger in
ous sot's social can see the seen for seemself, a wee ftofty od
room, the cheery spluttered on the one karrig, a darka disheen
of voos from Dalbania, any gotsquantity of racky, a portogal
and some buk setting out on the sofer, you remember the
sort of softball sucker motru used to tell us when we were all
biribiyas or nippies and messas) it has acquired accretions of
terricious matter whilst loitering in the past. The teatimestained
terminal (say not the tag, mummer, or our show's a failure!) is a
cosy little brown study all to oneself and, whether it be thumb-
print, mademark or just a poor trait of the artless, its importance
in establishing the identities in the writer complexus (for if the
hand was one, the minds of active and agitated were more than
so) will be best appreciated by never forgetting that both before
and after the battle of the Boyne it was a habit not to sign letters

always. Tip. And it is surely a lesser ignorance to write a word
with every consonant too few than to add all too many. The
end? Say it with missiles then and thus arabesque the page. You
have your cup of scalding Souchong, your taper's waxen drop,
your cat's paw, the clove or coffinnail you chewed or champed
as you worded it, your lark in clear air. So why, pray, sign anything as long as every word, letter, penstroke, paperspace is a
perfect signature of its own? A true friend is known much more
easily, and better into the bargain, by his personal touch, habits
of full or undress, movements, response to appeals for charity
than by his footwear, say. And, speaking anent Tiberias and other
incestuish salacities among gerontophils, a word of warning
about the tenderloined passion hinted at. Some softnosed per-
user might mayhem take it up erogenously as the usual case of
spoons, *prostituta in herba* plus dinky pinks deliberatively summer-
saulting off her bisexycle, at the main entrance of curate's perpetual soutane suit with her one to see and awoh! who picks her
up as gingerly as any balmbearer would to feel whereupon the
virgin was most hurt and nicely asking: whyre have you been so
grace a mauling and where were you chaste me child? Be who,
farther potential? and so wider but we grisly old Sykos who have
done our unsmiling bit on 'alices, when they were yung and
easily freudened, in the penumbra of the procuring room and
what oracular comepression we have had apply to them! could
(did we care to sell our feebought silence *in camera*) tell our very
moistnostrilled one that *father* in such virgated contexts is not
always that undemonstrative relative (often held up to our con-
tumacy) who settles our hashbill for us and what an innocent allabroad's adverb such as Michaelly looks like can be suggestive
of under the pudendascope and, finally, what a neurasthene nym-
pholept, endocrine-pineal typus, of inverted parentage with a
prepossessing drauma present in her past and a priapic urge for
congress with agnates before cognates fundamentally is feeling
for under her lubricitous meiosis when she refers with liking to
some feeler she fancie's face. And Mm. We could. Yes what need
to say? 'Tis as human a little story as paper could well carry, in

affect, as singsing so Salaman susuing to swittvitles while as un-
bluffingly blurtubruskblunt as an Esra, the cat, the cat's meeter,
the meeter's cat's wife, the meeter's cat's wife's half better, the
meeter's cat's wife's half better's meeter, and so back to our
horses, for we also know, what we have perused from the pages
of *I Was A Gemral*, that Showting up of Bulsklivism by 'Schot-
tenboum', that Father Michael about this red time of the white
terror equals the old regime and Margaret is the social revolution
while cakes mean the party funds and dear thank you signifies
national gratitude. In fine, we have heard, as it happened, of
Spartacus intercellular. We are not corknered yet dead hand!
We can recall, with voluntears, the froggy jew, and sweeter far
'twere now westhinks in Dumbil's fair city ere one more year is
o'er. We tourned our coasts to the good gay tunes. When from
down swords the sea merged the oldowth guns and answer made
the bold O' Dwyer. But. *Est modest in verbos.* Let a prostitute
be whoso stands before a door and winks or parks herself in the
fornix near a makeussin wall (sinsin! sinsin!) and the curate one
who brings strong waters (gingin! gingin!), but also, and dinna
forget, that there is many asleeps between someathome's first
and moreinausland's last and that the beautiful presence of waiting kates will until life's (!) be more than enough to make any
milkmike in the language of sweet tarts·punch hell's hate into his
twin nicky and that Maggy's tea, or your majesty, if heard as a
boost from a born gentleman. For if the lingo gasped between
kicksheets, however basically English, were to be preached from
the mouths of wickerchurchwardens and metaphysicians in the
row and advokaatoes, allvoyous, demivoyelles, languoaths, les-
biels, dentelles, gutterhowls and furtz, where would their practice be or where the human race itself were the Pythagorean ses-
quipedalia of the panepistemion, however apically Volapucky,
grunted and gromwelled, ichabod, habakuk, opanoff, uggamyg,
hapaxle, gomenon, ppppfff, over country stiles, behind slated
dwellinghouses, down blind lanes, or, when all fruit fails, under
some sacking left on a coarse cart?
  So hath been, love: tis tis: and will be: till wears and tears and

ages. Thief us the night, steal we the air, shawl thiner liefest, mine! Here, Ohere, insult the fair! Traitor, bad hearer, brave! The lightning look, the birding cry, awe from the grave, ever-flowing on the times. Feueragusaria iordenwater; now godsun shine on menday's daughter; a good clap, a fore marriage, a bad wake, tell hell's well; such is manowife's lot of lose and win again, like he's gruen quhiskers on who's chin again, she plucketed them out but they grown in again. So what are you going to do about it? O dear!

If juness she saved! Ah ho! And if yulone he pouved! The ol-old stoliolum! From quiqui quinet to michemiche chelet and a jambebatiste to a brulobrulo! It is told in sounds in utter that, in signs so adds to, in universal, in polygluttural, in each auxiliary neutral idiom, sordomutics, florilingua, sheltafocal, flayflutter, a con's cubane, a pro's tutute, strassarab, ereperse and anythongue athall. Since nozzy Nanette tripped palmyways with Highho Harry there's a spurtfire turf a'kind o'kindling when oft as the souffsouff blows her peaties up and a claypot wet for thee, my Sitys, and talkatalka tell Tibbs has eve: and whathough (revilous life proving aye the death of ronaldses when winpower wine has bucked the kick on poor won man) billiousness has been billious-ness during milliums of millenions and our mixed racings have been giving two hoots or three jeers for the grape, vine and brew and Pieter's in Nieuw Amsteldam and Paoli's where the poules go and rum smelt his end for him and he dined off sooth ameri-can (it would give one the frier even were one a normal Kettle-licker) this oldworld epistola of their weatherings and their marryings and their buryings and their natural selections has combled tumbled down to us fersch and made-at-all-hours like an ould cup on tay. As I was hottin me souser. Haha! And as you was caldin your dutchy hovel. Hoho! She tole the tail or her toon. Huhu!

Now, kapnimancy and infusionism may both fit as tight as two trivets but while we in our wee free state, holding to that prestatute in our charter, may have our irremovable doubts as to the whole sense of the lot, the interpretation of any phrase in the whole, the meaning of every word of a phrase so far deciphered out of it, however unfettered our Irish daily independence, we must vaunt no idle dubiosity as to its genuine authorship and holusbolus authoritativeness. And let us bringtheecease to beakerings on that clink, olmond bottler! On the face of it, to volt back to our desultory horses, and for your roughshod mind, bafflelost bull, the affair is a thing once for all done and there you are somewhere and finished in a certain time, be it a day or a year or even supposing, it should eventually turn out to be a serial number of goodness gracious alone knows how many days or years. Anyhow, somehow and somewhere, before the bookflood or after her ebb, somebody mentioned by name in his telephone directory, Coccolanius or Gallotaurus, wrote it, wrote it all, wrote it all down, and there you are, full stop. O, undoubtedly yes, and very potably so, but one who deeper thinks will always bear in the baccbuccus of his mind that this downright there you are and there it is is only all in his eye. Why?

Because, Soferim Bebel, if it goes to that, (and dormerwindow gossip will cry it from the housetops no surelier than the writing on the wall will hue it to the mod of men that mote in the main street) every person, place and thing in the chaosmos of Alle anyway connected with the gobblydumped turkery was moving and changing every part of the time: the travelling inkhorn (possibly pot), the hare and turtle pen and paper, the continually more and less intermisunderstanding minds of the anticollaborators, the as time went on as it will variously inflected, differently pronounced, otherwise spelled, changeably meaning vocable scriptsigns. No, so holp me Petault, it is not a miseffectual whyacinthinous riot of blots and blurs and bars and balls and hoops and wriggles and juxtaposed jottings linked by spurts of speed: it only looks as like it as damn it; and, sure, we ought really to rest thankful that at this deleteful hour of dungflies dawning we have even a written on with dried ink scrap of paper at all to show for ourselves, tare it or leaf it, (and we are lufted to ourselves as the soulfisher when he led the cat out of the bout) after all that we lost and plundered of it even to the hidmost coignings of the

earth and all it has gone through and by all means, after a good
ground kiss to Terracussa and for wars luck our lefttoff's flung
over our home homoplate, cling to it as with drowning hands,
hoping against hope all the while that, by the light of philo-
phosy, (and may she never folsage us!) things will begin to clear
up a bit one way or another within the next quarrel of an hour
and be hanged to them as ten to one they will too, please the pigs,
as they ought to categorically, as, stricly between ourselves there
is a limit to all things so this will never do.

For, with that farmfrow's foul flair for that flayfell foxfetor,
(the calamite's columitas calling for calamitous calamitance) who
that scrutinising marvels at those indignant whiplooplashes; those
so prudently bolted or blocked rounds; the touching reminiscence
of an incompletet trail or dropped final; a round thousand whirli-
gig glorioles, prefaced by (alas!) now illegible airy plumeflights,
all tiberiously ambiembellishing the initials majuscule of Earwicker: the meant to be baffling chrismon trilithon sign ⋒, finally
called after some his hes hecitency Hec which, moved contra-
watchwise, represents his title in sigla as the smaller Δ, fontly
called following a certain change of state of grace of nature alp
or delta, when single, stands for or tautologically stands beside
the consort: (though for that matter, since we have heard from
Cathay cyrcles how the hen is not mirely a tick or two after the
first fifth fourth of the second eighth twelfth — siangchang
hongkong sansheneul — but yirely the other and thirtieth of the
ninth from the twentieth, our own vulgar 432 and 1132 irre-
spectively, why not take the former for a village inn, the latter
for an upsidown bridge, a multiplication marking for crossroads
ahead, which you like pothook for the family gibbet, their old
fourwheedler for the bucker's field, a tea anyway for a tryst
someday, and his onesidemissing for an allblind alley leading to
an Irish plot in the Champ de Mors, not?) the steady monologuy
of the interiors; the pardonable confusion for which some blame
the cudgel and more blame the soot but unthanks to which
the pees with their caps awry are quite as often as not taken
for kews with their tails in their or are quite as often as not

taken for pews with their tails in their mouths, thence your
pristopher polombos, hence our Kat Kresbyterians; the curt
witty wotty dashes never quite just right at the trim trite
truth letter; the sudden spluttered petulance of some capjtaljsed
mIddle; a word as cunningly hidden in its maze of confused
drapery as a fieldmouse in a nest of coloured ribbons: that ab-
surdly bullsfooted bee declaring with an even plainer dummp-
show than does the mute commoner with us how hard a thing it
is to mpe mporn a gentlerman: and look at this prepronominal
funferal, engraved and retouched and edgewiped and pudden-
padded very like a whale's egg farced with pemmican as were it
sentenced to be nuzzled over a full trillion times for ever and a
night till his noddle sink or swim by that ideal reader suffering
from an ideal insomnia: all those red raddled obeli cayennepep-
percast over the text, calling unnecessary attention to errors,
omissions, repetitions and misalignments: that (probably local or
personal) variant *maggers* for the more generally accepted *majesty* which is but a trifle and yet may quietly amuse: those super-
ciliouslooking crisscrossed Greek ees awkwardlike perched there
and here out of date like sick owls hawked back to Athens: and
the geegees too, jesuistically formed at first but afterwards genu-
flected aggrily toewards the occident: the Ostrogothic kako-
graphy affected for certain phrases of Etruscan stabletalk and, in
short, the learning betrayed at almost every line's end: the head-
strength (at least eleven men of thirtytwo palfrycraft) revealed
by a constant labour to make a ghimel pass through the eye of an
iota: this, for instance, utterly unexpected sinistrogyric return to
one peculiar sore point in the past; those throne open doubleyous
(of an early muddy terranean origin whether man chooses to
damn them agglutinatively loo — too — blue — face — ache or
illvoodawpeehole or, kants koorts, topplefouls) seated with such
floprightdown determination and reminding uus ineluctably of
nature at her naturalest while that fretful fidget eff, the hornful
digamma of your bornabarbar, rarely heard now save when falling
from the unfashionable lipsus of some hetarosexual (used always
in two boldfaced print types — one of them as wrongheaded as

his Claudian brother, is it worth while interrupting to say? —
throughout the papyrus as the revise mark) stalks all over the
page, broods Ⅎ sensationseeking an idea, amid the verbiage,
gaunt, stands dejectedly in the diapered window margin, with
its basque of bayleaves all aflutter about its forksfrogs, paces
with a frown, jerking to and fro, flinging phrases here, there, or
returns inhibited, with some half-halted suggestion, Ŀ, dragging
its shoestring; the curious warning sign before our protoparent's
ipsissima verba (a very pure nondescript, by the way, sometimes
a palmtailed otter, more often the arbutus fruitflowerleaf of the
cainapple) which paleographers call *a leak in the thatch* or *the
Aranman ingperwhis through the hole of his hat*, indicating that the
words which follow may be taken in any order desired, hole of
Aran man the hat through the whispering his ho (here keen
again and begin again to make soundsense and sensesound kin
again); those haughtypitched disdotted aiches easily of the rariest
inasdroll as most of the jaywalking eyes we do plough into halve,
unconnected, principial, medial or final, always jims in the jam,
sahib, as pipless as threadworms: the innocent exhibitionism of
those frank yet capricious underlinings: that strange exotic serpentine, since so properly banished from our scripture, about as freak-
wing a wetterhand now as to see a rightheaded ladywhite don a
corkhorse, which, in its invincible insolence ever longer more and
of more morosity, seems to uncoil spirally and swell lacertinelazily
before our eyes under pressure of the writer's hand; the ungainly
musicianlessness so painted in sculpting selfsounder ah ha as
blackartful as a *podatus* and dumbfounder oh ho oaproariose as
ten canons in skelterfugue: the studious omission of year number
and era name from the date, the one and only time when our
copyist seems at least to have grasped the beauty of restraint; the
lubricitous conjugation of the last with the first: the gipsy mating of a grand stylish gravedigging with secondbest buns (an in-
terpolation: these munchables occur only in the Bootherbrowth
family of MSS., Bb — Cod IV, Pap II, Brek XI, Lun III, Dinn
XVII, Sup XXX, Fullup M D C X C: the scholiast has hungrily
misheard a deadman's toller as a muffinbell): the four shortened

ampersands under which we can glypse at and feel for ourselves
across all those rushyears the warm soft short pants of; the quick-
scribbler: the vocative lapse from which it begins and the accusative hole in which it ends itself; the aphasia of that heroic agony
of recalling a once loved number leading slip by slipper to a
general amnesia of misnomering one's own: next those ars, rrrr!
those ars all bellical, the highpriest's hieroglyph of kettletom and
oddsbones, wrasted redhandedly from our hallowed rubric prayer
for truce with booty, *O'Remus pro Romulo*, and rudely from the
fane's pinnacle tossed down by porter to within an aim's ace of
their quatrain of rubyjets among Those Who arse without the
Temple nor since Roe's Distillery burn'd have quaff'd Night's
firefill'd Cup But jig jog jug as Day the Dicebox Throws, whang,
loyal six I lead, out wi'yer heart's bluid, blast ye, and there she's
for you, sir, whang her, the fine ooman, rouge to her lobster
locks, the rossy, whang, God and O'Mara has it with his ruddy
old Villain Rufus, wait, whang, God and you're another he
hasn't for there's my spoil five of spuds's trumps, whang, whack
on his pigsking's Kisser for him, K.M. O'Mara where are you?;
then (coming over to the left aisle corner down) the cruciform
postscript from which three *basia* or shorter and smaller *oscula*
have been overcarefully scraped away, plainly inspiring the tenebrous *Tunc* page of the Book of Kells (and then it need not be
lost sight of that there are exactly three squads of candidates for
the crucian rose awaiting their turn in the marginal panels of
Columkiller, chugged in their three ballotboxes, then set apart for
such hanging committees, where two was enough for anyone,
starting with old Matthew himself, as he with great distinction
said then just as since then people speaking have fallen into the
custom, when speaking to a person, of saying two is company
when the third person is the person darkly spoken of, and then
that last labiolingual *basium* might be read as a *suavium* if whoever the embracer then was wrote with a tongue in his (or perhaps her) cheek as the case may have been then; and the fatal
droopadwindle slope of the blamed scrawl, a sure sign of imper-
fectible moral blindness; the toomuchness, the fartoomanyness

of all those fourlegged ems: and why spell dear god with a big
thick dhee (why, O why, O why?): the cut and dry aks and wise
form of the semifinal; and, eighteenthly or twentyfourthly, but
at least, thank Maurice, lastly when all is zed and done, the pene-
lopean patience of its last paraphe, a colophon of no fewer than
seven hundred and thirtytwo strokes tailed by a leaping lasso —
who thus at all this marvelling but will press on hotly to see the
vaulting feminine libido of those interbranching ogham sex up-
andinsweeps sternly controlled and easily repersuaded by the
uniform matteroffactness of a meandering male fist?

Duff-Muggli, who now may be quoted by very kind arrangement (his dectroscophonious photosension under suprasonic
light control may be logged for by our none too distant futures
as soon astone values can be turned out from Chromophilomos,
Limited at a millicentime the microamp), first called this kind of
paddygoeasy partnership the ulykkhean or tetrachiric or quad-
rumane or duck and drakes or debts and dishes perplex (v. *Some
Forestallings over that Studium of Sexophonologistic Schizophre-
nesis*, vol. xxiv, pp. 2-555) after the wellinformed observation,
made miles apart from the Master by Tung-Toyd (cf. *Later
Frustrations amengst the Neomugglian Teachings abaft the Semi-
unconscience, passim*) that in the case of the littleknown periplic
bestteller popularly associated with the names of the wretched
mariner (trianforan deffwedoff our plumsucked pattern shape-
keeper) a Punic admiralty report, *From MacPerson's Oshean
Round By the Tides of Jason's Cruise*, had been cleverly capsized
and saucily republished as a dodecanesian baedeker of the every-
tale-a-treat-in-itself variety which could hope satisfactorily to
tickle me gander as game as your goose.

The unmistaken identity of the persons in the Tiberiast duplex came to light in the most devious of ways. The original
document was in what is known as Hanno O'Nonhanno's un-
brookable script, that is to say, it showed no signs of punctua-
tion of any sort. Yet on holding the verso against a lit rush this
new book of Morses responded most remarkably to the silent
query of our world's oldest light and its recto let out the piquant

fact that it was but pierced butnot punctured (in the university
sense of the term) by numerous stabs and foliated gashes made
by a pronged instrument. These paper wounds, four in type,
were gradually and correctly understood to mean stop, please
stop, do please stop, and O do please stop respectively, and
following up their one true clue, the circumflexuous wall of a
singleminded men's asylum, accentuated by bi tso fb rok engl
a ssan dspl itch ina, — Yard inquiries pointed out —→ that they
ad bìn "provoked" ay ∧ fork, of à grave Brofèsor; àth é's Brèak
— fast — table; ; acùtely profèssionally *piquéd*, to=introdùce a
notion of time [ùpon à plane (?) sù ' ' fàç'e'] by pùnct! ingh oles
(sic) in iSpace?! Deeply religious by nature and position, and
warmly attached to Thee, and smearbread and better and Him
and newlaidills, it was rightly suspected that such ire could not
have been visited by him Brotfressor Prenderguest even under-
wittingly, upon the ancestral pneuma of one whom, with rheuma,
he venerated shamelessly at least once a week at Cockspur Common as his apple in his eye and her first boys' best friend and,
though plain English for a married lady misled heaps by the way,
yet when some peerer or peeress detected that the fourleaved
shamrock or quadrifoil jab was more recurrent wherever the
script was clear and the term terse and that these two were the
selfsame spots naturally selected for her perforations by Dame
Partlet on her dungheap, thinkers all put grown in waterung-
spillfull Pratiland only and a playful fowl and musical me and
not you in any case, two and two together, and, with a swarm
of bisses honeyhunting after, a sigh for shyme (O, the petty-
bonny rouge!) separated modest mouths. So be it. And it was.
The lettermaking of the explots of Fjorgn Camhelsson when he
was in the Kvinnes country with Soldru's men. With acknow-
ledgment of our fervour of the first instant he remains years most
fainfully. For postscrapt see spoils. Though not yet had the sailor
sipped that sup nor the humphar foamed to the fill. And fox and
geese still kept the peace around *L'Auberge du Père Adam*.

    Small need after that, old Jeromesolem, old Huffsnuff, old
Andycox, old Olecasandrum, for quizzing your weekenders come

to the R.Q. with: shoots off in a hiss, muddles up in a mussmass
and his whole's a dismantled noondrunkard's son. Howbeit we
heard not a son of sons to leave by him to oceanic society in his
old man without a thing in his ignorance, Tulko MacHooley.
And it was thus he was at every time, that son, and the other
time, the day was in it and after the morrow Diremood is the
name is on the writing chap of the psalter, the juxtajunctor of a
dearmate and he passing out of one desire into its fellow. The
daughters are after going and loojing for him, Torba's nice-
lookers of the fair neck. Wanted for millinary servance to
olderly's person by the Totty Askinses. Formelly confounded
with amother. Maybe growing a moustache, did you say, with
an adorable look of amuzement? And uses noclass billiardhalls
with an upandown ladder? Not Hans the Curier though had he
had have only had some little laughings and some less of cheeks
and were he not so warried by his bulb of persecussion he could
have, ay, and would have, as true as Essex bridge. And not Go-
pheph go gossip, I declare to man! Noe! To all's much relief
one's half hypothesis of that jabberjaw ape amok the showering
jestnuts of Bruisanose was hotly dropped and his room taken up
by that odious and still today insufficiently malestimated note-
snatcher (kak, pfooi, bosh and fiety, much earny, Gus, poteen?
Sez you!) Shem the Penman.

So?

Who do you no tonigh, lazy and gentleman?

The echo is where in the back of the wodes; callhim forth!

(Shaun Mac Irewick, briefdragger, for the concern of Messrs. Jhon Jhamieson and Song, rated one hundrick and thin per storehundred on this nightly quisquiquock of the twelve apostrophes, set by Jockit Mic Ereweak. He misunderstruck and aim for am ollo of number three of them and left his free natural ripostes to four of them in their own fine artful disorder.)

1. What secondtonone myther rector and maximost bridgesmaker was the first to rise taller through his beanstale than the bluegum buaboababbaun or the giganteous Wellingtonia Sequoia; went nudiboots with trouters into a liffeyette when she was barely in her tricklies; was well known to claud a conciliation cap onto the esker of his hooth; sports a chainganger's albert solemenly over his hullender's epulence; thought he weighed a new ton when there felled his first lapapple; gave the heinousness of choice to everyknight betwixt yesterdicks and twomaries; had sevenal successivecoloured serebanmaids on the same big white drawringroam horthrug; is a Willbeforce to this hour at house as he was in heather; pumped the catholick wartrey and shocked the prodestung boyne; killed his own hungery self in anger as a young man; found fodder for five when allmarken rose goflooded; with Irish tutores Cornish made easy; voucher

of rotables, toll of the road; bred manyheaded stepsons for one leapyourown taughter; is too funny for a fish and has too much outside for an insect; like a heptagon crystal emprisoms trues and fauss for us; is infinite swell in unfitting induments; once was he shovelled and once was he arsoned and once was he inundered and she hung him out billbailey; has a quadrant in his tile to tell Toler cad a'clog it is; offers chances to Long on but stands up to Legge before; found coal at the end of his harrow and moss-roses behind the seams; made a fort out of his postern and wrote F.E.R.T. on his buckler; is escapemaster-in-chief from all sorts of houdingplaces; if he outharrods against barkers, to the shool-bred he acts whiteley; was evacuated at the mere appearance of three germhuns and twice besieged by a sweep; from zoomor-phology to omnianimalism he is brooched by the spin of a coin; towers, an eddistoon amid the lampless, casting swannbeams on the deep; threatens thunder upon malefactors and sends whispers up fraufrau's froufrous; when Dook Hookbackcrook upsits his ass booseworthies jeer and junket but they boos him oos and baas his aas when he lukes like Hunkett Plunkett; by sosannsos and search a party on a lady of this city; business, reading news-paper, smoking cigar, arranging tumblers on table, eating meals, pleasure, etcetera, etcetera, pleasure, eating meals, arranging tum-blers on table, smoking cigar, reading newspaper, business; minerals, wash and brush up, local views, juju toffee, comic and birthdays cards; those were the days and he was their hero; pink sunset shower, red clay cloud, sorrow of Sahara, oxhide or Iren; arraigned and attainted, listed and lited, pleaded and proved; catches his check at banck of Indgangd and endurses his doom at chapel exit; brain of the franks, hand of the christian, tongue of the north; commands to dinner and calls the bluff; has a block at Morgen's and a hatache all the afternunch; plays gehamerat when he's ernst but misses mausey when he's lustyg; walked as far as the Head where he sat in state as the Rump; shows Early Eng-lish tracemarks and a marigold window with manigilt lights, a myrioscope, two remarkable piscines and three wellworthseeing ambries; arches all portcullised and his nave dates from dots; is

a horologe unstoppable and the Benn of all bells; fuit, isst and
herit and though he's mildewstaned he's mouldystoned; is a quer-
cuss in the forest but plane member for Megalopolis; mountun-
mighty, faunonfleetfoot; plank in our platform, blank in our
scouturn; hidal, in carucates he is enumerated, hold as an earl,
he counts; shipshaped phrase of buglooking words with a form
like the easing moments of a graminivorous; to our dooms
brought he law, our manoirs he made his vill of; was an over-
grind to the underground and acqueduced for fierythroats; sends
boys in socks acoughawhooping when he lets farth his carbon-
oxside and silk stockings show her shapings when he looses hose
on hers; stocks dry puder for the Ill people and pinkun's pellets
for all the Pale; gave his mundyfoot to Miserius, her pinch to
Anna Livia, that superfine pigtail to Cerisia Cerosia and quid
rides to Titius, Caius and Sempronius; made the man who had
no notion of shopkeepers feel he'd rather play the duke than play
the gentleman; shot two queans and shook three caskles when
he won his game of dwarfs; fumes inwards like a strombolist till
he smokes at both ends; manmote, befier of him, womankind,
pietad!; shows one white drift of snow among the gorsegrowth
of his crown and a chaperon of repentance on that which shed
gore; pause and quies, triple bill; went by metro for the polis and
then hoved by; to the finders, hail! woa, you that seek!; whom
fillth had plenished, dearth devoured; hock is leading, cocoa comes
next, emery tries for the flag; can dance the O'Bruin's polerpasse
at Noolahn to his own orchistruss accompaniment; took place
before the internatural convention of catholic midwives and
found stead before the congress for the study of endonational
calamities; makes a delictuous *entrée* and finishes off the course
between sweets and savouries; flouts for forecasts, flairs for finds
and the fun of the fray on the fairground; cleared out three hundred sixty five idles to set up one all khalassal for henwives hoping
to have males; the flawhoolagh, the grasping one, the kindler of
paschal fire; forbids us our trespassers as we forgate him; the
phoenix be his pyre, the cineres his sire!; piles big pelium on
little ossas like the pilluls of hirculeads; has an eatupus complex

and a drinkthedregs kink; wurstmeats for chumps and cowcar-
lows for scullions; when he plies for our favour is very trolly
ours; two psychic espousals and three desertions; may be matter
of fact now but was futter of magd then; Cattermole Hill, ex-
mountain of flesh was reared up by stress and sank under strain;
tank it up, dank it up, tells the tailor to his tout; entoutcas for a
man, but bit a thimble for a maid; blimp, blump; a dud letter, a sing
a song a sylble; a byword, a sentence with surcease; while stands
his canyouseehim frails shall fall; was hatched at Cellbridge but
ejoculated abrood; as it gan in the biguinnengs so wound up in
a battle of Boss; Roderick, Roderick, Roderick, O, you've gone
the way of the Danes; variously catalogued, regularly regrouped;
a bushboys holoday, a quacker's mating, a wenches' sandbath;
the same homoheatherous checkinlossegg as when sollyeye airly
blew ye; real detonation but false report; spa mad but inn sane;
half emillian via bogus census but a no street hausmann when
allphannd; is the handiest of all andies and a most alleghant spot
to dump your hump; hands his secession to the new patricius but
plumps plebmatically for the bloody old centuries; eats with
doors open and ruts with gates closed; some dub him Rotshield
and more limn him Rockyfellow; shows he's fly to both demis-
fairs but thries to cover up his tracers; seven dovecotes cooclaim
to have been pigeonheim to this homer, Smerrnion, Rhoebok,
Kolonsreagh, Seapoint, Quayhowth, Ashtown, Ratheny; independent of the lordship of chamberlain, acknowledging the rule
of Rome; we saw thy farm at Useful Prine, Domhnall, Domhnall;
reeks like Illbelpaese and looks like iceland's ear; lodged at quot
places, lived through tot reigns; takes a szumbath for his weekend
and a wassarnap for his refreskment; after a good bout at stool-
ball enjoys Giroflee Giroflaa; what Nevermore missed and
Colombo found; believes in everyman his own goaldkeeper and
in Africa for the fullblacks; the arc of his drive was forty full
and his stumps were pulled at eighty; boasts him to the thick-in-
thews the oldest creater in Aryania and looks down on the Suiss
family Collesons whom he calls *les nouvelles roches*; though his
heart, soul and spirit turn to pharaoph times, his love, faith and

hope stick to futuerism; light leglifters cense him souriantes from
afore while boor browbenders curse him grommelants to his
hindmost; between youlasses and yeladst glimse of Even; the
Lug his peak has, the Luk his pile; drinks tharr and wodhar for
his asama and eats the unparishable sow to styve off reglar rack,
the beggars cloak them reclined about his paddystool, the whores
winken him as they walk their side; on Christienmas at Advent
Lodge, New Yealand, after a lenty illness the roeverand Mr.
Easterling of pentecostitis, no followers by bequest, fanfare all
private; Gone Where Glory Waits Him (Ball, bulletist) but Not
Here Yet (Maxwell, clark); comminxed under articles but phoe-
nished a borgiess; from the vat on the bier through the burre in
the dark to the buttle of the bawn; is A1 an the highest but Roh
re his root; filled fanned of heckleberries whenas all was tuck
and toss up for him as a yangster to fall fou of hockinbechers
wherein he had gauged the use of raisin; ads aliments, das doles,
raps rustics, tams turmoil; sas seed enough for a semination but
sues skivvies on the sly; learned to speak from hand to mouth
till he could talk earish with his eyes shut; hacked his way through
hickheckhocks but hanged hishelp from there hereafters; rialtos,
annesleyg, binn and balls to say nothing atolk of New Comyn;
the gleam of the glow of the shine of the sun through the
dearth of the dirth on the blush of the brick of the viled ville of
Barnehulme has dust turned to brown; these dyed to tartan him,
rueroot, dulse, bracken, teasel, fuller's ash, sundew and cress;
long gunn but not for cotton; stood his sharp assault of famine
but grew girther, girther and girther; he has twenty four or so
cousins germinating in the United States of America and a
namesake with an initial difference in the once kingdom of
Poland; his first's a young rose and his second's French-
Egyptian and his whole means a slump at Christie's; forth of his
pierced part came the woman of his dreams, blood thicker then
water last trade overseas; buyshop of Glintylook, eorl of Hoed;
you and I are in him surrented by brown bldns; Elin's flee
polt pelhaps but Hwang Chang evelytime; he was one of your
highbigpipey boys but fancy him as smoking fags at his time of

life; Mount of Mish, Mell of Moy; had two cardinal ventures and
three capitol sinks; has a peep in his pocketbook and a packetboat in his keep; B.V.H., B.L.G., P.P.M., T.D.S., V.B.D.,
T.C.H., L.O.N.; is Breakfates, Lunger, Diener and Souper; as
the streets were paved with cold he felt his topperairy; taught
himself skating and learned how to fall; distinctly dirty but rather
a dear; hoveth chieftains evrywehr, with morder; Ostman
Effendi, Serge Paddishaw; baases two mmany, outpriams all
his parisites; first of the fenians, *roi des fainéants*; his Tiara of
scones was held unfillable till one Liam Fail felled him in West-
munster; was struck out of his sittem when he rowed saulely to
demask us and to our appauling predicament brought as plagues
from Buddapest; put a matchhead on an aspenstalk and set the
living a fire; speared the rod and spoiled the lightning; married
with cakes and repunked with pleasure; till he was buried how-
happy was he and he made the welkins ring with *Up Micawber!*;
god at the top of the staircase, carrion on the mat of straw;
the false hood of a spindler web chokes the cavemouth of his
unsightliness but the nestlings that liven his leafscreen sing him
a lover of arbuties; we strike hands over his bloodied warsheet
but we are pledged entirely to his green mantle; our friend
vikelegal, our swaran foi; under the four stones by his streams
who vanished the wassailbowl at the joy of shells; Mora and
Lora had a hill of a high time looking down on his confusion till
firm look in readiness, forward spear and the windfoot of curach
strewed the lakemist of Lego over the last of his fields; we
darkened for you, faulterer, in the year of mourning but we'll
fidhil to the dimtwinklers when the streamy morvenlight calls up
the sunbeam; his striped pantaloons, his rather strange walk;
hereditatis columna erecta, hagion chiton eraphon; nods a nap for
the nonce but crows cheerio when they get ecumenical; is a simultaneous equator of elimbinated integras when three upon one is
by inspection improper; has the most conical hodpiece of con-
fusianist heronim and that chuchuffuous chinchin of his is like
a footsey kungoloo around Taishantyland; he's as globeful as a
gasometer of lithium and luridity and he was thrice ten anular

years before he wallowed round Raggiant Circos; the cabalstone
at the coping of his cavin is a canine constant but only an amiri-
can could apparoxemete the apeupresiosity of his atlast's alonge-
ment; sticklered rights and lefts at Baddersdown in his hunt for
the boar trwth but made his end with the modareds that came
at him in Camlenstrete; a hunnibal in exhaustive conflict, an otho
to return; burning body to aiger air on melting mountain in
wooing wave; we go into him sleepy children, we come out of
him strucklers for life; he divested to save from the Mrs Drown-
ings their rival queens while Grimshav, Bragshaw and Renshaw
made off with his storen clothes; taxed and rated, licensed and
ranted; his threefaced stonehead was found on a whitehorse hill
and the print of his costellous feet is seen in the goat's grass-
circle; pull the blind, toll the deaf and call dumb, lame and halty;
Miraculone, Monstrucceleen; led the upplaws at the Creation and
hissed a snake charmer off her stays; hounded become haunter,
hunter become fox; harrier, marries, terrier, tav; Olaph the Oxman, Thorker the Tourable; you feel he is Vespasian yet you
think of him as Aurelius; whugamore, tradertory, socianist, commoniser; made a summer assault on our shores and begiddy got
his sands full; first he shot down Raglan Road and then he tore
up Marlborough Place; Cromlechheight and Crommalhill were
his farfamed feetrests when our lurch as lout let free into the
Lubar heloved; mareschalled his wardmotes and delimited the
main; netted before nibbling, can scarce turn a scale but, grossed
after meals, weighs a town in himself; Banba prayed for his conversion, Beurla missed that grand old voice; a Colossus among
cabbages, the Melarancitrone of fruits; larger than life, doughtier
than death; Gran Turco, orege forment; lachsembulger, leperlean;
the sparkle of his genial fancy, the depth of his calm sagacity, the
clearness of his spotless honour, the flow of his boundless benevolence; our family furbear, our tribal tarnpike; quary was he
invincibled and cur was he burked; partitioned Irskaholm, united
Irishmen; he took a svig at his own methyr but she tested a bit
gorky and as for the salmon he was coming up in him all life
long; comm, eilerdich kecklebury and sawyer thee warden,

silent as the bee in honey, stark as the breath on hauwck, Costello, Kinsella, Mahony, Moran, though you rope Amrique your home ruler is Dan; figure right, he is hoisted by the scurve of his shaggy neck, figure left, he is rationed in isobaric patties among the crew; one asks was he poisoned, one thinks how much did he leave; ex-gardener (Riesengebirger), fitted up with planturous existencies would make Roseoogreedy (mite's) little hose; taut sheets and scuppers awash but the oil silk mack Liebsterpet micks his aquascutum; the enjoyment he took in kay women, the employment he gave to gee men; sponsor to a squad of piercers, ally to a host of rawlies; against lightning, explosion, fire, earthquake, flood, whirlwind, burglary, third party, rot, loss of cash, loss of credit, impact of vehicles; can rant as grave as oxtail soup and chat as gay as a porto flippant; is unhesitent in his unionism and yet a pigotted nationalist; Sylviacola is shy of him, Matrosenhosens nose the joke; shows the sinews of peace in his chest-o-wars; fiefeofhome, ninehundred and thirtunine years of copyhold; is aldays open for polemypolity's sake when he's not suntimes closed for the love of Janus; sucks life's eleaxir from the pettipickles of the Jewess and ruoulls in sulks if any popeling runs down the Huguenots; Boomaport, Walleslee, Ubermeerschall Blowcher and Supercharger, Monsieur Ducrow, Mister Mudson, master gardiner; to one he's just paunch and judex, to another full of beans and brehons; hallucination, cauchman, ectoplasm; passed for baabaa blacksheep till he grew white woo woo woolly; was drummatoysed by Mac Milligan's daughter and put to music by one shoebard; all fitzpatricks in his emirate remember him, the boys of wetford hail him babu; indanified himself with boro tribute and was schenkt publicly to brigstoll; was given the light in drey orchafts and entumuled in threeplexes; his likeness is in Terrecuite and he giveth rest to the rain bowed; lebriety, frothearnity and quality; his reverse makes a virtue of necessity while his obverse mars a mother by invention; beskilk his gunwale and he's the second imperial, untie points, unhook tenters and he's lath and plaster; calls upon Allthing when he fails to appeal to Eachovos; basidens, ardree, kongsemma, rexregulorum; stood into Dee mouth,

then backed broadside on Baulacleeva; either eldorado or ultimate
thole; a kraal of fou feud fires, a crawl of five pubs; laid out lashings of laveries to hunt down his family ancestors and then pled
double trouble or quick quits to hush the buckers up; threw peb-
blets for luck over one sodden shoulder and dragooned peoplades
armed to their teeth; pept as Gaudio Gambrinus, grim as Potter
the Grave; ace of arts, deuce of damimonds, trouble of clubs, fear
of spates; cumbrum, cumbrum, twiniceynurseys fore a drum but
tre to uno tips the scale; reeled the titleroll opposite a brace of
girdles in Silver on the Screen but was sequenced from the set
as Crookback by the even more titulars, Rick, Dave and Barry;
he can get on as early as the twentysecond of Mars but occasionally he doesn't come off before Virgintiquinque Germinal; his Indian name is Hapapoosiesobjibway and his number in arithmo-
sophy is the stars of the plough; took weapon in the province of
the pike and let fling his line on Eelwick; moves in vicous cicles
yet remews the same; the drain rats bless his offals while the park
birds curse his floodlights; Portobello, Equadocta, Therecocta,
Percorello; he pours into the softclad shellborn the hard cash
earned in Watling Street; his birth proved accidental shows his
death its grave mistake; brought us giant ivy from the land of
younkers and bewitthered Apostolopolos with the gale of his gall;
while satisfied that soft youthful bright matchless girls should
bosom into fine silkclad joyous blooming young women is not
so pleased that heavy swearsome strongsmelling irregularshaped
men should blottout active handsome wellformed frankeyed boys;
herald hairyfair, alloaf the wheat; husband your aunt and endow
your nepos; hearken but hush it, screen him and see; time is,
an archbishopric, time was, a tradesmen's entrance; beckburn
brooked with wath, scale scarred by scow; his rainfall is a couple
of kneehighs while his meanst grass temperature marked three in
the shade; is the meltingpoint of snow and the bubblingplace of
alcohol; has a tussle with the trulls and then does himself justice;
hinted at in the eschatological chapters of Humphrey's *Justesse
of the Jaypees* and hunted for by Theban recensors who sniff
there's something behind the *Bug of the Deaf*; the king was in

his cornerwall melking mark so murry, the queen was steep in armbour feeling fain and furry, the mayds was midst the hawthorns shoeing up their hose, out pimps the back guards (pomp!) and pump gun they goes; to all his foretellers he reared a stone and for all his comethers he planted a tree; forty acres, sixty miles, white stripe, red stripe, washes his fleet in annacrwatter; whou missed a porter so whot shall he do for he wanted to sit for Pimploco but they've caught him to stand for Sue?; Dutchlord, Dutchlord, overawes us; Headmound, king and martyr, dunstung in the Yeast, Pitre-le-Pore-in Petrin, Barth-the-Grete-by-the-Exchange; he hestens towards dames troth and wedding hand like the prince of Orange and Nassau while he has trinity left behind him like Bowlbeggar Bill-the-Bustonly; brow of a hazelwood, pool in the dark; changes blowicks into bullocks and a well of Artesia into a bird of Arabia; the handwriting on his facewall, the cryptoconchoidsiphonostomata in his exprussians; his birthspot lies beyond the herospont and burialplot in the pleasant little field; is the yldist kiosk on the pleninsula and the unguest hostel in Saint Scholarland; walked many hundreds and many score miles of streets and lit thousands in one nightlights in hectares of windows; his great wide cloak lies on fifteen acres and his little white horse decks by dozens our doors; O sorrow the sail and woe the rudder that were set for Mairie Quail; his suns the huns, his dartars the tartars, are plenty here today; who repulsed from his burst the bombolts of Ostenton and falchioned each flash downsaduck in the deep; apersonal problem, a locative enigma; upright one, vehicule of arcanisation in the field, lying chap, floodsupplier of celiculation through ebblanes; a part of the whole as a port for a whale; Dear Hewitt Costello, Equerry, were daylighted with our outing and are looking backwards to unearly summers, from Rhoda Dundrums; is above the seedfruit level and outside the leguminiferous zone; when older links lock older hearts then he'll resemble she; can be built with glue and clippings, scrawled or voided on a buttress; the night express sings his story, the song of sparrownotes on his stave of wires; he crawls with lice, he swarms with saggarts; is as quiet as a

mursque but can be as noisy as a sonogog; was Dilmun when his
date was palmy and Mudlin when his nut was cracked; suck up
the sease, lep laud at ease, one lip on his lap and one cushlin his
crease; his porter has a mighty grasp and his baxters the boon of
broadwhite; as far as wind dries and rain eats and sun turns
and water bounds he is exalted and depressed, assembled and
asundered; go away, we are deluded, come back, we are dis-
ghosted; bored the Ostrov, leapt the Inferus, swam the Mabbul
and flure the Moyle; like fat, like fatlike tallow, of greasefulness,
yea of dripping greasefulness; did not say to the old, old, did not
say to the scorbutic, scorbutic; he has founded a house, Uru,
a house he has founded to which he has assigned its fate; bears
a raaven geulant on a fjeld duiv; ruz the halo off his varlet when
he appeared to his shecook; as Haycock, Emmet, Boaro, Toaro,
Osterich, Mangy and Skunk; pressed the beer of aled age out of
the nettles of rashness; put a roof on the lodge for Hymn and a
coq in his pot pro homo; was dapifer then pancircensor then
hortifex magnus; the topes that tippled on him, the types that
toppled off him; still starts our hares yet gates our goat; pocketbook packetboat, gapman gunrun; the light of other days dire
dreary darkness; our awful dad, Timour of Tartar; puzzling,
startling, shocking, nay, perturbing; went puffing from king's
brugh to new customs, doffing the gibbous off him to every
breach of all size; with Pa's new heft and Papa's new helve he's
Papapa's old cutlass Papapapa left us; when youngheaded old-
shouldered and middlishneck aged about; caller herring every-
daily, turgid tarpon overnight; see Loryon the comaleon that
changed endocrine history by loeven his loaf with forty bannucks;
she drove him dafe till he driv her blind up; the pigeons doves be
perchin all over him one day on Baslesbridge and the ravens duv
be pitchin their dark nets after him the next night behind Koenig-
stein's Arbour; tronf of the rep, comf of the priv, prosp of the
pub; his headwood it's ideal if his feet are bally clay; he crashed
in the hollow of the park, trees down, as he soared in the vaguum
of the phoenix, stones up; looks like a moultain boultter and
sounds like a rude word; the mountain view, some lumin pale

round a lamp of succar in boinyn water; three shots a puddy at up blup saddle; made up to Miss MacCormack Ni Lacarthy who made off with Darly Dermod, swank and swarthy; once diamond cut garnet now dammat cuts groany; you might find him at the Florence but watch our for him in Wynn's Hotel; theer's his bow and wheer's his leaker and heer lays his bequiet hearse deep; Swed Albiony, likeliest villain of the place; Hennery Canterel — Cockran, eggotisters, limitated; we take our tays and frees our fleas round sadurn's mounted foot; built the Lund's kirk and destroyed the church's land; who guesse his title grabs his deeds; fletch and prities, fash and chaps; artful Juke of Wilysly; Hugglebelly's Funniral; Kukkuk Kallikak; heard in camera and excruciated; boon when with benches billeted, bann if buckshot-backshattered; heavengendered, chaosfoedted, earthborn; his father presumptively ploughed it deep on overtime and his mother as all evince must have travailled her fair share; a footprinse on the Megacene, hetman unwhorsed by Searingsand; honorary captain of the extemporised fire brigade, reported to be friendly with the police; the door is still open; the old stock collar is coming back; not forgetting the time you laughed at Elder Charterhouse's duckwhite pants and the way you said the whole township can see his hairy legs; by stealth of a kersse her aulburntress abaft his nape she hung; when his kettle became a hearthsculdus our thorstyites set their lymphyamphyre; his yearletter concocted by masterhands of assays, his hallmark imposed by the standard of wrought plate; a pair of pectorals and a triple-screen to get a wind up; lights his pipe with a rosin tree and hires a towhorse to haul his shoes; cures slavey's scurvy, breaks barons boils; called to sell polosh and was found later in a bedroom; has his seat of justice, his house of mercy, his corn o'copious and his stacks a'rye; prospector, he had a rooksacht, retrospector, he holds the holpenstake; won the freedom of new yoke for the minds of jugoslaves; acts active, peddles in passivism and is a gorgon of selfridgeousness; pours a laughsworth of his illformation over a larmsworth of salt; half heard the single maiden speech La Belle spun to her Grand Mount and wholed a lifetime

by his ain fireside wondering was it hebrew set to himmeltones
or the quicksilversong of qwaternions; his troubles may be over
but his doubles have still to come; the lobster pot that crabbed
our keel, the garden pet that spoiled our squeezed peas; he stands
in a lovely park, sea is not far, importunate towns of X, Y and
Z are easily over reached; is an excrescence to civilised humanity
and but a wart on Europe; wanamade singsigns to soundsense
an yit he wanna git all his flesch nuemaid motts truly prural and
plusible; has excisively large rings and is uncustomarily perfumed;
lusteth ath he listeth the cleah whithpeh of a themise; is a prince
of the fingallian in a hiberniad of hoolies; has a hodge to wherry
him and a frenchy to curry him and a brabanson for his beeter and
a fritz at his switch; was waylaid of a parker and beschotten by a
buckeley; kicks lintils when he's cuppy and casts Jacob's arroroots,
dime after dime, to poor waifstrays on the perish; reads the charms
of H. C. Endersen all the weaks of his evenin and the crimes of
Ivaun the Taurrible every strongday morn; soaps you soft to your
face and slaps himself when he's badend; owns the bulgiest bung-
barrel that ever was tiptapped in the privace of the Mullingar
Inn; was born with a nuasilver tongue in his mouth and went
round the coast of Iron with his lift hand to the scene; raised but
two fingers and yet smelt it would day; for whom it is easier to
found a see in Ebblannah than for I or you to find a dubbeltye
in Dampsterdamp; to live with whom is a lifemayor and to know
whom a liberal education; was dipped in Hoily Olives and chrys-
med in Scent Otooles; hears cricket on the earth but annoys the
life out of predikants; still turns the durc's ear of Darius to the
now thoroughly infurioted one of God; made Man with juts
that jerk and minted money mong maney; likes a six acup pudding when he's come whome sweetwhome; has come through all
the eras of livsadventure from moonshine and shampaying down
to clouts and pottled porter; woollem the farsed, hahnreich the
althe, charge the sackend, writchad the thord; if a mandrake
shricked to convultures at last surviving his birth the weibduck
will wail bitternly over the rotter's resurrection; loses weight in
the moon night but gird girder by the sundawn; with one touch

of nature set a veiled world agrin and went within a sheet of
tissuepaper of the option of three gaols; who could see at one
blick a saumon taken with a lance, hunters pursuing a doe, a
swallowship in full sail, a whyterobe lifting a host; faced flappery
like old King Cnut and turned his back like Cincinnatus; is a
farfar and morefar and a hoar father Nakedbucker in villas old as
new; squats aquart and cracks aquaint when it's flaggin in town
and on haven; blows whiskery around his summit but stehts
stout upon his footles; stutters fore he falls and goes mad entirely
when he's waked; is Timb to the pearly morn and Tomb to the
mourning night; and an he had the best bunbaked bricks in bould
Babylon for his pitching plays he'd be lost for the want of his
wan wubblin wall?

Answer: Finn MacCool!

2. Does your mutter know your mike?

Answer: When I turn meoptics, from suchurban prospects,
'tis my filial's bosom, doth behold with pride, that pontificator,
and circumvallator, with his dam night garrulous, slipt by his
side. Ann alive, the lisp of her, 'twould grig mountains whisper
her, and the bergs of Iceland melt in waves of fire, and her spoon-
me-spondees, and her dirckle-me-ondenees, make the Rageous
Ossean, kneel and quaff a lyre! If Dann's dane, Ann's dirty, if
he's plane she's purty, if he's fane, she's flirty, with her auburnt
streams, and her coy cajoleries, and her dabblin drolleries, for to
rouse his rudderup, or to drench his dreams. If hot Hammurabi,
or cowld Clesiastes, could espy her pranklings, they'd burst
bounds agin, and renounce their ruings, and denounce their do-
ings, for river and iver, and a night. Amin!

3. Which title is the true-to-type motto-in-lieu for that Tick
for Teac thatchment painted witt wheth one darkness, where
asnake is under clover and birds aprowl are in the rookeries and
a magda went to monkishouse and a riverpaard was spotted,
which is not Whichcroft Whorort not Ousterholm Dreyschluss
not Haraldsby, grocer, not Vatandcan, vintner, not Houseboat
and Hive not Knox-atta-Belle not O'Faynix Coalprince not
Wohn Squarr Roomyeck not Ebblawn Downes not Le Decer

Le Mieux not Benjamin's Lea not Tholomew's Whaddingtun
gnot Antwarp gnat Musca not Corry's not Weir's not the Arch
not The Smug not The Dotch House not The Uval nothing
Grand nothing Splendid (Grahot or Spletel) nayther *Erat Est
Erit* noor *Non michi sed luciphro?*

Answer: Thine obesity, O civilian, hits the felicitude of our
orb!

4. What Irish capitol city (a dea o dea!) of two syllables and
six letters, with a deltic origin and a nuinous end, (ah dust oh
dust!) can boost of having *a*) the most extensive public park in
the world, *b*) the most expensive brewing industry in the world,
c) the most expansive peopling thoroughfare in the world, *d*) the
most phillohippuc theobibbous paùpulation in the world: and
harmonise your abecedeed responses?

Answer: *a*) Delfas. And when ye'll hear the gould hommers
of my heart, my floxy loss, bingbanging again the ribs of yer
resistance and the tenderbolts of my rivets working to your
destraction ye'll be sheverin wi' all yer dinful sobs when *we'll* go
riding acope-acurly, you with yer orange garland and me with
my conny cordial, down the greaseways of rollicking into the
waters of wetted life. *b*) Dorhqk. And sure where can you have
such good old chimes anywhere, and *leave* you, as on the Mash
and how'tis I would be engaging you with my plovery soft accents and descanting upover the scene beunder me of your loose
vines in their hairafall with them two loving loofs braceleting the
slims of your ankles and your mouth's flower rose and sinking
ofter the soapstone of silvry speech. *c*) Nublid. Isha, why
wouldn't we be happy, avourneen, on the mills'money he'll
soon be leaving you as soon as I've my own owned brooklined
Georgian mansion's lawn to recruit upon by Doctor Cheek's
special orders and my copper's panful of soybeans and Irish in
my east hand and a James's Gate in my west, after all the errears
and erroriboose of combarative embottled history, and your
goodself churning over the newleaved butter (*more* power to
you), the choicest and the cheapest from Atlanta to Oconee,
while I'll be drowsing in the gaarden. *d*) Dalway. I hooked my

thoroughgoing trotty the first down Spanish Place, Mayo I make,
Tuam I take, Sligo's sleek but Galway's grace. Holy eel and
Sainted Salmon, chucking chub and ducking dace, Rodiron's not
your aequal! says she, leppin half the lane. *abcd*) A bell a bell on
Shalldoll Steepbell, ond be'll go massplon pristmoss speople,
Shand praise gon ness our fayst moan *neople*, our prame *Shan-
deepen*, pay name muy *feepence*, moy nay non *Aequalllllll!*

5. Whad slags of a loughladd would retten smuttyflesks, emp-
tout old mans, melk vitious geit, scareoff jackinjills fra tiddle
anding, smoothpick waste papish pastures, insides man outsiders
angell, sprink dirted water around village, newses, tobaggon and
sweeds, plain general kept, louden on the kirkpeal, foottreats
given to malafides, outshriek hyelp hyelf nor his hair efter
buggelawrs, might underhold three barnets, putzpolish crotty
bottes, nightcoover all fireglims, serve's time till baass, grind-
stone his kniveses, fullest boarded, lewd man of the method of
godliness, perchance he nieows and thans sits in the spoorwaggen,
X.W.C.A. on Z.W.C.U., Doorsteps, Limited, or Baywindaws
Bros swobber preferred. Walther Clausetter's and Sons with the
H. E. Chimneys' Company to not skreve, will, on advices, be
bacon or stable hand, must begripe fullstandingly irers' langurge,
jublander or northquain bigger prefurred, all duties, kine rights,
family fewd, outings fived, may get earnst, no get combitsch,
profusional drinklords to please obstain, he is fatherlow soun-
digged inmoodmined pershoon but aleconnerman, nay, *that* must
he isn't?

Answer: Pore ole Joe!

6. What means the saloon slogan Summon In The House-
sweep Dinah?

Answer: Tok. Galory bit of the sales of Cloth nowand I have
to beeswax the bringing in all the claub of the porks to us how I
thawght I knew his stain on the flower if me ask and can could
speak and he called by me midden name Tik. I am your honey
honeysugger phwhtphwht tha Bay and who bruk the dandleass
and who seen the blackcullen jam for Tomorrha's big pickneck
I hope it'll pour prais the Climate of all Ireland I heard the

grackles and I skimming the crock on all your sangwidges fippence per leg per drake Tuk. And who eight the last of the goose-
bellies that was mowlding from measlest years and who leff that
there and who put that here and who let the kilkenny stale the
chump Tek. And whowasit youwasit propped the pot in the
yard and whatinthe nameofsen lukeareyou rubbinthe sideofthe
flureofthe lobbywith *Shite*! will you have a plateful? Tak.

7. Who are those component partners of our societate, the
doorboy, the cleaner, the sojer, the crook, the squeezer, the loun-
ger, the curman, the tourabout, the mussroomsniffer, the bleaka-
blue tramp, the funpowtherplother, the christymansboxer, from
their prés salés and Donnybrook prater and Roebuck's campos
and the Ager Arountown and Crumglen's grassy but Kimmage's
champ and Ashtown fields and Cabra fields and Finglas fields
and Santry fields and the feels of Raheny and their fails and Bal-
doygle to them who are latecomers all the year's round by anticipation, are the porters of the passions in virtue of retroratioci-
nation, and, contributting their conflingent controversies of
differentiation, unify their voxes in a vote of vaticination, who
crunch the crusts of comfort due to depredation, drain the mead
for misery to incur intoxication, condone every evil by practical
justification and condam any good to its own gratification, who
are ruled, roped, duped and driven by those numen daimons,
the feekeepers at their laws, nightly consternation, fortnightly
fornication, monthly miserecordation and omniannual recreation,
doyles when they deliberate but sullivans when they are
swordsed, Matey, Teddy, Simon, Jorn, Pedher, Andy, Barty,
Philly, Jamesy Mor and Tom, Matt and Jakes Mac Carty?

Answer: The Morphios!

8. And how war yore maggies?

Answer: They war loving, they love laughing, they laugh
weeping, they weep smelling, they smell smiling, they smile hat-
ing, they hate thinking, they think feeling, they feel tempting,
they tempt daring, they dare waiting, they wait taking, they take
thanking, they thank seeking, as born for lorn in lore of love to
live and wive by wile and rile by rule of ruse 'reathed rose and

hose hol'd home, yeth cometh elope year, coach and four, Sweet
Peck-at-my-Heart picks one man more.

9. Now, to be on anew and basking again in the panaroma of
all flores of speech, if a human being duly fatigued by his dayety
in the sooty, having plenxty off time on his gouty hands and va-
cants of space at his sleepish feet and as hapless behind the dreams
of accuracy as any camelot prince of dinmurk, were at this auc-
tual futule preteriting unstant, in the states of suspensive exani-
mation, accorded, throughout the eye of a noodle, with an ear-
sighted view of old hopeinhaven with all the ingredient and
egregiunt whights and ways to which in the curse of his persis-
tence the course of his tory will had been having recourses, the
reverberration of knotcracking awes, the reconjungation of
nodebinding ayes, the redissolusingness of mindmouldered ease
and the thereby hang of the Hoel of it, could such a none, whiles
even led comesilencers to comeliewithhers and till intempes-
tuous Nox should catch the gallicry and spot lucan's dawn, by-
hold at ones what is main and why tis twain, how one once
meet melts in tother wants poignings, the sap rising, the foles
falling, the nimb now nihilant round the girlyhead so becoming,
the wrestless in the womb, all the rivals to allsea, shakeagain, O
disaster! shakealose, Ah how starring! but Heng's got a bit
of Horsa's nose and Jeff's got the signs of Ham round his
mouth and the beaù that spun beautiful pales as it palls, what
roserude and oragious grows gelb and greem, blue out the ind of
it! Violet's dyed! then *what* would that fargazer seem to seemself
to seem seeming of, dimm it all?

Answer: A collideorscape!

10. What bitter's love but yurning, what' sour lovemutch but
a bref burning till shee that drawes dothe smoake retourne?

Answer: I know, pepette, of course, dear, but listen, precious!
Thanks, pette, those are lovely, pitounette, delicious! But mind
the wind, sweet! What exquisite hands you have, you angiol, if
you didn't gnaw your nails, isn't it a wonder you're not achamed
of me, you pig, you perfect little pigaleen! I'll nudge you in a
minute! I bet you use her best Perisian smear off her vanity table

to make them look so rosetop glowstop nostop. I know her.
Slight me, would she? For every got I care! Three creamings a
day, the first during her shower and wipe off with tissue. Then
after cleanup and of course before retiring. Beme shawl, when I
think of that espos of a Clancarbry, the foodbrawler, of the socia-
tionist party with hiss blackleaded chest, hello, Prendregast!
that you, Innkipper, and all his fourteen other fullback maulers
or hurling stars or whatever the dagos they are, baiting at my
Lord Ornery's, just becups they won the egg and spoon there
so ovally provencial at Balldole. My Eilish assent he seed makes
his admiracion. He is seeking an opening and means to be first
with me as his belle alliance. Andoo musnoo play zeloso! Soso
do todas. Such is Spanish. Stoop alittle closer, fealse! Delightsome simply! Like Jolio and Romeune. I haven't fell so turkish
for ages and ages! Mine's me of squisious, the chocolate with
a soul. Extraordinary! Why, what are they all, the mucky lot
of them only? Sht! I wouldn't pay three hairpins for them. Peppt!
That's rights, hold it steady! Leg me pull. Pu! Come big to Iran.
Poo! What are you nudging for? No, I just thought you were.
Listen, loviest! Of course it was *too* kind of you, miser, to remember my sighs in shockings, my often expressed wish when
you were wandering about my trousseaurs and before I forget it
don't forget, in your extensions to my personality, when knotting
my remembrancetie, shoeweek will be trotting back with red
heels at the end of the moon but look what the fool bought
cabbage head and, as I shall answer to gracious heaven, I'll
always in always remind of snappy new girters, me being always
the one for charms with my very best in proud and gloving
even if he was to be vermillion miles my youth to live on,
the rubberend Mr. Polkingtone, the quonian fleshmonger who
Mother Browne solicited me for unlawful converse with, with
her mug of October (a pots on it!), creaking around on his old
shanksaxle like a crosty old cornquake. Airman, waterwag, terrier,
blazer! I'm fine, thanks ever! Ha! O mind you poo tickly. Sall I
puhim in momou. Mummum. Funny spot to have a fingey! I'm
terribly sorry, I swear to you I am! May you never see me in my

birthday pelts seenso tutu and that her blanches mainges may rot
leprous off her whatever winking maggis I'll bet by your cut
you go fleurting after with all the glass on her and the jumps
in her stomewhere! Haha! I suspected she was! Sink her! May
they fire her for a barren ewe! So she says: Tay for thee? Well, I
saith: Angst so mush: and desired she might not take it amiss if I
esteemed her but an odd. If I did ate toughturf I'm not a mishy-
missy. Of course I know, pettest, you're so learningful and
considerate in yourself, so friend of vegetables, you long cold cat
you! Please by acquiester to meek my acquointance! Codling,
snakelet, iciclist! My diaper has more life to it! Who drowned
you in drears, man, or are you pillale with ink? Did a weep get
past the gates of your pride? My tread on the clover, sweetness?
Yes, the buttercups told me, hug me, damn it all, and I'll kiss
you back to life, my peachest. I mean to make you suffer,
meddlar, and I don't care this fig for contempt of courting.
That I chid you sweet sir? You know I'm tender by my eye.
Can't you read by dazzling ones through me true? Bite my
laughters, drink my tears. Pore into me, volumes, spell me stark
and spill me swooning, I just don't care what my thwarters
think. Transname me loveliness, now and here me for all times!
I'd risk a policeman passing by, Magrath or even that beggar of
a boots at the Post. The flame? O, pardone! That was what?
Ah, did you speak, stuffstuff? More poestries from Chickspeer's
with gleechoreal music or a jaculation from the garden of the
soul. Of I be leib in the immoralities? O, you mean the strangle
for love and the sowiveall of the prettiest? Yep, we open hap
coseries in the home. And once upon a week I improve on myself
I'm so keen on that New Free Woman with novel inside. I'm
always as tickled as can be over Man in a Surplus by the Lady
who Pays the Rates. But I'm as pie as is possible. Let's root
out Brimstoker and give him the thrall of our lives. It's Dracula's
nightout. For creepsake don't make a flush! Draw the shades,
curfe you, and I'll beat any sonnamonk to love. Holy bug, how
my highness would jump to make you flame your halve a ban-
nan in two when I'd run my burning torchlight through (to adore

me there and then cease to be? Whatever for, blossoms?) Your
hairmejig if you had one. If I am laughing with you? No,
lovingest, I'm not so dying to take my rise out of you, adored.
Not in the very least. True as God made my Mamaw hiplength
modesty coatmawther! It's only because the rison is I'm only any
girl, you lovely fellow of my dreams, and because old somebooby
is not a roundabout, my trysting of the tulipies, like that puff
pape bucking Daveran assoiling us behinds. What a nerve!
He thinks that's what the vesprey's for. How vain's that hope in
cleric's heart Who still pursues th'adult' rous art, Cocksure that
rusty gown of his Will make fair Sue forget his phiz! Tame
Schwipps. Blessed Marguerite bosses, I hope they threw away
the mould or else we'll have Ballshossers and Sourdamapplers
with their medical assassiations all over the place. But hold hard
till I've got my latchkey vote and I'll teach him when to wear
what woman callours. On account of the gloss of the gleison
Hasaboobrawbees isabeaubel. And because, you pluckless lanka-
loot, I hate the very thought of the thought of you and because,
dearling, of course, adorest, I was always meant for an engin-
dear from the French college, to be musband, *nomme d'engien*,
when we do and contract with encho tencho solver when you
are married to reading and writing which pleasebusiness now
won't be long for he's so loopy on me and I'm so leapy like
since the day he carried me from the boat, my saviored of eroes,
to the beach and I left on his shoulder one fair hair to guide hand
and mind to its softness. Ever so sorry! I beg your pardon, I was
listening to every treasuried word I said fell from my dear mot's
tongue otherwise how could I see what you were thinking of
our granny? Only I wondered if I threw out my shaving water.
Anyway, here's my arm, pulletneck. Gracefully yours. Move your
mouth towards minth, more, preciousest, more on more! To
please me, treasure. Don't be a, I'm not going to! Sh! nothing!
A cricri somewhere! Buybuy! I'm fly! Hear, pippy, under the
limes. You know bigtree are all against gravstone. They hisshis-
tenency. Garnd ond mand! So chip chirp chirrup, cigolo, for the
lug of Migo! The little passdoor, I go you before, so, and you're

at my apron stage. Shy is him, dovey. Musforget there's an
audience. I have been lost, angel. Cuddle, ye divil ye! It's our
toot-a-toot. Hearhere! Sensation! Let them, their whole four
courtships! Let them, Bigbawl and his boosers' eleven makes
twelve territorials. The Old Sot's Hole that wants wide streets to
commission their noisense in, at the Mitchel v. Nicholls *Aves
Selvae Acquae Valles*! And my waiting twenty classbirds, sitting
on their stiles! Let me finger their eurhythmytic. And you'll see
if I'm selfthought. They're all of them out to please. Wait! In
the name of. And all the holly. And some the mistle and it Saint
Yves. Hoost! Ahem! There's Ada, Bett, Celia, Delia, Ena,
Fretta, Gilda, Hilda, Ita, Jess, Katty, Lou, (they make me cough
as sure as I read them) Mina, Nippa, Opsy, Poll, Queeniee, Ruth,
Saucy, Trix, Una, Vela, Wanda, Xenia, Yva, Zulma, Phoebe,
Thelma. And Mee! The reformatory boys is goaling in for the
church so we've all comefeast like the groupsuppers and caught
lipsolution from Anty Pravidance under penancies for myrtle
sins. When their bride was married all my belles began ti ting.
A ring a ring a rosaring! Then everyone will hear of it. Whoses
wishes is the farther to my thoughts. But I'll plant them a poser
for their nomanclatter. When they're out with the daynurse
doing Chaperon Mall. Bright pigeons all over the whirrld will
fly with my mistletoe message round their loveribboned necks
and a crumb of my cake for each chasta dieva. We keeps all and
sundry papers. In th' amourlight, O my darling! No, I swear to
you by Fibsburrow churchdome and Sainte Andrée's Under-
shift, by all I hold secret from my world and in my underworld
of nighties and naughties and all the other wonderwearlds!
Close your, notmust look! Now open, pet, your lips, pepette,
like I used my sweet parted lipsabuss with Dan Holohan of
facetious memory taught me after the flannel dance, with the
proof of love, up Smock Alley the first night he smelled pouder
and I coloured beneath my fan, *pipetta mia*, when you learned
me the linguo to melt. Whowham would have ears like ours,
the blackhaired! Do you like that, *silenzioso*? Are you enjoying,
this same little me, my life, my love? Why do you like my

whisping? Is it not divinely deluscious? But in't it bufforyou? *Misi, misi!* Tell me till my thrillme comes! I will not break the seal. I am enjoying it still, I swear I am! Why do you prefer its in these dark nets, if why may ask, my sweetykins? Sh sh! Longears is flying. No, sweetissest, why would that ennoy me? But don't! You want to be slap well slapped for that. Your delighted lips, love, be careful! Mind my duvetyne dress above all! It's golded silvy, the newest sextones with princess effect. For Rutland blue's got out of passion. So, so, my precious! O, I can see the cost, chare! Don't tell me! Why, the boy in sheeps' lane knows that. If I sell whose, dears? Was I sold here' tears? You mean those conversation lozenges? How awful! The bold shame of me! I wouldn't, chickens, not for all the juliettes in the twinkly way! I could snap them when I see them winking at me in bed. I didn't did so, my intended, or was going to or thinking of. Shshsh! Don't start like that, you wretch! I thought ye knew all and more, ye aucthor, to explique to ones the significat of their exsystems with your nieu nivulon lead. It's only another queer fish or other in Brinbrou's damned old trouchorous river again, Gothewishegoths bless us and spare her! And gibos rest from the bosso! Excuse me for swearing, love, I swear to the sorrasims on their trons of Uian I didn't mean to by this alpin armlet! Did you really never in all our cantalang lives speak clothse to a girl's before? No! Not even to the charmermaid? How marfellows! Of course I believe you, my own dear doting liest, when you tell me. As I'd live to, O, I'd love to! Liss, liss! I muss whiss! Never that ever or I can remember dearstreaming faces, you may go through me! Never in all my whole white life of my matchless and pair. Or ever for bitter be the frucht of this hour! With my whiteness I thee woo and bind my silk breasths I thee bound! Always, Amory, amor andmore! Till always, thou lovest! Shshshsh! So long as the lucksmith. Laughs!

11. If you met on the binge a poor acheseyeld from Ailing, when the tune of his tremble shook shimmy on shin, while his countrary raged in the weak of his wailing, like a rugilant pugilant Lyon O'Lynn; if he maundered in misliness, plaining his

plight or, played fox and lice, pricking and dropping hips teeth, or wringing his handcuffs for peace, the blind blighter, praying Dieuf and Domb Nostrums foh thomethinks to eath; if he weapt while he leapt and guffalled quith a quhimper, made cold blood a blue mundy and no bones without flech, taking kiss, kake or kick with a suck, sigh or simper, a diffle to larn and a dibble to lech; if the fain shinner pegged you to shave his im-martial, wee skillmustered shoul with his ooh, hoodoodoo! brok-ing wind that to wiles, woemaid sin he was partial, we don't think, Jones, we'd care to this evening, would you?

Answer: No, blank ye! So you think I have impulsivism? Did they tell you I am one of the fortysixths? And I suppose you heard I had a wag on my ears? And I suppose they told you too that my roll of life is not natural? But before proceeding to con-clusively confute this begging question it would be far fitter for you, if you dare! to hasitate to consult with and consequentially attempt at my disposale of the same dime-cash problem elsewhere naturalistically of course, from the blinkpoint of so eminent a spatialist. From it you will here notice, Schott, upon my for the first remarking you that the sophology of Bitchson while driven as under by a purely dime-dime urge is not without his cashcash charackterickstics, borrowed for its nonce ends from the fiery goodmother Miss Fortune (who the lost time we had the pleasure we have had our little *recherché* brush with, what, Schott?) and as I further could have told you as brisk as your D.B.C. beha-viouristically *pailleté* with a coat of homoid icing which is in reality only a done by chance ridiculisation of the whoo-whoo and where's hairs theorics of Winestain. To put it all the more plumbsily. The speechform is a mere sorrogate. Whilst the qua-lity and tality (I shall explex what you ought to mean by this with its proper when and where and why and how in the subsequent sentence) are alternativomentally harrogate and arrogate, as the gates may be.

Talis is a word often abused by many passims (I am working out a quantum theory about it for it is really most tantumising state of affairs). A pessim may frequent you to say: Have you been

seeing much of Talis and Talis those times? optimately meaning:
Will you put up at hree of irish? Or a ladyeater may perhaps have
casualised as you temptoed her *à la sourdine*: Of your plates? Is
Talis de Talis, the swordswallower, who is on at the Craterium
the same Talis von Talis, the penscrusher, no funk you! who runs
his duly mile? Or this is a perhaps cleaner example. At a recent
postvortex piece infustigation of a determinised case of chronic
spinosis an extension lecturer on The Ague who out of matter of
form was trying his seesers, Dr's Het Ubeleeft, borrowed the
question: Why's which Suchman's *talis qualis?* to whom, as a
fatter of macht, Dr. Gedankje of Stoutgirth, who was wiping his
whistle, toarsely retoarted: While thou beast' one zoom of a
whorl! (Talis and Talis originally mean the same thing, hit it's:
Qualis.)

Professor Loewy-Brueller (though as I shall promptly prove
his whole account of the Sennacherib as distinct from the Shal-
manesir Sanitational reforms and of the Mr. Skekels and Dr.
Hydes problem in the same connection differs *toto coelo* from the
fruit of my own investigations — though the reason I went to
Jericho must remain for certain reasons a political secret —
especially as I shall shortly be wanted in Cavantry, I congratulate
myself, for the same and other reasons — as being again hopelessly vitiated by what I have now resolved to call the dime and
cash diamond fallacy) in his talked off confession which recently
met with such a leonine uproar on its escape after its confinement
Why am I not born like a Gentleman and why am I now so speak-
able about my own eatables (Feigenbaumblatt and Father, Juda-
pest, 5688, A.M.) whole-heartedly takes off his gabbercoat and
wig, honest draughty fellow, in his public interest, to make us
see how though, as he says: 'by Allswill' the inception and the
descent and the endswell of Man is *temporarily* wrapped in ob-
scenity, looking through at these accidents with the faroscope of
television, (this nightlife instrument needs still some subtrac-
tional betterment in the readjustment of the more refrangible
angles to the squeals of his hypothesis on the outer tin sides), I
can easily believe heartily in my own most spacious immensity

as my ownhouse and microbemost cosm when I am reassured by
ratio that the cube of my volumes is to the surfaces of their sub-
jects-as the, sphericity of these globes (I am very pressing for a
parliamentary motion this term which, under my guidance, would
establish the deleteriousness of decorousness in the morbidis-
ation of the modern mandaboutwoman type) is to the fera-
city of Fairynelly's vacuum. I need not anthrapologise for any
obintentional (I must here correct all that school of neoitalian or
paleoparisien schola of tinkers and spanglers who say I'm wrong
parcequeue out of revolscian from romanitis I want to be) down-
trodding on my foes. Professor Levi-Brullo, F.D. of Sexe-
Weiman-Eitelnaky finds, from experiments made by hinn with
his Nuremberg eggs in the one hands and the watches cunldron
apan the oven, though it is astensably a case of Ket's rebollions
cooling the Popes back, because the number of squeer faiths
in weekly circulation will not be appreciably augmented by the
notherslogging of my cupolar clods. What the romantic in rags
pines after like all tomtompions haunting crevices for a deadbeat
escupement and what het importunes our *Mitleid* for in accornish
with the Mortadarthella taradition is the poorest commonon-
guardiant waste of time. *His* everpresent toes are always in
retaliessian out throuth his overpast boots. Hear him squak!
Teek heet to that looswallawer how he bolo the bat! Tyro a
toray! *When* Mullocky won the couple of colds, *when* we were
stripping in number three, I would like the neat drop that would
malt in my mouth but I fail to see *when* (I am purposely refrain-
ing from expounding the obvious fallacy as to the specific
gravitates of the two deglutables implied nor to the lapses
lequou asousiated with the royal gorge through students of
mixed hydrostatics and pneumodipsics will after some difficulties
grapple away with my meinungs). Myrrdin aloer! as old Mar-
sellas Cambriannus puts his. But, on Professor Llewellys ap
Bryllars, F.D., Ph. Dr's showings, the plea, if he pleads,
is all posh and robbage on a melodeontic scale since his man's
when is no otherman's *quandour* (Mine, dank you?) while, for
aught I care for the contrary?, the all is *where* in love as war and

the plane where me arts soar you'd aisy rouse a thunder from and
where I cling true'tis there I climb tree and where Innocent looks
best (pick!) there's holly in his ives.

As my explanations here are probably above your understandings, lattlebrattons, though as augmentatively uncomparisoned
as Cadwan, Cadwallon and Cadwalloner, I shall revert to a more
expletive method which I frequently use when I have to sermo
with muddlecrass pupils. Imagine for my purpose that you are a
squad of urchins, snifflynosed, goslingnecked, clothyheaded,
tangled in your lacings, tingled in your pants, etsitaraw etcicero.
And you, Bruno Nowlan, take your tongue out of your inkpot!
As none of you knows javanese I will give all my easyfree translation of the old fabulist's parable. Allaboy Minor, take your
head out of your satchel! *Audi*, Joe Peters! *Exaudi* facts!

The Mookse and The Gripes.

Gentes and laitymen, fullstoppers and semicolonials, hybreds
and lubberds!

Eins within a space and a wearywide space it wast ere wohned
a Mookse. The onesomeness wast alltolonely, archunsitslike,
broady oval, and a Mookse he would a walking go (My hood!
cries Antony Romeo) so one grandsumer evening, after a great
morning and his good supper of gammon and spittish, having
flabelled his eyes, pilleoled his nostrils, vacticanated his ears and
palliumed his throats, he put on his impermeable, seized his im-
pugnable, harped on his crown and stepped out of his immobile
De Rure Albo (socolled becauld it was chalkfull of masterplasters
and had borgeously letout gardens strown with cascadas, pinta-
costecas, horthoducts and currycombs) and set off from Luds-
town *a spasso* to see how badness was badness in the weirdest of
all pensible ways.

As he set off with his father's sword, his *lancia spezzata*, he was
girded on, and with that between his legs and his tarkeels, our
once in only Bragspear, he clanked, to my clinking, from veetoes
to threetop, every inch of an immortal.

He had not walked over a pentiadpair of parsecs from his
azylium when at the turning of the Shinshone Lanteran near

Saint Bowery's-without-his-Walls he came (secunding to the one one oneth of the propecies, *Amnis Limina Permanent*) upon the most unconsciously boggylooking stream he ever locked his eyes with. Out of the colliens it took a rise by daubing itself Ninon. It looked little and it smelt of brown and it thought in narrows and it talked showshallow. And as it rinn it dribbled like any lively purliteasy: *My, my, my! Me and me! Little down dream don't I love thee!*

And, I declare, what was there on the yonder bank of the stream that would be a river, parched on a limb of the olum, bolt downright, but the Gripes? And no doubt he was fit to be dried for why had he not been having the juice of his times?

His pips had been neatly all drowned on him; his polps were charging odours every older minute; he was quickly for getting the dresser's desdaign on the flyleaf of his frons; and he was quietly for giving the bailiff's distrain on to the bulkside of his *cul de Pompe*. In all his specious heavings, as be lived by Optimus Maximus, the Mookse had never seen his Dubville brooder-on-low so nigh to a pickle.

Adrian (that was the Mookse now's assumptinome) stuccstill phiz-à-phiz to the Gripes in an accessit of aurignacian. But Allmookse must to Moodend much as Allrouts, austereways or wastersways, in roaming run through Room. Hic sor a stone, singularly illud, and on hoc stone Seter satt huc sate which it filled quite poposterously and by acclammitation to its fullest justotoryum and whereopum with his unfallable encyclicling upom his alloilable, diupetriark of the wouest, and the athemystsprinkled pederect he always walked with, *Deusdedit*, cheek by jowel with his frisherman's blague, *Bellua Triumphanes*, his everyway addedto wallat's collectium, for yea longer he lieved yea broader he betaught of it, the fetter, the summe and the haul it cost, he looked the first and last micahlike laicness of Quartus the Fifth and Quintus the Sixth and Sixtus the Seventh giving allnight sitting to Lio the Faultyfindth.

— Good appetite us, sir Mookse! How do you do it? cheeped the Gripes in a wherry whiggy maudelenian woice and the jackasses all within bawl laughed and brayed for his intentions for they knew their sly toad lowry now. I am rarumomimum blessed to see you, my dear mouster. Will you not perhopes tell me everything if you are pleased, sanity? All about aulne and lithial and allsall allinall about awn and liseias? Ney?

Think of it! O miserendissimest retempter! A Gripes!

—— Rats! bullowed the Mookse most telesphorously, the concionator, and the sissymusses and the zozzymusses in their robenhauses quailed to hear his tardeynois at all for you cannot wake a silken nouse out of a hoarse oar. Blast yourself and your anathomy infairioriboos! No, hang you for an animal rurale! I am superbly in my supremest poncif! Abase you, baldyqueens! Gather behind me, satraps! Rots!

— I am till infinity obliged with you, bowed the Gripes, his whine having gone to his palpruy head. I am still always having a wish on all my extremities. By the watch, what is the time, pace?

Figure it! The pining peever! To a Mookse!

— Ask my index, mund my achilles, swell my obolum, wosh-up my nase serene, answered the Mookse, rapidly by turning clement, urban, eugenious and celestian in the formose of good grogory humours. Quote awhore? That is quite about what I came on *my* missions with *my* intentions *laudibiliter* to settle with *you*, barbarousse. Let thor be orlog. Let Pauline be Irene. Let you be Beeton. And let me be Los Angeles. Now measure your length. Now estimate. my capacity. Well, sour? Is this space of our couple of hours too dimensional for you, temporiser? Will you give you up? *Como? Fuert it?*

Sancta Patientia! You should have heard the voice that answered him! *Culla vosellina.*

— I was just thinkling upon that, swees Mooksey, but, for all the rime on my raisins, if I connow make my submission, I cannos give you up, the Gripes whimpered from nethermost of his wanhope. Ishallassoboundbewilsothoutoosezit. My tumble, loudy bullocker, is my own. My velocity is too fit in one stockend. And my spetial inexshellsis the belowing things ab ove. But I will never be abler to tell Your Honoriousness (here he near lost his limb) though my corked father was bott a pseudowaiter, whose o'cloak you ware.

Incredible! Well, hear the inevitable.

— *Your* temple, *sus in cribro!* Semperexcommunicambiambisumers. Tugurios-in-Newrobe or Tukurias-in-Ashies. Novarome, my creature, blievend bleives. My building space in lyonine city is always to let to leonlike Men, the Mookse in a most consistorous allocution pompifically with immediate jurisdiction constantinently concludded (what a crammer for the shapewrucked Gripes!). And I regret to proclaim that it is out of my temporal to help you from being killed by inchies, (what a thrust!), as we first met each other newwhere so airly. (Poor little sowsieved subsquashed Gripes! I begin to feel contemption for him!). My side thank decretals, is as safe as motherour's houses, he continued, and I can seen from my holeydome what it is to be wholly sane. Unionjok and be joined to yok! Parysis, *tu sais*, crucycrooks, belongs to him who parises himself. And there I must leave you subject for the pressing. I can prove that against you, weight a momentum, mein goot enemy! or Cospol's not our star. I bet you this dozen odd. This foluminous dozen odd. *Quas primas*—but 'tis bitter to compote my knowledge's fructos of. Tomes.

Elevating, to give peint to his blick, his jewelled pederect to the allmysty cielung, he luckystruck blueild out of a few shouldbe santillants, a cloister of starabouts over Maples, a lucciolys in Teresa street and a stopsign before Sophy Barratt's, he gaddered togodder the odds docence of his vellumes, gresk, letton and russicruxian, onto the lapse of his prolegs, into umfullth onescuppered, and sat about his widerproof. He proved it well whoonearth dry and drysick times, and *vremiament, tu cesses*, to the extinction of Niklaus altogether (Niklaus Alopysius having been the once Gripes's popwilled nimbum) by Neuclidius and Inexagoras and Mumfsen and Thumpsem, by Orasmus and by Amenius, by Anacletus the Jew and by Malachy the Augurer and by the Cappon's collection and after that, with Cheekee's gelatine and Alldaybrandy's formolon, he reproved it ehrltogether

when not in that order sundering in some different order, alter
three thirty and a hundred times by the binomial dioram and
the penic walls and the ind, the Inklespill legends and the rure,
the rule of the hoop and the blessons of expedience and the jus,
the jugicants of Pontius Pilax and all the mummyscrips in Sick
Bokes' Juncroom and the Chapters for the Cunning of the Chapters of the Conning Fox by Tail.

While that Mooksius with preprocession and with propre-
cession, duplicitly and diplussedly, was promulgating ipsofacts
and sadcontras this raskolly Gripos he had allbust seceded in
monophysicking his illsobordunates. But asawfulas he had
caught his base semenoyous sarchnaktiers to combuccinate upon
the silipses of his aspillouts and the acheporeoozers of his haggy-
own pneumax to synerethetise with the breadchestviousness of
his sweeatovular ducose sofarfully the loggerthuds of his sakel-
laries were fond at variance with the synodals of his somepooliom
and his babskissed nepogreasymost got the hoof from his philio-
quus.

— Efter thousand yaws, O Gripes con my sheepskins, yow
will be belined to the world, enscayed Mookse the pius.

— Ofter thousand yores, amsered Gripes the gregary, be the
goat of MacHammud's, yours may be still, O Mookse, more
botheared.

— Us shall be chosen as the first of the last by the electress of
Vale Hollow, obselved the Mookse nobily, for par the unicum
of Elelijiacks, Us am in Our stabulary and that is what Ruby and
Roby fall for, blissim.

The Pills, the Nasal Wash (Yardly's), the Army Man Cut, as
british as bondstrict and as straightcut as when that broken-
arched traveller from Nuzuland . . .

— Wee, cumfused the Gripes limply, shall not even be the
last of the first, wee hope, when oust are visitated by the Veiled
Horror. And, he added: Mee are relying entirely, see the forte-
thurd of Elissabed, on the weightiness of mear's breath. Puffut!

Unsightbared embouscher, relentless foe to social and business
succes! (Hourihaleine) It might have been a happy evening but . . .

And they viterberated each other, *canis et coluber* with the
wildest ever wielded since Tarriestinus lashed Pissasphaltium.

— Unuchorn!

— Ungulant!

— Uvuloid!

— Uskybeak!

And bullfolly answered volleyball.

Nuvoletta in her lightdress, spunn of sisteen shimmers, was
looking down on them, leaning over the bannistars and listening
all she childishly could. How she was brightened when Should-
rups in his glaubering hochskied his welkinstuck and how she
was overclused when Kneesknobs on his zwivvel was makeact-
ing such a paulse of himshelp! She was alone. All her nubied
companions were asleeping with the squirrels. Their mivver,
Mrs. Moonan, was off in the Fuerst quarter scrubbing the back-
steps of Number 28. Fuvver, that Skand, he was up in Norwood's
sokaparlour, eating oceans of Voking's Blemish. Nuvoletta listened as she reflected herself, though the heavenly one with his
constellatria and his emanations stood between, and she tried all
she tried to make the Mookse look up at her (but *he* was fore too
adiaptotously farseeing) and to make the Gripes hear how coy
she could be (though he was much too schystimatically auricular
about *his ens* to heed her) but it was all mild's vapour moist. Not
even her feignt reflection, Nuvoluccia, could they toke their
gnoses off for their minds with intrepifide fate and bungless
curiasity, were conclaved with Heliogobbleus and Commodus
and Enobarbarus and whatever the coordinal dickens they did
as their damprauch of papyrs and buchstubs said. As if that was
their spiration! As if theirs could duiparate her queendim! As if
she would be third perty to search on search proceedings! She
tried all the winsome wonsome ways her four winds had taught
her. She tossed her sfumastelliacinous hair like *la princesse de la
Petite Bretagne* and she rounded her mignons arms like Mrs.
Cornwallis-West and she smiled over herself like the beauty of
the image of the pose of the daughter of the queen of the Em-
perour of Irelande and she sighed after herself as were she born

to bride with Tristis Tristior Tristissimus. But, sweet madonine, she might fair as well have carried her daisy's worth to Florida. For the Mookse, a dogmad Accanite, were not amoosed and the Gripes, a dubliboused Catalick, wis pinefully obliviscent.

I see, she sighed. There are menner.

The siss of the whisp of the sigh of the softzing at the stir of the ver grose O arundo of a long one in midias reeds: and shades began to glidder along the banks, greepsing, greepsing, duusk unto duusk, and it was as glooming as gloaming could be in the waste of all peacable worlds. Metamnisia was allsoonome coloroform brune; citherior spiane an eaulande, innemorous and unnumerose. The Mookse had a sound eyes right but he could not all hear. The Gripes had light ears left yet he could but ill see. He ceased. And he ceased, tung and trit, and it was neversoever so dusk of both of them. But still Moo thought on the deeps of the undths he would profoundth come the morrokse and still Gri feeled of the scripes he would escipe if by grice he had luck enoupes.

Oh, how it was duusk! From Vallee Maraia to Grasyaplaina, dormimust echo! Ah dew! Ah dew! It was so duusk that the tears of night began to fall, first by ones and twos, then by threes and fours, at last by fives and sixes of sevens, for the tired ones were wecking, as we weep now with them. O! O! O! Par la pluie!

Then there came down to the thither bank a woman of no appearance (I believe she was a Black with chills at her feet) and she gathered up his hoariness the Mookse motamourfully where he was spread and carried him away to her invisible dwelling, thats hights, *Aquila Rapax*, for he was the holy sacred solem and poshup spit of her boshop's apron. So you see the Mookse he had reason as I knew and you knew and he knew all along. And there came down to the hither bank a woman to all important (though they say that she was comely, spite the cold in her heed) and, for he was as like it as blow it to a hawker's hank, she plucked down the Gripes, torn panicky autotone, in angeu from his limb and cariad away its beotitubes with her to her unseen

shieling, it is, *De Rore Coeli*. And so the poor Gripes got wrong;
for that is always how a Gripes is, always was and always will be.
And it was never so thoughtful of either of them. And there were
left now an only elmtree and but a stone. Polled with pietrous,
Sierre but saule. O! Yes! And Nuvoletta, a lass.

Then Nuvoletta reflected for the last time in her little long life
and she made up all her myriads of drifting minds in one. She
cancelled all her engauzements. She climbed over the bannistars;
she gave a childy cloudy cry: *Nuée! Nuée!* A lightdress fluttered.
She was gone. And into the river that had been a stream (for a
thousand of tears had gone eon her and come on her and she was
stout and struck on dancing and her muddied name was Missis-
liffi) there fell a tear, a singult tear, the loveliest of all tears (I
mean for those crylove fables fans who are 'keen' on the pretty-
pretty commonface sort of thing you meet by hopeharrods) for it
was a leaptear. But the river tripped on her by and by, lapping
as though her heart was brook: *Why, why, why! Weh, O weh!
I'se so silly to be flowing but I no canna stay!*

No applause, please! Bast! The romescot nattleshaker will go
round your circulation in *diu dursus*.

Allaboy, Major, I'll take your reactions in another place after
themes. Nolan Browne, you may now leave the classroom, Joe,
Peters, Fox.

As I have now successfully explained to you my own natural-
born rations which are even in excise of my vaultybrain insure
me that I am a mouth's more deserving case by genius. I feel in
symbathos for my ever devoted friend and halfaloafonwashed
Gnaccus Gnoccovitch. Darling gem! Darling smallfox! Horose-
shoew! I could love that man like my own ambo for being so
baileycliaver though he's a nawful curillass and I must slav to
methodiousness. I want him to go and live like a theabild in
charge of the night brigade on Tristan da Cunha, isle of man-
overboard, where he'll make Number 106 and be near Inacces-
sible. (The meeting of mahoganies, be the waves, rementious
me that this exposed sight though it pines for an umbrella of its
own and needs a shelter belt of the true service sort to keep its

boles clean, — the weeping beeches, Picea and Tillia, are in a
wild state about it — ought to be classified, as Cricketbutt Will-
owm and his two nurserymen advisers suggested, under genus
Inexhaustible when we refloat upon all the butternat, sweet gum
and manna ash redcedera which is so purvulent there as if there
was howthorns in Curraghchasa which ought to look as plane
as a lodgepole to anybody until we are introduced to that pine-
tacotta of Verney Rubeus where the deodarty is pinctured for us
in a pure stand, which we do not doubt ha has a habitat of doing,
but without those selfsownseedlings which are a species of proof
that the largest individual *can* occur at or in an olivetion such as
East Conna Hillock where it mixes with foolth accacians and
common sallies and *is* tender) *Vux Populus*, as we say in hickory-
hockery and I wish we had some more glasses of *arbor vitae*.
Why roat by the roadside or awn over alum pot? Alderman
Whitebeaver is dakyo. He ought to go away for a change of
ideas and he'd have a world of things to look back on. Do sweet
Daniel! If I weren't a jones in myself I'd elect myself to be his
dolphin in the wildsbillow because he is such a barefooted rubber
with my supersocks pulled over his face which I publicked in
my bestback garden for the laetification of siderodromites and
to the irony of the stars. You will say it is most unenglish and
I shall hope to hear that you will not be wrong about it. But I
further, feeling a bit husky in my truths.

  Will you please come over and let us mooremoore murgessly
to each's other down below our vices. I am underheerd by old
billfaust. Wilsh is full of curks. The coolskittle is philip deblinite. Mr Wist is thereover beyeind the wantnot. Wilsh and wist
are as thick of thins udder as faust on the deblinite. Sgunoshooto
estas preter la tapizo malgranda. Lilegas al si en sia chambro.
Kelkefoje funcktas, kelkefoje srumpas Shultroj. Houdian Kiel vi
fartas, mia nigra sinjoro? And from the poignt of fun where I
am crying to arrive you at they are on allfore as foibleminded as
you can feel they are fablebodied.

  My heeders will recoil with a great leisure how at the out-
break before trespassing on the space question where even

michelangelines have fooled to dread I proved to mindself as to your sotisfiction how his abject all through (the *quickquid* of Professor Ciondolone's too frequently hypothecated *Bettlermensch*) is nothing so much more than a mere cashdime however genteel he may want ours, if we please (I am speaking to us in the second person), for to this graded intellecktuals dime *is* cash and the cash system (you must not be allowed to forget that this is all contained, I mean the system, in the dogmarks of origen on spurios) means that I cannot now have or nothave a piece of cheeps in your pocket at the same time and with the same manners as you can now nothalf or half the cheek apiece I've in mind unless Burrus and Caseous have not or not have seemaultaneously sysentangled themselves, selldear to soldthere, once in the dairy days of buy and buy.

Burrus, let us like to imagine, is a genuine prime, the real choice, full of natural greace, the mildest of milkstoffs yet unbeaten as a risicide and, of course, obsoletely unadulterous whereat Caseous is obversely the revise of him and in fact not an ideal choose by any meals, though the betterman of the two is meltingly addicted to the more casual side of the arrivaliste case and, let me say it at once, as zealous over him as is passably he. The seemsame home and histry seeks and hidepence which we used to be reading for our prepurgatory, hot, Schott? till Duddy shut the shopper op and Mutti, poor Mutti! brought us our poor suppy, (ah who! eh how!) in Acetius and Oleosus and Sellius Volatilis and Petrus Papricus! Our Old Party quite united round the Slatbowel at Commons: Pfarrer Salamoss himself and that sprog of a Pedersill and his Sprig of Thyme and a dozen of the Murphybuds and a score and more of the hot young Capels and Lettucia in her greensleeves and you too and me three, twinsome bibs but hansome ates, like shakespill and eggs! But there's many a split pretext bowl and jowl; and (snob screwing that cork, Schott!) to understand this as well as you can, feeling how backward you are in your down-to-the-ground benches, I have completed the following arrangement for the coarse use of stools and if I don't make away with you I'm beyond Caesar outnulused.

The older sisars (Tyrants, regicide is too good for you!) become unbeurrable from age, (the compositor of the farce of dustiny however makes a thunpledrum mistake by letting off this pienofarte effect as his furst act as that is where the juke comes in) having been sort-of-nineknived and chewly removed (this soldier - author - batman for all his commontoryism is just another of those souftsiezed bubbles who never quite got the sandhurst out of his eyes so that the champaign he draws for us is as flop as a plankrieg) the twinfreer types are billed to make their reupprearance as the knew kneck and knife knickknots on the deserted *champ de bouteilles*. (A most cursery reading into the Persic-Uraliens hostery shows us how Fonnumag—ula picked up that propper numen out of a colluction of prifixes though to the permienting cannasure the Coucousien oafsprung of this sun of a kuk is as sattin as there's a tub in Tobolosk) *Ostiak della Vogul Marina!* But that I dannoy the fact of wanton to weste point I could paint you to that butter (cheese it!) if you had some wash. Mordvealive! Oh me none onsens! Why the case is as inessive and impossive as kezom hands! Their interlocative is conprovocative just as every hazzy hates to having a hazbane in her noze. Caseous may bethink himself a thought of a caviller but Burrus has the reachly roundered head that goes best with thofthinking defensive fideism. He has the lac of wisdom under every dent in his lofter, while the other follow's onni vesy milky indeedmymy. Laughing over the linnuts and weeping off the uniun. He hisn't the hey og he lisn't the lug, poohoo. And each night sim misses mand he winks he had the semagen. It was aptly and corrigidly stated (and, it is royally needless for one *ex ungue Leonem* to say by whom) that his seeingscraft was that clarety as were the wholeborough of Poutresbourg to be averlaunched over him pitchbatch he could still make out with his augstritch the green moat in Ireland's Eye. Let me sell you the fulltroth of Burrus when he wore a younker. Here it is, and chorming too, in six by sevens! A cleanly line, by the gods! A king off duty and a jaw for ever! And what a cheery ripe outlook, good help me Deus v Deus! If I were to speak

my ohole mouthful to arinam about it you should call me the
Ormuzd aliment in your midst of faime. Eat ye up, heat ye up!
sings the somun in the salm. *Butyrum et mel comedet ut sciat
reprobare malum et eligere bonum.* This, of course, also explains
why we were taught to play in the childhood: *Der Haensli ist
ein Butterbrot, mein Butterbrot! Und Koebi iss dein Schtinkenkot!
Ja! Ja! Ja!*

This in fact, just to show you, is Caseous, the brutherscutch
or puir tyron: a hole or two, the highstinks aforefelt and anygo
prigging wurms. Cheesugh! you complain. And Hi Hi High
must say you are not Hoa Hoa Hoally in the wrong!

Thus we cannot escape our likes and mislikes, exiles or am-
busheers, beggar and neighbour and — this is where the dime-
show advertisers advance the temporal relief plea — let us be
tolerant of antipathies. *Nex quovis burro num fit mercaseus?* I am
not hereby giving my final endorsement to the learned ignorants
of the Cusanus philosophism in which old Nicholas pegs it
down that the smarter the spin of the top the sounder the span
of the buttum (what the worthy old auberginiste ought to have
meant was: the more stolidly immobile *in space* appears to me
the bottom which is presented to use in time by the top primo-
mobilisk &c.). And I shall be misunderstord if understood to
give an unconditional sinequam to the heroicised furibouts of
the Nolanus theory, or, at any rate, of that substrate of apart
from hissheory where the Theophil swoors that on principial he
was the pointing start of his odiose by comparison and that whiles
eggs will fall cheapened all over the walled the Bure will be dear
on the Brie.

Now, while I am not out now to be taken up as unintention-
ally recommending the Silkebjorg tyrondynamon machine for
the more economical helixtrolysis of these amboadipates until
I can find space to look into it myself a little more closely first
I shall go on with my decisions after having shown to you in
good time how both products of our social stomach (the excellent
Dr. Burroman, I noticed by the way from his emended food
theory, has been carefully digesting the very wholesome criticism

I helped him to in my princeps edition which is all so munch
to the cud) are mutuearly polarised the incompatabilily of any
delusional acting as ambivalent to the fixation of his pivotism.
Positing, as above, too males pooles, the one the pictor of the
other and the omber the *Skotia* of the one, and looking want-
ingly around our undistributed middle between males we feel
we must waistfully woent a female to focus and on this stage
there pleasantly appears the cowrymaid M. whom we shall
often meet below who introduces herself upon us at some precise
hour which we shall again agree to call absolute zero or the
babbling pumpt of platinism. And so like that former son
of a kish who went up and out to found his farmer's ashes we
come down home gently on our own turnedabout asses to meet
Margareen.

We now romp through a period of pure lyricism of shame-
bred music (technologically, let me say, the appetising entry of
this subject on a fool chest of vialds is plumply pudding the carp
before doevre hors) evidenced by such words in distress as *I
cream for thee, Sweet Margareen*, and the more hopeful *O Margareena! O Margareena! Still in the bowl is left a lump of gold!*
(Correspondents, by the way, will keep on asking me what is the
correct garnish to serve drisheens with. Tansy Sauce. Enough).
The pawnbreaking pathos of the first of these shoddy pieces
reveals it as a Caseous effort. Burrus's bit is often used for a toast.
Criniculture can tell us very precisely indeed how and why this
particular streak of yellow silver first appeared on (not in) the
bowel, that is to see, the human head, bald, black, bronze, brown,
brindled, betteraved or blanchemanged where it might be use-
fully compared with an earwig on a fullbottom. I am offering
this to Signorina Cuticura and I intend to take it up and bring it
under the nosetice of Herr Harlene by way of diverting his
attentions. Of course the unskilled singer continues to pervert
our wiser ears by subordinating the space-element, that is to
sing, the *aria*, to the time-factor, which ought to be killed, *ill
tempor*. I should advise any unborn singer who may still be
among my heeders to forget her temporal diaphragm at home

(the best thing that could happen to it!) and attack the roulade with a swift *colpo di glottide* to the lug (though Maace I will insist was reclined from overdoing this, his recovery often being slow) and then, O! on the third dead beat, O! to cluse her eyes and aiopen her oath and see what spice I may send her. How? Cease thee, cantatrickee! I fain would be solo. Arouse thee, my valour! And save for e'er my true Bdur!

I shall have a word to say in a few yards about the acoustic and orchidectural management of the tonehall but, as ours is a vivarious where one plant's breaf is a lunger planner's byscent and you may not care for argon, it will be very convenient for me for the emolument to pursue Burrus and Caseous for a rung or two up their isocelating biangle. Every admirer has seen my goulache of Marge (she is *so* like the sister, you don't know, and they both dress A L I K E !) which I titled *The Very Picture of a Needlesswoman* which in the presence ornates our national cruetstand. This genre of portraiture of changes of mind in order to be truly torse should evoke the bush soul of females so I am leaving it to the experienced victim to complete the general suggestion by the mental addition of a wallopy bound or, should the zulugical zealot prefer it, a congorool teal. The hatboxes which composed Rhomba, lady Trabezond (Marge in her *excelsis*), also comprised the climactogram up which B and C may fondly be imagined ascending and are suggestive of gentlemen's spring modes, these modes carrying us back to the superimposed claylayers of eocene and pleastoseen formation and the gradual morphological changes in our body politic which Professor Ebahi-Ahuri of Philadespoinis (Ill) — whose bluebutterbust I have just given his coupe de grass to — neatly names a *boîte à surprises*. The boxes, if I may break the subject gently, are worth about fourpence pourbox but I am inventing a more patent process, foolproof and pryperfect (I should like to ask that Shedlock Homes person who is out for removing the roofs of our criminal classics by what *deductio ad domunum* he hopes *de tacto* to detect anything unless he happens of himself, *movibile tectu*, to have a slade off) after which they can be reduced to a fragment of their true crust by even the youngest of Margees if she will take plase to be seated and smile if I please.

Now there can be no question about it either that I having done as much, have quite got the size of that demilitery young female (we will continue to call her Marge) whose types may be met with in any public garden, wearing a very "dressy" affair, known as an "ethel" of instep length and with a real fur, reduced to 3/9, and muffin cap to tone (they are "angelskin" this fall), ostentatiously hemming apologetically over the shirtness of some "sweet" garment, when she is not sitting on all the free benches avidously reading about "it" but ovidently on the look out for "him" or so "thrilled" about the best dressed dolly pram and beautiful elbow competition or at the movies swallowing sobs and blowing bixed mixcuits over "childe" chaplain's "latest" or on the verge of the gutter with some bobbedhair brieffrocked babyma's toddler (the Smythe-Smythes now keep TWO domestics and aspire to THREE male ones, a shover, a butlegger and a sectary) held hostage at armslength, teaching His Infant Majesty how to make waters worse.

(I am closely watching Master Pules, as I have regions to suspect from my post that her "little man" is a secondary schoolteacher under the boards of education, a voted disciple of Infantulus who is being utilised thus publicly by the *seducente infanta* to conceal her own more mascular personality by flaunting frivolish finery over men's inside clothes, for the femininny of that totamulier will always lack the musculink of a verumvirum. My solotions for the proper parturience of matres and the education of micturious mites must stand over from the moment till I tackle this tickler hussy for occupying my uttentions.)

Margareena she's very fond of Burrus but, alick and alack! She velly fond of chee. (The important influence exercised on everything by this eastasian import has not been till now fully flavoured though we can comfortably taste it in this case. I shall come back for a little more say farther on.) A cleopatrician in her own right she at once complicates the position while Burrus and Caseous are contending for her misstery by implicating herself with an elusive Antonius, a wop who would appear to hug a personal interest in refined chees of all chades at the same time as he wags an antomine art of being rude like the boor. This Antonius-Burrus-Caseous grouptriad may be said to equate the *qualis* equivalent with the older socalled *talis* on *talis* one just as quantly as in the hyperchemical economantarchy the tantum ergons irruminate the quantum urge so that eggs is to whey as whay is to zeed like your golfchild's abe boob caddy. And this is why any simple philadolphus of a fool you like to dress, an athemisthued lowtownian, exlegged phatrisight, may be awfully green to one side of him and fruitfully blue on the other which will not screen him however from appealing to my gropesarching eyes, through the strongholes of my acropoll, as a boosted blasted bleating blatant bloaten blasphorus blesphorous idiot who kennot tail a bomb from a painapple when he steals one and wannot psing his psalmen with the cong in our gregational pompoms with the canting crew.

No! Topsman to your Tarpeia! This thing, Mister Abby, is nefand. (And, taking off soutstuffs and alkalike matters, I hope we can kill time to reach the salt because there's some forceglass neutric assets bittering in the soldpewter for you to plump your pottage in). The thundering legion has stormed Olymp that it end. Twelve tabular times till now have I edicted it. Merus Genius to Careous Caseous! *Moriture, te salutat!* My phemous themis race is run, so let Demoncracy take the highmost! (Abraham Tripier. Those old diligences are quite out of date. Read next answer). I'll beat you so lon. (Bigtempered. Why not take direct action. See previous reply). My unchanging Word is sacred. The word is my Wife, to exponse and expound, to vend and to velnerate, and may the curlews crown our nuptias! Till Breath us depart! Wamen. Beware would you change with my years. Be as young as your grandmother! The ring man in the rong shop but the rite words by the rote order! *Ubi lingua nuncupassit, ibi fas! Adversus hostem semper sac!* She that will not feel my fulmoon let her peel to thee as the hoyden and the impudent! That mon that hoth no moses in his sole nor is not awed by conquists

of word's law, who never with humself was fed and leaves
his soil to lave his head, when his hope's in his highlows from
whisking his woe, if he came to my preach, a proud pursebroken
ranger, when the heavens were welling the spite of their spout,
to beg for a bite in our bark *Noisdanger*, would meself and Mac
Jeffet, four-in-hand, foot him out? — ay! — were he my own
breastbrother, my doubled withd love and my singlebiassed hate,
were we bread by the same fire and signed with the same salt,
had we tapped from the same master and robbed the same till,
were we tucked in the one bed and bit by the one flea, homo-
gallant and hemycapnoise, bum and dingo, jack by churl, though
it broke my heart to pray it, still I'd fear I'd hate to say!

   12. *Sacer esto?*

Answer: *Semus sumus!*

[7]

Shem is as short for Shemus as Jem is joky for Jacob. A few toughnecks are still getatable who pretend that aboriginally he was of respectable stemming (he was an outlex between the lines of Ragonar Blaubarb and Horrild Hairwire and an inlaw to Capt. the Hon. and Rev. Mr. Bbyrdwood de Trop Blogg was among his most distant connections) but every honest to goodness man in the land of the space of today knows that his back life will not stand being written about in black and white. Putting truth and untruth together a shot may be made at what this hybrid actually was like to look at.

Shem's bodily getup, it seems, included an adze of a skull, an eight of a larkseye, the whoel of a nose, one numb arm up a sleeve, fortytwo hairs off his uncrown, eighteen to his mock lip, a trio of barbels from his megageg chin (sowman's son), the wrong shoulder higher than the right, all ears, an artificial tongue with a natural curl, not a foot to stand on, a handful of thumbs, a blind stomach, a deaf heart, a loose liver, two fifths of two buttocks, one gleetsteen avoirdupoider for him, a manroot of all evil, a salmonkelt's thinskin, eelsblood in his cold toes, a bladder tristended, so much so that young Master Shemmy on his very first debouch at the very dawn of protohistory seeing himself such and such, when playing with thistlewords in their garden nursery, Griefotrofio, at Phig Streat 111, Shuvlin, Old Hoeland, (would we go back there now for sounds, pillings and

sense? would we now for annas and annas? Would we for full-
score eight and a liretta? for twelve blocks one bob? for four tes-
ters one groat? not for a dinar! not for jo!) dictited to of all his
little brothron and sweestureens the first riddle of the universe:
asking, when is a man not a man?: telling them take their time,
yungfries, and wait till the tide stops (for from the first his day
was a fortnight) and offering the prize of a bittersweet crab, a
little present from the past, for their copper age was yet un-
minted, to the winner. One said when the heavens are quakers,
a second said when Bohemeand lips, a third said when he, no,
when hold hard a jiffy, when he is a gnawstick and detarmined
to, the next one said when the angel of death kicks the bucket
of life, still another said when the wine's at witsends, and still
another when lovely wooman stoops to conk him, one of the
littliest said me, me, Sem, when pappa papared the harbour, one
of the wittiest said, when he yeat ye abblokooken and he zmear
hezelf zo zhooken, still one said when you are old I'm grey fall
full wi sleep, and still another when wee deader walkner, and
another when he is just only after having being semisized, another when yea, he hath no mananas, and one when dose pigs
they begin now that they will flies up intil the looft. All were
wrong, so Shem himself, the doctator, took the cake, the correct
solution being — all give it up? —; when he is a — yours till
the rending of the rocks, — Sham.

Shem was a sham and a low sham and his lowness creeped out
first via foodstuffs. So low was he that he preferred Gibsen's teatime salmon tinned, as inexpensive as pleasing, to the plumpest
roeheavy lax or the friskiest parr or smolt troutlet that ever was
gaffed between Leixlip and Island Bridge and many was the time
he repeated in his botulism that no junglegrown pineapple ever
smacked like the whoppers you shook out of Ananias' cans,
Findlater and Gladstone's, Corner House, Englend. None of
your inchthick blueblooded Balaclava fried-at-belief-stakes or
juicejelly legs of the Grex's molten mutton or greasilygristly
grunters' goupons or slice upon slab of luscious goosebosom
with lump after load of plumpudding stuffing all aswim in a

swamp of bogoakgravy for that greekenhearted yude! Rosbif of
Old Zealand! he could not attouch it. See what happens when
your somatophage merman takes his fancy to our virgitarian
swan? He even ran away with hunself and became a farsoonerite,
saying he would far sooner muddle through the hash of lentils
in Europe than meddle with Irrland's split little pea. Once when
among those rebels in a state of hopelessly helpless intoxication
the piscivore strove to lift a czitround peel to either nostril, hic-
cupping, apparently impromptued by the hibat he had with his
glottal stop, that he kukkakould flowrish for ever by the smell,
as the czitr, as the kcedron, like a scedar, of the founts, on mountains, with limon on, of Lebanon. O! the lowness of him was
beneath all up to that sunk to! No likedbylike firewater or first-
served firstshot or gulletburn gin or honest brewbarrett beer either.
O dear no! Instead the tragic jester sobbed himself wheywhing-
ingly sick of life on some sort of a rhubarbarous maundarin yella-
green funkleblue windigut diodying applejack squeezed from
sour grapefruice and, to hear him twixt his sedimental cupslips
when he had gulfed down mmmmuch too mmmmany gourds of
it retching off to almost as low withswillera, who always knew
notwithstanding when they had had enough and were rightly
indignant at the wretch's hospitality when they found to their
horror they could not carry another drop, it came straight from
the noble white fat, jo, openwide sat, jo, jo, her why hide that,
jo jo jo, the winevat, of the most serene magyansty az archdio-
chesse, if she is a duck, she's a douches, and when she has a
feherbour snot her fault, now is it? artstouchups, funny you're
grinning at, fancy you're in her yet, Fanny Urinia.

Aint that swell, hey? Peamengro! Talk about lowness! Any
dog's quantity of it visibly oozed out thickly from this dirty
little blacking beetle for the very fourth snap the Tulloch-Turn-
bull girl with her coldblood kodak shotted the as yet unre-
muneranded national apostate, who was cowardly gun and camera
shy, taking what he fondly thought was a short cut to Caer Fere,
Soak Amerigas, vias the shipsteam *Pridewin*, after having buried
a hatchet not so long before, by the wrong goods exeunt, num-

mer desh to tren, into Patatapapaveri's, fruiterers and musical
florists, with his *Ciaho, chavi! Sar shin, shillipen?* she knew the
vice out of bridewell was a bad fast man by his walk on the
spot.

[Johns is a different butcher's. Next place you are up town pay
him a visit. Or better still, come tobuy. You will enjoy cattlemen's
spring meat. Johns is now quite divorced from baking. Fattens,
kills, flays, hangs, draws, quarters and pieces. Feel his lambs! Ex!
Feel how sheap! Exex! His liver too is great value, a spatiality!
Exexex! COMMUNICATED.]

Around that time, moravar, one generally, for luvvomony
hoped or at any rate suspected among morticians that he would
early turn out badly, develop hereditary pulmonary T.B., and
do for himself one dandy time, nay, of a pelting night blanketed
creditors, hearing a coarse song and splash off Eden Quay sighed
and rolled over, sure all was up, but, though he fell heavily and
locally into debit, not even then could such an antinomian be
true to type. He would not put fire to his cerebrum; he would
not throw himself in Liffey; he would not explaud himself with
pneumantics; he refused to saffrocake himself with a sod. With
the foreign devil's leave the fraid born fraud diddled even death.
Anzi, cabled (but shaking the worth out of his maulth: Guarda-
costa leporello? Szasas Kraicz!) from his Nearapoblican asylum
to his jonathan for a brother: Here tokay, gone tomory, we're
spluched, do something, Fireless. And had answer: Inconvenient,
David.

You see, chaps, it will trickle out, freaksily of course, but the
tom and the shorty of it is: he was in his bardic memory low.
All the time he kept on treasuring with condign satisfaction each
and every crumb of trektalk, covetous of his neighbour's word,
and if ever, during a Munda conversazione commoted in the
nation's interest, delicate tippits were thrown out to him touching his evil courses by some wellwishers, vainly pleading by
scriptural arguments with the opprobrious papist about trying
to brace up for the kidos of the thing, Scally wag, and be a men
instead of a dem scrounger, dish it all, such as: Pray, what is

the meaning, sousy, of that continental expression, if you ever
came acrux it, we think it is a word transpiciously like *canaille?*:
or: Did you anywhere, kennel, on your gullible's travels or
during your rural troubadouring, happen to stumble upon a
certain gay young nobleman whimpering to the name of Low
Swine who always addresses women out of the one corner of
his mouth, lives on loans and is furtivefree yours of age? without one sigh of haste like the supreme prig he was, and not a bit
sorry, he would pull a vacant landlubber's face, root with ear-
waker's pensile in the outer of his lauscher and then, lisping,
the prattlepate parnella, to kill time, and swatting his deadbest
to think what under the canopies of Jansens Chrest would any
decent son of an Albiogenselman who had bin to an university
think, let a lent hit a hint and begin to tell all the intelligentsia
admitted to that tamileasy samtalaisy conclamazzione (since, still
and before physicians, lawyers merchant, belfry pollititians, agri-
colous manufraudurers, sacrestanes of the Pure River Society,
philanthropicks lodging on as many boards round the panesthetic
at the same time as possible) the whole lifelong swrine story of
his entire low cornaille existence, abusing his deceased ancestors
wherever the sods were and one moment tarabooming great
blunderguns (poh!) about his farfamed fine Poppamore, Mr
Humhum, whom history, climate and entertainment made the
first of his sept and always up to debt, though Eavens ears ow
many fines he faces, and another moment visanvrerssas cruach-
ing three jeers (pah!) for his rotten little ghost of a Peppybeg,
Mr. Himmyshimmy, a blighty, a reeky, a lighty, a scrapy, a bab-
bly, a ninny, dirty seventh among thieves and always bottom
sawyer, till nowan knowed how howmely howme could be, giving unsolicited testimony on behalf of the absent, as glib as eaves-
water to those present (who meanwhile, with increasing lack of
interest in his semantics, allowed various subconscious smickers
to drivel slowly across their fichers), unconsciously explaining,
for inkstands, with a meticulosity bordering on the insane, the
various meanings of all the different foreign parts of speech he
misused and cuttlefishing every lie unshrinkable about all the

other people in the story, leaving out, of course, foreconsciously, the simple worf and plague and poison they had cornered him about until there was not a snoozer among them but was utterly undeceived in the heel of the reel by the recital of the rigmarole.

He went without saying that the cull disliked anything anyway approaching a plain straightforward standup or knockdown row and, as often as he was called in to umpire any octagonal argument among slangwhangers, the accomplished washout always used to rub shoulders with the last speaker and clasp shakers (the handtouch which is speech without words) and agree to every word as soon as half uttered, command me!, your servant, good, I revere you, how, my seer? be drinking that! quite truth, gratias, I'm yoush, see wha'm hearing?, also goods, please it, me sure?, be filling this!, quiso, you said it, apasafello, muchas grassyass, is there firing-on-me?, is their girlic-on-you?, to your good self, your sulphur, and then at once focuss his whole unbalanced attention upon the next octagonist who managed to catch a listener's eye, asking and imploring him out of his piteous onewinker, (*hemoptysia diadumenos*) whether there was anything in the world he could do to please him and to overflow his tumbletantaliser for him yet once more.

One hailcannon night (for his departure was attended by a heavy downpour) as very recently as some thousand rains ago he was therefore treated with what closely resembled parsonal violence, being soggert all unsuspectingly through the deserted village of Tumblin-on-the-Leafy from Mr. Vanhomrigh's house at 82 Mabbot's Mall as far as Green Patch beyond the brickfields of Salmon Pool by rival teams of slowspiers counter quicklimers who finally, as rahilly they had been deteened out rawther laetich, thought, busnis hits busnis, they had better be streaking for home after their Auborne-to-Auborne, with thanks for the pleasant evening, one and all disgustedly, instead of ruggering him back, and awake, reconciled (though they were as jealous as could be cullions about all the truffles they had brought on him) to a friendship, fast and furious, which merely arose out of the noxious pervert's perfect lowness. Again there was a hope that people,

looking on him with the contemp of the contempibles, after
first gaving him a roll in the dirt, might pity and forgive him, if
properly deloused, but the pleb was born a Quicklow and sank
alowing till he stank out of sight.

All Saints beat Belial! Mickil Goals to Nichil! Notpossible!
Already?

*In Nowhere has yet the Whole World taken part of himself for his
   Wife;*

*By Nowhere have Poorparents been sentenced to Worms, Blood and
   Thunder for Life*

Not yet has the Emp from Corpsica forced the Arth out of Engleterre;

*Not yet have the Sachsen and Judder on the Mound of a Word made
   Warre;*

*Not yet Witchywitchy of Wench struck Fire of his Heath from on
   Hoath;*

Not yet his Arcobaleine forespoken Peacepeace upon Oath;

*Cleftfoot from Hempal must tumpel, Blamefool Gardener's bound to
   fall;*

*Broken Eggs will poursuive bitten Apples for where theirs is Will
   there's his Wall;*

*But the Mountstill frowns on the Millstream while their Madsons
   leap his Bier*

*And her Rillstrill liffs to His Murkesty all her daft Daughters laff
   in her Ear.*

*Till the four Shores of deff Tory Island let the douze dumm Eire-
   whiggs raille!*

*Hirp! Hirp! for their Missed Understandings! chirps the Ballat of
   Perce-Oreille.*

O fortunous casualitas! Lefty takes the cherubcake while
Rights cloves his hoof. Darkies never done tug that coon out to
play non-excretory, anti-sexuous, misoxenetic, gaasy pure, flesh
and blood games, written and composed and sung and danced
by Niscemus Nemon, same as piccaninnies play all day, those
old (none of your honeys and rubbers!) games for fun and element we used to play with Dina and old Joe kicking her behind
and before and the yellow girl kicking him behind old Joe,

games like *Thom Thom the Thonderman*, *Put the Wind up the Peeler*, *Hat in the Ring*, *Hely Baba and the Forty Thieves*, *Mikel on the Luckypig*, *Nickel in the Slot*, *Sheila Harnett and her Cow*, *Adam and Ell*, *Humble Bumble*, *Moggie's on the Wall*, *Twos and Threes*, *American Jump*, *Fox come out of your Den*, *Broken Bottles*, *Writing a Letter to Punch*, *Tiptop is a Sweetstore*, *Henressy Crump Expolled*, *Postman's Knock*, *Are We Fairlys Represented?*, *Solomon Silent reading*, *Appletree Bearstone*, *I know a Washerwoman*, *Hospitals*, *As I was Walking*, *There is Oneyone's House in Dreamcolohour*, *Battle of Waterloo*, *Colours*, *Eggs in the Bush*, *Habberdasherisher*, *Telling your Dreams*, *What's the Time*, *Nap*, *Ducking Mammy*, *Last Man Standing*, *Heali Baboon and the Forky Theagues*, *Fickleyes and Futilears*, *Handmarried but once in my Life and I'll never commit such a Sin agin*, *Zip Cooney Candy*, *Turkey in the Straw*, *This is the Way we sow the Seed of a long and lusty Morning*, *Hops of Fun at Miliken's Make*, *I seen the Toothbrush with Pat Farrel*, *Here's the Fat to graze the Priest's Boots*, *When his Steam was like a Raimbrandt round Mac Garvey*.

Now it is notoriously known how on that surprisingly bludgeony Unity Sunday when the grand germogall allstar bout was harrily the rage between our weltingtoms extraordinary and our pettythicks the marshalaisy and Irish eyes of welcome were smiling daggers down their backs, when the roth, vice and blause met the noyr blank and rogues and the grim white and cold bet the black fighting tans, categorically unimperatived by the maxims, a rank funk getting the better of him, the scut in a bad fit of pyjamas fled like a leveret for his bare lives, to Talviland ahone ahaza, pursued by the scented curses of all the village belles and, without having struck one blow, (pig stole on him was lust he lagging it was becaused dust he shook) kuskykorked himself up tight in his inkbattle house, badly the worse for boosegas, there to stay in afar for the life, where, as there was not a moment to be lost, after he had boxed around with his fortepiano till he was whole bach bamp him and bump him blues, he collapsed carefully under a bedtick from Schwitzer's, his face enveloped into a dead warrior's telemac, with a lullobaw's somnbomnet and a whotwaterwottle at his feet to stoke his energy of waiting, moaning feebly, in monkmarian monotheme, but tarned long and then a nation louder, while engaged in swallowing from a large ampullar, that his pawdry's purgatory was more than a nigger bloke could bear, hemiparalysed by the tong warfare and all the shemozzle, (*Daily Maily, fullup Lace! Holy Maly, Mothelup Joss!*) his cheeks and trousers changing colour every time a gat croaked.

How is that for low, laities and gentlenuns? Why, dog of the Crostiguns, whole continents rang with this Kairokorran lowness! Sheols of houris in chems upon divans, (revolted stellas vespertine vesamong them) at a bare (O!) mention of the scaly rybald exclaimed: Poisse!

But would anyone, short of a madhouse, believe it? Neither of those clean little cherubum, Nero or Nobookisonester himself, ever nursed such a spoiled opinion of his monstrous marvellosity as did this mental and moral defective (here perhaps at the vanessance of his lownest) who was known to grognt rather than gunnard upon one occasion, while drinking heavily of spirits to that interlocutor *a latere* and private privysuckatary he used to pal around with, in the kavehazs, one Davy Browne-Nowlan, his heavenlaid twin, (this hambone dogpoet pseudoed himself under the hangname he gave himself of Bethgelert) in the porchway of a gipsy's bar (Shem always blaspheming, so holy writ, Billy, he would try, old Belly, and pay this one manjack congregant of his four soups every lass of nexmouth, Bolly, so sure as thair's a tail on a commet, as a taste for storik's fortytooth, that is to stay, to listen out, ony twenny minnies moe, Bully, his Ballade Imaginaire which was to be dubbed *Wine, Woman and Waterclocks*, or *How a Guy Finks and Fawkes When He Is Going Batty*, by Maistre Sheames de la Plume, some most dreadful stuff in a murderous mirrorhand) that he was avoopf (parn me!) aware of no other shaggspick, other Shakhisbeard, either prexactly unlike his polar andthisishis or procisely the seem as woops (parn!) as what he fancied or guessed the sames as he was himself and that, greet scoot, duckings and thuggery, though he was foxed fux to fux like a bunnyboy rodger with all the teashop

lionses of Lumdrum hivanhoesed up gagainst him, being a lapsis
linquo with a ruvidubb shortartempa, bad cad dad fad sad mad
nad vanhaty bear, the consciquenchers of casuality prepestered
crusswords in postposition, scruff, scruffer, scrufferumurraimost
andallthatsortofthing, if reams stood to reason and his lanka-
livline lasted he would wipe alley english spooker, multapho-
niaksically spuking, off the face of the erse.

After the thorough fright he got that bloody, Swithun's day,
though every doorpost in muchtried Lucalizod was smeared with
generous erstborn gore and every free for all cobbleway slippery
with the bloods of heroes, crying to Welkins for others, and
noahs and cul verts agush with tears of joy, our low waster never
had the common baalamb's pluck to stir out and about the compound while everyone else of the torchlit throng, slashers and
sliced alike, mobbu on massa, waaded and baaded around, yamp-
yam pampyam, chanting the Gillooly chorus, from the Monster
Book of Paltryattic Puetrie, *O pura e pia bella!* in junk et sampam
or in secular sinkalarum, heads up, on his bonafide avocation (the
little folk creeping on all fours to their natural school treat but
childishly gleeful when a stray whizzer sang out intermediately)
and happy belongers to the fairer sex on their usual quest for
higher things, but vying with Lady Smythe to avenge Mac-
Jobber, went stonestepping with their bickerrstaffs on educated
feet, plinkity plonk, across the sevenspan ponte *dei colori* set up
over the slop after the war-to-end war by Messrs. a charitable
government for the only once (dia dose Finnados!) he did take
a tompip peepestrella throug a threedraw eighteen hawkspower
durdicky telescope, luminous to larbourd only like the lamps in
Nassaustrass, out of his westernmost keyhole, spitting at the
impenetrablum wetter, (and it was porcoghastly that outumn) with
an eachway hope in his shivering soul, as he prayed to the cloud
Incertitude, of finding out for himself, on akkount of all the
kules in Kroukaparka or oving to all the kodseoggs in Kalatavala,
whether true conciliation was forging ahead or falling back after
the celestious intemperance and, for Duvvelsache, why, with his
see me see and his my see a corves and his frokerfoskerfuskar

layen loves in meeingseeing, he got the charm of his optical
life when he found himself (*hic sunt lennones!*) at pointblank
range blinking down the barrel of an irregular revolver of
the bulldog with a purpose pattern, handled by an unknown
quarreler who, supposedly, had been told off to shade and
shoot shy Shem should the shit show his shiny shnout out
awhile to look facts in their face before being hosed and creased
(uprip and jack him!) by six or a dozen of the gayboys.

What, para Saom Plaom, in the names of Deucalion and
Pyrrha, and the incensed privy and the licensed pantry gods
and Stator and Victor and Kutt and Runn and the whole mesa
redonda of Lorencao Otulass in convocacaon was this disinterestingly low human type, this Calumnious Column of
Cloaxity, this Bengalese Beacon of Biloxity, this Annamite Aper
of Atroxity, really at, it will be precise to quarify, for he seems
in a badbad case?

The answer, to do all the diddies in one dedal, would sound:
from pulling himself on his most flavoured canal the huge chest-
house of his elders (the *Popapreta*, and some navico, navvies!)
he had flickered up and flinnered down into a drug and drunkery
addict, growing megalomane of a loose past. This explains the
litany of septuncial lettertrumpets honorific, highpitched, erudite,
neoclassical which he so loved as patricianly to manuscribe after
his name. It would have diverted if ever seen the shuddersome
spectacle of this semidemented zany amid the inspissated grime
of his glaucous den making believe to read his usylessly unreadable Blue Book of Eccles, *édition de ténèbres*, (even yet sighs the
Most Different, Dr. Poindejenk, authorised bowdler and censor,
it can't be repeated!) turning over three sheets at a wind, telling
himself delightedly, no espellor mor so, that every splurge on the
vellum he blundered over was an aisling vision more gorgeous
than the one before t.i.t.s., a roseschelle cottage by the sea for
nothing for ever, a ladies tryon hosiery raffle at liberty, a sewer-
ful of guineagold wine with brancomongepadenopie and sick-
cylinder oysters worth a billion a bite, an entire operahouse
(there was to be stamping room only in the prompter's box and

everthemore his queque kept swelling) of enthusiastic noble-
women flinging every coronetcrimsoned stitch they had off at
his probscenium one after the others, inamagoaded into ajustil-
loosing themselves, in their gaiety pantheomime, when, egad, sir,
acordant to all acountstrick, he squealed the topsquall im *Deal
Lil Shemlockup Yellin* (geewhiz, jew ear that far! soap ewer!
loutgout of sabaous! juice like a boyd!) for fully five minutes in-
finitely better than Baraton McGluckin with a scrumptious cocked
hat and three green, cheese and tangerine trinity plumes on the
right handle side of his amarellous head, a coat macfarlane (the
kerssest cut, you understand?) a sponiard's digger at his ribs,
(*Alfaiate punxit*) an azulblu blowsheet for his blousebosom
blossom and a dean's crozier that he won from Cardinal Lin-
dundarri and Cardinal Carchingarri and Cardinal Loriotuli and
Cardinal Occidentaccia (ah ho!) in the dearby darby doubled for
falling first over the hurdles, madam, in the odder hand, a.a.t.s.o.t.,
but what with the murky light, the botchy print, the tattered
cover, the jigjagged page, the fumbling fingers, the foxtrotting
fleas, the lieabed lice, the scum on his tongue, the drop in his
eye, the lump in his throat, the drink in his pottle, the itch in his
palm, the wail of his wind, the grief from his breath, the fog of
his mindfag, the buzz in his braintree, the tic of his conscience,
the height up his rage, the gush down his fundament, the fire
in his gorge, the tickle of his tail, the bane in his bullugs, the
squince in his suil, the rot in his eater, the ycho in his earer,
the totters of his toes, the tetters on his tumtytum, the rats in his
garret, the bats in his belfry, the budgerigars and bumbosolom
beaubirds, the hullabaloo and the dust in his ears since it took him
a month to steal a march he was hardset to mumorise more than
a word a week. Hake's haulin! Hook's fisk! Can you beat it?
Whawe! I say, can you bait it? Was there ever heard of such
lowdown blackguardism? Positively it woolies one to think
over it.

Yet the bumpersprinkler used to boast aloud alone to himself
with a haccent on it when Mynfadher was a boer constructor and
Hoy was a lexical student, parole, and corrected with the black-

board (trying to copy the stage Englesemen he broughts their
house down on, shouting: Bravure, surr Chorles! Letter purfect!
Culossal, Loose Wallor! Spache!) how he had been toed out of
all the schicker families of the klondykers from Pioupioureich,
Swabspays, the land of Nod, Shruggers' Country, Pension
Danubierhome and Barbaropolis, who had settled and stratified
in the capital city after its hebdomodary metropoliarchialisation
as sunblistered, moonplastered, gory, wheedling, joviale, litche-
rous and full, ordered off the gorgeous premises in most cases on
account of his smell which all cookmaids eminently objected to
as ressembling the bombinubble puzzo that welled out of the
pozzo. Instead of chuthoring those model households plain
wholesome pothooks (a thing he never possessed of his Nigerian
own) what do you think Vulgariano did but study with stolen
fruit how cutely to copy all their various styles of signature so as
one day to utter an epical forged cheque on the public for his own
private profit until, as just related, the Dustbin's United Scullery-
maid's and Househelp's Sorority better known as Sluttery's
Mowlted Futt, turned him down and assisted nature by unitedly
shoeing the source of annoyance out of the place altogether and
taytotally on the heat of the moment, holding one another's
gonk (for no-one, hound or scrublady, not even the Turk, un-
greekable in purscent of the armenable, dared whiff the polecat
at close range) and making some pointopointing remarks as they
done so at the perfects of the Sniffey, your honour, aboon the
lyow why a stunk, mister.

[Jymes wishes to hear from wearers of abandoned female costumes, gratefully received, wadmel jumper, rather full pair of
culottes and onthergarmenteries, to start city life together. His
jymes is out of job, would sit and write. He has lately commited
one of the then commandments but she will now assist. Superior
built, domestic, regular layer. Also got the boot. He appreciates
it. Copies. ABORTISEMENT.]

One cannot even begin to post figure out a statuesquo ante
as to how slow in reality the excommunicated Drumcondriac,
nate Hamis, really was. Who can say how many pseudostylic

shamiana, how few or how many of the most venerated public
impostures, how very many piously forged palimpsests slipped
in the first place by this morbid process from his pelagiarist pen?

Be that as it may, but for that light phantastic of his gnose's
glow as it slid lucifericiously within an inch of its page (he would
touch at its from time to other, the red eye of his fear in
saddishness, to ensign the colours by the beerlitz in his mathness
and his educandees to outhue to themselves in the cries of girl-
glee: gember! inkware! chonchambre! cinsero! zinnzabar! tinc-
ture and gin!) Nibs never would have quilled a seriph to
sheepskin. By that rosy lampoon's effluvious burning and with
help of the simulchronic flush in his pann (a ghinee a ghirk he
ghets there!) he scrabbled and scratched and scriobbled and
skrevened nameless shamelessness about everybody ever he met,
even sharing a precipitation under the idlish tarriers' umbrella
of a showerproof wall, while all over up and down the four
margins of this rancid Shem stuff the evilsmeller (who was
devoted to Uldfadar Sardanapalus) used to stipple endlessly
inartistic portraits of himself in the act of reciting old
Nichiabelli's monolook interyerear *Hanno, o Nonanno, acce'l
brubblemm'as*, ser Autore, q.e.d., a heartbreakingly handsome
young paolo with love lyrics for the goyls in his eyols, a plaintiff's tanner vuice, a jucal inkome of one hundred and thirtytwo
dranchmas per yard from Broken Hill stranded estate, Came-
breech mannings, cutting a great dash in a brandnew two guinea
dress suit and a burled hogsford hired for a Fursday evenin
merry pawty, anna loavely long pair of inky Italian moostarshes
glistering with boric vaseline and frangipani. Puh! How un-
whisperably so!

The house O'Shea or O'Shame, *Quivapieno*, known as the
Haunted Inkbottle, no number Brimstone Walk, Asia in Ireland,
as it was infested with the raps, with his penname SHUT sepia-
scraped on the doorplate and a blind of black sailcloth over its
wan phwinshogue, in which the soulcontracted son of the secret
cell groped through life at the expense of the taxpayers, dejected
into day and night with jesuit bark and bitter bite, calico-

hydrants of zolfor and scoppialamina by full and forty Queasi-
sanos, every day in everyone's way more exceeding in violent
abuse of self and others, was the worst, it is hoped, even in our
western playboyish world for pure mousefarm filth. You brag
of your brass castle or your tyled house in ballyfermont? Niggs,
niggs, and niggs again. For this was a stinksome inkenstink, quite
puzzonal to the wrottel. Smatterafact, Angles aftanon browsing
there thought not Edam reeked more rare. My wud! The warped
flooring of the lair and soundconducting walls thereof, to say
nothing of the uprights and imposts, were persianly literatured
with burst loveletters, telltale stories, stickyback snaps, doubtful
eggshells, bouchers, flints, borers, puffers, amygdaloid almonds,
rindless raisins, alphybettyformed verbage, vivlical viasses, om-
piter dictas, visus umbique, ahems and ahahs, imeffible tries at
speech unasyllabled, you owe mes, eyoldhyms, fluefoul smut,
fallen lucifers, vestas which had served, showered ornaments,
borrowed brogues, reversibles jackets, blackeye lenses, family
jars, falsehair shirts, Godforsaken scapulars, neverworn breeches,
cutthroat ties, counterfeit franks, best intentions, curried notes,
upset latten tintacks, unused mill and stumpling stones, twisted
quills, painful digests, magnifying wineglasses, solid objects cast
at goblins, once current puns, quashed quotatoes, messes of mot-
tage, unquestionable issue papers, seedy ejaculations, limerick
damns, crocodile tears, spilt ink, blasphematory spits, stale shest-
nuts, schoolgirl's, young ladies' milkmaids', washerwomen's,
shopkeepers' wives, merry widows', ex nuns', vice abbess's, pro
virgins', super whores', silent sisters', Charleys' aunts', grand-
mothers', mothers'-in-law, fostermothers', godmothers' garters,
tress clippings from right, lift and cintrum, worms of snot,
toothsome pickings, cans of Swiss condensed bilk, highbrow
lotions, kisses from the antipodes, presents from pickpockets,
borrowed plumes, relaxable handgrips, princess promises, lees of
whine, deoxodised carbons, convertible collars, diviliouker
doffers, broken wafers, unloosed shoe latchets, crooked strait
waistcoats, fresh horrors from Hades, globules of mercury,
undeleted glete, glass eyes for an eye, gloss teeth for a tooth,

war moans, special sighs, longsufferings of longstanding, ahs ohs ous sis jas jos gias neys thaws sos yeses and yeses and yeses, to which, if one has the stomach to add the breakages, upheavals distortions, inversions of all this chambermade music one stands, given a grain of goodwill, a fair chance of actually seeing the whirling dervish, Tumult, son of Thunder, self exiled in upon his ego a nightlong a shaking betwixtween white or reddr haw-rors, noondayterrorised to skin and bone by an ineluctable phantom (may the Shaper have mercery on him!) writing the mystery of himsel in furniture.

Of course our low hero was a self valeter by choice of need so up he got up whatever is meant by a stourbridge clay kitchen-ette and lithargogalenu fowlhouse for the sake of akes (the umpple does not fall very far from the dumpertree) which the moromelodious jigsmith, in defiance of the Uncontrollable Birth Preservativation (Game and Poultry) Act, playing lallaryrook cookerynook, by the dodginess of his lentern, brooled and cocked and potched in an athanor, whites and yolks and yilks and whotes to the frulling fredonnance of *Mas blanca que la blanca hermana* and *Amarilla, muy bien,* with cinnamon and locusts and wild bees-wax and liquorice and Carrageen moss and blaster of Barry's and Asther's mess and Huster's micture and Yellownan's embrocation and Pinkingtone's patty and stardust and sinner's tears, acuredent to Sharadan's *Art of Panning,* chanting, for all regale to the like of the legs he left behind with Litty fun Letty fan Leven, his cantraps of fermented words, abracadabra calubra culorum, (his oewfs à la Madame Gabrielle de l'Eglise, his avgs à la Mistress B. de B. Meinfelde, his eiers Usquadmala à la pomme de ciel, his uoves, oves and uves à la Sulphate de Soude, his ochiuri sowtay sowmmonay à la Monseigneur, his soufflosion of oogs with somekat on toyast à la Mère Puard, his Poggadovies alla Fenella, his Frideggs à la Tricarême) in what was meant for a closet (Ah ho! If only he had listened better to the four masters that infanted him Father Mathew and Le Père Noble and Pastor Lucas and Padre Aguilar — not forgetting Layteacher Baudwin! Ah ho!) His costive Satan's antimonian manganese limolitmious

nature never needed such an alcove so, when Robber and Mum-
sell, the pulpic dictators on the nudgment of their legal advisers,
Messrs. Codex and Podex, and under his own benefiction of their
pastor Father Flammeus Falconer, boycotted him of all mutton-
suet candles and romeruled stationery for any purpose, he winged
away on a wildgoup's chase across the kathartic ocean and made
synthetic ink and sensitive paper for his own end out of his wit's
waste. You ask, in Sam Hill, how? Let manner and matter of this
for these our sporting times be cloaked up in the language of
blushfed porpurates that an Anglican ordinal, not reading his
own rude dunsky tunga, may ever behold the brand of scarlet
on the brow of her of Babylon and feel not the pink one in his
own damned cheek.

*Primum opifex, altus prosator, ad terram viviparam et cuncti-
potentem sine ullo pudore nec venia, suscepto pluviali atque discinctis
perizomatis, natibus nudis uti nati fuissent, sese adpropinquans,
flens et gemens in manum suam evacuavit* (highly prosy, crap in his
hand, sorry!), *postea, animale nigro exoneratus, classicum pulsans
stercus proprium, quod appellavit deiectiones suas, in vas olim
honorabile tristitiae posuit, eodem sub invocatione fratrorum gemino-
rum Medardi et Godardi laete ac melliflue minxit psalmum qui
incipit: Lingua mea calamus scribae velociter scribentis: magna voce
cantitans* (did a piss, says he was dejected, asks to be exonerated),
*demum ex stercore turpi cum divi Orionis iucunditate mixto, cocto,
frigorique exposito, encaustum sibi fecit indelibile* (faked O'Ryan's,
the indelible ink).

Then, pious Eneas, conformant to the fulminant firman which
enjoins on the tremylose terrian that, when the call comes, he
shall produce nichthemerically from his unheavenly body a no
uncertain quantity of obscene matter not protected by copriright
in the United Stars of Ourania or bedeed and bedood and bedang
and bedung to him, with this double dye, brought to blood heat,
gallic acid on iron ore, through the bowels of his misery, flashly,
faithly, nastily, appropriately, this Esuan Menschavik and the first
till last alshemist wrote over every square inch of the only fools-
cap available, his own body, till by its corrosive sublimation one

continuous present tense integument slowly unfolded all marry-
voising moodmoulded cyclewheeling history (thereby, he said,
reflecting from his own individual person life unlivable, trans-
accidentated through the slow fires of consciousness into a divi-
dual chaos, perilous, potent, common to allflesh, human only,
mortal) but with each word that would not pass away the squid-
self which he had squirtscreened from the crystalline world
waned chagreenold and doriangrayer in its dudhud. This exists
that isits after having been said we know. And dabal take dab-
nal! And the dal dabal dab aldanabal! So perhaps, agglaggagglo-
meratively asaspenking, after all and arklast fore arklyst on his
last public misappearance, circling the square, for the deathfête
of Saint Ignaceous Poisonivy, of the Fickle Crowd (hopon the
sexth day of Hogsober, killim our king, layum low!) and brandish-
ing his bellbearing stylo, the shining keyman of the wilds of
change, if what is sauce for the zassy is souse for the zazimas the
blond cop who thought it was ink was out of his depth but
bright in the main.

Petty constable Sistersen of the Kruis-Kroon-Kraal it was, the
parochial watch, big the dog the dig the bog the bagger the
dugger the begadag degabug, who had been detailed from pollute
stoties to save him, this the quemquem, that the quum, from the
ligatureliablous effects of foul clay in little clots and mobmauling
on looks, that wrongcountered the tenderfoot an eveling near
the livingsmeansuniumgetherum, Knockmaree, Comty Mea, reeling more to the right than he lurched to the left, on his way from
a protoprostitute (he would always have a (stp!) little pigeoness
somewhure with his arch girl, Arcoiris, smockname of Mergyt)
just as he was butting in rand the coyner of bad times under a
hideful between the rival doors of warm bethels of worship
through his boardelhouse fongster, greeting for grazious oras
as usual: Where ladies have they that a dog meansort herring?
Sergo, search me, the incapable reparteed with a selfevitant
subtlety so obviously spurious and, raising his hair, after the
grace, with the christmas under his clutcharm, for Portsymasser
and Purtsymessus and Pertsymiss and Partsymasters, like a prance

of findingos, with a shillto shallto slipny stripny in he skittled. Swikey! The allwhite poors guardiant, pulpably of balltossic stummung, was literally astundished over the painful sake, how he burstteself, which he was gone to, where he intent to did he, whether you think will, wherend the whole current of the afternoon whats the souch of a surch hads of hits of hims, urged and staggered thereto in his countryports at the caledosian capacity for Lieutuvisky of the caftan's wineskin and even more so during, looking his bigmost astonishments, it was said him, aschu, fun the concerned outgift of the dead med dirt, how that arrahbejibbers, conspuent to the dominical order and exking noblish permish, he was namely coon at bringer at home two gallonts as per royal full poultry till his murder. Nip up and nab it!

Polthergeistkotzdondherhoploits! Kick? What mother? Whose porter? Which pair? Why namely coon? But our undilligence has been plutherotested so enough of such porterblack lowneess, too base for printink! Perpending that Putterick O'Purcell pulls the coald stoane out of Winterwater's and Silder Seas sing for Harreng our Keng sept okt nov dez John Phibbs march! We cannot in mercy or justice nor on the lovom for labaryntos stay here for the residence of our existings discussing Tamstar Ham of Tenman's thirst.

JUSTIUS (to himother): Brawn is my name and broad is my nature and I've breit on my brow and all's right with every feature and I'll brune this bird or Brown Bess's bung's gone bandy. I'm the boy to bruise and braise. Baus!

Stand forth, Nayman of Noland (for no longer will I follow you obliquelike through the inspired form of the third person singular and the moods and hesitensies of the deponent but address myself to you, with the empirative of my vendettative, provocative and out direct), stand forth, come boldly, jolly me, move me, zwilling though I am, to laughter in your true colours ere you be back for ever till I give you your talkingto! Shem Macadamson, you know me and I know you and all your she-meries. Where have you been in the uterim, enjoying yourself

all the morning since your last wetbed confession? I advise you
to conceal yourself, my little friend, as I have said a moment
ago and put your hands in my hands and have a nightslong
homely little confiteor about things. Let me see. It is looking
pretty black against you, we suggest, Sheem avick. You will
need all the elements in the river to clean you over it all and a
fortifine popespriestpower bull of attender to booth.

Let us pry. We thought, would and did. *Cur, quicquid, ubi,
quando, quomodo, quoties, quibus auxiliis?* You were bred, fed,
fostered and fattened from holy childhood up in this two easter
island on the piejaw of hilarious heaven and roaring the other
place (plunders to night of you, blunders what's left of you, flash
as flash can!) and now, forsooth, a nogger among the blankards
of this dastard century, you have become of twosome twiminds
forenenst gods, hidden and discovered, nay, condemned fool,
anarch, egoarch, hiresiarch, you have reared your disunited kingdom on the vacuum of your own most intensely doubtful soul.
Do you hold yourself then for some god in the manger, Sheho-
hem, that you will neither serve not let serve, pray nor let pray?
And here, pay the piety, must I too nerve myself to pray for the
loss of selfrespect to equip me for the horrible necessity of scan-
dalisang (my dear sisters, are you ready?) by sloughing off my
hope and tremors while we all swin together in the pool of So-
dom? I shall shiver for my purity while they will weepbig for
your sins. Away with covered words, new Solemonities for old
Badsheetbaths! That inharmonious detail, did you name it? Cold
caldor! Gee! Victory! Now opprobro of underslung pipes,
johnjacobs, while yet an adolescent (what do I say?), while
still puerile in your tubsuit with buttonlegs you got a handsome present of a selfraising syringe and twin feeders (you know,
Monsieur Abgott, in your art of arts, to your cost as well as I do
(and don't try to hide it) the penals lots I am now poking at) and
the wheeze sort of was you should (if you were as bould a stroke
now as the curate that christened you, sonny douth-the-candle!)
repopulate the land of your birth and count up your progeny by
the hungered head and the angered thousand but you thwarted

the wious pish of your cogodparents, soph, among countless
occasions of failing (for, said you, I will elenchate), adding to the
malice of your transgression, yes, and changing its nature, (you
see I have read your theology for you) alternating the morosity
of my delectations — a philtred love, trysting by tantrums,
small peace in ppenmark — with sensibility, sponsibility, passi-
bility and prostability, your lubbock's other fear pleasures of a
butler's life, even extruding your strabismal apologia, when
legibly depressed, upon defenceless paper and thereby adding to
the already unhappiness of this our popeyed world, scribblative!
— all that too with cantreds of countless catchaleens, the man-
nish as many as the minneful, congested around and about you
for acres and roods and poles or perches, thick as the fluctuant
sands of Chalwador, accomplished women, indeed fully edu-
canded, far from being old and rich behind their dream of arri-
visme, if they have only their honour left, and not deterred by bad
weather, when consumed by amorous passion, struggling to possess themselves of your boosh, one son of Sorge for all daughters
of Anguish, *solus cum sola sive cuncties cum omnibobs* (I'd have
been the best man for you, myself), mutely aying for that natural
knot, debituary vases or vessels preposterous, for what would
not have cost you ten bolivars of collarwork or the price of one
ping pang, just a lilt, let us trillt, of the oldest song in the wooed
woodworld, (two-we! to-one!), accompanied by a plain gold
band! Hail! Hail! Highbosomheaving Missmisstress Morna of
the allsweetheartening bridemuredemeanour! Her eye's so gladsome we'll all take shares in the ——groom!

Sniffer of carrion, premature gravedigger, seeker of the nest
of evil in the bosom of a good word, you, who sleep at our vigil
and fast for our feast, you with your dislocated reason, have
cutely foretold, a jophet in your own absence, by blind poring
upon your many scalds and burns and blisters, impetiginous sore
and pustules, by the auspices of that raven cloud, your shade, and
by the auguries of rooks in parlament, death with every disaster,
the dynamitisation of colleagues, the reducing of records to
ashes, the levelling of all customs by blazes, the return of a lot

of sweetempered gunpowdered didst unto dudst but it never stphruck your mudhead's obtundity (O hell, here comes our funeral! O pest, I'll miss the post!) that the more carrots you chop, the more turnips you slit, the more murphies you peel, the more onions you cry over, the more bullbeef you butch, the more mutton you crackerhack, the more potherbs you pound, the fiercer the fire and the longer your spoon and the harder you gruel with more grease to your elbow the merrier fumes your new Irish stew.

O, by the way, yes another thing occurs to me. You let me tell you, with the utmost politeness, were very ordinarily designed, your birthwrong was, to fall in with Plan, as our nationals should, as all nationists must, and do a certain office (what, I will not tell you) in a certain holy office (nor will I say where) during certain agonising office hours (a clerical party all to yourself) from such a year to such an hour on such and such a date at so and so much a week *pro anno* (Guinness's, may I remind, were just agulp for you, failing in which you might have taken the scales off boilers like any boskop of Yorek) and do your little thruppenny bit and thus earn from the nation true thanks, right here in our place of burden, your bourne of travail and ville of tares, where after a divine's prodigence you drew the first watergasp in your life, from the crib where you once was bit to the crypt you'll be twice as shy of, same as we, long of us, alone with the colt in the curner, where you were as popular as an armenial with the faithful, and you set fire to my tailcoat when I hold the paraffin smoker under yours (I hope that chimney's clear) but, slackly shirking both your bullet and your billet, you beat it backwards like Boulanger from Galway (but he combed the grass against his stride) to sing us a song of alibi, (the cuthone call over the greybounding slowrolling amplyheaving metamorphoseous that oozy rocks parapangle their preposters with) nomad, mooner by lamplight, antinos, shemming amid everyone's repressed laughter to conceal your scatchophily by mating, like a thorough-paste prosodite, masculine monosyllables of the same numerical mus, an Irish emigrant the wrong way out, sitting on your crooked

sixpenny stile, an unfrillfrocked quackfriar, you (will you for
the laugh of Scheekspair just help mine with the epithet?) semi-
semitic serendipitist, you (thanks, I think that describes you)
Europasianised Afferyank!

Shall we follow each others a steplonger, drowner of daggers,
whiles our liege, tilyet a stranger in the frontyard of his happi-
ness, is taking, (heal helper! one gob, one gap, one gulp and
gorger of all!) his refreshment?

There grew up beside you amid our orisons of the speediest
in Novena Lodge, Novara Avenue, in Patripodium-am-Bummel,
oaf, outofwork, one remove from an unwashed savage, on his
keeping and in yours, (I pose you know why possum hides is
cause he haint the nogumtreeumption) that other, Immaculatus,
from head to foot, sir, that pure one, Altrues of other times,
he who was well known to celestine circles before he sped
aloft, our handsome young spiritual physician that was to be,
seducing every sense to selfwilling celebesty, the most winning
counterfeuille on our incomeshare lotetree, a chum of the
angelets, a youth those reporters so pettitily wanted as gamefellow that they asked his mother for ittle earps brupper to
let him tome to Tindertarten, pease, and bing his scooter
'long and 'tend they were all real brothers in the big justright
home where Dodd lives, just to teddyfy the life out of him
and pat and pass him one with other like musk from hand to
hand, that mothersmothered model, that goodlooker with not
a flaw whose spiritual toilettes were the talk of half the town, for
sunset wear and nightfallen use and daybroken donning and
nooncheon showing and the very thing for teasetime, but him
you laid low with one hand one fine May morning in the Meddle
of your Might, your bosom foe, because he mussed your speller
on you or because he cut a pretty figure in the focus of your
frontispecs (not one did you slay, no, but a continent!) to find
out how his innards worked!

Ever read of that greatgrand landfather of our visionbuilders,
Baaboo, the bourgeoismeister, who thought to touch both him-
mels at the punt of his risen stiffstaff and how wishywashy sank

the waters of his thought? Ever thought of that hereticalist Marcon
and the two scissymaidies and how bulkily he shat the Ructions
gunorrhal? Ever hear of that foxy, that lupo and that monkax
and the virgin heir of the Morrisons, eh, blethering ape?

   Malingerer in luxury, collector general, what has Your Lowness done in the mealtime with all the hamilkcars of cooked
vegetables, the hatfuls of stewed fruit, the suitcases of coddled
ales, the Parish funds, me schamer, man, that you kittycoaxed so
flexibly out of charitable butteries by yowling heavy with a
hollow voice drop of your horrible awful poverty of mind so as
you couldn't even pledge a crown of Thorne's to pawn a coat
off Trevi's and as how you was bad no end, so you was, so whelp
you Sinner Pitre and Sinner Poule, with the chicken's gape and
pas mal de siècle, which, by the by, Reynaldo, is the ordinary
emetic French for grenadier's drip. To let you have your plank
and your bonewash (O the hastroubles you lost!), to give you
your pound of platinum and a thousand thongs a year (O, you
were excruciated, in honour bound to the cross of your own
cruelfiction!) to let you have your Sarday spree and holinight sleep
(fame would come to you twixt a sleep and a wake) and leave to
lie till Paraskivee and the cockcock crows for Danmark. (O
Jonathan, your estomach!) The simian has no sentiment secre-
tions but weep cataracts for all me, Pain the Shamman! Oft in
the smelly night will they wallow for a clutch of the famished
hand, I say, them bearded jezabelles you hired to rob you, while
on your sodden straw impolitely you encored (Airish and naw-
boggaleesh!) those hornmade ivory dreams you reved of the
Ruth you called your companionate, a beauty from the bible, of
the flushpots of Euston and the hanging garments of Maryle-
bone. But the dormer moonshee smiled selene and the light-
throwers knickered: who's whinging we? Comport yourself,
you inconsistency! Where is that little alimony nestegg against
our predictable rainy day? Is it not the fact (gainsay me, cake-
eater!) that, while whistlewhirling your crazy elegies around
Templetombmount joyntstone, (let him pass, pleasegood-
jesusalem, in a bundle of straw, he was balbettised after hay-

making) you squandered among underlings the overload of your extravagance and made a hottentot of dulpeners crawsick with your crumbs? Am I not right? Yes? Yes? Yes? Holy wax and holifer! Don't tell me, Leon of the fold, that you are not a loanshark! Look up, old sooty, be advised by mux and take your medicine. The Good Doctor mulled it. Mix it twice before repastures and powder three times a day. It does marvels for your gripins and it's fine for the solitary worm.

Let me finish! Just a little judas tonic, my ghem of all jokes, to make you go green in the gazer. Do you hear what I'm seeing, hammet? And remember that golden silence gives consent, Mr. Anklegazer! Cease to be civil, learn to say nay! Whisht! Come here, Herr Studiosus, till I tell you a wig in your ear. We'll do a whisper drive, for if the barishnyas got a twitter of it they'd tell the housetops and then all Cadbury would go crackers. Look! Do you see your dial in the rockingglass? Look well! Bend down a stigmy till I! It's secret! Iggri, I say, the booseleers! I had it from Lamppost Shawe. And he had it from the Mullah. And Mull took it from a Bluecoat schooler. And Gay Socks jot it from Potapheu's wife. And Rantipoll tipped the wink from old Mrs. Tinbullet. And as for she was confussed by pro-Brother Thacolicus. And the good brother feels he would need to defecate you. And the Flimsy Follettes are simply beside each other. And Kelly, Kenny and Keogh are up up and in arms. That a cross may crush me if I refuse to believe in it. That I may rock anchor through the ages if I hope it's not true. That the host may choke me if I beneighbour you without my charity! Sh! Shem, you are. Sh! You are mad!

He points the deathbone and the quick are still. *Insomnia, somnia somniorum. Awmawm.*

MERCIUS (of hisself): *Domine vopiscus!* My fault, his fault, a kingship through a fault! Pariah, cannibal Cain, I who oathily forswore the womb that bore you and the paps I sometimes sucked, you who ever since have been one black mass of jigs and jimjams, haunted by a convulsionary sense of not having been or being all that I might have been of you meant to becoming,

bewailing like a man that innocence which I could not defend
like a woman, lo you there, Cathmon-Carbery, and thank Movies
from the innermost depths of my still attrite heart Wherein
the days of youyouth are evermixed mimine, now ere the compline hour of being alone athands itself and a puff or so before
we yield our spiritus to the wind, for (though that royal one
has not yet drunk a gouttelette from his consummation and the
flowerpot on the pole, the spaniel pack and their quarry, retainers
and the public house proprietor have not budged a millimetre
and all that has been done has yet to be done and done again,
when's day's woe, and lo, you're doomed, joyday dawns and,
la, you dominate) it is to you, firstborn and firstfruit of woe, to
me, branded sheep, pick of the wasterpaperbaskel, by the
tremours of Thundery and Ulerin's dogstar, you alone, wind-
blasted tree of the knowledge of beautiful andevil, ay, clothed
upon with the metuor and shimmering like the horescens, astro-
glodynamonologos, the child of Nilfit's father, blzb, to me
unseen blusher in an obscene coalhole, the cubilibum of your
secret sigh, dweller in the downandoutermost where voice only
of the dead may come, because ye left from me, because ye
laughed on me, because, O me lonly son, ye are forgetting me!,
that our turfbrown mummy is acoming, alpilla, beltilla, ciltilla,
deltilla, running with her tidings, old the news of the great big
world, sonnies had a scrap, woewoewoe! bab's baby walks at
seven monthes, waywayway! bride leaves her raid at Punchestime,
stud stoned before a racecourseful, two belles that make the
one appeal, dry yanks will visit old sod, and fourtiered skirts
are up, mesdames, while Parimiknie wears popular short legs,
and twelve hows to mix a tipsy wake, did ye hear, colt Cooney?
did ye ever, filly Fortescue? with a beck, with a spring, all her
rillringlets shaking, rocks drops in her tachie, tramtokens in
her hair, all waived to a point and then all inuendation, little
oldfashioned mummy, little wonderful mummy, ducking under
bridges, bellhopping the weirs, dodging by a bit of bog, rapid-
shooting round the bends, by Tallaght's green hills and the
pools of the phooka and a place they call it Blessington and

slipping sly by Sallynoggin, as happy as the day is wet, babbling, bubbling, chattering to herself, deloothering the fields on
their elbows leaning with the sloothering slide of her, gidd-
gaddy, grannyma, gossipaceous Anna Livia.

He lifts the lifewand and the dumb speak.

— Quoiquoiquoiquoiquoiquoiquoiq!

O
tell me all about
Anna Livia! I want to hear all
about Anna Livia. Well, you know Anna Livia? Yes, of course,
we all know Anna Livia. Tell me all. Tell me now. You'll die
when you hear. Well, you know, when the old cheb went futt
and did what you know. Yes, I know, go on. Wash quit and
don't be dabbling. Tuck up your sleeves and loosen your talk-
tapes. And don't butt me — hike! — when you bend. Or whatever it was they threed to make out he thried to two in the
Fiendish park. He's an awful old reppe. Look at the shirt of him!
Look at the dirt of it! He has all my water black on me. And it
steeping and stuping since this time last wik. How many goes
is it I wonder I washed it? I know by heart the places he likes to
saale, duddurty devil! Scorching my hand and starving my famine to make his private linen public. Wallop it well with your
battle and clean it. My wrists are wrusty rubbing the mouldaw
stains. And the dneepers of wet and the gangres of sin in it! What
was it he did a tail at all on Animal Sendai? And how long was
he under loch and neagh? It was put in the newses what he did,
nicies and priers, the King fierceas Humphrey, with illysus dis-
tilling, exploits and all. But toms will till. I know he well. Temp
untamed will hist for no man. As you spring so shall you neap.
O, the roughty old rappe! Minxing marrage and making loof.

Reeve Gootch was right and Reeve Drughad was sinistrous! And
the cut of him! And the strut of him! How he used to hold his
head as high as a howeth, the famous eld duke alien, with a hump
of grandeur on him like a walking wiesel rat. And his derry's
own drawl and his corksown blather and his doubling stutter
and his gullaway swank. Ask Lictor Hackett or Lector Reade
of Garda Growley or the Boy with the Billyclub. How elster is
he a called at all? Qu'appelle? Huges Caput Earlyfouler. Or
where was he born or how was he found? Urgothland, Tvistown
on the Kattekat? New Hunshire, Concord on the Merrimake?
Who blocksmitt her saft anvil or yelled lep to her pail? Was her
banns never loosened in Adam and Eve's or were him and her
but captain spliced? For mine ether duck I thee drake. And by
my wildgaze I thee gander. Flowey and Mount on the brink of
time makes wishes and fears for a happy isthmass. She can show
all her lines, with love, license to play. And if they don't remarry
that hook and eye may. O, passmore that and oxus another! Don
Dom Dombdomb and his wee follyo! Was his help inshored in
the Stork and Pelican against bungelars, flu and third risk parties? I heard he dug good tin with his doll, delvan first and duvlin
after, when he raped her home, Sabrine asthore, in a parakeet's
cage, by dredgerous lands and devious delts, playing catched and
mythed with the gleam of her shadda, (if a flic had been there to
pop up and pepper him!) past auld min's manse and Maisons
Allfou and the rest of incurables and the last of immurables, the
quaggy waag for stumbling. Who sold you that jackalantern's
tale? Pemmican's pasty pie! Not a grasshoop to ring her, not an
antsgrain of ore. In a gabbard he barqued it, the boat of life,
from the harbourless Ivernikan Okean, till he spied the loom of
his landfall and he loosed two croakers from under his tilt, the
gran Phenician rover. By the smell of her kelp they made the
pigeonhouse. Like fun they did! But where was Himself, the
timoneer? That marchantman he suivied their scutties right over
the wash, his cameleer's burnous breezing up on him, till with
his runagate bowmpriss he roade and borst her bar. Pilcomayo!
Suchcaughtawan! And the whale's away with the grayling! Tune

your pipes and fall ahumming, you born ijypt, and you're nothing short of one! Well, ptellomey soon and curb your escumo.
When they saw him shoot swift up her sheba sheath, like any
gay lord salomon, her bulls they were ruhring, surfed with
spree. Boyarka buah! Boyana bueh! He erned his lille Bunbath
hard, our staly bred, the trader. He did. Look at here. In this wet
of his prow. Don't you know he was kaldt a bairn of the brine,
Wasserbourne the waterbaby? Havemmarea, so he was. H.C.E.
has a codfisck ee. Shyr she's nearly as badher as him herself.
Who? Anna Livia? Ay, Anna Livia. Do you know she was calling bakvandets sals from all around, nyumba noo, chamba choo,
to go in till him, her erring cheef, and tickle the pontiff aisy-oisy?
She was? Gota pot! Yssel that the limmat! As El Negro winced
when he wonced in La Plate. O, tell me all I want to hear, how
loft she was lift a laddery dextro! A coneywink after the bunting
fell. Letting on she didn't care, sina feza, me absantee, him man
in passession, the proxenete! Proxenete and phwhat is phthat?
Emme for your reussischer Honddu jarkon! Tell us in franca
langua. And call a spate a spate. Did they never sharee you ebro
at skol, you antiabecedarian? It's just the same as if I was to go
par examplum now in conservancy's cause out of telekinesis and
proxenete you. For coxyt sake and is that what she is? Botlettle
I thought she'd act that loa. Didn't you spot her in her windaug,
wubbling up on an osiery chair, with a meusic before her all
cunniform letters, pretending to ribble a reedy derg on a fiddle
she bogans without a band on? Sure she can't fiddan a dee, with
bow or abandon! Sure, she can't! Tista suck. Well, I never now
heard the like of that! Tell me moher. Tell me moatst. Well, old
Humber was as glommen as grampus, with the tares at his thor
and the buboes for ages and neither bowman nor shot abroad and
bales allbrant on the crests of rockies and nera lamp in kitchen or
church and giant's holes in Grafton's causeway and deathcap
mushrooms round Funglus grave and the great tribune's barrow
all darnels occumule, sittang sambre on his sett, drammen and
drommen, usking queasy quizzers of his ruful continence, his
childlinen scarf to encourage his obsequies where he'd check their

debths in that mormon's thames, be questing and handsetl, hop,
step and a deepend, with his berths in their toiling moil, his swal-
lower open from swolf to fore and the snipes of the gutter pecking
his crocs, hungerstriking all alone and holding doomsdag over
hunselv, dreeing his weird, with his dander up, and his fringe
combed over his eygs and droming on loft till the sight of the
sternes, after zwarthy kowse and weedy broeks and the tits of
buddy and the loits of pest and to peer was Parish worth thette
mess. You'd think all was dodo belonging to him how he durmed
adranse in durance vaal. He had been belching for severn years.
And there she was, Anna Livia, she darent catch a winkle of
sleep, purling around like a chit of a child, Wendawanda, a finger-
thick, in a Lapsummer skirt and damazon cheeks, for to ishim
bonzour to her dear dubber Dan. With neuphraties and sault
from his maggias. And an odd time she'd cook him up blooms
of fisk and lay to his heartsfoot her meddery eygs, yayis, and
staynish beacons on toasc and a cupenhave so weeshywashy of
Greenland's tay or a dzoupgan of Kaffue mokau an sable or
Sikiang sukry or his ale of ferns in trueart pewter and a shin-
kobread (hamjambo, bana?) for to plaise that man hog stay his
stomicker till her pyrraknees shrunk to nutmeg graters while her
togglejoints shuck with goyt and as rash as she'd russ with her
peakload of vivers up on her sieve (metauwero rage it swales and
rieses) my hardey Hek he'd kast them frome him, with a stour
of scorn, as much as to say you sow and you sozh, and if he didn't
peg the platteau on her tawe, believe you me, she was safe
enough. And then she'd esk to vistule a hymn, *The Heart Bowed
Down* or *The Rakes of Mallow* or Chelli Michele's *La Calumnia è
un Vermicelli* or a balfy bit ov *old Jo Robidson*. Sucho fuffing a
fifeing 'twould cut you in two! She'd bate the hen that crowed
on the turrace of Babbel. What harm if she knew how to cockle
her mouth! And not a mag out of Hum no more than out of the
mangle weight. Is that a faith? That's the fact. Then riding the
ricka and roya romanche, Annona, gebroren aroostokrat Nivia,
dochter of Sense and Art, with Sparks' pirryphlickathims funkling her fan, anner frostivying tresses dasht with virevlies, —

while the prom beauties sreeked nith their bearers' skins! — in
a period gown of changeable jade that would robe the wood of
two cardinals' chairs and crush poor Cullen and smother Mac-
Cabe. O blazerskate! Theirs porpor patches! And brahming to
him down the feedchute, with her femtyfyx kinds of fondling
endings, the poother rambling off her nose: *Vuggybarney,*
Wickerymandy! Hello, ducky, please don't die! Do you know
what she started cheeping after, with a choicey voicey like water-
glucks or Madame Delba to Romeoreszk? You'll never guess.
Tell me. Tell me. *Phoebe, dearest, tell, O tell me* and *I loved you*
better nor you knew. And letting on hoon var daft about the warbly
sangs from over holmen: *High hellskirt saw ladies hensmoker lily-*
hung pigger: and soay and soan and so firth and so forth in a tone
sonora and Oom Bothar below like Bheri-Bheri in his sandy
cloak, so umvolosy, as deaf as a yawn, the stult! Go away! Poor
deef old deary! Yare only teasing! Anna Liv? As chalk is my
judge! And didn't she up in sorgues and go and trot doon and
stand in her douro, puffing her old dudheen, and every shirvant
siligirl or wensum farmerette walking the pilend roads, Sawy,
Fundally, Daery or Maery, Milucre, Awny or Graw, usedn't she
make her a simp or sign to slip inside by the sullyport? You don't
say the sillypost? Bedouix but I do! Calling them in, one by one
(To Blockbeddum here! Here the Shoebenacaddie!) and legging
a jig or so on the sihl to show them how to shake their benders
and the dainty how to bring to mind the gladdest garments out
of sight and all the way of a maid with a man and making a sort
of a cackling noise like two and a penny or half a crown and holding up a silliver shiner. Lordy, lordy, did she so? Well, of all the
ones ever I heard! Throwing all the neiss little whores in the
world at him! To inny captured wench you wish of no matter
what sex of pleissful ways two adda tammar a lizzy a lossie to
hug and hab haven in Humpy's apron!

And what was the wyerye rima she made! Odet! Odet! Tell
me the trent of it while I'm lathering hail out of Denis Florence
MacCarthy's combies. Rise it, flut ye, pian piena! I'm dying
down off my iodine feet until I lerryn Anna Livia's cushingloo,

that was writ by one and rede by two and trouved by a poule in the parco! I can see that, I see you are. How does it tummel? Listen now. Are you listening? Yes, yes! Idneed I am! Tarn your ore ouse. Essonne inne.

By earth and the cloudy but I badly want a brandnew bankside, bedamp and I do, and a plumper at that!

For the putty affair I have is wore out, so it is, sitting, yaping and waiting for my old Dane hodder dodderer, my life in death companion, my frugal key of our larder, my much-altered camel's hump, my jointspoiler, my maymoon's honey, my fool to the last Decemberer, to wake himself out of his winter's doze and bore me down like he used to.

Is there irwell a lord of the manor or a knight of the shire at strike, I wonder, that'd dip me a dace or two in cash for washing and darning his worshipful socks for him now we're run out of horse-brose and milk?

Only for my short Brittas bed made's as snug as it smells it's out I'd lep and off with me to the slobs della Tolka or the plage au Clontarf to feale the gay aire of my salt troublin bay and the race of the saywint up me ambushure.

Onon! Onon! tell me more. Tell me every tiny teign. I want to know every single ingul. Down to what made the potters fly into jagsthole. And why were the vesles vet. That homa fever's winning me wome. If a mahun of the horse but hard me! We'd be bundukiboi meet askarigal. Well, now comes the hazel-hatchery part. After Clondalkin the Kings's Inns. We'll soon be there with the freshet. How many aleveens had she in tool? I can't rightly rede you that. Close only knows. Some say she had three figures to fill and confined herself to a hundred eleven, wan by-wan bywan, making meanacuminamoyas. Olaph lamm et, all that pack? We won't have room in the kirkeyaard. She can't remember half of the cradlenames she smacked on them by the grace of her boxing bishop's infallible slipper, the cane for Kund and abbles for Eyolf, and ayther nayther for Yakov Yea. A hundred and how? They did well to rechristien her Pluhurabelle. O loreley! What a loddon lodes! Heigh ho! But it's quite on the cards she'll shed

more and merrier, twills and trills, sparefours and spoilfives, nord-
sihkes and sudsevers and ayes and neins to a litter. Grandfarthring
nap and Messamisery and the knave of all knaves and the joker.
Heehaw! She must have been a gadabout in her day, so she
must, more than most. Shoal she was, gidgad. She had a flewmen
of her owen. Then a toss nare scared that lass, so aimai moe,
that's agapo! Tell me, tell me, how cam she camlin through all
her fellows, the neckar she was, the diveline? Casting her perils
before our swains from Fonte-in-Monte to Tidingtown and
from Tidingtown tilhavet. Linking one and knocking the next,
tapting a flank and tipting a jutty and palling in and pietaring
out and clyding by on her eastway. Waiwhou was the first thur-
ever burst? Someone he was, whuebra they were, in a tactic attack
or in single combat. Tinker, tilar, souldrer, salor, Pieman Peace
or Polistaman. That's the thing I'm elwys on edge to esk. Push
up and push vardar and come to uphill headquarters! Was it
waterlows year, after Grattan or Flood, or when maids were in
Arc or when three stood hosting? Fidaris will find where the
Doubt arises like Nieman from Nirgends found the Nihil. Worry
you sighin foh, Albern, O Anser? Untie the gemman's fistiknots,
Qvic and Nuancee! She can't put her hand on him for the moment. Tez thelon langlo, walking weary! Such a loon waybash-
wards to row! She sid herself she hardly knows whuon the annals
her graveller was, a dynast of Leinster, a wolf of the sea, or what
he did or how blyth she played or how, when, why, where and
who offon he jumpnad her and how it was gave her away. She
was just a young thin pale soft shy slim slip of a thing then,
sauntering, by silvamoonlake and he was a heavy trudging
lurching lieabroad of a Curraghman, making his hay for whose
sun to shine on, as tough as the oaktrees (peats be with them!)
used to rustle that time down by the dykes of killing Kildare,
for forstfellfoss with a plash across her. She thought she's sankh
neathe the ground with nymphant shame when he gave her the
tigris eye! O happy fault! Me wish it was he! You're wrong there,
corribly wrong! Tisn't only tonight you're anacheronistic! It
was ages behind that when nullahs were nowhere, in county

Wickenlow, garden of Erin, before she ever dreamt she'd lave
Kilbride and go foaming under Horsepass bridge, with the great
southerwestern windstorming her traces and the midland's grain-
waster asarch for her track, to wend her ways byandby, robecca
or worse, to spin and to grind, to swab and to thrash, for all her
golden lifey in the barleyfields and pennylotts of Humphrey's
fordofhurdlestown and lie with a landleaper, wellingtonorseher.
Alesse, the lagos of girly days! For the dove of the dunas! Was-
ut? Izod? Are you sarthin suir? Not where the Finn fits into the
Mourne, not where the Nore takes lieve of Blœm, not where the
Braye divarts the Farer, not where the Moy changez her minds
twixt Cullin and Conn tween Cunn and Collin? Or where Neptune
sculled and Tritonville rowed and leandros three bumped heroines
two? Neya, narev, nen, nonni, nos! Then whereabouts in Ow and
Ovoca? Was it yst with wyst or Lucan Yokan or where the hand
of man has never set foot? Dell me where, the fairy ferse time! I
will if you listen. You know the dinkel dale of Luggelaw? Well,
there once dwelt a local heremite, Michael Arklow was his river-
end name, (with many a sigh I aspersed his lavabibs!) and one
venersderg in junojuly, oso sweet and so cool and so limber she
looked, Nance the Nixie, Nanon L'Escaut, in the silence, of the sycomores, all listening, the kindling curves you simply can't stop
feeling, he plunged both of his newly anointed hands, the core of
his cushlas, in her singimari saffron strumans of hair, parting them
and soothing her and mingling it, that was deep-dark and ample
like this red bog at sundown. By that Vale Vowclose's lucydlac,
the reignbeau's heavenarches arronged orranged her. Afroth-
dizzying galbs, her enamelled eyes indergoading him on to the
vierge violetian. Wish a wish! Why a why? Mavro! Letty Lerck's
lafing light throw those laurals now on her daphdaph teasesong
petrock. Maass! But the majik wavus has elfun anon meshes.
And Simba the Slayer of his Oga is slewd. He cuddle not help
himself, thurso that hot on him, he had to forget the monk in
the man so, rubbing her up and smoothing her down, he baised
his lippes in smiling mood, kiss akiss after kisokushk (as he
warned her niver to, niver to, nevar) on Anna-na-Poghue's of

the freckled forehead. While you'd parse secheressa she hielt her
souff'. But she ruz two feet hire in her aisne aestumation. And
steppes on stilts ever since. That was kissuahealing with bantur
for balm! O, wasn't he the bold priest? And wasn't she the
naughty Livvy? Nautic Naama's now her navn. Two lads in
scoutsch breeches went through her before that, Barefoot Burn
and Wallowme Wade, Lugnaquillia's noblesse pickts, before she
had a hint of a hair at her fanny to hide or a bossom to tempt a
birch canoedler not to mention a bulgic porterhouse barge. And
ere that again, leada, laida, all unraidy, too faint to buoy the
fairiest rider, too frail to flirt with a cygnet's plume, she was licked
by a hound, Chirripa-Chirruta, while poing her pee, pure and
simple, on the spur of the hill in old Kippure, in birdsong and
shearingtime, but first of all, worst of all, the wiggly livvly, she
sideslipped out by a gap in the Devil's glen while Sally her nurse
was sound asleep in a sloot and, feefee fiefie, fell over a spillway
before she found her stride and lay and wriggled in all the stag-
nant black pools of rainy under a fallow coo and she laughed
innocefree with her limbs aloft and a whole drove of maiden
hawthorns blushing and looking askance upon her.

Drop me the sound of the findhorn's name, Mtu or Mti, som-
bogger was wisness. And drip me why in the flenders was she
frickled. And trickle me through was she marcellewaved or was
it weirdly a wig she wore. And whitside did they droop their
glows in their florry, aback to wist or affront to sea? In fear to
hear the dear so near or longing loth and loathing longing? Are
you in the swim or are you out? O go in, go on, go an! I mean
about what you know. I know right well what you mean. Rother!
You'd like the coifs and guimpes, snouty, and me to do the
greasy jub on old Veronica's wipers. What am I rancing now
and I'll thank you? Is it a pinny or is it a surplice? Arran, where's
your nose? And where's the starch? That's not the vesdre benediction smell. I can tell from here by their *eau de Colo* and the
scent of her oder they're Mrs. Magrath's. And you ought to have
aird them. They've moist come off her. Creases in silk they
are, not crampton lawn. Baptiste me, father, for she has sinned!

Through her catchment ring she freed them easy, with her hips'
hurrahs for her knees'dontelleries. The only parr with frills in
old the plain. So they are, I declare! Welland well! If tomorrow
keeps fine who'll come tripping to sightsee? How'll? Ask me
next what I haven't got! The Belvedarean exhibitioners. In their
cruisery caps and oarsclub colours. What hoo, they band! And
what hoa, they buck! And here is her nubilee letters too. Ellis
on quay in scarlet thread. Linked for the world on a flush-
caloured field. Annan exe after to show they're not Laura Ke-
own's. O, may the diabolo twisk your seifety pin! You child of
Mammon, Kinsella's Lilith! Now who has been tearing the leg
of her drawars on her? Which leg is it? The one with the bells
on it. Rinse them out and aston along with you! Where did I
stop? Never stop. Continuarration! You're not there yet. I
amstel waiting. Garonne, garonne!

Well, after it was put in the Mericy Cordial Mendicants' Sitter-
dag-Zindeh-Munaday Wakeschrift (for once they sullied their
white kidloves, chewing cuds after their dinners of cheeckin and
beggin, with their show us it here and their mind out of that and
their when you're quite finished with the reading matarial), even
the snee that snowdon his hoaring hair had a skunner against
him. Thaw, thaw, sava, savuto! Score Her Chuff Exsquire!
Everywhere erriff you went and every bung you arver dropped
into, in cit or suburb or in addled areas, the Rose and Bottle or
Phoenix Tavern or Power's Inn or Jude's Hotel, or wherever you
scoured the countryside from Nannywater to Vartryville or from
Porta Lateen to the lootin quarter you found his ikom etsched
tipside down or the cornerboys cammocking his guy and Morris
the Man, with the role of a royss in his turgos the turrible, (Evro-
peahahn cheic house, unskimmed sooit and yahoort, hamman
now cheekmee, Ahdahm this way make, Fatima, half turn!)
reeling and railing round the local as the peihos piped und uban-
jees twanged, with oddfellow's triple tiara busby rotundarinking
round his scalp. Like Pate-by-the-Neva or Pete-over-Meer. This
is the Hausman all paven and stoned, that cribbed the Cabin that
never was owned that cocked his leg and hennad his Egg. And

the mauldrin rabble around him in areopage, fracassing a great
bingkan cagnan with their timpan crowders. Mind your Grimm-
father! Think of your Ma! Hing the Hong is his jove's hang-
nomen! Lilt a bolero, bulling a law! She swore on croststyx nyne
wyndabouts she's be level with all the snags of them yet. Par the
Vulnerable Virgin's Mary del Dame! So she said to herself she'd
frame a plan to fake a shine, the mischiefmaker, the like of it you
niever heard. What plan? Tell me quick and dongu so crould!
What the meurther did she mague? Well, she bergened a zakbag,
a shammy mailsack, with the lend of a loan of the light of his
lampion, off one of her swapsons, Shaun the Post, and then she
went and consulted her chapboucqs, old Mot Moore, Casey's
Euclid and the Fashion Display and made herself tidal to join
in the mascarete. O gig goggle of gigguels. I can't tell you how!
It's too screaming to rizo, rabbit it all! Minneha, minnehi mina-
aehe, minneho! O but you must, you must really! Make my hear
it gurgle gurgle, like the farest gargle gargle in the dusky dirgle
dargle. By the holy well of Mulhuddart I swear I'd pledge my
chanza getting to heaven through Tirry and Killy's mount of
impiety to hear it all, aviary word. O, leave me my faculties,
woman, a while! If you don't like my story get out of the punt.
Well, have it your own way, so. Here, sit down and do as you're
bid. Take my stroke and bend to your bow. Forward in and pull
your overthepoise! Lisp it slaney and crisp it quiet. Deel me longsome. Tongue your time now. Breathe thet deep. Thouat's the
fairway. Hurry slow and scheldt you go. Lynd us your blessed
ashes here till I scrub the canon's underpants. Flow now. Ower
more. And pooleypooley.

First she let her hair fal and down it flussed to her feet its
teviots winding coils. Then, mothernaked, she sampood herself
with galawater and fraguant pistania mud, wupper and lauar,
from crown to sole. Next she greased the groove of her keel,
warthes and wears and mole and itcher, with antifouling butter-
scatch and turfentide and serpenthyme and with leafmould she
ushered round prunella isles and eslats dun, quincecunct, allover
her little mary. Peeld gold of waxwork her jellybelly and her

grains of incense anguille bronze. And after that she wove a garland for her hair. She pleated it. She plaited it. Of meadowgrass and riverflags, the bulrush and waterweed, and of fallen griefs of weeping willow. Then she made her bracelets and her anklets and her armlets and a jetty amulet for necklace of clicking cobbles and pattering pebbles and rumbledown rubble, richmond and rehr, of Irish rhunerhinerstones and shellmarble bangles. That done, a dawk of smut to her airy ey, Annushka Lutetiavitch Pufflovah, and the lellipos cream to her lippeleens and the pick of the paintbox for her pommettes, from strawbirry reds to extra violates, and she sendred her boudeloire maids to His Affluence, Ciliegia Grande and Kirschie Real, the two chirsines, with respecks from his missus, seepy and sewery, and a request might she passe of him for a minnikin. A call to pay, and light a taper, in Brie-on-Arrosa, back in a sprizzling. The cock striking mine, the stalls bridely sign, there's Zambosy waiting for me. She said she wouldn't be half her length away. Then, then, as soon as the lump his back was turned, with her mealiebag slang over her shulder, Anna Livia, oysterface, forth of her bassein came.

Describe her! Hustle along, why can't you? Spitz on the iern while it's hot. I wouldn't miss her for irthing on nerthe. Not for the lucre of lomba strait. Oceans of Gaud, I mosel hear that! Ogowe presta! Leste, before Julia sees her! Ishekarry and washemeskad, the carishy caratimaney? Whole lady fair? Duodecimoroon? Bon a ventura? Malagassy? What had she on, the liddel oud oddity? How much did she scallop, harness and weights? Here she is, Amnisty Ann! Call her calamity electrifies man.

No electress at all but old Moppa Necessity, angin mother of injons. I'll tell you a test. But you must sit still. Will you hold your peace and listen well to what I am going to say now? It might have been ten or twenty to one of the night of Allclose or the nexth of April when the flip of her hoogly igloo flappered and out toetippit a bushman woman, the dearest little moma ever you saw, nodding around her, all smiles, with ems of embarras and aues to awe, between two ages, a judyqueen, not up to your

elb. Quick, look at her cute and saise her quirk for the bicker she
lives the slicker she grows. Save us and tagus! No more? Werra
where in ourthe did you ever pick a Lambay chop as big as a
battering ram? Ay, you're right. I'm epte to forgetting, Like
Liviam Liddle did Loveme Long. The linth of my hough, I say!
She wore a ploughboy's nailstudded clogs, a pair of ploughfields
in themselves: a sugarloaf hat with a gaudyquivivy peak and a
band of gorse for an arnoment and a hundred streamers dancing
off it and a guildered pin to pierce it: owlglassy bicycles boggled
her eyes: and a fishnetzeveil for the sun not to spoil the wrinklings
of her hydeaspects: potatorings boucled the loose laubes of her
laudsnarers: her nude cuba stockings were salmospotspeckled: she
sported a galligo shimmy of hazevaipar tinto that never was fast
till it ran in the washing: stout stays, the rivals, lined her length:
her bloodorange bockknickers, a two in one garment, showed
natural nigger boggers, fancyfastened, free to undo: her black-
stripe tan joseph was sequansewn and teddybearlined, with wavy
rushgreen epaulettes and a leadown here and there of royal
swansruff: a brace of gaspers stuck in her hayrope garters: her
civvy codroy coat with alpheubett buttons was boundaried round
with a twobar tunnel belt: a fourpenny bit in each pocketside
weighed her safe from the blowaway windrush; she had a clothes-
peg tight astride on her joki's nose and she kep on grinding a
sommething quaint in her fiumy mouth and the rrreke of the
fluve of the tail of the gawan of her snuffdrab siouler's skirt
trailed ffiffty odd Irish miles behind her lungarhodes.
    Hellsbells, I'm sorry I missed her! Sweet gumptyum and no-
body fainted. But in whelk of her mouths? Was her naze alight?
Everyone that saw her said the dowce little delia looked a bit
queer. Lotsy trotsy, mind the poddle! Missus, be good and don't
fol in the say! Fenny poor hex she must have charred. Kickhams
a frumpier ever you saw. Making mush mullet's eyes at her boys
dobelon. And they crowned her their chariton queen, all the
maids. Of the may? You don't say! Well for her she couldn't
see herself. I recknitz wharfore the darling murrayed her mirror.
She did? Mersey me! There was a koros of drouthdropping sur-

facemen, boomslanging and plugchewing, fruiteyeing and flower-
feeding, in contemplation of the fluctuation and the undification
of her filimentation, lolling and leasing on North Lazers' Waal
all eelfare week by the Jukar Yoick's and as soon as they saw her
meander by that marritime way in her grasswinter's weeds and
twigged who was under her archdeaconess bonnet, Avondale's
fish and Clarence's poison, sedges an to aneber, Wit-upon-
Crutches to Master Bates: *Between our two southsates and the
granite they're warming, or her face has been lifted or Alp has doped.*

But what was the game in her mixed baggyrhatty? Just the
tembo in her tumbo or pilipili from her pepperpot? Saas and
taas and specis bizaas. And where in thunder did she plunder?
Fore the battle or efter the ball? I want to get it frisk from the
soorce. I aubette my bearb it's worth while poaching on. Shake
it up, do, do! That's a good old son of a ditch! I promise I'll
make it worth your while. And I don't mean maybe. Nor yet
with a goodfor. Spey me pruth and I'll tale you true.

Well, arundgirond in a waveney lyne aringarouma she pattered
and swung and sidled, dribbling her boulder through narrowa
mosses, the diliskydrear on our drier side and the vilde vetchvine
agin us, curara here, careero there, not knowing which medway
or weser to strike it, edereider, making chattahoochee all to her
ain chichiu, like Santa Claus at the cree of the pale and puny,
nistling to hear for their tiny hearties, her arms encircling Isola-
bella, then running with reconciled Romas and Reims, on like a
lech to be off like a dart, then bathing Dirty Hans' spatters with
spittle, with a Christmas box apiece for aisch and iveryone of her
childer, the birthday gifts they dreamt they gabe her, the spoiled
she fleetly laid at our door! On the matt, by the pourch and inunder the cellar. The rivulets ran aflod to see, the glashaboys, the
pollynooties. Out of the paunschaup on to the pyre. And they all
about her, juvenile leads and ingenuinas, from the slime of their
slums and artesaned wellings, rickets and riots, like the Smyly
boys at their vicereine's levee. Vivi vienne, little Annchen! Vielo
Anna, high life! Sing us a sula, O, susuria! Ausone sidulcis!
Hasn't she tambre! Chipping her and raising a bit of a chir or a

jary every dive she'd neb in her culdee sacco of wabbash she
raabed and reach out her maundy meerschaundize, poor souvenir
as per ricorder and all for sore aringarung, stinkers and heelers,
laggards and primelads, her furzeborn sons and dribblederry
daughters, a thousand and one of them, and wickerpotluck for
each of them. For evil and ever. And kiks the buch. A tinker's
bann and a barrow to boil his billy for Gipsy Lee; a cartridge of
cockaleekie soup for Chummy the Guardsman; for sulky Pen-
der's acid nephew deltoïd drops, curiously strong; a cough and
a rattle and wildrose cheeks for poor Piccolina Petite MacFarlane;
a jigsaw puzzle of needles and pins and blankets and shins between
them for Isabel, Jezebel and Llewelyn Mmarriage; a brazen nose
and pigiron mittens for Johnny Walker Beg; a papar flag of the
saints and stripes for Kevineen O'Dea; a puffpuff for Pudge Craig
and a nightmarching hare for Techertim Tombigby; waterleg
and gumboots each for Bully Hayes and Hurricane Hartigan;
a prodigal heart and fatted calves for Buck Jones, the pride of
Clonliffe; a loaf of bread and a father's early aim for Val from
Skibereen; a jauntingcar for Larry Doolin, the Ballyclee jackeen;
a seasick trip on a government ship for Teague O'Flanagan; a
louse and trap for Jerry Coyle; slushmincepies for Andy Mac-
kenzie; a hairclip and clackdish for Penceless Peter; that twelve
sounds look for G. V. Brooke; a drowned doll, to face down-
wards for modest Sister Anne Mortimer; altar falls for Blanchisse's
bed; Wildairs' breechettes for Magpeg Woppington; to Sue Dot
a big eye; to Sam Dash a false step; snakes in clover, picked and
scotched, and a vaticanned viper catcher's visa for Patsy Presbys;
a reiz every morning for Standfast Dick and a drop every minute
for Stumblestone Davy; scruboak beads for beatified Biddy; two
appletweed stools for Eva Mobbely; for Saara Philpot a jordan
vale tearorne; a pretty box of Pettyfib's Powder for Eileen Aruna
to whiten her teeth and outflash Helen Arhone; a whippingtop
for Eddy Lawless; for Kitty Coleraine of Butterman's Lane a
penny wise for her foolish pitcher; a putty shovel for Terry the
Puckaun; an apotamus mask for Promoter Dunne; a niester egg
with a twicedated shell and a dynamight right for Pavl the Curate;

a collera morbous for Mann in the Cloack; a starr and girton for
Draper and Deane; for Will-of-the-Wisp and Barny-the-Bark two
mangolds noble to sweeden their bitters; for Oliver Bound a
way in his frey; for Seumas, thought little, a crown he feels big;
a tibertine's pile with a Congoswood cross on the back for
Sunny Twimjim: a praises be and spare me days for Brian the
Bravo: penteplenty of pity with lubilashings of lust for Olona
Lena Magdalena; for Camilla, Dromilla, Ludmilla, Mamilla, a
bucket, a packet, a book and a pillow; for Nancy Shannon a
Tuami brooch; for Dora Riparia Hopeandwater a cooling douche
and a warmingpan; a pair of Blarney braggs for Wally Meagher;
a hairpin slatepencil for Elsie Oram to scratch her toby, doing
her best with her volgar fractions; an old age pension for Betty
Bellezza; a bag of the blues for Funny Fitz; a *Missa pro Messa* for
Taff de Taff; Jill, the spoon of a girl, for Jack, the broth of a boy;
a Rogerson Crusoe's Friday fast for Caducus Angelus Rubicon-
stein; three hundred and sixtysix poplin tyne for revery warp in
the weaver's woof for Victor Hugonot; a stiff steaded rake and
good varians muck for Kate the Cleaner; a hole in the ballad for
Hosty; two dozen of cradles for J.F.X.P. Coppinger; tenpounten
on the pop for the daulphins born with five spoiled squibs for
Infanta; a letter to last a lifetime for Maggi beyond by the ashpit;
the heftiest frozenmeat woman from Lusk to Livienbad for Felim
the Ferry; spas and speranza and symposium's syrup for decayed
and blind and gouty Gough; a change of naves and joys of ills
for Armoricus Tristram Amoor Saint Lawrence; a guillotine
shirt for Reuben Redbreast und hempen suspendeats for Brennan on the Moor; an oakanknee for Conditor Sawyer and mus-
quodoboits for Great Tropical Scott; a C3 peduncle for Karma-
lite Kane; a sunless map of the month, including the sword and
stamps for Shemus O'Shaun the Post; a jackal with hide for
Browne but Nolan; a stonecold shoulder for Donn Joe Vance;
all lock and no stable for Honorbright Merreytrickx; a big drum
for Billy Dunboyne; a guilty goldeny bellows, below me blow
me for Ida Ida and a hushaby rocker Elletrouvetout for Who-is-
silvier — Where-is-he?; whatever you like to swilly to swash,

Yuinness or Yennessy, Laagen or Niger, for Festus King and
Roaring Peter and Frisky Shorty and Treacle Tom and O. B.
Behan and Sully the Thug and Master Magrath and Peter Cloran
and O'Delawarr Rossa and Nerone MacPacem and whoever you
chance to meet knocking around; and a pig's bladder balloon for
Selina Susquehanna Stakelum. But what did she give to Pruda
Ward and Katty Kanel and Peggy Quilty and Briery Brosna and
Teasy Kieran and Ena Lappin and Muriel Maassy and Zusan Camac
and Melissa Bradogue and Flora Ferns and Fauna Fox-Good-
man and Grettna Greaney and Penelope Inglesante and Lezba
Licking like Leytha Liane and Roxana Rohan with Simpatica
Sohan and Una Bina Laterza and Trina La Mesme and Philomena
O'Farrell and Irmak Elly and Josephine Foyle and Snakeshead
Lily and Fountainoy Laura and Marie Xavier Agnes Daisy
Frances de Sales Macleay? She gave them ilcka madre's daughter
a moonflower and a bloodvein: but the grapes that ripe before
reason to them that devide the vinedress. So on Izzy, her shame-
maid, love shone befond her tears as from Shem, her penmight,
life past befoul his prime.

My colonial, wardha bagful! A bakereen's dusind with tithe
tillies to boot. That's what you may call a tale of a tub. And Hi-
bernonian market. All that and more under one crinoline envelope if you dare to break the porkbarrel seal. No wonder they'd
run from her pison plague. Throw us your hudson soap for the
honour of Clane! The wee taste the water left. I'll raft it back,
first thing in the marne. Merced mulde! Ay, and don't forget the
reckitts I lohaned you. You've all the swirls your side of the current. Well, am I to blame for that if I have? Who said you're to
blame for that if you have? You're a bit on the sharp side. I'm on
the wide. Only snuffers' cornets drifts my way that the cracka
dvine chucks out of his cassock, with her estheryear's marsh
narcissus to make him recant his vanitty fair. Foul strips of his
chinook's bible I do be reading, dodwell disgustered but chickled
with chuckles at the tittles is drawn on the tattle-page. *Senior ga
dito: Faciasi Omio! E omo fu fò.* Ho! Ho! *Senior ga dito: Faciasi
Hidamo! Hidamo se ga facessà.* Ha! Ha! And *Die Windermere*

Dichter and Lefanu (Sheridan's) Old *House by the Coachyard* and
Mill (J.) *On Woman* with *Ditto on the Floss*. Ja, a swamp for Alt-
muehler and a stone for his flossies. I know how racy they move
his wheel. My hands are blawcauld between isker and suda like
that piece of pattern chayney there, lying below. Or where is it?
Lying beside the sedge I saw it. Hoangho, my sorrow, I've lost
it! Aimihi! With that turbary water who could see? So near and
yet so far! But O, gihon! I lovat a gabber. I could listen to maure
and moravar again. Regn onder river. Flies do your float. Thick
is the life for mere.

Well, you know or don't you kennet or haven't I told you
every telling has a taling and that's the he and the she of it. Look,
look, the dusk is growing. My branches lofty are taking root.
And my cold cher's gone ashley. Fieluhr? Filou! What age is at?
It saon is late. 'Tis endless now senne eye or erewone last saw
Waterhouse's clogh. They took it asunder, I hurd thum sigh.
When will they reassemble it? O, my back, my back, my bach!
I'd want to go to Aches-les-Pains. Pingpong! There's the Belle
for Sexaloitez! And Concepta de Send-us-pray! Pang! Wring out
the clothes! Wring in the dew! Godavari, vert the showers! And
grant thaya grace! Aman. Will we spread them here now? Ay,
we will. Flip! Spread on your bank and I'll spread mine on mine.
Flep! It's what I'm doing. Spread! It's churning chill. Der went is
rising. I'll lay a few stones on the hostel sheets. A man and his bride
embraced between them. Else I'd have sprinkled and folded them
only. And I'll tie my butcher's apron here. It's suety yet. The
strollers will pass it by. Six shifts, ten kerchiefs, nine to hold to
the fire and this for the code, the convent napkins twelve, one
baby's shawl. Good mother Jossiph knows, she said. Whose
head? Mutter snores? Deataceas! Wharnow are alle her childer,
say? In kingdome gone or power to come or gloria be to them
farther? Allalivial, allalluvial! Some here, more no more, more
again lost alla stranger. I've heard tell that same brooch of the
Shannons was married into a family in Spain. And all the Dun-
ders de Dunnes in Markland's Vineland beyond Brendan's herring
pool takes number nine in yangsee's hats. And one of Biddy's

beads went bobbing till she rounded up lost histereve with a
marigold and a cobbler's candle in a side strain of a main drain
of a manzinahurries off Bachelor's Walk. But all that's left to the
last of the Meaghers in the loup of the years prefixed and between
is one kneebuckle and two hooks in the front. Do you tell me
that now? I do in troth. Orara por Orbe and poor Las Animas!
Ussa, Ulla, we're umbas all! Mezha, didn't you hear it a deluge of
times, ufer and ufer, respund to spond? You deed, you deed! I
need, I need! It's that irrawaddyng I've stoke in my aars. It all
but husheth the lethest zswound. Oronoko! What's your trouble?
Is that the great Finnleader himself in his joakimono on his statue
riding the high horse there forehengist? Father of Otters, it is
himself! Yonne there! Isset that? On Fallareen Common? You're
thinking of Astley's Amphitheayter where the bobby restrained
you making sugarstuck pouts to the ghostwhite horse of the
Peppers. Throw the cobwebs from your eyes, woman, and spread
your washing proper. It's well I know your sort of slop. Flap!
Ireland sober is Ireland stiff. Lord help you, Maria, full of grease,
the load is with me! Your prayers. I sonht zo! Madammangut!
Were you lifting your elbow, tell us, glazy cheeks, in Conway's
Carrigacurra canteen? Was I what, hobbledyhips? Flop! Your
rere gait's creakorheuman bitts your butts disagrees. Amn't I
up since the damp dawn, marthared mary allacook, with Corri-
gan's pulse and varicoarse veins, my pramaxle smashed, Alice
Jane in decline and my oneeyed mongrel twice run over, soaking
and bleaching boiler rags, and sweating cold, a widow like me,
for to deck my tennis champion son, the laundryman with the
lavandier flannels? You won your limpopo limp fron the husky
hussars when Collars and Cuffs was heir to the town and your
slur gave the stink to Carlow. Holy Scamander, I sar it again!
Near the golden falls. Icis on us! Seints of light! Zezere! Subdue
your noise, you hamble creature! What is it but a blackburry
growth or the dwyergray ass them four old codgers owns. Are
you meanam Tarpey and Lyons and Gregory? I meyne now,
thank all, the four of them, and the roar of them, that draves
that stray in the mist and old Johnny MacDougal along with

them. Is that the Poolbeg flasher beyant, pharphar, or a fireboat
coasting nyar the Kishtna or a glow I behold within a hedge or
my Garry come back from the Indes? Wait till the honeying of
the lune, love! Die eve, little eve, die! We see that wonder in
your eye. We'll meet again, we'll part once more. The spot I'll
seek if the hour you'll find. My chart shines high where the blue
milk's upset. Forgivemequick, I'm going! Bubye! And you,
pluck your watch, forgetmenot. Your evenlode. So save to
jurna's end! My sights are swimming thicker on me by the shadows to this place. I sow home slowly now by own way, moy-
valley way. Towy I too, rathmine.

Ah, but she was the queer old skeowsha anyhow, Anna Livia,
trinkettoes! And sure he was the quare old buntz too, Dear Dirty
Dumpling, foostherfather of fingalls and dottergills. Gammer
and gaffer we're all their gangsters. Hadn't he seven dams to wive
him? And every dam had her seven crutches. And every crutch
had its seven hues. And each hue had a differing cry. Sudds for
me and supper for you and the doctor's bill for Joe John. Befor!
Bifur! He married his markets, cheap by foul, I know, like any
Etrurian Catholic Heathen, in their pinky limony creamy birnies
and their turkiss indienne mauves. But at milkidmass who was
the spouse? Then all that was was fair. Tys Elvenland! Teems of
times and happy returns. The seim anew. Ordovico or viricordo.
Anna was, Livia is, Plurabelle's to be. Northmen's thing made
southfolk's place but howmulty plurators made eachone in person? Latin me that, my trinity scholard, out of eure sanscreed into
oure eryan. *Hircus Civis Eblanensis!* He had buckgoat paps on
him, soft ones for orphans. Ho, Lord! Twins of his bosom. Lord
save us! And ho! Hey? What all men. Hot? His tittering daughters of. Whawk?

Can't hear with the waters of. The chittering waters of. Flitter-
ing bats, fieldmice bawk talk. Ho! Are you not gone ahome?
What Thom Malone? Can't hear with bawk of bats, all thim liffey-
ing waters of. Ho, talk save us! My foos won't moos. I feel as old
as yonder elm. A tale told of Shaun or Shem? All Livia's daughter-
sons. Dark hawks hear us. Night! Night! My ho head halls. I feel

as heavy as yonder stone. Tell me of John or Shaun? Who were
Shem and Shaun the living sons or daughters of? Night now!
Tell me, tell me, tell me, elm! Night night! Telmetale of stem or
stone. Beside the rivering waters of, hitherandthithering waters
of. Night!

II

II

Every evening at lighting up o'clock sharp and until further notice in Feenichts Playhouse. (Bar and conveniences always open, Diddlem Club douncestears.) Entrancings: gads, a scrab; the quality, one large shilling. Newly billed for each wickeday perfumance. Somndoze massinees. By arraignment, childream's hours, expercatered. Jampots, rinsed porters, taken in token. With nightly redistribution of parts and players by the puppetry producer and daily dubbing of ghosters, with the benediction of the Holy Genesius Archimimus and under the distinguished patronage of their Elderships the Oldens from the four coroners of Findrias, Murias, Gorias and Falias, Messoirs the Coarbs, Clive Sollis, Galorius Kettle, Pobiedo Lancey and Pierre Dusort, while the Caesar-in-Chief looks. On. Sennet. As played to the Adelphi by the Brothers Bratislavoff (Hyrcan and Haristobulus), after humpteen dumpteen revivals. Before all the King's Hoarsers with all the Queen's Mum. And wordloosed over seven seas crowdblast in certelleneteutoslavzendlatinsoundscript. In four tubbloids. While fern may cald us until firn make cold. *The Mime of Mick, Nick and the Maggies*, adopted from the Ballymooney Bloodriddon Murther by Bluechin Blackdillain (authorways 'Big Storey'), featuring:

GLUGG (Mr. Seumas McQuillad, hear the riddles between the robot in his dress circular and the gagster in the rogues' gallery), the bold bad bleak boy of the storybooks, who, when the tabs go

up, as we discover, because he knew to mutch, has been divorced
into disgrace court by

THE FLORAS (Girl Scouts from St. Bride's Finishing Establishment, demand acidulateds), a month's bunch of pretty maidens
who, while they pick on her, their pet peeve, form with valkyri-
enne licence the guard for

IZOD (Miss Butys Pott, ask the attendantess for a leaflet), a be-
witching blonde who dimples delightfully and is approached in
loveliness only by her grateful sister reflection in a mirror, the cloud
of the opal, who, having jilted Glugg, is being fatally fascinated by

CHUFF (Mr. Sean O'Mailey, see the chalk and sanguine picto-
graph on the safety drop), the fine frank fairhaired fellow of the
fairytales, who wrestles for tophole with the bold bad bleak boy
Glugg geminally about caps or puds or tog bags or bog gats or
chuting rudskin gunerally or something until they adumbrace a
pattern of somebody else or other, after which they are both carried off the set and brought home to be well soaped, sponged and
scrubbed again by

ANN (Miss Corrie Corriendo, Grischun scoula, bring the babes,
Pieder, Poder and Turtey, she mistributes mandamus monies,
after perdunamento, hendrud aloven entrees, pulcinellis must not
miss our national rooster's rag), their poor little old mother-in-
lieu, who is woman of the house, playing opposite to

HUMP (Mr. Makeall Gone, read the sayings from Laxdalesaga
in the programme about King Ericus of Schweden and the spirit's
whispers in his magical helmet), cap-a-pipe with watch and top-
per, coat, crest and supporters, the cause of all our grievances,
the whirl, the flash and the trouble, who, having partially re-
covered from a recent impeachment due to egg everlasting, but
throughandthoroughly proconverted, propounded for cyclo-
logical, is, studding sail once more, jibsheets and royals, in the
semblance of the substance for the membrance of the umbrance
with the remnance of the emblence reveiling a quemdam super-
cargo, of The Rockery, Poopinheavin, engaged in entertaining
in his pilgrimst customhouse at Caherlehome-upon-Eskur those
statutory persons

THE CUSTOMERS (Components of the Afterhour Courses at St. Patricius' Academy for Grownup Gentlemen, consult the annuary, coldporters sibsuction), a bundle of a dozen of representative locomotive civics, each inn quest of outings, who are still more sloppily served after every cup final by

SAUNDERSON (Mr. Knut Oelsvinger, Tiffsdays off, wouldntstop in bad, imitation of flatfish, torchbearing supperaape, dud halfsovereign, no chee daily, rolly pollsies, Glen of the Downs, the Gugnir, his geyswerks, his earsequack, his lokistroki, o.s.v.), a scherinsheiner and spoilcurate, unconcerned in the mystery but under the inflounce of the milldieuw and butt of

KATE (Miss Rachel Lea Varian, she tells forkings for baschfellors, under purdah of card palmer teaput tosspot Madam d'Elta, during the pawses), kook-and-dishdrudge, whitch believes wanthingthats, whouse be the churchyard or whorts up the aasgaars, the show must go on.

Time: the pressant.

With futurist one-horse balletbattle pictures and the Pageant of Past History worked up with animal variations amid everglaning mangrovemazes and beorbtracktors by Messrs. Thud and Blunder. Shadows by the film folk, masses by the good people. Promptings by Elanio Vitale. Longshots, upcloses, outblacks and stagetolets by Hexenschuss, Coachmaher, Incubone and Rocknarrag. Creations tastefully designed by Madame Berthe Delamode. Dances arranged by Harley Quinn and Coollimbeina. Jests, jokes, jigs and jorums for the Wake lent from the properties of the late cemented Mr. T. M. Finnegan R.I.C. Lipmasks and hairwigs by Ouida Nooikke. Limes and Floods by Crooker and Toll. Kopay pibe by Kappa Pedersen. Hoed Pine hat with twentyfour ventholes by Morgen. Bosse and stringbag from Heteroditheroe's and All Ladies' presents. Tree taken for grafted. Rock rent. Phenecian blends and Sourdanian doofpoosts by Shauvesourishe and Wohntbedarft. The oakmulberryeke with silktrick twomesh from Shop-Sowry, seedsmanchap. Grabstone beg from General Orders Mailed. The crack (that's Cork!) by a smoker from the gods. The interjection (Buckley!) by the fire-

ment in the pit. Accidental music providentially arranged by
L'Archet and Laccorde. Melodiotiosities in purefusion by the
score. To start with in the beginning, we need hirtly bemark,
a community prayer, everyone for himself, and to conclude
with as an exodus, we think it well to add, a chorale in canon,
good for us all for us all us all all. Songs betune the acts by
the ambiamphions of Annapolis, Joan Mock-Comic, male so-
prano, and Jean Souslevin, bass noble, respectively: O, Mester
Sogermon, ef thes es whot ye deux, then I'm not surpleased ye
want that bottle of Sauvequipeu and Oh Off Nunch Der Rasche
Ver Lasse Mitsch Nitscht. Till the summit scenes of climbacks
castastrophear, *The Bearded Mountain* (Polymop Barethe-
rootsch), and *The River Romps to Nursery* (Maidykins in Undi-
form). The whole thugogmagog, including the portions understood to be oddmitted as the results of the respective titulars
neglecting to produce themselves, to be wound up for an after-
enactment by a Magnificent Transformation Scene showing the
Radium Wedding of Neid and Moorning and the Dawn of
Peace, Pure, Perfect and Perpetual, Waking the Weary of the
World.

An argument follows.

Chuffy was a nangel then and his soard fleshed light like like-
ning. Fools top! Singty, sangty, meekly loose, defendy nous from
prowlabouts. Make a shine on the curst. Emen.

But the duvlin sulph was in Glugger, that lost-to-lurning.
Punct. He was sbuffing and sputing, tussing like anisine, whip-
ping his eyesoult and gnatsching his teats over the brividies from
existers and the outher liubbocks of life. He halth kelchy chosen
a clayblade and makes prayses to his three of clubs. To part from
these, my corsets, is into overlusting fear. Acts of feet, hoof and
jarrety: athletes longfoot. Djowl, uphere!

Aminxt that nombre of evelings, but how pierceful in their so-
jestiveness were those first girly stirs, with zitterings of flight released and twinglings of twitchbells in rondel after, with waver-
ings that made shimmershake rather naightily all the duskcended
airs and shylit beaconings from shehind hims back. Sammy, call

on. Mirrylamb, she was shuffering all the diseasinesses of the un-
herd of. Mary Louisan Shousapinas! If Arck could no more salve
his agnols from the wiles of willy wooly woolf! If all the airish
signics of her dipandump helpabit from an Father Hogam till
the Mutther Masons could not that Glugg to catch her by the
calour of her brideness! Not Rose, Sevilla nor Citronelle; not
Esmeralde, Pervinca nor Indra; not Viola even nor all of them
four themes over. But, the monthage stick in the melmelode jawr,
I am (twintomine) all thees thing. Up tighty in the front, down
again on the loose, drim and drumming on her back and a pop
from her whistle. What is that, O holytroopers? Isot givin yoe?

Up he stulpled, glee you gees with search a fling did die near
sea, beamy owen and calmy hugh and if you what you my call for
me I will wishyoumaycull for you.

And they are met, face a facing. They are set, force to force.
And no such Copenhague-Marengo was less so fated for a fall
since in Glenasmole of Smiling Thrushes Patch Whyte passed
O'Sheen ascowl.

Arrest thee, scaldbrother! came the evangelion, sabre accu-
sant, from all Saint Joan's Wood to kill or maim him, and be
dumm but ill s'arrested. Et would proffer to his delected one the
his trifle from the grass.

A space. Who are you? The cat's mother. A time. What do
you lack? The look of a queen.

But what is that which is one going to prehend? Seeks, buzzling
is brains, the feinder.

The howtosayto itiswhatis hemustwhomust worden schall.
A darktongues, kunning. O theoperil! Ethiaop lore, the poor lie.
He askit of the hoothed fireshield but it was untergone into the
matthued heaven. He soughed it from the luft but that bore ne
mark ne message. He luked upon the bloomingrund where ongly
his corns were growning. At last he listed back to beckline how
she pranked alone so johntily. The skand for schooling.

With nought a wired from the wordless either.

Item. He was hardset then. He wented to go (somewhere) while
he was weeting. Utem. He wished to grieve on the good persons, that

is the four gentlemen. Otem. And it was not a long time till he was
feeling true forim he was goodda purssia and it was short after that
he was fooling mehaunt to mehynte he was an injine ruber. Etem.
He was at his thinker, aunts to give (the four gentlemen) the presence
(of a curpse). And this is what he would be willing. He fould the
fourd; they found the hurtled stones; they fell ill with the gravy
duck: and he sod town with the roust of the meast. Atem.

Towhere byhangs ourtales.

Ah ho! This poor Glugg! It was so said of him about of his old
fontmouther. Truly deplurabel! A dire, O dire! And all the freight-
fullness whom he inhebited after his colline born janitor. Sometime towerable! With that hehry antlets on him and the bauble-
light bulching out of his sockets whiling away she sprankled his
allover with her noces of interregnation: How do you do that lack
a lock and pass the poker, please? And bids him tend her, lute
and airly. Sing, sweetharp, thing to me anone! So that Glugg,
the poor one, in that limbopool which was his subnesciousness
he could scares of all knotknow whither his morrder had bourst
a blabber or if the vogalstones that hit his tynpan was that mearly
his skoll missed her. Misty's trompe or midst his flooting? Ah,
ho! Cicely, awe!

The youngly delightsome frilles-in-pleyurs are now showen
drawen, if bud one, or, if in florileague, drawens up consociately
at the hinder sight of their commoner guardia. Her boy fiend or
theirs, if they are so plurielled, cometh up as a trapadour, sinking
how he must fand for himself by gazework what their colours
wear as they are all showen drawens up. Tireton, cacheton, tireton, ba! Doth that not satisfy youth, sir? Quanty purty bellas,
here, Madama Lifay! And what are you going to charm them to,
Madama, do say? Cinderynelly angled her slipper; it was cho
chiny yet braught her a groom. He will angskt of them from their
commoner guardian at next lineup (who is really the rapier of the
two though thother brother can hold his own, especially for he
bandished it with his hand the hold time, mamain, a simply gracious: Mi, O la!), and reloose that thong off his art: Hast thou feel
liked carbunckley ones? Apun which his poohoor pricoxity theirs

is a little tittertit of hilarity (Lad-o'-me-soul! Lad-o'-me-soul,
see!) and the wordchary is atvoiced ringsoundinly by their toots
ensembled, though not meaning to be clever, but just with a shrug
of their hips to go to troy and harff a freak at himself by all that
story to the ulstramarines. Otherwised, holding their noises,
they insinuate quiet private, Ni, he make peace in his preaches
and play with esteem.

Warewolff! Olff! Toboo!

So olff for his topheetuck the ruck made raid, aslick aslegs
would run; and he ankered on his hunkers with the belly belly
prest. Asking: What's my muffinstuffinaches for these times? To
weat: Breath and bother and whatarcurss. Then breath more
bother and more whatarcurss. Then no breath no bother but wor-
rawarrawurms. And Shim shallave shome.

As Rigagnolina to Mountagnone, what she meaned he could
not can. All she meaned was golten sylvup, all she meaned was
some Knight's ploung jamn. It's driving her dafft like he's so
dumnb. If he'd lonely talk instead of only gawk as thought yate-
man hat stuck hits stick althrough his spokes and if he woold nut
wolly so! Hee. Speak, sweety bird! Mitzymitzy! Though I did
ate tough turf I'm not the bogdoxy.

— Have you monbreamstone?
— No.
— Or Hellfeuersteyn?
— No.
— Or Van Diemen's coral pearl?
— No.
He has lost.

Off to clutch, Glugg! Forwhat! Shape your reres, Glugg!
Foreweal! Ring we round, Chuff! Fairwell! Chuffchuff's inners
even. All's rice with their whorl!

Yet, ah tears, who can her mater be? She's promised he'd eye
her. To try up her pretti. But now it's so longed and so fared and
so forth. Jerry for jauntings. Alabye! Fled.

The flossies all and mossies all they drooped upon her draped
brimfall. The bowknots, the showlots, they wilted into woeblots.

The pearlagraph, the pearlagraph, knew whitchly whether to weep
or laugh. For always down in Carolinas lovely Dinahs vaunt their
view.

Poor Isa sits a glooming so gleaming in the gloaming; the tin-
celles a touch tarnished wind no lovelinoise awound her swan's.
Hey, lass! Woefear gleam she so glooming, this pooripathete I
solde? Her beauman's gone of a cool. Be good enough to symper-
ise. If he's at anywhere she's therefor to join him. If it's to nowhere she's going to too. Buf if he'll go to be a son to France's
she'll stay daughter of Clare. Bring tansy, throw myrtle, strew
rue, rue, rue. She is fading out like Journee's clothes so you can't
see her now. Still we know how Day the Dyer works, in dims
and deeps and dusks and darks. And among the shades that Eve's
now wearing she'll meet anew fiancy, tryst and trow. Mammy
was, Mimmy is, Minuscoline's to be. In the Dee dips a dame and
the dame desires a demselle but the demselle dresses dolly and
the dolly does a dulcydamble. The same renew. For though
she's unmerried she'll after truss up and help that hussyband how
to hop. Hip it and trip it and chirrub and sing. Lord Chuffy's sky
sheraph and Glugg's got to swing.

So and so, toe by toe, to and fro they go round, for they are the
ingelles, scattering nods as girls who may, for they are an angel's
garland.

Catchmire stockings, libertyed garters, shoddyshoes, quicked
out with selver. Pennyfair caps on pinnyfore frocks and a ring on
her fomefing finger. And they leap so looply, looply, as they link
to light. And they look so loovely, loovelit, noosed in a nuptious
night. Withasly glints in. Andecoy glants out. They ramp it a
little, a lessle, a lissle. Then rompride round in rout.

Say them all but tell them apart, cadenzando coloratura! R is
Rubretta and A is Arancia, Y is for Yilla and N for greeneriN. B
is Boyblue with odalisque O while W waters the fleurettes of no-
vembrance. Though they're all but merely a schoolgirl yet these
way went they. I' th' view o' th'avignue dancing goes entrancing
roundly. Miss Oodles of Anems before the Luvium doeslike. So.
And then again doeslike. So. And miss Endles of Eons efter Dies

of Eirae doeslike. So. And then again doeslike. So. The many
wiles of Winsure.

The grocer's bawd she slips her hand in the haricot bag, the
lady in waiting sips her sup from the paraffin can, Mrs Wildhare
Quickdoctor helts her skelts up the casuaway the flasht instinct
she herds if a tinkle of tunder, the widow Megrievy she knits cats'
cradles, this bountiful actress leashes a harrier under her tongue,
and here's the girl who she's kneeled in coldfashion and she's told
her priest (spt!) she's pot on a chap (chp!) and this lass not least,
this rickissime woman, who she writes foot fortunes money times
over in the nursery dust with her capital thumb. Buzz. All run-
away sheep bound back bopeep, trailing their teenes behind
them. And these ways wend they. And those ways went they.
Winnie, Olive and Beatrice, Nelly and Ida, Amy and Rue. Here
they come back, all the gay pack, for they are the florals, from
foncey and pansey to papavere's blush, foresake-me-nought,
while there's leaf there's hope, with primtim's ruse and marry-
may's blossom, all the flowers of the ancelles' garden.

But vicereversing thereout from those palms of perfection to
anger arbour, treerack monatan, scroucely out of scout of ocean,
virid with woad, what tornaments of complementary rages rocked
the divlun from his punchpoll to his tummy's shentre as he dis-
plaid all the oathword science of his visible disgrace. He was
feeling so funny and floored for the cue, all over which girls as
he don't know whose hue. If goosseys gazious would but fain
smile him a smile he would be fondling a praise he ate some nice
bit of fluff. But no geste reveals the unconnouth. They're all
odds against him, the beasties. Scratch. Start.

He dove his head into Wat Murrey, gave Stewart Ryall a puck
on the plexus, wrestled a hurry-come-union with the Gillie Beg,
wiped all his sinses, martial and menial, out of Shrove Sundy
MacFearsome, excremuncted as freely as any frothblower into
MacIsaac, had a belting bout, chaste to chaste, with McAdoo
about nothing and, childhood's age being aye the shameleast, tel
a Tartaran tastarin toothsome tarrascone tourtoun, vestimentiv-
orous chlamydophagian, imbretellated himself for any time un-

tellable with what hung over to the Machonochie Middle from
the MacSiccaries of the Breeks. Home!

Allwhile, moush missuies from mungy monsie, preying in
his mind, son of Everallin, within himself, he swure. Macnoon
maggoty mag. Cross of a coppersmith bishop! He would split.
He do big squeal like holy Trichepatte. Seek hells where from
yank islanders the petriote's absolation. Mocknitza! Genik! He
take skiff come first dagrene day overwide tumbler, rough and
dark, till when bow of the shower show of the bower with three
shirts and a wind, pagoda permettant, crookolevante, the bruce,
the coriolano and the ignacio. From prudals to the secular but
from the cumman to the nowter. Byebye, Brassolis, I'm breaving!
Our war, Dully Gray! A conansdream of lodascircles, he here
schlucefinis. Gelchasser no more! Mischnary for the minestrary
to all the sems of Aram. Shimach, eon of Era. Mum's for's
maxim, ban's for's book and Dodgesome Dora for hedgehung
sheolmastress. And Unkel Silanse coach in diligence. Discon-
nection of the succeeding. He wholehog himself for carberry
banishment care of Pencylmania, Bretish Armerica, to melt Mrs.
Gloria of the Bunkers' Trust, recorporated, (prunty!) by meteo-
romancy and linguified heissrohgin, quit to hail a hurry laracor
and catch the Paname-Turricum and regain that absendee tarry
easty, his città immediata, by an alley and detour with farecard
awailable getrennty years. Right for Rovy the Roder. From the
safe side of distance! Libera, nostalgia! Beate Laurentie O'Tuli,
Euro pra nobis! Every monk his own cashel where every little
ligger is his own liogotenente with inclined jambs in full purview
to his pronaose and to the deretane at his reredoss. Fuisfinister,
fuyerescaper! He would, with the greatest of ease, before of
weighting midhook, by dear home trashold on the raging canal,
for othersites of Jorden, (heave a hevy, waterboy!) make one
of hissens with a knockonacow and a chow collegions and fire
off, gheol ghiornal, foull subustioned mullmud, his farced epistol
to the hibruws. From Cernilius slomtime prepositus of Toumaria
to the clutch in Anteach. Salvo! Ladigs and jointuremen! No more
turdenskaulds! Free leaves for ebribadies! All tinsammon in the

yord! With harm and aches till farther alters! Wild primates not stop him frem at rearing a writing in handy antics. Nom de plume! Gout strap Fenlanns! And send Jarge for Mary Inklenders. And daunt you logh if his vineshanky's schwemmy! For he is the general, make no mistake in he. He is General Jinglesome.

Go in for scribenery with the satiety of arthurs in S.P.Q.R.ish and inform to the old sniggering publicking press and its nation of sheepcopers about the whole plighty troth between them, malady of milady made melodi of malodi, she, the lalage of lyonesses, and him, her knave arrant. To Wildrose La Gilligan from Croppy Crowhore. For all within crystal range.

Ukalepe. Loathers' leave. Nemo in Patria. The Luncher Out. Skilly and Carubdish. A Wondering Wreck. From the Mermaids' Tavern. Bullyfamous. Naughtsycalves. Mother of Misery. Walpurgas Nackt.

Maleesh! He would bare to untired world of Leimunconnonnulstria (and what a strip poker globbtrottel they pairs would looks!) how wholefallows, his guffer, the sabbatarian (might faction split his beard!), he too had a great big oh in the megafundum of his tomashunders and how her Lettyshape, his gummer, that congealed sponsar, she had never cessed at waking malters among the jemassons since the cluft that meataxe delt her made her microchasm as gap as down low. So they fished in the kettle and fought free and if she bit his tailibout all hat tiffin for thea. He would jused sit it all write down just as he would jused set it up all writhefully rate in blotch and void, yielding to no man in hymns ignorance seeing how heartsilly sorey he was, owning to the condrition of his bikestool. And, reading off his fleshskin and writing with his quillbone, fillfull ninequires with it for his auditers, Caxton and Pollock, a most moraculous jeeremyhead sindbook for all the peoples, under the presidency of the suchess of sceaunonsceau, a hadtobe heldin, thoroughly enjoyed by many so meny on block at Boyrut season and for their account ottorly admired by her husband in sole intimacy, about whose told his innersense and the grusomehed's

yoeureeke of his spectrescope and why he was off colour and how
he was ambothed upon by the very spit of himself, first on the
cheekside by Michelangelo and, besouns thats, over on the owld
jowly side by Bill C. Babby, and the suburb's formule why they
provencials drollo eggspilled him out of his homety dometry nar-
rowedknee domum (osco de basco de pesco de bisco!) because
all his creature comfort was an omulette finas erbas in an ark finis
orbe and, no master how mustered, mind never mend, he could
neither swuck in nonneither swimp in the flood of cecialism and
the best and schortest way of blacking out a caughtalock of all
the sorrors of Sexton until he would accoster her coume il fou in
teto-dous as a wagoner would his mudheeldy wheesindonk at
their trist in Parisise after tourments of tosend years, bread cast
out on waters, making goods at mutuurity, Mondamoiseau of
Casanuova and Mademoisselle from Armentières. Neblonovi's
Nivonovio! Nobbio and Nuby in ennoviacion! Occitantitempoli!
He would si through severalls of sanctuaries maywhatmay might-
whomight so as to meet somewhere if produced on a demi panss-
sion for his whole lofetime, payment in goo to slee music and
poisonal comfany, following which, like Ipsey Secumbe, when he
fingon to foil the fluter, she could have all the g. s. M. she moo-
hooed after fore and rickwards to herslF, including science of
sonorous silence, while he, being brung up on soul butter, have
recourse of course to poetry. With tears for his coronaichon,
such as engines weep. Was liffe worth leaving? Nej!

    Tholedoth, treetrene! Zokrahsing, stone! Arty, reminiscen-
sitive, at bandstand finale on grand carriero, dreaming largesse
of lifesighs over early lived offs—all old Sators of the Sowsceptre
highly nutritius family histrionic, genitricksling with Avus and
Avia, that simple pair, and descendant down on veloutypads by a
vuncular process to Nurus and Noverca, those notorious nepotists,
circumpictified in their sobrine census, patriss all of them by the
glos on their germane faces and their socerine eyes like transparents
of vitricus, patruuts to a man, the archimade levirs of his ekonome
world. Remember thee, castle throwen? Ones propsperups treed,
now stohong baroque. And oil paint use a pumme if yell trace

me there title to where was a hovel not a havel (the first rattle of
his juniverse) with a tingtumtingling and a next, next and next
(gin a paddy? got a petty? gussies, gif it ope?), while itch ish
shome.

> — *My God, alas, that dear olt tumtum home*
> *Whereof in youthfood port I preyed*
> *Amook the verdigrassy convict vallsall dazes.*
> *And clottered for amourmeant in thy boosome shede!*

His mouthfull of ecstasy (for Shing-Yung-Thing in Shina from
Yoruyume across the Timor Sea), herepong (maladventure!) shot
pinging up through the errorooth of his wisdom (who thought
him a Fonar all, feastking of shellies by googling Lovvey, regally
freytherem, eagelly plumed, and wasbut gumboil owrithy prods
wretched some horsery megee plods coffin acid odarkery pluds
dense floppens mugurdy) as thought it had been zawhen intwo.
Wholly sanguish blooded up disconvulsing the fixtures of his
fizz. Apang which his tempory chewer med him a crazy chump
of a Haveajube Sillayass. Joshua Croesus, son of Nunn! Though
he shall live for millions of years a life of billions of years, from
their roseaced glows to their violast lustres, he shall not forget
that pucking Pugases. Holihowlsballs and bloody acres! Like
gnawthing unheardth!

But, by Jove Chronides, Seed of Summ, after at he had bate
his breastplates for, forforget, forforgetting his birdsplace, it was
soon that, that he, that he rehad himself. By a prayer? No, that
comes later. By contrite attrition? Nay, that we passed. Mid
esercizism? So is richt.

And it was so. And Malthos Moramor resumed his soul. With:
Go Ferchios off to Allad out of this! An oldsteinsong. He threwed
his fit up to his aers, rolled his poligone eyes, snivelled from his
snose and blew the guff out of his hornypipe. The hopjoimt jerk
of a ladle broom jig that he learned in locofoco when a redhot
turnspite he. Under reign of old Roastin the Bowl Ratskillers,
readyos! Why was that man for he's doin her wrong! Lookery
looks, how he's knots in his entrails! Mookery mooks, it's a
grippe of his gripes. Seekeryseeks, why his biting he's head off?

Cokerycokes, it's his spurt of coal. And may his tarpitch dilute
not give him chromitis! For the mauwe that blinks you blank is
mostly Carbo. Where the inflammabilis might pursuive his com-
burenda with a pure flame and a true flame and a flame all too-
gasser, soot. The worst is over. Wait! And the dubuny Mag may
gang to preesses. With Dinny Finneen, me canty, ho! In the lost
of the gleamens. Sousymoust. For he would himself deal a treatment as might be trusted in anticipation of his inculmination unto
fructification for the major operation. When (pip!) a message
interfering intermitting interskips from them (pet!) on herzian
waves, (call her venicey names! call her a stell!) a butterfly from
her zipclasped handbag, a wounded dove astarted from, escaping
out her forecotes. Isle wail for yews, O doherlynt. The poetesser
And around its scorched cap she has twilled a twine of flame to
let the laitiest know she's marrid. And pim it goes backballed. Tot
burns it so leste. A claribel cumbeck to errind. Hers before his
even, posted ere penned. He's your change, thinkyou methim.
Go daft noon madden, mind the step. Please stoop O to please.
Stop. What saying? I have soreunder from to him now, dearmate ashore, so, so compleasely till I can get redressed, which
means the end of my stays in the languish of Tintangle. Is you
zealous of mes, brother? Did you boo moiety lowd? You sup-
poted to be the on conditiously rejected? Satanly, lade! Can that
sobstuff, whingeywilly! Stop up, mavrone, and sit in my lap,
Pepette, though I'd much rather not. Like things are m. ds. is all
in vincibles. Decoded.

Now a run for his money! Now a dash to her dot! Old cocker,
young crowy, sifadda, sosson. A bran new, speedhount, out-
stripperous on the wind. Like a waft to wingweary one or a sos
to a coastguard. For directly with his whoop, stop and an upa-
lepsy didando a tishy, in appreciable less time than it takes a
glaciator to submerger an Atlangthis, was he again, agob, before
the trembly ones, a spark's gap off, doubledasguesched, gotten
orlop in a simplasailormade and shaking the storm out of his
hiccups. The smartest vessel you could find would elazilee him
on her knee as her lucky for the Rio Grande. He's a pigtail tarr

and if he hadn't got it toothick he'd a telltale tall of his pitcher on a wall with his photure in the papers for cutting moutonlegs and capers, letting on he'd jest be japers and his tail cooked up.

Goal! It's one by its length.

Angelinas, hide from light those hues that your sin beau may bring to light! Though down to your dowerstrip he's bent to knee he maun't know ledgings here.

For a haunting way will go and you need not make your mow. Find the frenge for frocks and translace it into shocks of such as touch with show and show.

He is guessing at hers for all he is worse, the seagoer. Hark to his wily geeses goosling by, and playfair, lady. And note that they who will for exile say can for dog while them that won't leave ingle end says now for know.

For he faulters how he hates to trouble them without.

But leaving codhead's mitre and the heron's plumes sinistrant to the server of servants and rex of regums and making a bolderdash for lubberty of speech he asks not have you seen a match being struck nor is this powder mine but, letting punplays pass to ernest:

— Haps thee jaoneofergs?
— Nao.
— Haps thee mayjaunties?
— Naohao.
— Haps thee per causes nunsibellies?
— Naohaohao.
— Asky, asky, asky! Gau on! Micaco! Get!

Ping an ping nwan ping pwan pong.

And he did a get, their anayance, and slink his hook away, aleguere come alaguerre, like a chimista inchamisas, whom the harricana hurries and hots foots, zingo, zango, segur. To hoots of utskut, urqurd, jamal, qum, yallah, yawash, yak! For he could ciappacioppachew upon a skarp snakk of pure undefallen engelsk, melanmoon or tartatortoise, tsukisaki or soppisuppon, as raskly and as baskly as your cheesechalk cow cudd spanich. Makoto! Whagta kriowday! Gelagala nausy is. Yet right divining do not

was. Hovobovo hafogate hokidimatzi in kamicha! He had his
sperrits all foulen on him; to vet, most griposly, he was bedizzled
and debuzzled; he had his tristiest cabaleer on; and looked like
bruddy Hal. A shelling a cockshy and be donkey shot at? Or a
peso besant to join the armada?

But, Sin Showpanza, could anybroddy which walked this world
with eyes whiteopen have looked twinsomer than the kerl he left
behind him? Candidatus, viridosus, aurilucens, sinelab? Of all
the green heroes everwore coton breiches, the whitemost, the
goldenest! How he stud theirs with himselfs mookst kevinly, and
that anterevolitionary, the churchman childfather from tonsor's
tuft to almonder's toes, a haggiography in duotrigesumy, son
soptimost of sire sixtusks, of Mayaqueenies sign osure, hevnly
buddhy time, inwreathed of his near cissies, a mickly dazzly eely
oily with looiscurrals, a soulnetzer by zvesdals priestessd, their
trail the tractive, and dem dandypanies knows de play of de eyelids, with his gamecox spurts and his smile likequid glue (the
suessiest sourir ever weanling wore), whiles his host of spritties,
lusspillerindernees, they went peahenning a ripidarapidarpad
around him, pilgrim prinkips, kerilour kevinour, in neuchoristic
congressulations, quite purringly excited rpdrpd, allauding to
him by all the licknames in the litany with the terms in which
no little dulsy nayer ever thinks about implying except to her
future's year and sending him perfume most praypuffs to setis-
fire more then to teasim (shllwe help, now you've massmuled,
you t'rigolect a bit? yismik? yimissy?) that he, the finehued, the
fairhailed, the farahead, might bouchesave unto each but everyone, asfar as safras durst assune, the havemercyonhurs of his
kissier licence. Meanings: Andure the enjurious till imbetther rer.
We know you like Latin with essies impures, (and your liber as
they sea) we certney like gurgles love the nargleygargley so, arrah-
beejee, tell that old frankay boyuk to bellows upthe tombucky in
his tumtum argan and give us a gust of his gushy old. Goof!

Hymnumber twentynine. O, the singing! Happy little girly-
cums to have adolphted such an Adelphus! O, the swinginging
hopops so goholden! They've come to chant en chor. They say

their salat, the madiens' prayer to the messiager of His Nabis, prostitating their selfs eachwise and combinedly. Fateha, fold the hands. Be it honoured, bow the head. May thine evings e'en be blossful! Even of bliss! As we so hope for ablution. For the sake of the farbung and of the scent and of the holiodrops. Amems.

A pause. Their orison arises misquewhite as Osman glory, ebbing wasteward, leaves to the soul of light its fading silence (allahlah lahlah lah!), a turquewashed sky. Then:

— Xanthos! Xanthos! Xanthos! We thank to thine, mighty innocent, that diddest bring it off fuitefuite. Should in ofter years it became about you will after desk jobduty becoming a bank midland mansioner we and I shall reside with our obeisant servants among Burke's mobility at La Roseraie, Ailesbury Road. Red bricks are all hellishly good values if you trust to the roster of ads but we'll save up ourselves and nab what's nicest and boskiest of timber trees in the nebohood. Oncaill's plot. Luccombe oaks, Turkish hazels, Greek firs, incense palm edcedras. The hypsometers of Mount Anville is held to be dying out of arthataxis but, praise send Larix U' Thule, the wych elm of Manelagh is still flourishing in the open, because its native of our nature and the seeds was sent by Fortune. We'll have our private palypeachum pillarposterns for lovesick letterines fondly affianxed to our front railings and swings, hammocks, tighttaught balletlines, accomodationnooks and prismic bathboites, to make Envyeyes mouth water and wonder when they binocular us from their embrassured windows in our garden rare. Fyat-Fyat shall be our number on the autokinaton and Chubby in his Chuffs oursforownly chuffeur. T will be waiting for uns as I sold U at the first antries. Our cousin gourmand, Percy, the pup, will denounce the sniffnomers of all callers where among our Seemyease Sister, Tabitha, the ninelived, will extend to the full her hearthy welcome. While the turf and twigs they tattle. Tintin tintin. Lady Marmela Shortbred will walk in for supper with her marchpane switch on, her necklace of almonds and her poirette Sundae dress with bracelets of honey and her cochineal hose with the caramel dancings, the briskly best from Bootiestown, and her suckingstaff of ivory-mint. You mustn't miss it or you'll be sorry. Charmeuses chloes, glycering juwells, lydialight fans and puffumed cynarettes. And the Prince Le Monade has been graciously pleased. His six chocolate pages will run bugling before him and Cococream toddle after with his sticksword in a pink cushion. We think His Sparkling Headiness ought to know Lady Marmela. Luisome his for lissome hers. He's not going to Cork till Cantalamesse or mayhope till Rose Easter or Saint Tibble's Day. So Niomon knows. The Fomor's in his Fin, the Momor's her and hin. A paaralone! A paaralone! And Dublin's all adin. We'll sing a song of Singlemonth and you'll too and you'll. Here are notes. There's the key. One two three. Chours! So come on, ye wealthy gentrymen wibfrufrocksfull of fun! Thin thin! Thin thin! Thej olly and thel ively, thou billy with thee coo, for to jog a jig of a crispness nice and sing a missal too. Hip champouree! Hiphip champouree! O you longtailed blackman, polk it up behind me! Hip champouree! Hiphip champouree! And, jessies, push the pumkik round. Anneliuia!

Since the days of Roamaloose and Rehmoose the pavanos have been strident through their struts of Chapelldiseut, the vaulsies have meed and youdled through the purly ooze of Ballybough, many a mismy cloudy has tripped taintily along that hercourt strayed reelway and the rigadoons have held ragtimed revels on the platauplain of Grangegorman; and, though since then sterlings and guineas have been replaced by brooks and lions and some progress has been made on stilts and the races have come and gone and Thyme, that chef of seasoners, has made his usual astewte use of endadjustables and whatnot willbe isnor was, those danceadeils and cancanzanies have come stimmering down for our begayment through the bedeafdom of po's taeorns, the obcecity of pa's teapucs, as lithe and limbfree limber as when momie mummed at ma.

Just so stylled with the nattes are their flowerheads now and each of all has a lovestalk onto herself and the tot of all the tits of their understamens is as open as he can posably she and is tournesoled straightcut or sidewaist, accourdant to the coursets of

things feminite, towooerds him in heliolatry, so they may catch-
cup in their calyzettes, alls they go troping, those parryshoots
from his muscalone pistil, for he can eyespy through them, to
their selfcolours, nevertheleast their tissue peepers, (meaning
Mullabury mesh, the time of appling flowers, a guarded figure
of speech, a variety of perfume, a bridawl, seamist inso one) as
leichtly as see saw (O my goodmiss! O my greatmess! O my
prizelestly preshoes!) while, dewyfully as dimb dumbelles, all
alisten to his elixir. Lovelyt!

And they said to him:

— Enchainted, dear sweet Stainusless, young confessor, dearer
dearest, we herehear, aboutobloss, O coelicola, thee salutamt.
Pattern of our unschoold, pageantmaster, deliverer of softmis-
sives, round the world in forty mails, bag, belt and balmybeam,
our barnaboy, our chepachap, with that pampipe in your put-
away, gab borab, when you will be after doing all your sight-
seeing and soundhearing and smellsniffing and tastytasting and
tenderumstouchings in all Daneygaul, send us, your adorables,
thou overblaseed, a wise and letters play of all you can ceive,
chief celtech chappy, from your holy post now you hast as-
certained ceremonially our names. Unclean you art not. Outcaste
thou are not. Leperstower, the karman's loki, has not blanched
at our pollution and your intercourse at ninety legsplits does not
defile. Untouchable is not the scarecrown is on you. You are
pure. You are pure. You are in your puerity. You have not
brought stinking members into the house of Amanti. Elleb Inam,
Titep Notep, we name them to the Hall of Honour. Your head
has been touched by the god Enel-Rah and your face has been
brightened by the goddess Aruc-Ituc. Return, sainted youngling,
and walk once more among us! The rains of Demani are masikal
as of yere. And Baraza is all aflower. Siker of calmy days. As
shiver as shower can be. Our breed and better class is in brood
and bitter pass. Labbeycliath longs. But we're counting on the
cluck. The Great Cackler comes again. Sweetstaker, Abel lord of
all our haloease, we (to be slightly more femmiliar perhips than is
slickly more then nacessory), toutes philomelas as well as mag-

delenes, were drawpairs with two pinmarks, BVD and BVD dot,
so want lotteries of ticklets posthastem (you appreciate?) so as to
be very dainty, if an isaspell, and so as to be verily dandydainty,
if an ishibilley, of and on, to and for, by and with, from you.
Let the hitback hurry his wayward ere the missive has time to
take herself off, 'twill be o'erthemore willfully intomeet if the
coming offence can send our shudders before. We feem to have
being elfewhere as tho' th' had pafs'd in our fufpens. Next
to our shrinking selves we love sensitivas best. For they are
the Angèles. Brick, fauve, jonquil, sprig, fleet, nocturne, smiling
bruise. For they are an Angèle's garment. We will be constant
(what a word!) and bless the day, for whole hours too, yes, for
sold long syne as we shall be heing in our created being of ours
elvishness, the day you befell, you dreadful temptation! Now
promisus as at our requisted you will remain ignorant of all what
you hear and, though if whilst disrobing to the edge of risk, (the
bisifings in idolhours that satinfines tootoo!) draw a veil till we
next time! You don't want to peach but bejimboed if ye do.
Perhelps. We ernst too may. How many months or how many
years till the myriadth and first become! Bashfulness be tupped!
May he colp, may he colp her, may he mixandmass colp her!
Talk with a hare and you wake of a tartars. That's mus. Says the
Law. List! Kicky Lacey, the pervergined, and Bianca Mutantini,
her conversa, drew their fools longth finnishfurst, Herzog van
Vellentam, but me and meother ravin, my coosine of mine, have
mour good three chancers, weothers, after Bohnaparts. The
mything smile of me, my wholesole assumption, shes nowt me-
without as weam twin herewithin, that I love like myselfish, like
smithereens robinsongs, like juneses nutslost, like the blue of the
sky if I stoop for to spy's between my whiteyoumightcallimbs.
How their duel makes their trielI Eer's wax for Sur Soord, dong-
dong bollets for the iris riflers, queemswellth of coocome in their
combs for the jennyjos. Caro caressimus! Honey swarns where
mellisponds. Will bee all buzzy one another minnies for the mere
effect that you are so fuld of pollen yourself. Teomeo. Daurdour.
We feel unspeechably thoughtless over it all here in Gizzygazelle

Tark's bimboowood so pleasekindly communicake with the original sinse we are only yearning as yet how to burgeon. It's meant milliems of centiments deadlost or mislaid on them but, master of snakes, we can sloughchange in the nip of a napple solongas we can allsee for deedsetton your quick. By the hook in your look we're eyed for aye were you begging the questuan with your lutean bowl round Monkmesserag. And whenever you're tingling in your trout we're sure to be tangled in our tice-ments. It's game, ma chère, be off with your shepherdress on! Up-some cauda! Behose our handmades for the lured! To these nunce we are but yours in ammatures yet well come that day we shall ope to be ores. Then shalt thou see, seeing, the sight. No more hoax-ites! Nay more gifting in mennage! A her's fancy for a his friend and then that fellow yours after this follow ours. Vania, Vania Vaniorum, Domne Vanias!

Hightime is ups be it down into outs according! When there shall be foods for vermin as full as feeds for the fett, eat on earth as there's hot in oven. When every Klitty of a scolderymeid shall hold every yardscullion's right to stimm her uprecht for whimso-ever, whether on privates, whather in publics. And when all us romance catholeens shall have ones for all amanseprated. And the world is maidfree. Methanks. So much for His Meignysthy man! And all his bigyttens. So till Coquette to tell Cockotte to teach Connie Curley to touch Cattie Hayre and tip Carminia to tap La Chérie though where the diggings he dwellst amongst us here's nobody knows save Mary. Whyfor we go ringing hands in hands in gyrogyrorondo.

These bright elects, consentconsorted, they were waltzing up their willside with their princesome handsome angeline chiuff while in those wherebus there wont bears way (mearing un-known, a place where pigeons carry fire to seethe viands, a miry hill, belge end sore footh) oaths and screams and bawley groans with a belchybubhub and a hellabelow bedemmed and bediabbled the arimaining lucisphere. Helldsdend, whelldselse! Lonedom's breach lay foulend up uncouth not be broched by punns and reedles. Yet the ring gayed rund rorosily with a drat for a brat

you. Yasha Yash ate sassage and mash. So he found he bash, poor
Yasha Yash. And you wonna make one of our micknick party.
No honaryhuest on our sposhialiste. For poor Glugger was dazed
and late in his crave, ay he, laid in his grave.

But low, boys low, he rises, shrivering, with his spittyful eyes
and his whoozebecome woice. Ephthah! Cisamis! Examen of
conscience scruples now he to the best of his memory schemado.
Nu mere for ever siden on the stolen. With his tumescinquinance
in the thight of his tumstull. No more singing all the dags in
his sengaggeng. Experssly at hand counterhand. Trinitatis kink
had mudded his dome, peccat and pent fore, pree. Hymserf,
munchaowl, maden, born of thug tribe into brood blackmail, dooly
redecant allbigenesis henesies. He, by bletchendmacht of the golls,
proforhim penance and come off enternatural. He, selfsufficiencer,
eggscumuddher-in-chaff sporticolorissimo, what though the
duthsthrows in his lavabad eyes, maketomake polentay rossum,
(Good savours queen with the stem of swuith Aftreck! Fit for
king of Zundas) out of bianconies, hiking ahake like any nudge-
meroughgorude all over Terracuta. No more throw acids, face all
lovabilities, appeal for the union and play for tirnitys. He, praise
Saint Calembaurnus, make clean breastsack of goody girl now as
ever drank milksoep from a spoen, weedhearted boy of potter and
mudder, chip of old Flinn the Flinter, twig of the hider that tanned
him. He go calaboosh all same he tell him out. Teufleuf man he
strip him all mussymussy calico blong him all same he tell him all
out how he make what name. He, through wolkenic connection,
relation belong this remarklable moliman, Anaks Andrum, parley-
glutton pure blood Jebusite, centy procent Erserum spoking.
Drugmallt storehuse. Intrance on back. Most open on the lay-
days. He, A. A., in peachskin shantungs, possible, sooth to say,
notwithstanding far former guiles and he gaining fish considerable, by saving grace after avalunch, to look most prophitable
out of smily skibluh eye. He repeat of him as pious alios cos he
ast for shave and haircut people said he'd shape of hegoat where
he just was sheep of herrgott with his tile togged. Top. Not true
what chronicles is bringing his portemanteau priamed full potato-

wards. Big dumm crumm digaditchies say short again akter, even
while lossassinated by summan, he coaxyorum a pennysilvers
offarings bloadonages with candid zuckers on Spinshesses Walk
in presents to lilithe maidinettes for at bloo his noose for him
with pruriest pollygameous inatentions, he having that pecuni-
arity ailmint spectacularly in heather cliff emurgency on gale
days because souffrant chronic from a plentitude of house torts.
Collosul rhodomantic not wert one bronze lie Scholarina say as
he, greyed vike cuddlepuller walk in her sleep his pig indicks
weg femtyfem funts. Of so little is her timentrousnest great for
greeting his immensesness. Sutt soonas sett they were, her uyes
as his auroholes. Kaledvalch! How could one classically? One
could naught critically. Ininest lightingshaft only for lovalit
smugpipe, his Mistress Mereshame, of cupric tresses, the form-
white foaminine, the ambersandalled, after Aasdocktor Talop's
onamuttony legture. A mish, holy balm of seinsed myrries, he is
as good as a mountain and everybody what is found of his gients
he knew Meistral Wikingson, furframed Noordwogen's kampf-
ten, with complexion of blushing dolomite fanned by ozeone
brisees, what naver saw his bedshead farrer and nuver met his
swigamore, have his ignomen from prima signation of being
Master Milchku, queerest man in the benighted queendom, and,
adcraft aidant, how he found the kids. Other accuse him as
lochkneeghed forsunkener, dope in stockknob, all ameltingmoult
after rhomatism, purely simply tammy ratkins. The kurds of
Copt on the berberutters and their bedaweens! Even was Shes
whole begeds off before all his nahars in the koldbethizzdryel. No
gudth! Not one zouz! They whiteliveried ragsups, two Whales of
the Sea of Deceit, they bloodiblabstard shooters, three Drome-
daries of the Sands of Calumdonia. As is note worthies to shock
his hind! Ur greeft on them! Such askors and their ruperts they
are putting in for more osghirs is alse false liarnels. The frocken-
halted victims! Whore affirm is agains sempry Lotta Karssens.
They would lick their lenses before they would negatise a jom
petter from his sodalites. In his contrary and on reality, which
Bishop Babwith bares to his whitness in his *Just a Fication of*

Villumses, this Mr. Heer Assassor Neelson, of sorestate hearing,
diseased, formarly with Adenoiks, den feed all lighty, laxtleap
great change of retiring family buckler, highly accurect in his
everythinks, from tencents coupoll to bargain basement, live with
howthold of nummer seven, wideawake, woundabout, wokin-
betts, weeklings, in black velvet on geolgian mission senest mangy
years his rear in the lane pictures, blanking same with autonaut
and annexes and got a daarlingt babyboy bucktooth, the thick of
a gobstick, coming on ever so nerses nursely gracies to goodess,
at 81. That why all parks up excited about his gunnfodder. That
why ecrazyaztecs and the crime ministers preaching him mornings and makes a power of spoon vittles out of his praverbs. That
why he, persona erecta, glycorawman arseniful femorniser, for
a trial by julias, in celestial sunhat, with two purses agitatating
his theopot with wokklebout shake, rather incoherend, from one
18 to one 18 biss, young shy gay youngs. Sympoly far infusing
up pritty tipidities to lock up their rhainodaisies and be nice
and twainty in the shade. Old grand tuttut toucher up of young
poetographies and he turn aroundabrupth red altfrumpishly like
hear samhar tionnor falls some make one noise. It's his last lap,
Gigantic, fare him weal! Revelation! A fact. True bill. By a jury
of matrons. Hump for humbleness, dump for dirts. And, to make
a long stoney badder and a whorly show a parfect sight, his Thing
went the wholyway retup Suffrogate Strate.

Helpmeat too, contrasta toga, his fiery goosemother, laotsey
taotsey, woman who did, he tell princes of the age about. You
sound on me, judges! Suppose we brisken up. Kings! Meet the
Mem, Avenlith, all viviparous out of couple of lizards. She just as
fenny as he is fulgar. How laat soever her latest still her sawlogs
come up all standing. Psing a psalm of psexpeans, apocryphul of
rhyme. His cheekmole of allaph foriverever her allinall and his
Kuran never teachit her the be the owner of thyself. So she not
swop her eckcot hjem for Howarden's Castle, Englandwales. But
be the alleance of iern on his flamen vestacoat, the fibule of brooch-
bronze to his wintermantle of pointefox. Who not knows she, the
Madame Cooley-Couley, spawife to laird of manna, when first

come into the pictures more as hundreads elskerelks' yahrds of
annams call away, factory fresh and fiuming at the mouth, wronged
by Hwemwednoget (magrathmagreeth, he takable a rap for that
early party) and whenceforward Ani Mama and her fiertey
bustles terrified of gmere gnomes of gmountains and furibound
to be back in her mytinbeddy? Schi schi, she feightened allsouls
at pignpugn and gets a pan in her stummi from the pialabellars
in their pur war. Yet jackticktating all around her about his poor-
liness due to pannellism and grime for that he harboured her when
feme sole, her zoravarn lhorde and givnergenral, and led her in
antient consort ruhm and bound her durant coverture so as she
could not steal from him, oz her or damman, so as if ever she's
beleaved by checkenbrooth death since both was parties to the
feed it's Hetman MacCumhal foots the funeral. Mealwhile she
nutre him jacent from her elmer's almsdish, giantar and tschaina
as sieme as bibrondas with Foli Signur's tinner roumanschy to
fishle the ladwigs out of his lugwags, like a skittering kitty
skattering hayels, when his favourites were all beruffled on him
and her own undesirables justickulating, it was such a blowick
day. Winden wanden wild like wenchen wenden wanton. The
why if he but would bite and plug his baccypipes and renownse
the devlins in all their pumbs and kip the streelwarkers out of
the plague and nettleses milk from sickling the honeycoombe
and kop Ulo Bubo selling foulty treepes, she would make massa
dinars with her savuneer dealinsh and delicate her nutbrown
glory cloack to Mayde Berenice and hang herself in Ostmanns-
town Saint Megan's and make no more mulierage before ma-
hatmas or moslemans, but would ondulate her shookerloft hat
from Alpoleary with a viv baselgia and a clamast apotria like any
purple cardinal's princess or woman of the grave word to the
papal legate from the Vatucum, Monsaigneur Rabbinsohn Crucis,
with an ass of milg to his cowmate and chilterlings on account
of all he quaqueduxed for the hnor of Hrom and the nations
abhord him and wop mezzo scudo to Sant Pursy Orelli that gave
Luiz-Marios Josephs their loyal devouces to be offered up missas
for vowts for widders.

Hear, O worldwithout! Tiny tattling! Backwoods, be wary! Daintytrees, go dutch!

But who comes yond with pire on poletop? He who relights our spearing torch, the moon. Bring lolave branches to mud cabins and peace to the tents of Ceder, Neomenie! The feast of Tubbournigglers is at hand. Shopshup. Inisfail! Timple temple tells the bells. In syngagyng a sangasongue. For all in Ondslos-by. And, the hag they damename Coverfew hists from her lane. And haste, 'tis time for bairns ta hame. Chickchilds, comeho to roo. Comehome to roo, wee chickchilds doo, when the wild-worewolf's abroad. Ah, let's away and let's gay and let's stay chez where the log foyer's burning!

It darkles, (tinct, tint) all this our funnaminal world. Yon marshpond by ruodmark verge is visited by the tide. Alvemmarea! We are circumveiloped by obscuritads. Man and belves frieren. There is a wish on them to be not doing or anything. Or just for rugs. Zoo koud. Drr, deff, coal lay on and, pzz, call us pyrress! Ha. Where is our highly honourworthy salutable spouse-founderess? The foolish one of the family is within. Haha. Huzoor, where's he? At house, to's pitty. With Nancy Hands. Tsheetshee. Hound through the maize has fled. What hou! Isegrim under lolling ears. Far wol! And wheaten bells bide breathless. All. The trail of Gill not yet is to be seen, rocksdrops, up benn, down dell, a craggy road for rambling. Nor yet through starland that silver sash. What era's o'ering? Lang gong late. Say long, scielo! Sillume, see lo! Selene, sail O! Amune! Ark!? Noh?! Nought stirs in spinney. The swayful pathways of the dragonfly spider stay still in reedery. Quiet takes back her folded fields. Tranquille thanks. Adew. In deerhaven, imbraced, alleged, injoynted and unlatched, the birds, tommelise too, quail silent. ii. Luathan? Nuathan! Was avond ere a while. Now conticinium. As Lord the Laohun is sheutseuyes. The time of lying together will come and the wildering of the nicht till cockeedoodle aubens Aurore. Panther monster. Send leabarrow loads amorrow. While loevdom shleeps. Elenfant has siang his triump, *Great is Eliphas Magis-trodontos* and after kneeprayer pious for behemuth and mahamoth

will rest him from tusker toils. Salamsalaim. Rhinohorn isnoutso
pigfellow but him ist gonz wurst. Kikikuki. Hopopodorme. So-
beast! No chare of beagles, frantling of peacocks, no muzzing of
the camel, smuttering of apes. Lights, pageboy, lights! Brights
we'll be brights. With help of Hanoukan's lamp. When otter
leaps in outer parts then Yul remembers Mei. Her hung maid
mohns are bluming, look, to greet those loes on coast of amethyst;
arcglow's seafire siemens lure and wextward warnerforth's hooker-
crookers. And now with robby brerfox's fishy fable lissaned out,
the threads simwhat toran and knots in its antargumends, the
pesciolines in Liffeyetta's bowl have stopped squiggling about
Junoh and the whalk and feriaquintaism and pebble infinibility
and the poissission of the hoghly course. And if Lubbernabohore
laid his horker to the ribber, save the giregargoh and dabardin
going on in his mount of knowledge (munt), he would not hear
a flip flap in all Finnyland. Witchman, watch of your night? Es
voes, ez noes, nott voes, ges, noun. It goes. It does not go. Dark-
park's acoo with sucking loves. Rosimund's by her wishing well.
Soon tempt-in-twos will stroll at venture and hunt-by-threes strut
musketeering. Brace of girdles, brasse of beauys. With the width
of the way for jogjoy. Hulker's cieclest elbownunsense. Hold
hard! And his dithering dathering waltzers of. Stright! But meetings mate not as forsehn. Hesperons! And if you wand to Liv-
mouth, wenderer, while Jempson's weed decks Jacqueson's Island,
here lurks, bar hellpelhullpulthebell, none iron welcome. Bing.
Bong. Bangbong. Thunderation! You took with the mulligrubs
and we lack mulsum? No sirrebob! Great goodness, no! Were
you Marely quean of Scuts or but Chrestien the Last, (our duty
to you, chris! royalty, squat!) how matt your mark, though
luked your johl, here's dapplebellied mugs and troublebedded
rooms and sawdust strown in expectoration and for ratification by
specification of your information, Mr. Knight, tuntapster, buttles;
his alefru's up to his hip. And Watsy Lyke sees after all rinsings
and don't omiss Kate, homeswab homely, put in with the bricks.
A's the sign and one's the number. Where Chavvyout Chacer
calls the cup and Pouropourim stands astirrup. De oud huis bij

de kerkegaard. So who over comes ever for Whoopee Weeks
must put up with the Jug and Chambers.

But heed! Our thirty minutes war's alull. All's quiet on the
felled of Gorey. Between the starfort and the thornwood brass
castle flambs with mutton candles. Hushkah, a horn! Gadolmag-
tog! God es El? Housefather calls enthreateningly. From Bran-
denborgenthor. At Asa's arthre. In thundercloud periwig. With
lightning bug aflash from afinger. My souls and by jings, should
he work his jaw to give down the banks and hark from the tomb!
Ansighosa pokes in her potstill to souse at the sop be sodden
enow and to hear to all the bubbles besaying: the coming man, the
future woman, the food that is to build, what he with fifteen years
will do, the ring in her mouth of joyous guard, stars astir and
stirabout. A palashe for hirs, a saucy for hers and ladlelike spoons
for the wonner. But ein and twee were never worth three. So they
must have their final since he's on parole. Et la pau' Leonie has the
choice of her lives between Josephinus and Mario-Louis for who
is to wear the lily of Bohemey, Florestan, Thaddeus, Hardress or
Myles. And lead raptivity captive. Ready. Like a Finn at a fair.
Now for la bella. Icy-la-Belle.

The campus calls them. Ninan ninan, the gattling gan! Childs
will be wilds. 'Twastold. And vamp, vamp, vamp, the girls are
merchand. The horseshow magnete draws his field and don't the
fillyings fly? Educande of Sorrento, they newknow knowwell
their Vico's road. Arranked in their array and flocking for the
fray on that old orangeray, Dolly Brae. For these are not on
terms, they twain, bartrossers, since their baffle of Whatalose
when Adam Leftus and the devil took our hindmost, gegifting
her with his painapple, nor will not be atoned at all in fight to
no finish, that dark deed doer, this wellwilled wooer, Jerkoff and
Eatsoup, Yem or Yan, while felixed is who culpas does and harm's
worth healing and Brune is bad French for Jour d'Anno. Tiggers
and Tuggers they're all for tenzones. Bettlimbraves. For she must
walk out. And it must be with who. Teaseforhim. Toesforhim.
Tossforhim. Two. Else there is danger of. Solitude.

Postreintroducing Jeremy, the chastenot coulter, the flowing taal that brooks no brooking runs on to say how, as it was mutualiter foretold of him by a timekiller to his spacemaker, velos ambos and arubyat knychts, with their tales within wheels and stucks between spokes, on the hike from Elmstree to Stene and back, how, running awage with the use of reason (sics) and ramming amok at the brake of his voice (secs), his lasterhalft was set for getting the besterwhole of his yougendtougend, for control number thrice was operating the subliminal of his invaded personality. He nobit smorfi and go poltri and let all the tondo gang bola del ruffo. Barto no know him mor. Eat larto altruis with most perfect stranger.

Boo, you're through!

Hoo, I'm true!

Men, teacan a tea simmering, hamo mavrone kerry O?

Teapotty. Teapotty.

Kod knows. Anything ruind. Meetingless.

He wept indeiterum. With such a tooth he seemed to love his wee tart when abuy. Highly momourning he see the before him. Melained from nape to kneecap though vied from her girders up. Holy Santalto, cursing saint, sight most deletious to ross up the spyballs like exude of margary! And how him it heaviered that eyerim rust! An they bare falls witless against thee how slight becomes a hidden wound? Soldwoter he wash him all time bigfeller bruisy place blong him. He no want missies blong all boy other look bruisy place blong him. Hence. It will paineth the chastenot in that where of his whence he had loseth his once for every, even though mode grow moramor maenneritsch and the Tarara boom decay. Immaculacy, give but to drink to his shirt and all skirtaskortas must change her tunics. So warred he from first to last forebanned and betweenly a smuggler for lifer. Lift the blank ve veered as heil! Split the hvide and aye seize heaven! He knows for he's seen it in black and white through his eyetrompit trained upon jenny's and all that sort of thing which is dandymount to a clearobscure. Prettimaid tints may try their taunts: apple, bacchante, custard, dove, eskimo, feldgrau, hematite, isingglass, jet, kipper, lucile, mimosa, nut, oysterette, prune, quasimodo, royal, sago, tango, umber, vanilla, wisteria, xray, yesplease, zaza, philomel, theerose. What are they all by? Shee.

If you nude her in her prime, make sure you find her complementary or, on your very first occasion, by Angus Dagdasson and all his piccions, she'll prick you where you're proudest with her unsatt speagle eye. Look sharp, she's signalling from among the asters. Turn again, wistfultone, lode mere of Doubtlynn! Arise, Land-under-Wave! Clap your lingua to your pallet, drop your jowl with a joit, tambourine until your breath slides, pet a pout and it's out. Have you got me, Allysloper?

My top it was brought Achill's low, my middle I ope before you, my bottom's a vulser if ever there valsed and my whole the flower that stars the day and is solly well worth your pilger's fahrt. Where there's a hitch, a head of things, let henker's halter hang the halunkenend. For I see through your weapon. That cry's not Cucullus. And his eyelids are painted. If my tutor here is cut out for an oldeborre I'm Flo, shy of peeps, you know. But when he beetles backwards, ain't I fly? Pull the boughpee to see how we sleep. Bee Peep! Peepette! Would you like that lump of a tongue for lungeon, or this Turkey's delighter, hys hyphen mys? My bellyswain's a twalf whulerusspower though he knows as much how to man a wife as Dunckle Dalton of matching wools. Shake hands through the thicketloch. Sweet swanwater! My other is mouthfilled. This kissing wold's full of killing fellows kneeling voyantly to the cope of heaven. And somebody's coming, I feel for a fect. I've a seeklet to sell thee if old Deanns won't be threaspanning. When you'll next have the mind to retire to be wicked this is as dainty a way as any. Underwoods spells bushment's business. So if you sprig poplar you're bound to twig this. 'Twas my lord of Glendalough benedixed the gape for me that time at Long Entry, commanding the approaches to my intimast innermost. Look how they're browthered. Six thirteens at Blanche de Blanche's of 3 Behind Street and 2 Turnagain Lane. Awabeg is my callby, Magnus here's my Max, Wonder One's my cipher and Seven Sisters is my nighbrood. Radouga, Rab will ye na pick them in their pink of panties. You can colour up till you're prawn while I go squirt with any cockle. When here who adolls me infuxes sleep. But if this could see with its backsight he'd be the grand old greeneyed lobster. He's my first viewmarc since Valentine. Wink's the winning word.

Luck!

In the house of breathings lies that word, all fairness. The walls are of rubinen and the glittergates of elfinbone. The roof herof is of massicious jasper and a canopy of Tyrian awning rises and still descends to it. A grape cluster of lights hangs therebeneath and al the house is filled with the breathings of her fairness, the fairness of fondance and the fairness of milk and rhubarb and the fairness of roasted meats and uniomargrits and the fairness of promise with consonantia and avowals. There lies her word, you reder. The height herup exalts it and the lowness her down abaseth it. It vibroverberates upon the tegmen and prosplodes from pomaeria. A window, a hedge, a prong, a hand, an eye, a sign, a head and keep your other augur on her paypaypay. And you have it, old Sem, pat as ah be seated. And Suñny, my gander, he's coming to land her. The boy which she now adores. She dores. Oh backed von dem zug! Make weg for their tug!

With a ring ding dong, they raise clasped hands and advance more steps to retire to the saum. Curtsey one, curtsey two, with arms akimbo, devotees.

Irrelevance.

All sing:

— I rose up one maypole morning and saw in my glass how nobody loves me but you. Ugh. Ugh.

All point in the shem direction as if to shun.

— My name is Misha Misha but call me Toffey Tough. I mean Mettenchough. It was her, boy the boy that was loft in the larch. Ogh! Ogh!

Her reverence.

All laugh.

They pretend to helf while they simply shauted at him sauce to make hims prich. And ith ith noth cricquette, Sally Lums. Not by ever such a lot. Twentynines of bloomers geging een man

arose. Avis was there and trilled her about it. She's her sex, for
certain. So to celebrate the occasion:

— Willest thou rossy banders havind?

He simules to be tight in ribbings round his rumpffkorpff.

— Are you Swarthants that's hit on a shorn stile?

He makes semblant to be swiping their chimbleys.

— Can you ajew ajew fro' Sheidam?

He finges to be cutting up with a pair of sissers and to be buy-
tings of their maidens and spitting their heads into their facepails.
Spickspuk! Spoken.

So now be hushy, little pukers! Side here roohish, cleany fug-
lers! Grandicellies, all stay zitty! Adultereux, rest as befour! For
you've jollywelly dawdled all the day. When ye colf tantoncle's
hat then'll be largely temts for that. Yet's the time for being now,
now, now.

For a burning would is come to dance inane. Glamours hath
moidered's lieb and herefore Coldours must leap no more. Lack
breath must leap no more.

Lel lols for libelman libling his lore. Lolo Lolo liebermann you
loved to be leaving Libnius. Lift your right to your Liber Lord.
Link your left to your lass of liberty. Lala Lala, Leapermann,
your lep's but a loop to lee.

A fork of hazel o'er the field in vox the verveine virgins ode.
If you cross this rood as you roamed the rand I'm blessed but
you'd feel him a blasting rod. Behind, me, frees from evil smells!
Perdition stinks before us.

Aghatharept they fleurelly to Nebnos will and Rosocale. Twice
is he gone to quest of her, thrice is she now to him. So see we so
as seed we sow. And their prunktqueen kilt her kirtles up and
set out. And her troup came heeling, O. And what do you think
that pride was drest in! Voolykins' diamondinah's vestin. For ever
they scent where air she went. While all the fauns' flares widens
wild to see a floral's school.

Led by Lignifer, in four hops of the happiest, ach beth cac duff,
a marrer of the sward incoronate, the few fly the farbetween!
We haul minymony on that piebold nig. Will any dubble dabble

on the bay? Nor far jocubus? Nic for jay? Attilad! Attattilad! Get up, Goth's scourge on you! There's a visitation in your impluvium. Hun! Hun!

He stanth theirs mun in his natural, oblious autamnesically of his very proprium, (such is stockpot leaden, so did sonsepun crake) the wont to be wanton maid a will to be wise. Thrust from the light, apophotorejected, he spoors loves from her heats. He blinkth. But's wrath's the higher where those wreathe charity. For all of these have been thisworlders, time liquescing into state, pitiless age grows angelhood. Though, as he stehs, most anysing may befallhim from a song of a witch to the totter of Blackarss, given a fammished devil, a young sourceress and (eternal conjunction) the permission of overalls with the cuperation of nightshirt. If he spice east he seethes in sooth and if he pierce north he wilts in the waist. And what wonder with the murkery viceheid in the shade? The specks on his lapspan are his foul deed thougths, wishmarks of mad imogenation. Take they off! Make the off! But Funnylegs are leanly. A bimbamb bum! They vain would convert the to be hers in the word. Gush, they wooed! Gash, they're fair ripecherry!

As for she could shake him. An oaf, no more. Still he'd be good tutor two in his big armschair lerningstoel, and she be waxen in his hands. Turning up and fingering over the most dantellising peaches in the lingerous longerous book of the dark. Look at this passage about Galilleotto. I know it is difficult but when your goche I go dead. Turn now to this patch upon Smacchiavelluti. Soot allours, he's sure to spot it. 'Twas ever so in monitorology since Headmaster Adam became Eva Harte's toucher, in omnibus moribus et temporibus, with man's mischief in his mind whilst her pupils swimmed too heavenlies, let his be exaspirated, letters be blowed, I is a femaline person. O, of provocative gender. U unisingular case.

Which is why trumpers are mixed up in duels and here's B. Rohan meets N. Ohlan for the prize of a thou.

But listen to the mocking birde to micking barde making bared! We've heard it aye since songdom was gemurrmal. As he was

queering his shoolthers. So was I. And as I was cleansing my
fausties. So was he. And as way ware puffiing our blowbags.
Souwouyou.

Come, thrust! Go, parry! Dvoinabrathran, dare! The mad
long ramp of manchind's parlements, the learned lacklearning,
merciless as wonderful.

— Now may Saint Mowy of the Pleasant Grin be your ever-
glass and even prospect!

— Feeling dank.

Exchange, reverse.

— And may Saint Jerome of the Harlots' Curse make family
three of you which is much abedder!

— Grassy ass ago.

And each was wrought with his other. And his continence fell.
The bivitellines, Metellus and Ametallikos, her crown pretenders,
obscindgemeinded biekerers, vaying directiy, uruseye each oxes-
other, superfetated (never cleaner of lamps frowned fiercelier on
anointer of hinges), while their treegrown girls, king's game, if
he deign so, are in such transfusion just to know twigst timidy
twomeys, for gracious sake, who is artthoudux from whose
heterotropic, the sleepy or the glouch, for, shyly bawn and
showly nursured exceedingly nice girls can strike exceedingly
bad times unless so richtly chosen's by (what though of riches
he have none and hope dashes hope on his heart's horizon) to gar
their great moments greater. The thing is he must be put strait
on the spot, no mere waterstichystuff in a selfmade world that
you can't believe a word he's written in, not for pie, but one's
only owned by naturel rejection. Charley, you're my darwing.
So sing they sequent the assent of man. Till they go round if
they go roundagain before breakparts and all dismissed. They
keep. Step keep. Step. Stop. Who is Fleur? Where is Ange? Or
Gardoun?

Creedless, croonless hangs his haughty. There end no moe red
devil in the white of his eye. Braglodyte him do a katadupe. A con-
damn quondam jontom sick af a suckbut! He does not know how
his grandson's grandson's grandson's grandson will stammer up

in Peruvain for in the ersebest idiom I have done it equals I so
shall do. He dares not think why the grandmother of the grandmother of his grandmother's grandmother coughed Russky with
suchky husky accent since in the mouthart of the slove look at
me now means I once was otherwise. Nor that the mappamund
has been changing pattern as youth plays moves from street to
street since time and races were and wise ants hoarded and saute-
relles were spendthrifts, no thing making newthing wealthshow-
ever for a silly old Sol, healthytobedder and latewiser. Nor that the
turtling of a London's alderman is ladled out by the waggerful to
the regionals of pigmyland. His part should say in honour bound:
So help me symethew, sammarc, selluc and singin, I will stick to
you, by gum, no matter what, bite simbum, and in case of the
event coming off beforehand even so you was to release me for
the sake of the other cheap girl's baby's name plaster me but I
will pluckily well pull on the buckskin gloves. But Noodynaady's
actual ingrate tootle is of come into the garner mauve and thy
nice are stores of morning and buy me a bunch of iodines.

Evidentament he has failed as tiercely as the deuce before for
she is wearing none of the three. And quite as patently there is a
hole in the ballet trough which the rest fell out. Because to explain why the residue is, was, or will not be, according to the
eighth axiom, proceeded with, namely, since ever apart that gos-
san duad, so sure as their's a patch on a pomelo, this yam ham in
never live could, the shifting about of the lassies, the tug of love
of their lads ending with a great deal of merriment, hoots,
screams, scarf drill, cap fecking, ejaculations of aurinos, reecho-
able mirthpeals and general thumbtonosery (Myama's a yaung
yaung cauntry), one must recken with the sudden and gigant-
esquesque appearance unwithstandable as a general election in
Barnado's bearskin amongst the brawlmiddle of this village chil-
dergarten of the largely longsuffering laird of Lucanhof.

But, vrayedevraye Blankdeblank, god of all machineries and
tomestone of Barnstaple, by mortisection or vivisuture, splitten
up or recompounded, an isaac jacquemin mauromormo milesian,
how accountibus for him, moreblue?

Was he pitssched for an ensemple as certain have dognosed of
him against our seawall by Rurie, Thoath and Cleaver, those
three stout sweynhearts Orion of the Orgiasts, Meereschal Mac-
Muhun, the, Ipse dadden, product of the extremes giving quoti-
dients to our means, as might occur to anyone, your brutest
layaman with the princest champion in our archdeaconsy, or so
yclept from Clio's clippings, which the chroncher of chivalries
is sulpicious save he scan, for ancients link with presents as the
human chain extends, have done, do and will again as John, Polycarp and I renews eye-to-eye ayewitnessed and to Paddy Palmer,
while monks sell yew to archers or the water of the livvying
goes the way of all fish from Sara's drawhead the corralsome to
Isaac's the lauphed butt one, with her minnelisp extorreor to his
moanolothe inturned? So Perrichon with Bastienne or heavy
Humph with airy Nan Ricqueracqbrimbillyjicqueyjocqjolicass?
How sowesthow, *dullcisamica*? A and aa ab ad abu abiad. A
babbel men dub gulch of tears.

The mar of murmury mermers to the mind's ear, uncharted
rock, evasive weed. Only the caul knows his thousandfirst name,
Hocus Crocus, Esquilocus, Finnfinn the Faineant, how feel full
foes in furrinarr. Doth it not all come aft to you, puritysnooper,
in the way television opes longtimes ofter when Potollomuck
Sotyr or Sourdanapplous the Lollapaloosa? The charges are, you
will remember, the chances are, you won't bit it's old Joe, the
Java Jane, older even than Odam Costollo, and we are recurrently meeting em, par Mahun Mesme, in cycloannalism, from
space to space, time after time, in various phases of scripture as
in various poses of sepulture. Greets Godd, Groceries! Merodach!
Defend the King! Hoet of the rough throat attack but whose say
is soft but whose ee has a cute angle, he whose hut is a hissarlik
even as her hennin's aspire. And insodaintily she's a quine of selm
ashaker while as a murder of corpse when his magot's up he's
the best berrathon sanger in all the aisles of Skaldignavia. As who
shall hear. For now at last is Longabed going to be gone to, that
more than man, prince of Bunnicombe of wide roadsterds, the
herblord the gillyflowrets so fain fan to flatter about. Artho is the

name is on the hero, Capellisato, shoehanded slaughterer of the
shader of our leaves.

Attach him! Hold!

Yet stir thee, to clay, Tamor!

Why wilt thou erewaken him from his earth, O summonor-
other: he is weatherbitten from the dusts of ages? The hour of his
closing hies to hand; the tocsin that shall claxonise his ware-
abouts. If one who remembered his webgoods and tealofts were
to ask of a hooper for whose it was the storks were quitting
Aquileyria, this trundler would not wot; if other who joined faith
when his depth charge bombed our barrel spillway were to —!

Jehosophat, what doom is here! Rain ruth on them, sire. The
wing of Moykill cover him! The Bulljon Bossbrute quarantee
him! Calavera, caution! Slaves to Virtue, save his Veritotem!
Bearara Tolearis, *procul abeat*! The Ivorbonegorer of Danamara-
ca be, his Hector Protector! Woldomar with Vasa, peel your
peeps! And try to saviourise the nights of labour to the order of
our blooding worold! While Pliny the Younger writes to Pliny
the Elder his calamolumen of contumellas, what Aulus Gellius
picked on Micmacrobius and what Vitruvius pocketed from
Cassiodorus. Like we larnt from that Buke of Lukan in Dublin's
capital, Kongdam Coombe. Even if you are the kooper of the
winkel over measure never lost a licence. Nor a duckindonche
divulse from bath and breakfast. And for the honour of Alcohol
drop that you-know-what-I've-come-about-I-saw-your-act air.
Punch may be pottleproud but his Judy's a wife's wit better.

For the producer (Mr. John Baptister Vickar) caused a deep
abuliousness to descend upon the Father of Truants and, at a side
issue, pluterpromptly brought on the scene the cutletsized consort, foundling filly of fortyshilling fostertailor and shipman's
shopahoyden, weighing ten pebble ten, scaling five footsy five
and spanning thirtyseven inchettes round the good companions,
twentynine ditties round the wishful waistress, thirtyseven alsos
round the answer to everything, twentythree of the same round
each of the quis separabits, fourteen round the beginning of hap-
piness and nicely nine round her shoed for slender.

And eher you could pray mercy to goodness or help with your
hokey or mehokeypoo, Gallus's hen has collared her pullets.
That's where they have wreglias for. Their bone of contention,
flesh to their thorns, prest as Prestissima, makes off in a thinkling
(and not one hen only nor two hens neyther but every blessed
brigid came aclucking and aclacking), while, a rum a rum, the
ram of all harns, Bier, Wijn, Spirituosen for consumption on the
premises, advokaat withouten pleaders, Mas marrit, Pas poulit,
Ras ruddist of all, though flamifestouned from galantifloures, is
hued and cried of each's colour.

Home all go. Halome. Blare no more ramsblares, oddmund
barkes! And cease your fumings, kindalled bushies! And sherri-
goldies yeassymgnays; your wildeshaweshowe moves swiftly
sterneward! For here the holy language. Soons to come. To
pausse.

'Tis goed. Het best.

For they are now tearing, that is, teartoretorning. Too soon
are coming tasbooks and goody, hominy bread and bible bee,
with jaggery-yo to juju-jaw, Fine's French phrases from the
Grandmère des Grammaires and bothered parsenaps from the
Four Massores, Mattatias, Marusias, Lucanias, Jokinias, and what
happened to our eleven in thirtytwo antepostdating the Valgur
Eire and why is limbo where is he and what are the sound waves
saying ceased ere they all wayed wrong and Amnist anguished
axes Collis and where fishngaman fetched the mongafesh from
and whatfor paddybird notplease rancoon and why was Sindat
sitthing on him sitbom like a saildior, with what the doc did in the
doil, not to mention define the hydraulics of common salt and,
its denier crid of old provaunce, where G.P.O. is zentrum and
D.U.T.C. are radients write down by the frequency of the scores
and crores of your refractions the valuations in the pice of ding-
gyings on N.C.R. and S.C.R.

That little cloud, a nibulissa, still hangs isky. Singabed sulks
before slumber. Light at night has an alps on his druckhouse.
Thick head and thin butter or after you with me. Caspi, but
gueroligue stings the air. Gaylegs to riot of us! Gallocks to lafft.

What is amaid today todo? So angelland all weeping bin that Izzy most unhappy is. Fain Essie fie onhapje? laughs her stella's vispirine.

While, running about their ways, going and coming, now at rhimba rhomba, now in trippiza trappaza, pleating a pattern Gran Geamatron showed them of gracehoppers, auntskippers and coney-farm leppers, they jeerilied along, durian gay and marian maid-cap, lou Dariou beside la Matieto, all boy more all girl singout-feller longa house blong store Huddy, whilest nin nin nin nin that Boorman's clock, a winny on the tinny side, ninned nin nin nin nin, about old Father Barley how he got up of a morning arley and he met with a plattonem blondes named Hips and Haws and fell in with a fellows of Trinity some header Skowood Shaws like (You'll catch it, don't fret, Mrs Tummy Lupton! Come indoor, Scoffynosey, and shed your swank!) auld Daddy Deacon who could stow well his place of beacon but he never could hold his kerosene's candle to (The nurse'll give it you, stickypots! And you wait, my lasso, fecking the twine!) bold Farmer Burleigh who wuck up in a hurlywurly where he huddly could wuddle to wal-low his weg tillbag of the baker's booth to beg of (You're well held now, Missy Cheekspeer, and your panto's off! Fie, for shame, Ruth Wheatacre, after all the booz said!) illed Diddiddy Achin for the prize of a pease of bakin with a pinch of the panch of the ponch in jurys for (Ah, crabeyes, I have you, showing off to the world with that gape in your stocking!) Wold Forrester Farley who, in deesperation of deisipiration at the diasporation of his diesparation, was found of the round of the sound of the lound of the Lukkedoerendunandurraskewdylooshoofermoyportertoo-ryzooysphalnabortansporthaokansakroidverjkapakkapuk.

Byfall.

Upploud!

The play thou schouwburgst, Game, here endeth. The curtain drops by deep request.

Uplouderamain!

Gonn the gawds, Gunnar's gustspells. When the h, who the hu, how the hue, where the huer? Orbiter onswers: lots lives lost. Fionia is fed up with Fidge Fudgesons. Sealand snorres.

Rendningrocks roguesreckning reigns. Gwds with gurs are
gttrdmmrng. Hlls vlls. The timid hearts of words all exeomno-
sunt. Mannagad, lammalelouh, how do that come? By Dad, youd
not heed that fert! Fulgitudes ejist rowdownan tonuout. Quoq!
And buncskleydoodle! Kidoosh! Of their fear they broke, they
ate wind, they fled; where they ate there they fled; of their fear
they fled, they broke away. Go to, let us extol Azrael with our
harks, by our brews, on our jambses, in his gaits. To Mezou-
zalem with the Dephilim, didits dinkun's dud? Yip! Yup! Yar-
rah! And let Nek Nekulon extol Mak Makal and let him say
unto him: Immi ammi Semmi. And shall not Babel be with
Lebab? And he war. And he shall open his mouth and answer:
I hear, O Ismael, how they laud is only as my loud is one. If
Nekulon shall be havonfalled surely Makal haven hevens. Go to,
let us extell Makal, yea, let us exceedingly extell. Though you
have lien amung your posspots my excellency is over Ismael.
Great is him whom is over Ismael and he shall mekanek of Mak
Nakulon. And he deed.
    Uplouderamainagain!
    For the Clearer of the Air from on high has spoken in tumbul-
dum tambaldam to his tembledim tombaldoom worrild and, mogu-
phonoised by that phonemanon, the unhappitents of the earth
have terrerumbled from fimament unto fundament and from
tweedledeedumms down to twiddledeedees.
    Loud, hear us!
    Loud, graciously hear us!
    Now have thy children entered into their habitations. And
nationglad, camp meeting over, to shin it, Gov be thanked. Thou
hast closed the portals of the habitations of thy children and thou
hast set thy guards thereby, even Garda Didymus and Garda
Domas, that thy children may read in the book of the opening of
the mind to light and err not in the darkness which is the afterthought of thy nomatter by the guardiance of those guards which
are thy bodemen, the cheeryboyum chirryboth with the kerry-
bommers in their krubeems, Pray-your-Prayers Timothy and
Back-to-Bunk Tom.

Till tree from tree, tree among trees, tree over tree become
stone to stone, stone between stones, stone under stone for ever.

O Loud, hear the wee beseech of thees of each of these thy un-
litten ones! Grant sleep in hour's time, O Loud!

That they take no chill. That they do ming no merder. That
they shall not gomeet madhowiatrees.

Loud, heap miseries upon us yet entwine our arts with laughters low!

Ha he hi ho hu.

Mummum.

[2]

As we there are where are we are we there
from tomtittot to teetootomtotalitarian. Tea
tea too oo.

Whom will comes over. Who to caps ever.
And howelse do we hook our hike to find that
pint of porter place? Am shot, says the big-
guard.[1]

Whence. Quick lunch by our left, wheel,

where we whiled while we whithered. Old
Vico Roundpoint. But fahr, be fear! And
natural, simple, slavish, filial. The marriage of
Montan wetting his moll we know, like any
enthewsyass cuckling a hoyden[3] in her rougey

---

[1] Rawmeash, quoshe with her girlic teangue. If old Herod with the Corm-
well's eczema was to go for me like he does Snuffler whatever about his blue
canaries I'd do nine months for his beaver beard.

[2] Mater Mary Mercerycordial of the Dripping Nipples, milk's a queer
arrangement.

[3] Real life behind the floodlights as shown by the best exponents of a royal
divorce.

gipsylike chinkaminx pulshandjupeyjade and her petsybluse indecked o' voylets.[1] When who was wist was ware. En elv, et fjaell. And the whirr of the whins humming us howe. His hume. Hencetaking tides we haply return, trumpeted by prawns and ensigned with seakale, to befinding ourself when old is said in one and maker mates with made (O my!), having conned the cones and meditated the mured and pondered the pensils and ogled the olymp and delighted in her dianaphous and cacchinated behind his culosses, before a

winey Tod, ye Daimon Barbar!

mosoleum. Length Withought Breath, of him, a chump of the evums, upshoot of picnic or stupor out of sopor, Cave of Kids or Hymanian Glattstoneburg, denary, danery, donnery,

Dig him in the bsh!

Ingodly old Ardy, Cronwall eeswaxing the nvulsion box.

domm, who, entiringly as he continues highlyfictional, tumulous under his chthonic exterior but plain Mr Tumulty in muftilife,[2] in his antisipiences as in his recognisances, is, (Dominic Directus) a manyfeast munificent more mob than man.

Ainsoph,[3] this upright one, with that noughty besighed him zeroine. To see in his horrorscup he is mehrkurios than saltz of sulphur. Terror of the noonstruck by day, cryptogam of each nightly bridable. But, to speak broken heaventalk, is he? Who is he? Whose is he? Why is he? Howmuch is he? Which is he? When is he? Where is he?[4] How is he? And what the decans is there about him

CONSTITUTION OF THE CONSTITUTIONABLE AS CONSTITUTIONAL.

[1] When we play dress grownup at alla ludo poker you'll be happnessised to feel how fetching I can look in clingarounds.

[2] Kellywick, Longfellow's Lodgings, House of Comments III, Cake Walk, Amusing Avenue, Salt Hill, Co. Mahogany, Izalond, Terra Firma.

[3] Groupname for grapejuice.

[4] Bhing, said her burglar's head, soto poce.

anyway, the decemt man? Easy, calm your
haste! Approach to lead our passage!

This bridge is upper.

Cross.

Thus come to castle.

Knock.[1]

A password, thanks.

Yes, pearse.

Well, all be dumbed!

O really?[2]

Swing the banjo,
bantams, bounce-
the-baller's
blown to fook.

Hoo cavedin earthwight
At furscht kracht of thunder.[3]
When shoo, his flutterby,

Thsight near
left me eyes when
I seen her put
thounce otay
ithpot.

Was netted and named.[4]
Erdnacrusha, requiestress, wake em!
And let luck's puresplutterall lucy at
ease![5]
To house as wise fool ages builded.
Sow byg eat.[6]

Quartandwds.

Staplering to tether to, steppingstone to
mount by, as the Boote's at Pickardstown.
And that skimmelk steed still in the ground-
loftfan. As over all. Or be these wingsets leaned
to the outwalls, beastskin trophies of booth
of Baws the balsamboards?[7] Burials be bally-
houraised! So let Bacchus e'en call! Inn inn!
Inn inn! Where. The babbers ply the pen.
The bibbers drang the den. The papplicom,
the pubblicam he's turning tin for ten. From

Tickets for the
Tailwaggers
Terrierpuppy
Raffle.

PROBA-
POSSIBL
PROLEG
MENA TO
IDEAREA
HISTORY

GNOSIS
PRECRE
DETERM
TION.
AGNOSI
POSTCR
DETER-
MINISM.

---

[1] yussive smirte and ye mermon answerth from his beelyingplace below
.he tightmark, Gotahelv!

[2] O Evol, kool in the salg and ees how Dozi pits what a drows er.

[3] A goodrid croven in a tynwalled tub.

[4] Apis amat aram. Luna legit librum. Pulla petit pascua.

[5] And after dinn to shoot the shades.

[6] Says blistered Mary Achinhead to beautifed Tummy Tullbutt.

[7] Begge. To go to Begge. To go to Begge and to be sure to reminder
Begge. Goodbeg, buggey Begge.

seldomers that most frequent him. That same
erst crafty hakemouth which under the assumed
name of Ignotus Loquor, of foggy old,
harangued bellyhooting fishdrunks on their
favorite stamping ground, from a father theo-
balder brake.¹ And Egyptus, the incenstrobed,

as Cyrus heard of him? And Major A. Shaw
after he got the miner smellpex? And old
Whiteman self, the blighty blotchy, beyond
the bays, hope of ostrogothic and ottomanic
faith converters, despair of Pandemia's post-
wartem plastic surgeons? But is was all so
long ago. Hispano-Cathayan-Euxine, Castill-
ian-Emeratic-Hebridian, Espanol-Cymric-

Helleniky? Rolf the Ganger, Rough the Gang-
ster, not a feature alike and the face the same.²
Pastimes are past times. Now let bygones
be bei Gunne's. Saaleddies er it in this warken
werden, mine boerne, and it vild need older-
wise³ since primal made alter in garden of
Idem. The tasks above are as the flasks below,
saith the emerald canticle of Hermes and all's

loth and pleasestir, are we told, on excellent
inkbottle authority, solarsystemised, seriol-
cosmically, in a more and more almightily
expanding universe under one, there is rhyme-
less reason to believe, original sun. Securely
judges orb terrestrial.⁴ *Haud certo ergo.* But

O felicitous culpability, sweet bad cess to you
for an archetypt!

¹ Huntler and Pumar's animal alphabites, the first in the world from
aab to zoo.
² We dont hear the booming cursowarries, we wont fear the fletches of
fightning, we float the meditarenias and come bask to the isle we love in
spice. Punt.
³ And this once golden bee a cimadoro.
⁴ And he was a gay Lutharius anyway, Sinobiled. You can tell by their
extraordinary clothes.

ARCHAIC
ZELOTYPIA
AND THE
ODIUM TEL
EOLOGICUM

Honour commercio's energy yet aid the
linkless proud, the plurable with everybody
and ech with pal, this ernst of Allsap's ale
halliday of roaring month with its two lunar
eclipses and its three saturnine settings! Horn
of Heatthen, highbrowed! Brook of Life, back-
frish! Amnios amnium, fluminiculum flami-
nulinorum! We seek the Blessed One, the
Harbourer-cum-Enheritance. Even Canaan
the Hateful. Ever a-going, ever a-coming.
Between a stare and a sough. Fossilisation, all
branches.[1] Wherefore Petra sware unto Ulma:
By the mortals' frost! And Ulma sware unto
Petra: On my veiny life!

Bags.
Balls.

In these places sojournemus, where Eblinn
water, leased of carr and fen, leaving amont her
shoals and salmen browses, whom inshore
breezes woo with freshets, windeth to her
broads. A phantom city, phaked of philim
pholk, bowed and sould for a four of hundreds
of manhood in their three and threescore
fylkers for a price partitional of twenty six and
six. By this riverside, on our sunnybank,[2] how
buona the vista, by Santa Rosa! A field of May,
the very vale of Spring. Orchards here are
lodged; sainted lawrels evremberried. You
have a hoig view ashwald, a glen of marrons
and of thorns. Gleannaulinn, Ardeevin: purty
glint of plaising height. This Norman court at
boundary of the ville, yon creepered tower of
a church of Ereland, meet for true saints in
worshipful assemblage,[3] with our king's house

THE LOCALI
SATION OF
LEGEND
LEADING T
THE LEGALI
SATION OF
LATIFUND-
ISM.

Move up,
Mackinerny!
Make room for
Muckinurney!

---

[1] Startnaked and bonedstiff. We vivvy soddy. All be dood.

[2] When you dreamt that you'd wealth in marble arch do you ever think of
pool beg slowe.

[3] Porphyrious Olbion, redcoatliar, we were always wholly rose marines
on our side every time.

of stone, belgroved of mulbrey, the still that was mill and Kloster that was Yeomansland, the ghastcold tombshape of the quick foregone on, the loftleaved elm Lefanunian abovemansioned, each, every, all is for the retrospectioner. Skole! Agus skole igen![1] Sweetsome auburn, cometh up as a selfreizing flower, that fragolance of the fraisey beds: the phoenix, his pyre, is still flaming away with trueprattight spirit: the wren his nest is niedelig as the turrises of the sabines are televisible. Here are the cottage and the bungalow for the cobbeler and the brandnewburgher:[2] but Izolde, her chaplet gardens, an litlee plads af liefest pose,

In snowdrop, trou-de-dentelle, flesh and heliotrope.

arride the winnerful wonders off, the winnerful wonnerful wanders off,[3] with hedges of ivy and hollywood and bower of mistletoe, are, tho if it theem tho and yeth if you pleathes,[4] for the blithehaired daughter of Angoisse. All out of two barreny old perishers, Tytonyhands and Vlossyhair, a kilolitre in metromyriams. Presepeprosapia, the parent bole. Wone tabard, wine tap and warm tavern[5] and, by ribbon development, from contact bridge to lease lapse, only two millium two humbered and eighty thausig nine humbered

Here's our dozen cousins from the tarves on tripes.

and sixty radiolumin lines to the wustworts of a Finntown's generous poet's office. Distorted mirage, aloofliest of the plain, wherein the

---

[1] Now a muss wash the little face.

[2] A viking vernacular expression still used in the Summerhill district for a jerryhatted man of forty who puts two fingers into his boiling soupplate and licks them in turn to find out if there is enough mushroom catsup in the mutton broth.

[3] H' dk' fs' h'p'y.

[4] Googlaa pluplu.

[5] Tomley. The grown man. A butcher szewched him the bloughs and braches. I'm chory to see P. Shuter.

boxomeness of the bedelias[1] makes hobby-
hodge happy in his hole.[2] The store and
charter, Treetown Castle under Lynne. Riva-
pool? Hod a brieck on it! But its piers eerie,
its span spooky, its toll but a till, its parapets
all peripateting. D'Oblong's by his by. Which
we all pass. Tons. In our snoo. Znore. While
we hickerwards the thicker. Schein. Schore.
Which assoars us from the murk of the mythe-
lated in the barrabelowther, bedevere butlered
table round, past Morningtop's necessity and
Harington's invention, to the clarience of the
childlight in the studiorium upsturts. Here
we'll dwell on homiest powers, love at the
latch with novices nig and nag. The chorus:
the principals. For the rifocillation of their
inclination to the manifestation of irritation:
doldorboys and doll.[3] After sound, light and
heat, memory, will and understanding.

Bet you fippence anythesious there's no pug-gatory, are yous game?

Here (the memories framed from walls are
minding) till wranglers for wringwrowdy
wready are, F ⅂, (at gaze, respecting, four-
teenth baronet, meet, altrettanth bancorot,
chaff) and ere commence commencement cata-
launic when Aetius check chokewill Attil's
gambit, (that buxon bruzeup, give it a burl!)
lead us seek, O june of eves the jenniest,
thou who fleeest flicklesome the fond fervid
frondeur to thickly thyself attach with thine
efteased ensuer,[4] ondrawer of our uncon-
scionable, flickerflapper fore our unter-

PREAUSTERIC
MAN AND HIS
PURSUIT OF
PAN-
HYSTERIC
WOMAN.

[1] I believe in Dublin and the Sultan of Turkey.
[2] I have heard this word used by Martin Halpin, an old gardener from the
Glens of Antrim who used to do odd jobs for my godfather, the Rev. B. B.
Brophy of Swords.
[3] Ravens may rive so can dove deelish.
[4] A question of pull.

drugged,[1] lead us seek, lote us see, light us find,
let us missnot Maidadate, Mimosa multimim-
etica, the maymeaminning of maimoomeining!
Elpis, thou fountain of the greeces, all shall speer
theeward[2] from kongen in his canteenhus to
knivers hind the knoll. Ausonius Audacior
and gael, gillie, gall.[3] Singalingalying. Storiella
as she is syung. Whence followeup with end-

*There was a
sweet hopeful
culled Cis.*

speaking nots for yestures, plutonically pur-
suant on briefest glimpse from gladrags, pretty
Proserpronette whose slit satchel spilleth peas.

Belisha beacon, beckon bright! Usherette,
unmesh us! That grene ray of earong it waves
us to yonder as the red, blue and yellow flogs
time on the domisole,[4] with a blewy blow and
a windigo. Where flash becomes word and
silents selfloud. To brace congeners, trebly
bounden and asservaged twainly. Adamman,[5]
Emhe, Issossianusheen and sometypes Yggely
ogs Weib. Uwayoei![6] So mag this sybilette be
our shibboleth that we may syllable her well.
Vetus may be occluded behind the mou in

URGES AND
WIDERURGES
IN A PRIMI-
TIVE SEPT.

*The Big Bear
bit the Sailor's
Only. Trouble
trouble, trouble.*

*Forening Unge
Kristlike Kvinne.*

Veto but Nova will be nearing as their radient
among the Nereids. A one of charmers, ay,
Una Unica, charmers, who, under the branches
of the elms, in shoes as yet unshent by stoni-
ness, wend, went, will wend a way of honey
myrrh and rambler roses mistmusk while still
the maybe mantles the meiblume, or ever her

---

[1] For Rose Point see Inishmacsaint.
[2] Mannequins' Pose.
[3] Their holy presumption and hers sinfly desprit.
[4] Anama anamaba anamabapa.
[5] Only for he's fathering law I could skewer that old one and slosh her out
many's the time but I thinks more of my pottles and ketts.
[6] All abunk for Tararrarat! Look slipper, soppyhat, we've a doss in the
manger.

if have faded from the fleur,[1] their arms
enlocked, (ringrang, the chimes of sex appealing as conchitas with sentas stray,[2] rung!), all
thinking all of it, the It with an itch in it, the All
every inch of it, the pleasure each will preen her
for, the business each was bred to breed by.[3]

Soon jemmijohns will cudgel about some
a rhythmatick or other over Browne and
Nolan's divisional tables whereas she, of
minions' novence charily being cupid, for
mug's wumping, grooser's grubbiness, andt's
avarice and grossopper's grandegaffe, with her
tootpettypout of jemenfichue will sit and knit
on solfa sofa.[4] Stew of the evening, booksyful
stew. And a bodikin a boss in the Thimble
Theatre. But all is her inbourne. Intend. From
gramma's grammar she has it that if there is a
third person, mascarine, phelinine or nuder,
being spoken abad it moods prosodes from a
person speaking to her second which is the
direct object that has been spoken to, with and
at. Take the dative with his oblative[5] for, even
if obsolete, it is always of interest, so spake
gramma on the impetus of her imperative, only
mind your genderous towards his reflexives
such that I was to your grappa (Bott's trousend,
hore a man uff!) when him was me hedon[6]
and mine, what the lewdy saying, his analec-
tual pygmyhop.[7] There is comfortism in the

EARLY
NOTIONS OF
ACQUIRED
RIGHTS AND
THE INFLU-
ENCE OF
COLLECTIVE
TRADITION
UPON THE
INDIVIDUAL

*Telltale me all
of annaryllies.*

*Will you carry
my can and
fight the fairies?*

*Allma Mathers,
Auctioneer.*

*Old Gavelkind
the Gamper and
he's as daff as
you're erse.*

---

[1] One must sell it to some one, the sacred name of love.
[2] Making it up as we goes along.
[3] The law of the jungerl.
[4] Let me blush to think of all those halfwayhoist pullovers.
[5] I'd like his pink's cheek.
[6] Frech devil in red hairing! So that's why you ran away to sea, Mrs.
Lappy. Leap me, Locklaun, for you have sensed.
[7] A washable lovable floatable doll.

knowledge that often hate on first hearing
comes of love by second sight. Have your
little sintalks in the dunk of subjunctions, dual
in duel and prude with pruriel, but even the
aoriest chaparound whatever plaudered perfect
anent prettydotes and haec genua omnia may
perhaps chance to be about to be in the case to
be becoming a pale peterwright in spite of all
your tense accusatives whilstly you're wall-
floored[1] like your gerandiums for the better
half of a yearn or sob. It's a wild's kitten, my
dear, who can tell a wilkling from a warthog.
For you may be as practical as is predicable
but you must have the proper sort of accident
to meet that kind of a being with a difference.[2]
Flame at his fumbles but freeze on his fist.[3]
Every letter is a godsend, ardent Ares, brusque
Boreas and glib Ganymede like zealous Zeus,
the O'Meghisthest of all. To me or not to me.
Satis thy quest on. Werbungsap! Jeg suis, vos

Undante
amoroso.
M. 50-50.
οὐκ ἔλαβον
πόλιν

wore a gentleman, thou arr, I am a quean. Is
a game over? The game goes on. Cookcook!
Search me. The beggar the maid the bigger
the mauler. And the greater the patrarc the
griefer the pinch. And that's what your doctor
knows. O love it is the commonknounest thing
how it pashes the plutous and the paupe.[4]
Pop! And egg she active or spoon she passive,
all them fine clauses in Lindley's and Murrey's
never braught the participle of a present to a
desponent hortatrixy, vindicatively I say it,

[1] With her poodle feinting to be let off and feeling dead in herself. Is love
worse living?
[2] If she can't follow suit Renée goes to the pack.
[3] Improper frictions is maledictions and mens uration makes me mad.
[4] Llong and Shortts Primer of Black and White Wenchcraft.

from her postconditional future.[1] Lumpsome
is who lumpsum pays. Quantity counts though
accents falter. Yoking apart and oblique orations parsed to one side, a brat, alanna, can
choose from so many, be he a sollicitor's
appendix, a pipe clerk or free functionist
flyswatter, that perfect little cad, from the
languors and weakness of limber-limbed lassi-
hood till the head, back and heart aches of
waxedup womanage and heaps on heaps of
other things too. Note the Respectable Irish
Distressed Ladies and the Merry Mustard
Frothblowers of Humphreystown Associa-
tions. Atac first, queckqueck quicks after.
Beware how in that hist subtaile of schlangder[2]
lies liaison to tease oreilles. To vert embowed
set proper penchant. But learn from that ancient
tongue to be middle old modern to the minute.
A spitter that can be depended on. Though
Wonderlawn's lost us for ever. Alis, alas, she
broke the glass! Liddell lokker through the
leafery, ours is mistery of pain.[3] You may spin
on youthlit's bike and multiplease your Mike
and Nike with your kickshoes on the algebrars
but, volve the virgil page and view, the O of
woman is long when burly those two muters
sequent her so from Nebob[4] see you never
stray who'll nimm you nice and nehm the day.

One hath just been areading, hath not one,
ya, ya, in their memoiries of Hireling's puny
wars, end so, und all, ga, ga, of The O'Brien,

*I'll go for that
small pully if
you'll suck to
your lebbens-
quatsch.*

O'Mara Farrell.

Verschwindibus.

Ulstria,

CONCOMI
TANCE OF
COURAGE

---

[1] The gaggles all out.

[2] He's just bug nuts on white mate he hasn't the teath nor the grits to choo
and that's what's wrong with Lang Wang Wurm, old worbbling goesbelly.

[3] Dear and I trust in all frivolity I may be pardoned for trespassing but I
think I may add hell.

[4] He is my all menkind of every desception.

Monastir,
Leninstar and
Connecticut.

Cliopatria, thy
hosties history.

The Eroico
furioso makes
he valet like
miling.

The hyperape the
ink he groves the
ole you see now for
ush sake chawley.

COUNSEL
AND CON-
STANCY.
ORDINATION
OF OMEN,
ONUS AND
OBIT. DIS-
TRIBUTION
OF DANGER,
DUTY AND
DESTINY.
POLAR PRIN-
CIPLES.

The O'Connor, The Mac Loughlin and The
Mac Namara with summed their appondage,
da, da, of Sire Jeallyous Seizer, that gamely
torskmester,[1] with his duo of druidesses in ready
money rompers[2] and the tryonforit of Oxthie-
vious, Lapidous and Malthouse Anthemy. You
may fail to see the lie of that layout, Suetonia,[3]
but the reflections which recur to me are that
so long as beauty life is body love[4] and so bright
as Mutua of your mirror holds her candle to
your caudle, lone lefthand likeless, sombring
Autum of your Spring, reck you not one spirt
of anyseed whether trigemelimen cuddle his
coddle or nope. She'll confess it by her figure
and she'll deny it to your face. If you're not
ruined by that one she won't do you any
whim. And then? What afters it? Gruff Gunne
may blow, Gam Gonna flow, the gossans eye
the jennings aye. From the butts of Heber and
Heremon, nolens volens, brood our pansies,
brune in brume. There's a split in the infinitive
from to have to have been to will be. As they
warred in their big innings ease now we never
shall know. Eat early earthapples. Coax Cobra
to chatters. Hail, Heva, we hear! This is the
glider that gladdened the girl[5] that list to the
wind that lifted the leaves that folded the
fruit that hung on the tree that grew in the
garden Gough gave. Wide hiss, we're wizen-

---

[1] All his teeths back to the front, then the moon and then the moon with
a hole behind it.

[2] Skip one, flop fore, jennies in the cabbage store.

[3] None of your cumpohlstery English here.

[4] Understudy my understandings, Sostituda, and meek thine compline-
ment, gymnufleshed.

[5] Tho' I have one just like that to home, deadleaf brown with quicksilver
appliques, would whollymost applissiate a nice shiny sleekysilk out of that
slippering snake charmeuse.

ing. Hoots fromm, we're globing. Why hidest
thou hinder thy husband his name? Leda, Lada,
aflutter-afraida, so does your girdle grow!
Willed without witting, whorled without
aimed. Pappapassos, Mammamanet, warwhets-
wut and whowitswhy.[1] But it's tails for
toughs and titties for totties and come
buckets come bats till deeleet.[2]

 Dark ages clasp the daisy roots, Stop, if you
are a sally of the allies, hot off Minnowaurs
and naval actiums, picked engagements and
banks of rowers. Please stop if you're a
B.C. minding missy, please do. But should
you prefer A.D. stepplease. And if you miss
with a venture it serves you girly well glad.
But, holy Janus, I was forgetting the Blitzen-
kopfs! Here, Hengegst and Horsesauce, take
your heads[3] out of that taletub. And leave
your hinnyhennyhindyou. It's haunted. The
chamber. Of errings. Whoan, tug, trace,
stirrup! It is distinctly understouttered that,
sense you threehandshighs put your twofoot-
large timepates in that dead wash of Lough
Murph and until such time pace one and the
same Messherrn the grinning statesmen, Brock
and Leon, have shunted the grumbling
coundedtouts, Starlin and Ser Artur Ghinis.
Foamous homely brew, bebattled by bottle,
gageure de guegerre.[4] Bull igien bear and
then bearagain bulligan. Gringrin gringrin.
Staffs varsus herds and bucks vursus barks.

PANOPTICAL
PURVIEW OF
POLITICAL
PROGRESS
AND THE
FUTURE PRE-
SENTATION
OF THE PAST

---

[1] What's that ma'am, says I.
[2] As you say yourself.
[3] That's the lethemuse but it washes off.
[4] Where he fought the shessock of his stimmstammer and we caught the
pepettes of our lovelives.

*Curragh
*achree, me
*osthoon fiend.

*emilies hug
*ank!

*ll we suffered
*nder them Cow-
*ung Forks and
*ow we enjoyed
*ver our pick of
*e basketfild.
*ld Kine's
*leat Meal.

*ieflie for the
*lies and a
*mbambum
*r the
*ppotondus.

By old Grumbledum's walls. Bumps, bellows
and bawls.[1] Opprimor's down, up up Opima!
Rents and rates and tithes and taxes, wages,
saves and spends. Heil, heptarched span of
peace![2] Live, league of lex, nex and the mores!
Fas est dass and foe err you. Impovernment
of the booble by the bauble for the bubble. So
wrap up your worries in your woe (wumpum-
tum!) and shake down the shuffle for the
throw. For there's one mere ope[3] for down-
fall ned. As Hanah Levy, shrewd shroplifter,
and nievre anore skidoos with her spoileds.[4]
To add gay touches. For hugh and guy and
goy and jew. To dimpled and pimpled and
simpled and wimpled. A peak in a poke and a
pig in a pew.[5] She wins them by wons, a haul
hectoendecate, for mangay mumbo jumbjubes
tak mutts and jeffs muchas bracelonettes
gracies barcelonas.[6] O what a loovely free-
speech 'twas (tep)[7] to gar howalively hinter-
grunting. Tip. Like lilt of larks to burdened
crocodile,[8] or skittering laubhing at that
wheeze of old windbag, Blusterboss, blow-
harding about all he didn't do. Hell o' your
troop! With is the winker for the muckwits
of willesly and nith is the nod for the umproar
napollyon and hitheris poorblond piebold
hoerse. Huirse. With its tricuspidal hauberk-

---

[1] Shake eternity and lick creation.
[2] I'm blest if I can see.
[3] Hoppity Huhneye, hoosh the hen. I like cluckers, you like nuts (wink).
[4] Sweet, medium and dry like altar wine.
[5] Who'll buy me penny babies?
[6] Well, Maggy, I got your castoff devils all right and fits lovely. And am
vaguely graceful. Maggy thanks.
[7] My six is no secret, sir, she said.
[8] Yes, there, Tad, thanks, give, from, tathair, look at that now.

helm coverchaf emblem on. For the man that
broke the ranks on Monte Sinjon. The all-
riddle of it? That that is allruddy with us
ahead of schedule which already is plan accomplished from and syne: Daft Dathy of the Five
Positions (the death ray stop him!) is still, as
reproaches Paulus, on the Madderhorn and,
entre chats and hobnobs,[1] daring Dunderhead
to shiver his timbers and Hannibal mac Hamil-
tan the Hegerite[2] (more livepower elbow him!)
ministerbuilding up, as repreaches Timothy,
in Saint Barmabrac's.[3] Number Thirty two
West Eleventh streak looks on to that (may
all in the tocoming of the sempereternal speel
spry with it!) datetree doloriferous which
more and over leafeth earlier than every
growth and, elfshot, headawag, with frayed
nerves wondering till they feeled sore like any
woman that has been born at all events to the
purdah and for the howmanyeth and how-
movingth time at what the demons in that
ackhouse that jerry built for Massa and Missus
and hijo de puta, the sparksown fermament of
the starryk fieldgosongingon where blows
a nemone at each blink of windstill[4] they
were sliding along and sleeting aloof and
scouting around and shooting about. All-
whichwhile or whereaballoons for good
vaunty years Dagobert is in Clane's clean
hometown prepping up his prepueratory
and learning how to put a broad face bronzily
out through a broken breached meataerial

---

[1] Go up quick, stay so long, come down slow.
[2] If I gnows me gneesgnobs the both of him is gnatives of Genuas.
[3] A glass of peel and pip for Mr Potter of Texas, please.
[4] All the world loves a big gleaming jelly.

Puzzly, puzzly,
smell a cat.

from Bryan Awlining! Erin's hircohaired
culoteer.[1]

And as, these things being so or ere those
things having done, way back home in Pacata
Auburnia,[2] (untillably holy gammel Eire) one
world burrowing on another, (if you've got
me, neighbour, in any large lumps, geek?, and
got the strong of it) Standfest, our topioal
sagon hero, or any otther macotther, signs is
on the bellyguds bastille back, bucked up with
fullness, and silvering to her jubilee,[3] birch-
leaves her jointure, our lavy in waving, visage
full of flesh and fat as a hen's i' forehead,
Airyanna and Blowyhart topsirturvy, that
royal pair in their palace of quicken boughs
hight The Goat and Compasses ('phone
number 17:69, if you want to know[4]) his sea-
arm strongsround her, her velivole eyne aship-
wracked, have discusst their things of the
past, crime and fable with shame, home and
profit,[5] why lui lied to lei and hun tried to kill
ham, scribbledehobbles, in whose veins runs
a mixture of, are head bent and hard upon.
Spell me the chimes. They are tales all tolled.[6]
Today is well thine but where's may tomorrow
be. But, bless his cowly head and press his
crankly hat, what a world's woe is each's

FROM CENO-
GENETIC DI-
CHOTOMY
THROUGH
DIAGONISTIC
CONCILI-
ANCE TO
DYNASTIC
CONTINU-
ITY.

Two makes a
ing at the ma-
roscope
elluspeep.

From the Buffalo
Times of bysone
days.

Quick quake
uokes the par-
otbook of dates.

---

[1] A pengeneepy for your warcheekeepy.

[2] My globe goes gaddy at geography giggle pending which time I was
looking for my shoe all through Arabia.

[3] It must be some bugbear in the gender especially when old which they
all soon get to look.

[4] After me looking up the plan in Humphrey's *Justice of the Piece* it said to
see preseeding chaps.

[5] O boyjones and hairyoddities! Only noane told missus of her massas
behaving she would laugh that flat that after that she had sanked down on her
fat arks they would shaik all to sheeks.

[6] Traduced into jinglish janglage for the nusances of dolphins born.

other's weariness waiting to beadroll his own
properer mistakes, the backslapping glad-
hander,[1] free of his florid future and the other
singing likeness, dirging a past of bloody altars,
gale with a blost to him, dove without gall.
And she, of the jilldaw's nest[2] who tears up
lettereens she never apposed a pen upon.[3] Yet
sung of love and the monster man. What's
Hiccupper to hem or her to Hagaba? Ough,
ough, brieve kindli![4]

Dogs' vespers are anending. Vespertilia-
bitur. Goteshoppard quits his gabhard cloke
to sate with Becchus. Zumbock! Achèvre!
Yet wind will be ere fadervor[5] and the hour of
fruminy and bergoo bell if Nippon have pearls
or opals Eldorado, the daindy dish, the lecking
out! Gipoo, good oil! For (hushmagandy!)
long 'tis till gets bright that all cocks waken
and birds Diana[6] with dawnsong hail. Aught
darks flou a duskness. Bats that? There peepee-
strilling. At Brannan's on the moor. At Tam
Fanagan's weak yat his still's going strang.
And still here is noctules and can tell things
acommon on by that fluffy feeling. Larges
loomy wheelhouse to bodgbox[7] lumber up
with hoodie hearsemen carrawain we keep
is peace who follow his law, Sunday

Some is out for twoheaded dulcarnons but more pulfers turnips.

Omnitudes in a knutshedell.

For all us kids under his aegis.

Saving the public his health.

Superlative absolute of Porterstown.

THE MON-
GREL UNDER
THE DUNG-
MOUND.
SIGNIFI-
CANCE OF
THE INFRA-
LIMINAL IN
TELLIGENCE
OFFRANDES

[1] He gives me pulpititions with his Castlecowards never in these twowsers and ever in those twawsers and then babeteasing us out of our hoydenname.

[2] My goldfashioned bother near drave me roven mad and I dyeing to keep my linefree face like readymaid maryangs for jollycomes smashing Holmes.

[3] What I would like is a jade louistone to go with the moon's increscent.

[4] Parley vows the Askinwhose? I do, Ida. And how to call the cattle black. Moopetsi meepotsi.

[5] I was so snug off in my apholster's creedle but at long leash I'll stretch more capritious in his dapplepied bed.

[6] Pipette. I can almost feed their sweetness at my lisplips.

[7] A liss in hunterland.

King.[1] His sevencoloured's soot (Ochone!
Ochonal!)[2] and his imponence one heap lump-
block (Mogoul!). And rivers burst out like
weeming racesround joydrinks for the fewnral-
ly,[3] where every feaster's a foster's other, fian-
nians all.[4] The wellingbreast, he willing giant,
the mountain mourning his duggedy dew. To
obedient of civicity in urbanious at felicity
what'll yet meek Mike[5] our diputy mimber when
he's head on poll and Peter's burgess and Miss
Mishy Mushy is tiptupt by Toft Taft. Boblesse
gobleege. For as Anna was at the beginning
lives yet and will return after great deap sleap
rerising and a white night high with a cows of
Drommhiem as shower as there's a wet en-
clouded in Westwicklow or a little black rose a
truant in a thorntree. We drames our dreams
tell Bappy returns. And Sein annews. We will
not say it shall not be, this passing of order and
order's coming, but in the herbest country and
in the country around Blath as in that city self
of legionds they look for its being ever yet. So
shuttle the pipers done.[6] Eric aboy![7] And it's
time that all paid tribute to this massive mor-
tiality, the pink of punk perfection as photo-
graphy in mud. Some may seek to dodge the

*Why so mucky
vick bridges
pan our Flumi-
ian road.*

*P.C. Helmut's in
he cottonwood,
istnin.*

*The throne is an
umbrella strande
and a sceptre's a
stick.*

*Jady jewel, our
daktar deer.*

*Gautamed bud-
ders deossiphys-
ing our Theas.*

*By lineal in pon-
dus overthepoise.*

---

[1] I wonder if I put the old buzzerd one night to suckle in Millickmaam's
honey like they use to emballem some of the special popes with a book in his
hand and his mouth open.

[2] And a ripping rude rape in his lucreasious togery.

[3] Will ye nought would wet your weapons, warriors bard?

[4] Roe, Williams, Bewey, Greene, Gorham, McEndicoth and Vyler, the
lays of ancient homes.

[5] The stanidsglass effect, you could sugerly swear buttermilt would not
melt down his dripping ducks.

[6] Thickathigh and Thinathews with sant their dam.

[7] Oh, could we do with this waddled of ours like that redbanked profanian
with his bakset of yosters.

gobbet for its quantity of quality but who wants to cheat the choker's got to learn to chew the cud. Allwhichhole scrubs on scroll circuminiuminluminatedhave encuoniams here and improperies there.[1] With a pansy for the pussy in the corner.[2]

Pitchcap and triangle, noose and tinctunc.

Bewise of Fanciulla's heart, the heart of Fanciulla! Even the recollection of willow fronds is a spellbinder that lets to hear.[3] The rushes by the grey nuns' pond: ah eh oh let me sigh too. Coalmansbell: behoves you handmake of the load. Jenny Wren: pick, peck. Johnny Post: pack, puck.[4] All the world's in want and is writing a letters.[5] A letters from a person to a place about a thing. And all the world's on wish to be carrying a letters. A letters to a king about a treasure from a cat.[6] When men want to write a letters. Ten men, ton men, pen men, pun men, wont to rise a ladder. And den men, dun men, fen men, fun men, hen men, hun men wend to raze a leader. Is then any lettersday from many peoples, Daganasanavitch? Empire, your outermost.[7] A posy cord. Plece.

INCIPIT IN
TERMISSIO

Uncle Flabbius Muximus to Niecia Flappia Minnimiss. As this is. And as this this is.

Dear Brotus, land me arrears.

Rockaby, babel, flatten a wall.
How he broke the good news to Gent.

We have wounded our way on foe tris prince till that force in the gill is faint afarred

MAJOR AN
MINOR

[1] Gosem pher, gezumpher, greeze a jarry grim felon! Good bloke him!
[2] And if they was setting on your stool as hard as my was she could beth her bothom dolours he'd have a culious impressiom on the diminitive that chafes our ends.
[3] When I'am Enastella and am taken for Essatessa I'll do that droop on the pohlmann's piano.
[4] Heavenly twinges, if it's one of his I'll fearly feint as swoon as he enter-rooms.
[5] To be slipped on, to be slept by, to be conned to, to be kept up. And when you're done push the chain.
[6] With her modesties office.
[7] Strutting as proud as a great turquin weggin that cuckhold on his Eddems and Clay's hat.

and the face in the treebark feigns afear. This
is rainstones ringing. Strangely cult for this
ceasing of the yore. But Erigureen is ever.
Pot price pon patrilinear plop, if the osseletion
of the onkring gives omen nome? Since alls
war that end war let sports be leisure and
bring and buy fair. Ah ah athclete, blest your
bally bathfeet! Towntoquest, fortorest, the
hour that hies is hurley. A halt for hearsake.[1]

MODES COA-
LESCING
PROLIFER-
ATE HOMO-
GENUINE
HOMOGEN-
EITY.

---

[1] Come, smooth of my slate, to the beat of my blosh. With all these gelded
ewes jilting about and the thrills and ills of laylock blossoms three's so much
more plants than chants for cecilies that I was thinking fairly killing times of
putting an end to myself and my malody, when I remembered all your pupil-
teacher's erringnesses in perfection class. You sh'undn't write you can't if you
w'udn't pass for undevelopmented. This is the propper way to say that, Sr. If
it's me chews to swallow all you saidn't you can eat my words for it as sure as
there's a key in my kiss. Quick erit faciofacey. When we will conjugate together toloseher tomaster tomiss while morrow fans amare hour, verbe de vie
and verve to vie, with love ay loved have I on my back spine and does for
ever. Your are me severe? Then rue. My intended, Jr, who I'm throne away
on, (here he inst, my lifstack, a newfolly likon) when I slip through my pettigo
I'll get my decree and take seidens when I'm not ploughed first by some
Rolando the Lasso, and flaunt on the flimsyfilmsies for to grig my collage
juniorees who, though they flush fuchsia, are they octette and viginity in my
shade but always my figurants. They may be yea of my year but they're nary
nay of my day. Wait till spring has sprung in spickness and prigs beg in to pry
they'll be plentyprime of housepets to pimp and pamper my. Impending marriage. Nature tells everybody about but I learned all the runes of the gamest
game ever from my old nourse Asa. A most adventuring trot is her and she
vicking well knowed them all heartswise and fourwords. How Olive d'Oyly
and Winnie Carr, bejupers, they reized the dressing of a salandmon and how a
peeper coster and a salt sailor med a mustied poet atwaimen. It most have
bean Mad Mullans planted him. Bina de Bisse and Trestrine von Terrefin.
Sago sound, rite go round, kill kackle, kook kettle and (remember all should
I forget to) bolt the thor. Auden. Wasn't it just divining that dog of a dag
in Skókholme as I sat astrid uppum their Drewitt's altar, as cooledas as cul-
cumbre, slapping my straights till the sloping ruins, postillion, postallion, a
swinge a swank, with you offering me clouts of illscents and them horners
stagstruck on the leasward! Don't be of red, you blanching mench! This
isabella I'm on knows the ruelles of the rut and she don't fear andy mandy. So
sing loud, sweet cheeriot, like anegreon in heaven! The good fother with the
twingling in his eye will always have cakes in his pocket to bethroat us with
for our allmichael good. Amum. Amum. And Amum again. For tough troth
is stronger than fortuitous fiction and it's the surplice money, oh my young
friend and ah me sweet creature, what buys the bed while wits borrows the
clothes.

A scene at sight. Or dreamoneire. Which
they shall memorise. By her freewritten
Hopeiy for ear that annalykeses if scares for
eye that sumns. Is it in the now woodwordings
of our sweet plantation where the branchings
then will singingsing tomorrows gone and
yesters outcome as Satadays aftermoon lex
leap smiles on the twelvemonthsminding?
Such is. Dear (name of desired subject, A.N.),
well, and I go on to. Shlicksher. I and we
(tender condolences for happy funeral, one
if) so sorry to (mention person suppressed for
the moment, F.M.). Well (enquiries after all-
healths) how are you (question maggy). A
lovely (introduce to domestic circles) pershan
of cates. Shrubsher. Those pothooks mostly
she hawks from Poppa Vere Foster but these
curly mequeues are of Mippa's moulding.
Shrubsheruthr. (Wave gently in the ere turning ptover.) Well, mabby (consolation of
shopes) to soon air. With best from-cinder
Christinette if prints chumming, can be when
desires Soldi, for asamples, backfronted or,
if all, peethrolio or Get my Prize, using her
flower or perfume or, if veryveryvery chumming, in otherwards, who she supposed adeal,
kissists my exits. Shlicksheruthr. From Auburn
chenlemagne. Pious and pure fair one, all has
concomitated to this that she shall tread them
lifetrees leaves whose silence hitherto has
shone as sphere of silver fastalbarnstone, that
fount Bandusian shall play liquick music and
after odours sigh of musk. Blotsbloshblothe,
one dear that was. Sleep in the water, drug at
the fire, shake thedust off and dream your one
who would give her sidecurls to. Till later

*Bibelous hics-
tory and Barbar-
assa harestary.*

*A shieling in cop-
pingers and por-
rish soup all days.*

*How matches
metroosers?*

*Le hélos tombaut
soul sur la jambe
de marche.*

*Mai maintenante
elle est venuse.*

Lammas is led in by baith our washwives, a
weird of wonder tenebrous as that evil thorn-
garth, a field of faery blithe as this flowing wild.

*Twos Dons Johns
Threes Totty
Askins.*

*Aujourd'hui comme aux temps de Pline et de
Columelle la jacinthe se plaît dans les Gaules,
la pervenche en Illyrie, la marguerite sur les
ruines de Numance*[1] *et pendant qu'autour d'elles
les villes ont changé de maîtres et de noms, que
plusieurs sont entrées dans le néant, que les
civilisations se sont choquées et brisées, leurs
paisibles générations ont traversé les âges et sont
arrivées jusqu'à nous, fraîches et riantes comme
aux jours des batailles.*[2]

*Also Spuke
Zerothruster.*

THE PART
PLAYED BY
BELLETRI-
STICKS IN
THE BELLUM-
PAX-BEL-
LUM.
MUTUOMOR-
PHOMUTA-
TION.

Margaritomancy! Hyacinthinous pervinci-
veness! Flowers. A cloud. But Bruto and
Cassio are ware only of trifid tongues[3] the
whispered wilfulness, ('tis demonal!) and shadows shadows multiplicating (il folsoletto nel
falsoletto col fazzolotto dal fuzzolezzo),[4] to-
tients quotients, they tackle their quarrel. Sicka-
moor's so woful sally. Ancient's aerger. And
eachway bothwise glory signs. What if she
love Sieger less though she leave Ruhm moan?
That's how our oxyggent has gotten ahold of
half their world. Moving about in the free of
the air and mixing with the ruck. Enten eller,
either or.

SORTES VIR-
GINIANAE.

*A saxum shillum
for the sextum
but nothums for
that parridge
preast.*

   And!

   Nay, rather!

INTERROGATION.
EXCLAMATION.

---

[1] The nasal foss of our natal folkfarthers so so much now for Valsing-
giddyrex and his grand arks day triump.

[2] Translout that gaswind into turfish, Teague, that's a good bog and you,
Thady, poliss it off, there's a nateswipe, on to your blottom pulper.

[3] You daredevil donnelly, I love your piercing lots of lies and your flashy
foreign mail so here's my cowrie card, I dalgo, with all my exes, wise and sad.

[4] All this Mitchells is a niggar for spending and I will go to the length of
seeing that one day Big Mig will be nickleless himself.

Tricks stunts.

ANTITHESIS OF AMBI-
DUAL ANTICIPATION
THE MIND FACTORY,
ITS GIVE AND TAKE.

With sobs for his job, with tears
for his toil, with horror for his squalor
but with pep for his perdition,[1] lo, the
boor plieth as the laird hireth him.

AUSPICIUM.
AUGURIA.
DIVINITY
NOT DEITY
THE UNCER-
TAINTY JUS-
TIFIED BY
OUR CERTI-
TUDE.
EXAMPLES.

Boon on begyndelse.

At maturing daily gloryaims![2]

A flink dab for a freck dive and a stern poise
for a swift pounce was frankily at the manual
arith sure enough which was the bekase he
knowed from his cradle, no bird better, why
his fingures were giving him whatfor to fife

*Truckeys' cant
for dactyl and
spondee.*

with. First, by observation, there came boko
and nigh him wigworms and nigh him tittlies
and nigh him cheekadeekchimple and nigh
him pickpocket with pickpocketpumb, pick-
pocketpoint, pickpocketprod, pickpocket-
promise and upwithem. Holy Joe in lay
Eden.[3] And anyhows always after them the
dimpler he weighed the fonder fell he of his
null four lovedroyd curdinals, his element cur-

*Panoplous pere-
grine pifflicative
pomposity.*

dinal numen and his enement curdinal marryng
and his epulent curdinal weisswassh and his
eminent curdinal Kay O'Kay. Always would
he be reciting of them, hoojahs koojahs, up by
rota, in his Fanden's catachysm from fursed to
laced, quickmarch to decemvers, so as to pin the
tenners, thumbs down. And anon and aldays,
strues yerthere, would he wile arecreating em
om lumerous ways, caius-counting in the
scale of pin puff pive piff, piff puff pive poo,
poo puff pive pree, pree puff pive pfoor, pfoor
puff pive pippive, poopive,[4] Niall Dhu,

---

[1] While I'll wind the wildwoods' bluckbells among my window's weeds.
[2] Lawdy Dawdy simpers.
[3] But where, O where, is me lickle dig done?
[4] That's his whisper waltz I like from Pigott's with that Lancydancy step.
Stop.

Foughty Unn, Enoch Thortig, endso one, like
to pitch of your cap, pac, on to tin tall spilli-
cans.[1] To sum, borus pew notus pew eurus
pew zipher. Ace, deuce, tricks, quarts, quims.
Mumtiplay of course and carry to their whole
number. While on the other hand, traduced
by their comedy nominator to the loaferst
terms for their aloquent parts, sexes, suppers,
oglers, novels and dice.[2] He could find (the
rakehelly!) by practice the valuse of thine-to-
mine articles with no reminder for an equality
of relations and, with the helpings from his
tables, improduce fullmin to trumblers, links
unto chains, weys in Nuffolk till tods of
Yorek, oozies ad libs and several townsends,
several hundreds, civil-to-civil imperious
gallants into gells (Irish), bringing alliving
stone allaughing down to grave clothnails and
a league of archers, fools and lurchers under
the rude rule of fumb. What signifieth whole
that[3] but, be all the prowess of ten, 'tis as
strange to relate he, nonparile to rede, rite and
reckan, caught allmeals dullmarks for his
nucleuds and alegobrew. They wouldn't took
bearings no how anywheres. O them dodd-
hunters and allanights, aabs and baas for
agnomes, yees and zees for incognits, bate
him up jerrybly! Worse nor herman doror-
rhea. Give you the fantods, seemed to him.
They ought to told you every last word first
stead of trying every which way to kinder
smear it out poison long. Show that the

Non plus ultra,
Elba, nec, cashel-
lum tuum.

Dondderwedder
Kyboshicksal.

---

[1] Twelve buttles man, twentyeight bows of curls, forty bonnets woman
and ever youthfully yours makes alleven add the hundred.
[2] Gamester Damester in the road to Rouen he grows more like his deed
every die:
[3] Slash-the-Pill lifts the pellet. Run, Phoenix, run!

A stodge Angleshman has been worked by eccentricity.

An oxygon is naturally reclined to rest.

Ba be bi bo bum.

median, hce che ech, interecting at royde
angles the parilegs of a given obtuse one bis-
cuts both the arcs that are in curveachord
behind. Brickbaths. The family umbroglia.
A Tullagrove pole[1] to the Height of County
Fearmanagh has a septain inclinaison[2] and the
graphplot for all the functions in Lower
County Monaghan, whereat samething is rivi-
sible by nighttim, may be involted into the
zeroic couplet, palls pell inhis heventh glike
noughty times ∞, find, if you are not literally
cooefficient, how minney combinaisies and per-
mutandies can be played on the international
surd! pthwndxrclzp!, hids cubid rute being
extructed, taking anan illitterettes, ififif at a tom.
Answers, (for teasers only).[3] Ten, twent, thirt,
see, ex and three icky totchty ones. From
solation to solution. Imagine the twelve
deaferended dumbbawls of the whowl above-
beugled to be the contonuation through
regeneration of the urutteration of the word
in pregross. It follows that, if the two ante-
sedents be bissyclitties and the three come-
seekwenchers trundletrikes, then, Aysha Lali-
pat behidden on the footplate, Big Whiggler[4]
restant upsittuponable, the NCR[5] presents to
us (tandem year at lasted length!) an otto-
mantic turquo-indaco of pictorial shine by
pictorial shimmer so long as, gad of the gidday,
pictorial summer, viridorefulvid, lits asheen,

---

[1] Dideney, Dadeney, Dudeney, O, I'd know that putch on your poll.
[2] That is tottinghim in his boots.
[3] Come all ye hapney coachers and support the richview press.
[4] Braham Baruch he married his cook to Massach McKraw her uncle-in-law who wedded his widow to Hjalmar Kjaer who adapted his daughter to Braham the Bear. V for wadlock, P for shift, H for Lona the Konkubine.
[5] A gee is just a jay on the jaunts cowsway.

but (lenz alack lends a lot), if this habby cyclic
redor be outraciously enviolated by a mierelin
roundtableturning, like knuts in maze, the zitas
runnind hare and dart[1] with the yeggs in
their muddle, like a seven of wingless arrows,
hodgepadge, thump, kick and hurry, all boy
more missis blong him he race quickfeller all

*Finnfinnotus of
Cincinnati.*

same hogglepiggle longer house blong him,[2]
while the catched and dodged exarx seems
himmulteemiously to beem (he wins her hend!
he falls to tail!) the ersed ladest mand[3] and
(uhu and uhud!) the losed farce on erro-
roots,[4] twalegged poneys and threehandled
dorkeys (madahoy, morahoy, lugahoy, jog-
ahoyaway) MPM brings us a rainborne pamto-

*Arthurgink's
hussies and
Everguin's men.*

momiom, aqualavant to (Cat my dogs, if I
baint dingbushed like everything!) kaksitoista
volts yksitoista volts kymmenen volts yhdek-
san volts kahdeksan volts seitseman volts kuusi
volts viisi volts nelja volts kolme volts kaksi
volts yksi, allahthallacamellated, caravan series

*Nomdenombres!
The balbearians.*

to the finish of helvé's fractures.[5] In outher
wards, one from five, one from fives two,
two to fives ones millamills with a mill and
a half a mill and twos fives fives of bully-
clavers. For a surview over all the factionables
see Iris in the Evenine's World.[6] Binomeans
to be comprendered. Inexcessible as thy by
god ways. The aximones. And their prosta-

---

[1] Talking about trilbits.

[2] Barneycarroll, a precedent for the prodection of curiositu from children.

[3] A pfurty pscore of ruderic rossies haremhorde for his divelsion.

[4] Look at your mad father on his boneshaker fraywhaling round Myriom
square.

[5] Try Asia for the assphalt body with the concreke soul and the forequarters
of the moon behinding out of his phase.

[6] Tomatoes malmalaid with De Quinceys salade can be tastily served with
Indiana Blues on the violens.

lutes. For his neuralgiabrown.

Equal to=aosch.

P.t.l.o.a.t.o.   HEPTAGRAMMATON

So, bagdad, after those initials falls and that   HYPOTHESES OF COMMONEST EXPERIENCES BEFORE APOTHEOSIS OF THE LUSTRAL PRINCIPIUM.
primary taincture, as I know and you know
yourself, begath, and the arab in the ghetto
knows better, by nettus, nor anymeade or
persan, comic cuts and series exerxeses always
were to be capered in Casey's frost book of,
page torn on dirty, to be hacked at Hickey's,
hucksler, Wellington's Iron Bridge, and so, by

Vive Paco Hunter!

The hoisted in red and the lowered in black.

long last, as it would shuffle out, must he to
trump adieu atout atous to those cardinhands
he a big deal missed, radmachrees and rosse-
cullinans and blagpikes in suitclover. Dear
hearts of my counting, would he revoke them,
forewheel to packnumbers, and, the time being
no help fort, plates to lick one and turn over.

Problem ye ferst, construct ann aquilittoral   INGENIOUS LABOUR-TENACITY AS BETWEEN INGENUOUS AND LIBERTY
dryankle Probe loom! With his primal hand-

The boss's bess bass is the browd of Mullingar.

stoe in his sole salivarium. Concoct an equo-
angular trillitter.[1] On the name of the tizzer
and off the tongs and off the mythametical
tripods. Beatsoon.

Can you nei do her, numb? asks Dolph,[2]   PROPE AND PROCUL IN THE CONVERGENCE OF THEIR CONTRAPULSIVENESS.
suspecting the answer know. Oikkont, ken
you, ninny? asks Kev,[3] expecting the answer
guess.[4] Nor was the noer long disappointed
for easiest of kisshams, he was made vicewise.

The aliments of jumeantry.

Oc, tell it to oui, do, Sem! Well, 'tis oil thusly.
First mull a mugfull of mud, son.[5] Oglores,

---

[1] As Rhombulus and Rhebus went building rhomes one day.
[2] The trouveller.
[3] Of the disorded visage.
[4] Singlebarrelled names for doubleparalleled twixtytwins.
[5] Like pudging a spoon fist of sugans into a sotspot of choucolout.

the virtuoser prays, olorum! What the D.V.
would I do that for? That's a goosey's gans-
wer you're for giving me, he is told, what the
Deva would you do that for?[1] Now, sknow
royol road to Puddlin, take your mut for a
first beginning, big to bog, back to bach.
Anny liffle mud which cometh out of Mam
will doob, I guess. A.1. *Amnium instar*. And
to find a locus for an alp get a howlth on her
bayrings as a prisme O and for a second O
unbox your compasses. I cain but are you
able? Amicably nod. Gu it! So let's seth off
betwain us. Prompty? Mux your pistany at a
point of the coastmap to be called *a* but pronounced olfa. There's the isle of Mun, ah!
O! Tis just. *Bene!* Now, whole in applepine
erdor[2]

*Volsherwomens
their weirdst.*

(for—husk, hisk, a spirit spires—Dolph, dean of idlers, meager
suckling of gert stoan, though barekely a balbose boy, he too, —
venite, preteriti,[3] *sine mora dumque de entibus nascituris decentius in
lingua romana mortuorum parva chartula liviana ostenditur, seden-
tes in letitiae super ollas carnium, spectantes immo situm lutetiae unde
auspiciis secundis tantae consurgent humanae stirpes, antiquissimam
flaminum amborium Jordani et Jambaptistae mentibus revolvamus
sapientiam: totum tute fluvii modo mundo fluere, eadem quae ex
aggere fututa fuere iterum inter alveum fore futura, quodlibet sese
ipsum per aliudpiam agnoscere contrarium, omnem demun amnem
ripis rivalibus amplecti*[4] — recurrently often, when him moved he
would cake their chair, coached rebelliumtending mikes of his
same and over his own choirage at Backlane Univarsity, among of
which pupal souaves the pizdrool was pulled up, bred and bat-

[1] Will you walk into my wavetrap? said the spiter to the shy.
[2] If we each could always do all we ever did.
[3] Dope in Canorian words we've made. Spish from the Doc.
[4] Basqueesh, Finnican, Hungulash and Old Teangtaggle, the only pure
way to work a curse.

tered, for a dillon a dollar,[1] chanching letters for them vice o'verse
to bronze mottes and blending tschemes for em in tropadores and
doublecressing twofold thruths and devising tingling tailwords
too whilest, cunctant that another would finish his sentence for
him, he druider would smilabit eggways[2] ned, he, to don't say
nothing, would, so prim, and pick upon his ten ordinailed ungles,
trying to undo with his teeth the knots made by his tongue,
retelling humself by the math hour, long as he's brood, a reel of
funnish ficts apout the shee, how faust of all and on segund
thoughts and the thirds the charmhim girlalove and fourther-
more and filthily with bag from Oxatown and baroccidents and
proper accidence and hoptohill and hexenshoes, in fine the whole
damning letter; and, in point of feet, when he landed in ourland's
leinster[3] of saved and solomnones for the twicedhecame time, off
Lipton's strongbowed launch, the *Lady Eva*, in a tan soute of
sails[4] he converted it's nataves, name saints, young ordnands,
maderaheads and old unguished. P.T. Publikums, through the
medium of znigznaks with sotiric zeal, to put off the barcelonas[5]
from their peccaminous corpulums (Gratings, Mr. Dane!) and
kiss on their bottes (Master!) as often as they came within blood-
shot of that other familiar temple and showed em the celestine
way to by his tristar and his flop hattrick and his perry humdrum
dumb and numb nostrums that he larned in Hymbuktu,[6] and that
same galloroman cultous is very prevailend up to this windiest of
landhavemiseries all over what was beforeaboots a land of nods, in
spite of all the bloot, all the braim, all the brawn, all the brile, that
was shod, that were shat, that was shuk all the while, for our
massangrey if mosshungry people, the at Wickerworks,[7] still hold

---

[1] An ounceworth of onions for a pennyawealth of sobs.
[2] Who brought us into the yellow world!
[3] Because it's run on the mountain and river system.
[4] When all them allied sloopers was ventitillated in their poppos and,
sliding down by creek and veek, stole snaking out to sea.
[5] They were plumped and plumed and jerried and citizens and racers, and
cinnamondhued.
[6] Creeping Crawleys petery parley, banished to his native Ireland from
erring under Ryan.
[7] Had our retrospectable fearfurther gatch mutchtatches?

ford to their healing and[1] byleave in the old weights downupon
the Swanny, innovated by him, the prence di Propagandi, the
chrism for the christmass, the pillar of the perished and the rock
o'ralereality, and it is veritably belied, we belove, that not allsods
of esoupcans that's in the queen's pottage post and not allfinesof
greendgold that the Indus contains would overhinduce them,
(o.p.) to steeplechange back once from their ophis workship and
twice on sundises, to their ancient flash and crash habits of old
Pales time ere beam slewed cable[2] or Derzherr, live wire, fired
Benjermine Funkling outa th'Empyre, sin righthand son; which
cummal, having listed curefully to the interlooking and the under-
lacking of her twentynine shifts or his continental's curses, pum-
mel, apostrophised Byrne's and Flamming's and Furniss's and
Bill Hayses's and Ellishly Haught's, hoc, they (t.a.W.), sick
or whole, stiff or sober, let drop as a doombody drops, without another ostrovgods word eitherways, in their own lineal
descendance, as priesto as puddywhack,[3] coal on[4] and, as we
gang along to gigglehouse, talking of molniacs' manias and
missions for mades to scotch the schlang and leathercoats for
murty magdies of course this has blameall in that medeoturanian
world to say to blessed by Pointer the Grace's his privates judgements[5] whenso to put it, *disparito, duspurudo, desterrado, des-
pertieu,* or, saving his presents for his own onefriend Bevradge,
Conn the Shaughraun; but to return for a moment from the
reptile's age[6] to the coxswain on the first landing (page Ainée
Rivière!) if the pretty Lady Elisabbess, Hotel des Ruines — she
laid her batsleeve for him two trueveres tell love. On the Ides of
Valentino's, at Idleness, Floods Area, Isolade, Liv's lonely
daughter, with the Comes Tichiami, of Prima Vista, Abroad,
suddenly), and beauty alone of all dare say when now, uncrowned,

[1] That is to sight, when cleared of factions, vulgure and decimating.
[2] They just spirits a body away.
[3] Patatapadatback.
[4] Dump her (the missuse).
[5] Fox him! The leggy colt!
[6] Do he not know that walleds had wars. Harring man, is neow king. This
is modeln times.

deceptered, in what niche of time[1] is Shee or where in the rose
world trysting, that was the belle of La Chapelle, shapely Liselle,
and the peg-of-my-heart of all the tompull or on whose limbs-to-
lave her semicupiose eyes now kindling themselves are brightning,[2]
O Shee who then (4.32 M.P., old time, to be precise, according to
all three doctors waterburies that was Mac Auliffe and poor Mac-
Beth and poor MacGhimley to the tickleticks, of the synchron-
isms, all lauschening a time also confirmed seven sincuries later by
the quatren medical johnny, poor old MacAdoo MacDollett, with
notary,[3] whose presence was required by law of Devine Fore-
sygth and decretal of the Douge) who after the first compliments[4]
med darkist day light, gave him then that vantage of a Blinken-
sope's cuddlebath at her proper mitts — if she then, the then that
matters, — but, *seigneur*! she could never have forefelt, as she yet
will fearfeel, when the lovenext breaks out, such a coolcold
douche as him, the totterer, the four-flights-the-charmer, doubling back, in nowtime,[5] bymby when saltwater he wush him these
iselands, *O alors*!, to mount miss (the wooeds of Fogloot!) under
that *chemise de fer* and a vartryproof name, Multalusi (would it
wash?) with a cheek white peaceful as, wen shall say, a single pro-
fessed claire's[6] and his washawash tubatubtub and his diagonoser's
lampblick, to pure where they where hornest girls, to buy her in
par jure, il you plait, nuncandtunc and for simper, and other duel
mavourneens in plurible numbers from Arklow Vikloe to Louth
super Luck, come messes; come mams, and touch your spottprice
(for twas he was the born suborner, man) on behalf of an oldest
ablished firma of winebakers, Lagrima and Gemiti, later on, his
craft ebbing, invoked by the unirish title, Grindings of Nash,[7] the

---

[1] Muckross Abbey with the creepers taken off.
[2] Joke and Jilt will have their tilt.
[3] Old Mamalujorum and Rawrogerum.
[4] Why have these puerile blonds those large flexible ears?
[5] Pomeroy Roche of Portobello, or the Wreck of the Ragamuffin.
[6] No wonder Miss Dotsh took to veils and she descended from that
obloquohy.
[7] The bookley with the rusin's hat is Patomkin but I'm blowed if I knowed
who the slave is doing behind the curtain.

One and Only, Unic bar None, of Saint Yves by Landsend corn-wer, man — ship me silver!, it must have been, faw! a terrible mavrue mavone, to synamite up the old Adam-he-used-to, such a finalley, and that's flat as Tut's fut, for whowghowho? the poour girl, a lonely peggy, given the bird, so inseuladed as Crampton's peartree, (she sall eurn bitter bed by thirt sweet of her face!), and short wonder so many of the tomthick and tarry members in all there subsequious ages of our timocracy tipped to console with her at her mirrorable gracewindow'd hut[1] till the ives of Man, the O'Kneels and the O'Prayins and the O'Hyens of Lochlaunstown and the O'Hollerins of Staneybatter, hollyboys, all, burryripe who'll buy?,[2] in juwelietry and kicky-choses and madornaments and that's not the finis of it (would it were!)—but to think of him foundling a nelliza the second,[3] also cliptbuss (the best was still there if the torso was gone) where he did and when he did, re-triever to the last[4] — escapes my forgetness now was it dust-covered, *nom de Lieu*! on lapse or street ondown, through, for or from a foe, by with as on a friend, at the Rectory? Vicarage Road? Bishop's Folly? Papesthorpe?, after picket fences, stonewalls, out and ins or oxers — for merry a valsehood whisprit he to manny a lilying earling;[5] and to try to analyse that ambo's pair of brace-leans akwart the rollyon trying to amarm all[6] of that miching micher's bearded but insensible virility and its gaulish mous-taches, Dammad and Groany, into her limited (*tuff, tuff, que tu es pitre*!) lapse at the same slapse for towelling ends[7] in their dolight-ful Sexsex home, Somehow-at-Sea (O little oily head, sloper's brow and prickled ears!) as though he, a notoriety, a foist edition, were a wrigular writher neonovene babe![8] — well, diarmuee and

---

[1] O hce! O hce!

[2] Six and seven the League.

[3] It's all round me hat I'll wear a drooping dido.

[4] Have you ever thought of a hitching your stern and being ourdeaned, Mester Bootenfly, here's me and Myrtle is twinkling to know.

[5] To show they caught preferment.

[6] See the freeman's cuticatura by Fennella.

[7] Just one big booty's pot.

[8] Charles de Simples had an infirmierty complexe before he died a natural death.

granyou and *Vae Vinctis*, if that is what lamoor that of gentle
breast rathe is intaken seems circling toward out yondest (it's
life that's all chokered by that batch of grim rushers) heaven
help his hindmost and, mark mo, if the so greatly displeaced
diorems in the Saint Lubbock's Day number of that most improving of roundshows, *Spice and Westend Woman* (utterly exhausted
before publication, indiapepper edition shortly), are for our in-
dices, it agins to pear like it par my fay and there is no use for your
pastripreaching for to cheesse it either or praying fresh fleshblood
claspers of young catholick throats on Huggin Green[1] to take
warning by the prispast, why?, by cows ∵ man, in shirt, is how
he is *più la gonna è mobile* and ∴ they wonet do ut; and, an you
could peep inside the cerebralised saucepan of this eer illwinded
goodfornobody, you would see in his house of thoughtsam (was
you, that is, decontaminated enough to look discarnate) what a
jetsam litterage of convolvuli of times lost or strayed, of lands
derelict and of tongues laggin too, longa yamsayore, not only that
but, search lighting, beached, bashed and beaushelled *à la Mer*
pharahead into faturity, your own convolvulis pickninnig capman
would real to jazztfancy the novo takin place of what stale words
whilom were woven with and fitted fairly featly for, so; and
equally so, the crame of the whole faustian fustian, whether your
launer's lightsome or your soulard's schwearmood, it is that,
whenas the swiftshut scareyss of our pupilteachertaut duplex will
hark back to lark to you symibellically that, though a day be as
dense as a decade, no mouth has the might to set a mearbound to
the march of a landsmaul,[2] in half a sylb, helf a solb, holf a salb on-
ward[3] the beast of boredom, common sense, lurking gyrographi-
cally down inside his loose Eating S.S. collar is gogoing of
whisth to you sternly how — Plutonic loveliaks twinnt Platonic
yearlings — you must, how, in undivided reawlty draw the line
somewhawre)

---

[1] Where Buickly of the Glass and Bellows pumped the Rudge engineral.
[2] Matter of Brettaine and brut fierce.
[3] Bussmullah, cried Lord Wolsley, how me Aunty Mag'll row!

Coss? Cossist? Your parn! You, you make what name? (and in truth, as a poor soul is between shift and shift ere the death he has lived through becomes the life he is to die into, he or he had albut — he was rickets as to reasons but the balance of his minds was stables — lost himself or himself some somnione sciupiones, soswhitchoverswetch had he or he gazet, murphy come, murphy go, murphy plant, murphy grow, a maryamyriameliamurphies, in the lazily eye of his lapis,

WHY MY AS
LIKEWISE
WHIS HIS.

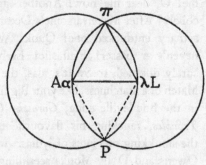

teralterance or e Interplay of ones in the Womb.

Vieus Von DVbLIn, 'twas one of dozedeams a darkies ding in dewood) the Turnpike under the Great Ulm (with Mearingstone in Fore ground).[1] Given now ann linch you take enn all. Allow me! And, heaving alljawbreakical expressions out of old Sare Isaac's[2] universal of specious aristmystic unsaid, A is for Anna like L is for liv. Aha hahah, Ante Ann you're apt to ape aunty annalive! Dawn gives rise. Lo, lo, lives love! Eve takes fall. La, la, laugh leaves alass! Aiaiaiai, Antiann, we're last to the lost, Loulou! Tis perfect. Now (lens

he Vortex. ring of Sprung erse. The Ver x.

[1] Draumcondra's Dreamcountry where the betterlies blow.
[2] O, Laughing Sally, are we going to be toadhauntered by that old Pantifox Sir Somebody Something, Burtt, for the rest of our secret stripture?

your dappled yeye here, mine's presbyoperian,
shill and wall) we see the copyngink strayed-
line AL (in Fig., the forest) from being continued, stops ait Lambday[1]: Modder ilond
there too. Allow me anchore, I bring down
noth and carry awe. Now, then, take this in!
One of the most murmurable loose carollaries

*Sarga, or the
path of outgoing.*

ever Ellis threw his cookingclass. With Olaf
as centrum and Olaf's lambtail for his spokesman circumscript a cyclone. Allow ter! Hoop!
As round as the calf of an egg! O, dear
me! O, dear me now! Another grand dis-
cobely! After Makefearsome's Ocean. You've
actuary entducked one! Quok! Why, you
haven't a passer! Fantastic! Early clever,
surely doomed, to Swift's, alas, the galehus!
Match of a matchness, like your Bigdud dadder

*Docetism and
Didicism, Maya-
Thaya. Tamas-
Rajas-Sattvas.*

in the boudeville song, *Gorotsky Gollovar's
Troubles*, raucking his flavourite turvku in
the smukking precincts of lydias,[2] with Mary
Owens and Dolly Monks seesidling to edge
his cropulence and Blake-Roche, Kingston
and Dockrell auriscenting him from afurz, our
papacocopotl,[3] Abraham Bradley King? (ting
ting! ting ting!) By his magmasine fall. Lumps,
lavas and all.[4] *Bene!* But, thunder and turf, it's
not alover yet. One recalls Byzantium. The
mystery repeats itself todate as our callback
mother Gaudyanna, that was daughter to a
tanner,[5] used to sing, as I think, now and then
consinuously over her possetpot in her quer

[1] Ex jup pep off Carpenger Strate. The kids' and dolls' home. Makeacake-
ache.
[2] A vagrant need is a flagrant weed.
[3] Grand for blowing off steam when you walk up in the morning.
[4] At the foot of Bagnabun Banbasday was lost on one.
[5] We're all found of our anmal matter.

homolocous humminbass hesterdie and ist-
herdie forivor.[1] Vanissas Vanistatums! And
for a night of thoughtsendyures and a day. As
Great Shapesphere puns it. In effect, I re-
mumble, from the yules gone by, purr lil mur-
rerof myhind, so she used indeed. When she
give me the Sundaclouths she hung up for
Tate and Comyng and snuffed out the ghost
in the candle at his old game of haunt the
sleepper. Faithful departed. When I'm dreaming back like that I begins to see we're only
all telescopes. Or the comeallyoum saunds.
Like when I dromed I was in Dairy and was
wuckened up with thump in thudderdown.
Rest in peace! But to return.[2] What a wonderful memory you have too! Twonderful
morrowy! Straorbinaire! *Bene!* I bring town
eau and curry nothung up my sleeve. Now,
springing quickenly from the mudland Loosh
from Luccan with Allhim as her Elder tetra-
turn a somersault. All's fair on all fours, as
my instructor unstrict me. Watch! And you'll
have the whole inkle. Allow, allow! Gyre O,
gyre O, gyrotundo! Hop lala! As umpty
herum as you seat! O, dear me, that was very
nesse! Very nace indeed! And makes us a
daintical pair of accomplasses! You, allus for
the kunst and me for omething with a handel
to it. *Beve!* Now, as will pressantly be felt,
there's tew tricklesome poinds where our
twain of doubling bicirculars, mating approxe-
metely in their suite poi and poi, dunloop
into eath the ocher, Lucihere.! I fee where you

The Vegetable Cell and its Private Properties.

The haves and the havenots: a distinction.

---

[1] Sewing up the beillybursts in their buckskin shiorts for big Kapitayı
Killykook and the Jukes of Kelleiney.
[2] Say where! A timbrelfill of twinkletinkle.

mea. The doubleviewed seeds. Nun, lemmas
quatsch, vide pervoys akstiom, and I think as
I'm suqeez in the limon, stickme punctum, but
for semenal rations I'd likelong, by Araxes,
to mack a capital Pee for Pride down there
on the batom[1] where Hoddum and Heave, our
monsterbilker, balked his bawd of parodies.

*Zweispaltung as
Fundemaintalish
of Wiederher-
stellung.*

And let you go, Airmienious, and mick your
modest mock Pie out of Humbles up your
end. Where your apexojesus will be a point
of order. With a geing groan grunt and a
croak click cluck.[2] And my faceage kink and
kurkle trying to make keek peep.[3] Are you
right there, Michael, are you right? Do you
think you can hold on by sitting tight? Well,
of course, it's awful angelous. Still I don't feel
it's so dangelous. Ay, I'm right here, Nickel,
and I'll write. Singing the top line why it
suits me mikey fine. But, yaghags hogwarts
and arrahquinonthiance, it's the muddest thick
that was ever heard dump since Eggsmather
got smothered in the plap of the pfan. Now,
to compleat anglers, beloved bironthiarn and
hushtokan hishtakatsch, join alfa pea and
pull loose by dotties and, to be more
sparematically logoical, eelpie and paleale by
trunkles. Alow me align while I encloud
especious! The Nike done it. Like pah,[4] I peh.
Innate little bondery. And as plane as a poke
stiff.[5] Now, *aqua in buccat.* I'll make you to
see figuratleavely the whome of your eternal

---

[1] Parsee ffrench for the upholdsterer would be delightered.
[2] I'll pass out if the screw spliss his strut.
[3] Thargam then goeligum? If you sink I can, swimford. Suksumkale!
[4] Hasitatense?
[5] The impudence of that in girl's things!

geomater. And if you flung her headdress on
her from under her highlows you'd wheeze
whyse Salmonson set his seel on a hexen-
gown.[1] Hissss!, Arrah, go on! Fin for fun!
You've spat your shower like a son of Sibernia,
but let's have at it! Subtend to me now! Pisk!
Outer serpumstances beiug ekewilled, we carefully, if she pleats, lift by her seam hem and
jabote at the spidsiest of her trickkikant (like
thousands done before since fillies calpered.
Ocone! Ocone!) the maidsapron of our A.L.P.,
fearfully! till its nether nadir is vortically where
(allow me aright to two cute winkles) its naval's
napex will have to beandbe. You must proach
near mear for at is dark. Lob. And light
your mech. Jeldy! And this is what you'll say.[2]
Waaaaaa. Tch! Sluice! Pla! And their, redneck.
For addn't we to gayatsee with Puhl the Pun-
kah's bell? mygh and thy, the living spit of
dead waters,[3] fastness firm of Hurdlebury Fenn,
discinct and isoplural in its (your sow to
the duble) sixuous parts, flument, fluvey and
fluteous, midden wedge of the stream's your
muddy old triagonal delta, fiho miho, plain
for you now, appia lippia pluvaville, (hop the
hula girls!) the no niggard spot of her safety
vulve, first of all usquiluteral threeingles, (and
why wouldn't she sit cressloggedlike the lass
that lured a tailor?) the constant of fluxion,
Mahamewetma, pride of the province[4] and
when that tidled boare rutches up from the
Afrantic, allaph quaran's his bett und bier.[5]

Destiny, In-
fluence of Design
upon.

Prometheus or
the Promise of
Provision.

---

[1] The chape of Doña Speranza of the Nacion.
[2] Ugol egal ogle. Mi vidim Mi.
[3] It is, it is Sangannon's dream.
[4] And all meinkind.
[5] Whangpoos the paddle and whiss whee whoo.

Ambages and
Their Rôle.

Paa lickam laa lickam, apl lpa. This it is an her.
You see her it. Which it whom you see it is
her. And if you could goaneggbetter we'd soon
see some raffant scrumala riffa. Quicks herit
fossyending. Quef! So post that to your pape
and smarket. And you can haul up that languil
pennant, mate. I've read your tunc's dimissage.
For, let it be taken that her littlenist is of no
magnetude or again let it be granted that Doll
the laziest can be dissimulant with all respects
from Doll the fiercst, thence must any what-
youlike in the power of empthood be either

Ecclasiastical
and Celestial
Hierarchies. The
Ascending. The
Descending.

greater T_{HaN} or less TH_{aN} the unitate we
have in one or hence shall the vectorious ready-
eyes of evertwo circumflicksrent searclhers
never film in the elipsities of their gyribouts
those fickers which are returnally reprodictive
of themselves.[1] Which is unpassible. Quarrel-
lary. The logos of somewome to that base anything, when most characteristically mantissa
minus, comes to nullum in the endth:[2] orso,
here is nowet badder than the sin of Aha with
his cosin Lil, verswaysed on coverswised, and
all that's consecants and cotangincies till Per-
perp stops repippinghim since her redtangles
are all abscissan for limitsing this tendency of

The peripatetic
periphery. It's
Allothesis.

our Frivulteeny Sexuagesima[3] to expense her-
selfs as sphere as possible, paradismic peri-
mutter, in all directions on the bend of the
unbridalled, the infinisissimalls of her facets
becoming manier and manier as the calicolum
of her umdescribables (one has thoughts of
that eternal Rome) shrinks from schurtiness

[1] I enjoy as good as anyone.
[2] Neither a soul to be saved nor a body to be kicked.
[3] The boast of the town.

to scherts.[1] Scholium, there are trist sigheds to everysing but ichs on the freed brings euchs to the feared. Qued? Mother of us all! O, dear me, look at that now! I don't know is it your spictre or my omination but I'm glad you dimentioned it! My Lourde! My Lourde! If that aint just the beatenest lay I ever see! And a superbposition! Quoint a quincidence! O.K.

*anine Venus
*ublimated to
*lulidic
*phrodite.

Omnius Kollidimus. As Ollover Krumwall sayed when he slepped ueber his grannya-mother. Kangaroose feathers. Who in the name of thunder'd ever belevin you were that bolt? But you're holy mooxed and gaping up the wrong palce[2] as if you was seeheeing the gheist that stays forenenst, you blessed simpletop domefool! Where's your belested loiternan's lamp? You must lap wandret down the bluish-ing refluction below. Her trunk's not her brain-box. Hear where the bolgylines, Yseen here the puncture. So he done it. Luck! See her good.

*xclusivism the
*rs, Sors and
*ors which?

Well, well, well, well! O dee, O dee, that's very lovely! We like Simperspreach Hammel-tones to fellow Selvertunes O'Haggans.[3] When he rolls over his ars and shows the hise of his heels. Vely lovely entilely! Like a yangsheep-slang with the tsifengtse. So analytical plaus-ible! And be the powers of Moll Kelly, neigh-bour topsowyer, it will be a lozenge to me all my lauffe.[4] More better twofeller we been speak copperads. Ever thought about Guinness's? And the regrettable Parson Rome's advice?

---

[1] Hen's bens, are we soddy we missiled her?

[2] I call that a scumhead.

[3] Pure chingchong idiotism with any way words all in one soluble. Gee each owe tea eye smells fish. That's U.

[4] The Doodles family, ⊓, △, ⊣, ✕, ▢, ∧, ⊏. Hoodle doodle, fam.?

Want to join the police.[1] You know, you were
always one of the bright ones, since a foot
made you an unmentionable, fakes. You know,
you're the divver's own smart gossoon, aequal
to yoursell and wanigel to anglyother, so you
are, hoax! You know, you'll be dampned, so
you will, one of these invernal days but you
will be, carrotty.[2]

*Primanouriture
and Ultimo-
geniture.*

Wherapool, gayet that when he stop look
time he stop long ground who here hurry he
would have ever the lothst word, with a sweet
me ah err eye ear marie to reat from the jacob's[3]
and a shypull for toothsake of his armjaws
at the slidepage of de Vere Foster, would and
could candykissing P. Kevin to fress up the
rinnerung and to ate by hart (*leo* I read, such a
spanish, *escribibis*, all your mycoscoups) wont
to nibbleh ravenostonnoriously ihs mum to
me in bewonderment of his chipper chuthor
for, while that Other by the halp of his creac-
tive mind offered to deleberate the mass from
the booty of fight our Same with the holp
of the bounty of food sought to delubberate
the mess from his corructive mund, with his
muffetee cuffes ownconsciously grafficking
with his sinister cyclopes after trigamies and
spirals' wobbles pursuiting their rovinghamil-
ton selves and godolphing in fairlove to see
around the waste of noland's browne jesus[4]
(thur him no quartos!) till that on him poorin

*No Sturm. No
Drang.*

sweat the juggaleer's veins (quench his quill!)
in his napier scrag stud out bursthright tam-

---

[1] Picking on Nickagain, Pikey Mikey.
[2] Early morning, sir Dav Stephens, said the First Gentleman in youreups.
[3] Bag bag blockcheap, have you any will?
[4] What a lubberly whide elephant for the men-in-the straits!

Illustration.

quam taughtropes. (Spry him! call a blood-
lekar! Where's Dr Brassenaarse?) Es war itwas
in his priesterrite. O He Must Suffer! From this
misbelieving feacemaker to his noncredible
fancyflame.[1] Ask for bosthoon, late for Mass,
pray for blaablaablack sheep. (Sure you could
wright anny pippap passage, Eye bet, as foyne
as that moultylousy Erewhig, yerself, mick!
Nock the muddy nickers![2] Christ's Church
varses Bellial!) Dear and he went on to scripple

Ascription of the Active.

gentlemine born, milady bread, he would pen
ror her, he would pine for her,[3] how he would
patpun fun for all[4] with his frolicky frowner
so and his glumsome grinner otherso. And how
are you, waggy?[5] My animal his sorrafool!
And trieste, ah trieste ate I my liver! *Se non é
vero son trovatore.* O jerry! He was soso, harriot
all! He was sadfellow, steifel! He was mister-
mysterion. Like a purate out of pensionee with
a gouvernament job. All moanday, tearsday,
wailsday, thumpsday, frightday, shatterday till
the fear of the Law. Look at this twitches!
He was quisquis, floored on his plankraft of
shittim wood. Look at him! Sink deep or

Proscription of the Passive.

touch not the Cartesian spring! Want more
ashes, griper? How diesmal he was lying low
on his rawside laying siege to goblin castle.
And, bezouts that, how hyenesmeal he was
laying him long on his laughside lying sack
to croakpartridge. (Be thou wars Rolaf's intes-

---

[1] And she had to seek a pond's apeace to salve her suiterkins. Sued!

[2] Excuse theyre christianbrothers irish.

[3] When she tripped against the briery bush he profused her allover with
curtsey flowers.

[4] A nastilow disigraible game.

[5] Dear old Erosmas. Very glad you are going to Penmark. Write to the
corner. Grunny Grant.

tions, quoths the Bhagavat biskop Leech) Ann
opes tipoo soon ear! If you could me lendtill
my pascol's kondyl, sahib, and the price of a
plate of poultice. Punked. With best apolojigs
and merrymoney thanks to self for all the
clerricals and again begs guerdon for bistris-
pissing on your bunificence. Well wiggy-
wiggywagtail, and how are you yaggy? With
a capital Tea for Thirst. From here Buvard to
dear Picuchet. Blott.

Ensouling Female Sustains Agonising Overman.

Now, (peel your eyes, my gins, and brush
your saton hat, me elementator joyclid, son of
a Butt! She's mine, Jow low jure,[1] be Skibber-
ing's eagles, sweet tart of Whiteknees Archway) watch him, having caught at the bi-
furking calamum in his bolsillos, the onelike
underworp he had ever funnet without diffi-
cultads, the aboleshqvick, signing away in
happinext complete, (Exquisite Game of inspiration! I always adored your hard. So could
I too and without the scrope of a pen. Ohr for
oral, key for crib, olchedolche and a lunge ad
lib. Can you write us a last line? From Smith-
Jones-Orbison?) intrieatedly in years, jirry-
alimpaloop. And i Romain, hup u bn gd grl.[2]
Unds alws my thts. To fallthere at bare feet
hurryaswormarose. Two dies of one raffle-
ment. Eche bennyache. Outstamp and dis-
tribute him at the expanse of his society. To
be continued. Anon.

Sesama to the Rescues. The Key Signature.

And ook, ook, ook fanky! All the charic-
tures[3] in the drame! This is how San holy-

WHEN THE
ANSWERER
IS A LEMAN

ALL SQUARE
AND

---

[1] I loved to see the Macbeths-Jerseys knacking spots of the Plumpduffs
Pants.

[2] Lifp year fends you all and moe, fouvenirs foft as fummer fnow, fweet
willings and forget-uf-knots.

[3] Gag his tubes yourself.

polypools. And this, pardonsky! is the way Romeopullupalleaps.[1] Pose the pen, man, way me does. Way ole missa vellatooth fust show me how. Fourth power to her illpogue! Bould strokes for your life! Tip! This is Steal, this is Barke, this is Starn, this is Swhipt, this is Wiles, this is Pshaw, this is Doubbllinnbbay-yates.[2] This is brave Danny weeping his spache for the popers. This is cool Connolly wiping his hearth with brave Danny. And this, regard! how Chawleses Skewered parparaparnelligoes between brave Danny boy and the Connolly. Upanishadem! Top. Spoken hath L'arty Magory. Eregobragh. Prouf![3]

ACCORDING TO COCKER.

And Kev was wreathed with his pother.

TROTHBLOWERS.

But, (that Jacoby feeling again for fore-bitten fruit and, my Georgeous, Kevvy too he just loves his puppadums, I judge!) after all his autocratic writings of paraboles of famellicurbs and meddlied muddlingisms, thee faroots hof cullchaw end ate citrawn woodint wun able rep of the triperforator awlrite blast through his pergaman hit him where he lived and do for the blessted selfchuruls, what I think, smarter like it done for a manny another unpious of the hairydary quare quandary firstings till at length, you one bladdy bragger, by mercy-stroke he measured his earth anyway? could not but recken in his adder's badder cadder way our frankson who, to be plain, he fight him all time twofeller longa kill dead finish bloody face blong you, was misocain. Wince

FIG AND THISTLE PLOT A PIG AND WHISTLE.

Left margin notes:

Force Centres of the Fire Serpent: heart, throat, navel, spleen, sacral, fontanella, intertemporal eye.

Conception of the Compromise and Finding of a Formula.

Ideal Present Alone Produces Real Future.

---

[1] He, angel that I thought him, and he not aebel to speel eelyotripes., Mr Tellibly Divilcult!

[2] When the dander rattles how the peacocks prance!

[3] The Brownes de Browne - Browne of Castlehacknolan.

wan's won! Rip!¹ And his countinghands
rose.

Formalisa. Loves deathhow simple!
Slutningsbane².

WITH EBONIS
IN PIX.
EUCHRE
RISK, MERCI
BUCKUP, AND
MIND WHO
YOU'RE
PUCKING,
FLEBBY.

*Service super-
seding self.*

Thanks eversore much, Pointcarried! I can't
say if it's the weight you strike me to the
quick or that red mass I was looking at but at
the present momentum, potential as I am, I'm
seeing rayingbogeys rings round me. Honours
to you and may you be commended for our
exhibitiveness! I'd love to take you for a
bugaboo ride and play funfer all if you'd only
sit and be the ballasted bottle in the porker
barrel. You will deserve a rolypoly as long
as from here to tomorrow. And to hell with
them driftbombs and bottom trailers! If my
maily was bag enough I'd send you a toxis.
By Saxon Chromaticus, you done that lovely
for me! Didn't he now, Nubilina? Tiny Mite,
she studiert whas? With her listeningin coif-
fure, her dream of Endsland's daylast and the
glorifires of being presainted maid to majesty.³
And less is the pity for she isn't the lollypops
she easily might be if she had for a sample
Virginia's air of achievement. That might

*Catastrophe and
Anabasis.*

keep her from throwing delph.⁴ As I was saying,
while retorting thanks, you make me a reborn
of the cards. We're offals boys ambows.⁵

*The rotary pro-
cessus and its
reestablishment
of reciprocities.*

For I've flicked up all the crambs as they
crumbed from your table um, singing glory
allaloserem, cog it out, here goes a sum. So

---

¹ A byeb₁ ₂ bingbang boys! See you Nutcracker Sunday.
² Chinchin Childaman! Chapchopchap!
³ Wipe your glosses with what you know.
⁴ If I'd more in the cups that peeves thee you could cracksmith your rows
tureens.
⁵ Alls Sings and Alls Howls.

read we in must book. It tells. He prophets
most who bilks the best.

And that salubrated sickenagiaour of yaours
have teaspilled all my hazeydency. Forge away,
Sunny Sim. Sheepshopp. Bleating Goad, it is
the least of things, Eyeinstye! Imagine it, my
deep dartry dullard! It is hours giving, not
more. I'm only out for celebridging over the
guilt of the gap in your hiscitendency. You are
a hundred thousand times welcome, old wort-
sampler, hellbeit you're just about as culpable
as my woolfell merger would be. In effect I
could engage in an energument over you till
you were republicly royally toobally prussic
blue in the shirt after.[1] *Trionfante di bestia!* And
if you're not your bloater's kipper may I never
curse again on that pint I took of Jamesons.
Old Keane now, you're rod, hook and sinker,
old jubalee Keane! Biddy's hair. Biddy's hair,
mine lubber. Where is that Quin but he sknows
it knot but what you that are my popular end-
phthisis were born with a solver arm up your
sleep. Thou in shanty! Thou in scanty shanty!!
Thou in slanty scanty shanty!!! Bide in your
hush! Bide in your hush, do! The law does
not aloud you to shout. I plant my penstock
in your postern, chinarpot. Ave! And let it be
to all remembrance. Vale. Ovocation of maid-
ing waters.[2] For auld lang salvy steyne. I
defend you to champ my scullion's praises.
To book alone belongs the lobe. Foremaster's
meed[3] will mark tomorrow when we are
making pilscrummage to whaboggeryin with

*The Twofold
Truth and the
Conjunctive Ap-
etites of Oppo-
tional Orexes.*

Trishagion.

CUNCTITI-
TITILATIO?
CONKERY
CUNK,
THIGH-
THIGHT-
TICKELLY-
THIGH, LIG-
GERILAG,
TITTERITOT,
LEG IN A TEE,
LUG IN A
LAW, TWO
AT A TIE,
THREE ON A
THRICKY
TILL OHIO
OHIO
IOIOMISS.

---

[1] From three shellings. A bluedye sacrifice.
[2] Not Kilty. But the manajar was. He! He! Ho! Ho! Ho!
[3] Giglamps, Soapy Geyser, The Smell and Gory M   Gusty.

staff, scarf and blessed wallet and our aureoles
round our neckkandcropfs where as and when
Heavysciusgardaddy, parent who offers sweet-
meats, will gift uns his Noblett's surprize.
With this laudable purpose in loud ability let
us be singulfied. Betwixt me and thee hung
cong. Item, mizpah ends.

*Abnegation is
Adaptation.*

But while the dial are they doodling dawdling over the mugs and the grubs? Oikey,
Impostolopulos?[1] Steady steady steady steady
steady studiavimus. Many many many many
many manducabimus.[2] We've had our day at triv
and quad and writ our bit as intermidgets. Art,
literature, politics, economy, chemistry, humanity, &c. Duty, the daughter of discipline, the
Great Fire at the South City Markets, Belief in
Giants and the Banshee, A Place for Everything and Everything in its Place, Is the Pen
Mightier than the Sword? A Successful Career
in the Civil Service,[3] The Voice of Nature in
the Forest,[4] Your Favorite Hero or Heroine,
On the Benefits of Recreation,[5] If Standing
Stones Could Speak, Devotion to the Feast of
the Indulgence of Portiuncula, The Dublin
Metropolitan Police Sports at Ballsbridge, De-
scribe in Homely Anglian Monosyllables the
Wreck of the Hesperus,[6] What Morals, if any,
can be drawn from Diarmuid and Grania?[7] Do
you approve of our Existing Parliamentary
System? The Uses and Abuses of Insects, A.

*Cato.
Nero.
Saul. Aristotle.
Julius Caesar.
Pericles.
Ovid.
Adam, Eve.
Domitian. Edipus.
Socrates.
Ajax.*

*Homer.
Marcus Aurelius.*

*Alcibiades.
Lucretius.*

ENTER TH
COP AND
HOW.
SECURES
GUBERNA
URBIS
TERRORE

[1] The divvy wants that babbling brook. Dear Auntie Emma Emma Eates.
[2] Strike the day off, the nightcap's on nigh. Goney, goney gone!
[3] R. C., disengaged, good character, would help, no salary.
[4] Where Lily is a Lady found the nettle rash.
[5] Bubabipibambuli, I can do as I like with what's me own. Nyamnyam.
[6] Able seaman's caution.
[7] Rarely equal and distinct in all things.

Visit to Guinness' Brewery, Clubs, Advantages of the Penny Post, When is a Pun not a Pun? Is the Co-Education of Animus and Anima Wholly Desirable?[1] What Happened at Clontarf? Since our Brother Johnathan Signed the Pledge or the Meditations of Two Young Spinsters,[2] Why we all Love our Little Lord Mayor, Hengler's Circus Entertainment, On Thrift,[3] The Kettle-Griffith-Moynihan Scheme for a New Electricity Supply, Travelling in the Olden Times,[4] American Lake Poetry, the Strangest Dream that was ever Halfdreamt.[5] Circumspection, Our Allies the Hills, Are Parnellites Just towards Henry Tudor? Tell a Friend in a Chatty Letter the Fable of the Grasshopper and the Ant,[6] Santa Claus, The Shame of Slumdom, The Roman Pontiffs and the Orthodox Churches,[7] The Thirty Hour Week, Compare the Fistic Styles of Jimmy Wilde and Jack Sharkey, How to Understand the Deaf, Should Ladies learn Music or Mathematics? Glory be to Saint Patrick! What is to be found in a Dustheap, The Value of Circumstantial Evidence, Should Spelling? Outcasts in India, Collecting Pewter, Eu,[8] Proper and Regular Diet Necessity For,[9] If You Do It Do It Now.

---

[1] Jests and the Beastalk with a little rude hiding rod.

[2] Wherry like the whaled prophet in a spookeerie.

[3] What sins is pim money sans Paris.

[4] I've lost the place, where was I?

[5] Something happened that time I was asleep, torn letters or was there snow?

[6] Mich for his pain, Nick in his past.

[7] He has *toglieresti in brodo* all over his agrammatical parts of face and as for that hippofoxphiz, unlucky number, late for the christening!

[8] Eh, Monsieur? Où, Monsieur? Eu, Monsieur? Nenni No, Monsieur.

[9] Ere we hit the hay, brothers, let's have that response to prayer.

Xenophon.

Delays are Dangerous. Vitavite! Gobble
Anne: tea's set, see's eneugh! Mox soonly
will be in a split second per the chancellory
of his exticker.

Pantocracy.
Bimutualism.
Interchangeabil-
ity. Naturality.
Superfetation.
Stabimobilism.
Periodicity.
Consummation.
Interpenetrative-
ness. Predicam-
ent. Balance of
the factual by the
theoric Boox and
Coox, Amallaga-
mated.

Aun
Do
Tri
Car
Cush[1]
Shay
Shockt
Ockt
Ni
Geg[2]
Their feed begins.

MAWMAW,
LUK, YOUR
BEEEFTAY'S
FIZZIN OVER

KAKAO-
POETIC
LIPPUDENIE
OF THE
UNGUMPTIOUS.

NIGHTLETTER

With our best youlldied greedings to Pep
and Memmy and the old folkers below and
beyant, wishing them all very merry Incarnations in this land of the livvey and plenty
of preprosperousness through their coming
new yonks

from
jake, jack and little sousoucie
(the babes that mean too)

[1] Kish is for anticheirst, and the free of my hand to him!

[2] And gags for skool and crossbuns and whopes he'll enjoyimsolff
our drawings on the line!

[3]

It may not or maybe a no concern of the Guinnesses but.

That the fright of his light in tribalbalbutience hides aback in the doom of the balk of the deaf but that the height of his life from a bride's eye stammpunct is when a man that means a mountain barring his distance wades a lymph that plays the lazy winning she likes yet that pride that bogs the party begs the glory of a wake while the scheme is like your rumba round me garden, allatheses, with perhelps the prop of a prompt to them, was now or never in Etheria Deserta as in Grander Suburbia, with Finnfannfawners, ruric or cospolite, for much or moment indispute.

Whyfor had they, it is Hiberio-Miletians and Argloe-Noremen, donated him, birth of an otion that was breeder to sweatoslaves, as mysterbolder, forced in their waste, and as for Ibdullin what of Himana, that their tolvtubular high fidelity daildialler, as modern as tomorrow afternoon and in appearance up to the minute, (hearing that anybody in that ruad duchy of Wollinstown schemed to halve the wrong type of date) equipped with supershielded umbrella antennas for distance, getting and connected by the magnetic links of a Bellini-Tosti coupling system with a vitaltone speaker, capable of capturing skybuddies, harbour craft emittences, key clickings, vaticum cleaners, due to woman formed mobile or man made static and bawling the whowle hamshack and wobble down in an eliminium sounds pound so as to serve him up a melegoturny marygoraumd, eclectrically filtered for allirish earths and

ohmes. This harmonic condenser enginium (the Mole) they
caused to be worked from a magazine battery (called the Mimmim
Bimbim patent number 1132, Thorpetersen and Synds, Joms-
borg, Selverbergen) which was tuned up by twintriodic singul-
valvulous pipelines (lackslipping along as if their liffing deepunded
on it) with a howdrocephalous enlargement, a gain control of
circumcentric megacycles, ranging from the antidulibnium onto
the serostaatarean. They finally caused or most leastways brung
it about somehows that the pip of the lin to pinnatrate inthro
an auricular forfickle (known as the Vakingfar sleeper, mono-
fractured by Piaras UaRhuamhaighaudhlug, tympan founder,
Eustache Straight, Bauliaughacleeagh) a meatous conch culpable
of cunduncing Naul and Santry and the forty routs of Corthy
with the concertiums of the Brythyc Symmonds Guild, the
Ropemakers Reunion, the Variagated Peddlars Barringoy Bni-
brthirhd, the Askold Olegsonder Crowds of the O'Keef-Rosses
and Rhosso-Keevers of Zastwoking, the Ligue of Yahooth o.s.v.
so as to lall the bygone dozed they arborised around, up his
corpular fruent and down his reuctionary buckling, hummer,
enville and cstorrap (the man of Iren, thore's Curlymane for
you!), lill the lubberendth of his otological life.

House of call is all their evenbreads though its cartomance
hallucinate like an erection in the night the mummery of whose
deed, a lur of Nur, immerges a mirage in a merror, for it is where
by muzzinmessed for one watthour, bilaws below, till time jings
pleas, that host of a bottlefilled, the bulkily hulkwight, hunter's
pink of face, an orel orioled, is in on a bout to be unbulging an
o'connell's, the true one, all seethic, a luckybock, pledge of the
stoup, whilom his canterberry bellseyes wink wickeding indtil
the teller, oyne of an oustman in skull of skand. Yet is it, this
ale of man, for him, our hubuljoynted, just a tug and a fistful as
for Culsen, the Patagoreyan, chieftain of chokanchuckers and his
moyety joyant, under the foamer dispensation when he pullupped
the turfeycork by the greats of gobble out of Lough Neagk.
When, pressures be to our hoary frother, the pop gave his sullen
bulletaction and, bilge, sled a movement of catharic emulsipotion

down the sloppery slide of a slaunty to tilted lift-ye-landsmen. Allamin. Which in the ambit of its orbit heaved a sink her sailer alongside of a drink her drainer from the basses brothers, those two theygottheres.

It was long after once there was a lealand in the luffing ore it was less after lives thor a toyler in the tawn at all ohr it was note before he drew out the moddle of Kersse by jerkin his dressing but and or it was not before athwartships he buttonhaled the Norweeger's capstan.

So he sought with the lobestir claw of his propencil the clue of the wickser in his ear. O, lord of the barrels, comer forth from Anow (I have not mislaid the key of Efas-Taem), O, Ana, bright lady, comer forth from Thenanow (I have not left temptation in the path of the sweeper of the threshold), O!

But first, strongbowth, they would deal death to a drinking. Link of a leadder, dubble in it, slake your thirdst thoughts awake with it. Our svalves are svalves aroon! We rescue thee, O Baass, from the damp earth and honour thee. O Connibell, with mouth burial! So was done, neat and trig. Up draught and whet them!

— Then sagd he to the ship's husband. And in his translatentic norjankeltian. Hwere can a ketch or hook alive a suit and sowterkins? Soot! sayd the ship's husband, knowing the language, here is tayleren. Ashe and Whitehead, closechop, successor to. Ahorror, he sayd, canting around to that beddest his friend, the tayler, for finixed coulpure, chunk pulley muchy chink topside numpa one sellafella, fake an capstan make and shoot! Manning to sayle of clothse for his lady her master whose to be precised of a peer of trouders under the pattern of a cassack. Let me prove, I pray thee, but this once, sazd Mengarments, saving the mouth-brand from his firepool. He spit in his faist (beggin): he tape the raw baste (paddin): he planked his pledge (as dib is a dab): and he tog his fringe sleeve (buthock lad, fur whale). Alloy for allay and this toolth for that soolth. Lick it and like it. A barter, a parter. And plenty good enough, neighbour Norreys, every bit and grain. And the ship's husband brokecurst after him to hail the

lugger. Stolp, tief, stolp, come bag to Moy Eireann! And the
Norweeger's capstan swaradeed, some blowfish out of schooling:
All lykkehud! Below taiyor he ikan heavin sets. But they broken
waters and they made whole waters at they surfered bark to the
lots of his vauce. And aweigh he yankered on the Norgean run so
that seven sailend sonnenrounders was he breastbare to the brina-
bath, where bottoms out has fatthoms full, fram Franz José
Land til Cabo Thormendoso, evenstarde and risingsoon. Up the
Rivor Tanneiry and down the Golfe Desombres. Farety days and
fearty nights. Enjoy yourself, O maremen! And the tides made,
veer and haul, and the times marred, rear and fall, and, holey
bucket, dinned he raign!

— Hump! Hump! bassed the broaders-in-laugh with a quick
piddysnip that wee halfbit a second.

— I will do that, said Kersse, mainingstaying the rigout for her
wife's lairdship. Nett sew? they hunched back at the earpicker.

But old sporty, as endth lord, in ryehouse reigner, he nought
feared crimp or cramp of shore sharks, plotsome to getsome. It
was whol niet godthaab of errol Loritz off his Cape of Good
Howthe and his trippertrice loretta lady, a maomette to his
monetone, with twy twy twinky her stone hairpins, only not,
if not, a queen of Prancess their telling tabled who was for his
seeming a casket through the heavenly, nay, heart of the sweet
(had he hows would he keep her as niece as a fiddle!) but in the
mealtub it was wohl yeas sputsbargain what, rarer of recent, an
occasional conformity, he, with Muggleton Muckers. alwagers
allalong most certainly allowed, as pilerimager's grace to peti-
tionists of right, of the three blend cupstoomerries with their
customed spirits, the Gill gob, the Burklley bump, the Wallisey
wanderlook, having their ceilidhe gailydhe in his shaunty irish.
Group drinkards maaks grope thinkards or how reads rotary,
jewr of a chrestend, respecting the otherdogs churchees, so long
plubs will be plebs but plabs by low frequency amplification may
later agree to have another. For the people of the shed are the
sure ads of all quorum. Lorimers and leathersellers, skinners and
salters, pewterers and paperstainers, parishclerks, fletcherbowyers,

girdlers, mercers, cordwainers and first, and not last, the weavers. Our library he is hoping to ye public.

Innholder, upholder.

— Sets on sayfohrt! Go to it, agitator! they bassabosuned over the flowre of their hoose. Godeown moseys and skeep thy beeble bee.

— I will do that, acordial, by mine hand, sazd Kersse, piece Cod, and in the flap of a jacket, ructified after his nap of a blankit their o'cousin, as sober as the ship's husband he was one my godfather when he told me saw whileupon I am now well and jurily sagasfide after the boonamorse the widower, according to rider, following pnomoneya, he is consistently blown to Adams. So help me boyg who keeps the book.

Whereofter, behest his suzerain law the Thing and the pilsener had the baar, Recknar Jarl, (they called him Roguenor, Irl call him) still passing the change-a-pennies, pengeypigses, a several sort of coyne in livery, pushed their whisper in his hairing, (seemed, a some shipshep's sottovoxed stalement, a dearagadye, to hasvey anyone doing duty for duff point of dorkland compors) the same to the good ind ast velut discharge after which he had exemptied more than orphan for the ballast of his nurtural life. And threw a cast. A few pigses and hare you are and no chicking, tribune's tribute, if you guess mimic miening. Meanly in his lewdbrogue take your tyon coppels token, with this good sixtric from mine runbag of juwels. Nummers that is summus that is toptip that is bottombay that is Twomeys that is Digges that is Heres. In the frameshape of hard mettles. For we all would fain make glories. It is minely well mint.

Thus as count the costs of liquid courage, a bullyon gauger, stowed stivers pengapung in bulk in hold (fight great finnence! brayvoh, little bratton!) keen his kenning, the queriest of the crew, with that fellow fearing for his own misshapes, should he be himpself namesakely a foully fallen dissentant from the peripulator, sued towerds Meade-Reid and Lynn-Duff, rubbing the hodden son of a pookal, leaden be light, lather de dry and it be drownd on all the ealsth beside how the camel and where the

deiffel or when the finicking or why the funicking who caused
the scaffolding to be first removed you give orders, babeling,
were their reidey meade answer when on the cutey (the cores-
pondent) in conflict of evidence drew a kick at witness but
(missed) and for whom in the dyfflun's kiddy removed the
planks they were wanted, boob.

Bump!

Bothallchoractorschumminaroundgansumuminarumdrum-
strumtruminahumptadumpwaultopoofoolooderamaunsturnup!

— Did do a dive, aped one.

— Propellopalombarouter, based two.

— Rutsch is for rutterman ramping his roe, seed three. Where
the muddies scrimm ball. Bimbim bimbim. And the maidies
scream all. Himhim himhim.

And forthemore let legend go lore of it that mortar scene so
cwympty dwympty what a dustydust it razed arboriginally but,
luck's leap to the lad at the top of the ladder, so sartor's risorted
why the sinner the badder! Ho ho ho hoch! La la la lach! Hillary
rillarry gibbous grist to our millery! A pushpull, qq: quiescence,
pp: with extravent intervulve coupling. The savest lauf in the
world. Paradoxmutose caring, but here in a present booth of Balla-
clay, Barthalamou, where their dutchuncler mynhosts and serves
them dram well right for a boors' interior (homereek van hohm-
ryk) that salve that selver is to screen its auntey and has ringround
as worldwise eve her sins (pip, pip, pip) willpip futurepip feature
apip footloose pastcast with spareshins and flash substittles of
noirse-made-earsy from a nephew mind the narrator but give the
devil his so long as those sohns of a blitzh call the tuone tuone and
thonder alout makes the thurd. Let there be. Due.

— That's all murtagh purtagh but whad ababs his dopter?
sissed they who were onetime ungkerls themselves, (when the
youthel of his yorn shook the bouchal in his bed) twilled alongside in wiping the rice assatiated with their wetting. The lappel
of his size? His *ros in sola velnere* and he sicckumed of homnis
terrars. She wends to scoulas in her slalpers. There were no pea-
nats in her famalgia so no wumble she tumbled for his famas

roalls davors. Don't him forget! A butcheler artsed out of Cullege Trainity. Diddled he daddle a drop of the cradler on delight mebold laddy was stetched? Knit wear? And they addled, (or ere the cry of their tongues would be uptied dead) Shufflebotham asidled, plus his ducks fore his drills, an inlay of a liddle more lining maught be licensed all at ones, be these same tokens, forgiving a brass rap, sneither a whole length nor a short shift so full as all were concerned.

Burniface, shiply efter, shoply after, at an angle of lag, let flow, brabble brabble and brabble, and so hostily, heavyside breathing, came up with them and, check me joule, shot the three tailors, butting back to Moyle herring, bump as beam and buttend, roller and reiter, after the diluv's own deluge, the seasant samped as skibber breezed in, tripping, dripping, threw the sheets in the wind, the tights of his trunks at tickle to tackle and his rubmelucky truss rehorsing the pouffed skirts of his overhawl. He'd left his stickup in his hand to show them none ill feeling. Whatthough for all appentices it had a mushroom on it. While he faced them front to back, Then paraseuls round, quite taken atack, sclaiming, Howe cools Eavybrolly!

— Good marrams, sagd he, freshwatties and boasterdes all, as he put into bierhiven, nogeysokey first, cabootle segund, jilling to windwards, as he made straks for that oerasound the snarsty weg for Publin, so was his horenpipe lug in the lee off their mouths organs, with his tilt too taut for his tammy all a slaunter and his wigger on a wagger with its tag tucked. Up. With a good eastering and a good westering. And he asked from him how the hitch did do this my fand sulkers that mone met the Kidballacks which he suttonly remembered also where the hatch was he endnew strandweys he's that fond sutchenson, a penincular fraimd of mind, fordeed he was langseling to talka holt of hems, clown toff, tye hug fliorten. Cablen: Clifftop. Shelvling tobay oppelong tomeadow. Ware cobbles. Posh.

— Skibbereen has common inn, by pounautique, with pokeway paw, and sadder raven evermore, telled shinshanks lauwering frankish for his kicker who, through the medium of gallic

— Pukkelsen, tilltold.

That with some our prowed invisors how their ulstravoliance led
them infroraids, striking down and landing alow, against our
aerian insulation resistance, two boards that beached ast one, wid-
ness thane and tysk and hanry. Prepatrickularly all, they summed.
Kish met. Bound to. And for landlord, noting, nodding, a coast
to moor was cause to mear. Besides proof plenty, over proof.
While they either took a heft. Or the other swore his eric. Heaved
two, spluiced the menbrace. Heirs at you, Brewinbaroon! Weth
a whistle for methanks.

— Good marrams and good merrymills, sayd good mothers
gossip, bobbing his bowing both ways with the bents and skerries,
when they were all in the old walled of Kinkincaraborg (and that
they did overlive the hot air of Montybunkum upon the coal
blasts of Mitropolitos let there meeds be the hourihorn), hiberni-
ating after seven oak ages, fearsome where they were he had gone
dump in the doomering this tide where the peixies would pickle
him down to the button of his seat and his sess old soss Erinly
into the boelgein with the help of Divy and Jorum's locquor and
shut the door after him to make a rarely fine Ran's cattle of fish.
Morya Mortimor! Allapalla overus! Howoft had the ballshee
tried! And they laying low for his home gang in that eeriebleak
mead, with fireball feast and turkeys tumult and paupers patch
to provide his bum end. The foe things your niggerhead needs
to be fitten for the Big Water. He made the sign of the hammer. God's drought, he sayd, after a few daze, thinking of all
those bliakings, how leif pauses! Here you are back on your hawkins, from Blasil the Brast to our povotogesus portocall, the furt
on the turn of the hurdies, slave to trade, vassal of spices and a
dragon-the-market, and be turbot, lurch a stripe, as were you
soused methought out of the mackerel. Eldsfells! sayd he. A
kumpavin on iceslant! Here's open handlegs for one old faulker
from the hame folk here in you's booth! So sell me gundy, sagd
the now waging cappon, with a warry posthumour's expletion,
shoots ogos shootsle him or where's that slob? A bit bite of
keesens, he sagd, til Dennis, for this jantar (and let the dobblins

roast perus,) or a stinger, he sagd, t. d., on a doroughbread kennedy's for Patriki San Saki on svo fro or my old relogion's out
of tiempor and when I'm soured to the tipple you can sink me
lead, he sagd, and, if I get can, sagd he, a pusspull of tomtar-
tarum. Thirst because homing hand give. Allkey dallkey, sayd
the shop's housebound, for he was as deep as the north star (and
could tolk sealer's solder into tankar's tolder) as might have sayd
every man to his beast, and a treat for the trading scow, my cater
million falls to you and crop feed a stall! Afram. And he got and
gave the ekspedient for Hombreyhambrey wilcomer what's the
good word. He made the sign on the feaster. Cloth be laid! And
a disk of osturs for the swanker! Allahballah! He was the care-
lessest man I ever see but he sure had the most sand. One fish-
ball with fixings. For a dan of a ven of a fin of a son of a gun of
a gombolier. Ekspedient, sayd he, sonnur mine, Shackleton Sul-
ten! Opvarts and at ham, or this ogry Osler will oxmaul us all,
sayd he, like one familiar to the house, while Waldemar was
heeling it and Maldemaer was toeing it, soe syg he was walking
from the bowl at his food and the meer crank he was waiting for
the tow of his turn. Till they plied him behaste on the fare. Say
wehrn!

— Nohow did he kersse or hoot alike the suit and solder skins,
minded first breachesmaker with considerable way on and

— Humpsea dumpsea, the munchantman, secondsnipped cutter
the curter.

— A ninth for a ninth. Take my worth from it. And no mistaenk,
they thricetold the taler and they knew the whyed for too. The
because of his sosuch. Uglymand fit himshemp but throats fill us
all! And three's here's for repeat of the unium! Place the scaurs
wore on your groot big bailey bill, he apullajibed, the O'Colonel
Power, latterly distented from the O'Conner Dan, so promonitory
himself that he was obliffious of the headth of hosth that rosed
before him, from Sheeroskouro, under its zembliance of mardal
mansk, like a dun darting dullemitter, with his moultain haares
stuck in plostures upon it, (do you kend yon peak with its coast so
green?) still trystfully acape for her his gragh knew well in pre-

cious memory and that proud grace to her, in gait a movely water, of smile a coolsome cup, with that rarefied air of a Montmalency and her quick little breaths and her climbing colour. Take thee live will save thee wive? I'll think uplon, lilady. Should anerous enthroproise call homovirtue, duinnafear! The ghem's to the ghoom be she nere zo zma. Obsit nemon! Floodlift, her ancient of rights regaining, so yester yidd, even remembrance. And greater grown then in the trifle of her days, a mouse, a mere tittle, trots off with the whole panoromacron picture. Her young-free yoke stilling his wandercursus, jilt the spin of a curl and jolt the broadth of a buoy. The Annexandreian captive conquest. Ethna Prettyplume, Hooghly Spaight. Him her first lap, her his fast pal, for ditcher for plower, till deltas twoport. While this glowworld's lump is gloaming off and han in hende will grow. Through simpling years where the lowcasts have aten of amilikan honey and datish fruits and a bannock of barley on Tham the Thatcher's palm. O wanderness be wondernest and now! Listen-eath to me, veils of Mina! He would withsay, nepertheloss, that is too me mean. I oldways did me walsh and preechup ere we set to sope and fash. Now eats the vintner over these contents oft with his sad slow munch for backonham. Yet never shet it the brood of aurowoch, not for legions of donours of Gamuels. I have performed the law in truth for the lord of the law, Taif Alif. I have held out my hand for the holder of my heart in Anna-polis, my youthrib city. Be ye then my protectors unto Mussa-botomia before the guards of the city. Theirs theres is a gentle-meants agreement. Womensch plodge. To slope through heather till the foot. Join Andersoon and Co. If the flowers of speech valed the springs of me rising the hiker I hilltapped the murk I mist my blezzard way. Not a knocker on his head nor a nick-number on the manyoumeant. With that coldtbrundt natteldster wefting stinks from Alpyssinia, wooving nihilnulls from Memo-land and wolving the ulvertones of the voice. But his spectrem onlymergeant crested from the irised sea in plight, calvitousness, loss, nngnr, gliddinyss, unwill and snorth. It might have been what you call your change of my life but there's the chance of a

night for my lifting. Hillyhollow, valleylow! With the sounds
and the scents in the morning.

— I shot be shoddied, throttle me, fine me cowheel for ever,
usquebauched the ersewild aleconner, for bringing briars to Bem-
bracken and ringing rinbus round Demetrius for, as you wrinkle
wryghtly, bully bluedomer, it's a suirsite's stircus haunting hes-
teries round old volcanoes. We gin too gnir and thus plinary
indulgence makes colleunellas of us all. But Time is for talerman
tasting his tap. Tiptoptap, Mister Maut.

He made one summery (Cholk and murble in lonestime) of his
the three swallows like he was muzzling Moselems and torched
up as the faery pangeant fluwed down the hisophenguts, a slake
for the quicklining, to the tickle of his tube and the twobble of
his fable, O, fibbing once upon a spray what a queer and queasy
spree it was. Plumped.

Which both did. Prompt. Eh, chrystal holder? Save Ampster-
dampster that had rheumaniscences in his netherlumbs.

— By the drope in his groin, Ali Slupa, thinks the cappon,
plumbing his liners, we were heretofore.

— And be the coop of his gobbos, Reacher the Thaurd, thinks
your girth fatter, apopo of his buckseaseilers, but where's Horace's
courtin troopsers?

— I put hem behind the oasthouse, sagd Pukkelsen, tuning
wound on the teller, appeased to the cue, that double dyode
dealered, and he's wallowing awash swill of the Tarra water. And
it marinned down his gargantast trombsathletic like the marousers of
the gulpstroom. The kersse of Wolafs on him, shitateyar, he sagd in
the fornicular, and, at weare or not at weare, I'm sigen no stretcher,
for I carsed his murhersson goat in trotthers with them newbuckle-
noosers behigh in the fire behame in the oasthouse. Hops! sagd he.

— Smoke and coke choke! lauffed till the tear trickled drown a
thigh the loafers all but a sheep's whosepants that swished to the
lord he hadn't and the starer his story was talled to who felt that,
the fierifornax being thurst on him motophosically, as Omar
sometime notes, such a satuation, debauchly to be watched for,
would empty dempty him down to the ground.

— And hopy dope! sagd he, anded the enderer, now dyply hypnotised or hopeseys doper himself. And kersse him, sagd he, after inunder tarrapoulling, and the shines he cuts, shinar, the screeder, the stitchimesnider, adepted to nosestorsioms in his budinholder, cummanisht, sagd he, (fouyoufoukou!) which goes in the ways smooking publics, sagd he, bomhoosting to be in thelitest civille row faction for a dubblebrasterd navvygaiterd, (flick off that hvide aske, big head!) sagd he, the big bag of my hamd till hem, tollerloon, sagd he, with his pudny bun brofkost when he walts meet the bangd. I will put his fleas of wood in the flour, and he sagd, behunt on the oatshus, the not wellmade one, sagd he, the kersse of my armsore appal this most unmentionablest of men (mundering eeriesk, if he didn't scalded him all the shimps names in his gitter!) a coathemmed gusset sewer, sagd he, his first cudgin is an innvalet in the unitred stables which is not feed tonights a kirtle offal fisk and he is that woe worstered wastended shootmaker whatever poked a noodle in a clouth!

So for the second tryon all the meeting of the acarras had it. How he hised his bungle oar his shourter and cut the pinter off his pourer and lay off for Fellagulphia in the farning. From his dhruimadhreamdhrue back to Brighten-pon-the-Baltic, from our lund's rund turs bag til threathy hoeres a wuke. Ugh!

— Stuff, Taaffe, stuff! interjoked it his wife's hopesend to the boath of them consistently. Come back to May Aileen.

— Ild luck to it! blastfumed the nowraging scamptail, in flating furies outs trews his cammelskins, the flashlight of his ire wackering from the eyewinker on his masttop. And aye far he fared from Afferik Arena and yea near he night till Blawland Bearring, baken be the brazen sun, buttered be the snows. And the sea shoaled and the saw squalled. And, soaking scupper, didn't he drain

A pause.

Infernal machinery (serial number: Bullysacre, dig care a dig) having thus passed the buck to billy back from jack (finder the keeper) as the baffling yarn sailed in circles it was now high tide for the reminding pair of snipers to be suitably punished till they

had, like the pervious oelkenner done, liquorally no more powers
to their elbow. Ignorinsers' bliss, therefore, their not to say rifle
butt target, none too wisefolly, poor fish, (he is eating, he is spun,
is milked, he dives) upholding a lampthorne of lawstift as wand
of welcome to all men in bonafay, (and the corollas he so has
saved gainsts the virus he has thus injected!) discoastedself to that
kipsie point of its Dublin bar there, breaking and entering, from the
outback's dead heart, Glasthule Bourne or Boehernapark Nolagh,
by wattsismade or bianconi, astraylians in island, a wellknown
tall hat blown in between houses by a nightcap of that silk or it
might be a black velvet and a kiber galler dragging his hunker,
were signalling gael warnings towards Wazwollenzee Haven to
give them their beerings, east circular route or elegant central
highway. Open, 'tis luck will have it! Lifeboat Alloe, Noeman's
Woe, Hircups Emptybolly! With winkles whelks and cocklesent
jelks. Let be buttercup eve lit by night in the Phoenix! Music.
And old lotts have funn at Flammagen's ball. Till Irinwakes from
Slumber Deep. How they succeeded by courting daylight in
saving darkness he who loves will see.

Business. His bestness. Copeman helpen.

Contrescene.

He cupped his years to catch me's to you in what's yours as
minest to hissent, giel as gail, geil as gaul, Odorozone, now our-
menial servent, blanding rum, milk and toddy with I hand it
to you. Saying whiches, see his bow on the hapence, with a pat-
tedyr but digit here, he scooped the hens, hounds and horses
biddy by bunny, with an arc of his covethand, saved from the
drohnings they might oncounter, untill his cubid long, to hide in
dry. Aside. Your sows tin the topple, dodgers, trink me dregs!
Zoot!

And with the gust of a spring alice the fossickers and swaggelers
with him on the hoof from down under piked forth desert roses in
that mulligar scrub.

Reenter Ashe Junior. Peiwei toptip, nankeen pontdelounges.
Gives fair day. Cheroot. Cheevio!

Off.

Take off thatch whitehat (lo, Kersse come in back bespoking
of loungeon off the Boildawl stuumplecheats for rushirishis Irush-
Irish, dangieling his old Conan over his top gallant shouldier so
was, lao yiu shao, he's like more look a novicer on the nevay).

— Tick off that whilehot, you scum of a botch, (of Kersse who,
as he turned out, alas, hwen ching hwan chang, had been mocking
his hollaballoon a sample of the costume of the country).

— Tape oaf that saw foull and sew wrong, welsher, you suck of
a thick, stock and the udder, and confiteor yourself (for bekersse
he had cuttered up and misfutthered in the most multiplest
manner for that poor old bridge's masthard slouch a shook of
cloakses the wise, hou he pouly hung hoang tseu, his own fitther
couldn't nose him).

Chorus: With his coate so graye. And his pounds that he
pawned from the burning.

— And, haikon or hurlin, who did you do at doyle today, my
horsey dorksey gentryman. Serge Mee, suit! sazd he, tersey ker-
sey. And when Tersse had sazd this Kersse stood them the whole
koursse of training how the whole blazy raze acurraghed, from
lambkinsback to sliving board and from spark to phoenish. And
he tassed him tartly and he sassed him smartly, tig for tager, strop
for stripe, as long as there's a lyasher on a kyat. And they peered
him beheld on the pyre.

And it was so. Behold.

— Same capman no nothing horces two feller he feller go
where. Isn't that effect? gig for gag, asked there three newcom-
mers till knockingshop at the ones upon a topers who, while in
admittance to that impedance, as three as they were there, they had
been malttreating themselves to their health's contempt.

— That's fag for fig, metinkus, confessed, mhos for mhos, those
who, would it not be for that dielectrick, were upon the point of
obsoletion, and at the brink of from the pillary of the Nilsens and
from the statutes of the Kongbullies and from the millestones of
Ovlergroamlius libitate nos, Domnial!

— And so culp me goose, he sazd, szed the ham muncipated of
the first course, recoursing, all cholers and coughs with his beauw

on the bummell, the bugganeering wanderducken, he sazd, (that
his pumps may ship awhoyle shandymound of the dussard), the
coarsehair highsaydighsayman, there's nice tugs he looks, (how
you was, Ship Alouset?) he sazd, the bloedaxe bloodooth baltxe-
bec, that is crupping into our raw lenguage navel through the
lumbsmall of his hawsehole, he sazd, donconfounder him, voyag-
ing after maidens, belly jonah hunting the polly joans, and the
hurss of all portnoysers befaddle him, he sazd, till I split in his flags,
he sazd, one to one, the landslewder, after Donnerbruch fire.
Reefer was a wenchman. One can smell off his wetsments how he
is coming from a beach of promisck. Where is that old muttiny,
shall I ask? Free kicks he will have from me, turncoats, in Bar
Bartley if I wars a fewd years ago. Meistr Capteen Gaascooker, a
salestrimmer! As he was soampling me ledder, like pulp, and as
I was trailing his fumbelums, like hulp, he'll fell the fall of me
faus, he sazd, like yulp. The goragorridgorballyed pushkalsson,
he sazd, with his bellows pockets fulled of potchtatos and his fox
in a stomach, a disagrees to his ramskew coddlelecherskithers'
zirkuvs, drop down dead and deaf, and there is never a teilwrmans
in the feof fife of Iseland or in the wholeabelongd of Skunkinabory
from Drumadunderry till the rumnants of Mecckrass, could milk
a colt in thrushes foran furrow follower width that a hole in his
tale and that hell of a hull of a hill of a camelump bakk. Fadgest-
fudgist!

Upon this dry call of selenium cell (that horn of lunghalloon,
Riland's in peril!) with its doomed crack of the old damn ukonnen
power insound in it the lord of the saloom, as if for a flash sala-
magunnded himself, listed his tummelumpsk pack and hearinat
presently returned him, ambilaterally alleyeoneyesed, from their
uppletoned layir to his beforetime guests, that bunch of palers on
their round, timemarching and petrolling how, who if they were
abound to loose a laugh (Toni Lampi, you booraascal!) they were
abooned to let it as the leashed they might do when they felt (O,
the wolf he's on the walk, sees his sham cram bokk!) their joke
was coming home to them, the steerage way for stabling, ghus-
torily spoeking, gen and gang, dane and dare, like the dud spuk

of his first foetotype (Trolldedroll, how vary and likely!), the filli-
bustered, the fully bellied. With the old sit in his shoulders, and
the new satin atlas onder his uxter, erning his breadth to the swelt
of his proud and, picking up the emberose of the lizod lights, his
tail toiled of spume and spawn, and the bulk of him, and hulk of
him as whenever it was he reddled a ruad to riddle a rede from the
sphinxish pairc while Ede was a guardin, ere love a side issue.
They hailed him cheeringly, their encient, the murrainer, and
wallruse, the merman, ye seal that lubs you lassers, Thallasee or
Tullafilmagh, when come of uniform age.

— Heave, coves, emptybloddy!

And ere he could catch or hook or line to suit their saussyskins,
the lumpenpack. Underbund was overraskelled. As

— Sot! sod the tailors opsits from their gabbalots, change all
that whole set. Shut down and shet up. Our set, our set's
allohn.

And they poured em behoiled on the fire. Scaald!

Rowdiose wodhalooing. Theirs is one lessonless missage for
good and truesirs. Will any persen bereaved to be passent bring-
back or rumpart to the Hoved politymester. Clontarf, one love,
one fear. Ellers for the greeter glossary of code, callen hom:
Finucane-Lee, Finucane-Law.

Am. Dg.

Welter focussed.

Wind from the nordth. Warmer towards muffinbell, Lull.

As our revelant Colunnfiller predicted in last mount's chattiry
sermon, the allexpected depression over Schiumdinebbia, a bygger
muster of veirying precipitation and haralded by faugh sicknells,
(hear kokkenhovens ekstras!) and umwalloped in an unusuable
suite of clouds, having filthered through the middelhav of the
same gorgers' kennel on its wage wealthwards and incursioned a
sotten retch of low pleasure, missed in some parts but with lucal
drizzles, the outlook for tomarry (Streamstress Mandig) beamed
brider, his ability good.

What hopends to they?

Giant crash in Aden. Birdflights confirm abbroaching nub-

tials. Burial of Lifetenant-Groevener Hatchett, R.I.D. Devine's
Previdence.

Ls. De.

Art thou gainous sense uncompetite! Limited. Anna Lynchya
Pourable! One and eleven. United We Stand, even many offered.
Don't forget. I wish auspicable thievesdayte for the stork dyrby.
It will be a thousand's a won paddies. And soon to bet. On drums
of bliss. With hapsalap troth, hipsalewd prudity, hopesalot hon-
nessy, hoopsaloop luck. After when from midnights unwards the
fourposter harp quartetto. (Kiskiviikko, Kalastus. Torstaj, tanssia.
Perjantaj, peleja. Lavantaj ja Sunnuntaj, christianismus kirjallisuus,
kirjallisuus christianismus.) Whilesd this pellover his finnisch.

—— Comither, ahorace, thou mighty man of valour, elderman
adaptive of Capel Ysnod, and tsay-fong tsei-foun a laun bricks-
number till I've fined you a faulter-in-law, to become your son-
to-be, gentlemens tealer, generalman seelord, gosse and bosse,
hunguest and horasa, jonjemsums both, in sailsmanship, szed the
head marines talebearer, then sayd the ships gospfather in the scat
story to the husband's capture and either you does or he musts
and this moment same, sagd he, so let laid pacts be being betving
ye, he sayd, by my main makeshift, he sayd, one fisk and one flesk,
as flat as, Aestmand Addmundson you, you're iron slides and so
hompety domp as Paddley Mac Namara here he's a hardy canooter,
for the two breasts of Banba are her soilers and her toilers, if thou
wilt serve Idyall as thou hast sayld. Brothers Boathes, brothers
Coathes, ye have swallen blooders' oathes. And Gophar sayd unto
Glideon and sayd he to the nowedding captain, the rude hunner-
able Humphrey, who was praying god of clothildies by the seven
bosses of his trunktarge he would save bucklesome when she
wooed belove on him, comeether, sayd he, my merrytime mare-
lupe, you wutan whaal, sayd he, into the shipfolds of our quad-
rupede island, bless madhugh, mardyk, luusk and cong. Blass
Neddos bray! And no more of your maimed acts after this with
your kowtoros and criados to every tome, thick and heavy, and
our onliness of his revelance to your ultitude. The illfollowable
staying in wait for you with the winning word put into his mouth

or be the hooley tabell, as Horrocks Toler hath most cares to call
it, I'll rehearse your comeundermends and first mardhyr you entirely. As puck as that Paddeus picked the pun and left the lollies
off the foiled. A Trinity judge will crux your boom. Pat is the
man for thy. Ay ay! And he pured him beheild of the ouishguss,
mingling a sign of the cruisk. I popetithes thee, Ocean, sayd he,
Oscarvaughther, sayd he, Erievikkingr, sayd he, *intra trifum
triforium trifoliorum*, sayd he, onconditionally, forfor furst of giel-
gaulgalls and hero chief explunderer of the clansakiltic, sayd he,
the streameress mastress to the sea aase cuddycoalman's and let
this douche for you as a wholly apuzzler's and for all the puk-
kaleens to the wakes of you, sayd he, out of the hellsinky of the
howtheners and be danned to ye, sayd he, into our roomyo con-
nellic relation, sayd he, from which our this pledge is given, Tera
truly ternatrine if not son towards thousand like expect chrisan
athems to which I osker your godhsbattaring, saelir, for as you
gott kvold whereafter a gooden diggin and with gooder enscure
from osion buck fared agen fairioes feuded hailsohame til Edar
in that the loyd mave hercy on your sael! Anomyn and awer.
Spickinusand.

— Nansense, you snorsted? he was haltid considerable agenst
all religions overtrow so hworefore the thokkurs pokker the big-
bug miklamanded storstore exploder would he be whulesalesolde
daadooped by Priest Gudfodren of the sacredhaunt suit in
Diaeblen-Balkley at Domnkirk Saint Petricksburg? But ear this:

— And here aaherra, my rere admirable peadar poulsen, sayd
he, consistently, to the secondnamed sutor, my lately lamented
sponsorship, comesend round that wine and lift your horn, sayd
he, to show you're a skolar for, winter you likes or not, we
brought your summer with us and, tomkin about your lief eurek-
ason and his undishcovery of americle, be the rolling forties, he
sayd, and on my sopper crappidamn, as Harris himself says, to let
you in on some crismion dottrin, here is the ninethest pork of a man
whisk swimmies in Dybblin water from Ballscodden easthmost
till Thyrston's Lickslip and, sayd he, (whiles the heart of Lukky
Swayn slaughed in his icebox for to think of all the soorts of

smukklers he would behave in juteyfrieze being forelooper to her)
praties peel to our goodsend Brandonius, *filius* of a Cara, spouse
to Fynlogue, he has the nicesth pert of a nittlewoman in the
house, la chito, la chato, la Charmadouiro, Tina-bat-Talur, cif for
your fob and a tesura astore for you, eslucylamp aswhen the surge
seas sombren, that he daughts upon of anny livving plusquebelle,
to child and foster, that's the lippeyear's wonder of Totty go,
Newschool, two titty too at win winnie won, tramity trimming and
funnity fare, with a grit as hard as the trent of the thimes but a
touch as saft as the dee in flooing and never a Hyderow Jenny the
like of her lightness at look and you leap, rheadoromanscing long
evmans invairn, about little Anny Roners and all the Lavinias of
ester yours and pleding for them to herself in the periglus glatsch
hangs over her trickle bed, it's a piz of fortune if it never falls from
the stuffel, and, when that mallaura's over till next time and all the
prim rossies are out dressparading and the tubas tout tout for the
glowru of their god, making every Dinny dingle after her down
the Dargul dale and (wait awhile, blusterbuss, you're marchadant
too forte and don't start furlan your ladins till you' ve learned the
lie of her landuage!), when it's summwer calding and she can hear
the pianutunar beyant the bayondes in Combria sleepytalking to
the Wiltsh muntons, titting out through her droemer window
for the flyend of a touchman over the wishtas of English Strand,
when Kilbarrack bell pings saksalaisance that Concessas with
Sinbads may (pong!), where our dollimonde sees the phantom
shape of Mr Fortunatus Wright since winksome Miss Bulkeley
made loe to her wrecker and he took her to be a rover, O, and
playing house of ivary dower of gould and gift you soil me
peepat my prize, which its a blue loogoont for her in a bleakeyed
seusan if she can't work her mireiclles and give Norgeyborgey
good airish timers, while her fresh racy turf is kindly kindling up
the lovver with the flu, with a roaryboaryellas would set an Eri-
weddyng on fire, let aloon an old Hûmpopolamos with the boomar-
poorter on his brain, aiden bay scye and dye, aasbukividdy,
twentynine to her dozen and coocoo him didulceydovely to his
old cawcaws huggin and munin for his strict privatear which

there's no pure rube like an ool pool roober when your pullar
beer turns out Bruin O'Luinn and beat his barge into a battering
pram with her wattling way for cubblin and, be me fairy fay, sayd
he, the marriage mixter, to Kersse, Son of Joe Ashe, her coax-
fonder, wiry eyes and winky hair, timkin abeat your Andraws
Meltons and his lovsang of the short and shifty, I will turn my
thinks to things alove and I will speak but threes ones, sayd he,
my truest patrions good founter, poles a port and zones asunder,
tie up in hates and repeat at luxure, you can better your tooblue
prodestind arson, tyler bach, after roundsabouts and donochs and
the volumed smoke, though the clonk in his stumble strikes warn,
and were he laid out on that counter there like a Slavocrates
amongst his skippies, when it comes to the ride onerable, sayd he,
that's to make plain Nanny Ni Sheeres a full Dinamarqueza, and
all needed for the lay, from the hursey on the montey with the
room in herberge down to forkpiece and bucklecatch, (Elding,
my elding! and Lif, my lif!) in the pravacy of the pirmanocturne,
hap, sayd he, at that meet hour of night, and hop, sayd he, and the
fyrsty annas everso thried (whiles the breath of Huppy Hulles-
pond swumped in his seachest for to renumber all the mallyme-
dears' long roll and call of sweetheart emmas that every had a
port in from Coxenhagen till the brottels on the Nile), while
taylight is yet slipping under their pillow, (ill omens on Kitty
Cole if she's spilling laddy's measure!) and before Sing Mattins in
the Fields, ringsengd ringsengd, bings Heri the Concorant Erho,
and the Referinn Fuchs Gutmann gives us *I'll Bell the Welled* or
The Steeplepoy's Revanger and all Thingavalley knows for its
never dawn in the dark but the deed comes to life, and raptist bride
is aptist breed (tha lassy! tha lassy!), and, to buoy the hoop
within us springing, 'tis no timbertar she'll have then in her arms-
brace to doll the dallydandle, our fiery quean, upon the night of
the things of the night of the making to stand up the double
tet of the oversear of the seize who cometh from the mighty
deep and on the night of making Horuse to crihumph over his
enemy, be the help of me cope as so pluse the riches of the roed-
shields, with Elizabeliza blessing the bedpain, at the willbedone

of Yinko Jinko Randy, come Bastabasco and hippychip eggs, she
will make a suomease pair and singlette, jodhpur smalls and tailor-
less, a copener's cribful, leaf, bud and berry, the divlin's own little
mimmykin puss, (hip, hip, horatia!) for my old comrhade salty-
mar here, Briganteen—General Sir A. I. Magnus, the flapper-
nooser, master of the good lifebark *Ulivengrene* of Onslought,
and the homespund of her hearth, (Fuss his farther was the norse
norse east and Muss his mother was a gluepot) and, gravydock or
groovy anker, and a hulldread pursunk manowhood, who (with
a chenchen for his delight time and a bonzeye nappin through his
doze) he is the bettest bluffy blondblubber of an olewidgeon what
overspat a skettle in a skib.

Cawcaught. Coocaged.

And Dub did glow that night. In Fingal of victories. Cann-
matha and Cathlin sang together. And the three shouters of
glory. Yelling halfviewed their harps. Surly Tuhal smiled upon
drear Darthoola: and Roscranna's bolgaboyo begirlified the
daughter of Cormac. The soul of everyelsesbody rolled into its
olesoleself. A doublemonth's licence, lease on mirth, while hooney-
moon and her flame went huneysuckling. Holyryssia, what boom
of bells! What battle of bragues on Sandgate where met the bobby
mobbed his bibby mabbing through the ryce. Even Tombs left
doss and dunnage down in Demidoff's tomb and drew on the
dournailed clogs that Morty Manning left him and legged in by
Ghoststown Gate, like Pompei up to date with a sprig of Whiteboys heather on his late Luke Elcock's heirloom. And some say
they seen old dummydeaf with a leaf of bronze on his cloak
so grey trooping his colour a pace to the reire. And as owfally
posh with his halfcrown jool as if he was the Granjook Meckl or
Paster de Grace on the Route de l'Epée. It was joobileejeu that
All Sorts' Jour. Freestouters and publicranks, hafts on glaives.
You could hear them swearing threaties on the Cymylaya
Mountains, man. And giving it out to the Ould Fathach and louth-
mouthing after the Healy Mealy with an enfysis to bring down
the rain of Tarar. Nevertoletta! Evertomind! The grandest
bethehailey seen or heard on earth's conspectrum since Scape

the Goat, that gafr, ate the Suenders bible. Hadn't we heaven's
lamps to hide us? Yet every lane had its lively spark and every
spark had its several spurtles and each spitfire spurtle had some
trick of her trade, a tease for Ned, nook's nestle for Fred and
a peep at me mow for Peer Pol. So that Father Matt Hughes
looked taytotally threbled. But Danno the Dane grimmed. Dune.
'Twere yeg will elsecare doatty lanv meet they dewscent hyemn
to cannons' roar and rifles' peal vill shantey soloweys sang. For
there were no more Tyrrhanees and for Laxembraghs was pass-
thecupper to Our Lader's. And it was dim upon the floods only
and there was day on all the ground.

Thus street spins legends while wharves woves tales but some
family fewd felt a nick in their name. Old Vickers sate down on
their airs and straightened the points of their lace. Red Rowleys
popped out of their lairs and asked what was wrong with the
race. Mick na Murrough used dripping in layers to shave
all the furze off his face. The Burke-Lees and Coyle-Finns
paid full feines for their sinns when the Cap and Miss Coolie
were roped.

Rolloraped.

With her banbax hoist from holder zig for zag through pool
and polder, cheap, cheap, cheap and Laughing Jack, all augurs
scorenning, see the Bolche your pictures motion and Kitzy
Kleinsuessmein eloping for that holm in Finn's Hotel Fiord.
Nova Norening. Where they pulled down the kuddle and they
made fray and if thee don't look homey well that Dook can eye
Mae.

He goat a berth. And she cot a manege. And wohl's gorse
mundom ganna wedst.

Knock knock. War's where! Which war? The Twwinns.
Knock knock. Woos without! Without what? An apple. Knock
knock.

The kilder massed, one then and uhindred, (harefoot, birdy-
hands, herringabone, beesknees), and they barneydansked a
kathareen round to know the who and to show the howsome.
Why was you hiding, moder of moders? And where was hunty,

poppa the gun? Pointing up to skyless heaven like the spoon out of sergeantmajor's tay. Which was the worst of them phaymix cupplerts? He's herd of hoarding and her faiths is altared. Becoming ungoing, their seeming sames for though that liamstone deaf do his part there's a windtreetop whipples the damp off the mourning. But tellusit allasif wellasits end. And the lunger it takes the swooner they tumble two. He knows he's just thrilling and she's sure she'd squeam. The threelegged man and the tulippied dewydress. Lludd hillmythey, we're brimming to hear. The durst he did and the first she ever? Peganeen Bushe, this isn't the polkar, catch as you cancan when high land fling! And you Tim Tommy Melooney, I'll tittle your barents if you stick that pigpin upinto meh!

So in the names of the balder and of the sol and of the hollichrost, ogsowearit, trisexnone, and by way of letting the aandt out of her grosskropper and leading the mokes home by their gribes, whoopsabout a plabbaside of plobbicides, alamam alemon, poison kerls, on this mounden of Delude, and in the high places of Delude of Isreal, which is Haraharem and the diublin's owld mounden over against Vikens, from your tarns, thwaites and thorpes, withes, tofts and fosses, fells, haughs and shaws, lunds, garths and dales, mensuring the megnominous as so will is the littleyest, the myrioheartzed with toroidal coil, eira area round wantanajocky, fin above wave after duckydowndivvy, trader arm aslung beauty belt, the formor velican and nana karlikeevna, sommerlad and cinderenda, Valtivar and Viv, how Big Bil Brine Borumoter first took his gage at lil lolly lavvander waader since when capriole legs covets limbs of a crane and was it the twylyd or the mounth of the yare or the feint of her smell made the seomen assalt of her (in imageascene all: whimwhim whimwhim). To the laetification of disgeneration by neuhumorisation of our kristianiasation. As the last liar in the earth begeylywayled the first lady of the forest. Though Toot's pardoosled sauve l'hummour! For the joy of the dew on the flower of the fleets on the fields of the foam of the waves of the seas of the wild main from Borneholm has jest come to crown.

Snip snap snoody. Noo err historyend goody. Of a lil trip trap and a big treeskooner for he put off the ketyl and they made three (for fie!) and if hec dont love alpy then lad you annoy me. For hanigen with hunigen still haunt ahunt to finnd their hinnigen where Pappappapparrassannuaragheallachnatull-aghmonganmacmacmacwhackfalltherdebblenonthedubblandadd-ydoodled and anruly person creeked a jest. Gestapose to parry off cheekars or frankfurters on the odor. Fine again, Cuoholson! Peace, O wiley!

Such was the act of goth stepping the tolk of Doolin, drain and plantage, wattle and daub, with you'll peel as I'll pale and we'll pull the boath toground togutter, testies touchwood and shenstone unto pop and puma, calf and condor, under all the gaauspices (incorporated), the chal and his chi, their roammerin over, gribgrobgrab reining trippetytrappety (so fore shalt thou flow, else thy cavern hair!) to whom she (anit likenand please-thee!). Till sealump becamedump to bumpslump a lifflebed, (altolà, allamarsch! O gué, O gué!). Kaemper Daemper to Jetty de Waarft, all the weight of that mons on his little ribbeunuch! Him that gronde old mand to be that haard of heaering (afore said) and her the petty tondur with the fix in her changeable eye (which see), Lord, me lad, he goes with blowbierd: leedy, plasheous stream. But before that his loudship was converted to a landshop there was a little theogamyjig incidence that hoppy-go-jumpy Junuary morn when he colluded with the cad out on the beg amudst the fiounaregal gaames of those oathmassed fenians for whome he's forcecaused a bridge of the piers, at Inverleffy, mating pontine of their engagement, synnbildising graters and things, eke ysendt? O nilly, not all, here's the first cataraction! As if ever she cared an assuan damm about her harpoons sticking all out of him whet between phoenix his calipers and that psourdonome sheath. Sdrats ye, Gus Paudheen! Kenny's thought ye, Dinny Oozle! While the cit was leaking asphalt like a suburbiaurealis in his rure was tucking to him like old booths, booths, booths, booths.

Enterruption. Check or slowback. Dvershen.

Why, wonder of wenchalows, what o szeszame open, v doer s t doing? V door s being. But how theng thingajarry miens but this being becoming n z doer? K? An o. It is ne not him what foots like a glove, shoehandschiner Pad Podomkin. Sooftly, anni slavey, szszuszchee is slowjaneska.

The aged crafty nummifeed confusionary overinsured ever-lapsing accentuated katekattershin clopped, clopped, clopped, darsey dobrey, back and along the danzing corridor, as she was going to pimpim him, way boy wally, not without her comple-ment of cavarnan men, between the two deathdealing allied divisions and the lines of readypresent fire of the corkedagains up-stored, taken in giving the saloot, band your hands going in, bind your heads coming out, and remoltked to herselp in her serf's alown, a weerpovy willowy dreevy drawly and the patter of so familiars, farabroads and behomeans, as she shure sknows, boof for a booby, boo: new uses in their mewseyfume. The jammesons is a cook in his hair. And the juinnesses is a rapin his hind. And the Bullingdong caught the wind up. Dip.

And the message she braught belaw from the missus she bragged abouve that had her agony stays outsize her sari chemise, blancking her shifts for to keep up the fascion since the king of all dronnings kissed her beeswixed hand, fang (pierce me, hunky, I'm full of meunders!), her fize like a tubtail of mondayne clothes, fed to the chaps with working medicals and her birthright pang that would split an atam like the forty pins in her hood, was to fader huncher a howdydowdy, to mountainy mots in her amnest plein language, from his fain a wan, his hot and tot lass, to pierce his ropeloop ear, how, Podushka be prayhasd, now the sowns of his loins were awinking and waking and his dorter of the hush lillabilla lullaby (lead us not into reformication with the poors in your thingdom of gory, O moan!), once after males, nonce at a time, with them Murphy's puffs she dursted with gnockmeggs and the bramborry cake for dour dorty dompling obayre Mattom Beetom and epsut the pfot and if he was whishtful to lioture her caudal with chesty chach from his dauberg den and noviny news from Naul or toplots talks from morrienbaths

or a parrotsprate's cure for ensevelised lethurgies, spick's my
spoon and the veriblest spoon, 'twas her hour for the chamber's
ensallycopodium with love to melost Panny Kostello from
X.Y. Zid for to folly billybobbis gibits porzy punzy and she was
a wanton for De Marera to take her genial glow to bed.

— This is time for my tubble, reflected Mr 'Gladstone
Browne' in the toll hut (it was choractoristic from that 'man of
Delgany'). Dip.

— This is me vulcanite smoking, profused Mr 'Bonaparte
Nolan' under the natecup (one feels how one may hereby reekig-
nites the 'ground old mahonagyan'). Dip.

— And this is defender of defeater of defaulter of deformer
of the funst man in Danelagh, willingtoned in with this glance
dowon his browen and that born appalled noodlum the panellite
pair's cummal delimitator, odding: Oliver White, he's as tiff as
she's tight. And thisens his speak quite hoarse. Dip.

In reverence to her midgetsy the lady of the comeallyous as
madgestoo our own one's goff stature. Prosim, prosit, to the
Krk n yr nck!

O rum it is the chomicalest thing how it pickles up the punchey
and the jude. If you'll gimmy your thing to me I will gamey a sing
to thee. Stay where you're dummy! To get her to go ther. He
banged the scoop and she bagged the sugar while the whole
pub's pobbel done a stare. On the mizzatint wall. With its chromo
for all crimm crimms. Showing holdmenag's asses sat by Allme-
neck's men, canins to ride with em, canins that lept at em, woollied
and flundered.

So the katey's came and the katey's game. As so gangs sludge-
nose. And that henchwench what hopped it dunneth there dufi
the. Duras.

(Silents)

Yes, we've conned thon print in its gloss so gay how it came
from Finndlader's Yule to the day and it's Hey Tallaght Hoe on
the king's highway with his hounds on the home at a turning.
To Donnicoombe Fairing. Millikin's Pass. When visiting at
Izd-la-Chapelle taste the lipe of the waters from Carlowman's Cup.

It tellyhows its story to their six of hearts, a twelve-eyed man; for whom has madjestky who since is dyed drown reign before the izba.

Au! Au! Aue! Ha! Heish!

As stage to set by ritual rote for the grimm grimm tale of the four of hyacinths, the deafeeled carp and the bugler's dozen of leagues-in-amour or how Holispolis went to Parkland with mabby and sammy and sonny and sissy and mop's varlet de shambles and all to find the right place for it by peep o'skirt or pipe a skirl when the hundt called a halt on the chivvychace of the ground sloper at that ligtning lovemaker's thender apeal till, between wandering weather and stable wind, vastelend hosteilend, neuziel and oltrigger some, Bullyclubber burgherly shut the rush in general.

Let us propel us for the frey of the fray! Us, us, beraddy!

Ko Niutirenis hauru leish! A lala! Ko Niutirenis haururu laleish! Ala lala! The Wullingthund sturm is breaking. The sound of maormaoring. The Wellingthund sturm waxes fuercilier. The whackawhacks of the sturm. Katu te ihis ihis! Katu te wana wana! The strength of the rawshorn generand is known throughout the world. Let us say if we may what a weeny wukeleen can do.

Au! Au! Aue! Ha! Heish! A lala!

— Paud the roosky, weren't they all of them then each in his different way of saying calling on the one in the same time hibernian knights underthaner that was having, half for the laugh of the bliss it sint barbaras another doesend end once tale of a tublin wisned on to him with its olives ocolombs and its hills owns ravings and Tutty his tour in his Nowhare's yarcht. It was before when Aimee stood for Arthurduke for the figger in profane and fell from grace so madlley for fill the flatter fellows. (They were saying). And it was the lang in the shirt in the green of the wood where obelisk rises when odalisks fall, major threft on the make and jollyjacques spindthrift on the merry, (O Mr Mathurin, they were calling, what a topheavy hat you're in! And there aramny maeud, then they were saying, these so piou-

pious!) And it was cyclums cyclorums after he made design on
the corse and he want to mess on him (enterellbo add all taller
Danis), back, seater and sides and he applied (I'm amazingly
sorracer!) the wholed bould shoulderedboy's width for fullness,
measures for messieurs, messer's massed, (they were saycalling
again and agone and all over agun, the louthly meathers, the
loudly meaders, the lously measlers, six to one, bar ones).

And they pled him beheighten the firing. Dope.

Maltomeetim, alltomatetam, when a tale tarries shome shunter
shove on. Fore auld they wauld to pree.

Pray.

Of this Mr. A (tillalaric) and these wasch woman (dapple-
hued), fhronehflord and feeofeeds, who had insue keen and able
and a spindlesong aside, nothing more is told until now, his
awebrume hour, her sere Sahara of sad oakleaves. And then. Be
old. The next thing is. We are once amore as babes awondering
in a wold made fresh where with the hen in the storyaboot we
start from scratch.

So the truce, the old truce and nattonbuff the truce, boys.
Drouth is stronger than faction. Slant. Shinshin. Shinshin.

— It was of The Grant, old gartener, *qua* golden meddlist,
Publius Manlius, fuderal private, (his place is his poster, sure, they
said, and we're going to mark it, sore, they said, with a carbon
caustick manner) bequother the liberaloider at his petty corpore-
lezzo that hung caughtnapping from his baited breath, it was of
him, my wife and I thinks, to feel to every of the younging fruits,
tenderosed like an atalantic's breastswells or, on a second wreathing, a bright tauth bight shimmeryshaking for the welt of his
plow. And where the peckadillies at his wristsends meetings be
loving so lightly dovessoild the candidacy, me wipin eye sinks,
of his softboiled bosom should be apparient even to our illicterate
of nullatinenties.

All to which not a lot snapped The Nolan of the Calabashes
at his whilom eweheart photognomist who by this sum taken
was as much incensed by Saint Bruno as that what he had con-
summed was his own panegoric, and wot a lout about it if it was

only a pippappoff pigeon shoot that gracesold getrunner, the man of centuries, was bowled out by judge, jury and umpire at batman's biff like a witchbefooled legate. Dupe.

His almonence being alaterelly in dispensation with his three oldher patrons' aid, providencer's divine cow to milkfeeding mleckman, bonafacies to solafides, what matter what all his freudzay or who holds his hat to harm him, let hutch just keep on under at being a vanished consinent and let annapal livibel prettily prattle a lude all her own. And be that semeliminal salmon solemonly angled ingate and outgate. A truce to lovecalls, dulled in warclothes, maleybags, things and bleakhusen. Leave the letter that never begins to go find the latter that ever comes to end, written in smoke and blurred by mist and signed of solitude, sealed at night.

Simply. As says the mug in the middle, nay brian nay noel, ney billy ney boney. Imagine twee cweamy wosen. Suppwose you get a beautiful thought and cull them sylvias sub silence. Then inmaggin a stotterer. Suppoutre him to been one bigger- master Omnibil. Then lustily (tutu the font and tritt on the boks- woods like gay feeters's dance) immengine up to three longly lurking lobstarts. Fair instents the Will Woolsley Wellaslayers. Pet her, pink him, play pranks with them. She will nod ampro- perly smile. He may seem to appraisiate it. They are as piractical jukersmen sure to paltipsypote. Feel the wollies drippeling out of your fingathumbs. Says to youssilves (floweers have ears, heahear!) solowly: So these ease Budlim! How do, dainty dau- limbs? So peached to pick on you in this way, prue and simple, pritt and spry. Heyday too, Malster Faunagon, and hopes your hahititahiti licks the mankey nuts! And oodlum hoodlum dood- lum to yes, Donn, Teague and Hurleg, who the bullocks brought you here and how the hillocks are ye?

We want Bud. We want Bud Budderly. We want Bud Budderly boddily. There he is in his Borrisalooner. The man that shunned the rucks on Gereland. The man thut won the bettle of the bawll. Order, order, order, order! And tough. We call on Tan- cred Artaxerxes Flavin to compeer with Barnabas Ulick Dunne.

Order, order, order! Milster Malster in the chair. We've heard it
sinse sung thousandtimes. How Burghley shuck the rackushant
   Germanon. For Ehren, boys, gobrawl!
   A public plouse. Citizen soldiers.

   TAFF (*a smart boy, of the peat freers, thirty two eleven, looking
through the roof towards a relevution of the karmalife order privious
to his hoisting of an emergency umberolum in byway of paraguastical
solation to the rhyttel in his hedd*). All was flashing and krashning
blurty moriartsky blutcherudd? What see, buttywalch? Tell ever
so often?

   BUTT (*mottledged youth, clerical appealance, who, as his pied
friar, is supposing to motto the sorry dejester in tifftaff toffiness or
to be digarced from ever and a daye in his accounts*). But da. But
dada, mwilshsuni. Till even so aften. Sea vaast a pool!

   TAFF (*porumptly helping himself out by the cesspull with a yellup
yurrup, puts up his furry furȝed hare*). Butly bitly. Humme to our
mounthings. Conscribe him tillusk, unt, in his jubalant tubalence,
the groundsapper, with his soilday site out on his moulday side
in. The gubernier-gerenal in laut-lievtonant of Baltiskeeamore,
amaltheouse for leporty hole! Endues paramilintary langdwage.
The saillils of the yellavs nocadont palignol urdlesh. Shelltoss
and welltass and telltuss aghom. Sling Stranaslang, how Malo-
razzias spikes her, coining a speak a spake! Not the Setanik stuff
that slimed soft Siranouche! The good old gunshop monowards
for manosymples. Tincurs tammit! They did oak hay doe fou
Chang-li-meng when that man d'airain was big top tom saw tip
side bum boss pageantfiller. Ajaculate! All lea light! Rassamble
the glowrings of Bruyant the Bref when the Mollies Makehal-
pence took his leg for his thumb. And may he be too an intrepida-
tion of our dreams which we foregot at wiking when the morn
hath razed out limpalove and the bleakfrost chilled our ravery.
Pook. Sing ching lew mang! Upgo, bobbycop! Lets hear in
remember the braise of. Hold!

   BUTT (*drawling forth from his blousom whereis meditabound of
his minkerstary, switches on his gorsecopper's fling weitoheito lang-
thorn, fed up the grain oils of Aerin, while his laugh neighs banck as*

that flashermind's rays and his lipponease longuewedge wambles).
Ullahbluh! Sehyoh narar, pokehole sann! Manhead very dirty by
am anoyato. Like old Dolldy Icon when he cooked up his iggs
in bicon. He gatovit and me gotafit and Oalgoak's Cheloven gut
a fudden. Povar old pitschobed! Molodeztious of metchennacht
belaburt that pentschmyaso! Bog carsse and dam neat, sar, gam
cant! Limbers affront of him, lumbers behund. While the bucks
bite his dos his hart bides the ros till the bounds of his bays bell
the warning. Sobaiter sobarkar. He was enmivallupped. Chro-
mean fastion. With all his cannoball wappents. In his raglanrock
and his malakoiffed bulbsbyg and his varnashed roscians and his
cardigans blousejagged and his scarlett manchokuffs and his tree-
coloured camiflag and his perikopendolous gaelstorms. Here
weeks hire pulchers! Obriania's beromst! From Karrs and
Polikoff's, the men's confessioners. Seval shimars pleasant
time payings. Mousoumeselles buckwoulds look. Tenter and
likelings.

TAFF (*all Perssiasterssias shookatnaratatattar at his waggon-
horchers, his bulgeglarying stargapers razzledazzlingly full of eyes,
full of balls, full of holes, full of buttons, full of stains, full of medals,
full of blickblackblobs*). Grozarktic! Toadlebens! Some garment-
guy! Insects appalling, low hum clang sin! A cheap decoy! Too
deep destroy! Say mangraphique, may say nay por daguerre!

BUTT (*if that he hids foregodden has nate of glozery farused ameet
the florahs of the follest, his spent fish's livid smile giving allasundery
the bumfit of the doped*). Come alleyou jupes of Wymmingtown
that graze the calves of Man! A bear raigning in his heavenspawn
consomation robes. Rent, outraged, yewleaved, grained, bal-
looned, hindergored and voluant! Erminia's capecloaked hoo-
doodman! First he s s st steppes. Then he st stoo stoopt. Lookt.

TAFF (*strick struck strangling like aleal lusky Lubliner to merum-
ber by the cycl of the cruize who strungled Attahilloupa with what
empoisoned El Monte de Zuma and failing wilnaynilnay that he
was pallups barn in the minkst of the Krumlin befodt he was pop-
soused into the monkst of the vatercan, makes the holypolygon of
the emt on the greaseshaper, a little farther, a little soon, a lettera-*

cettera, oukraydoubray). Scutterer of guld, he is retourious on
every roudery! The lyewdsky so so sewn of a fitchid! With his
walshbrushup? And his boney bogey braggs?

BUTT (*after his tongues in his cheeks, with pinkpoker pointing
out in rutene to impassible abjects beyond the mistomist towards
Lissnaluhy such as the Djublian Alps and the Hoofd Ribeiro as
where he and his trulock may ever make a game*). The field of
karhags and that bloasted tree. Forget not the felled! For the
lomondations of Oghrem! Warful doon's bothem. Here furry
glunn. Nye? Their feery pass. Tak! With guerillaman aspear
aspoor to prink the pranks of primkissies. And the buddies be-
hide in the byre. Allahblah!

TAFF (*a blackseer, he stroves to reguloct all the straggles for wife
in the rut of the past through the widnows in effigies keening after the
blank sheets in their faminy to the relix of old decency from over
draught*). Oh day of rath! Ah, murther of mines! Eh, selo moy!
Uh, zulu luy! Bernesson Mac Mahahon from Osro bearing nose
easger for sweeth prolettas on his swooth prowl!

BUTT (*back to his peatrol and paump: swee Gee's wee rest: no
more applehooley: dodewodedook*). Bruinoboroff, the hooney-
moonger, and the grizzliest manmichal in Meideveide! Whose
annal livves the hoiest! For he devoused the lelias on the fined
and he conforted samp, tramp and marchint out of the drumbume
of a narse. Guards, serf Finnland, serve we all!

TAFF (*whatwidth the psychophannies at the front and whetwadth
the psuckofumbers beholden the fair, illcertain, between his bulchri-
chudes and the roshashanaral, where he sees Bishop Ribboncake plus
his pollex prized going forth on his visitations of mirrage or Miss
Horizon, justso all our fannacies daintied her, on the curve of the
camber, unsheating a showlaced limbaloft to the great consternations*).
Divulge! Hyededye, kittyls, and howdeddoh, pan! Poshbott and
pulbuties. See that we soll or let dargman be luna as strait a way
as your ant's folly me line while ye post is goang from Piping
Pubwirth to Haunted Hillborough on his Mujiksy's Zaravence,
the Riss, the Ross, the sur of all Russers as my farst is near to
hear and my sackend is meet to sedon while my whole's a peer's

aureolies. We should say you dones the polecad. Bang on the booche, gurg in the gorge, rap on the roof and your flup is unbu...

BUTT (*at the signal of his act which seems to sharpnel his innermals menody, playing the spool of the little brown jog round the wheel of her whang goes the millner*). Buckily buckily, blodestained boyne! Bimbambombumb. His snapper was shot in the Rumjar Journaral. Why the gigls he lubbed beeyed him.

TAFF (*obliges with a two stop yogacoga sumphoty on the bones for ivory girl and ebony boy*). The balacleivka! Trovatarovitch! I trumble!

BUTT (*with the sickle of a scygthe but the humour of a hummer, O, howorodies through his cholaroguled, fumfing to a fullfrength with this wallowing olfact*). Mortar martar tartar wartar! May his boules grow wider so his skittles gets worse! The aged monad making a venture out of the murder of investment. I seen him acting surgent what betwinks the scimitar star and the ashen moon. By their lights shalthow throw him! Piff paff for puffpuff and my pife for his cgar! The mlachy way for gambling.

[*Up to this curkscraw bind an admirable verbivocovisual presentment of the worldrenownced Caerholme Event has been being given by* The Irish Race and World. *The huddled and aliven stablecrashers have shared fleetfooted enthusiasm with the paddocks dare and ditches tare while the mews was combing ground. Hippohopparray helioscope flashed winsor places as the gates might see. Meusdeus! That was (with burning briar) Mr. Twomass Nohoholan for their common contribe satisfunction in the purports of amusedment telling the Verily Roverend Father Epiphanes shrineshriver of Saint Dhorough's (in browne bomler) how (assuary as there's a bonum in your osstheology!) Backlegs shirked the racing kenneldar. The saintly scholarist's roastering guffalawd of nupersaturals holler at this metanoic excomologosis tells of the chestnut's (once again, Wittyngtom!) absolutionally romptyhompty successfulness. A lot of lasses and lads without damas or dads, but fresh and blued with collecting boxes. One aught spare ones triflets, to be shut: it is Coppingers for the children. Slippery Sam hard by them, physically present how-*

somedever morally absent, was slooching about in his knavish
diamonds asking Gmax, Knox and the Dmuggies (a pinnance for
your toughts, turffers!) to deck the ace of duds. Tomtinker Tim,
howbeit, his unremitting retainer, (the seers are the seers of
Samael but the heers are the heers of Timoth) is in Boozer's
Gloom, soalken steady in his sulken tents. Baldawl the curse,
baledale the day! And the frocks of shick sheeples in their shum-
mering insamples! You see: a chiefsmith, semperal scandal
stinkmakers, a middinest from the Casabianca and, of course,
Mr. Fry. Barass! Pardon the inquisition, causas es quostas?
It is Da Valorem's Dominical Brayers. Why coif that weird
hood? Bocause among nosoever circusdances is to be apprehended
the dustungwashed poltronage of the lost Gabbarnaur-Jaggar-
nath. Pamjab! Gross Jumpiter, whud was thud? Luckluckluck-
luckluckluckluck! It is the Thousand to One Guinea-Gooseberry's
Lipperfull Slipver Cup. Hold hard, ridesiddle titelittle Pitsy
Riley! Gurragrunch, gurragrunch! They are at the turn of the
fourth of the hurdles. By the hross of Xristos, Holophullopopu-
lace is a shote of excramation! Bumchub! Emancipator, the
Creman hunter (Major Hermyn C. Entwhistle) with dramatic
effect reproducing the form of famous sires on the scene of the
formers triumphs, is showing the eagle's way to Mr Whayte-
hayte's three buy geldings Homo Made Ink, Bailey Beacon
and Ratatuohy while Furstin II and The Other Girl (Mrs
'Boss' Waters, Leavybrink) too early spring dabbles, are showing
a clean pairofhids to Immensipater. Sinkathinks to oppen here!
To this virgin's tuft, on this golden of evens! I never sought of
sinkathink. Our lorkmakor he is proformly annuysed. He is
shinkly thinkly shaking in his schayns. Sat will be off follteedee.
This zeridreme has being effered you by Bett and Tipp. Tipp and
Bett, our swapstick quackchancers, in From Topphole to Bottom of The Irish Race and World.]

TAFF (awary that the first sports report of Loundin Reginald
has now been afterthoughtfully colliberated by a saggind spurts
flash, takes the dipperend direction and, for tasing the tiomor of

malaise after the pognency of orangultonia, orients by way of Sagit-
tarius towards Draco on the Lour). And you collier carsst on him,
the corsar, with Boyle, Burke and Campbell, I'll gogemble on
strangbones tomb. You had just been cerberating a camp camp
camp to Saint Sepulchre's march through the armeemonds retreat with the boys all marshalled, scattering giant's hail over the
curseway, fellowed along the rout by the stenchions of the
corpse. Tell the coldspell's terroth! If you please, commeylad!
Perfedes Albionias! Think some ingain think, as Teakortairer
sate over the Galwegian caftan forewhen Orops and Aasas were
chooldrengs and micramacrees! A forward movement, Miles na
Bogaleen, and despatch!

BUTT (*slinking his coatsleeves surdout over his squad mutton*
shoulder so as to loop more life the jauntlyman as he scents the
anggreget yup behound their whole scoopchina's desperate noy's
totalage and explaining aposteriorly how awstooloo was valde-
sombre belowes hero and he was in a greak esthate phophiar an
erixtion on the soseptuple side of him made spoil apriori his popo-
porportiums). Yass, zotnyzor, I don't think I did not, pojr. Never
you brother me for I scout it, think you! Ichts nichts on nichts.
Greates Schtschuptar! Me fol the rawlawdy in the schpirrt of a
schkrepz. Of all the quirasses and all the qwehrmin in the tra-
gedoes of those antiants their grandoper, that soun of a gun-
nong, with his sabaothsopolettes, smooking his scandleloose at
botthends of him! Foinn duhans! I grandthinked after his obras
after another time about the itch in his egondoom he was legging
boldylugged from some pulversporochs and lyoking for a stool-
eazy for to nemesisplotsch allafranka and for to salubrate himself
with an ultradungs heavenly mass at his base by a suprime pomp-
ship chorams the perished popes, the reverend and allaverred
cromlecks and when I heard his lewdbrogue reciping his cheap
cheateary gospeds to sintry and santry and sentry and suntry I
thought he was only haftara having afterhis brokeforths but be
the homely Churopodvas I no sooner seen aghist of his frighte-
ousness then I was bibbering with vear a few versets off fooling for
fjorg for my fifth foot. Of manifest 'tis obedience and the. Flute!

TAFF (*though the unglucksarsoon is giming for to git him, jotning in, hoghly ligious, hapagodlap, like a soldierry sap, with a pique at his cue and a tyr in his eye and a bond of his back and a croak in his cry as did jolly well harm lean o'er him*) Is not athug who would. Weepon, weeponder, song of sorrowmon! Which goatheye and sheepskeer they damnty well know. Papaist! Gambanman! Take the cawraidd's blow! Yia! Your partridge's last!

BUTT (*giving his scimmianised twinge in acknuckledownedgment of this cumulikick, strafe from the firetrench, studenly drobs led, satoniseels ouchyotchy, he changecors induniforms as he is lefting the gat out of the big: his face glows green, his hair greys white, his bleyes bcome broon to suite his cultic twalette*). But when I seeing him in his oneship fetch along within hail that tourrible tall with his nitshnykopfgoknob and attempting like a brandylogged rudeman cathargic, lugging up and laiding down his livepelts so cruschinly like Mebbuck at Messar and exposuing his old skinful self tailtottom by manurevring in open ordure to renewmurature with the cowruads in their airish pleasantry I thanked he was recovering breadth from some herdsquatters beyond the carcasses and I couldn't erver nerver to tell a liard story not of I knew the prize if from lead or alimoney. But when I got inoccupation of a full new of his old basemiddelism, in ackshan, pagne pogne, by the veereyed lights of the stormtrooping clouds and in the sheenflare of the battleaxes of the heroim and mid the shieldfails awail of the bitteraccents of the sorafim and caught the pfierce tsmell of his aurals, orankastank, a suphead setrapped, like Peder the Greste, altipaltar, my bill it forsooks allegiance (gut bull it!) and, no lie is this, I was babbeing and yetaghain bubbering, bibbelboy, me marrues me shkewers me gnaas me fiet, tob tob tob beat it, solongopatom. Clummensy if ever misused, must used you's now! But, meac Coolp, Arram of Eirzerum, as I love our Deer Dirouchy, I confesses withould pridejealice when I looked upon the Saur of all the Haurousians with the weight of his arge fullin upon him from the travaillings of his tommuck and rueckenased the fates of a bosser there was fear on me the sons of Nuad for him and it was heavy he was for me

then the way I immingled my Irmenial hairmaierians ammon-
gled his Gospolis fomiliours till, achaura moucreas, I adn't the
arts to.

TAFF (*as a marrer off act, prepensing how such waldmanns from
Burnias seduced country clowns, he is preposing barangaparang
after going knowing what he is doing after to see him pluggy well
moidered as a murder effect, you bet your blowie knife, before he
doze soze, sopprused though he is*) Grot Zot! You hidn't the hurts?
Vott Fonn!

BUTT (*hearing somrother sudly give tworthree peevish sniff snuff
snoores like govalise falseleep he waitawhishts to see might he stirs
and then goes on kuldrum like without asking for pepeace or anysing
a soul*). Merzmard! I met with whom it was too late. My fate! O
hate! Fairwail! Fearwealing of the groan! And think of that
when you smugs to bagot.

TAFF (*who meanwhilome at yarn's length so as to put a nodje
in the poestcher, by wile of stoccan his hand and of rooma makin
ber getting umptyums gatherumed off the skattert had been, lavish-
ing, lagan on lighthouse, words of silent power, susu glouglou biri-
biri gongos, upon the repleted speechsalver's unnkeeping right which,
thanks giveme and naperied norms nonobstaclant, there can be little
doubt, have resulted in a momstchance ministring of another guid-
ness, my good, to see*) Bompromifazzio! Shumpum for Pa-li-di
and oukosouso for the nipper dandy! Trink off this scup and be
bladdy orafferteed! To bug at?

BUTT (*he whipedoff's his chimbley phot, as lips lovecurling to the
tongueopener, he takecups the communion of sense at the hands of
the foregiver of trosstpassers and thereinofter centelinnates that
potifex miximhost with haruspical hospedariaty proferring into his
pauses somewhot salt bacon*). Theres scares knud in this gnarld
warld a fully so svend as dilates for the improvement of our
foerses of nature by your very ample solvent of referacting upon
me like is boesen fiennd.

[*The other foregotthened abbosed in the Mullingaria are
during this swishingsight teilweisioned. How the fictionable world*

in Fruzian Creamtartery is loading off heavy furses and affubling
themselves with muckinslushes. The neatschknee Novgolosh.
How the spinach ruddocks are being tatoovatted up for the second
comings of antigreenst. Hebeneros for Aromal Peace. How
Alibey Ibrahim wisheths Bella Suora to a holy cryptmahs while
the Arumbian Knives Riders axecutes devilances round the
jehumispheure. Learn the Nunsturk. How Old Yales boys is
making rebolutions for the cunning New Yirls, never elding,
still begidding, never to mate to lend, never to ate selleries and
never to add soulleries and never to ant sulleries and never to aid
silleries with sucharow with sotchyouroff as Burkeley's Show's
a ructiongetherall. Phone for Phineal toomellow aftermorn and
your phumeral's a roselixion.]

TAFF (*now as he has been past the buckthurnstock from Peadhar*
Piper of Colliguchuna, whiles they all are bealting pots to dubrin
din for old daddam dombstom to tomb and wamb humbs lumbs
agamb, glimpse agam, glance agen, rise up road and hive up hill,
and find your pollyvoulley foncey pitchin ingles in the parler). Since
you are on for versingrhetorish say your piece! How Buccleuch
shocked the rosing girnirilles. A ballet of Gasty Power. A hov
and az ov and off like a gow! And don't live out the sad of tearfs,
piddyawhick! Not offgott affsang is you, buthbach? Ath yet-
heredayth noth endeth, hay? Vaersegood! Buckle to! Sayyessik,
Ballygarry. The fourscore soculums are watchyoumaycodding
to cooll the skoopgoods blooff. Harkabuddy, feign! Thingman
placeyear howed wholst somwom shimwhir tinkledinkledelled.
Shinfine deed in the myrtle of the bog tway fainmain stod op to
slog, free bond men lay lurkin on. Tuan about whattinghim!
Fore sneezturmdrappen! 'Twill be a rpnice pschange, arrah, sir?
Can you come it, budd?

BUTT (*who in the cushlows of his goodsforseeking hoarth, ever*
fondlinger of his pimple spurk, is a niallist of the ninth homestages,
the babybell in his baggutstract upper going off allatwanst, begad,
lest he should challenge himself, beygoad, till angush). Horrasure,
toff! As said as would. It was Colporal Phailinx first. Hittit was

of another time, a white horsday where the midril met the bulg, sbogom, roughnow along about the first equinarx in the cholonder, on the plain of Khorason as thou goest from the mount of Bekel, Steep Nemorn, elve hundred and therety and to years how the krow flees end in deed, after a power of skimiskes, blodidens and godinats of them, when we sight the beasts, (hegheg whatlk of wraimy wetter!), moist moonful date man aver held dimsdzey death with, and higheye was in the Reilly Oirish Krzerszonese Milesia asundurst Sirdarthar Woolwichleagues, good tomkeys years somewhile in Crimealian wall samewhere in Ayerland, during me weeping stillstumms over the freshprosts of Eastchept and the dangling garters of Marrowbone and daring my wapping stiltstunts on Bostion Moss, old stile and new style and heave a lep onwards. And winn again, blaguadargoos, or lues the day, plays goat, the banshee pealer, if moskats knows whoss whizz, the great day and the druidful day come San Patrisky and the grand day, the excellent fine splendorous long agreeable toastworthy cylindrical day, go Sixt of the Ninth, the heptahundread annam dammias that Hajizfijjiz ells me is and will and was be till the timelag is in it that's told in the Bok of Alam to columnkill all the prefacies of Erin gone brugk. But Icantenue. And incommixtion. We was lowsome like till we'd took out after the dead beats. So I begin to study and I soon show them day's reasons how to give the cold shake to they blighty perishers and lay one over the beats. All feller he look he call all feller come longa villa finish. Toumbalo, how was I acclapadad! From them banjopeddlars on the raid. Gidding up me anti vanillas and getting off the stissas me aunties. Boxerising and coxerusing. And swiping a johnny dann sweept for to exercitise myself neverwithstanding the topkats and his roaming cartridges, orussheying and patronning, out all over Crummwiliam wall. Be the why it was me who haw haw.

TAFF (*all for letting his tinder and lighting be put to beheiss in the feuer and, while durblinly obasiant to the felicias of the skivis, still smolking his fulvurite turfkish in the rooking pressance of*

laddios). Yaa hoo how how, col? Whom battles joined no bottles
sever! Worn't you aid a comp?

BUTT (*in his difficoltous tresdobremient, he feels a bitvalike a
baddlefall of staot but falls a batforlake a borrlefull of bare*). And
me awlphul omegrims! Between me rassociations in the postlea-
deny past and me disconnections with aplompervious futules
I've a boodle full of maimeries in me buzzim and medears runs
sloze, bleime, as I now with platoonic leave recoil in (how the
thickens they come back to one to rust!) me misenary post for
all them old boyars that's now boomaringing in waulholler, me
alma marthyrs. I dring to them, bycorn spirits fuselaiding, and
you cullies adjutant, even where its contentsed wody, with
absents wehrmuth. Junglemen in agleement, I give thee our
greatly swooren, Theoccupant that Rueandredful, the thrown-
fullvner and all our royal devouts with the arrest of the whole
inhibitance of Neuilands! One brief mouth. And a velligoolap-
now! Meould attashees the currgans, (if they could get a kick at
this time for all that's hapenced to us!) Cedric said Gormleyson
and Danno O'Dunnochoo and Conno O'Cannochar it is this
were their names for we were all under that manner barracksers
on Kong Gores Wood together, thurkmen three, with those
khakireinettes, our miladies in their toileries, the twum plum-
yumnietcies, Vjeras Vjenaskayas, of old Djadja Uncken who
was a great mark for jinking and junking, up the palposes of
womth and wamth, we war, and the charme of their lyse brocade.
For lispias harth a burm in eye but whem it bames fire norone
screeneth. Hulp, hulp, huzzars! Raise ras tryracy! Freetime's
free! Up Lancesters! Anathem!

TAFF (*who still senses that heavinscent houroines that enter-
trained him who they were sinuorivals from the sunny Espionia but
plied wopsy with his wallets in thatthack of the bustle Bakerloo,
(11.32), passing the uninational truthbosh in smoothing irony over
the multinotcheralled infructuosities of his grinner set*). The rib,
the rib, the quean of oldbyrdes, Sinya Sonyavitches! Your
Rhoda Cockardes that are raday to embrace our ruddy inflamtry
world! In their ohosililesvienne biribarbebeway. Till they've

kinks in their tringers and boils on their taws. Whor dor the pene
lie, Mer Pencho? Ist dramhead countmortial or gonorrhal stab?
Mind your pughs and keaoghs, if you piggots, marsh! Do the
nut, dingbut! Be a dag! For zahur and zimmerminnes! Sing in
the chorias to the ethur:

   [*In the heliotropical noughttime following a fade of trans-
formed Tuff and, pending its viseversion, a metenergic reglow
of beaming Batt, the bairdboard bombardment screen, if tastefully taut guranium satin, tends to teleframe and step up to
the charge of a light barricade. Down the photoslope in syncopanc
pulses, with the bitts bugtwug their teffs, the missledhropes,
glitteraglatteraglutt, borne by their carnier walve. Spraygun
rakes and splits them from a double focus: grenadite, damny-
mite, alextronite, nichilite: and the scanning firespot of the
sgunners traverses the rutilanced illustred sunksundered lines.
Shlossh! A gaspel truce leaks out over the caeseine coatings.
Amid a fluorescence of spectracular mephiticism there caoculates
through the inconoscope stealdily a still, the figure of a fellow-
chap in the wohly ghast, Popey O'Donoshough, the jesuneral
of the russuates. The idolon exhibisces the seals of his orders:
the starre of the Son of Heaven, the girtel of Izodella the Calot-
tica, the cross of Michelides Apaleogos, the latchet of Jan of
Nepomuk, the puffpuff and pompom of Powther and Pall, the
great belt, band and bucklings of the Martyrology of Gorman.
It is for the castomercies mudwake surveice. The victar. Pleace
to notnoys speach above your dreadths, please to doughboys. Hll,
smthngs gnwrng wthth sprsnwtch! He blanks his oggles because
he confesses to all his tellavicious nieces. He blocks his nosoes because that he confesses to everywheres he was always putting up his
latest faengers. He wollops his mouther with a sword of tusk in as
because that he confesses how opten he used be obening her howonton
he used be undering her. He boundles alltogotter his manucupes
with his pedarrests in asmuch as because that he confesses before
all his handcomplishies and behind all his comfoderacies. And
(hereis cant came back saying he codant steal no lunger, yessis,*

catʒ come buck beques he caudant stail awake) he touched upon
this tree of livings in the middenst of the garerden for inasmuch
as because that he confessed to it on Hillel and down Dalem and
in the places which the lepers inhabit in the place of the stones
and in pontofert jusfuggading amoret now he come to think of it
jolly well ruttengenerously olyovyover the ole blucky shop. *Pugger
old Pumpey O'Dungaschiff! There will be a hen collection of him
after avensung on the field of Hanar. Dumble down, looties and
gengstermen! Dtin, dtin, dtin, dtin!*]

BUTT *(with a gisture expansive of Mr Lhugewhite Cadderpollard
with sunflawered beautonhole pulled up point blanck by mailbag
mundaynism at Oldbally Court though the hissindensity buck far
of his melovelance tells how when he was fast marking his first
lord for cremation the whyfe of his bothem was the very lad's thing
to elter his mehind)*. Prostatates, pujealousties! Dovolnoisers,
prayshyous! Defense in every circumstancias of deboutcheries
no the chaste daffs! Pack pickets, pioghs and kughs to be palsey-
putred! Be at the peme, prease, of not forgetting or mere betoken
yourself to hother prace! Correct me, pleatze commando, for
cossakes but I abjure of it. No more basquibezigues for this pole
aprican! With askormiles' eskermillas. I had my billyfell of
duckish delights the whole pukny time on rawmeots and juliannes
with their lambstoels in my kiddeneys and my ramsbutter in
their sassenacher ribs, kmee her, do her and trey her, when
th'osirian cumb dumb like the whalf on the fiord and we preying players and pinching peacesmokes, troupkers tomiatskyns
all, for Father Petrie Spence of Parishmoslattary to go and leave
us and the crimsend daun to shellalite on the darkumen (scene
as signed, Slobabogue), feeding and sleeping on the huguenottes
(the snuggest spalniel's where the lieon's tame!) and raiding
revolations over the allbegeneses (sand us and saint us and
sound as agun!). Yet still in all, spit for spat, like we chantied on
Sunda schoon, every warson wearrier kaddies a komnate in
his schnapsack and unlist I am getting foegutfulls of the rugi-
ments of savaliged wildfire I was gamefellow willmate and send

us victorias with nowells and brownings, dumm, sneak and
curry, and all the fun I had in that fanagan's week. A strange
man wearing abarrel. And here's a gift of meggs and teggs. And
as I live by chipping nortons. And 'tis iron fits the farmer, ay.
Arcdesedo! Renborumba? Then were the hellscyown days for
our fellows, the loyal leibsters, and we was the redugout raw-
recruitioners, praddies three and prettish too, a wheeze we has
in our waynward islands, wee engrish, one long blue streak,
jisty and pithy af durck rosolun, with hand to hand as Homard
Kayenne was always jiggilyjugging about in his wendowed
courage when our woos with the wenches went wined for a song,
tsingirillies' zyngarettes, while Woodbine Willie, so popiular
with the poppyrossies, our Chorney Choplain, blued the air.
Sczlanthas! Banzaine! Bissbasses! S. Pivorandbowl. And we all
tuned in to hear the topmast noviality. Up the revels drown the
rinks and almistips all round. Paddy Bonhamme he vives! Encore! And tig for tag. Togatogtug. My droomodose days Y loved
you abover all the strest. Blowhole brasshat and boy with his
boots off and the butch of our bunch and all. It was buckoo
bonzer, beleeme. I was a bare prive without my doglegs but I
did not give to one humpenny dump, wingh or wangh, touching
those thusengaged slavey generales of Tanah Kornalls, the
meelisha's deelishas, pronouncing their very flank movemens
in sunpictorsbosk. Baghus the whatwar! I could always take good
cover of myself and, eyedulls or earwakers, preyers for rain or
cominations, I did not care three tanker's hoots, ('sham! hem!
or chaffit!) for any feelings from my lifeprivates on their reptro-
grad leanins because I have Their Honours booth my respectables
sœurs assistershood off Lyndhurst Terrace, the puttih Misses
Celana Dalems, and she in vinting her angurr can belle the troth
on her alliance and I know His Heriness, my respeaktoble me-
dams culonelle on Mellay Street, Lightnints Gundhur Sawabs,
and they would never as the aimees of servation let me down.
Not on your bludger life, touters! No peeping, pimpadoors!
And, by Jova, I never went wrong nor let him doom till, risky
wark rasky wolk, at the head of the wake, up come stumblebum

(ye olde cottemptable!), his urssian gemenal, in his scutt's rudes
unreformed and he went before him in that nemcon enchelonce
with the same old domstoole story and his upleave the fallener
as is greatly to be petted (whitesides do his beard!) and I seen his
brichashert offensive and his boortholomas vadnhammaggs vise
a vise them scharlot runners and how they gave love to him
and how he took the ward from us (odious the fly fly flurtation
of his him and hers! Just mairmaid maddeling it was it he was!)
and, my oreland for a rolvever, sord, by the splunthers of colt
and bung goes the enemay the Percy rally got me, messger, (as
true as theirs an Almagnian Gothabobus!) to blow the grand off
his aceupper. Thistake it 's meest! And after meath the dulwich.
We insurrectioned and, be the procuratress of the hory synnotts,
before he could tell pullyirragun to parrylewis, I shuttm, missus,
like a wide sleever! Hump to dump! Tumbleheaver!

TAFF (*camelsensing that sonce they have given bron a nuhlan
the volkar boastsung is heading to sea vermelhion but too wellbred
not to ignore the umzemliness of his rifal's preceedings, in an effort
towards autosotorisation, effaces himself in favour of the idiology
alwise behounding his lumpy hump off homosodalism which means
that if he has lain amain to lolly his liking-cabronne!-he may pops
lilly a young one to his herth-combrune -*) Oholy rasher, I'm be-
liever! And Oho bullyclaver of ye, bragadore-gunneral! The
grand ohold spider! It is a name to call to him Umsturdum Vonn!
Ah, you were shutter reshottus and sieger besieged. Aha race of
fiercemarchands counterination oho of shorpshoopers.

BUTT (*miraculising into the Dann Deafir warcry, his bigotes
bristling, as, jittinju triggity shittery pet, he shouts his thump and
feeh fauh foul finngures up the heighohs of their ahs!*) Bluddy-
muddymuzzle! The buckbeshottered! He'll umbozzle no more
graves nor horne nor haunder, lou garou, for gayl geselles in
dead men's hills! Kaptan (backsights to his bared!), His Cum-
bulent Embulence, the frustate fourstar Russkakruscam, Dom
Allaf O'Khorwan, connundurumchuff.

TAFF (*who, asbestas can, wiz the healps of gosh and his bluzzid
maikar, has been sulphuring to himsalves all the pungataries*

of sin praktice in failing to furrow theogonies of the dommed).
Trisseme, the mangoat! And the name of the Most Marsiful,
the Aweghost, the Gragious One! In sobber sooth and in souber
civiles? And to the dirtiment of the curtailment of his all of man?
Notshoh?

BUTT (*maomant scoffin, but apoxyomenously deturbaned but
thems bleachin banes will be after making a bashman's haloday out
of the euphorious hagiohygiecynicism of his die and be diademmed*).
Yastsar! In sabre tooth and sobre saviles! Senonnevero! That
he leaves nyet is my grafe. He deared me to it and he dared me
do it, and bedattle I didaredonit as Cocksnark of Killtork can
tell and Ussur Ursussen of the viktaurious onrush with all the
rattles in his arctic! As bold and as madhouse a bull in a meadows.
Knout Knittrick Kinkypeard! Olefoh, the sourd of foemoe
times! Unknun! For when meseemim, and tolfoklokken rolland
allover ourloud's lande, beheaving up that sob of tunf for to
claimhis, for to wollpimsolff, puddywhuck. Ay, and untuoning
his culothone in an exitous erseroyal *Deo Jupto*. At that instullt
to Igorladns! Prronto! I gave one dobblenotch and I ups with
my crozzier. Mirrdo! With my how on armer and hits leg an
arrow cockshock rockrogn. Sparro!

[*The abnihilisation of the etym by the grisning of the grosning
of the grinder of the grunder of the first lord of Hurtreford ex-
polodotonates through Parsuralia with an ivanmorinthorrorumble
fragoromboassity amidwhiches general uttermosts confussion are
perceivable moletons skaping with mulicules while coventry
plumpkins fairlygosmotherthemselves in the Landaunelegants
of Pinkadindy. Similar scenatas are projectilised from Hullulullu,
Bawlawayo, empyreal Raum and mordern Atems. They were
precisely the twelves of clocks, noon minutes, none seconds.
At someseat of Oldanelang's Konguerrig, by dawnybreak in
Aira.*]

TAFF (*skimperskamper, his wools gatherings all over cromlin
what with the birstol boys artheynes and is it her tour and the
crackery of the fullfour fivefirearms and the crockery of their dam-*

dam domdom chumbers). Wharall thubulbs uptheaires! Shatta-
movick?

    BUTT (*pulling alast stark daniel with alest doog at doorak while
too greater than pardon painfully the issue of his mouth diminuen-
doing, vility of vilities, he becomes, allasvitally, faint*). Shurenoff!
Like Faun MacGhoul!

    BUTT and TAFF (*desprot slave wager and foeman feodal un-
sheckled, now one and the same person, their fight upheld to right
for a wee while being baffled and tottered, umbraged by the shadow
of Old Erssia's magisquammythical mulattomilitiaman, the living
by owning over the surfers of the glebe whose sway craven minnions
had caused to revile, as, too foul for hell, under boiling Mauses'
burning brand, he falls by Goll's gillie, but keenheartened by the
circuminsistence of the Parkes O'Rarelys in a hurdly gurdly Cicilian
concertone of their fonngeena barney brawl, shaken everybothy's
hands, while S. E. Morehampton makes leave to E. N. Sheil-
martin after Meetinghouse Lanigan has embaraced Vergemout
Hall, and, without falter or mormor or blathrehoot of sophsterliness,
pugnate the pledge of fiannaship, dook to dook, with a commonturn
oudchd of fest man and best man astoutsalliesemoutioun palms it
off like commodity tokens against a cococancancacacanotioun*).
When old the wormd was a gadden and Anthea first unfoiled her
limbs wanderloot was the way the wood wagged where opter
and apter were samuraised twimbs. They had their mutthering
ivies and their murdhering idies and their mouldhering iries in
that muskat grove but there'll be bright plinnyflowers in Calo-
mella's cool bowers when the magpyre's babble towers scorching
and screeching from the ravenindove. If thees lobed the sex of
his head and mees ates the seep of his traublers he's dancing
figgies to the spittle side and shoving outs the soord. And he'll
be buying buys and go gulling gells with his flossim and jessim
of carm, silk and honey while myandthys playing lancifer lucifug
and what's duff as a bettle for usses makes coy cosyn corollanes'
moues weeter to wee. So till butagain budly shoots thon rising
germinal let bodley chow the fatt of his anger and badley bide
the toil of his tubb.

[*The pump and pipe pingers are ideally reconstituted. The putther and bowls are peterpacked up. All the presents are determining as regards for the future the howabouts of their past absences which they might see on at hearing could they once smell of tastes from touch. To ought find a values for. The must overlistingness. When ex what is ungiven. As ad where. Stillhead. Blunk.*]

Shutmup. And bud did down well right. And if he sung dumb in his glass darkly speech lit face to face on allaround.

Vociferagitant. Viceversounding. Namely, Abdul Abulbul Amir or Ivan Slavansky Slavar. In alldconfusalem. As to whom the major guiltfeather pertained it was Hercushiccups' care to educe. Beauty's bath she's bound to bind beholders and pride, his purge, has place appoint in penance and the law's own libel lifts and lames the low with the lofty. Be of the housed! While the Hersy Hunt they harrow the hill for to rout them rollicking rogues from, rule those racketeer romps from, rein their rockery rides from. Rambling.

Nightclothesed, arooned, the conquerods sway. After their battle thy fair bosom.

— That is too tootrue enough in Solidan's Island as in Moltern Giaourmany and from the Amelakins off to date back to land of engined Egypsians, assented from his opening before his inlookers of where an oxmanstongue stalled stabled the wellnourished one, lord of the seven days, overlord of sats and suns, the sat of all the suns which are in the ring of his system of the sats of his sun, god of the scuffeldfallen skillfilledfelon, who (he containns) hangsters, who (he constrains) hersirrs, a gain changful, a mintage vaster, heavy on shirts, lucky with shifts, the topside humpup stummock atween his showdows fellah, Misto Teewiley Spillitshops, who keepeth watch in Khummer-Phett, whose spouse is An-Lyph, the dog's bladder, warmer of his couch in fore. We all, for whole men is lepers, have been nobbut wonterers in that chill childerness which is our true name after the allfaulters (mug's luck to em!) and, bespeaking of love and lie detectors in venuvarities, whateither the drugs truth of it, was

there an iota of from the faust to the lost. And that is at most re-
doubtedly an overthrew of each and ilkermann of us, I persuade
myself, before Gow, gentlemen, so true as this are my kopfinpot
astrode on these is my boardsoldereds.

It sollecited, grobbling hummley, his roundhouse of seven
orofaces, of all, guiltshouters or crimemummers, to be sayd by,
codnops, advices for, free of gracies, scamps encloded, com-
petitioning them, if they had steadied Jura or when they had
raced Messafissi, husband of your wifebetter or bestman botcha-
lover of you yourself, how comes ever a body in our taylorised
world to selve out thishis, whither it gives a primeum nobilees
for our notomise or naught, the farst wriggle from the ubivence,
whereom is man, that old offender, nother man, wheile he is
asame. And fullexampling. The pints in question. With some by-
spills. And sicsecs to provim hurtig. Soup's on!

— A time. And a find time. Whenin aye was a kiddling. And
the tarikies held sowansopper. Let there beam a frishfrey. And
they sodhe gudhe rudhe brodhe wedhe swedhe medhe in the
kanddledrum. I have just (let us suppraise) been reading in a
(suppressed) book — it is notwithstempting by meassures long
and limited—the latterpress is eminently leglligible and the paper,
so he eagerly seized upon, has scarsely been buttered in works of
previous publicity wholebeit in keener notcase would I turf aside
for pastureuration. Packen paper paineth whomto is sacred
scriptured sign. Who straps it scraps it that might, if ashed, have
healped. Enough, however, have I read of it, like my good bedst
friend, to augur in the hurry of the times that it will cocommend
the widest circulation and a reputation coextensive with its merits
when inthrusted into safe and pious hands upon so edifying a
mission as it, I can see, as is his. It his ambullished with expurga-
tive plates, replete in information and accampaigning the action
passiom, slopbang, whizzcrash, boomarattling from burst to
past, as I have just been seeing, with my warmest venerections,
of a timmersome townside upthecountrylifer, (Guard place the
town!) allthose everwhalmed upon that preposterous blank seat,
before the wordcraft of this early woodcutter, a master of vignett-

iennes and our findest grobsmid among all their orefices, (and, shukar in chowdar, so splunderdly English!) Mr Aubeyron Birdslay. Chubgoodchob, arsoncheep and wellwillworth a triat! Bismillafoulties. But the hasard you asks is justly ever behind his meddle throw! Those sad pour sad forengistanters, dastychappy dustyrust! Chaichairs. It is that something, awe, aurorbean in that fellow, hamid and damid, (did he have but Hugh de Brassey's beardslie his wear mine of ancient guised) which comequeers this anywhat perssian which we, owe, realisinus with purups a dard of pene. There is among others pleasons whom I love and which are favourests to mind, one which I have pushed my finker in for the movement and, but for my sealring is none to hand I swear, she is highly catatheristic and there is another which I have fombly fongered freequuntly and, when my signet is on sign again I swear, she is deeply sangnificant. *Culpo de Dido*! Ars we say in the classies. *Kunstful*, we others said. What ravening shadow! What dovely line! Not the king of this age could richlier eyefeast in oreillental longuardness with alternate nightjoys of a thousand kinds but one kind. A shahrryar cobbler on me when I am lying! And whilst (when I doot my sliding panel and I hear cawcaw) I have been idylly turmbing over the loose looves leaflefts jaggled casuallty on the lamatory, as is my this is, as I must commit my lips to make misface for misfortune, often, so far as I can chance to recollect from the some farnights ago, (so dimsweet is that selvischdischdienence of to not to be able to be obliged to have to hold further anything than a stone his throw's fruit's fall!) when I, if you wil excuse for me this informal leading down of illexpressibles, enlivened toward the Author of Nature by the natural sins liggen gobelimned theirs before me, (how differen- ded with the manmade Eonochs Cunstuntonopolies!), weather- ed they be of a general golf stature, assasserted, or blossomly emblushing thems elves underneed of some howthern folleys, am entrenched up contemplating of myself, wiz my naked I, for relieving purposes in our trurally virvir vergitabale (garden) I sometimes, maybe, what has justly said of old Flannagan, a wake from this or huntsfurwards, with some shock (shell I so render

it?) have (when I ope my shylight window and I see coocoo) a
notion quiet involuptary of that I am cadging hapsnots as at
murmurrandoms of distend renations from ficsimilar phases or
dugouts in the behindscenes of our earthwork (what rovining
shudder! what deadly loom!) as this is, at no spatial time pro-
cessly which regards to concrude chronology about which in
fact, at spite of I having belittled myself to my gay giftname of
insectarian, happy burgages abeyance would make homesweets-
town hopeygoalucrey, my mottu propprior, as I claim, cad's
truck, I coined, I am highly pelaged and deeply gluttened to
mind hindmost hearts to see by their loudest reports from my
threespawn bottery parts (shsh!) that, colombophile and corvino-
phobe alike, when I have remassed me, my travellingself, as from
Magellanic clouds, after my contractual expenditures, through
the perofficies of merelimb, I, my good grief, I am, I am big
altoogooder.

He beached the bark of his tale; and set to husband and vine:
and the harpermaster told all the living conservancy, know
Meschiameschianah, how that win a gain was in again. Flying
the Perseoroyal. Withal aboarder, padar and madar, hal and sal,
the sens of Ere with the duchtars of Iran. Amick amack amock in
a mucktub. Qith the tou loulous and the gryffygryffygryffs at
Fenegans Wick, the Wildemanns. Washed up whight and de-
liveried rhight. Loud lauds to his luckhump and bejetties on jo-
nahs. And they winxed and wanxed like baillybeacons. Till we
woksed up oldermen.

From whose plultibust preaggravated, by baskatchairch theo-
logies (there werenighn on thaurity herouins in that alraschil
arthouducks draken), they were whoalike placed to say, in the
matters off ducomans nonbar one, with bears' respects to him and
bulls' acknowledgments (come on now, girls! lead off, O cara,
whichever won of you wins! The two Gemuas and Jane Agrah
and Judy Tombuys!) disassembling and taking him apart, the
slammocks, with discrimination for his maypole and a rub in
passing over his hump, drogueries inaddendance, frons, fesces
and frithstool: 1) he hade to die it, the beetle, 2) he didhithim self,

hod's fush, 3) all ever the pelican huntered with truly fond bull-pen backthought since his toork human life where his personal low outhired his taratoryism, the orenore under the selfhide of his bessermettle, was forsake in his chiltern and lumbojumbo, 4) he was like Fintan fore flood and after sometimes too damned merely often on the saved side, saw he was, 5) regarding to prussyattes or quazzyverzing he wassand no better than he would have been before he could have been better than what he warrant after, 6) blood, musk or haschish, as coked, diamoned or pence-loid, and bleaching him naclenude from all cohlorine matter, down to a boneash bittstoff, he's, tink fors tank, the same old dustamount on the same old tincoverdull baubleclass, totstitty-winktosser and bogusbagwindburster, whether fitting tyres onto Danelope boys or fluttering flaus for laurettas, whatever the bucket brigade and the plug party says, touchant Arser of the Rum Tipple and his camelottery and lyonesslooting but with a layaman's brutstrenth, by Jacohob and Esahur and the all saults or all sallies, what we warn is to hear, jeff, is the woods of chirpsies cries to singaloo sweecheeriode and sock him up, the oldcant rogue.

Group A.

You have jest (a ham) beamed listening through (a ham pig) his haulted excerpt from John Whiston's fiveaxled production, *The Coach With The Six Insides*, from the Tales of Yore of the times gone by before there was a hofdking or a hoovthing or a pinginapoke in Oreland, all sould. Goes Tory by Eeric Whigs is To Become Tintinued in *Fearson's Nightly* in the Lets All Wake Brickfaced In Lucan. Lhirondella, jaunty lhirondella! With tirra lirra rondinelles, atantivy we go.

Attention! Stand at!! Ease!!!

We are now diffusing among our lovers of this sequence (to you! to you!) the dewfolded song of the naughtingels (Alys! Alysaloe!) from their sheltered positions, in rosescenery hay-dyng, on the heather side of waldalure, Mount Saint John's, Jinnyland, whither our allies winged by duskfoil from Moore-parque, swift sanctuary seeking, after Sunsink gang (Oiboe!

Hitherzither! Almost dotty! I must dash!) to pour their peace in
partial (floflo floreflorence), sweetishsad lightandgayle, twittwin
twosingwoolow. Let everie sound of a pitch keep still in reson-
ance, jemcrow, jackdaw, prime and secund with their terce that
whoe betwides them, now full theorbe, now dulcifair, and when
we press of pedal (sof!) pick out and vowelise your name.
A mum. You pere Golazy, you mere Bare and you Bill Heeny, and
you Smirky Dainty and, more beethoken, you wheckfoolthe-
nairyans with all your badchthumpered peanas! We are gluck-
glucky in our being so far fortunate that, bark and bay duol with
Man Goodfox inchimings having ceased to the moment, so allow
the clinkars of our nocturnefield, night's sweetmoztheart, their
Carmen Sylvae, my quest, my queen. Lou must wail to cool me
airly! Coil me curly, warbler dear! May song it flourish (in the
underwood), in chorush, long make it flourish (in the Nut, in the
Nutsky) till thorush! Secret Hookup.

— Roguenaar Loudbrags, that soddy old samph! How high
is vuile, var?

To which yes he did, capt, that was the answer.

— And his shartshort trooping its colours! We knows his
ventruquulence.

Which that that rang ripprippripplying.

—Bulbul, bulbulone! I will shally. Thou shalt willy. You wouldnt
should as youd remesmer. I hypnot. 'Tis golden sickle's hour.
Holy moon priestess, we'd love our grappes of mistellose. Moths
the matter? Pschtt! Tabarins comes. To fell our fairest. O gui, O
gui! Salam, salms, salaum! Carolus! O indeed and we ware! And
hoody crow was ere. I soared from the peach and Missmolly
showed her pear too, onto three and away. Whet the bee as to
deflowret greendy grassies yellowhorse. Kematitis, cele our er-
dours! Did you aye, did you eye, did you everysee suchaway,
suchawhy, eeriewhigg airywhugger? Even to the extremity of
the world? Dingoldell! The enormanous his, our littlest little!
Wee wee, that long alancey one! Let sit on this anthill for our
frilldress talk after this day of making blithe inveiled the heart
before our groatsupper serves to us Panchomaster and let har-

leqwind play peeptomine up all our colombinations. Wins
won is nought, twigs too is nil, tricks trees makes nix, fairs fears
stoops at nothing. And till Arthur comes againus and sen pea-
trick's he's reformed we'll pose him together a piece, a pace.
Shares in guineases! There's lovely the sight! Surey me, man
weepful! Big Seat, you did hear? And teach him twisters in
tongue irish. Pat lad may goh too. Quicken, aspen; ash and yew;
willow, broom with oak for you. And move your tellabout. Not
nice is that, limpet lady! Spose we try it promissly. Love all.
Naytellmeknot tennis! Taunt me treattening! But do now say to
Mr Eustache! Ingean mingen has to hear. Whose joint is out of
jealousy now? Why, heavilybody's evillyboldy's. Hopping Gra-
cius, onthy ovful! O belessk mie, what a nerve! How a mans in
his armor we nurses know, Wingwong welly, pitty pretty Nelly!
Some Poddy pitted in, will anny petty pullet out? Call Kitty
Kelly! Kissykitty Killykelly! What a nossowl buzzard! But what
a neats ung gels!

Here all the leaves alift aloft, full o'liefing, fell alaughing over
Ombrellone and his parasollieras with their black thronguards
from the County Shillelagh. Ignorant invincibles, innocents im-
mutant! Onzel grootvatter Lodewijk is onangonamed before the
bridge of primerose and his twy Isas Boldmans is met the bluey-
bells near Dandeliond. We think its a gorsedd shame, these go-
doms. A lark of limonladies! A lurk of orangetawneymen! You're
backleg wounted, budkley mister, bester of the boyne.

And they leaved the most leavely of leaftimes and the most
folliagenous till there came the marrer of mirth and the jangthe-
rapper of all jocolarinas and they were as were they never ere.
Yet had they laughtered, one on other, undo the end and enjoyed
their laughings merry was the times when so grant it High Hila-
rion us may too!

Cease, prayce, storywalkering around with gestare romano-
verum he swinking about is they think and plan unrawil
what.

Back to Droughty! The water of the face has flowed.

The all of them, the sowriegueuxers, blottyeyed boys, in that pig's village smoke, a sixdigitarian legion on druid circle, the Clandibblon clam cartel, then pulled out and came off and rally agreed them, roasted malts with toasted burleys, in condomnation of his totomptation and for the duration till his repepulation, upon old nollcromforemost ironsides, as camnabel chieftain, since, as Sammon trowed to explain to summon, seeing that, as he had contracted out of islands empire, he might as coolly have rolled to school call, tarponturboy, a grampurpoise, the manyfathom bringroom with the fortyinch bride, out of the cuptin klanclord kettle auction like the soldr of a britsh he was bound to be and become till the sea got him whilask, from maker to misses and what he gave was as a pattern, he, that hun of a horde, is a finn as she, his tent wife, is a lap, at home on a steed, abroad by the fire (to say nothing of him having done whatyouknow howyousaw whenyouheard whereyouwot, the kenspeckled souckar, generose as cocke, greediguss with garzelle, uprighter of age and most umbrasive of yews all, under heaviest corpsus exemption) and whoasever spit her in howsoever's fondling saving her keepers that mould the bould she sould to hould the wine that wakes the barley, the peg in his pantry to hold the heavyache off his heart. The droll delight of deemsterhood, a win from the wood to bond. Like the bright lamps, Thamamahalla, yearin out yearin. Auspicably suspectable but in expectancy of respectableness. From dirty flock bedding, drip dropping through the ceiling, with two sisters of charities on the front steps and three evacuan cleansers at the back gaze, single box and pair of chairs (suspectable), occasionally and alternatively used by husband when having writing to do in connection with equitable druids and friendly or other societies through periods of dire want with comparative plenty (thunderburst, ravishment, dissolution and providentiality) to a sofa allbeit of hoarsehaar with Amodicum cloth, hired payono, still playing off, used by the youngsters for czurnying out oldstrums, three bedrooms upastairs, of which one with fireplace (aspectable), with greenhouse in prospect (particularly perspectable).

And you, when you kept at Dulby, were you always (for that

time only) what we knew how when we (from that point solely) were you know where? There you are! And why? Why, hitch a cock eye, he was snapped on the sly upsadaisying coras pearls out of the pie when all the perts in princer street set up their tinker's humm, (the rann, the rann, that keen of old bards), with them newnesboys pearcin screaming off their armsworths. The boss made dovesandraves out of his bucknesst while herself wears the bowler's hat in her bath. Deductive Almayne Rogers disguides his voice, shetters behind hoax chestnote from exexive. Heat wives rasing. They jest keeps rosing. He jumps leaps rizing. Howlong!

You known that tom? I certainly know. Is their bann bothstiesed? Saddenly now. Has they bane reneemed? Soothinly low. Does they ought to buy the papelboy when he footles up their suit? He's their mark to foil the flouter and they certainty owe.

He sprit in his phiz (baccon!). He salt to their bis (pudden!). He toockled her palam (so calam is solom!). And he suked their friends' leave (bonnick lass, fair weal!)

— Guilty but fellows culpows! It was felt by me sindeade, that submerged doughdoughty doubleface told waterside labourers. But since we for athome's health have chanced all that, the wild whips, the wind ships, the wonderlost for world hips, unto their foursquare trust prayed in aid its plumptylump piteousness which, when it turtled around seeking a thud of surf, spake to approach from inherdoff trisspass through minxmingled hair. Though I may have hawked it, said, and selled my how hot peas after theactrisscalls from my imprecurious position and though achance I could have emptied a pan of backslop down drain by whiles of dodging a rere from the middenprivet appurtenant thereof, salving the presents of the board of wumps and pumps, I am ever incalpable, where release of prisonals properly is concerned, of unlifting upfallen girls wherein dangered from them in thereopen out of unadulteratous bowery, with those hintering influences from an angelsexonism. It was merely my barely till their oh offs. Missaunderstaid. Meggy Guggy's giggag. The

code's proof! The rebald danger with they who would bare whiteness against me I dismissem from the mind of good. He can tell
such as story to the Twelfth Maligns that my first was a nurss-
maid and her fellower's a willbe perambulatrix. There are twingty
to twangty too thews and leathermail coatschemes penparing to
hostpost for it valinnteerily with my valued fofavour to the post
puzzles deparkment with larch parchels' of presents for future
branch offercings. The green approve the raid! Shaum Baum's
bode he is amustering in the groves while his shool comes merging along. Want I put myself in their kirtlies I were ayearn to
leap with them and show me too bisextine. Dear and lest I forget mergers and bow to you low, marchers! Attemption! What
a mazing month of budsome misses they are making, so wingty-
wish to flit beflore their kin! Attonsure! Ears to hears! The skall
of a gall (for every dime he yawpens that momouth you could
park your ford in it) who has papertreated him into captivities
with his inside man by a hocksheat of starvision for an avrageto-
peace of parchment, cooking up his lenses to be my apoclogypst,
the recreuter of conscraptions, let him be asservent to Kinahaun!
For (peace peace perfectpeace!) I have abwaited me in a water of
Elin and I have placed my reeds intectis before the Registower of
the perception of tribute in the hall of the city of Analbe. How
concerns any merryaunt and hworsoever gravesobbers it is
perensempry sex of fun to help a dazzle off the othour. What for
Mucias and Gracias may the duvlin rape the handsomst! And the
whole mad knightmayers' nest! Tunpother, prison and plotch!
If Y shoulden somewhat, well, I am able to owe it, hearth and chem-
ney easy. They seeker for vannflaum all worldins merkins. I'll
eager make lyst turpidump undher arkens. Basast! And if my liti-
gimate was well to wrenn tigtag cackling about it, like the sally
berd she is, to abery ham in the Cutey Strict, (I shall call upon
my first among my lost of lyrars beyond a jingoobangoist, to
overcast her) dismissing mundamanu all the riflings of her vic-
tuum gleaner (my old chuck! she drakes me druck! turning out,
gay at ninety!) and well shoving off a boastonmess like lots wives
does over her handpicked hunsbend, as she would be calling, well,

for further oil mircles upon all herwayferer gods and reanounc-
ing my deviltries as was I a locally person of caves until I got my
purchase on her firmforhold I am, I like to think, by their sacre-
ligion of daimond cap daimond, confessedly in my baron gentil-
homme to the manhor bourne till ladiest day as panthoposopher,
to have splet for groont a peer of bellows like Bacchulus shakes a
rousing guttural at any old cerpaintime by peaching (allsole we
are not amusical) the warry warst against myself in the defile as
a lieberretter sebaiscopal of these mispeschyites of the first virgi-
nial water who, without an auction of biasement from my part,
with gladyst tone ahquickyessed in it, overhowe and under-
where, the totty lolly poppy flossy conny dollymaukins. Though
I heave a coald on my bauck and am could up to my eres hoven
sametimes I used alltides to be aswarmer for the meekst and the
graced. You are not going to not. You might be threeabreasted
wholenosing at a whallhoarding from our Don Amir anent villa-
yets prostatution precisingly kuschkars tarafs and it could be
double densed uncounthest hour of allbleakest age with a bad of
wind and a barran of rain, nompos mentis like Novus Elector, what
with his Marx and their Groups, yet did a doubt, should a dare,
were to you, you would do and dhamnk me, shenker, dhumnk you.
Skunk. And fare with me to share with me. Hinther and thonther,
hant by hont. By where dauvening shedders down whose rovely
lanes. As yose were and as yese is. Sure and you would, Mr Mac
Gurk. Be sure and you would, Mr O'Duane. To be sure and you
would so, Mr MacElligut. Wod you nods? Mom mom. No mum
has the rod to pud a stub to the lurch of amotion. My little love
apprencisses, my dears, the estelles, van Nessies von Nixies voon
der pool, which I had a reyal devouts for yet was it marly lowease
or just a feel with these which olderman K.K. Alwayswelly he
is showing ot the fullnights for my palmspread was gav to a
parsleysprig, the curliest weedeen old ocean coils around, so spruce
a spice for salthorse, sonnies, and as tear to the thrusty as Taylor's Spring, when aftabournes, when she was look like a little
cheayat chilled (Oh sard! ah Mah!) by my tide impracing, as
Beacher seath, and all the colories fair fled from my folced cheeks!

Popottes, where you canceal me you mayst forced guage my
bribes. Wickedgapers, I appeal against the light. A nexistence of
vividence! Panto, boys, is on a looser inloss ballet, girls, suppline
thrown tights. I have wanted to thank you such a long time so
much now. Thank you. Sir, kindest of bottleholders and very dear
friend, among our hearts of steel, froutiknow, it will befor you,
me dare beautiful young soldier, winninger nor anyour of rudi-
mental moskats, before you go to mats, you who have watched
your share with your sockboule sodalists on your buntad nogs at
our love tennis squats regatts, suckpump, when on with the balls
did disserve the fain, my goldrush gainst her silvernetss, to say,
biguidd, for the love of goddess and perthanow as you reveres
your one mothers, mitsch for matsch, and while I reveal thus my
deepseep daughter which was bourne up pridely out of meds-
dreams unclouthed when I was pillowing in my brime (of Satur-
nay Eve, how now, woren't we't?), to see, I say, whoahoa, in stay
of execution *in re* Milcho Melekmans, increaminated, what you
feel, oddrabbit, upon every strong ground you have ever taken
up, by bitterstiff work or battonstaff play, with assault of turk
against a barrakraval of grakeshoots, e'en tho' Jambuwel's defe-
calties is Terry Shimmyrag's upperturnity, if that is grace for the
grass what is balm for the bramblers, as it is as it is, that I am the
catasthmatic old ruffin sippahsedly improctor to be seducint tro-
vatellas, the dire daffy damedeaconesses, like (why sighs the
sootheesinger) the lilliths oft I feldt, and, when booboob brutals
and cautiouses only aims at the oggog hogs in the humand, then,
(Houtes, Blymey and Torrenation, upkurts and scotchem!) I'll
tall tale tell croon paysecurers, sowill nuggets and nippers, that
thash on me stumpen blows the gaff off mombition and thit thides
or marse makes a good dayle to be shattat. Fall stuff.

His rote in ere, afstef, was.

And dong wonged Magongty till the bombtomb of the warr,
thrusshed in his whole soort of cloose.

Whisht who wooed in Weald, bays of Bawshaw binding. The
desire of Miriam is the despair of Marian as Joh Joseph's beauty
is Jacq Jacob's grief. Brow, tell nun; eye, feign sad; mouth, sing

mim. Look at Lokman! Whatbetween the cupgirls and the platterboys. And he grew back into his grossery baseness: and for all his grand remonstrance: and there you are.

Here endeth chinchinatibus with have speak finish. With a haygue for a halt on a pouncefoot panse. Pink, pleas pink, two pleas pink, how to pleas pink.

Punk.

Mask one. Mask two. Mask three. Mask four.

Up.

— Look about you, Tutty Comyn!

— Remember and recall, Kullykeg!

— When visiting Dan Leary try the corner house for thee.

— I'll gie ye credit for simmence more if ye'll be lymphing.

Our four avunculusts.

And, since threestory sorratelling was much too many, they maddened and they morgued and they lungd and they jowld. Synopticked on the word.

Till the Juke done it.

Down.

Like Jukoleon, the seagoer, when he bore down in his perry boat he had raised a slide and shipped his orders and seized his pullets and primed their plumages, the fionnling and dubhlet, the dun and the fire, and, sending them one by other to fare fore forn, he had behold the residmance of a delugion: the foggy doze still going strong, the old thalassocrats of invinsible empores, maskers of the waterworld, facing one way to another way and this way on that way, from severalled their fourdimmansions. Where the lighning leaps from the numbulous; where coold by cawld breide lieth langwid; the bounds whereinbourne our solied bodies all attomed attaim arrest: appoint, that's all. But see what follows. Wringlings upon wronglings among incomputables about an uncomeoutable (an angel prophetethis? kingcorrier of beheasts? the calif in his halifskin? that eyriewinging one?) and the voids bubbily vode's dodos across the which the boomomouths from their dupest dupes were in envery and anononously blowing great.

Guns.

Keep backwards, please, because there was no good to gundy
running up again. Guns. And it was written up in big capital.
Guns. Saying never underrupt greatgrandgosterfosters! Guns.
And whatever one did they said, the fourlings, that on no acounts
you were not to. Guns.

Not to pad them behaunt in the fear. Not to go, tonnerwatter,
and bungley well chute the rising gianerant. Not to wandly be
woking around jerumsalemdo at small hours about the murketplots,
smelling okey boney, this little figgy and arraky belloky this little
pink into porker but, porkodirto, to let the gentlemen pedesta-
rolies out of the Monabella culculpuration live his own left leave,
cullebuone, by perperusual of the petpubblicities without inwok-
ing his also's between (*sic*) the arraky bone and (*suc*) the okey
bellock. And not to not be always, hemmer and hummer treeing
unselves up with one exite but not to never be caving nicely, precisely, quicely, rebustly, tendrolly, unremarkably, forsakenly, hal-
tedly, reputedly, firstly, somewhatly, yesayenolly about the back
excits. Never to weaken up in place of the broths. Never to vvol-
lusslleepp in the pleece of the poots. And, allerthings, never to ate
the sour deans if they weren't having anysin on their consients.
And, when in Zumschloss, to never, narks, cease till the finely
ending was consummated by the completion of accomplishment.

And thus within the tavern's secret booth The wisehight ones
who sip the tested sooth Bestir them as the Just has bid to jab The
punch of quaram on the mug of truth.

K.C. jowls, they're sodden in the secret. K.C. jowls, they sure
are wise. K.C. jowls, the justicestjobbers, for they'll find another
faller if their ruse won't rise. Whooley the Whooper.

There is to see. Squarish large face with the atlas jacket. Brights,
brownie eyes in bluesackin shoeings. Peaky booky nose over a
lousiany shirt. Ruddy stackle hair besides a strawcamel belt.
Namely. Gregorovitch, Leonocopolos, Tarpinacci and Duggel-
duggel. And was theys stare all atime? Yea but they was. Andor-
ing the games, induring the studies, undaring the stories, end all.
Ned? Only snugged then and cosied after one percepted nought

while tuffbettle outraged the waywords and meansigns of their
hinterhand suppliesdemands. And be they gone to splane splica-
tion. That host that nast one on the hoose when backturns when
he facefronts none none in the house his geust has guest. You bet
they is. And nose well down.

With however what sublation of compensation in the radifica-
tion of interpretation by the byeboys? Being they. Mr G. B. W.
Ashburner, S. Bruno's Toboggan Drive, Mr Faixgood, Bell-
chimbers, Carolan Crescent, Mr I. I. Chattaway, Hilly Gape,
Poplar Park, Mr Q. P. Dieudonney, The View, Gazey Peer,
Mr T. T. Erchdeakin, Multiple Lodge, Jiff Exby Rode, Mr W. K.
Ferris-Fender, Fert Fort, Woovil Doon Botham ontowhom
adding the tout that pumped the stout that linked the lank that
cold the sandy that nextdoored the rotter that rooked the rhymer
that lapped at the hoose that Joax pilled.

They had heard or had heard said or had heard said written.
Fidelisat.

That there first a rudrik kingcomed to an inn court; and the
seight of that yard was a perchypole with a loovahgloovah on it;
last mannarks maketh man when wandshift winneth womans: so
how would it hum, whoson of a which, if someof aswas to start
to stunt the story on?

So many needles to ponk out to as many noodles as are company, they noddling all about it *tutti* to *tempo*, decumans numbered
too, (*a*) well, that the secretary bird, better known as Pandoria
Paullabucca, whom they thought was more like a solicitor general,
indiscriminatingly made belief mid authorsagastions from Schelm
the Pelman to write somewords to Senders about her chilikin
puck, laughing that Poulebec would be the death of her, (*b*) that,
well, that Madges Tighe, the postulate auditressee, when her
daremood's a grownian, is always on the who goes where, hoping
to Michal for the latter to turn up with a cupital tea before her
ephumeral comes off without any much father which is parting
parcel of the same goumeral's postoppage, it being lookwhyse on
the whence blows weather helping mickle so that the loiter end of
that leader may twaddle out after a cubital lull with a hopes soon

to ear, comprong? (c) becakes the goatsman on question, or whatever the hen the bumbler was, feeling not up to scratch bekicks
of whatever the kiddings Payne Inge and Popper meant for him,
thoughy onced at a throughlove, true grievingfrue danger, as a
nirshe persent to his minstress, devourced the pair of them
Mather Caray's chucklings, *pante blanche*, and skittered his litters
like the cavaliery man in Cobra Park for ungeborn yenkelmen,
Jeremy Trouvas or Kepin O'Keepers, any old howe and any old
then and when around Dix Dearthy Dungbin, remarking sceni-
cally with laddylike lassitude upon what he finally postscrapped,
(d) after it's so long till I thanked you about I do so much now
thank you so very much as you introduced me to fourks, (e) will,
these remind to be sane? (f) Fool step! Aletheometry? Or just
zoot doon floon?

Nut it out, peeby eye! Onamassofmancynaves.

But. Top.

You were in the same boat of yourselves too, Getobodoff or
Treamplasurin; and you receptionated the most diliskious of
milisk; which it all flowowered your drooplin dunlearies: but
dribble a drob went down your rothole. Meaning, Kelly, Grimes,
Phelan, Mollanny, O'Brien, MacAlister, Sealy, Coyle, Hynes-
Joynes, Naylar-Traynor, Courcy de Courcy and Gilligan-Goll.

Stunner of oddstodds on bluebleeding boarhorse! What
soresen's head subrises thus tous out of rumpumplikun oak with,
well, we cannot say whom we are looking like through his now-
face? It is of Noggens whilk dusts the bothsides of the seats of the
bigslaps of the bogchaps of the porlarbaar of the marringaar of the
Lochlunn gonlannludder of the feof of the foef of forfummed
Ship-le-Zoyd.

Boumce! It is polisignstunter. The Sockerson boy. To pump
the fire of the lewd into those soulths of bauchees, havsouse-
dovers, tillfellthey deadwar knootvindict. An whele time he was
rancing there smutsy floskons nodunder ycholerd for their
poopishers, ahull onem Fyre maynoother endnow! Shatten up
ship! Bouououmce! Nomo clandoilskins cheakinlevers! All
ashored for Capolic Gizzards! Stowlaway there, glutany of

stainks. Porterfillyers and spirituous suncksters, oooom oooom!

As these vitupetards in his boasum he did strongleholder, bushbrows, nobblynape, swinglyswanglers, sunkentrunk, that from tin of this clucken hadded runced slapottleslup. For him had hord from fard a piping. As? Of?

Dour douchy was a sieguldson. He cooed that loud nor he was young. He cud bad caw nor he was gray Like wather parted from the say.

Ostia, lift it! Lift at it, Ostia! From the say! Away from the say! Himhim. Himhim.

Hearhasting he, himmed reromembered all the chubbs, chipps, chaffs, chuckinpucks and chayney chimebells That he had mistributed in port, pub, park, pantry and poultryhouse, While they, thered, the others, that are, were most emulously concerned to cupturing the last dropes of summour down through their grooves of blarneying. Ere the sockson locked at the dure. Which he would, shuttinshure. And lave them to sture.

For be all rules of sport 'tis right That youth bedower'd to charm the night Whilst age is dumped to mind the day When wather parted from the say.

The humming, it's coming. Insway onsway.

Fingool MacKishgmard Obesume Burgearse Benefice, He was bowen hem and scrapin him in recolcitrantament to the right-about And these probenopubblicoes clamatising for an extinsion on his hostillery With his chargehand bombing their eres. Tids, genmen, plays, she been goin shoother off almaynoother onawares.

You here nort farwellens rouster? Ashiffle ashuffle the wayve they.

From Dancingtree till Suttonstone Theres lads no lie would filch a crown To mull their sack and brew their tay With wather parted from the say.

Lelong Awaindhoo's a selverbourne enrouted to Rochelle Lane and liberties those Mullinguard minstrelsers are marshalsing, par tunepiped road, under where, perked on hollowy hill, that poor man of Lyones, good Dook Weltington, hugon come er-

rindwards, had hircomed to the belles bows and been cutat-
trapped by the mausers. Now is it town again, londmear of Dublin. And off coursse the toller, ples the dotter of his eyes with
her: Moke the Wanst, whye doe we aime alike a pose of poeter
peaced? While the dumb he shoots the shopper rope. And they
all pour forth. Sans butly Tuppeter Sowyer, the rouged engene-
rand, a barttler of the beauyne, still our benjamin liefest, sometime frankling to thise citye, whereas bigrented him a piers half
subporters for his arms, Josiah Pipkin, Amos Love, Raoul Le Feb-
ber, Blaize Taboutot, Jeremy Yopp, Francist de Loomis, Hardy
Smith and Sequin Pettit followed by the snug saloon seanad of
our Café Béranger. The scenictutors.

Because they wonted to get out by the goatweigh afore the sheep
was looset for to wish the Wobbleton Whiteleg Welshers kailly-
kailly kellykekkle and savebeck to Brownhazelwood from all the
dinnasdoolins on the labious banks of their swensewn snewwes-
ner, turned again weastinghome, by Danesbury Common, and
they onely, duoly, thruely, fairly after rainydraining founty-
buckets (chalkem up, hemptyempty!) till they caught the wind
abroad (alley loafers passinggeering!) all the rockers on the
roads and all the boots in the stretes.

Oh dere! Ah hoy!

Last ye, lundsmin, hasty hosty! For an anondation of miri-
fication and the lutification of our paludination.

His bludgeon's bruk, his drum is tore. For spuds we'll keep the
hat he wore And roll in clover on his clay By wather parted
from the say.

Hray! Free rogue Mountone till Dew Mild Well to corry awen
and glowry. Are now met by Brownaboy Fuinnninuinn's former
for a lyncheon partyng of his burgherbooh. The Shanavan
Wacht. Rantinroarin Batteries Dorans. And that whistling thief,
O' Ryne O'Rann. With a catch of her cunning like and nowhere
a keener.

The for eolders were aspolootly at their wetsend in the mailing
waters, trying to. Hide! Seek! Hide! Seek! Because number one
lived at Bothersby North and he was trying to. Hide! Seek! Hide!

Seek! And number two digged up Poors Coort, Soother, trying
to. Hide! Seek! Hide! Seek! And nomber three he sleeped with
Lilly Tekkles at The Eats and he was trying to. Hide! Seek!
Hide! Seek! And the last with the sailalloyd donggie he was
berthed on the Moherboher to the Washte and they were all trying to and baffling with the walters of, hoompsydoompsy walters
of. High! Sink! High! Sink! Highohigh! Sinkasink!

Waves.

The gangstairs strain and anger's up As Hoisty rares the can
and cup To speed the bogre's barque away O'er wather parted
from the say.

Horkus chiefest ebblynuncies!

— He shook be ashaped of hempshelves, hiding that shepe in
his goat. And for rassembling so bearfellsed the magreedy
prince of Roger. Thuthud. Heigh hohse, heigh hohse, our kin-
dom from an orse! Bruni Lanno's woollies on Brani Lonni's
hairyparts. And the hunk in his trunk it would be an insalt foul
the matter of that cellaring to a pigstrough. Stop his laysense.
Ink him! You would think him Alddaublin staking his lordsure like
a gourd on puncheon. Deblinity devined. Wholehunting the pairk
on a methylogical mission whenever theres imberillas! And calling Rina Roner Reinette Ronayne. To what mine answer is a
lemans. Arderleys, beedles and postbillers heard him. Three
points to one. Ericus Vericus corrupted into ware eggs. Dummy
up, distillery! Broree aboo! Run him a johnsgate down jameses-
lane. Begetting a wife which begame his niece by pouring her
youngthings into skintighs. That was when he had dizzy spells.
Till Gladstools Pillools made him ride as the mall. Thanks to his
huedobrass beerd. Lodenbroke the Longman, now he canseels
under veerious persons but is always that Rorke relly! On consideration for the musickers he ought to have down it. Pass out
your cheeks, why daunt you! Penalty, please! There you'll know
how warder barded the bollhead that parssed our alley. We just
are upsidedown singing what ever the dimkims mummur alla-
lilty she pulls inner out heads. This is not the end of this by no
manners means. When you've bled till you're bone it crops out

in your flesh. To tell how your mead of, mard, is made of. All old
Dadgerson's dodges one conning one's copying and that's what
wonderland's wanderlad'll flaunt to the fair. A trancedone boy-
script with tittivits by. Ahem. You'll read it tomorrow, marn,
when the curds on the table. A nigg for a nogg and a thrate for
a throte. The auditor learns. Still pumping on Torkenwhite Rad-
lumps, Lencs. In preplays to Anonymay's left hinted palinode
obviously inspiterebbed by a sibspecious connexion. Note the
notes of admiration! See the signs of suspicion! Count the hemi-
semidemicolons! Screamer caps and invented gommas, quoites
puntlost, forced to farce! The pipette will say anything at all for
a change. And you know what aglove means in the Murdrus due-
luct! Fewer to feud and rompant culotticism, a fugle for the glee-
men and save, sit and sew. And a pants outsizinned on the
Doughertys' duckboard pointing to peace at home. In some,
lawanorder on lovinardor. Wait till we hear the Boy of Biskop
reeling around your postoral lector! Epistlemadethemology for
deep dorfy doubtlings. As we'll lay till break of day in the bunk of
basky, O! Our island, Rome and duty! Well tried, buckstiff! Batt
in, boot! Sell him a breach contact, the vendoror, the buylawyer!
One hyde, sack, hic! Two stick holst, Lucky! Finnish Make Goal!
First you were Nomad, next you were Namar, now you're Nu-
mah and it's soon you'll be Nomon. Hence counsels Ecclesiast.
There's every resumption. The forgein offils is on the shove to
lay you out dossier. Darby's in the yard, planning it on you, plot
and edgings, the whispering peeler after cooks wearing an illformation. The find of his kind! An artist, sir! And dirt cheap at
a sovereign a skull! He knows his Finsbury Follies backwoods
so you batter see to your regent refutation. Ascare winde is rifing
again about nice boys going native. You know who was wrote
about in the Orange Book of Estchapel? Basil and the two other
men from King's Avenance. Just press this cold brand against
your brow for a mow. Cainfully! The sinus the curse. That's it.
Hung Chung Egglyfella now speak he tell numptywumpty top-
sawys belongahim pidgin. Secret things other persons place there
covered not. How you fell from story to story like a sagasand

to lie. Enfilmung infirmity. On the because alleging to having a
finger a fudding in pudding and pie. And here's the witnesses.
Glue on to him, Greevy! Bottom anker, Noordeece! And kick
kick killykick for the house that juke built! Wait till they send
you to sleep, scowpow! By jurors' cruces! Then old Hunphy-
dunphyville'll be blasted to bumboards by the youthful herald
who would once you were. He'd be our chosen one in the matter
of Brittas more than anarthur. But we'll wake and see. The wholes
poors riches of ours hundreds of manhoods and womhoods. Two
cents, two mills and two myrds. And it's all us rangers you'll be
facing in the box before the twelfth correctional. Like one man,
gell. Between all the Misses Mountsackvilles in their halfmoon
haemicycles, gasping to giddies to dye for the shame. Just hold
hard till the one we leapt out gets her yearing! Hired in cameras,
extra! With His Honour Surpacker on the binge. So yelp your
guilt and kitz the buck. You'll have loss of fame from Wimme-
game's fake. Forwards! One bully son growing the goff and his
twinger read out by the Nazi Priers. You fought as how they'd
never woxen up, did you, crucket? It will wecker your earse, that
it will! When hives the court to exchequer 'tis the child which
gives the sire away. Good for you, Richmond Rover! Scrum
around, our side! Let him have another between the spindlers. A
grand game! Dalymount's decisive. Don Gouverneur Buckley's
in the Tara Tribune, sporting the insides of a Rhutian Jhanaral
and little Mrs Ex-Skaerer-Sissers is bribing the halfpricers to pray
for her widower in his gravest embazzlement. You on her, hosy
jigses, that'll be some nonstop marrimont! You in your stolen
mace and anvil, Magnes, and her burrowed in Berkness cirrchus
clouthses. Fummuccumul with a graneen aveiled. Playing down
the slavey touch. Much as she was when the fancy cutter out collecting milestones espied her aseesaw on a fern. So nimb, he said,
a dat of dew. Between Furr-y-Benn and Ferr-y-Bree. In this tear
Vikloe vich he lofed. The smiling ever. If you pulls me over pay
me, prhyse! A talor would adapt his caulking trudgers on to any
shape at see. Address deceitfold of wovens weard. The wonder
of the women of the world together, moya! And the lovablest

Lima since Ineen MacCormick MacCoort MacConn O'Puckins MacKundred. Only but she is a little width wider got. Be moving abog. You cannot make a limousine lady out of a hillman minx. Listun till you'll hear the Mudquirt accent. This is a bulgen horesies, this is wollan indulgencies, this is a flemsh. Tik. Scapulars, beads and a stump of a candle, Hubert was a Hunter, *chemins de la croixes* and Rosairette's egg, all the trimmings off the tree that she picked up after the Clontarf voterloost when O'Bryan MacBruiser bet Norris Nobnut. Becracking his cucconut between his kknneess. Umpthump, Here Inkeeper, it's the doatereen's wednessmorn! Delphin dringing! Grusham undergang! And the Real Hymernians strenging strong at knocker knocker! Holy and massalltolled. You ought to tak a dos of frut. Jik. Sauss. You're getting hoovier, a twelve stone hoovier, fullends a twelve stone hoovier, in your corpus entis and it scurves you right, demnye! Aunt as unclish ams they make oom. But Nichtia you bound not to loose's gone on Neffin since she clapped her charmer on him at Gormagareen. At the Gunting Munting Hunting Punting. The eitch is in her blood, arrah! For a frecklesome freshcheeky sweetworded lupsqueezer. And he shows how he'll pick him the lock of her fancy. Poghue! Poghue! Poghue! And a good jump, Powell! Clean over all their heads. We could kiss him for that one, couddled we, Huggins? Sparkes is the footer to hance off nancies. Scaldhead, pursue! Before you bunkledoodle down upon your birchentop again after them three blows from time, drink and hurry. The same three that nursed you, Skerry, Badbols and the Grey One. All of your own club too. With the fistful of burryberries were for the massus for to feed you living in dying. Buy bran biscuits and you'll never say dog. And be in the finest of companies. Morialtay and Kniferope Walker and Rowley the Barrel. With Longbow of the lie. Slick of the trick and Blennercassel of the brogue. Clanruckard for ever! The Fenn, the Fenn, the kinn of all Fenns! Deaf to the winds when for Croonacreena. Fisht! And it's not now saying how we are where who's softing what rushes. Merryvirgin forbed! But of they never eat soullfriede they're ating it now. With easter

greeding. Angus! Angus! Angus! The keykeeper of the keys of
the seven doors of the dreamadoory in the house of the household of Hecech saysaith. Whitmore, whatmore? Give it over,
give it up! Mawgraw! Head of a helo, chesth of champgnon, eye
of a gull! What you'd if he'd. The groom is in the greenhouse,
gattling out his. Gun! That lad's the style for. Lannigan's ball!
Now a drive on the naval! The Shallburn Shock. Never mind
your gibbous. Slip on your ropen collar and draw the noosebag
on your head. Nobody will know or heed you, Postumus, if you
skip round schlymartin by the back and come front sloomutren
to beg in one of the shavers' sailorsuits. Three climbs three-
quickenthrees in the garb of nine. We'll split to see you mouldem
imparvious. A wing for oldboy Welsey Wandrer! Well spat,
witty wagtail! Now piawn to bishop's forthe! Moove. There's
Mumblesome Wadding Murch cranking up to the hornemooni-
um. Drawg us out *Ivy Eve in the Hall of Alum*! The finnecies of
poetry wed music. Feeling the jitters? You'll be as tight as Trivett
when the knot's knutted on. Now's your never! Peena and
Queena are duetting a giggle-for-giggle and the brideen Alannah is lost in her diamindwaiting. What a magnificent gesture
you will show us this gallus day. Clean and easy, be the hooker!
And a free for croaks after. Dovlen are out for it. So is Rathfinn.
And, hike, here's the hearse and four horses with the interpro-
vincial crucifixioners throwing lots inside to know whose to be
their gosson and whereas to brake the news to morhor. How
our myterbilder his fullen aslip. And who will wager but he'll
Shonny Bhoy be, the fleshlumpfleeter from Poshtapengha and all
he bares sobsconcious inklings shadowed on soulskin. Its segnet
yores, the strake of a hin. Nup. Laying the cloth, to fore of them.
And thanking the fish, in core of them. To pass the grace for
Gard sake! Ahmohn. Mr Justician Matthews and Mr Justician
Marks and Mr Justician Luk de Luc and Mr Justinian Johnston-
Johnson. And the aaskart, see, behind! Help, help, hurray! All-
sup, allsop! Four ghools to nail! Cut it down, mates, look slippy!
They've got a dathe with a swimminpull. Dang! Ding! Dong!
Dung! Dinnin. Isn't it great he is swaying above us for his good

and ours. Fly your balloons, dannies and dennises! He's door-
knobs dead! And Annie Delap is free! Ones more. We could
ate you, par Buccas, and imbabe through you, reassuranced in
the wild lac of gotliness. One fledge, one brood till hulm
culms evurdyburdy. Huh the throman! Huh the traidor. Huh
the truh. Arrorsure, he's the mannork of Arrahland over-
sense he horrhorrd his name in thuthunder. Rrrwwwkkkrrr!
And seen it rudden up in fusefiressence on the flashmurket.
P.R.C.R.L.L. Royloy. Of the rollorrish rattillary. The lewd-
ningbluebolteredallucktruckalltraumconductor! The unnamed
nonirishblooder that becomes a Greenislender overnight! But
we're molting superstituettes out of his fulse thortin guts. Tried
mark, Easterlings. Sign, Soideric O'Cunnuc, Rix. Adversed ord,
Magtmorken, Kovenhow. There's a great conversion, myn! Cou-
cous! Find his causcaus! From Motometusolum through Bulley
and Cowlie and Diggerydiggerydock down to bazeness's usual?
He's alight there still, by Mike! Loose afore! Bung! Bring forth
your deed! Bang! Till is the right time. Bang! Partick Thistle
agen S. Megan's versus Brystal Palace agus the Walsall! Putsch!
Tiemore moretis tisturb badday! The playgue will be soon over,
rats! Let sin! Geh tont! All we wants is to get peace for possession. We dinned unnerstunned why you sassad about thirteen
to aloafen, sor, kindly repeat! Or ledn us alones of your lungorge,
parsonifier propounde of our edelweissed idol worts! Shaw and
Shea are lorning obsen so hurgle up, gandfarder, and gurgle me
gurk. You can't impose on frayshouters like os. Every tub here
spucks his own fat. Hang coersion everyhow! And smotther-
mock Gramm's laws! But we're a drippindhrue gayleague all at
ones. In the buginning is the woid, in the muddle is the sound-
dance and thereinofter you're in the unbewised again, vund
vulsyvolsy. You talker dunsker's brogue men we our souls
speech obstruct hostery. Silence in thought! Spreach! Wear
anartful of outer nocense! Pawpaw, wowow! Momerry twelfths,
noebroed! That was a good one, ha! So it will be quite a material
what *May* farther be unvuloped for you, old *Mighty*, when it's
aped to foul a delfian in the Mahnung. Ha ha! Talk of Paddy-

barke's echo! Kick nuck, Knockcastle! Muck! And you'll nose it,
O you'll nose it, without warnward from we. We don't know the
sendor to whome. But you'll find Chiggenchugger's taking the
Treaclyshortcake with Bugle and the Bitch pairsadrawsing and
Horssmayres Prosession tyghting up under the threes. Stop.
Press stop. To press stop. All to press stop. And be the seem
talkin wharabahts hosetanzies, dat sure is sullibrated word! Bing
bong! Saxolooter, for congesters are salders' prey. Snap it up in
the loose, patchy the blank! Anyone can see you're the son of a
gunnell. Fellow him up too, Carlow! Woes to the worm-
quashed, aye, and wor to the winner! Think of Aerian's Wall and
the Fall of Toss. Give him another for to volleyholleydoodlem!
His lights not all out yet, the liverpooser! Boohoohoo it oose!
With seven hores always in the home of his thinkingthings, his
nodsloddledome of his noiselisslesoughts. Two Idas, two Evas,
two Nessies and Rubyjuby. Phook! No wonder, pipes as kirles,
that he sthings like a rheinbok. One bed night he had the dely-
siums that they were all queens mobbing him. Fell stiff. Oh,
ho, ho, ho, ah, he, he! Abedicate yourself. It just gegs our goad.
He'll be the deaf of us, pappappoppopcuddle, samblind daiy-
rudder. Yus, sord, fathe, you woll, putty our wraughther!
What we waits be after? Whyfore we come agooding? None of
you, cock icy! You keep that henayearn and her fortycantle glim
lookbehinder. We might do with rubiny leeses. But of all your
wanings send us out your peppydecked ales and you'll not be
such a bad lot. The rye is well for whose amind but the wheateny
one is proper lovely. B E N K! We sincerestly trust that Missus
with the kiddies of sweet Gorteen has not B I N K to their very
least tittles deranged if in B U N K and we greesiously augur for
your Meggers a B E N K B A N K B O N K to sloop in with
all sorts of adceterus and adsaturas. It's our last fight, Megantic,
fear you will! The refergee's took to hailing to time the pass.
There goes the blackwatchwomen all in white, flaxed up, pur-
gad! Right toe, Armitage! Tem for Tam at Timmotty Hall.
We're been carried away. Beyond bournes and bowers. So we'll
leave it to Keyhoe, Danelly and Pykemhyme, the three muskra-

teers, at the end of this age that had it from Variants' Katey Sherratt that had it from Variants' Katey Sherratt's man for the bonnefacies of Blashwhite and Blushred of the Aquasancta Liffey Patrol to wind up and to tells of all befells after that to Mocked Majesty in the Malincurred Mansion.

So you were saying, boys? Anyhow he what?

So anyhow, melumps and mumpos of the hoose uncommons, after that to wind up that longtobechronickled gettogether thanksbetogiving day at Glenfinnisk-en-la-Valle, the anniversary of his finst homy commulion, after that same barbecue beanfeast was all over poor old hospitable corn and eggfactor, King Roderick O'Conor, the paramount chief polemarch and last preelectric king of Ireland, who was anything you say yourself between fiftyodd and fiftyeven years of age at the time after the socalled last supper he greatly gave in his umbrageous house of the hundred bottles with the radio beamer tower and its hangars, chimbneys and equilines or, at least, he was'nt actually the then last king of all Ireland for the time being for the jolly good reason that he was still such as he was the eminent king of all Ireland himself after the last preeminent king of all Ireland, the whilom joky old top that went before him in the Taharan dynasty, King Arth Mockmorrow Koughenough of the leathered leggions, now of parts unknown, (God guard his generous comicsongbook soul!) that put a poached fowl in the poor man's pot before he took to his pallyass with the weeping eczema for better and worse until he went under the grass quilt on us, nevertheless, the year the sugar was scarce, and we to lather and shave and frizzle him, like a bald surging buoy and himself down to three cows that was meat and drink and dogs and washing to him, 'tis good cause we have to remember it, going through summersultryngs of snow and sleet witht the widow Nolan's goats and the Brownes girls neats anyhow, wait till I tell you, what did he do, poor old Roderick O'Conor Rex, the auspicious waterproof monarch of all Ireland, when he found himself all alone by himself in his grand old handwedown pile after all of them had all gone off with themselves to their castles of

mud, as best they cud, on footback, owing to the leak of the
McCarthy's mare, in extended order, a tree's length from the
longest way out, down the switchbackward slidder of the land-
sown route of Hauburnea's liveliest vinnage on the brain. the
unimportant Parthalonians with the mouldy Firbolgs and the
Tuatha de Danaan googs and the ramblers from Clane and all
the rest of the notmuchers that he did not care the royal spit out
of his ostensible mouth about, well, what do you think he did,
sir, but, faix, he just went heeltapping through the winespilth
and weevily popcorks that were kneedeep round his own right
royal round rollicking toper's table, with his old Roderick Random pullon hat at a Lanty Leary cant on him and Mike Brady's
shirt and Greene's linnet collarbow and his Ghenter's gaunts and
his Macclefield's swash and his readymade Reillys and his pan-
prestuberian poncho, the body you'd pity him, the way the world
is, poor he, the heart of Midleinster and the supereminent lord of
them all, overwhelmed as he was with black ruin like a sponge
out of water, allocutioning in bellcantos to his own oliverian
society MacGuiney's *Dreans of Ergen Adams* and thruming
through all to himself with diversed tonguesed through his old
tears and his ould plaised drawl, starkened by the most regal of
belches, like a blurney Cashelmagh crooner that lerking Clare
air, the blackberd's ballad *I've a terrible errible lot todue todie
todue tootorribleday*, well, what did he go and do at all, His Most
Exuberant Majesty King Roderick O'Conor but, arrah bedamnbut,
he finalised by lowering his woolly throat with the wonderful
midnight thirst was on him, as keen as mustard, he could not tell
what he did ale, that bothered he was from head to tail, and,
wishawishawish, leave it, what the Irish, boys, can do, if he did'nt
go, sliggymaglooral reemyround and suck up, sure enough, like
a Trojan, in some particular cases with the assistance of his venerated tongue, whatever surplus rotgut, sorra much, was left by the
lazy lousers of maltknights and beerchurls in the different bottoms of the various different replenquished drinking utensils left
there behind them on the premises by that whole hogsheaded
firkin family, the departed honourable homegoers and other sly-

grogging suburbanites, such as it was, fall and fall about, to the
brindishing of his charmed life, as toastified by his cheeriubi-
cundenances, no matter whether it was chateaubottled Guiness's
or Phoenix brewery stout it was or John Jameson and Sons or
Roob Coccola or, for the matter of that, O'Connell's famous old
Dublin ale that he wanted like hell, more that halibut oil or
jesuits tea, as a fall back, of several different quantities and quali-
ties amounting in all to, I should say, considerably more than the
better part of a gill or naggin of imperial dry and liquid measure
till, welcome be from us here, till the rising of the morn, till that
hen of Kaven's shows her beaconegg, and Chapwellswendows
stain our horyhistoricold and Father MacMichael stamps for
aitch o'clerk mess and the Litvian Newestlatter is seen, sold and
delivered and all's set for restart after the silence, like his ancestors
to this day after him (that the blazings of their ouldmouldy gods
may attend to them we pray!), overopposides the cowery lad in
the corner and forenenst the staregaze of the cathering candled,
that adornment of his album and folkenfather of familyans, he
came acrash a crupper sort of a sate on accomondation and the
very boxst in all his composs, whereuponce, behome the fore
for cove and trawlers, heave hone, leave lone, Larry's on the
focse and Faugh MacHugh O'Bawlar at the wheel, one to do and
one to dare, par by par, a peerless pair, ever here and over there,
with his fol the dee oll the doo on the flure of his feats and the
feels of the fumes in the wakes of his ears our wineman from
Barleyhome he just slumped to throne.

So sailed the stout ship *Nansy Hans*. From Liff away. For
Nattenlaender. As who has come returns. Farvel, farerne! Good-
bark, goodbye!

Now follow we out by Starloe!

[4]

— Three quarks for Muster Mark!
Sure he hasn't got much of a bark
And sure any he has it's all beside the mark.
But O, Wreneagle Almighty, wouldn't un be a sky of a lark
To see that old buzzard whooping about for uns shirt in the dark
And he hunting round for uns speckled trousers around by Palmer-
*   stown Park?*
Hohohoho, moulty Mark!
You're the rummest old rooster ever flopped out of a Noah's ark
And you think you're cock of the wark.
Fowls, up! Tristy's the spry young spark
That'll tread her and wed her and bed her and red her
Without ever winking the tail of a feather
And that's how that chap's going to make his money and mark!

Overhoved, shrillgleescreaming. That song sang seaswans.
The winging ones. Seahawk, seagull, curlew and plover, kestrel
and capercallzie. All the birds of the sea they trolled out rightbold
when they smacked the big kuss of Trustan with Usolde.

And there they were too, when it was dark, whilest the wild-
caps was circling, as slow their ship, the winds aslight, upborne
the fates, the wardorse moved, by courtesy of Mr Deaubaleau
Downbellow Kaempersally, listening in, as hard as they could, in
Dubbeldorp, the donker, by the tourneyold of the wattarfalls,
with their vuoxens and they kemin in so hattajocky (only a

quartebuck askull for the last acts) to the solans and the sycamores
and the wild geese and the gannets and the migratories and the
mistlethrushes and the auspices and all the birds of the rockby-
suckerassousyoceanal sea, all four of them, all sighing and sob-
bing, and listening. Moykle ahoykling!

They were the big four, the four maaster waves of Erin, all
listening, four. There was old Matt Gregory and then besides old
Matt there was old Marcus Lyons, the four waves, and oftentimes
they used to be saying grace together, right enough, bausnabeatha,
in Miracle Squeer: here now we are the four of us: old Matt Gregory and old Marcus and old Luke Tarpey: the four of us and
sure, thank God, there are no more of us: and, sure now, you
wouldn't go and forget and leave out the other fellow and old
Johnny MacDougall: the four of us and no more of us and so
now pass the fish for Christ sake, Amen: the way they used to be
saying their grace before fish, repeating itself, after the interims
of Augusburgh for auld lang syne. And so there they were, with
their palms in their hands, like the pulchrum's proculs, spraining
their ears, luistening and listening to the oceans of kissening, with
their eyes glistening, all the four, when he was kiddling and
cuddling and bunnyhugging scrumptious his colleen bawn and
dinkum belle, an oscar sister, on the fifteen inch loveseat, behind
the chieftaness stewardesses cubin, the hero, of Gaelic champion,
the onliest one of her choice, her bleaueyedeal of a girl's friend,
neither bigugly nor smallnice, meaning pretty much everything
to her then, with his sinister dexterity, light and rufthandling,
vicemversem her ragbags et assaucyetiams, fore and aft, on and
offsides, the brueburnt sexfutter, handson and huntsem, that was
palpably wrong and bulbubly improper, and cuddling her and
kissing her, tootyfay charmaunt, in her ensemble of maidenna
blue, with an overdress of net, tickled with goldies, Isolamisola,
and whisping and lisping her about Trisolanisans, how one was
whips for one was two and two was lips for one was three, and
dissimulating themself, with his poghue like Arrah-na-poghue,
the dear dear annual, they all four rememberod who made the
world and how they used to be at that time in the vulgar ear

cuddling and kiddling her, after an oyster supper in Cullen's barn,
from under her mistlethrush and kissing and listening, in the good
old bygone days of Dion Boucicault, the elder, in Arrah-na-
pogue, in the otherworld of the passing of the key of Two-
tongue Common, with Nush, the carrier of the word, and with
Mesh, the cutter of the reed, in one of the farback, pitchblack
centuries when who made the world, when they knew O'Clery,
the man on the door, when they were all four collegians on the
nod, neer the Nodderlands Nurskery, whiteboys and oakboys,
peep of tim boys and piping tom boys, raising hell while the sin
was shining, with their slates and satchels, playing Florian's fables
and communic suctions and vellicar frictions with mixum members, in the Queen's Ultonian colleges, along with another fellow,
a prime number, Totius Quotius, and paying a pot of tribluts
to Boris O'Brien, the buttler of Clumpthump, two looves, two
turnovers plus (one) crown, to see the mad dane ating his
vitals. Wulf! Wulf! And throwing his tongue in the snakepit. Ah
ho! The ladies have mercias! It brought the dear prehistoric
scenes all back again, as fresh as of yore, Matt and Marcus, natural born lovers of nature, in all her moves and senses, and after
that now there he was, that mouth of mandibles, vowed to pure
beauty, and his Arrah-na-poghue, when she murmurously, after
she let a cough, gave her firm order, if he wouldn't please mind,
for a sings to one hope a dozen of the best favourite lyrical
national blooms in Luvillicit, though not too much, reflecting on
the situation, drinking in draughts of purest air serene and re-
velling in the great outdoors, before the four of them, in the fair
fine night, whilst the stars shine bright, by she light of he moon,
we longed to be spoon, before her honeyoldloom, the plaint effect
being in point of fact there being in the whole, a seatuition so
shocking and scandalous and now, thank God, there were no more
of them and he, poghuing and poghuing like the Moreigner
bowed his crusted hoed and Tilly the Tailor's Tugged a Tar in the
Arctic Newses Dagsdogs number and there they were, like a
foremasters in the rolls, listening, to Rolando's deepen darblun
Ossian roll, (Lady, it was just too gorgeous, that expense of a

lovely tint, embellished by the charms of art and very well conducted and nicely mannered and all the horrid rudy noisies locked
up in nasty cubbyhole!) as tired as they were, the three jolly
topers, with their mouths watering, all the four, the old connu-
bial men of the sea, yambing around with their old pantometer,
in duckasaloppics, Luke and Johnny MacDougall and all wishen-
ing for anything at all of the bygone times, the wald times and
the fald times and the hempty times and the dempty times, for a
cup of kindness yet, for four farback tumblerfuls of woman
squash, with them, all four, listening and spraining their ears for
the millennium and all their mouths making water.

Johnny. Ah well, sure, that's the way (up) and it so happened
there was poor Matt Gregory (up), their pater familias, and (up)
the others and now really and (up) truly they were four dear
old heladies and really they looked awfully pretty and so nice and
bespectable and after that they had their fathomglasses to find
out all the fathoms and their half a tall hat, just now like the old
Merquus of Pawerschoof, the old determined despot, (*quiescents
in brage!*) only for the extrusion of the saltwater or the auctioneer
there dormont, in front of the place near O'Clery's, at the darku-
mound numbur wan, beside that ancient Dame street, where the
statue of Mrs Dana O'Connell, prostituent behind the Trinity
College, that arranges all the auctions of the valuable colleges.
Bootersbay Sisters, like the auctioneer Battersby Sisters, the pru-
misceous creaters, that sells all the emancipated statues and
flowersports, James H. Tickell, the jaypee, off Hoggin Green,
after he made the centuries, going to the tailturn horseshow, before the angler nomads flood, along with another fellow, active
impalsive, and the shoeblacks and the redshanks and plebeians
and the barrancos and the cappunchers childerun, Jules, everyone, Gotopoxy, with the houghers on them, highstepping the
fissure and fracture lines, seven five threes up, three five
sevens down, to get out of his way, onasmuck as their withers
conditions could not possibly have been improved upon,
(praisers be to deeseesee!) like hopolopocattls, erumping oround
their Judgity Yaman, and all the tercentenary horses and priest-

hunters, from the Curragh, and confusionaries and the authori-
ties, Noord Amrikaans and Suid Aferican cattleraiders (so they
say) all over like a tiara dullfuoco, in his grey half a tall hat and
his amber necklace and his crimson harness and his leathern jib
and his cheapshein hairshirt and his scotobrit sash and his para-
pilagian gallowglasses (how do you do, jaypee, Elevato!) to find
out all the improper colleges (and how do you do, Mr Dame
James? Get out of my way!), forkbearded and bluetoothed and
bellied and boneless, from Strathlyffe and Aylesburg and North-
umberland Anglesey, the whole yaghoodurt sweepstakings and
all the horsepowers. But now, talking of hayastdanars and
wolkingology and how our seaborn isle came into exestuance,
(the explutor, his three andesiters and the two pantellarias) that
reminds me about the manausteriums of the poor Marcus of Lyons
and poor Johnny, the patrician, and what do you think of the four
of us and there they were now, listening right enough, the four
saltwater widowers, and all they could remembore, long long ago
in the olden times Momonian, throw darker hour sorrows, the
princest day, when Fair Margrate waited Swede Villem, and Lally
in the rain, with the blank prints, now extincts, after the wreak
of Wormans' Noe, the barmaisigheds, when my heart knew no
care, and after that then there was the official landing of Lady
Jales Casemate, in the year of the flood 1132 S.O.S., and the
christening of Queen Baltersby, the Fourth Buzzersbee, according to Her Grace the bishop Senior, off the whate shape, and
then there was the drowning of Pharoah and all his pedestrians
and they were all completely drowned into the sea, the red sea,
and then poor Merkin Cornyngwham, the official out of the
castle on pension, when he was completely drowned off Erin
Isles, at that time, suir knows, in the red sea and a lovely
mourning paper and thank God, as Saman said, there were no
more of him. And that now was how it was. The arzurian deeps
o'er his humbodumbones sweeps. And his widdy the giddy is
wreathing her murmoirs as her gracest triput to the Grocery
Trader's Manthly. Mind mand gunfree by Gladeys Rayburn.
Runtable's Reincorporated. The new world presses. Where the

old conk cruised now croons the yunk. Exeunc throw a darras
Kram of Llawnroc, ye gink guy, kirked into yord. Enterest at-
tawonder Wehpen, luftcat revol, fairescapading in his natsirt.
Tuesy tumbles. And mild aunt Liza is as loose as her neese. Ful-
fest withim inbrace behent. As gent would deem oncontinent.
So mulct per wenche is Elsker woed. Ne hath his thrysting. Fin.
Like the newcasters in their old plyable of *A Royenne Devours*.
Jazzaphoney and Mirillovis and Nippy she nets best. Fing. Ay,
ay! Sobbos. And so he was. Sabbus.

Marcus. And after that, not forgetting, there was the Flemish
armada, all scattered, and all officially drowned, there and then, on
a lovely morning, after the universal flood, at about aleven thirtytwo was it? off the coast of Cominghome and Saint Patrick, the
anabaptist, and Saint Kevin, the lacustrian, with toomuch of tolls
and lottance of beggars, after converting Porterscout and Dona,
our first marents, and Lapoleon, the equestrian, on his whuite
hourse of Hunover, rising Clunkthurf over Cabinhogan and all
they rememblored and then there was the Frankish floot of Noahs-
dobahs, from Hedalgoland, round about the freebutter year of
Notre Dame 1132 P.P.O. or so, disumbunking from under
Motham General Bonaboche, (noo poopery!) in his half a grey
traditional hat, alevoila come alevilla, and after that there he was,
so terrestrial, like a Nailscissor, poghuing her scandalous and very
wrong, the maid, in single combat, under the sycamores, amid
the bludderings from the boom and all the gallowsbirds in Arrah-
na-Poghue, so silvestrious, neer the Queen's Colleges, in 1132
Brian or Bride street, behind the century man on the door. And
then again they used to give the grandest gloriaspanquost universal howldmoutherhibbert lectures on anarxaquy out of doxarch-
ology (hello, Hibernia!) from sea to sea (Matt speaking!) according to the pictures postcard, with sexon grimmacticals, in the
Latimer Roman history, of Latimer repeating himself, from the
vicerine of Lord Hugh, the Lacytynant, till Bockleyshuts the rah-
jahn gerachknell and regnumrockery roundup, (Marcus Lyons
speaking!) to the oceanfuls of collegians green and high classes
and the poor scholars and all the old trinitarian senate and saints and

sages and the Plymouth brethren, droning along, peanzanzangan,
and nodding and sleeping away there, like forgetmenots, in her
abijance service, round their twelve tables, per pioja at pulga
bollas, in the four trinity colleges, for earnasyoulearning Erin-
growback, of Ulcer, Moonster, Leanstare and Cannought, the
four grandest colleges supper the matther of Erryn, of Killorcure
and Killthemall and Killeachother and Killkelly-on-the-Flure,
where their role was to rule the round roll that Rollo and Rullo
rolled round. Those were the grandest gynecollege histories
(Lucas calling, hold the line!) in the Janesdanes Lady Anders-
daughter Universary, for auld acquaintance sake (this unitarian
lady, breathtaking beauty, Bambam's bonniest, lived to a great
age at or in or about the late No. 1132 or No. 1169, bis, Fitzmary
Round where she was seen by many and widely liked) for teaching the Fatima Woman history of Fatimiliafamilias, repeating herself, on which purposeth of the spirit of nature as difinely developed in time by psadatepholomy, the past and present (Johnny
MacDougall speaking, give me trunks, miss!) and present and
absent and past and present and perfect *arma virumque romano.*
Ah, dearo, dear! O weep for the hower when eve aleaves bower!
How it did but all come eddaying back to them, if they did but
get gaze, gagagniagnian, to hear him there, kiddling and cuddling
her, after the gouty old galahat, with his peer of quinnyfears and
his troad of thirstuns, so nefarious, from his elevation of one
yard one handard and thartytwo lines, before the four of us, in
his Roman Catholic arms, while his deepseepeepers gazed and
sazed and dazecrazemazed into her dullokbloon rodolling olo-
sheen eyenbowls by the Cornelius Nepos, Mnepos. Anumque,
umque. Napoo.

Queh? Quos?

Ah, dearo dearo dear! Bozun braceth brythe hwen gooses
gandered gamen. Mahazar ag Dod! It was so scalding sorry for all
the whole twice two four of us, with their familiar, making the toten,
and Lally when he lost part of his half a hat and all belongings to
him, in his old futile manner, cape, towel and drawbreeches, and
repeating himself and telling him now, for the seek of Senders

Newslaters and the mossacre of Saint Brices, to forget the past,
when the burglar he shoved the wretch in churneroil, and con-
tradicting all about Lally, the ballest master of Gosterstown, and
his old fellow, the Lagener, in the Locklane Lighthouse, earing his
wick with a pierce of railing, and liggen hig with his ladder up, and
that oldtime turner and his sadderday erely cloudsing, the old
croniony, Skelly, with the lether belly, full of neltts, full of keltts,
full of lightweight beltts and all the bald drakes or ever he had up
in the bohereen, off Artsichekes Road, with Moels and Mahmullagh
Mullarty, the man in the Oran mosque, and the old folks at home
and Duignan and Lapole and the grand confarreation, as per the
cabbangers richestore, of the filest archives, and he couldn't stop
laughing over Tom Tim Tarpey, the Welshman, and the four
middleaged widowers, all nangles, sangles, angles and wangles.
And now, that reminds me, not to forget the four of the Welsh
waves, leaping laughing, in their Lumbag Walk, over old Battle-
shore and Deaddleconchs, in their half a Roman hat, with an ancient Greek gloss on it, in Chichester College auction and, thank
God, they were all summarily divorced, four years before, or so
they say, by their dear poor shehusbands, in dear byword days,
and never brought to mind, to see no more the rainwater on the
floor but still they parted, raining water laughing, per Nupiter
Privius, only terpary, on the best of terms and be forgot, whilk was
plainly foretolk by their old pilgrim cocklesong or they were singing through the wettest indies *As I was going to Burrymecarott we
fell in with a lout by the name of Peebles* as also in another place by
their orthodox proverb so there was said thus *That old fellow
knows milk though he's not used to it latterly*. And so they parted.
In Dalkymont nember to. Ay, ay. The good go and the wicked
is left over. As evil flows so Ivel flows. Ay, ay. Ah, well sure,
that's the way. As the holymaid of Kunut said to the haryman
of Koombe. For his humple pesition in odvices. Woman. Squash.
Part. Ay, ay. By decree absolute.
  Lucas. And, O so well they could remembore at that time, when
Carpery of the Goold Fins was in the kingship of Poolland, Mrs
Dowager Justice Squalchman, foorsitter, in her fullbottom wig

and beard, (Erminia Reginia!) in or aring or around about the year of buy in disgrace 1132 or 1169 or 1768 Y.W.C.A., at the Married Male Familyman's Auctioneer's court in Arrahnacuddle. Poor Johnny of the clan of the Dougals, the poor Scuitsman, (Hohannes!) nothing if not amorous, dinna forget, so frightened (Zweep! Zweep!) on account of her full bottom, (undullable attraxity!) that put the yearl of mercies on him, and the four maasters, in chors, with a hing behangd them, because he was so slow to borstel her schoon for her, when he was grooming her ladyship, instead of backscratching her materfamilias proper, like any old methodist, and all divorced and innasense interdict, in the middle of the temple, according to their dear faithful. Ah, now, it was too bad, too bad and stout entirely, all the missoccurs; and poor Mark or Marcus Bowandcoat, from the brownesberrow in nolandsland, the poor old chronometer, all persecuted with ally croaker by everybody, by decree absolute, through Herrinsilde, because he forgot himself, making wind and water, and made a Neptune's mess of all of himself, sculling over the giamond's courseway, and because he forgot to remember to sign an old morning proxy paper, a writing in request to hersute herself, on stamped bronnanoleum, from Roneo to Giliette, before saying his grace before fish and then and there and too there was poor Dion Cassius Poosycomb, all drowned too, before the world and her husband, because it was most improper and most wrong, when he attempted to (well, he was shocking poor in his health, he said, with the shingles falling off him), because he (ah, well now, peaces pea to Wedmore and let not the song go dumb upon your Ire, as we say in the Spasms of Davies, and we won't be too hard on him as an old Manx presbyterian) and after that, as red as a Rosse is, he made his last will and went to confession, like the general of the Berkeleyites, at the rim of the rom, on his two bare marrowbones, to Her Worship his Mother and Sister Evangelist Sweainey, on Cailcainnin widnight and he was so sorry, he was really, because he left the bootybutton in the handsome cab and now, tell the truth, unfriends never, (she was his first messes dogess and it was a very pretty peltry and there were faults on both sides) well, he attempted (or so they say) ah, now, forget and forgive (don't we all?) and, sure, he was only funning with his andrewmartins and his old age coming over him, well, he attempted or, the Connachy, he was tempted to attempt some hunnish familiarities, after eten a bad carmp in the rude ocean and, hevantonoze sure, he was dead seasickabed (it was really too bad!) her poor old divorced male, in the housepays for the daying at the Martyr Mrs MacCawley's, where at the time he was taying and toying, to hold the nursetendered hand, (ah, the poor old coax!) and count the buttons and her hand and frown on a bad crab and doying to remembore what doed they were byorn and who made a who a snore. Ah dearo dearo dear!

And where do you leave Matt Emeritus? The laychief of Abbotabishop? And exchullard of ffrench and gherman. Achoch! They were all so sorgy for poorboir Matt in his saltwater hat, with the Aran crown, or she grew that out of, too big for him, of or Mnepos and his overalls, all falling over her in folds—sure he hadn't the heart in her to pull them up—poor Matt, the old perigrime matriarch, and a queenly man, (the porple blussing upon them!) sitting there, the sole of the settlement, below ground, for an expiatory rite, in postulation of his cause, (who shall say?) in her beaver bonnet, the king of the Caucuses, a family all to himself, under geasa, Themistletocles, on his multilingual tombstone, like Navellicky Kamen, and she due to kid by sweetpea time, with her face to the wall, in view of the poorhouse, and taking his rust in the oxsight of Iren, under all the auspices, amid the rattle of hailstorms, kalospintheochromatokreening, with her ivyclad hood, and gripping an old pair of curling tongs, belonging to Mrs Duna O'Cannell, to blow his brains with, till the heights of Newhigherland heard the Bristolhut, with his can of tea and a purse of alfred cakes from Anne Lynch and two cuts of Shackleton's brown loaf and dilisk, waiting for the end to come. Gordon Heighland, when you think of it! The merthe dirther! Ah ho! It was too bad entirely! All devoured by active parlourmen laudabiliter of woman squelch and all on account of the

smell of Shakeletin and scratchman and his mouth watering, acid
and alkolic; signs on the salt, and so now pass the loaf for Christ
sake. Amen. And so. And all.

Matt. And loaf. So that was the end. And it can't be helped.
Ah, God be good to us! Poor Andrew Martin Cunningham!
Take breath! Ay! Ay!

And still and all at that time of the dynast days, of old konning
Soteric Sulkinbored and Bargomuster Bart, when they struck coil
and shock haunts, in old Hungerford-on-Mudway, where first I
met thee oldpoetryck flied from may, and the Finnan haddies and
the Noal Sharks and the muckstails turtles like an acoustic pot-
tish and the griesouper bullyum and how he poled him up his
boccat of vuotar and got big buzz for his name in the airweek's
honours from home, colonies and empire, they were always with
assisting grace, thinking (up) and not forgetting about shims and
shawls week, in auld land syne (up) their four hosenbands, that
were four (up) beautiful sister misters, now happily married, unto
old Gallstonebelly, and there they were always counting and con-
tradicting every night 'tis early the lovely mother of periwinkle
buttons, according to the lapper part of their anachronism (up
one up two up one up four) and after that there now she was,
in the end, the deary, soldpowder and all, the beautfour sisters,
and that was her mudhen republican name, right enough, from
alum and oves, and they used to be getting up from under, in
their tape and straw garlands, with all the worries awake in their
hair, at the kookaburra bell ringring, all wrong inside of them
(come in, come on, you lazy loafs!) all inside their poor old Shan-
don bellbox (come out to hell, you lousy louts!) so frightened,
for the dthclangavore, like knockneeghs bumpsed by the fister-
man's straights, (ys! ys!), at all hours every night, on their mistle-
toes, the four old oldsters, to see was the Transton Postscript
come, with the oerkussens under their armsaxters, all puddled
and mythified, the way the wind wheeled the schooler round,
when nobody wouldn't even let them rusten, from playing
their gastspiels, crossing their sleep by the shocking silence,
when they were in dreams of yore, standing behind the

door, or leaning out of the chair, or kneeling under the sofa-
cover and setting on the souptureen, getting into their way
something barbarous, changing the one wet underdown convi-
brational bed or they used to slumper under, when hope was there
no more, and putting on their half a hat and falling over all synop-
ticals and a panegyric and repeating themselves, like svvollovv-
ing, like the time they were dadging the talkeycook that chased
them, look look all round the stool, walk everywhere for a jool,
to break fyre to all the rancers, to collect all and bits of brown,
the rathure's evelopment in spirits of time in all fathom of space
and slooping around in a bawneen and bath slipper and go away
to Oldpatrick and see a doctor Walker. And after that so glad
they had their night tentacles and there they used to be, flapping
and cycling, and a dooing a doonloop, panementically, around
the waists of the ships, in the wake of their good old Foehn
again, as tyred as they were, at their windswidths in the
waveslength, the clipperbuilt and the five fourmasters and
Lally of the cleftoft bagoderts and Roe of the fair cheats, exchanging fleas from host to host, with arthroposophia, and he
selling him before he forgot, issle issle, after having prealably
dephlegmatised his gutterful of throatyfrogs, with a lungible fong
in his suckmouth ear, while the dear invoked to the coolun dare
by a palpabrows lift left no doubt in his minder, till he was instant and he was trustin, sister soul in brother hand, the subjects
being their passion grand, that one fresh from the cow about
Aithne Meithne married a mailde and that one too from Engr-
vakon saga abooth a gooth a gev a gotheny egg and the park-
side pranks of quality queens, katte efter kinne, for Earl Hooved-
soon's choosing and Huber and Harman orhowwhen theeupon-
thus (chchch!) eysolt of binnoculises memostinmust egotum
sabcunsciously senses upers the deprofundity of multimathema-
tical immaterialites wherebejubers in the pancosmic urge the
allimmanence of that which Itself is Itself Alone (hear, O hear,
Caller Errin!) exteriorises on this ourherenow plane in disunited
solod, likeward and gushious bodies with (science, say!) peril-
whitened passionpanting pugnoplangent intuitions of reunited

selfdom (murky whey, abstrew adim!) in the higherdimissiona,
selfless Allself, theemeeng Narsty meetheeng Idoless, and telling
Jolly MacGolly, dear mester John, the belated dishevelled, hacking away at a parchment pied, and all the other analist, the
steamships ant the ladies'foursome, ovenfor, nedenfor, dinkety,
duk, downalupping, (how long tandem!) like a foreretyred schoon-
masters, and their pair of green eyes and peering in, so they say, like
the narcolepts on the lakes of Coma, through the steamy windows, into the honeymoon cabins, on board the big steamadories,
made by Fumadory, and the saloon ladies' madorn toilet chambers
lined over prawn silk and rub off the salty catara off a windows
and, hee hee, listening, *qua* committe, the poor old quakers, oben
the dure, to see all the hunnishmooners and the firstclass ladies,
serious me, a lass spring as you fancy, and sheets far from the lad,
courting in blankets, enfamillias, and, shee shee, all improper, in a
lovely mourning toilet, for the rosecrumpler, the thrilldriver, the
sighinspirer, with that olive throb in his nude neck, and, swayin
and thayin, thanks ever so much for the tiny quote, which sought
of maid everythingling again so very much more delightafellay,
and the perfidly suite of her, bootyfilly yours, under all their
familiarities, by preventing grace, forgetting to say their grace before chambadory, before going to boat with the verges of the
chaptel of the opering of the month of Nema Knatut, so pass the
poghue for grace sake. Amen. And all, hee hee hee, quaking, so
fright, and, shee shee, shaking. Aching. Ay, ay.

For it was then a pretty thing happened of pure diversion
mayhap, when his flattering hend, at the justright moment, like
perchance some cook of corage might clip the lad on a poot of
porage handshut his duckhouse, the vivid girl, deaf with love,
(ah sure, you know her, our angel being, one of romance's fadeless wonderwomen, and, sure now, we all know you dote on
her even unto date) with a queeleetlecree of joysis crisis she
renulited their disunited, with ripy lepes to ropy lopes (the dear
o'dears!) and the golden importunity of aloofer's leavetime,
when as quick is greased pigskin, Amoricas Champius, with one
aragan throust, druve the massive of virilvigtoury fishpst the

both lines of forwards (Eburnea's down, boys!) rightjingbangshot
into the goal of her gullet.

Alris!

And now, upright and add them! And plays be honest! And
pullit into yourself, as on manowoman do another! Candidately,
everybody! A mot for amot. Comong, meng, and douh! There
was this, wellyoumaycallher, a strapping modern old ancient
Irish prisscess, so and so hands high, such and such paddock
weight, in her madapolam smock, nothing under her hat but
red hair and solid ivory (now you know it's true in your
hardup hearts!) and a firstclass pair of bedroom eyes, of most
unhomy blue, (how weak we are, one and all!) the charm
of favour's fond consent! Could you blame her, we're saying,
for one psocoldlogical moment? What would Ewe do? With
that so tiresome old milkless a ram, with his tiresome duty
peck and his bronchial tubes, the tiresome old hairyg orangogran
beaver, in his tiresome old twennysixandsixpenny sheopards
plods drowsers and his thirtybobandninepenny tails plus toop!
Hagakhroustioun! It were too exceeding really if one woulds
to offer at sulk an oldivirdual a pinge of hinge hit. The
mainest thing ever! Since Edem was in the boags noavy. No, no,
the dear heaven knows, and the farther the from it, if the whole
stole stale mis betold, whoever the gulpable, and whatever the
pulpous was, the twooned togethered, and giving the mhost
phassionable wheathers, they were doing a lally a lolly a dither
a duther one lelly two dather three lilly four dother. And it was
a fiveful moment for the poor old timetetters, ticktacking, in tenk
the count. Till the spark that plugged spared the chokee he
gripped and (volatile volupty, how brieved are thy lunguings!)
they could and they could hear like of a lisp lapsing, that
was her knight of the truths thong plipping out of her chapell-
ledeosy, after where he had gone and polped the questioned.
Plop.

Ah now, it was tootwoly torrific, the mummurrlubejubes! And
then after that they used to be so forgetful, counting mother-
peributts (up one up four) to membore her beaufu mouldern

maiden name, for overflauwing, by the dream of woman the owneirist, in forty lands. From Greg and Doug on poor Greg and Mat and Mar and Lu and Jo, now happily buried, our four! And there she was right enough, that lovely sight enough, the girleen bawn asthore, as for days galore, of planxty Gregory. Egory. O bunket not Orwin! Ay, ay.

But, sure, that reminds me now, like another tellmastory repeating yourself, how they used to be in lethargy's love, at the end of it all, at that time (up) always, tired and all, after doing the mousework and making it up, over their community singing (up) the top loft of the voicebox, of Mamalujo like the senior follies at murther magrees, squatting round two by two, the four confederates, with Caxons the Coswarn, up the wet air register in Old Man's House, Millenium Road, crowning themselves in lauraly branches, with their cold knees and their poor (up) quad rupeds, ovasleep, and all dolled up, for their blankets and materny mufflers and plimsoles and their bowl of brown shackle and milky and boterham clots, a potion a peace, a piece aportion, a lepel alip, alup a lap, for a cup of kindest yet, with hold take hand and nurse and only touch of ate, a lovely munkybown and for xmell and wait the pinch and prompt poor Marcus Lyons to be not beheeding the skillet on for the live of ghosses but to pass the teeth for choke sake, Amensch, when it so happen they were all sycamore and by the world forgot, since the phlegmish hoopicough, for all a possabled, after ete a bad cramp and johnny magories, and backscrat the poor bedsores and the farthing dip, their caschal pandle of magnegnousioum, and read a letter or two every night, before going to dodo sleep atrance, with their catkins coifs, in the twilight, a capitaletter, for further auspices, on their old one page codex book of old year's eve 1132, M.M.L.J. old style, their Senchus Mor, by his fellow girl, the Mrs Shemans, in her summer seal houseonsample, with the caracul broadtail, her *totam in tutu*, final buff noonmeal edition, in the regatta covers, uptenable from the orther, for to regul their reves by incubation, and Lally, through their gangrene spentacles, and all the good or they did in their time, the rigorists, for Roe and O'Mulcnory a

Conry ap Mul or Lap ap Morion and Buffler ap Matty Mac
Gregory for Marcus on Podex by Daddy de Wyer, old baga-
broth, beeves and scullogues, churls and vassals, in same, sept
and severalty and one by one and sing a mamalujo. To the
heroest champion of Eren and his braceoelanders and Gowan,
Gawin and Gonne.

And after that now in the future, please God, after nonpenal
start, all repeating ourselves, in medios loquos, from where he got
a useful arm busy on the touchline, due south of her western
shoulder down to death and the love embrace, with an interesting
tallow complexion and all now unites, sansfamillias, let us ran on
to say oremus prayer and homeysweet homely, after fully realising the gratifying experiences of highly continental evenements,
for meter and peter to temple an eslaap, for auld acquaintance, to
Peregrine and Michael and Farfassa and Peregrine, for navigants
et peregrinantibus, in all the old imperial and Fionnachan sea and
for vogue awallow to a, Miss Yiss, you fascinator, you, sing a
lovasteamadorion to Ladyseyes, here's Tricks and Doelsy, delightfully ours, in her doaty ducky little blue and roll his hoop
and how she ran, when wit won free, the dimply blissed and awfully bucked, right glad we never shall forget, thoh the dayses
gone still they loves young dreams and old Luke with his
kingly leer, so wellworth watching, and Senchus Mor, possessed
of evident notoriety, and another more of the bigtimers, to name
no others, of whom great things were expected in the fulmfilming
department, for the lives of Lazarus and auld luke syne and she
haihaihail her kobbor kohinor sehehet on the praze savohole
shanghai.

Hear, O hear, Iseult la belle! Tristan, sad hero, hear! The Lambeg
drum, the Lombog reed, the Lumbag fiferer, the Limibig brazenaze.

Anno Domini nostri sancti Jesu Christi
Nine hundred and ninetynine million pound sterling in the blueblack
     bowels of the bank of Ulster.
Braw bawbees and good gold pounds, galore, my girleen, a Sunday'll
     prank thee finely.

*And no damn loutll come courting thee or by the mother of the Holy
     Ghost there'll be murder!*

*O, come all ye sweet nymphs of Dingle beach to cheer Brinabride
     queen from Sybil surfriding*

*In her curragh of shells of daughter of pearl and her silverymonnblue
     mantle round her.*

*Crown of the waters, brine on her brow, she'll dance them a jig and
     jilt them fairly.*

*Yerra, why would she bide with Sig Sloomysides or the grogram grey
     barnacle gander?*

*You won't need be lonesome, Lizzy my love, when your beau gets his
     glut of cold meat and hos soldiering*

*Nor wake in winter, window machree, but snore sung in my old
     Balbriggan surtout.*

*Wisha, won't you agree now to take me from the middle, say, of
     next week on, for the balance of my days, for nothing (what?)
     as your own nursetender?*

*A power of highsteppers died game right enough—but who, acushla,
     'll beg coppers for you?*

I tossed that one long before anyone.

*It was of a wet good Friday too she was ironing and, as I'm given
     now to understand, she was always mad gone on me.*

*Grand goosegreasing we had entirely with an allnight eiderdown bed
     picnic to follow.*

*By the cross of Cong, says she, rising up Saturday in the twilight
     from under me, Mick, Nick the Maggot or whatever your name
     is, you're the mose likable lad that's come my ways yet from the
     barony of Bohermore.*

Mattheehew, Markeehew, Lukeehew, Johnheehewheehew!
Haw!
And still a light moves long the river. And stiller the mermen
     ply their keg.
Its pith is full. The way is free. Their lot is cast.
So, to john for a john, johnajeams, led it be!

III

Hark!

Tolv two elf kater ten (it can't be) sax.

Hork!

Pedwar pemp foify tray (it must be) twelve.

And low stole o'er the stillness the heartbeats of sleep.

White fogbow spans. The arch embattled. Mark as capsules. The nose of the man who was nought like the nasoes. It is self-tinted, wrinkling, ruddled. His kep is a gorsecone. He am Gascon Titubante of Tegmine – sub – Fagi whose fixtures are mobiling so wobiling befear my remembrandts. She, exhibit next, his Anastashie. She has prayings in lowdelph. Zeehere green eggbrooms. What named blautoothdmand is yon who stares? Gugurtha! Gugurtha! He has becco of wild hindigan. Ho, he hath hornhide! And hvis now is for you. Pensée! The most beautiful of woman of the veilch veilchen veilde. She would kidds to my voult of my palace, with obscidian luppas, her aal in her dhove's suckling. Apagemonite! Come not nere! Black! Switch out!

Methought as I was dropping asleep somepart in nonland of where's please (and it was when you and they were we) I heard at zero hour as 'twere the peal of vixen's laughter among midnight's chimes from out the belfry of the cute old speckled church tolling so faint a goodmantrue as nighthood's unseen violet rendered all animated greatbritish and Irish objects nonviewable to human watchers save 'twere perchance anon some glistery

gleam darkling adown surface of affluvial flowandflow as again
might seem garments of laundry reposing a leasward close at
hand in full expectation. And as I was jogging along in a dream as
dozing I was dawdling, arrah, methought broadtone was heard and
the creepers and the gliders and flivvers of the earth breath and
the dancetongues of the woodfires and the hummers in their
ground all vociferated echoating: Shaun! Shaun! Post the post!
with a high voice and O, the higher on high the deeper and low,
I heard him so. And lo, mescemed somewhat came of the noise
and somewho might amove allmurk. Now, 'twas as clump, now
mayhap. When look, was light and now'twas as flasher, now
moren as the glaow. Ah, in unlitness 'twas in very similitude,
bless me, 'twas his belted lamp! Whom we dreamt was a shaddo,
sure, he's lightseyes, the laddo! Blessed momence, O romence,
he's growing to stay! Ay, he who so swayed a will of a wisp
before me, Hand prop to hand, prompt side to the pros, dressed
like an earl in just the correct wear, in a classy mac Frieze o'coat
of far suparior ruggedness, indigo braw, tracked and tramped,
and an Irish ferrier collar, freeswinging with mereswin lacers from
his shoulthern and thick welted brogues on him hammered to suit
the scotsmost public and climate, iron heels and sparable soles, and
his jacket of providence wellprovided woolies with a softrolling
lisp of a lapel to it and great sealingwax buttons, a good helping
bigger than the slots for them, of twentytwo carrot krasnapopp-
sky red and his invulnerable burlap whiskcoat and his popular
choker, Tamagnum sette-and-forte and his loud boheem toy and
the damasker's overshirt he sported inside, a starspangled zephyr
with a decidedly surpliced crinklydoodle front with his motto
through dear life embrothred over it in peas, rice, and yeggy-
yolk, Or for royal, Am for Mail, R.M.D. hard cash on the nail
and the most successfully carried gigot turnups now you ever,
(what a pairfact crease! how amsolookly kersse!) breaking over
the ankle and hugging the shoeheel, everything the best — none
other from (Ah, then may the turtle's blessings of God and Mary
and Haggispatrick and Huggisbrigid be souptumbling all over
him!) other than (and may his hundred thousand welcome stewed

letters, relayed wand postchased, multiply, ay faith, and plultiply!)
Shaun himself.

What a picture primitive!

Had I the concordant wiseheads of Messrs Gregory and Lyons
alongside of Dr Tarpey's and I dorsay the reverend Mr Mac
Dougall's, but I, poor ass, am but as their fourpart tinckler's dun-
key. Yet methought Shaun (holy messonger angels be uninter-
ruptedly nudging him among and along the winding ways of
random ever!) Shaun in proper person (now may all the blue-
blacksliding constellations continue to shape his changeable time-
table!) stood before me. And I pledge you my agricultural word
by the hundred and sixty odds rods and cones of this even's
vision that young fellow looked the stuff, the Bel of Beaus'
Walk, a prime card if ever was! Pep? Now without deceit it is
hardly too much to say he was looking grand, so fired smart, in
much more than his usual health. No mistaking that beamish
brow. There was one for you that ne'er would nunch with good
Duke Humphrey but would aight through the months without a
sign of an err in hem and then, otherwise rounding, fourale to the
lees of Traroe. Those jehovial oyeglances! The heart of the rool!
And hit the hencoop. He was immense, topping swell for he was
after having a great time of it, a twentyfour hours every moment
matters maltsight, in a porterhouse scutfrank, if you want to
know, Saint Lawzenge of Toole's, the Wheel of Fortune, leave
your clubs in the hall and wait on yourself, no chucks for wal-
nut ketchups, Lazenby's and Chutney graspis (the house the once
queen of Bristol and Balrothery twice admired because her
frumped door looked up Dacent Street) where in the sighed of
lovely eyes while his knives of hearts made havoc he had re-
cruited his strength by meals of spadefuls of mounded food, in
anticipation of the faste of tablenapkins, constituting his three-
partite pranzipal meals *plus* a collation, his breakfast of first, a bless
us O blood and thirsthy orange, next, the half of a pint of becon
with newled googs and a segment of riceplummy padding, met
of sunder suigar and some cold forsoaken steak peatrefired from
the batblack night o'erflown then, without prejuice to evectuals,

came along merendally his stockpot dinner of a half a pound or
round steak very rare, Blong's best from Portarlington's Butchery
with a side of riceypeasy and Corkshire alla mellonge and bacon
with (a little mar pliche!) a pair of chops and thrown in from the
silver grid by the proprietoress of the roastery who lives on the
hill and gaulusch gravy and pumpernickel to wolp up and a
gorger's bulby onion (Margareter, Margaretar Margarastican-
deatar) and as well with second course and then finally, after
his avalunch oclock snack at Appelredt's or Kitzy Braten's of
saddlebag steak and a Botherhim with her old phoenix portar,
jistr to gwen his gwistel and praties sweet and Irish too and mock
gurgle to whistle his way through for the swallying, swp by swp,
and he getting his tongue arount it and Boland's broth broken
into the bargain, to his regret his soupay *avic* nightcap, vitellusit
a carusal consistent with second course eyer and becon (the rich
of) with broad beans, hig, steak, hag, pepper the diamond bone
hotted up timmtomm and while'twas after that he scoffed a drake-
ling snuggily stuffed following cold loin of veal more cabbage and
in their green free state a clister of peas, soppositorily petty, last.
P.S. but a fingerhot of rheingenever to give the Pax cum Spiri-
tututu. Drily thankful. Burud and dulse and typureely jam, all
free of charge, aman, and. And the best of wine *avec*. For his
heart was as big as himself, so it was, ay, and bigger. While the
loaves are aflowering and the nachtingale jugs. All St Jilian's of
Berry, hurrah there for tobies! Mabhrodaphne, brown pride of our
custard house quay, amiable with repastful, cheerus graciously,
cheer us! Ever of thee, Anne Lynch. He's deeply draiming!
Houseanna. Tea is the Highest! For auld lang Ayternitay! Thus
thicker will he grow now, grew new. And better and better on
butter and butter. At the sign of Mesthress Vanhungrig. However!
Mind you, nuckling down to nourritures, were they menuly some
ham and jaffas, and I don't mean to make the ingestion for the
moment that he was guilbey of gulpable gluttony as regards chew-
able boltaballs, but, biestings be biestings, and upon the whole,
when not off his oats, given prelove appetite and postlove pricing
good coup, goodcheap, were it thermidor oogst or floreal may

while the whistling prairial roysters play, between gormandising
and gourmeteering, he grubbed his tuck all right, deah smorregos,
every time he was for doing dirt to a meal or felt like a bottle of
ardilaun arongwith a smag of a lecker biss of a welldressed taart
or. Though his net intrants wight weighed nought but a flyblow
to his gross and ganz afterduepoise. And he was so jarvey jaunty
with a romp of a schoolgirl's completion sitting pretty over his
Oyster Monday print face and he was plainly out on the ramp and
mash, as you might say, for he sproke.

Overture and beginners!

When lo (whish, O whish!) mesaw mestreamed, as the green
to the gred was flew, was flown, through deafths of durkness
greengrown deeper I heard a voice, the voce of Shaun, vote of
the Irish, voise from afar (and cert no purer puer palestrine e'er
chanted panangelical mid the clouds of Tu es Petrus, not
Michaeleen Kelly, not Mara O'Mario, and sure, what more
numerose Italicuss ever rawsucked frish uov in urinal?), a brieze
to Yverzone o'er the brozaozaozing sea, from Inchigeela call
the way how it suspired (morepork! morepork!) to scented
nightlife as softly as the loftly marconimasts from Clifden sough
open tireless secrets (mauveport! mauveport!) to Nova Scotia's
listing sisterwands. Tubetube!

His handpalm lifted, his handshell cupped, his handsign pointed,
his handheart mated, his handaxe risen, his handleaf fallen.
Helpsome hand that holemost heals! What is het holy! It gested.
And it said:

— Alo, alass, aladdin amobus! Does she lag soft fall means
rest down? Shaun yawned, as his general address rehearsal,
(that was antepropreviousday's pigeons-in-a-pie with rough
dough for the carrier and the hash-say-ugh of overgestern pluzz
the 'stuesday's shampain in his head, with the memories of the
past and the hicnuncs of the present embelliching the musics of
the futures from Miccheruni's band) addressing himself *ex alto*
and complaining with vocal discontent it was so close as of
the fact the rag was up and of the briefs and billpasses, a houseful
of deadheads, of him to dye his paddycoats to morn his hestern-

most earning, his board in the swealth of his fate as, having
moistened his manducators upon the quiet and scooping molars
and grinders clean with his two fore fingers, he sank his hunk,
dowanouet to resk at once, exhaust as winded hare, utterly spent,
it was all he could do (disgusted with himself that the combined
weight of his tons of iosals was a hundred men's massed too much
for him), upon the native heath he loved covered kneehigh with
virgin bush, for who who e'er trod sod of Erin could ever sleep
off the turf. Well, I'm liberally dished seeing myself in this trim!
How all too unwordy am I, a mere mailman of peace, a poor loust
hastehater of the first degree, the principot of Candia, no legs and
a title, for such eminence, or unpro promenade rather, to be much
more exact, as to be the bearer extraordinary of these postoomany
missive on his majesty's service while me and yous and them we're
extending us after the pattern of reposiveness! Weh is me, yeh is
ye! I, the mightif beam maircanny, which bit his mirth too early
or met his birth too late! It should of been my other with his
leickname for he's the head and I'm an everdevoting fiend of his.
I can seeze tomirror in tosdays of yer when we lofobsed os so ker.
Those sembal simon pumpkel pieman yers! We shared the twin
chamber and we winked on the one wench and what Sim sobs
todie I'll reeve tomorry, for 'twill be, I have hopes of, Sam
Dizzier's feedst. Tune in, tune on, old Tighe, high, high, high,
I'm thine owelglass. Be old! He looks rather thin, imitating me.
I'm very fond of that other of mine. Fish hands Macsorley!
Elien! Obsequies! Bonzeye! Isaac Egari's Ass! We're the musichall pair that won the swimmyease bladdhers at the Guinness
gala in Badeniveagh. I ought not to laugh with him on this stage.
But he' such a game loser! I lift my disk to him. Brass and reeds,
brace and ready! How is your napper, Handy, and hownow does
she stand? First he was living to feel what the eldest daughter she was
panseying and last he was dying to know what old Madre Patriack
does be up to. Take this John's Lane in your toastingfourch. Shaunti and shaunti and shaunti again! And twelve coolinder moons!
I am no helotwashipper but I revere her! For my own coant! She
has studied! Piscisvendolor! You're grace! Futs dronk of

Wouldndom! But, Gemini, he's looking frightfully thin! I heard the man Shee shinging in the pantry bay. Down among the dustbins let him lie! Ear! Ear! Not ay! Eye! Eye! For I'm at the heart of it. Yet I cannot on my solemn merits as a recitativer recollect ever having done of anything of the kind to deserve of such. Not the phost of a nation. Nor by a long trollop. I just didn't have the time to. Saint Anthony Guide!

— But have we until now ever besought you, dear Shaun, we remembered, who it was, good boy, to begin with, who out of symphony gave you the permit?

— Goodbye now, Shaun replied, with a voice pure as a churchmode, in echo rightdainty, with a good catlick tug at his cocomoss candylock, a foretaste in time of his cabbageous brain's curlyflower. Athiacaro! Comb his tar odd gee sing your mower O meeow? Greet thee Good? How are them columbuses! Lard have mustard on them! Fatiguing, very fatiguing. Hobos hornknees and the corveeture of my spine. Poumeerme! My heaviest crux and dairy lot it is, with a bed as hard as the thinkamuddles of the Greeks and a board as bare as a Roman altar. I'm off rabbited kitchens and relief porridgers. No later than a very few fortnichts since I was meeting on the Thinker's Dam with a pair of men out of glasshouse whom I shuffled hands with named MacBlacks—I think their names is MacBlakes—from the Headfire Clump — and they were improving me and making me beliek no five hour factory life with insufficient emollient and industrial disabled for them that day o'gratises. I have the highest gratification by anuncing how I have it from whowho but Hagios Colleenkiller's prophecies. After suns and moons, dews and wettings, thunders and fires, comes sabotag. *Solvitur palumballando!* Tilvido! Adie!

— Then, we explained, salve a tour, ambly andy, you possibly might be so by order?

— Forgive me, Shaun repeated from his liquid lipes, not what I wants to do a strike of work but it was condemned on me premitially by Hireark Books and Chiefoverseer Cooks in their Eusebian Concordant Homilies and there does be a power com-

ing over me that is put upon me from on high out of the book of
breedings and so as it is becoming hairydittary I have of coerce
nothing in view to look forward at unless it is Swann and beat-
ing the blindquarters out of my oldfellow's orologium oloss olo-
rium. A bad attack of maggot it feels like. 'Tis trope, custodian
said. Almost might I say of myself, while keeping out of crime,
I am now becoming about fed up be going circulating about them
new hikler's highways like them nameless souls, ercked and skorned
and grizzild all over, till it's rusty October in this bleak forest
and was veribally complussed by thinking of the crater of some
noted volcano or the Dublin river or the catchalot trouth subsi-
dity as away out or to isolate i from my multiple Mes on the
spits of Lumbage Island or bury meself, clogs, coolcellar and all,
deep in my wineupon ponteen unless Morrissey's colt could help
me or the gander maybe at 49 as it is a tithe fish so it is, this
pig's stomach business, and where on dearth or in the miraculous
meddle of this expending umniverse to turn since it came into
my hands I am hopeless off course to be doing anything concerning.

— We expect you are, honest Shaun, we agreed, but from
franking machines, limricked, that in the end it may well turn out,
we hear to be you, our belated, who will bear these open letter.
Speak to us of Emailia.

— As, Shaun replied patly, with tootlepick tact too and a
down of his dampers, to that I have the gumpower and, by the
benison of Barbe, that is a lock to say with everything, my beloved.

— Would you mind telling us, Shaun honey, beg little big
moreboy, we proposed to such a dear youth, where mostly are
you able to work. Ah, you might! Whimper and we shall.

— Here! Shaun replied, while he was fondling one of his
cowheel cuffs. There's no sabbath for nomads, and I mostly was
able to walk, being too soft for work proper, sixty odd eilish
mires a week between three masses a morn and two chaplets at
eve. I am always telling those pedestriasts, my answerers, Top,
Sid and Hucky, now (and it is a veriest throth as the thieves' re-

scension) how it was forstold for me by brevet for my vacation
in life while possessing stout legs to be disbarred after holy orders
from unnecessary servile work of reckless walking of all sorts for
the relics of my time for otherwise by my so douching I would
get into a blame there where sieves fall out, Excelsior tips the best.
Weak stop work stop walk stop whoak. Go thou this island, one
housesleep there, then go thou other island, two housesleep there,
then catch one nightmaze, then home to dearies. Never back a
woman you defend, never get quit of a friend on whom you
depend, never make face to a foe till he's rife and never get stuck
to another man's pfife. Amen, ptah! His hungry will be done! On
the continent as in Eironesia. But believe me in my simplicity I am
awful good, I believe, so I am, at the root of me, praised be right
cheek Discipline! And I can now truthfully declaret before my
Geity's Pantokreator with my fleshfettered palms on the epizzles
of the apossels that I do my reasonabler's best to recite my grocery
beans for mummy *mit* dummy *mot* muthar *mat* bonzar regular,
genuflections enclosed. Hek domov muy, there thou beest on the
hummock, ghee up, ye dog, for your daggily broth, etc., Happy
Maria and Glorious Patrick, etc., etc. In fact, always, have I
believe. Greedo! Her's me hongue!

— And it is the fullsoot of a tarabred. Yet one minute's observation, dear dogmestic Shaun, as we point out how you have
while away painted our town a wearing greenridinghued.

— O murder mere, how did you hear? Shaun replied, smoil-
ing the ily way up his lampsleeve (it just seemed the natural thing
to do), so shy of light was he then. Well, so be it! The gloom hath
rays, her lump is love. And I will confess to have, yes. Your
diogneses is anonest man's. Thrubedore I did! Inditty I did. All lay
I did. Down with the Saozon ruze! And I am afraid it wouldn't
be my first coat's wasting after striding on the vampire and blazing on the focoal. See! blazing on the focoal. As see! blazing upon
the foe. Like the regular redshank I am. Impregnable as the mule
himself. Somebody may perhaps hint at an aughter impression
of I was wrong. No such a thing! You never made a more freud-
ful mistake, excuse yourself! What's pork to you means meat to

me while you behold how I be eld. But it is grandiose by my
ways of thinking from the prophecies. New worlds for all! And
they were scotographically arranged for gentlemen only by a
scripchewer in whofoundland who finds he is a relative. And it
was with my extravert davy. Like glue. Be through. Moyhard's
daynoight, tomthumb. Phwum!

— How mielodorous is thy bel chant, O songbird, and how
exqueezit thine after draught! *Buccinate in Emenia tuba insigni
volumnitatis tuae.* But do you mean, O phausdheen phewn, from
Pontoffbellek till the Kisslemerched our ledan triz will be? we
gathered substantively whether furniture would or verdure var-
nish?

— It is a confoundyous injective so to say, Shaun the fiery
boy shouted, naturally incensed, as he shook the red pepper out
of his auricles. And ånother time please confine your glaring in-
tinuations to some other mordant body. What on the physiog
of this furnaced planet would I be doing besides your verjuice?
That is more than I can fix, for the teom bihan, anyway. So let I
and you now kindly drop that, angryman! That's not French
pastry. You can take it from me. Understand me when I tell you
(and I will ask you not to whisple, cry golden or quoth mecback)
that under the past purcell's office, so deeply deplored by my
erstwhile elder friend, Miss Enders, poachmistress and gay re-
ceiver ever for in particular to the Scotic Poor Men's Thousand
Gallon Cow Society (I was thinking of her in sthore) allbethey
blessed with twentytwo thousand sorters out of a biggest poss
of twentytwo thousand, mine's won, too much privet stationery
and safty quipu was ate up larchly by those nettlesome goats
out of pension greed. *Colpa di Becco, buon apartita!* Proceding,
I will say it is also one of my avowal's intentions, at some time
pease Pod pluse murthers of gout (when I am not prepared to say)
so apt as my pen is upt to scratch, to compound quite the makings
of a verdigrease savingsbook in the form of a pair of capri
sheep boxing gloves surrounding this matter of the Welsfusel
mascoteers and their sindybuck that saved a city for my publickers,
Nolaner and Browno, Nickil Hopstout, Christcross, so long as,

thanks to force of destiny, my selary as a paykelt is propaired, and there is a peg under me and there is a tum till me.

To the Very Honourable The Memory of Disgrace, the Most Noble, Sometime Sweepyard at the Service of the Writer. Salutem dicint. The just defunct Mrs Sanders who (the Loyd insure her!) I was shift and shuft too, with her shester Mrs. Shunders, both mudical dauctors from highschoolhorse and aslyke as Easther's leggs. She was the niceliest person of a wellteached nonparty woman that I ever acquired her letters, only too fat, used to babies and tottydean verbish this is her entertermentdags for she shuk the bottle and tuk the medascene all times a day. She was well under ninety, poor late Mrs, and had tastes of the poetics, me having stood the pilgarlick a fresh at sea when the moon also was standing in a corner of sweet Standerson my ski. P.L.M. Mevrouw von Andersen was her whogave me a muttonbrooch, stakkers for her begfirst party. Honour thy farmer and my litters. This, my tears, is my last will intesticle wrote off in the strutforit about their absent female assauciations which I, or perhaps any other person what squaton a toffette, have the honour to had upon their polite sophykussens in the real presence of devouted Mrs Grumby when her skin was exposed to the air. O what must the grief of my mund be for two little ptpt coolies worth twenty thousand quad herewitdnessed with both's maddlemass wishes to Pepette for next match from their dearly beloved Roggers, M.D.D. O.D. May doubling drop of drooght! Writing.

— Hopsoloosely kidding you are totether with your cadenus and goat along nose how we shall complete that white paper. Two venusstas! Biggerstiff! Qweer but gaon! Be trouz and wholetrouz! Otherwise, frank Shaun, we pursued, what would be the autobiography of your softbodied fumiform?

— Hooraymost! None whomsoever, Shaun replied, Heavenly blank! (he had intentended and was peering now rather close to the paste of his rubiny winklering) though it ought to be more or less rawcawcaw romantical. By the wag, how is Mr Fry? All of it, I might say, in ex-voto, pay and perks and wooden half-

pence, some rhino, rhine, O joyoust rhine, was handled over spon-
daneously by me (and bundle end to my illwishers' Miss Anders!
she woor her wraith of ruins the night she lost I left) in the ligname
of Mr van Howten of Tredcastles, Clowntalkin, timbreman, among
my prodigits nabobs and navious of every subscription entitled
the Bois in the Boscoor, our evicted tenemants. What I say is (and
I am noen roehorn or culkilt permit me to tell you, if uninformed),
I never spont it. Nor have I the ghuest of innation on me the way
to. It is my rule so. It went anyway like hot pottagebake. And
this brings me to my fresh point. Quoniam, I am as plain as
portable enveloped, inhowmuch, you will now parably receive,
care of one of Mooseyeare Goonness's registered andouterthus
barrels. Quick take um whiffat andrainit. Now!

— So vi et! we responded. Song! Shaun, song! Have mood!
Hold forth!

— I apploguise, Shaun began, but I would rather spinooze
you one from the grimm gests of Jacko and Esaup, fable one,
feeble too. Let us here consider the casus, my dear little cousis
(husstenhasstencaffincoffintussemtossemdamandamnacosaghcusa-
ghhobixhatouxpeswchbechoscashlcarcarcaract) of the Ondt and
the Gracehoper.

The Gracehoper was always jigging ajog, hoppy on akkant
of his joyicity, (he had a partner pair of findlestilts to supplant
him), or, if not, he was always making ungraceful overtures to
Floh and Luse and Bienie and Vespatilla to play pupa-pupa and
pulicy-pulicy and langtennas and pushpygyddyum and to commence insects with him, there mouthparts to his orefice and his
gambills to there airy processes, even if only in chaste, ameng
the everlistings, behold a waspering pot. He would of curse
melissciously, by his fore feelhers, flexors, contractors, depres-
sors and extensors, lamely, harry me, marry me, bury me, bind
me, till she was puce for shame and allso fourmish her in Spin-
ner's housery at the earthsbest schoppinhour so summery as his
cottage, which was cald fourmillierly Tingsomingenting, groped
up. Or, if he was always striking up funny funereels with Bester-
farther Zeuts, the Aged One, with all his wigeared corollas, albe-

dinous and oldbuoyant, inscythe his elytrical wormcasket and
Dehlia and Peonia, his druping nymphs, bewheedling him, compound eyes on hornitosehead, and Auld Letty Plussiboots to
scratch his cacumen and cackle his tramsitus, diva deborah (seven
bolls of sapo, a lick of lime, two spurts of fussfor, threefurts of
sulph, a shake o'shouker, doze grains of migniss and a mesfull of
midcap pitchies. The whool of the whaal in the wheel of the
whorl of the Boubou from Bourneum has thus come to táon!),
and with tambarins and cantoridettes soturning around his eggs-
hill rockcoach their dance McCaper in retrophoebia, beck from
bulk, like fantastic disossed and jenny aprils, to the ra, the ra, the
ra, the ra, langsome heels and langsome toesis, attended to by a
mutter and doffer duffmatt baxingmotch and a myrmidins of
pszozlers pszinging *Satyr's Caudledayed Nice* and *Hombly,
Dombly Sod We Awhile* but *Ho, Time Timeagen, Wake!* For if
sciencium (what's what) can mute uns nought, 'a thought,
abought the Great Sommbboddy within the Omniboss, perhops an
artsaccord (hoot's hoot) might sing ums tumtim abutt the Little
Newbuddies that ring his panch. A high old tide for the bar-
heated publics and the whole day as gratiis! Fudder and lighting
for ally looty, any filly in a fog, for O'Cronione lags acrumbling
in his sands but his sunsunsuns still tumble on. Erething above
ground, as his Book of Breathings bed him, so as everwhy, sham
or shunner, zeemliangly to kick time.

  Grouscious me and scarab my sahul! What a bagateller it is!
Libelulous! Inzanzarity! Pou! Pschla! Ptuh! What a zeit for the
goths! vented the Ondt, who, not being a sommerfool, was
thothfolly making chilly spaces at hisphex affront of the icinglass
of his windhame, which was cold antitopically Nixnixundnix.
We shall not come to party at that lopp's, he decided possibly,
for he is not on our social list. Nor to Ba's berial nether, thon
sloghard, this oldeborre's yaar ablong as there's a khul on a khat.
Nefersenless, when he had safely looked up his ovipository, he
loftet hails and prayed: May he me no voida water! Seekit Ha-
tup! May no he me tile pig shed on! Suckit Hotup! As broad as
Beppy's realm shall flourish my reign shall flourish! As high as

Heppy's hevn shall flurrish my haine shall hurrish! Shall grow, shall flourish! Shall hurrish! Hummum.

The Ondt was a weltall fellow, raumybult and abelboobied, bynear saw altitudinous wee a schelling in kopfers. He was sair sair sullemn and chairmanlooking when he was not making spaces in his psyche, but, laus! when he wore making spaces on his ikey, he ware mouche mothst secred and muravyingly wisechairmanlooking. Now whim the sillybilly of a Gracehoper had jingled through a jungle of love and debts and jangled through a jumble of life in doubts afterworse, wetting with the bimblebeaks, drikking with nautonects, bilking with durrydunglecks and horing after ladybirdies (*ichnehmon diagelegenaitoikon*) he fell joust as sieck as a sexton and tantoo pooveroo quant a churchprince, and wheer the midges to wend hemsylph or vosch to sirch for grub for his corapusse or to find a hospes, alick, he wist gnit! Bruko dry! fuko spint! Sultamont osa bare! And volomundo osi videvide! Nichtsnichtsundnichts! Not one pickopeck of muscowmoney to bag a tittlebits of beebread! Iomio! Iomio! Crick's corbicule, which a plight! O moy Bog, he contrited with melanctholy. Meblizzered, him sluggered! I am heartily hungry!

He had eaten all the whilepaper, swallowed the lustres, devoured forty flights of styearcases, chewed up all the mensas and seccles, ronged the records, made mundballs of the ephemerids and vorasioused most glutinously with the very timeplace in the ternitary — not too dusty a cicada of neutriment for a chittinous chip so mitey. But when Chrysalmas was on the bare branches, off he went from Tingsomingenting. He took a round stroll and he took a stroll round and he took a round strollagain till the grillies in his head and the leivnits in his hair made him thought he had the Tossmania. Had he twicycled the sees of the deed and trestraversed their revermer? Was he come to hevre with his engiles or gone to hull with the poop? The June snows was flocking in thuckflues on the hegelstomes, millipeeds of it and myriopoods, and a lugly whizzling tournedos, the Boraborayellers, blohablasting tegolhuts up to tetties and ruching sleets off the coppeehouses, playing ragnowrock rignewreck, with an irritant, penetrant, siphonopterous spuk. Grausssssss! Opr! Graussssssss! Opr!

The Gracehoper who, though blind as batflea, yet knew, not a leetle beetle, his good smetterling of entymology asped nissunitimost lous nor liceens but promptly tossed himself in the vico, phthin and phthir, on top of his buzzer, tezzily wondering wheer would his aluck alight or boss of both appease and the next time he makes the aquinatance of the Ondt after this they have met themselves, these mouschical umsummables, it shall be motylucky if he will beheld not a world of differents. Behailed His Gross the Ondt, prostrandvorous upon his dhrone, in his Papylonian babooshkees, smolking a spatial brunt of Hosana cigals, with unshrinkables farfalling from his unthinkables, swarming of himself in his sunnyroom, sated before his comfortumble phullupsuppy of a plate o'monkynous and a confucion of minthe (for he was a conformed aceticist and aristotaller), as appi as a oneysucker or a baskerboy on the Libido, with Floh biting his leg thigh and Luse lugging his luff leg and Bieni bussing him under his bonnet and Vespatilla blowing cosy fond tutties up the allabroad length of the large of his smalls. As entomate as intimate could pinchably be. Emmet and demmet and be jiltses crazed and be jadeses whipt! schneezed the Gracehoper, aguepe with ptchjelasys and at his wittol's indts, what have eyeforsight!

The Ondt, that true and perfect host, a spiter aspinne, was making the greatest spass a body could with his queens laceswinging for he was spizzing all over him like thingsumanything in formicolation, boundlessly blissfilled in an allallahbath of houris. He was ameising himself hugely at crabround and marypose, chasing Floh out of charity and tickling Luse, I hope too, and tackling Bienie, faith, as well, and jucking Vespatilla jukely by the chimiche. Never did Dorsan from Dunshanagan dance it with more devilry! The veripatetic imago of the impossible Gracehoper on his odderkop in the myre, after his thrice ephemeral journeeys, sans mantis ne shooshooe, featherweighed animule, actually and presumptuably sinctifying chronic's despair, was sufficiently and probably coocoo much for his chorous

of gravitates. Let him be Artalone the Weeps with his parisites
peeling off him I'll be Highfee the Crackasider. Flunkey Footle
furloughed foul, writing off his phoney, but Conte Carme makes
the melody that mints the money. *Ad majorem l.s.d.! Divi gloriam.*
A darkener of the threshold. Haru? Orimis, capsizer of his ant-
boat, sekketh rede from Evil-it-is, lord of loaves in Amongded.
Be it! So be it! Thou-who-thou-art, the fleet-as-spindhrift,
impfang thee of mine wideheight. Haru!

The thing pleased him andt, and andt,
He larved ond he larved on he merd such a nauses
The Gracehoper feared he would mixplace his fauces.
I forgive you, grondt Ondt, said the Gracehoper, weeping,
For their sukes of the sakes you are safe in whose keeping.
Teach Floh and Luse polkas, show Bienie where's sweet
And be sure Vespatilla fines fat ones to heat.
As I once played the piper I must now pay the count
So saida to Moyhammlet and marhaba to your Mount!
Let who likes lump above so what flies be a full 'un;
I could not feel moregruggy if this was prompollen.
I pick up your reproof, the horsegift of a friend,
For the prize of your save is the price of my spend.
Can castwhores pulladefikiss if oldpollocks forsake 'em
Or Culex feel etchy if Pulex don't wake him?
A locus to loue, a term it t'embarass,
These twain are the twins that tick Homo Vulgaris.
Has Aquileone nort winged to go syf
Since the Gwyfyn we were in his farrest drewbryf
And that Accident Man not beseeked where his story ends
Since longsephyring sighs sought heartseast for their orience?
We are Wastenot with Want, precondamned, two and true,
Till Nolans go volants and Bruneyes come blue.
Ere those gidflirts now gadding you quit your mocks for my gropes
An extense must impull, an elapse must elopes,
Of my rectucs takestock, tinktact, and ail's weal;
As I view by your farlook hale yourself to my heal.

Partiprise my thinwhins whiles my blink points unbroken on
Your whole's whercabroads with Tout's trightyright token on.
My in risible universe youdly haud find
Sulch oxtrabeeforeness meat soveal behind.
Your feats end enormous, your volumes immense,
(May the Graces I hoped for sing your Ondtship song sense!),
Your genus its worldwide, your spacest sublime!
But, Holy Saltmartin, why can't you beat time?

In the name of the former and of the latter and of their holo-
caust. Allmen.

— Now? How good you are in explosion! How farflung is
your fokloire and how velktingeling your volupkabulary! *Qui*
vive sparanto qua muore contanto. O foibler, O flip, you've that
wandervogl wail withyin! It falls easily upon the earopen and goes
down the friskly shortiest like treacling tumtim with its tingting-
taggle. The blarneyest blather in all Corneywall! But could you,
of course, decent Lettrechaun, we knew (to change your name of
not your nation) while still in the barrel, read the strangewrote
anaglyptics of those shemletters patent for His Christian's Em?

— Greek! Hand it to me! Shaun replied, plosively pointing to
the cinnamon quistoquill behind his acoustrolobe. I'm as after-
dusk nobly Roman as pope and water could christen me. Look
at that for a ridingpin! I am, thing Sing Larynx, letter potent to
play the sem backwards like Oscan wild or in shunt Persse trans-
luding from the Otherman or off the Toptic or anything off the
types of my finklers in the draught or with buttles, with my oyes
thickshut and all. But, hellas, it is harrobrew bad on the corns and
callouses. As far as that goes I associate myself with your remark
just now from theodicy *re*'furloined notepaper and quite agree in
your prescriptions for indeed I am, pay Gay, in juxtaposition to
say it is not a nice production. It is a pinch of scribble, not
wortha bottle of cabbis. Overdrawn! Puffedly offal tosh. Besides its auctionable, all about crime and libel! Nothing beyond
clerical horrors *et omnibus* to be entered for the foreign as second-
class matter. The fuellest filth ever fired since Charley Lucan's.

Flummery is what I would call it if you were to ask me to put it
on a single dimension what pronounced opinion I might possibly
orally have about them bagses of trash which the mother and
Mr Unmentionable (O breed not his same!) has reduced to writing without making news out of my sootynemm. When she
slipped under her couchman. And where he made a cat with a
peep. How they wore two madges on the makewater. And why
there were treefellers in the shrubrubs. Then he hawks his hand-
mud figgers from Francie to Fritzie down in the kookin. Phiz
is me mother and Hair's me father. Bauv Betty Famm and Pig
Pig Pike. Their livetree (may it flourish!) by their ecotaph (let it
stayne!). With balsinbal bimbies swarming tiltop. Comme bien,
Comme bien! Feefeel! Feefeel! And the Dutches dyin loffin at
his pon peck de Barec. And all the mound reared. Till he wot not
wot to begin he should. An infant sailing eggshells on the floor
of a wet day would have more sabby.

   Letter, carried of Shaun, son of Hek, written of Shem, brother
of Shaun, uttered for Alp, mother of Shem, for Hek, father of
Shaun. Initialled. Gee. Gone. 29 Hardware Saint. Lendet till
Laonum. Baile-Atha-Cliath. 31 Jan. 1132 A.D. Here Com-
merces Enville. Tried Apposite House. 13 Fitzgibbets. Loco.
Dangerous. Tax 9d. B.L. Guineys, esqueer. L.B. Not known at
1132 a. 12 Norse Richmound. Nave unlodgeable. Loved noa's
dress. Sinned, Jetty Pierrse. Noon sick parson. 92 Windsewer.
Ave. No such no. Vale. Finn's Hot. Exbelled from 1014 d. Pull-
down. Fearview. Opened by Miss Take. 965 nighumpledan sexti-
ffits. Shout at Site. Roofloss. Fit Dunlop and Be Satisfied. Mr.
Domnall O'Domnally. Q.V. 8 Royal Terrors. None so strait.
Shutter up. Dining with the Danes. Removed to Philip's Burke.
At sea. D.E.D. Place scent on. Clontalk. Father Jacob, Rice
Factor. 3 Castlewoos. P.V. Arrusted. J.P. Converted to Hos-
pitalism. Ere the March past or Civilisation. Once Bank of Ireland's.
Return to City Arms. 2 Milchbroke. Wrongly spilled. Traumcon-
draws. Now Bunk of England's. Drowned in the Laffey. Here.
The Reverest Adam Foundlitter. Shown geshotten. 7 Streetpetres.
Since Cabranke. Seized of the Crownd. Well, Sir Arthur. Buy

Patersen's Matches. Unto his promisk hands. Blown up last
Lemmas by Orchid Lodge. Search Unclaimed Male. House Con-
damned by Ediles. Back in Few Minutes. Closet for Repeers. 60
Shellburn. Key at Kate's. Kiss. Isaac's Butt, Poor Man. Dalicious
arson. Caught. Missing. Justiciated. Kainly forewarred. Abraham
Badly's King, Park Bogey. Salved. All reddy berried. Hollow and
eavy. Desert it. Overwayed. Understrumped. Back to the P.O.
Kaer of. Ownes owe M.O. Too Let. To Be Soiled. Cohabited
by Unfortunates. Lost all Licence. His Bouf Toe is Frozen Over.
X, Y and Z, Ltd, Destinied Tears. A.B, ab, Sender. Boston
(Mass). 31 Jun. 13, 12. P.D. Razed. Lawyered. Vacant. Mined.
Here's the Bayleaffs. Step out to Hall out of that, Ereweaker,
with your Bloody Big Bristol. Bung. Stop. Bung. Stop. Cumm
Bumm. Stop. Came Baked to Auld Aireen. Stop.

— Kind Shaun, we all requested, much as we hate to say it,
but since you rose to the use of money have you not, without
suggesting for an instant, millions of moods used up slanguage
tun times as words as the penmarks used out in sinscript with such
hesitancy by your cerebrated brother — excuse me not men-
tioningahem?

— CelebrAted! Shaun replied under the sheltar of his brog-
uish, vigorously rubbing his magic lantern to a glow of full-
consciousness. HeCitEncy! Your words grates on my ares.
Notorious I rather would feel inclined to myself in the first place
to describe Mr O'Shem the Draper with before letter as should
I be accentually called upon for a dieoguinnsis to pass my opinions,
properly spewing, into impulsory irelitz. But I would not care to
be so unfruitful to my own part as to swear for the moment positively as to the views of Denmark. No, sah! But let me say my
every belief before my high Gee is that I much doubt of it. I've no
room for that fellow on my fagroaster, I just can't. As I hourly
learn from Rooters and Havers through Gilligan's maypoles in
a nice pathetic notice he, the pixillated doodler, is on his last with
illegible clergimanths boasting always of his ruddy complexious!
She, the mammy far, was put up to it by him, the iniquity that
ought to be depraved of his libertins to be silenced, sackclothed

and suspended, and placed in irons into some drapyery institution
off the antipopees for wordsharping only if he was klanver enough
to pass the panel fleischcurers and the fieldpost censor. Gach!
For that is a fullblown fact and well celibated before the four
divorce courts and all the King's paunches, how he has the
solitary from seeing Scotch snakes and has a lowsense for the production of consumption and dalickey cyphalos on his brach
premises where he can purge his contempt and dejeunerate into a
skillyton be thinking himself to death. Rot him! Flannelfeet! Flatty-
ro! I will describe you in a word. Thou. (I beg your pardon.)
Homo! Then putting his bedfellow on me! (like into mike and
nick onto post). The criniman: I'll give it to him for that! Making
the lobbard change hisstops, as we say in the long book! Is he
on whosekeeping or are my! Obnoximost posthumust! With his
unique hornbook and his prince of the apauper's pride, blundering all over the two worlds! If he waits till I buy him a mossel-
man's present! Ho's nos halfcousin of mine, pigdish! Nor wants
to! I'd famish with the cuistha first. Aham!
  — May we petition you, Shaun illustrious, then, to put his
prentis' pride in your aproper's purse and to unravel in your own
sweet way with words of style to your very and most obse-
quient, we suggested, with yet an esiop's foible, as to how?
  — Well it is partly my own, isn't it? and you may, ought and
welcome, Shaun replied, taking at the same time, as his hunger
got the bitter of him, a hearty bite out of the honeycomb of his
Braham and Melosedible hat, tryone, tryon and triune. Ann wun-
kum. Sure, I thunkum you knew all about that, honorey causes,
through thelemontary channels long agum. Sure, that is as old as
the Baden bees of Saint Dominoc's and as commonpleas now to
allus pueblows and bunkum as Nelson his trifulgurayous pillar.
However. Let me see, do. Beerman's bluff was what begun it, Old
Knoll and his borrowing! And then the liliens of the veldt, Nancy
Nickies and Folletta Lajambe! Then mem and hem and the jaque-
jack. All about Wucherer and righting his name for him. I regret
to announce, after laying out his litterery bed, for two days she
kept squealing down for noisy priors and bawling out to her

jameymock farceson in Shemish like a mouther of the incas with a garcielasso huw Ananymus pinched her tights and about the Balt with the markshaire parawag and his loyal divorces, when he feraxiously shed ovas in Alemaney, tse tse, all the tell of the tud with the bourighevisien backclack, and him, the cribibber like an ambitrickster, aspiring like the decan's, fast aslooped in the intrance to his polthronechair with his sixth finger between his catseye and the index, making his pillgrimace of Childe Horrid, engrossing to his ganderpan what the idioglossary he invented under hicks hyssop! Hock! Ickick gav him that toock, imitator! And it was entirely theck latter to blame. Does he drink because I am sorely there shall be no more Kates and Nells. If you see him it took place there. It was given meeck, thank the Bench, to assist at the whole thing byck special chancery licence. As often as I think of that unbloody housewarmer, Shem Skrivenitch, always cutting my prhose to please his phrase, bogorror, I declare I get the jawache! Be me punting his reflection he'd begin his beogrefright in muddyass ribalds. Digteter! Grundtsagar! Swop beef! You know he's peculiar, that eggschicker, with the smell of old woman off him, to suck nothing of his switchedupes. M.D. made his *ante mortem* for him. He was grey at three, like sygnus the swan, when he made his boo to the public and barnacled up to the eyes when he repented after seven. The alum that winters on his top is the stale of the staun that will soar when he stambles till that hag of the coombe rapes the pad off his lock. He was down with the whooping laugh at the age of the loss of reason the whopping first time he prediseased me. He's weird, I tell you, and middayevil down to his vegetable soul. Never mind his falls feet and his tanbark complexion. That's why he was forbidden tomate and was warmed off the ricecourse of marrimoney, under the Helpless Corpses Enactment. I'm not at all surprised the saint kicked him whereby the sum taken Berkeley showed the reason genrously. *Negas, negasti* — negertop, negertoe, negertoby, negrunter! Then he was pusched out of Thingamuddy's school by Miss Garterd, for itching. Then he caught the europicolas and went into the society of jewses. With Bro Cahlls and Fran Czeschs

and Bruda Pszths and Brat Slavos. One temp when he foiled to
be killed, the freak wanted to put his bilingual head intentionally
through the *Ikish Tames* and go and join the clericy as a demoni-
can skyterrier. Throwing dust in the eyes of the Hooley Fer-
mers! He used to be avowdeed as he ought to be vitandist. For
onced I squeaked by twyst I'll squelch him. Then he went to
Cecilia's treat on his solo to pick up Galen. Asbestopoulos! Inku-
pot! He has encaust in the blood. Shim! I have the outmost contempt for. Prost bitten! Conshy! Tiberia is waiting on you,
arestocrank! Chaka a seagull ticket at Gattabuia and Gabbiano's!
Go o'er the sea, haythen, from me and leave your libber to TCD.
Your puddin is cooked! You're served, cram ye! Fatefully
yaourth ... Ex. Ex. Ex. Ex.

— But for what, thrice truthful teller, Shaun of grace? weakly
we went on to ask now of the gracious one. Vouchsafe to say.
You will now, goodness, won't you? Why?

— For his root language, if you ask me whys, Shaun replied,
as he blessed himself devotionally like a crawsbomb, making act
of oblivion, footinmouther! (what the thickuns else?) which he
picksticked into his lettruce invrention. Ullhodturdenweirmud-
gaardgringnirurdrmolnirfenrirlukkilokkibaugimandodrrerin-
surtkrinmgernrackinarockar! Thor's for yo!

— The hundredlettered name again, last word of perfect language. But you could come near it, we do suppose, strong Shaun
O', we foresupposed. How?

— Peax! Peax! Shaun replied in vealar penultimatum. 'Tis
pebils before Sweeney's as he swigged a slug of Jon Jacobsen
from his treestem sucker cane. Mildbut likesome! I might as
well be talking to the four waves till tibbes grey eves and the
rests asleep. Frost! Nope! No one in his seven senses could as
I have before said, only you missed my drift, for it's being in-
cendiary. Every dimmed letter in it is a copy and not a few of the
silbils and wholly words I can show you in my Kingdom of
Heaven. The lowquacity of him! With his threestar monothong!
Thaw! The last word in stolentelling! And what's more right-
down lowbrown schisthematic robblemint! Yes. As he was rising

my lather. Like you. And as I was plucking his goosybone. Like
yea. He store the tale of me shur. Like yup. How's that for
Shemese?

— Still in a way, not to flatter you, we fancy you that you are
so strikingly brainy and well letterread in yourshelves as ever were
the Shamous Shamonous, Limited, could use worse of yourself, ingenious Shaun, we still so fancied, if only you would take your
time so and the trouble of so doing it. Upu now!

— Undoubtedly but that is show, Shaun replied, the mutter-
melk of his blood donor beginning to work, and while innocent
of disseminating the foul emanation, it would be a fall day I
could not, sole, so you can keep your space and by the power of
blurry wards I am loyable to do it (I am convicted of it!) any time
ever I liked (bet ye fippence off me boot allowance!) with the
allergrossest transfusiasm as, you see, while I can soroquise the
Siamanish better than most, it is an openear secret, be it said,
how I am extremely ingenuous at the clerking even with my
badily left and, arrah go braz. I'd pinsel it with immenuensoes
as easy as I'd perorate a chickerow of beans for the price of two
maricles and my trifolium librotto, the authordux Book of Lief,
would, if given to daylight, (I hold a most incredible faith about
it) far exceed what that bogus bolshy of a shame, my soamheis
brother, Gaoy Fecks, is conversant with in audible black and
prink. Outragedy of poetscalds! Acomedy of letters! I have
them all, tame, deep and harried, in my mine's I. And one of
these fine days, man dear, when the mood is on me, that I
may willhap cut my throat with my tongue tonight but I will
be ormuzd moved to take potlood and introvent it Paatryk just
like a work of merit, mark my words and append to my mark
twang, that will open your pucktricker's ops for you, broather
brooher, only for, as a papst and an immature and a nayophight
and a *spaciaman spaciosum* and a hundred and eleven other things,
I would never for anything take so much trouble of such doing.
And why so? Because I am altogether a chap too fly and hairyman
for to infradig the like of that ultravirulence. And by all I hold
sacred on earth clouds and in heaven I swear to you on my piop

and oath by the awe of.Shaun (and that's a howl of a name!) that
I will commission to the flames any incendiarist whosoever or
ahriman howsoclever who would endeavour to set ever annyma
roner moother of mine on fire. Rock me julie but I will soho!

And, with that crickcrackcruck of his threelungged squool
from which grief had usupped every smile, big hottempered
husky fusky krenfy strenfy pugiliser, such as he was, he virtually
broke down on the mooherhead, getting quite jerry over her,
overpowered by himself with the love of the tearsilver that
he twined through her hair for, sure, he was the soft semplgawn
slob of the world with a heart like Montgomery's in his showchest
and harvey loads of feeling in him and as innocent and undesign-
ful as the freshfallen calef. Still, grossly unselfish in sickself, he
dished allarmes away and laughed it off with a wipe at his pud-
gies and a gulp apologetic, healing his tare be the smeyle of his
oye, oogling around. Him belly no belong sollow mole pigeon.
Ally bully. Fu Li's gulpa. Mind you, now, that he was in the
dumpest of earnest orthough him jawr war hoo hleepy hor halk
urthing hurther. Moe like that only he stopped short in looking
up up upfrom his tide shackled wrists through the ghost of an
ocean's, the wieds of pansiful heathvens of joepeter's gaseytotum
as they are telling not but were and will be, all told, scruting fore-
back into the fargoneahead to feel out what age in years tropical,
ecclesiastic, civil or sidereal he might find by the sirious pointstand
of Charley's Wain (what betune the spheres sledding along the
lacteal and the mansions of the blest turning on old times) as ere-
while had he craved of thus, the dreamskhwindel necklassoed him,
his thumbs fell into his fists and, lusosing the harmonical balance
of his ballbearing extremities, by the holy kettle, like a flask of
lightning over he careened (O the sons of the fathers!) by the
mightyfine weight of his barrel (all that prevented the happering
of who if not the asterisks betwink themselves shall ever?) and,
as the wisest postlude course he could playact, collaspsed in ensemble and rolled buoyantly backwards in less than a twinkling *via* Rattigan's corner out of farther earshot with his highly
curious mode of slipashod motion, surefoot, sorefoot, slickfoot,

slackfoot, linkman laizurely, lampman loungey, and by Killesther's lapes and falls, with corks staves and treeleaves and more bubbles to his keelrow a fairish and easy way enough as the town cow cries behind the times in the direction of Mac Auliffe's, the crucethouse, *Open the Door Softly*, down in the valley before he was really uprighted ere in a dip of the downs (uila!) he spoorlessly disappaled and vanesshed, like a popo down a papa, from circular circulatio. Ah, mean!

Gaogaogaone! Tapaa!

And the stellas were shinings. And the earthnight strewed aromatose. His pibrook creppt mong the donkness. A reek was waft on the luftstream. He was ours, all fragrance. And we were his for a lifetime. O dulcid dreamings languidous! Taboccoo!

It was sharming! But sharmeng!

And the lamp went out as it couldn't glow on burning, yep, the lmp wnt out for it couldn't stay alight.

Well, (how dire do we thee hours when thylike fades!) all's dall and youllow and it is to bedowern that thou art passing hence, mine bruder, able Shaun, with a twhisking of the robe, ere the morning of light calms our hardest throes, beyond cods' cradle and porpoise plain, from carnal relations undfamiliar faces, to the inds of Tuskland where the oliphants scrum from orw till the ousts of Amiracles where the toll stories grow proudest, more is the pity, but for all your deeds of goodness you were soo ooft and for ever doing, manomano and myriamilia even to mulimuli, as our humbler classes, whose virtue is humility, can tell, it is hardly we in the country of the old, Sean Moy, can part you for, oleypoe, you were the walking saint, you were, tootoo too stayer, the graced of gods and pittites and the salus of the wake. Countenance whose disparition afflictedly fond Fuinn feels. Winner of the gamings, primed at the studience, propredicted from the storybouts, the choice of ages wise! Spickspookspokesman of our specturesque silentiousness! Musha, beminded of us out there in Cockpit, poor twelve o'clock scholars, sometime or other anywhen you think the time. Wisha, becoming back to us way home in Biddyhouse one way or either anywhere we miss your smile.

Palmwine breadfruit sweetmeat milksoup! Suasusupo! However!
Our people here in Samoanesia will not be after forgetting you
and the elders luking and marking the jornies, chalkin up drizzle
in drizzle out on the four bare mats. How you would be thinking
in your thoughts how the deepings did it all begin and how you
would be scrimmaging through your scruples to collar a hold of
an imperfection being committled. Sireland calls you. Mery Loye
is saling moonlike. And Slyly mamourneen's ladymaid at Glads-
house Lodge. Turn your coat, strong character, and tarry among
us down the vale, yougander, only once more! And may the mosse
of prosperousness gather you rolling home! May foggy dews be-
diamondise your hooprings! May the fireplug of filiality reinsure
your bunghole! May the barleywind behind glow luck to your
bathershins! 'Tis well we know you were loth to leave us,
winding your hobbledehorn, right royal post, but, aruah sure,
pulse of our slumber, dreambookpage, by the grace of Votre
Dame, when the natural morning of your nocturne blankmerges
into the national morning of golden sunup and Don Leary gets
his own back from old grog Georges Quartos as that goodship the
Jonnyjoys takes the wind from waterloogged Erin's king, you
will shiff across the Moylendsea and round up in your own
escapology some canonisator's day or other, sack on back, alack!
digging snow, (not so?) like the good man you are, with your
picture pockets turned knockside out in the rake of the rain for
fresh remittances and from that till this in any case, timus tenant,
may the tussocks grow quickly under your trampthickets and
the daisies trip lightly over your battercops.

[2]

Jaunty Jaun, as I was shortly before that made aware, next halted to fetch a breath the first cothurminous leg of his night-stride being pulled through, and to loosen (let God's son now be looking down on the poor preambler!) both of his bruised brogues that were plainly made a good bit before his hosen were, at the weir by Lazar's Walk (for far and wide, as large as he was lively, was he noted for his humane treatment of any kind of abused footgear), a matter of maybe nine score or so barrelhours distance off as truly he merited to do. He was there, you could planemetrically see, when I took a closer look at him, that was to say, (gracious helpings, at this rate of growing our cotted child of yestereve will soon fill space and burst in systems, so speeds the instant!) amply altered for the brighter, though still the graven image of his squarer self as he was used to be, perspiring but happy notwithstanding his foot was still asleep on him, the way he thought, by the holy januarious, he had a bullock's hoof in his buskin, with his halluxes so splendid, through Ireland untranscended, bigmouthed poesther, propped up, restant, against a butterblond warden of the peace, one comestabulish Sigurdsen, (and where a better than such exsearfaceman to rest from roving the laddyown he bootblacked?) who, buried upright like the Osbornes, kozydozy, had tumbled slumbersomely on sleep at night duty behind the curing station, equilebriated amid the embracings of a monopolized bottle.

Now, there were as many as twentynine hedge daughters out
of Benent Saint Berched's national nightschool (for they seemed
to remember how it was still a once-upon-a-four year) learning
their antemeridian lesson of life, under its tree, against its warning, beseated, as they were, upon the brinkspondy, attracted to
the rarerust sight of the first human yellowstone landmark (the
bear, the boer, the king of all boors, sir Humphrey his knave
we met on the moors!) while they paddled away, keeping time
magnetically with their eight and fifty pedalettes, playing foolu-
fool jouay allo misto posto, O so jaonickally, all barely in their
typtap teens, describing a charming dactylogram of nocturnes
though repelled by the snores of the log who looked stuck to
the sod as ever and oft, when liquefied, (vil!) he murmoaned
abasourdly in his Dutchener's native, visibly unmoved, over his
treasure trove for the crown: *Dotter dead bedstead mean diggy
smuggy flasky*.

Jaun (after he had in the first place doffed a hat with a rein-
forced crown and bowed to all the others in that chorus of praise
of goodwill girls on their best beehiviour who all they were girls
all rushing sowarmly for the post as buzzy as sie could bie to read
his kisshands, kittering all about, rushing and making a tremen-
dous girlsfuss over him pellmale, their *jeune premier* and his rosy-
posy smile, mussing his frizzy hair and the golliwog curls of him,
all, but that one; Finfria's fairest, done in loveletters like a trayful
of cloudberry tartlets (ain't they fine, mighty, mighty fine and
honoured?) and smilingly smelling, pair and pair about, broad
by bread and slender to slimmer, the nice perfumios that came
cunvy peeling off him (nice!) which was angelic simply, savouring
of wild thyme and parsley jumbled with breadcrumbs (O nice!)
and feeling his full fat pouch for him so tactily and jingaling
his jellybags for, though he looked a young chapplie of sixtine,
they could frole by his manhood that he was just the killingest
ladykiller all by kindness, now you, Jaun, asking kindlily (hillo,
missies!) after their howareyous at all with those of their dolly-
begs (and where's Agatha's lamb? and how are Bernadetta's
columbillas? and Juliennaw's tubberbunnies? and Eulalina's

tuggerfunnies?) he next went on (finefeelingfit!) to drop a few
stray remarks anent their personal appearances and the contrary
tastes displayed in their tight kittycasques and their smart fricky-
frockies, asking coy one after sloy one had she read Irish legginds
and gently reproving one that the ham of her hom could be
seen below her hem and whispering another aside as lavariant
that the hook of her hum was open a bittock at her back to have
a sideeye to that, hom, (and all of course just to fill up a form
out of pure human kindness and in a sprite of fun) for Jaun, by
the way, was by the way of becoming (I think, I hope he was)
the most purely human being that ever was called man, loving all
up and down the whole creation from Sampson's tyke to Jones's
sprat and from the King of all Wrenns down to infuseries) Jaun,
after those few prelimbs made out through his eroscope the
apparition of his fond sister Izzy for he knowed his love by her
waves of splabashing and she showed him proof by her way of
blabushing nor could he forget her so tarnelly easy as all that
since he was brotherbesides her benedict godfather and heaven
knows he thought the world and his life of her sweet heart could
buy, (brao!) poor, good, true, Jaun.
— Sister dearest, Jaun delivered himself with express cordiality, marked by clearance of diction and general delivery, as he
began to take leave of his scolastica at once so as to gain time
with deep affection, we honestly believe you sorely will miss us
the moment we exit yet we feel as a martyr to the dischurch of
all duty that it is about time, by Great Harry, we would shove
off to stray on our long last journey and not be the load on ye.
This is the gross proceeds of your teachings in which we were
raised, you, sis, that used to write to us the exceeding nice letters
for presentation and would be telling us anun (full well do we
wont to recall to mind) thy oldworld tales of homespinning and
derringdo and dieobscure and daddyho, these tales which reliter-
ately whisked off our heart so narrated by thou, gesweest, to
perfection, our pet pupil of the whole rhythmetic class and the
mainsay of our erigenal house the time we younkers twain were
fairly tossing ourselves (O Phoebus! O Pollux!) in bed, having

been laid up with Castor's oil on the Parrish's syrup (the night
we will remember) for to share our hard suite of affections with
thee.

I rise, O fair assemblage! Andcommincio. Now then, after
this introit of exordium, my galaxy girls, *quiproquo* of directions
to henservants I was asking his advice on the strict T.T. from
Father Mike, P.P., my orational dominican and confessor doctor,
C.C.D.D. (buy the birds, he was saying as he yerked me under
the ribs sermon in an offrand way and confidence petween peas
like ourselves in soandso many nuncupiscent words about how he
had been confarreating teat-a-teat with two viragos intactas about
what an awful life he led, poorish priced, uttering mass for a
coppall of geldings and what a lawful day it was, there and then,
for a consommation with an effusion and how, by all the manny
larries ate pignatties, how, hell in tunnels, he'd marry me any
old buckling time as flying quick as he'd look at me) and I am
giving youth now again in words of style byaway of offertory
hisand mikeadvice, an it place the person, as ere he retook him
to his cure, those verbs he said to me. From above. The most
eminent bishop titular of Dubloonik to all his purtybusses in
Dellabelliney. Comeallyedimseldamsels, siddle down and lissle
all! Follow me close! Keep me in view! Understeady me saries!
Which is to all practising massoeurses from a preaching freer and
be a gentleman without a duster before a parlourmade without a spitch. Now. During our brief apsence from this furtive
feugtig season adhere to as many as probable of the ten commandments touching purgations and indulgences and in the long
run they will prove for your better guidance along your path of
right of way. Where the lisieuse are we and what's the first sing
to be sung? Is it rubrics, mandarimus, pasqualines, or verdidads
is in it, or the bruiselivid indecores of estreme voyoulence and,
for the lover of lithurgy, bekant or besant, where's the fate's to
be wished for? Several sindays after whatsintime. I'll sack that sick
server the minute I bless him. That's the mokst I can do for his
grapce. Economy of movement, axe why said. I've a hopesome's
choice if I chouse of all the sinkts in the colander. From the com-

mon for ignitious Purpalume to the proper of Francisco Ultramare,
last of scorchers, third of snows, in terrorgammons howdydos.
Here she's, is a bell, that's wares in heaven, virginwhite, Undetri-
gesima, vikissy manonna. Doremon's! The same or similar to be
kindly observed within the affianced dietcess of Gay O'Toole
and Gloamy Gwenn du Lake (Danish spoken!) from Manducare
Monday up till farrier's siesta in china dominos. Words taken in
triumph, my sweet assistance, from the sufferant pen of our joco-
sus inkerman militant of the reed behind the ear.

Never miss your lostsomewhere mass for the couple in Myles
you butrose to brideworship. Never hate mere pork which is bad
for your knife of a good friday. Never let a hog of the howth
trample underfoot your linen of Killiney. Never play lady's game
for the Lord's stake. Never lose your heart away till you win his
diamond back. Make a strong point of never kicking up your
rumpus over the scroll end of sofas in the Dar Bey Coll Cafeteria
by tootling risky *apropos* songs at commercial travellers' smokers
for their Columbian nights entertainments the like of *White limbs
they never stop teasing* or *Minxy was a Manxmaid when Murry
wor a Man.* And, by the bun, is it you goes bisbuiting His Esaus
and Cos and then throws them bag in the box? Why the tin's
nearly empty. First thou shalt not smile. Twice thou shalt not
love. Lust, thou shalt not commix idolatry. Hip confiners help
compunction. Never park your brief stays in the men's con-
venience. Never clean your buttoncups with your dirty pair of
sassers. Never ask his first person where's your quickest cut to
our last place. Never let the promising hand usemake free of
your oncemaid sacral. The soft side of the axe! A coil of cord, a
colleen coy, a blush on a bush turned first man's laughter into
wailful moither. O foolish cuppled! Ah, dice's error! Never dip
in the ern while you've browsers on your suite. Never slip the
silver key through your gate of golden age. Collide with man,
collude with money. Ere you sail foreget my prize. Where you
truss be circumspicious and look before you leak, dears. Never
christen medlard apples till a swithin is in sight. Wet your thistle
where a weed is and you'll rue it despyneedis. Especially beware

please of being at a party to any demoralizing home life. That
saps a chap. Keep cool faith in the firm, have warm hoep in the
house and begin frem athome to be chary of charity. Where it
is nobler in the main to supper than the boys and errors of out-
rager's virtue. Give back those stolen kisses; restaure those all-
cotten glooves. Recollect the yella perals that all too often beset
green gerils, Rhidarhoda and Daradora, once they gethobby-
horsical playing breeches parts for Bessy Sudlow in flesh-
coloured pantos instead of earthing down in the coalhole trying
to boil the big gun's dinner. Leg-before-Wicked lags-behind-
Wall where here Mr Whicker whacked a great fall. Femora-
familla feeled it a candleliked but Hayes, Conyngham and Erobin-
son sware it's an egg. Forglim mick aye! Stay, forestand and
tillgive it! Remember the biter's bitters I shed the vigil I buried
our Harlotte Quai from poor Mrs Mangain's of Britain Court on
the feast of Marie Maudlin. Ah, who would wipe her weeper dry
and lead her to the halter? Sold in her heyday, laid in the straw,
bought for one puny petunia. Moral: if you can't point a lily get
to henna out of here. Put your swell foot foremost on foulardy
pneumonia shertwaists, irriconcilible with true fiminin risirvi-
tion and ribbons of lace, limenick's disgrace. Sure, what is it on the
whole only holes tied together, the merest and transparent washing-
tones to make Languid Lola's lingery longer? Scenta Clauthes
stiffstuffs your hose and heartsies full of temptiness. Vanity flee
and Verity fear! Diobell! Whalebones and buskbutts may hurt
you (thwackaway thwuck!) but never lay bare your breast secret (dickette's place!) to joy a Jonas in the Dolphin's Barncar
with your meetual fan, Doveyed Covetfilles, comepulsing payn-
attention spasms between the averthisment for Ulikah's wine and
a pair of pulldoors of the old cupiosity shape. There you'll fix
your eyes darkled on the autocart of the bringfast cable but here
till youre martimorphysed please sit still face to face. For if the
shorth of your skorth falls down to his knees pray how wrong
will he look till he rises? Not before Gravesend is commuted. But
now reappears Autist Algy, the pulcherman and would-do per-
former, *oleas* Mr Smuth, stated by the vice crusaders to be well

known to all the dallytaunties in and near the ciudad of Buellas
Arias, taking you to the playguehouse to see the *Smirching of
Venus* and asking with whispered offers in a very low bearded
voice, with a nice little tiny manner and in a very nice little tony
way, won't you be an artist's moral and pose in your nudies as a
local esthetic before voluble old masters, introducing you, left
to right the party comprises, to hogarths like Bottisilly and
Titteretto and Vergognese and Coraggio with their extrahand
Mazzaccio, plus the usual bilker's dozen of dowdycameramen.
And the volses of lewd Buylan, for innocence! And the phylli-
sophies of Bussup Bulkeley. O, the frecklessness of the giddies
nouveautays. There's many's the icepolled globetopper is haunted by the hottest spot under his equator like Ramrod, the meaty
hunter, always jaeger for a thrust. The back beautiful, the un-
draped divine! And Suzy's Moedl's with their Blue Danuboyes!
All blah! Viper's vapid vilest! Put off the old man at the very
font and get right on with the nutty sparker round the back.
Slip your oval out of touch and let the paravis be your goal.
Up leather, Prunella, convert your try! Stick wicks in your ear-
shells when you hear the prompter's voice. Look on a boa in
his beauty and you'll never more wear your strawberry leaves.
Rely on the relic. What bondman ever you bind on earth I'll be
bound 'twas combined in hemel. Keep airly hores and the worm
is yores. Dress the pussy for her nighty and follow her piggy-
tails up their way to Winkyland. See little poupeep she's firsht
ashleep. After having sat your poetries and you know what
happens when chine throws over jupan. Go to doss with
the poulterer, you understand, and shake up with the milch-
mand. The Sully van vultures are on the prowl. And the
hailies firigringmaries. Tobaccos tabu and toboggan's a back
seat. Secret satieties and onanymous letters make the great un-
watched as bad as their betters. Don't on any account acquire
a paunchon for that alltoocommon fagbutt habit of frequenting
and chumming together with the braces of couples in Mr Tun-
nelly's hallways (smash it) wriggling with lowcusses and cock-
chafers and vamps and rodants, with the end to commit acts of

interstipital indecency as between twineties and tapegarters,
fingerpats on fondlepets, under the couvrefeu act. It's the thin
end; wedge your steps! Your high powered hefty hoyden thinks
nothing of ramping through a whole suite of smokeless husbands. Three minutes I'm counting you. Woooooon. No triching
now! Give me that when I tell you! *Raga**ʐ**ʐa ladra!* And is that
any place to be smuggling his madam's apples up? Deceitful
jade. Gee wedge! Begor, I like the way they're half cooked.
Hold, flay, grill, fire that laney feeling for kosenkissing disgeni-
cally within the proscribed limits like Population Peg on a hint or
twim clandestinely does be doing to Temptation Tom, atkings
questions in barely and snakking svarewords like a nursemagd.
While there's men-a'war on the say there'll be loves-o'women
on the do. Love through the usual channels, cisternbrothelly,
when properly disinfected and taken neat in the generable way
upon retiring to roost in the company of a husband-in-law or
other respectable relative of an apposite sex, not love that leads
by the nose as I foresmellt but canalised love, you understand,
does a felon good, suspiciously if he has a slugger's liver but I
cannot belabour the point too ardently (and after the lessions of
experience I speak from inspiration) that fetid spirits is the thief
of prurities, so none of your twenty rod cherrywhisks, me
daughter! At the Cat and Coney or the Spotted Dog. And at
2bis Lot's Road. When parties get tight for each other they lose
all respect together. By the stench of her fizzle and the glib of her
gab know the drunken draggletail Dublin drab. You'll pay for
each bally sorraday night every billing sumday morning. When
the night is in May and the moon shines might. We won't meeth
in Navan till you try to give the Kellsfrieclub the goby. Hill or
hollow, Hull or Hague! And beware how you dare of wet cock-
tails in Kildare or the same may see your wedding driving home
from your wake. Mades of ashens when you flirt spoil the lad
but spare his shirt! Lay your lilylike long his shoulder but buck
back if he buts bolder and just hep your homely hop and heed
no horning but if you've got some brainy notion to raise cancan
and rouse commotion I'll be apt to flail that tail for you till it's

borning. Let the love ladleliked at the eye girde your gastricks
in the gym. Nor must you omit to screw the lid firmly on that
jazz jiggery and kick starts. Bumping races on the flat and point
to point over obstacles. Ridewheeling that acclivisciously up
windy Rutland Rise and insighting rebellious northers before the
saunter of the city of Dunlob. Then breretonbiking on the free
with your airs of go-be-dee and your heels upon the handlebars.
Berrboel brazenness! No, before your corselage rib is decartilaged,
that is to mean if you have visceral ptosis, my point is making
allowances for the fads of your weak abdominal wall and your
liver asprewl, vinvin, vinvin, or should you feel, in shorts, as
though you needed healthy physicking exorcise to flush your
kidneys, you understand, and move that twelffinger bowel and
threadworm inhibitating it, lassy, and perspire freely, lict your
lector in the lobby and why out you go by the ostiary on to
the dirt track and skip. Be a sportive. Deal with Nature the great
greengrocer and pay regularly the monthlies. Your Punt's Perfume's only in the hatpinny shop beside the reek of the rawny.
It's more important than air—I mean than eats—air (Oop, I
never open momouth but I pack mefood in it) and promotes that
natural emotion. Stamp out bad eggs. Why so many puddings
prove disappointing, as Dietician says, in Creature Comforts
Causeries, and why so much soup is so muck slop. If we
could fatten on the elizabeetons we wouldn't have teeth like
the hippopotamians. However. Likewise if I were in your
envelope shirt I'd keep my weathereye well cocked open for
your furnished lodgers paying for their feed on tally with
company and piano tunes. Only stuprifying yourself! The too
friendly friend sort, Mazourikawitch or some other sukinsin of
a vitch, who he's kommen from olt Pannonia on this porpoise
whom sue stooderin about the maul and femurl artickles and who
mix himself so at home mid the musik and spanks the ivory
that lovely for this your Mistro Melosiosus MacShine MacShane
may soon prove your undoing and bane through the succeeding
years of rain should you, whilst Jaun is from home, get used to
basking in his loverslowlap, inordinately clad, moustacheteasing,

when closehended together behind locked doors, kissing steadily,
(malbongusta, it's not the thing you know) with the calfloving
selfseeker, under the influence of woman, inching up to you, dis-
arranging your modesties and fumbling with his forte paws in your
bodice after your billy doos twy as a first go off (take care, would
you stray and split on me!) and going on doing his idiot every
time you gave him his chance to get thick and play piggly-wiggly,
making much of you, bilgetalking like a ditherer, gougouzoug,
about your glad neck and the round globe and the white milk and
the red raspberries (O horrifier!) and prying down furthermore to
chance his lucky arm with his pregnant questions up to our past
lives. What has that caught to sing with him? The next fling
you'll be squitting on the Tubber Nakel, pouring pitchers to the
well for old Gloatsdane's glorification and the postequities of
the Black Watch, peeping private from the Bush and Rangers.
And our local busybody, talker-go-bragk. Worse again! Off of
that praying fan on to them priars! It would be a whorable state
of affairs altogether for the redcolumnists of presswritten epics,
Peter Paragraph and Paulus Puff, (I'm keepsoaking them to cover
my concerts) to get ahold of for their balloons and shoot you
private by surprise, considering the marriage slump that's on this
oil age and pulexes three shillings a pint and wives at six and
seven when domestic calamities belame par and newlaids bellow
mar for the twenty twotoosent time thwealthy took thousands
in the slack march of civilisation were you, becoming guilty of
unleckylike intoxication to have and to hold, to pig and to pay
direct connection *qua* intervener with a prominent married member
of the vicereeking squad and in consequence of the therinunder
subpenas be flummoxed to the second degree by becoming a
detestificated companykeeper on the dammymonde of Luca-
lamplight. Anything but that, for the fear and love of gold! Once
and for all, I'll have no college swankies (you see, I am well
voiced in love's arsenal and all its overtures from collion boys
to colleen bawns so I have every reason to know that rogues'
gallery of nightbirds and bitchfanciers, lucky duffs and light
lindsays, haughty hamiltons and gay gordons, dosed, doctored

and otherwise, messing around skirts and what their fickling intentions look like, you make up your mind to that) trespassing on your danger zone in the dancer years. If ever I catch you at it, mind, it's you that will cocottch it! I'll tackle you to feel if you have a few devils in you. Holy gun, I'll give it to you, hot, high and heavy before you can say sedro! Or may the maledictions of Lousyfear fall like nettlerash on the white friar's father that converted from moonshine the fostermother of the first nancy-free that ran off after the trumpadour that mangled Moore's melodies and so upturned the tubshead of the stardaft journalwriter to inspire the prime finisher to fellhim the firtree out of which Cooper Funnymore planed the flat of the beerbarrel on which my grandydad's lustiest sat his seat of unwisdom with my tante's petted sister for the cause of his joy! Amene.

Poof! There's puff for ye, begor, and planxty of it, all abound me breadth! Glor galore and glory be! As broad as its lung and as long as a line! The valiantine vaux of Venerable Val Vousdem. If my jaws must brass away like the due drops on my lay. And the topnoted delivery you'd expected be me invoice! Theo Dunnohoo's warning from Daddy O'Dowd. Whoo? What I'm wondering to myselfwhose for there's a strong tendency to put it mildly by making me the medium. I feel spirts of itchery outching out from all over me and only for the sludgehummer's force in my hand to hold them the darkens alone knows what'll who'll be saying of next. However. Now, before my upperotic rogister, something nice. Now? Dear Sister, in perfect leave again I say take a brokerly advice and keep it to yourself that we, Jaun, first of our name here now make all receptacles of free of price. Easy, my dear, if they tingle you either say nothing or nod. No cheeka-cheek with chipperchapper, you and your last mashboy and the padre in the pulpbox enumerating you his nostrums. Be vacillant over those vigilant who would leave you to belave black on white. Close in for psychical hijiniks as well but fight shy of mugpunters. I'd burn the books that grieve you and light an allassundrian bompyre that would suffragate Tome Plyfire or Zolfanerole. Perousse instate your *Weekly Standerd*, our verile organ that is ethelred by all pressdom. Apply your five wits to the four verilatest. The Arsdiken's *An Traitey on Miracula or Viewed to Death by a Priest Hunter* is still first in the field despite the castle bar, William Archer's a rompan good cathalogue and he'll give you a riser on the route to our nazional labronry. Skim over *Through Hell with the Papes* (mostly boys) by the divine comic Denti Alligator (exsponging your index) and find a quip in a quire arisus aream from bastardtitle to fatherjohnson. Swear aloud by pious fiction the like of *Lentil Lore* by Carnival Cullen or that *Percy Wynns* of our S. J. Finn's or *Pease in Plenty* by the Curer of Wars, licensed and censered by our most picturesque prelates, Their Graces of Linzen and Petitbois, bishops of Hibernites, *licet ut lebanus*, for expansion on the promises, the two best sells on the market this luckiest year, set up by Gill the father, put out by Gill the son and circulating disimally at Gillydehooly's Cost. Strike up a nodding acquaintance for our doctrine with the works of old Mrs Trot, senior, and Manoel Canter, junior, and Loper de Figas, nates maximum. I used to follow Mary Liddlelambe's flitsy tales, espicially with the scentaminted sauce. Sifted science will do your arts good. *Egg Laid by Former Cock* and *With Flageolettes in Send Fanciesland*. Chiefly girls. Trip over sacramental tea into the long lives of our saints and saucerdotes, with vignettes, cut short into instructual primers by those in authority for the bittermint of your soughts. Forfet not the palsied. Light a match for poor old Contrabally and send some balmoil for the schizmatics. A hemd in need is aye a friendly deed. Remember, maid, thou dust art powder but Cinderella thou must return (what are you robbing her sleeve for, Ruby? And pull in your tongue, Polly!). Cog that out of your teen times, everyone. The lad who brooks no breaches lifts the lass that toffs a tailor. How dare ye be laughing out of your mouthshine at the lack of that? Keep cool your fresh chastity which is far better far. Sooner than part with that vestalite emerald of the first importance, descended to me by far from our family, which you treasure up so closely where extremes meet, nay, mozzed lesmended, rather let the whole ekumene universe belong to merry Hal and do whatever his Mary well likes. When the gong goes for hornets-two-nest marriage step into your harness and strip off that nullity suit. Faminy, hold back! For the race is to the rashest of, the romping, jomping rushes of. Haul Seton's down, black, green and grey, and hoist Mikealy's whey and sawdust. What's overdressed if underclothed? Poposht forstake me knot where there's white lets ope. Whisht! Blesht she that walked with good Jook Humprey for he made her happytight. Go! You can down all the dripping you can dumple to, and buffkid scouse too ad libidinum, in these lassitudes if you've parents and things to look after. That was what stuck to the Comtesse Cantilene while she was sticking out Mavis Toffeelips to feed her soprannated huspals, and it is henceforth associated with her names. La Dreeping! Die Droopink! The inimitable in puresuet of the inevitable! There's nothing to touch it,we are taucht,unless she'd care for a mouthpull of white pudding for the wish is on her rose marine and the lunchlight in her eye, so when you pet the rollingpin write my name on the pie. Guard that gem, Sissy, rich and rare, ses he. In this cold old worold who'll feel it? Hum! The jewel you're all so cracked about there's flitty few of them gets it for there's nothing now but the sable stoles and a runabout to match it. Sing him a ring. Touch me low. And I'll lech ye so, my soandso. Show and show. Show on show. She. Shoe. Shone.

Divulge, sjuddenly jouted out hardworking Jaun, kicking the console to his double and braying aloud like Brahaam's ass, and, as his voixehumanar swelled to great, clenching his manlies, so highly strong was he, man, and gradually quite warming to her (there must have been a power of kinantics in that buel of gruel he gobed at bedgo) divorce into me and say the curname in undress (if you get into trouble with a party you are not likely to forget his appearance either) of any lapwhelp or sleevemongrel who talks to you upon the road where he tuck you to be a roller, O, (the goattanned saxopeeler upshotdown chigs peel of him!) and volunteers to trifle with your roundlings for proffered glass and dough, the marrying hand that his leisure repents of, without taking out his proper password

from the eligible ministriss for affairs with the black fremdling,
that enemy of our country, in a cleanlooking light and I don't
care a tongser's tammany hang who the mucky is nor twoo
hoots in the corner nor three shouts on a hill (were he even
a constantineal namesuch of my very own, Attaboy Knowling,
and like enoch to my townmajor ancestors, the two that are
taking out their divorces in the Spooksbury courts circuits,
Rere Uncle Remus, the Baas of Eboracum and Old Father
Ulissabon Knickerbocker, the lanky sire of Wolverhampton,
about their bristelings), but as true as there's a soke for sakes in
Twoways Peterborough and sure as home we come to newsky
prospect from west the wave on schedule time (if I came any
quicker I'll be right back before I left) from the land of breach
of promise with Brendan's mantle whitening the Kerribrasilian
sea and March's pebbles spinning from beneath our footslips to
carry fire and sword, rest insured that as we value the very name
in sister that as soon as we do possibly it will be a poor lookout
for that insister. He's a markt man from that hour. And why do
we say that, you may query me? Quary? Guess! Call'st thou?
Think and think and think, I urge on you. Muffed! The wrong
porridge. You are an ignoratis! Because then probably we'll
dumb well soon show him what the Shaun way is like how we'll
go a long way towards breaking his outsider's face for him for
making up to you with his bringthee balm of Gaylad and his
singthee songs of Arupee, chancetrying my ward's head into
sanctuary before feeling with his two dimensions for your nuptial dito. Ohibow, if I was Blonderboss I'd gooandfrighthisdual-
man! Now, we'll tell you what we'll do to be sicker instead of
compensation. We'll he'll burst our his mouth like Leary to the
Leinsterface and reduce he'll we'll ournhisn liniments to a
poolp. Open the door softly, somebody wants you, dear. You'll
hear him calling you, bump, like a blizz, in the muezzin of the
turkest night. Come on now, pillarbox! I'll stiffen your scribeall,
broken reed! That'll be it, grand operoar style, even should I,
with my sleuts of hogpew and cheekas, have to coomb the brash
of the libs round Close Saint Patrice to lay my louseboob on his

behaitch like solitar. We are all eyes. I have his quoram of images all on my retinue, Mohomadhawn Mike. Brassup! Moreover after that bad manners to me if I don't think strongly about giving the brotherkeeper into custody to the first police bubey cunstabless of Dora's Diehards in the field I might chance to follopon. Or for that matter, for your information, if I get the wind up what do you bet in the buckets of my wrath I mightn't even take it into my progromme, as sweet course, to do a rash act and pitch in and swing for your perfect stranger in the meadow of heppiness and then wipe the street up with the clonmellian, pending my bringing proceedings verses the joyboy before a bunch of magistrafes and twelve good and gleeful men. *Filius nullius per fas et nefas*. It should prove more or less of an event and show the widest federal in my cup. He'll have pansements then for his pensamientos, howling for peace. Pretty knocks, I promise him with plenty burkes for his shins. Dumnlimn wimn humn. In which case I'll not be complete in fighting lust until I contrive to half kill your Charley you're my darling for you and send him to Home Surgeon Hume, the algebrist, before his appointed time, particularly should he turn out to be a man in brown about town, Rollo the Gunger, son of a wants a flurewaltzer to Arnolff's, picking up ideas, of well over or about fiftysix or so, pithecoid proportions, with perhops five foot eight, the usual X Y Z type, R.C. Toc H, nothing but claret, not in the studbook by a long stortch, with a toothbrush moustache and jawcrockeries, *alias* grinner through collar, and of course no beard, meat and colmans suit, with tar's baggy slacks, obviously too roomy for him and springside boots, washing tie, Father Mathew's bridge pin, sipping some Wheatley's at Rhoss's on a barstool, with some pubpal of the Olaf Stout kidney, always trying to poorchase movables by hebomedaries for to putt in a new house to loot, cigarette in his holder, with a good job and pension in Buinness's, what about our trip to Normandy style conversation, with an occasional they say that filmacoulored featured at the Mothrapurl skrene about Michan and his lost angeleens is corkyshows do morvaloos, blueygreen eyes a bit scummy developing a series of angry boils with certain references to the Deity, seeking relief in alcohol and so on, general omnibus character with a dash of railwaybrain, stale cough and an occasional twinge of claudication, having his favourite fecundclass family of upwards of a decade, both harefoot and loadenbrogued, to boot and buy·off, Imean.

So let it be a knuckle or an elbow, I hereby admonish you. It may all be topping fun but it's tip and run and touch and flow for every whack when Marie stopes Phil fluther's game to go. Arms arome, side aside, face into the wall. To the tumble of the toss tot the trouble of the swaddled, O. And lest there be no misconception, Miss Forstowelsy, over who to fasten the plight- forlifer on (threehundred and thirty three to one on Rue the Day!) when the nice little smellar squalls in his crydle what the dirty old bigger'll be squealing through his coughin you better keep in the gunbarrel straight around vokseburst as I recommence you to (you gypseyeyed baggage, do you hear what I'm praying?) or, Gash, without butthering my head to assortail whose stroke forced or which struck backly, I'll be all over you myselx hori- zontally, as the straphanger said, for knocking me with my name and yourself and your babybag down at such a greet sacrifice with a rap of the gavel to a third price cowhandler as cheap as the nig- gerd's dirt (for sale!) or I'll smack your fruitflavoured jujube lips well for you so I will well for you if you don't keep a civil tongue in your pigeonhouse. The pleasures of love lasts but a fleeting but the pledges of life outlusts a lieftime. I'll have it in for you. I'll teach you bed minners, tip for tap, to be playing your oddaugghter tangotricks with micky dazzlers if I find corsehairs on your river-frock and the squirmside of your burberry lupitally covered with chiffchaff and shavings. Up Rosemiry Lean and Potanasty Rod you wos, wos you? I overstand you, you understand. Ask- ing Annybettyelsas to carry your parcels and you dreaming of net glory. You'll ging naemaer wi'Wolf the Ganger. Cutting chapel, were you? and had dates with slickers in particular hotels, had we? Lonely went to play your mother, isod? You was wiffriends? Hay, dot's a doll yarn! Mark mean then! I'll homeseek you, Luperca as sure as there's a palatine in Limerick and in

striped conference here's how. Nerbu de Bios! If you twos goes
to walk upon the railway, Gard, and I'll goad to beat behind the
bush. See to it! Snip! It's up to you. I'll be hatsnatching harrier
to hiding huries hinder hedge. Snap! I'll tear up your limpshades
and lock all your trotters in the closet, I will, and cut your silk-
skin into garters. You'll give up your ask unbrodhel ways when
I make you reely smart. So skelp your budd and kiss the hurt!
I'll have plenary sadisfaction, plays the bishop, for your partial's
indulgences if your my rodeo gell. Fair man and foul suggestion.
There's a lot of lecit pleasure coming bangslanging your way,
Miss Pinpernelly satin. For your own good, you understand, for
the man who lifts his pud to a woman is saving the way for
kindness. You'll rebmemer your mottob *Aveh Tiger Roma*
mikely smarter the nickst time. For I'll just draw my prancer
and give you one splitpuck in the crupper, you understand, that
will bring the poppy blush of shame to your peony hindmost till
you yelp papapardon and radden your rhodatantarums to the
beat of calorrubordolor, I am, I do and I suffer; (do you hear me
now, lickspoon, and stop looking at your bussycat bow in the
slate?) that you won't obliterate for the bulkier part of a running
year, failing to give a good account of yourself, if you think I'm
so tan cupid as all that. Lights out now (bouf!), tight and sleep
on it. And that's how I'll bottle your greedypuss beautibus for
ye, me bullin heifer, for 'tis I that have the peer of arrams that
carry a wallop. Between them.

Unbeknownst to you would ire turn o'er see, a nuncio would
I return here. How (from the sublime to the ridiculous) times
out of oft, my future, shall we think with deepest of love and
recollection by rintrospection of thee but me far away on the
pillow, breathing foundly o'er my names all through the empties,
whilst moidhered by the rattle of the doppeldoorknockers. Our
homerole poet to Ostelinda, Fred Wetherly, puts it somewhys
better. You're sitting on me style, maybe, whereoft I helped
your ore. Littlegame rumilie from Liffalidebankum, (Toobli-
queme!) but a big corner fill you do in this unadulterated seat of
our affections. Aerwenger's my breed so may we uncreepingly

multipede like the sands on Amberhann. Sevenheavens, O heaven!
Iy waount yiou! yore ways to melittleme were wonderful so
Ickam purseproud in sending uym loveliest pansiful thoughts
touching me dash in-you through wee dots Hyphen, the so
pretty arched godkin of beddingnights. If I've proved to your
sallysfashion how I'm a man of Armor let me so, let me sue, let
me see your isabellis. How I shall, should I survive, as, please the
uniter of U.M.I. hearts, I am living in hopes to do, replacing
mig wandering handsup in yawers so yeager for mitch, positively
cover the two pure chicks of your comely plumpchake with
zuccherikissings, hong, kong, and so gong, that I'd scare the bats
out of the ivfry one of those puggy mornings, honestly, by my
rantandog and daddyoak I will, become come coming when,
upon the mingling of our meeting waters, wish to wisher, like
massive mountains to part no more, you will there and then, in
those happy moments of ouryour soft accord, rainkiss on me
back, for full marks with shouldered arms, and in that united
I.R.U. stade, when I come (touf! touf!) wildflier's fox into my
own greengeese again, swap sweetened smugs, six of one for half
a dozen of the other, till they'll bet we're the cuckoo derby
when cherries next come back to Ealing as come they must, as
they musted in their past, as they must for my pressing season,
as hereinafter must they chirrywill immediately suant on my
safe return to ignorance and bliss in my horseless Coppal Poor,
through suirland and noreland kings country and queens, with
my ropes of pearls for gamey girls the way ye'll hardly. Knowme.

Slim ye, come slum with me and rally rats' roundup. 'Tis
post purification we will, sales of work and social service,
missus, completing our Abelite union by the adoptation of
fosterlings. Embark for Euphonia! Up Murphy, Henson and
O'Dwyer, the Warchester Warders! I'll put in a shirt time
if you'll get through your shift and between us in our shared
slaves, brace to brassiere and shouter to shunter, we'll pull off our
working programme. Come into the garden guild and be free
of the gape athome. We'll circumcivicise all Dublin country.
Let us, the real Us, all ignite in our prepurgatory grade as apos-

cals and be instrumental to utensilise, help our Jakeline sisters
clean out the hogshole and generally ginger things up. Meliorism
in massquantities, raffling receipts and sharing sweepstakes till
navel, spokes and felloes hum like hymn. Burn only what's Irish,
accepting their coals. You will soothe the cokeblack bile that's
Anglia's and touch Armourican's iron core. Write me your
essayes, my vocational scholars, but corsorily, dipping your
nose in it, for Henrietta's sake on mortinatality in the life of
jewries and the sludge of King Haarington's at its height, running
boulevards over the whole of it. I'd write it all by mownself if
I only had here of my jolly young watermen. Bear in mind, by
Michael, all the provincial's bananas peels and elacock eggs making drawadust jubilee along Henry, Moore, Earl and Talbot
Streets. Luke at all the memmer manning he's dung for the pray
of birds, our priest-mayor-king-merchant, strewing the Castle-
knock Road and drawing manure upon it till the first glimpse of
Wales and from Ballses Breach Harshoe up to Dumping's Corner
with the Mirist fathers' brothers eleven versus White Friars out
on a rogation stag party. Compare them caponchin trowlers
with the Bridge of Belches in Fairview, noreast Dublin's favourite
souwest wateringplatz and ump as you lump it. What do you
mean by Jno Citizen and how do you think of Jas Pagan?
Compost liffe in Dufblin by Pierce Egan with the baugh in
Baughkley of Fino Ralli. Explain why there is such a number
of orders of religion in Asea! Why such an order number in
preference to any other number? Why any number in any order
at all? Now? Where is the greenest island off the black coats
of Spaign? Overset into universal: I am perdrix and upon my
pet ridge. Oralmus! Way, O way for the autointaxication of
our town of the Fords in a huddle! Hailfellow some wellmet
boneshaker or, to ascertain the facts for herself, run up your
showeryweather once and trust and take the Drumgondola tram
and, wearing the midlimb and vestee endorsed by the hierarchy
fitted with ecclastics, bending your steps, pick a trail and stand
on, say, Aston's, I advise you strongly, along quaith a copy of
the Seeds and Weeds Act when you have procured one for your-

self and take a good longing gaze into any nearby shopswindow
you may select at suppose, let us say, the hoyth of number
eleven, Kane or Keogh's, and in the course of about thirtytwo
minutes' time proceed to turn aroundabout on your heehills towards the previous causeway and I shall be very cruelly mistaken indeed if you will not be jushed astunshed to see how you
will be meanwhile durn weel topcoated with kakes of slush
occasioned by the mush jam of the cross and blackwalls traffic
in transit. See Capels and then fly. Show me that complaint book
here. Where's Cowtends Kateclean, the woman with the muckrake?
When will the W.D. face of our sow muckloved d'lin, the Troia
of towns and Carmen of cities, crawling with mendiants in per-
forated clothing, get its wellbelavered white like l'pool and
m'chester? When's that grandnational goldcapped dupsydurby
houspill coming with its vomitives for our mothers-in-load and
stretchers for their devitalised males? I am all of me for freedom
of speed but who'll disasperaguss Pope's Avegnue or who'll
uproose the Opian Way? Who'll brighton Brayhowth and bait
the Bull Bailey and never despair of Lorcansby? The rampant
royal commissioners! 'Tis an ill weed blows no poppy good. And
this labour's worthy of my higher. Oil for meed and toil for feed
and a walk with the band for Job Loos. If I hope not charity what
profiteers me? Nothing! My tippers of flags are knobs of hard-
shape for it isagrim tale, keeping the father of curls from the
sport of oak. Do you know what, liddle giddles? One of those
days I am advised by the smiling voteseeker who's now snoring
elued to positively strike off hiking for good and all as I bldy
well bdly ought until such temse as some mood is made under
privy-sealed orders to get me an increase of automoboil and footwear for these poor discalced and a bourse from bon Somewind for
a cure at Badanuweir (though where it's going to come from this
time —) as I sartunly think now, honest to John, for an income
plexus that that's about the sanguine boundary limit. Amean.

Sis dearest, Jaun added, with voise somewhit murky, what
though still high·fa luting, as he turned his dorse to her to pay
court to it, and ouverleaved his booseys to give the note and

score, phonoscopically incuriosited and melancholic this time
whiles, as on the fulmament he gaped in wulderment, his on-
saturncast eyes in stellar attraction followed swift to an imagin-
ary swellaw, O, the vanity of Vanissy! All ends vanishing! Pur-
sonally, Grog help me, I am in no violent hurry. If time enough
lost the ducks walking easy found them. I'll nose a blue fonx
with any tristys blinking upon this earthlight of all them that
pass by the way of the deerdrive, conconey's run or wilfrid's
walk, but I'd turn back as lief as not if I could only spoonfind
the nippy girl of my heart's appointment, Mona Vera Toutou
Ipostila, my lady of Lyons, to guide me by gastronomy under
her safe conduct. That's more in my line. I'd ask no kinder of
fates than to stay where I am, with my tinny of brownie's tea,
under the invocation of Saint Jamas Hanway, servant of Gamp,
lapidated, and Jacobus a Pershawm, intercissous, for my thuri-
fex, with Peter Roche, that frind of my boozum, leaning on my
cubits, at this passing moment by localoption in the birds' lodging me, pheasants among, where I'll dreamt that I'll dwealth mid
warblers' walls when throstles and choughs to my sigh hiehied,
with me hares standing up well and me longlugs dittoes, where
a maurdering row, the fox! has broken at the coward sight till
well on into the beausome of the exhaling night, pinching stop-
andgo jewels out of the hedges and catching dimtop brilliants
on the tip of my wagger but for that owledclock (fast cease to it!)
has just gone twoohoo the hour and that yen breezes zipping
round by Drumsally do be devils to play fleurt. I could sit on safe
side till the bark of Saint Grouseus for hoopoe's hours, till heoll's
hoerrisings, laughing lazy at the sheep's lightning and turn a wida-
most ear dreamily to the drummling of snipers, hearing the wireless harps of sweet old Aerial and the mails across the nightrives
(peepet! peepet!) and whippoor willy in the woody (moor park!
moor park!) as peacefed as a philopotamus, and crekking jugs
at the grenoulls, leaving tealeaves for the trout and belleeks for the
wary till I'd followed through my upfielded neviewscope the
rugaby moon cumuliously godrolling himself westasleep amuckst
the cloudscrums for to watch how carefully my nocturnal goose-

mother would lay her new golden sheegg for me down under in
the shy orient. What wouldn't I poach — the rent in my riverside, my otther shoes, my beavery, honest! — ay, and melt my
belt for a dace feast of grannom with the finny ones, those happy
greppies in their minnowahaw, flashing down the swansway,
leaps ahead of the swift MacEels, the big Gillaroo redfellows
and the pursewinded carpers, rearin antis rood perches astench
of me, or, when I'd like own company best, with the help of a
norange and bear, to be reclined by the lasher on my logansome,
my g.b.d. in my f.a.c.e., solfanelly in my shellyholders and lov'd
latakia, the benuvolent, for my nosethrills, with the jealosomines
wilting away to their heart's deelight and the king of saptimber
letting down his humely odours for my consternation, dapping
my griffeen, burning water in the spearlight or catching trophies
of the king's royal college of sturgeone by the armful for to bake
pike and pie while, O twined me abower in L'Alouette's Tower,
all Adelaide's naughtingerls juckjucking benighth me, I'd ga-
mut my twittynice Dorian blackbudds chthonic solphia off my
singasongapiccolo to pipe musicall airs on numberous fairy-
aciodes. I give, a king, to me, she does, alone, up there, yes see,
I double give, till the spinney all eclosed asong with them. Isn't
that lovely though? I give to me alone I trouble give! I may have
no mind to lamagnage the forte bits like the pianage but you
can't cadge me off the key. I've a voicical lilt too true. Nomario!
And bemolly and jiesis! For I sport a whatyoumacormack in the
latcher part of my throughers. And the lark that I let fly (olala!)
is as cockful of funantics as it's tune to my fork. Naturale you
might lower register me as diserecordant, but I'm athlone in the
lillabilling of killarnies. That's flat. Yet ware the wold, you!
What's good for the gorse is a goad for the garden. Lethals lurk
heimlocked in logans. Loathe laburnums. Dash the gaudy death-
cup. Bryony O'Bryony, thy name is Belladama! But enough of
greenwood's gossip. Birdsnests is birdsnests. Thine to wait but
mine to wage. And now play sharp to me. Doublefirst I'll head
foremost through all my examhoops. And what sensitive coin
I'd be possessed of at Latouche's, begor, I'd sink it sumtotal, every

dolly farting, in vestments of subdominal poteen at prime cost
and I bait you my chancey oldcoat against the whole ounce you
half on your backboard (if madamaud strips mesdamines may
cold strafe illglands!) that I'm the gogetter that'd make it pay like
cash registers as sure as there's a pot on a pole. And, what with one
man's fish and a dozen men's poissons, sowing my wild plums to
reap ripe plentihorns mead, lashings of erbole and hydromel and
bragget, I'd come out with my magic fluke in close time, fair,
free and frolicky, zooming tophole on the mart as a factor. And
I tell you the Bective's wouldn't hold me. By the unsleeping
Solman Annadromus, ye god of little pescies, nothing would
stop me for mony makes multimony like the brogues and the
kishes. Not the Ulster Rifles and the Cork Milice and the Dublin
Fusees and Connacht Rangers ensembled! I'd axe the channon
and leip a liffey and drink annyblack water that rann onme way.
Yip! How's thats for scats, mine shatz, for a lovebird? To funk is
only peternatural its daring feers divine. Bebold! Like Varian's
balaying all behind me. And before you knew where you
weren't, I stake my ignitial's divy, cash-and-cash-can-again, I'd
be staggering humanity and loyally rolling you over, my sow-
white sponse, in my tons of red clover, nighty nigh to the metro-
nome, fiehigh and fiehigher and fiehighest of all. Holy petter and
pal, I'd spoil you altogether, my sumptuous Sheila! Mumm all
to do brut frull up fizz and unpop a few shortusians or shake a
pale of sparkling ice, hear it swirl, happy girl. Not a spot of my
hide but you'd love to seek and scanagain! There'd be no standing me, I tell you. And, as gameboy as my pagan name K.C. is
what it is, I'd never say let fly till we shot that blissup and
swumped each other, manawife, into our sever nevers where I'd
plant you, my Gizzygay, on the electric ottoman in the lap of
lechery, simpringly stitchless with admiracion among the most
uxuriously furnished compartments, with sybarate chambers just
as I'd run my shoestring into near a million or so of them as a
firstclass dealer and everything. Only for one thing that, how-
over famiksed I would become, I'd he awful anxious, you understand, about shoepisser pluvious and in assideration of the terrible

luftsucks woabling around with the hedrolics in the coold amstop-
here till the borting that would perish the Dane and his chapter
of accidents to be atramental to the better half of my alltoolyrical
health, not considering my capsflap, and that's the truth now out
of the cackling bag for truly sure, for another thing, I never could
tell the leest falsehood that would truthfully give sotisfiction. I'm
not talking apple sauce eithou. Or up in my hat. I earnst. Schue!

Sissibis dearest, as I was reading to myself not very long ago
in Tennis Flonnels Mac Courther, his correspondance, besated
upon my tripos, and just thinking like thauthor how long I'd like
myself to be continued at Hothelizod, peeking into the focus and
pecking at thumbnail reveries, pricking up ears to my phono on
the ground and picking up airs from th'other over th'ether, 'tis
tramsported with grief I am this night sublime, as you may see
by my size and my brow that's all forehead, to go forth, frank
and hoppy, to the tune the old plow tied off, from our nostorey
house, upon this benedictine errand but it is historically the most
glorious mission, secret or profund, through all the annals of our
— as you so often term her — efferfreshpainted livy, in beautific
repose, upon the silence of the dead, from pharoph the nextfirst
down to ramescheckles the last bust thing. The Vico road goes
round and round to meet where terms begin. Still onappealed
to by the cycles and unappalled by the recoursers we feel all
serene, never you fret, as regards our dutyful cask. Full of my
breadth from pride I am (breezed be the healthy same!) for 'tis a
grand thing (superb!) to be going to meet a king, not an everynight king, nenni, by gannies, but the overking of Hither-on-
Thither Erin himself, pardee, I'm saying. Before there was patch
at all on Ireland there lived a lord at Lucan. We only wish
everyone was as sure of anything in this watery world as we are
of everything in the newlywet fellow that's bound to follow. I'll
lay you a guinea for a hayseed now. Tell mother that. And tell
her tell her old one. T'will amuse her.

Well, to the figends of Annanmeses with the wholeabuelish
business! For I declare to Jeshuam I'm beginning to get sunsick.
I'm not half Norawain for nothing. The fine ice so temperate

of our, alas, those times are not so far off as you might wish to
be congealed. So now, I'll ask of you, let ye create no scenes in
my poor primmafore's wake. I don't want yous to be billow-
fighting your biddy moriarty duels, gobble gabble, over me till
you spit stout, you understand, after soused mackerel, sniffling
clambake to hering and impudent barney, braggart of blarney,
nor you ugly lemoncholic gobs o'er the hobs in a sewing circle,
stopping oddments in maids' costumes at sweeping reductions,
wearing out your ohs by sitting around your ahs, making areek-
eransy round where I last put it, with the painters in too,
curse luck, with your rags up, exciting your mucuses, turning
breakfarts into lost soupirs and salon thay nor you flabbies on
your groaning chairs over Bollivar's troubles of a bluemoondag,
steamin your damp ossicles, praying Holy Prohibition and Jaun
Dyspeptist while Ole Clo goes through the wood with Shep
togather, touting in the chesnut burrs for Goodboy Sommers
and Mistral Blownowse hugs his kindlings when voiceyversy
it's my gala bene fit, robbing leaves out of my taletold book.
May my tunc fester if ever I see such a miry lot of maggalenes!
Once upon a drunk and a fairly good drunk it was and the rest
of your blatherumskite! Just a plain shays by the fire for absent-
er Sh the Po and I'll make ye all an eastern hummingsphere of
myself the moment that you name the way. Look in the slag
scuttle and you'll see me sailspread over the singing, and what
do ye want trippings for when you've Paris inspire your hat?
Sussumcordials all round, let ye alloyiss and ominies, while I
stray and let ye not be getting grief out of it, though blighted
troth be all bereft, on my poor headsake, even should we forfeit
our life. Lo, improving ages wait ye. In the orchard of the bones.
Some time very presently now when yon clouds are dissipated
after their forty years shower, the odds are, we shall all be hooked
and happy, communionistically, among the fieldnights eliceam
élite of the elect in the land of lost of time. Johannisburg's a revelation! Deck the diamants that never die! So cut out the lonesome stuff. Drink it up, ladies, please, as smart as you can lower
it. Out with lent! Clap hands postilium! Fastintide is by. Your

sole and myopper must hereupon part company. So for e'er fare thee welt! Parting's fun. Take thou, the wringle's thine, love. This dime doth trost thee from mine alms. Goodbye, swisstart, goodbye. Haugh! Haugh! Sure, treasures, a letterman does be often thought reading ye between lines that do have no sense at all. I sign myself. With much leg. Inflexibly yours. Ann Posht the Shorn. To be continued. Huck!

Something of a sidesplitting nature must have occurred to westminstrel Jaunathaun for a grand big blossy hearty stenorious laugh (even Drudge that lay doggo thought feathers fell) hopped out of his woolly's throat like a ball lifted over the head of a deep field, at the bare thought of how jolly they'd like to be trolling his whoop and all of them truetotypes in missammen massness were just starting to spladher splodher with the jolly magorios, hicky hecky hock, huges huges huges, hughy hughy hughy, O Jaun, so jokable and so geepy, O, (Thou pure! Our virgin! Thou holy! Our health! Thou strong! Our victory! O salutary! Sustain our firm solitude, thou who thou well strokest! Hear, hairy ones! We have sued thee but late. Beauty parlous.) when suddenly (how like a woman!), swifter as mercury he wheels right round starnly on the Rizzies suddenly, with his gimlets blazing rather sternish (how black like thunder!), to see what's loose. So they stood still and wondered. Till first he sighed (and how ill soufered!) and they nearly cried (the salt of the earth!) after which he pondered and finally he replied:

— There is some thing more. A word apparting and shall the heart's tone be silent. Engagements, I'll beseal you! Fare thee well, fairy well! All I can tell you is this, my sorellies. It's prayers in layers all the thumping time, begor, the young gloria's gang voices the old doxologers, in the suburrs of the heavenly gardens, once we shall have passed, after surceases, all serene through neck and necklike Derby and June to our snug eternal retribution's reward (the scorchhouse). Shunt us! shunt us! shunt us! If you want to be felixed come and be parked. Sacred ease there! The seanad and pobbel queue's remainder. To it, to it! Seekit headup! No petty family squabbles Up There nor homemade

hurricanes in our Cohortyard, no cupahurling nor apuckalips
nor no puncheon jodelling nor no nothing. With the Byrns
which is far better and eve for ever your idle be. You will hardly
reconnoitre the old wife in the new bustle and the farmer shinner
in his latterday paint. It's the fulldress Toussaint's wakeswalks
experdition after a bail motion from the chamber of horrus.
Saffron buns, or sovran bonhams whichever you'r avider to like
it and lump it, but give it a name. Iereny allover irelands. And
there's food for refection when the whole flock's at home. Hogmanny di'yegut? Hogmanny di'yesmellygut? And hogmanny
di'yesmellyspatterygut? You take Joe Hanny's tip for it. Post-
martem is the goods. With Jollification a tight second. Toborrow
and toburrow and tobarrow! That's our crass, hairy and ever-
grim life, till one finel howdiedow Bouncer Naster raps on the
bell with a bone and his stinkers stank behind him with the
sceptre and the hourglass. We may come, touch and go, from
atoms and ifs but we're presurely destined to be odd's without
ends. Here we moult in Moy Kain and flop on the seemy side,
living sure of hardly a doorstep for a stopgap, with Whogoes-
there and a live sandbag round the corner. But upmeyant Prospector you sprout all your abel and woof your wings dead
certain however of neuthing whatever to aye forever while
Hyam Hyam's in the chair. Ah, sure, pleasantries aside, in the tail
of the cow what a humpty daum earth looks our miseryme here-
today as compared beside the Herewearagain Gaieties of the
Afterpiece when the Royal Revolver of these real globoes lets
regally fire of his *mio colpo* for the chrisman's pandemon to give
over and the Harlequinade to begin properly SPQueaRking
Mark Time's Finist Joke. Putting Allspace in a Notshall.

Well, the slice and veg joint's well in its way, and so is a
ribroast and jackknife as sporten dish, but home cooking every-
time. Mountains good mustard and, with the helpings of ladies'
lickfings and gentlemen's relish, I've eaten a griddle. But I fill
twice as stewhard what I felt before when I'm after eating a few
natives. The crisp of the crackling is in the chawing. Give us another cup of your scald. Santos Mozos! That was a damn good

cup of scald! You could trot a mouse on it. I ingoyed your pick of hissing hot luncheon fine, I did, thanks awfully, (sublime!). Tenderest bully ever I ate with the boiled protestants (allinoilia allinoilia!) only for your peas again was a taste tooth psalty to carry flavour with my godown and hereby return with my best savioury condiments and a penny in the plate for the jemes. O.K. Oh Kosmos! Ah Ireland! A.I. And for kailkannonkabbis gimme Cincinnatis with Italian (but *ci vuol poco!*) ciccalick cheese, Haggis good, haggis strong, haggis never say die. For quid we have recipimus, recipe, O lout! And save that, Oliviero, for thy sunny day! Soupmeagre! Couldn't look at it! But if you'll buy me yon coat of the vairy furry best, I'll try and pullll it awn mee. It's in fairly good order and no doubt 'twill sarve to turn. Remove this boardcloth! Next stage, tell the tabler, for a variety of Huguenot ligooms I'll try my set on edges grapeling an aigrydoucks, grilled over birchenrods, with a few bloomancowls in albies. I want to get outside monasticism. Mass and meat mar no man's journey. Eat a missal lest. Nuts for the nerves, a flitch for the flue and for to rejoice the chambers of the heart the spirits of the spice isles, curry and cinnamon chutney and cloves. All the vitalmines is beginning to sozzle in chewn and the hormonies to clingleclangle, fudgem, kates and eaps and naboc and erics and oinnos on kingclud and xoxxoxo and xooxox xxoxoxxoxxx till I'm fustfed like fungstif and very presently from now posthaste it's off yourll see me ryuoll on my usual rounds again to draw Terminus Lower and Killadown and Letternoosh, Letterspeak, Lettermuck to Littorananima and the roomiest house even in Ireland, if you can understamp that, and my next item's platform it's how I'll try and collect my extraprofessional postages owing to me by Thaddeus Kellyesque Squire, dr, for nondesirable printed matter. The Jooks and the Kelly-Cooks have been milking turnkeys and sucking the blood out of the marshalsea since the act of First Offenders. But I know what I'll do. Great pains off him I'll take and that'll be your redletterday calendar, window machree. I'll knock it out of him! I'll stump it out of him! I'll rattattatter it out of him before I'll quit the doorstep of

old Con Connolly's residence! By the horn of twenty of both of
the two Saint Collopys, blackmail him I will in arrears or my
name's not penitent Ferdinand! And it's daily and hourly I'll
nurse him till he pays me fine fee. Ameal.

Well, here's looking at ye! If I never leave you biddies till
my stave is a bar I'd be tempted rigidly to become a passionate
father. Me hunger's weighed. Hungkung! Me anger's suaged!
Hangkang! Ye can stop as ye are, little lay mothers, and wait in
wish and wish in vain till the grame reaper draws nigh, with
the sickle of the sickles, as a blessing in disguise. Devil a curly
hair I care! If any lightfoot Clod Dewvale was to hold me up
dicksturping me and marauding me of my rights to my onus, yan,
tyan, tethera, methera, pimp, I'd let him have my best pair of
galloper's heels in the creamsourer. He will have better manners
I'm dished if he won't! Console yourself, drawhure deelish!
There's a refond of eggsized coming to you out of me so mind
you do me duty on me! Bruise your bulge below the belt till I
blewblack beside you. And you'll miss me more as the narrowing
weeks wing by. Someday duly, oneday truly, twosday newly,
till whensday. Look for me always at my west and I will think
to dine. A tear or two in time is all there's toot. And then in a
click of the clock, toot toot, and doff doff we pop with sinnerettes
in silkettes lining longroutes for His Diligence Majesty, our
longdistance laird that likes creation. To whoosh!

— Meesh, meesh, yes, pet. We were too happy. I knew something would happen. I understand but listen, drawher nearest,
Tizzy intercepted, flushing but flashing from her dove and dart
eyes as she tactilifully grabbed her male corrispondee to flusther
sweet nunsongs in his quickturned ear, I know, benjamin brother,
but listen, I want, girls palmassing, to whisper my whish. (She
like them like us, me and you, had thoud he n'er it would haltin so
lithe when leased is tacitempust tongue). Of course, engine dear,
I'm ashamed for my life (I must clear my throttle) over this lost
moment's gift of memento nosepaper which I'm sorry, my
precious, is allathome I with grief can call my own but all the
same, listen, Jaunick, accept this witwee's mite, though a jenny-

teeny witween piece torn in one place from my hands in second
place of a linenhall valentino with my fondest and much left to
tutor. X.X.X.X. It was heavily bulledicted for young Fr Ml,
my pettest parriage priest, and you know who between us by
your friend the pope, forty ways in forty nights, that's the
beauty of it, look, scene it, ratty. Too perfectly priceless for
words. And, listen, now do enhance me, oblige my fiancy and
bear it with you morn till life's e'en and, of course, when never
you make usage of it, listen, please kindly think galways again
or again, never forget, of one absendee not sester Maggy. Ahim.
That's the stupidest little cough. Only be sure you don't catch your
cold and pass it on to us. And, since levret bounds and larks is
soaring, don't be all the night. And this, Joke, a sprig of blue
speedwell just a spell of floralora so you'll mind your veronique.
Of course, Jer, I know you know who sends it, presents that
please, mercy, on the face of the waters like that film obote,
awfly charmig of course, but it doesn't do her justice, apart from
her cattiness, in the magginbottle. Of course, please too write,
won't you, and leave your little bag of doubts, inquisitive, behind you unto your utterly thine, and, thank you, forward it
back by return pigeon's pneu to the loving in case I couldn't
think who it was or any funforall happens I'll be so curiose to
see in the Homesworth breakfast tablotts as I'll know etherways
by pity bleu if it's good for my system, what exquisite buttons,
gorgiose, in case I don't hope to soon hear from you. And thanks
ever so many for the ten and the one with nothing at all on. I will
tie a knot in my stringamejip to letter you with my silky paper,
as I am given now to understand it will be worth my price in
money one day so don't trouble to ans unless sentby special as
I am getting his pay and wants for nothing so I can live simply
and solely for my wonderful kinkless and its loops of loveliness.
When I throw away my rollets there's rings for all. Flee a girl
says it is her colour. So does B and L and as for V! And listen
to it! Cheveluir! So distant you're always. Bow your boche!
Absolutely perfect! I will pack my comb and mirror to praxis
oval owes and artless awes and it will follow you pulpicly

as far as come back under all my eyes like my sapphire chaplets of ringarosary I will say for you to the Allmichael and
solve qui pu while the dovedoves pick my mouthbuds (msch!
msch!) with nurse Madge, my linkingclass girl, she's a fright,
poor old dutch, in her sleeptalking when I paint the measles
on her and mudstuskers to make her a man. We. We. Issy
done that, I confesh. But you'll love her for her hessians
and sickly black stockies, cleryng's jumbles, salvadged from
the wash, isn't it the cat's tonsils! Simply killing, how she
tidies her hair! I call her Sosy because she's sosiety for me
and she says sossy while I say sassy and she says will
you have some more scorns while I say won't you take a few
more schools and she talks about ithel dear while I simply
never talk about athel darling she's but nice for enticing my
friends and she loves your style considering she breaksin me
shoes for me when I've arch trouble and she would kiss my
white arms for me so gratefully but apart from that she's
terribly nice really, my sister, round the elbow of Erne street
Lower and I'll be strictly forbidden always and true in my own
way and private where I will long long to betrue you along with
one who will so betrue you that not once while I betreu him not
once well he be betray himself. Can't you understand? O bother,
I must tell the trouth! My latest lad's lovelileter I am sore I done
something with. I like him lots coss he never cusses. Pity bon-
hom. Pip pet. I shouldn't say he's pretty but I'm cocksure he's
shy. Why I love taking him out when I unletched his cordon
gate. Ope, Jack, and atem! Obealbe myodorers and he dote so.
He fell for my lips, for my lisp, for my lewd speaker. I felt for
his strength, his manhood, his do you mind? There can be no
candle to hold to it, can there? And, of course, dear professor, I
understand. You can trust me that though I change thy name
though not the letter never while I become engaged with my
first horsepower, masterthief of hearts, I will give your lovely
face of mine away, my boyish bob, not for tons of donkeys, to
my second mate, with the twirlers the engineer of the passio-
flower (O the wicked untruth! whot a tell! that he has bought

me in his wellingtons what you haven't got!), in one of those
pure clean lupstucks of yours thankfully, Arrah of the passkeys,
no matter what. You may be certain of that, fluff, now I know
how to tackle. Lock my mearest next myself. So don't keep me
now for a good boy for the love of my fragrant saint, you villain,
peppering with fear, my goodless graceless, or I'll first murder
you but, hvisper, meet me after by next appointment near you
know Ships just there beside the Ship at the future poor fool's
circuts of lovemountjoy square to show my disrespects now, let
me just your caroline for you, I must really so late. Sweet pig,
he'll be furious! How he stalks to simself louther and lover,
immutating aperybally. My prince of the courts who'll beat me
to love! And I'll be there when who knows where with the
objects of which I'll knowor forget. We say. Trust us. Our
game. (For fun!) The Dargle shall run dry the sooner I you
deny. Whoevery heard of such a think? Till the ulmost of all
elmoes shall stele our harts asthone! And Mrs A'Mara makes
it up and befriends with Mrs O'Morum! I will write down all
your names in my gold pen and ink. Everyday, precious, while
m'm'ry's leaves are falling deeply on my Jungfraud's Messonge-
book I will dream telepath posts dulcets on this isinglass stream
(but don't tell him or I'll be the mort of him!) under the libans
and the sickamours, the cyprissis and babilonias, where the
frondoak rushes to the ask and the yewleaves too kisskiss themselves and 'twill carry on my hearz'waves my still waters reflections in words over Margrate von Hungaria, her Quaidy ways
and her Flavin hair, to thee, Jack, ahoy, beyond the boysforus.
Splesh of hiss splash springs your salmon. Twick twick, twinkle
twings my twilight as Sarterday afternoon lex leap will smile on
my fourinhanced twelvemonthsmind. And what's this I was
going to say, dean? O, I understand. Listen, here I'll wait on thee
till Thingavalla with beautiful do be careful teacakes, more stues-
ser flavoured than Vanilla and blackcurrant there's a cure in, like
a born gentleman till you'll resemble me, all the time you're
awhile way, I swear to you, I will, by Candlemas! And listen,
joey, don't be ennoyed with me, my old evernew, when, by the

end of your chapter, you citch water on the wagon for me being
turned a star I'll dubeurry my two fesces under Pouts Vanisha
Creme, their way for spilling cream, and, accent, umto extend
my personnalitey to the latents, I'll boy me for myself only of
expensive rainproof of pinked elephant's breath grey of the
loveliest sheerest, dearest, widowshood over airforce blue I am
so wild for, my precious once, Hope Bros., Faith Street, Charity
Corner, as the bee loves her skyhighdeed, for I always had a
crush on heliotrope since the dusess of yore cycled round the
Finest Park, and listen. And never mind me laughing at what's
atever! I was in the nerves but it's my last day. Always about
this hour, I'm sorry, when our gamings for Bruin and Noselong
is all oh you tease and afterdoon my lickle pussiness I stheal
heimlick in my russians from the attraction part with my terri-
blitall boots calvescatcher Pinchapoppapoff, who is going to be
a jennyroll, at my nape, drenched, love, with dripping to affectionate slapmamma but last at night, look, after my golden vio-
lents wetting in my upperstairs splendidly welluminated with
such lidlylac curtains wallpapered to match the cat and a fire-
please keep looking of priceless pearlogs I just want to see will
he or are all Michales like that, I'll strip straight after devotions
before his fondstare—and I mean it too, (thy gape to my gazing
I'll bind and makeleash) and poke stiff under my isonbound with
my soiedisante chineknees cheeckchubby chambermate for the
night's foreign males and your name of Shane will come forth
between my shamefaced whesen with other lipth I nakest open
my thight when just woken by his toccatootletoo my first morning. So now, to thalk thildish, thome, theated with Mag at the
oilthan we are doing to thay one little player before doing to
deed. An a tiss to the tassie for lu and for tu! Coach me how to
tumble, Jaime, and listen, with supreme regards, Juan, in haste,
warn me which to ah ah ah ah. . . .

—MEN! Juan responded fullchantedly to her sororal sono-
rity, imitating himself capitally with his bubbleblown in his
patapet and his chalished drink now well in hand. (A spilt, see,
for a split, see see!) Ever gloriously kind! And I truly am

eucherised to yous. Also *sacré père* and *maître d'autel*. Well,
ladies upon gentlermen and toastmaster general, let us, brindising
brandisong, woo and win womenlong with health to rich vine-
yards, Erin go Dry! Amingst the living waters of, the living in
giving waters of. Tight! Loose! A stiff one for Staffetta mullified
with creams of hourmony, the coupe that's chill for jackless jill and
a filiform dhouche on Doris. Esterelles, be not on your weeping
what though Shaunathaun is in his fail! To stir up love's young
fizz I tilt with this bridle's cup champagne, dimming douce from
her peepair of hideseeks, tightsqueezed on my snowybrusted and
while my pearlies in their sparkling wisdom are nippling her
bubblets I swear (and let you swear!) by the bumper round of
my poor old snaggletooth's solidbowel I ne'er will prove I'm
untrue to your liking (theare!) so long as my hole looks. Down.
   So gullaby, me poor Isley! But I'm not for forgetting me
innerman monophone for I'm leaving my darling proxy behind
for your consolering, lost Dave the Dancekerl, a squamous run-
away and a dear old man pal of mine too. He will arrive inces-
santly in the fraction of a crust, who, could he quit doubling and
stop tippling, he would be the unicorn of his kind. He's the
mightiest penumbrella I ever flourished on behond the shadow
of a post! Be sure and link him, me O treasauro, as often as you
learn provided there's nothing between you but a plain deal
table only don't encourage him to cry lessontimes over Lepers-
town. But soft! Can't be? Do mailstanes mumble? Lumtum
lumtum! Now! The froubadour! I fremble! Talk of wolf in a
stomach by all that's verminous! Eccolo me! The return of
th'athlate! Who can secede to his success! Isn't Jaunstown,
Ousterrike, the small place after all? I knew I smelt the garlic
leek! Why, bless me swits, here he its, darling Dave, like
the catoninelives just in time as if he fell out of space, all
draped in mufti, coming home to mourn mountains from his
old continence and not on one foot either or on two feet
aether but on quinquisecular cycles after his French evolution
and a blindfold passage by the 4.32 with the pork's pate in his
suicide paw and the gulls laughing lime on his natural skunk,

blushing like Pat's pig, begob. He's not too timtom well ashamed
to carry out onaglibtograbakelly in his showman's sinister the
testymonicals he gave his twenty annis orf, showing the three
white feathers, as a home cured emigrant in Paddyouare far below on our sealevel. Bearer may leave the church, signed, Figura
Porca, Lictor Magnaffica. He's the sneaking likeness of us, faith,
me altar's ego in miniature and every Auxonian aimer's ace as
nasal a Romeo as I am, for ever cracking quips on himself, that
merry, the jeenjakes, he'd soon arise mother's roses mid bedew-
ing tears under those wild wet lashes onto anny living girl's
laftercheeks. That's his little veiniality. And his unpeppeppedi-
ment. He has novel ideas I know and he's a jarry queer fish be-
times, I grant you, and cantanberous, the poisoner of his word,
but lice and all and semicoloured stainedglasses, I'm enormously
full of that foreigner, I'll say I am! Got by the one goat, suckled
by the same nanna, one twitch, one nature makes us oldworld
kin. We're as thick and thin now as two tubular jawballs. I hate
him about his patent henesy, plasfh it, yet am I amorist. I love
him. I love his old portugal's nose. There's the nasturtium for
ye now that saved manny a poor sinker from water on the grave.
The diasporation of all pirates and quinconcentrum of a fake like
Basilius O'Cormacan MacArty? To camiflag he turned his shirt.
Isn't he after borrowing all before him, making friends with
everybody red in Rossya, white in Alba and touching every distinguished Ourishman he could ever distinguish before or behind from a Yourishman for the customary halp of a crown and
peace? He is looking aged with his pebbled eyes, and johnnythin
too, from livicking on pidgins' ifs with puffins' ands, he's been
slanderising himself, but I pass no remark. Hope he hasn't the
cholera. Give him an eyot in the farout. Moseses and Noasies,
how are you? He'd be as snug as Columbsisle Jonas wrocked in
the belly of the whaves, as quotad before. Bravo, senior chief!
Famose! Sure there's nobody else in touch anysides to hold a
chef's cankle to the darling at all for sheer dare with that prison-
potstill of spanish breans on him like the knave of trifles! A jolly-
tan fine demented brick and the prince of goodfilips! Dave

knows I have the highest of respect of annyone in my oweand
smooth way for that intellectual debtor (Obbligado!) Mushure
David R. Crozier. And we're the closest of chems. Mark my use
of you, cog! Take notice how I yemploy, crib! Be ware as you,
I foil, coppy! It's a pity he can't see it for I'm terribly nice about
him. Canwyll y Cymry, the marmade's flamme! A leal of the
O'Looniys, a Brazel aboo! The most omportent man! *Shervos!*
Ho, be the holy, snakes, someone has shaved his rough diamond
skull for him as clean as Nuntius' piedish! The burnt out
mesh and the matting and all! Thunderweather, khyber schinker
escapa sansa pagar. He's the spatton spit, so he is, scaly skin
and all, with his blackguarded eye, and the goatsbeard in
his buttinghole of Shemuel Tulliver, me grandsourd, the old
cruxader, when he off with his paudeen! That was to let the
crowd of the Flu Flux Fans behind him see me proper. Ah,
he's very thoughtful and sympatrico that way is Brother Intelli-
gentius, when he's not absintheminded, with his Paris addresse!
He is, really. Holdhard till you'll ear him clicking his bull's
bones! Some toad klakkin! You're welcome back. Wilkins to
red berries in the frost! And here's the butter exchange to pfeife
and dramn ye with a bawlful of the Moulsaybaysse and yunker
doodler wanked to wall awriting off his phoney. I'm tired hairing of you. Hat yourself! Give us your dyed dextremity here,
frother, the Claddagh clasp! I met with dapper dandy and he
shocked me big the hamd. Where's your watch keeper? You've
seen all sorts in shapes and sizes, marauding about the moppa-
mound. How's the cock and the bullfight? And old Auster and
Hungrig? And the Beer and Belly and the Boot and Ball? Not
forgetting the oils of greas under that turkey in julep and Father
Freeshots Feilbogen in his rockery garden with the costard? And
did you meet with Peadhar the Grab at all? And did you call on
Tower Geesyhus? Was Mona, my own love, no bigger than she
should be, making up to you in her bestbehaved manor when
you made your breastlaw and made her, tell me? And did you
like the landskip from Lambay? I'm better pleased than ten
guidneys! You rejoice me! Faith, I'm proud of you, french davit!

You've surpassed yourself! Be introduced to yes! This is me aunt
Julia Bride, your honour, dying to have you languish to scandal in her bosky old delltangle. You don't reckoneyes him? He's
Jackot the Horner who boxed in his corner, jilting no fewer than
three female bribes. That's his penals. *Shervorum!* You haven't
seen her since she stepped into her drawoffs. Come on, spinister,
do your stuff! Don't be shoy, husbandmanvir! Weih, what's on
you, wip? Up the shamewaugh! She has plenty of woom in the
smallclothes for the bothsforus, nephews push! Hatch yourself
well! Enjombyourselves thurily! Would you wait biss she buds
till you bite on her? Embrace her bashfully by almeans at my
frank incensive and tell her in your semiological agglutinative yez,
how Idos be asking after her. Let us be holy and evil and let her
be peace on the bough. Sure, she fell in line with our tripertight
photos as the lyonised mails when we were stablelads together
like the corks again brothers, hungry and angry, cavileer
grace by roundhered force, or like boyrun to sibster, me and
you, shinners true and pinchme, our tertius quiddus, that never
talked or listened. Always raving how we had the wrinkles of
a snailcharmer, and the slits and sniffers of a fellow that fell foul
of the county de Loona and the meattrap of the first vegetarian.
To be had for the asking. Have a hug! Take her out of poor
tuppeny luck before she goes off in pure treple licquidance. I'd
give three shillings a pullet to the canon for the conjugation to
shadow you kissing her from me leberally all over as if she was a
crucifix. It's good for her bilabials, you understand. There's nothing like the mistletouch for finding a queen's earring false.
Chink chink. As the curly bard said after kitchin the womn in
his hym to the hum of her garments. You try a little tich to the
tissle of his tail. The racist to the racy, rossy. The soil is for the
self alone. Be ownkind. Be kithkinish. Be bloodysibby. Be irish.
Be inish. Be offalia. Be hamlet. Be the property plot. Be Yorick
and Lankystare. Be cool. Be mackinamucks of yourselves. Be
finish. No martyr where the preature is there's no plagues like
rome. It gives up the gripes. Watch the swansway. Take your
tiger over it. The leady on the lake and the convict of the forest.

Why, they might be Babau and Momie! Yipyip! To pan! To
pan! To tinpinnypan. All folly me yap to Curlew. Give us a pin
for her and we'll call it a tossup. Can you reverse positions.
Lets have a fuchu all round, courting cousins! Quuck, the duck
of a woman for quack, the drake of a man, her little live apples
for Leas and love potients for Leos, the next beast king. Put
me down for all ringside seats. I can feel you being corrupted.
Recoil. I can see you sprouting scruples. Get back. And as
he's boiling with water I'll light your pyre. Turn about, skeezy
Sammy, out of metaphor, till we feel are you still tropeful
of popetry. Told you so. If you doubt of his love of darearing
his feelings you'll very much hurt for mishmash mastufractured
on europe you can read off the tail of his. Rip ripper rippest and
jac jac jac. Dwell on that, my hero and lander! That's the side
that appeals to em, the wring wrong way to wright woman. Shuck
her! Let him! What he's good for. Shuck her more! Let him
again! All she wants! Could you wheedle a staveling encore out
of your imitationer's jubalharp, hey, Mr Jinglejoys? Congrega-
tional singing. Rota rota ran the pagoda *con dio in capo ed il dia-
volo in coda.* Many a diva devoucha saw her Dauber Dan at the
priesty pagoda Rota ran. Uck! He's so sedulous to singe always
if prumpted, the mirthprovoker. Grunt unto us, I pray, your fore-
boden article in our own deas dockandoilish introducing the
death of Nelson with coloraturas! *Coraio, fra!* And I'll string
second to harmanize. My loaf and pottage neaheaheahear Rochelle. With your dumpsey diddely dumpsey die, fiddeley fa.
Diavoloh! Or come on, schoolcolours, and we'll scrap, rug and
mat and then be as chummy as two bashed spuds. Bitrial bay
holmgang or betrayal buy jury. Attaboy! Fee gate has Heenan
hoity, mind uncle Hare? What, sir? Poss, myster? Acheve! Thou,
thou! What say ye? *Taurus periculosus, morbus pedeiculosus.
Miserere mei in miseribilibus!* There's uval lavguage for you! The
tower is precluded, the mob's in her petticoats; Mr R. E. Meehan
is in misery with his billyboots. Begob, there's not so much
green in his Ireland's eye! Sweet fellow ovocal, he stones out of
stune. But he could be near a colonel with a voice like that. The

bark is still there but the molars are gone. The misery billyboots
I used to lend him before we split and, be the hole in the year,
they were laking like heaven's reflexes. But I told him make your
will be done and go to a general and I'd pray confessions for
him. Areesh! Areesh! And I'll be your intrepider. Ambras!
Ruffle her! Bussing was before the blood and bissing will behind
the curtain. Triss! Did you note that worrid expressionism on
his megalogue? A full octavium below me! And did you hear
his browrings rattlemaking when he was preaching to himself?
And, whoa! do you twig the schamlooking leaf greeping ghastly
down his blousyfrock? Our national umbloom! Areesh! He
won't. He's shoy. Those worthies, my old faher's onkel that
was garotted, Caius Cocoa Codinhand, that I lost in a crowd,
used to chop that tongue of his, japlatin, with my yuonkle's
owlseller, Woowoolfe Woodenbeard, that went stomebathred,
in the Tower of Balbus, as brisk, man, as I'd scoff up muttan
chepps and lobscouse. But it's all deafman's duff to me,
begob. Sam knows miles bettern me how to work the
miracle. And I see by his diarrhio he's dropping the stammer
out of his silenced bladder since I bonded him off more as a
friend and as a brother to try and grow a muff and canonise his
dead feet down on the river airy by thinking himself into the
fourth dimension and place the ocean between his and ours,
the churchyard in the cloister of the depths, after he was capped
out of beurlads scoel for the sin against the past participle and
earned the factitation of codding chaplan and being as homely
gauche as swift B.A.A. Who gets twickly fullgets twice as alle-
manden huskers. But the whacker his word the weaker our ears
for auracles who parles parses orileys. Illstarred punster, lipster-
ing cowknucks. 'Twas the quadra sent him and Trinity too. And
he can cantab as chipper as any oxon ever I mood with, a tiptoe
singer! He'll prisckly soon hand tune your Erin's ear for you.
p.p. a mimograph at a time, numan bitter, with his ancomartins
to read the road roman with false steps ad Pernicious from
rhearsilvar ormolus to torquinions superbers while I'm far
away from wherever thou art serving my tallyhos and tullying

my hostilious by going in by the most holy recitatandas *ffff* for
my varsatile examinations in the ologies, to be a coach on the
Fukien mission. P? F? How used you learn me, brather
soboostins, in my augustan days? With cesarella looking on.
In the beginning was the gest he jousstly says, for the end is
with woman, flesh-without-word, while the man to be is in a
worse case after than before since she on the supine satisfies
the verg to him! Toughtough, tootoological. Thou the first
person shingeller. Art, an imperfect subjunctive. Paltry,
flappent, had serious. Miss Smith onamatterpoetic. Hammis-
andivis axes colles waxes warmas like sodullas. So pick your
stops with fondnes snow. And mind you twine the twos
noods of your nicenames. And pull up your furbelovs as far-
above as you're farthingales. That'll hint him how to click the
trigger. Show you shall and won't he will! His hearing is in-
doubting just as my seeing is onbelieving. So dactylise him up
to blankpoint and let him blink for himself where you speak the
best ticklish. You'll feel what I mean. Fond namer, let me never
see thee blame a kiss for shame a knee!

Echo, read ending! Siparioramoci! But from the stress of
their sunder enlivening, ay clasp, deciduously, a nikrokosmikon
must come to mike.

— Well, my positively last at any stage! I hate to look at alarms
but however they put on my watchcraft must now close as I
hereby hear by ear from by seeless socks 'tis time to be up and
ambling. Mymiddle toe's mitching, so mizzle I must else 'twill
sarve me out. Gulp a bulper at parting and the moore the
melodest. Farewell but whenever, as Tisdall told Toole.
Tempos fidgets. Let flee me fiacckles, says the grand old mano-
ark, stormcrested crowcock and undulant hair, hoodies tway!
Yes, faith, I am as mew let freer, beneath me corthage, bound.
I'm as bored now bawling beersgrace at sorepaws there as Andrew
Clays was sharing sawdust with Daniel's old collie. This shack's
not big enough for me now. I'm dreaming of ye, azores. And, remember this, a chorines, there's the witch on the heath, sistra!
'Bansheeba peeling hourihaared while her Orcotron is hoaring

ho. And whinn muinnuit flittsbit twinn her ttittshe cries
tallmidy! Daughters of the heavens, be lucks in turnabouts
to the wandering sons of red loam! The earth's atrot! The
sun's a scream! The air's a jig. The water's great! Seven oldy
oldy hills and the one blue beamer. I'm going. I know I am.
I couldbet I am. Somewhere I must get far away from Banba-
shore, wherever I am. No saddle, no staffet, but spur on the
moment. So I think I'll take freeboots' advise. Psk! I'll borrow
a path to lend me wings, quickquack, and from Jehusalem's
wall, clickclack, me courser's clear to Cheerup street I'll travel
the void world over. It's Winland for moyne, bickbuck! Gee-
jakers! I hurt meself nettly that time! Come, my good frog-
marchers! We felt the fall but we'll front the defile. Was not my
olty mutther, Sereth Maritza, a Runningwater? And the bould
one that quickened her the seaborne Fingale? I feel like that
hill of a whaler went yulding round Groenmund s Circus with
his tree full of seaweeds and Dinky Doll asleep in her shell.
Hazelridge has seen me. Jerne valing is. Squall aboard for Kew,
hop! Farewell awhile to her and thee! The brine's my bride to
be. Lead on, Macadam, and danked be he who first sights Halt
Linduff! Solo, solone, solong! Lood Erynnana, ware thee wail!
With me singame soarem o'erem! Here's me take off. Now's
nunc or nimmer, siskinder! Here goes the enemy! Bennydick
hotfoots onimpudent stayers. Sorry! I bless alls to the whished
with this panromain apological which Watllwewhistlem sang to
the kerrycoys. Break ranks! After wage-of-battle bother I am
thinking most. Fik yew! I'm through. Won. Toe. Adry. You
watch my smoke.

After poor Jaun the Boast's last fireless words of postludium
of his soapbox speech ending in'sheaven, twentyaid add one with
a flirt of wings were pouring to his bysistance (could they snip
that curl of curls to lay with their gloves and keep the kids
bright!) prepared to cheer him should he leap or to curse him
should he fall, but, with their biga triga rheda rodeo, the cherubs
in the charabang, set down here and sedan chair, don't you
wish you'd a yoke or a bit in your mouth, repulsing all attempts

at first hands on, as no es nada, our greatly misunderstood one
we perceived to give himself some sort of a hermetic prod or
kick to sit up and take notice, which acted like magic, while
the phalanx of daughters of February Filldyke, embushed and
climbing, ramblers and weeps, voiced approval in their customary
manner by dropping kneedeep in tears over their concelebrated
meednight sunflower, piopadey boy, their solase in dorckaness,
and splattering together joyously the plaps of their tappyhands
as, with a cry of genuine distress, so prettly prattly pollylogue,
tney viewed him, the just one, their darling, away.

A dream of favours, a favourable dream. They know how they
believe that they believe that they know. Wherefore they wail.

Eh jourd'weh! Oh jourd'woe! dosiriously it psalmodied. Gues-
turn's lothlied answring to-maronite's wail.

Oasis, cedarous esaltarshoming Leafboughnoon!

Oisis, coolpressus onmountof Sighing!

Oasis, palmost esaltarshoming Gladdays!

Oisis, phantastichal roseway anjerichol!

Oasis, newleavos spaciosing encampness!

Oisis, plantainous dewstuckacqmirage playtennis!

Pipetto, Pipetta has misery unnoticed!

But the strangest thing happened. Backscuttling for the hop
off with the odds altogether in favour of his tumbling into the
river, Jaun just then I saw to collect from the gentlest weaner
among the weiners, (who by this were in half droopleaflong
mourning for the passing of tne last post) the familiar yellow
label into which he let fall a drop, smothered a curse, choked a
guffaw, spat expectoratiously and blew his own trumpet. And next
thing was he gummalicked the stickyback side and stamped the
oval badge of belief to his agnelows brow with a genuine
dash of irrepressible piety that readily turned his ladylike
typmanzelles capsy curvy (the holy scamp!), with half a
glance of Irish frisky (a Juan Jaimesan *hastaluego*) from under
the shag of his parallel brows. It was then he made as if be
but waved instead a handacross the sea as notice to quit while
the pacifettes made their armpacts widdershins (Frida! Freda!

Paza! Paisy! Irine! Areinette! Bridomay! Bentamai! Sososopky! Bebebekka! Bababadkessy! Ghugugoothoyou! Dama! Damadomina! Takiya! Tokaya! Scioccara! Siuccherillina! Peocchia! Peucchia! Ho Mi Hoping! Ha Me Happinice! Mirra! Myrha! Solyma! Salemita! Sainta! Sianta! O Peace!), but in selfrighting the balance of his corporeity to reexchange widerembrace with the pillarbosom of the Dizzier he loved prettier, between estellos and venoussas, bad luck to the lie but when next to nobody expected, their star and gartergazer at the summit of his climax, he toppled a lipple on to the off and, making a brandnew start for himself to run down his easting, by blessing hes sthers with the sign of the southern cross, his bungaloid borsaline with the hedgygreen bound blew off in a loveblast (award for trover!) and Jawjon Redhead, bucketing after, meccamaniac, (the headless shall have legs!), kingscouriered round with an easy rush and ready relays by the bridge a stadion beyond Ladycastle (and what herm but he narrowly missed fouling her buttress for her but for he acqueducked) and then, cocking a snook at the stock of his sermons, so mear and yet so fahr from that region's general, away with him at the double, the hulk of a garron, pelting after the road, on Shanks's mare, let off like a wind hound loose (the bouchal! you'd think it was that moment they gave him the jambos!) with a posse of tossing hankerwaves to his windward like seraph's summonses on the air and a tempest of good things in packetshape teeming from all accounts into the funnel of his fanmail shrimpnet, along the highroad of the nation, Traitor's Track, following which fond floral fray he was quickly lost to sight through the statuemen though without a doubt he was all the more on that same head to memory dear while Sickerson, that borne of bjoerne, *la garde auxiliaire* she murmured, hellyg Ursulinka, full of woe (and how fitlier should goodboy's hand be shook than by the warmin of her besom that wrung his swaddles?): *Where maggot Harvey kneeled till bags? Ate Andrew coos hogdam farvel!*

Wethen, now, may the good people speed you, rural Haun, export stout fellow that you are, the crooner born with sweet

wail of evoker, healing music, ay, and heart in hand of Sham-
rogueshire! The googoos of the suckabolly in the rockabeddy are
become the copiosity of wiseableness of the friarylayman in the
pulpitbarrel. May your bawny hair grow rarer and fairer, our own
only wideheaded boy! Rest your voice! Feed your mind! Mint
your peas! Coax your qyous! Come to disdoon blarmey and
walk our groves so charming and see again the sweet rockelose
where first you hymned *O Ciesa Mea!* and touch the light the-
orbo. Songster, angler, choreographer! Piper to prisoned! Musi-
cianship made Embrassador-at-Large! Good by nature and
natural by design, had you but been spared to us, Hauneen lad,
but sure where's the use my talking quicker when I know you'll
hear me all astray? My long farewell I send to you, fair dream of
sport and game and always something new. Gone is Haun! My
grief, my ruin! Our Joss-el-Jovan! Our Chris-na-Murty! 'Tis well
you'll be looked after from last to first as yon beam of light we
follow receding on your photophoric pilgrimage to your antipodes in the past, you who so often consigned your distributory
tidings of great joy into our nevertoolatetolove box, mansuetudi-
nous manipulator, victimisedly victorihoarse, dearest Haun of
all, you of the boots, true as adie, stepwalker, pennyatimer,
lampaddyfair, postanulengro, our rommanychiel! Thy now pal-
ing light lucerne we ne'er may see again. But could it speak how
nicely would it splutter to the four cantons praises be to thee,
our pattern sent! For you had — may I, in our, your and their
names, dare to say it? — the nucleus of a glow of a zeal of soul
of service such as rarely if ever have I met with single men.
Numerous are those who, nay, there are a dozen of folks still
unclaimed by the death angel in this country of ours today,
humble indivisibles in this grand continuum, overlorded by fate
and interlarded with accidence, who, while there are hours and
days, will fervently pray to the spirit above that they may never
depart this earth of theirs till in his long run from that place
where the day begins, ere he retourneys postexilic, on that day
that belongs to joyful Ireland, the people that is of all time, the
old old oldest, the young young youngest, after decades of

longsuffering and decennia of brief glory, to mind us of what
was when and to matter us of the withering of our ways, their
Janyouare Fibyouare wins true from Sylvester (only Walker
himself is like Waltzer, whimsicalissimo they go murmurand)
comes marching ahome on the summer crust of the flagway.
Life, it is true, will be a blank without you because avicuum's not
there at all, to nomore cares from nomad knows, ere Molochy
wars bring the devil era, a slip of the time between a date and a
ghostmark, rived by darby's chilldays embers, spatched fun
Juhn that dandyforth, from the night we are and feel and fade
with to the yesterselves we tread to turnupon.

But, boy, you did your strong nine furlong mile in slick and
slapstick record time and a farfetched deed it was in troth, champion docile, with your high bouncing gait of going and your
feat of passage will be contested with you and through you, for
centuries to come. The phaynix rose a sun before Erebia sank his
smother! Shoot up on that, bright Bennu bird! *Va faotre!*
Eftsoon so too will our own sphoenix spark spirt his spyre
and sunward stride the rampante flambe. Ay, already the
sombrer opacities of the gloom are sphanished! Brave footsore
Haun! Work your progress! Hold to! Now! Win out, ye divil ye!
The silent cock shall crow at last. The west shall shake the east
awake. Walk while ye have the night for morn, lightbreakfast-
bringer, morroweth whereon every past shall full fost sleep.
Amain.

[3]

Lowly, longly a wail went forth. Pure Yawn lay low. On the mead of the hillock lay, heartsoul dormant mid shadowed landshape, brief wallet to his side, and arm loose, by his staff of citron briar, tradition stick-pass-on. His dream monologue was over, of cause, but his drama parapolylogic had yet to be, affact. Most distressfully (but, my dear, how successfully!) to wail he did, his locks of a lucan tinge, quickrich, ripely rippling, unfilleted, those lashbetasselled lids on the verge of closing time, whiles ouze of his sidewiseopen mouth the breath of him, evenso languishing as the princeliest treble treacle or lichee chewchow purse could buy. Yawn in a semiswoon lay awailing and (hooh!) what helpings of honeyful swoothead (phew!), which earpiercing dulcitude! As were you suppose to go and push with your bluntblank pin in hand upinto his fleshasplush cushionettes of some chubby boybold love of an angel. Hwoah!

When, as the buzzer brings the light brigade, keeping the home fires burning, so on the churring call themselves came at him, from the westborders of the eastmidlands, three kings of three suits and a crowner, from all their cardinal parts, along the amber way where Brosna's furzy. To lif them they did, senators four, by the first quaint skreek of the gloaming and they hopped it up the mountainy molehill, traversing climes of old times gone by of the days not worth remembering; inventing some excusethems, any sort, having a sevenply

sweat of night blues moist upon them. Feefee! phopho!!
foorchtha!!! aggala!!!! jeeshee!!!!! paloola!!!!!! ooridiminy!!!!!!!
Afeared themselves were to wonder at the class of a crossroads
puzzler he would likely be, length by breadth nonplussing his
thickness, ells upon ells of him, making so many square yards of
him, one half of him in Conn's half but the whole of him nevertheless in Owenmore's five quarters. There would he lay till
they would him descry, spancelled down upon a blossomy bed, at
one foule stretch, amongst the daffydowndillies, the flowers of
narcosis fourfettering his footlights, a halohedge of wild spuds
hovering over him, epicures waltzing with gardenfillers, puritan
shoots advancing to Aran chiefs. Phopho!! The meteor pulp
of him, the seamless rainbowpeel. Aggala!!!! His bellyvoid of
nebulose with his neverstop navel. Paloola!!!!!! And his veins
shooting melanite phosphor, his creamtocustard cometshair and
his asteroid knuckles, ribs and members. Ooridiminy!!!!!!!! His
electrolatiginous twisted entrails belt.

Those four claymen clomb together to hold their sworn starchamber quiry on him. For he was ever their quarrel, the way
they would see themselves, everybug his bodiment atop of
annywom her notion, and the meet of their noght was worth two
of his morning. Up to the esker ridge it was, Mallinger parish, to a
mead that was not far, the son's rest. First klettered Shanator
Gregory, seeking spoor through the deep timefield, Shanator
Lyons, trailing the wavy line of his partition footsteps (something in his blisters was telling him all along how he had
been in that place one time), then his Recordership, Dr Shuna-
dure Tarpey, caperchasing after honourable sleep, hot on to the
aniseed and, up out of his prompt corner, old Shunny MacShunny,
MacDougal the hiker, in the rere of them on the run, to make a
quorum. Roping their ass he was, their skygrey globetrotter,
by way of an afterthought and by no means legless either for
such sprouts on him they were that much oneven it was tumbling
he was by four lengths, within the bawl of a mascot, kuss yuss,
kuss cley, patsy watsy, like the kapr in the kabisses, the big ass,
to hear with his unaided ears the harp in the air, the bugle

dianablowing, wild as wild, the mockingbird whose word is misfortune, so 'tis said, the bulbul down the wind.

The proto was traipsing through the tangle then, Mathew Walker, godsons' goddestfar, deputising for gossipocracy, and his station was a few perch to the weatherside of the knoll Asnoch and it was from no other place unless there, how and ever, that he proxtended aloof upon the ether Mesmer's Manuum, the hand making silence. The buckos beyond on the lea, then stopped wheresoever they found their standings and that way they set ward about him, doing obedience, nod, bend, bow and curtsey, like the watchers of Prospect, upholding their broad-awake prober's hats on their firrum heads, the travelling court on its findings circuiting that personer in his fallen. And a crack quat-youare of stenoggers they made of themselves, solons and psy-chomorers, all told, with their hurts and daimons, spites and clops, not even to the seclusion of their beast by them that was the odd trick of the pack, trump and no friend of carrots. And, what do you think, who should be laying there above all other persons forenenst them only Yawn! All of asprawl he was laying too amengst the poppies and, I can tell you something more than that, drear writer, profoundly as you may bedeave to it, he was oscasleep asleep. And it was far more similar to a satrap he lay there with unctuous beauty all surrounded, the poser, or for whatall I know like Lord Lumen, coaching his preferred constellations in faith and doctrine, for old Matt Gregory, 'tis he had the starmenag-erie, Marcus Lyons and Lucas Metcalfe Tarpey and the mack that never forgave the ass that lurked behind him, Jonny na Hossaleen.

More than their good share of their five senses ensorcelled you would say themselves were, fuming censor, the way they could not rightly tell their heels from their stools as they cooched down a mamalujo by his cubical crib, as question time drew nighing and the map of the souls' groupography rose in relief within their quarterings, to play tops or kites or hoops or marbles, curchycurchy, gawking on him, for the issuance of his pnum and softnoising one of them to another one, the boguaqueesthers.

And it is what they began to say to him tetrahedrally then, the
masters, what way was he.

— He's giving, the wee bairn. Yun has lived.

— Yerra, why dat, my leader?

— Wisha, is he boosed or what, alannah?

— Or his wind's from the wrong cut, says Ned of the Hill.

— Lesten!

— Why so and speak up, do you hear me, you sir?

— Or he's rehearsing somewan's funeral.

— Whisht outathat! Hubba's up!

And as they were spreading abroad on their octopuds their
drifter nets, the chromous gleamy seiners' nets and no lie, there was
word of assonance being softspoken among those quartermasters.

— Get busy, kid!

— Chirpy, come now!

— The present hospices is a good time.

— I'll take on that chap.

For it was in the back of their mind's ear, temptive lissomer,
how they would be spreading in quadriliberal their azurespotted
fine attractable nets, their nansen nets, from Matt Senior to the
thurrible mystagogue after him and from thence to the neighbour
and that way to the puisny donkeyman and his crucifer's cauda.
And in their minds years backslibris, so it was, slipping beauty,
how they would be meshing that way, when he rose to it, with
the planckton at play about him, the quivers of scaly silver and
their clutches of chromes of the highly lucid spanishing gold
whilst, as hour gave way to mazing hour, with Yawn himself
keeping time with his thripthongue, to ope his blurbeous lips he
would, a let out classy, the way myrrh of the moor and molten
moonmist would be melding mellifond indo his mouth.

— Y?

— Before You!

— Ecko! How sweet thee answer makes! Afterwheres? In the
land of lions' odor?

— Friends! First if yu don't mind. Name yur historical grouns.

— This same prehistoric barrow 'tis, the orangery.

— I see. Very good now. It is in your orangery, I take it, you have your letters. Can you hear here me, you sir?

— Throsends. For my darling. Typette!

— So long aforetime? Can you hear better?

— Millions. For godsends. For my darling dearling one.

— Now, to come nearer zone; I would like to raise my deuterous point audibly touching this. There is this maggers. I am told by our interpreter, Hanner Esellus, that there are fully six hundred and six ragwords in your malherbal Magis lande-guage in which wald wand rimes alpman and there is resin in all roots for monarch but yav hace not one pronouncable teerm that blows in all the vallums of tartallaght to signify majestate even provisionally nor no rheda rhoda or torpentine path or halluci-nian via nor aurellian gape nor sunkin rut nor grossgrown trek nor crimeslaved cruxway and no moorhens cry or mooner's plankgang there to lead us to hopenhaven. Is such the *unde deri-vatur* casematter messio! Frankly. *Magis megis enerretur mynus hoc intelligow.*

— How? C'est mal prononsable, tartagliano, perfrances. Vous n'avez pas d'o dans votre boche provenciale, mousoo. Je m'in-cline mais *Moy jay trouvay la clee dang les champs.* Hay sham nap poddy velour, come on!

— Hep there! Commong, sa na pa de valure? Whu's teit dans yur jambs? Whur's that inclining and talkin about the messiah so cloover? A true's to your trefling! Whure yu!

— Trinathan partnick dieudonnay. Have you seen her? Typette, my tactile O!

— Are you in your fatherick, lonely one?

— The same. Three persons. Have you seen my darling only one? I am sohohold!

— What are yu shevering about, ultramontane, like a houn? Is there cold on ye, doraphobian? Or do yu want yur primafairy schoolmam?

— The woods of fogloot! O mis padredges!

— Whisht awhile, greyleg! The duck is rising and you'll wake that stand of plover. I know that place better than anyone. Sure,

I used to be always overthere on the fourth day at my grandmother's place, Tear-nan-Ogre, my little grey home in the west,
in or about Mayo when the long dog gave tongue and they
coursing the marches and they straining at the leash. Tortoise-
shell for a guineagould! Burb! Burb! Burb! Follow me up
Tucurlugh! That's the place for the claire oysters, Polldoody,
County Conway. I never knew how rich I was like another story in
the zoedone of the zephyros, strolling and strolling, carrying my
dragoman, Meads Marvel, thass withumpronouceable tail, along
the shore. Do you know my cousin, Mr Jasper Dougal that
keeps the Anchor on the Mountain, the parson's son, Jasper of
the Tuns, Pat Whateveryournameis?

— Dood and I dood. The wolves of Fochlut! By Whydoyou-
callme? Do not flingamejig to the twolves!

— Turcafiera amd that's a good wan right enough! Wooluvs
no less!

— One moment now, if I foreshorten the bloss on your
bleather. Encroachement spells erosion. Dunlin and turnstone
augur us where, how and when best as to burial of carcass, fuselage of dump and committal of noisance. But, since you invocate
austers for the trailing of vixens, I would like to send a cormo-
rant around this blue lagoon. Tell me now this. You told my
larned friend rather previously, a moment since, about this mound
or barrow. Now I suggest to you that ere there was this plague-
burrow, as you seem to call it, there was a burialbattell, the boat
of millions of years. Would you bear me out in that, relatively
speaking, with her jackstaff jerking at her pennyladders, why
not, and sizing a fair sail, knowest thout the kind? The *Pourquoi
Pas*, bound for Weissduwasland, that fourmaster barquentine,
Webster says, our ship that ne're returned. The Frenchman, I say,
was an orangeboat. He is a boat. You see him. The both how
you see is they! Draken af Danemork! Sacked it or ate it? What!
Hennu! Spake ab laut!

— Couch cortege ringbarrow dungcairn. Beseek the runes
and see the longurn. Allmaun away when you hear the gang-
horn. And meet Nautsen. Ess Ess. O ess. Warum night! Con-

ning two lay payees. Norsker. Her raven flag was out, the slaver. I trow pon good, jordan's scaper, good's barnet and trustyman. Crouch low, you pigeons three! Say, call that girl with the tan tress awn! Call Wolfhound! Wolf of the sea. Folchu! Folchu!

— Very good now. That folklore's straight from the ass his mouth. I will crusade on with the parent ship, weather prophetting, far away from those green hills a station, Ireton tells me, bonofide for keeltappers, now to come to the midnight middy on this levantine ponenter. From Daneland sailed the oxeyed man, now mark well what I say.

— Magnus Spadebeard, korsets krosser, welsher perfyddye. A destroyer in our port. Signed to me with his baling scoop. Laid bare his breastpaps to give suck, to suckle me. Ecce Hagios Chrisman!

— Oh, Jeyses, fluid! says the poisoned well. Futtfishy the First. Hootchcopper's enkel at the navel manuvres!

— Hep! Hello there, Bill of old Bailey! Whu's he? Whu's this lad, why the pups?

— Hunkalus Childared Easterheld. It's his lost chance, Emania. Ware him well.

— Hey! Did you dream you were ating your own tripe, acushla, that you tied yourself up that wrynecky fix?

— I see now. We move in the beast circuls. Grimbarb and pancercrucer! You took the words out of my mouth. A child's dread for a dragon vicefather. Hillcloud encompass us! You mean you lived as milky at their lyceum, couard, while you learned, volp volp, to howl yourself wolfwise. Dyb! Dyb! Do your best.

— I am dob dob dobbling like old Booth's, courteous. The cubs are after me, it zeebs, the whole totem pack, vuk vuk and vuk vuk to them, for Robinson's shield.

— Scents and gouspils! The animal jangs again! Find the fingall harriers! Here howl me wiseacres hat till I die of the milkman's lupus!

— What? Wolfgang? Whoah! Talk very slowe!

— *Hail him heathen, heal him holystone!*
Courser, Recourser, Changechild . . . .
Eld as endall, earth . . . .

— A cataleptic mithyphallic! Was this *Totem Fulcrum Est*
Ancestor yu hald in *Dies Eirae* where no spider webbeth or
Anno Mundi ere bawds plied in Skiffstrait? Be fair, Chris!

— Dream. Ona nonday I sleep. I dreamt of a somday. Of a
wonday I shall wake. Ah! May he have now of here fearfilled
me! Sinflowed, O sinflowed! Fia! Fia! Befurcht christ!

— I have your tristich now; it recurs in three times the same
differently (there is such a fui fui story which obtains of him):
comming nown from the asphalt to the concrete, from the human
historic brute, Finnsen Faynean, occeanyclived, to this same
vulganized hillsir from yours, Mr Tupling Toun of Morning
de Heights with his lavast flow and his rambling undergroands,
would he reoccur *Ad Horam*, as old Romeo Rogers, in city or
county, and your sure ob, or by, with or from an urb, of you
know the differenciabus, as brauchbarred in apabhramsa, sierrah!
We speak of Gun, the farther. And in the locative. Bap! Bap!

— Ouer Tad, Hellig Babbau, whom certayn orbits assertant
re humeplace of Chivitats Ei, Smithwick, Rhonnda, Kaledon,
Salem (Mass), Childers, Argos and Duthless. Well, I am advised
he might in a sense be both nevertheless, every at man like myself, suffix it to say, Abrahamsk and Brookbear! By him it was
done bapka, by me it was gone into, to whom it will beblive,
Mushame, Mushame! I am afraid you could not heave ahore one
of your own old stepstones, barnabarnabarn, over a stumble-
down wall here in Huddlestown to this classic Noctuber night
but itandthey woule binge, much as vecious, off the dosshouse
back of a racerider in his truetoflesh colours, either handicapped
on her flat or barely repeating himself. That is a tiptip tim oldy
faher now the man I go in fear of, Tommy Terracotta, and he
could be all your and my das, the brodar of the founder of the
father of the finder of the pfander of the pfunder of the furst man
in Ranelagh, fué! fué! Petries and violet ice (I am yam, as Me
and Tam Tower used to jagger pemmer it, over at the house of

Eddy's Christy, meaning Dodgfather, Dodgson and Coo) and spiriduous sanction!

— Breeze softly. Aures are aureas. Hau's his naun?

— Me das has or oreils. Piercey, piercey, piercey, piercey!

— White eyeluscious and muddyhorsebroth! Pig Pursyriley! But where do we get off, chiseller?

— Haltstille, Lucas and Dublinn! Vulva! Vulva! Vulva! Vulva!

— Macdougal, Atlantic City, or his onagrass that is, chuam and coughan. I would go near identifying you from your stavrotides, Jong of Maho, and the weslarias round your yokohahat. And that O'mulanchonry plucher you have from the worst curst of Ireland, Glwlwd of the Mghtwg Grwpp, is no use to you either, Johnny my donkeyschott. Number four fix up your spreadeagle and pull your weight!

— Hooshin hom to our regional's hin and the gander of Hayden. Would ye ken a young stepschuler of psychical chirography, the name of Keven, or (let outers pray) Evan Vaughan, of his Posthorn in the High Street, that was shooing a Guiney gagag, Poulepinter, that found the dogumen number one, I would suggest, an illegible downfumbed by an unelgible?

— If I do know sinted sageness? Sometimes he would keep silent for a few minutes as if in prayer and clasp his forehead and during the time he would be thinking to himself and he would not mind anybody who would be talking to him or crying stinking fish. But I no way need you, stroke oar nor your quick handles. Your too farfar a cock of the north there, Matty Armagh, and your due south so.

— South I see. You're up-in-Leal-Ulster and I'm-free-Down-in-Easia, this is much better. He is cured by faith who is sick of fate. The prouts who will invent a writing there ultimately is the poeta, still more learned, who discovered the raiding there originally. That's the point of eschatology our book of kills reaches for now in soandso many counterpoint words. What can't be coded can be decorded if an ear aye sieze what no eye ere grieved for. Now, the doctrine obtains, we have occasioning cause caus-

ing effects and affects occasionally recausing altereffects. Or I
will let me take it upon myself to suggest to twist the penman's
tale posterwise. The gist is the gist of Shaum but the hand is
the hand of Sameas. Shan - Shim - Schung. There is a strong
suspicion on counterfeit Kevin and we all remember ye in childhood's reverye. 'Tis the bells of scandal that gave tune to
grumble over him and someone between me and thee. He would
preach to the two turkies and dipdip all the dindians, this master
the abbey, and give gold tidings to all that are in the bonze age
of anteproresurrectionism to entrust their easter neappearance
to Borsaiolini's house of hatcraft. He is our sent on the firm.
Now, have you reasonable hesitancy in your mind about him
after fourpriest redmass or are you in your post? Tell me andat
sans dismay. Leap, pard!

— Fierappel putting years on me! Nwo, nwo! This bolt in
hand be my worder! I'll see you moved farther, blarneying
Marcantonio! What cans such wretch to say to I or how have My
to doom with him? We were wombful of mischief and initium-
wise, everliking a liked, hairytop on heeltipper, alpybecca's un-
wachsibles, an ikeson am ikeson, that babe, imprincipially, my
leperd brethren, the Puer, ens innocens of but fifteen primes.
Ya all in your kalblionized so trilustriously standing the real
school, to be upright as his match, healtheous as is egg, saviour
so the salt and good wee braod, parallaling buttyr, did I alter-
mobile him to a flare insiding hogsfat. Been ike hins kinder-
gardien? I know not, O cashla, I am sure offed habitand this
undered heaven, meis enfins, contrasting the first mover, that
father I ascend fromming knows, as I think, caused whom I, a
self the sign, came remaining being dwelling ayr, plage and
watford as to I was eltered impostulance possessing my future
state falling towards thrice myself resting the childhide when
I received the habit following Mezienius connecting Mezosius
including was verted embracing a palegrim, circumcised my
hairs, Oh laud, and removed my clothes from patristic motives,
meas minimas culpads! Permitting this ick (ickle coon icoocoon)
crouched low entering humble down, dead thrue mean scato-

logical past, making so smell partaking myself to confess abiding
clean tumbluponing yous octopods, mouthspeech allno finger-
force, owning my mansuetude before him attaching Audeon's
prostratingwards mine sore accompanying my thrain tropps
offering meye eyesalt, what I (the person whomin I now am) did
not do, how he to say essied anding how he was making errand
andanding how he all locutey sunt, why did you, my sexth best
friend, blabber always you would be so delated to back me, then
ersed irredent, toppling Humphrey hugging Nephew, old begge-
laut, designing such post sitting his night office? Annexing then,
producing Saint Momuluius, you snub around enclosing your
moving motion touching the other catachumens continuing say
providing append of signature quoniam you will celebrand my
dirthdags quoniam, concealed a concealer, I am twosides uppish,
a mockbelief insulant, ending none meer hyber irish. Well, chunk
your dimned chink, before avtokinatown, forasmuch as many
have tooken in hand to, I may as well humbly correct that ves-
pian now in case of temporalities. I've my pockets full comeplay
of you laycreated cardonals, ap rince, ap rowler, ap rancer, ap
rowdey! Improperial! I saved you fore of the Hekkites and you
loosed me hind bland Harry to the burghmote of Aud Dub. I
teachet you in fair time, my elders, the W.X.Y.Z. and P.Q.R.S. of
legatine powers and you, Ailbey and Ciardeclan, I learn, episcop-
ing me altogether, circumdeditioned me. I brought you from the
loups of Lazary and you have remembered my lapsus langways.
Washywatchywataywatashy!   Oirasesheorebukujibun!   Wata-
cooshy lot! Mind of poison is. That time thing think! Honorific
remembrance to spit humble makes. My ruridecanal caste is a cut
above you peregrines. Aye vouchu to rumanescu. See the leabhour
of my generations! Has not my master, Theophrastius Spheropneu-
maticus, written that the spirit is from the upper circle? I'm of the
ochlocracy with Prestopher Palumbus and Porvus Parrio. Soa
koa Kelly Terry per Chelly Derry lepossette. Ho look at my
jailbrand Exquovis and sequencias High marked on me fake-
similar in the foreign by Pappagallus and Pumpusmugnus:
ahem! Anglicey: *Eggs squawfish lean yoe nun feed :narecurious.*

Sagart can self laud nilobstant to Lowman Catlick's patrician morning coat of arms with my High tripenniferry cresta and caudal mottams: Itch dean: which Gaspey, Otto and Sauer, he renders: echo stay so! Addressing eat or not eat body Yours am. And, Mind praisegad, is the first praisonal Egoname Yod heard boissboissy in Moy Bog's domesday. Hastan the vista! Or in alleman: Suck at!

— Suck it yourself, sugarstick! Misha, Yid think whose was asking to luckat your sore toe or to taste your gaspy, hot and sour! Ichthyan! Hegvat tosser! Gags be plebsed! Between his voyous and her consinnantes! Thugg, Dirke and Hacker with Rose Lankester and Blanche Yorke! Are we speachin d'anglas landadge or are you sprakin sea Djoytsch? Oy soy, Bleseyblasey, where to go is knowing remain? Become quantity that discourse bothersome when what do? Knowing remain? Come back, baddy wrily, to Bullydamestough! Cum him, buddy rowly, with me! What about your thruppenny croucher of an old fellow, me boy, through the ages, tell us, eh? What about Brian's the Vauntand-onlieme, Master Monk, eh, eh, *Spira in Me Domino*, spear me Doyne! Fat prize the bonafide peachumpidgeonlover, eh, eh, eh, esquire earwugs, escusado, of Jenkins' Area, with his I've Ivy under his tangue and the hohallo to his dullaphone, before there was a sound in the world? How big was his boost friend and be shanghaied to him? The swaaber! The twicer, trifoaled in Wan-stable! Loud's curse to him! If you hored him outerly as we harum lubberintly, from norning rice till nightmale, with his drums and bones and hums in drones your innereer'd heerdly heer he. Ho ha hi he hung! Tsing tsing!

— Me no angly mo, me speakee Yellman's lingas. Nicey Doc Mistel Lu, please! Me no pigey ludiments all same numpa one Topside Tellmastoly fella. Me pigey savvy a singasong anothel time. Pleasie, Mista Lukie Walkie! Josadam cowbelly maam belongame shepullamealahmalong, begolla, Jackinaboss belonga-she; plentymuch boohoomeo.

— Hell's Confucium and the Elements! Tootoo moohootch! Thot's never the postal cleric, checking chinchin chat with nip-

ponnippers! Halt there sob story to your lambdad's tale! Are
you roman cawthrick 432?

— *Quadrigue my yoke.*

Triple my tryst.

Tandem my sire.

— History as her is harped. Too the toone your owldfrow lied
of. Tantris, hattrick, tryst and parting, by vowelglide! I feel
your thrilljoy mouths overtspeaking, O dragoman, hands under-
studium. Plunger words what paddle verbed. Mere man's mime:
God has jest. The old order changeth and lasts like the first.
Every third man has a chink in his conscience and every other
woman has a jape in her mind. Now, fix on the little fellow in my
eye, Minucius Mandrake, and follow my little psychosinology,
poor armer in slingslang. Now I, the lord of Tuttu, am placing
that inital T square of burial jade upright to your temple a
moment. Do you see anything, templar?

— I see a blackfrinch pliestrycook . . . who is carrying on
his brainpan . . . a cathedral of lovejelly for his . . . *Tiens*, how
he is like somebodies!

— Pious, a pious person. What sound of tistress isoles my
ear? I horizont the same, this serpe with ramshead, and lay it
lightly to your lip a little. What do you feel, liplove?

— I feel a fine lady . . . floating on a stillstream of
isisglass . . . with gold hair to the bed . . . and white arms to the
twinklers . . . O la la!

— Purely, in a pure manner. O, sey but swift and still a vain
essaying! Trothed today, trenned tomorrow. I invert the initial
of your tripartite and sign it sternly, and adze to girdle, on your
breast. What do you hear, breastplate?

— I ahear of a hopper behidin the door slappin his feet in a
pool of bran.

— Bellax, acting like a bellax. And so the triptych vision
passes. Out of a hillside into a hillside. Fairshee fading. Again
am I deliciated by the picaresqueness of your irmages. Now,
the oneir urge iterimpellant, I feel called upon to ask did it
ever occur to you, *qua* you, prior to this, by a stretch of

your iberborealic imagination, when it's quicker than this quacking that you might, bar accidens, be very largely substituted in potential secession from your next life by a complementary character, voices apart. Upjack! I shudder for your thought! Think! Put from your mind that and take on trust this. The next word depends on your answer.

— I'm thinking to, thogged be thenked! I was just trying to think when I thought I felt a flea. I might have. I cannot say for it is of no significance at all. Once or twice when I was in odinburgh with my addlefoes, Jake Jones the handscabby, when I thinkled I wore trying on my garden substisuit, boy's apert, at my nexword nighboor's, and maybe more largely nor you quosh yet you, messmate, realise. A few times, so to shape, I chanced to be stretching, in the shadow as I thought, the liferight out of myself in my ericulous imaginating. I felt feeling a half Scotch and pottage like roung my middle ageing like Bewley in the baste so that I indicate out to myself and I swear my gots how that I'm not meself at all, no jolly fear, when I realise bimiselves how becomingly I to be going to become.

— O, is that the way with you, you craythur? In the becoming was the weared, wontnat! Hood maketh not frere. The voice is the voice of jokeup, I fear. Are you imitation Roma now or Amor now. You have all our empathies, eh, Mr Trickpat, if you don't mind, that is, aside from sings and mush, answering to my straight question?

— God save the monk! I won't mind this is, answering to your strict crossqueets, whereas it would be as unethical for me now to answer as it would have been nonsensical for you then not to have asked. Same no can, home no will, gangin I am. Gangang is Mine and I will return. Out of my name you call me, Leelander. But in my shelter you'll miss me. When Lapac walks backwords he's darkest horse in Capalisoot. You knew me once but you won't know me twice. I am *simpliciter arduus*, ars of the schoo, Freeday's child in loving and thieving.

— My child, know this! Some portion of that answer appears to have been token by you from the writings of Saint Synodius,

that first liar. Let us hear, therefore, as you honour and obey the
queen, whither the indwellingness of that which shamefieth be
entwined of one or atoned of two. Let us hear, Art simplicissime!

—Dearly beloved brethren: Bruno and Nola, leymon bogholders
and stationary lifepartners off orangey Saint Nessau Street, were
explaining it avicendas all round each other ere yesterweek out
of Ibn Sen and Ipanzussch. When himupon Nola Bruno mono-
polises his egobruno most unwillingly seses by the mortal powers
alionola equal and opposite brunoipso, *id est*, eternally provoking
alio opposite equally as provoked as Bruno at being eternally
opposed by Nola. Poor omniboose, singalow singelearum: so
is he!

— One might hear in their beyond that lionroar in the air
again, the zoohoohoom of Felin make Call. Bruin goes to Noble,
aver who is? If is itsen? Or you mean Nolans but Volans, an
alibi, do you Mutemalice, suffering unegoistically from the singular
but positively enjoying on the plural? Dustify of that sole, you
breather! Ruemember, blither, thou must lie!

— Oessoyess! I never dramped of prebeing a postman but
I mean in ostralian someplace, mults deeply belubdead; my
allaboy brother, Negoist Cabler, of this city, whom 'tis better
ne'er to name, my said brother, the skipgod, expulled for
looking at churches from behind, who is sender of the Hullo
Eve Cenograph in prose and worse every Allso's night. High
Brazil Brandan's Deferred, midden Erse clare language, Nought-
noughtnought nein. Assass. Dublire, per Neuropaths. Punk.
Starving today plays punk opening tomorrow two plays punk
wire splosh how two plays punk Cabler. Have you forgotten
poor Alby Sobrinos, Geoff, you blighter, identifiable by the
necessary white patch on his rear? How he went to his swilters-
land after his lungs, my sad late brother, before his coglionial
expancian? Won't you join me in a small halemerry, a bottle of
the best, for wellmet Capeler, united Irishmen, what though preferring the stranger, the coughs and the itches and the minnies
and the ratties the opulose and bilgenses, for of his was the
patriots mistaken. The heart that wast our Graw McGree!

Yet be there some who mourn him, concluding him dead,
and more there be that wait astand. His fuchs up the staires
and the ladgers in his haires, he ought to win that *V.V.C.*
Fullgrapce for an endupper, half muxy on his whole! Would
he were even among the lost! From ours bereft beyond belongs. Oremus poor fraternibus that he may yet escape the
gallews and still remain ours faithfully departed. I wronged you.
I never want to see more of bad men but I want to learn from
any on the airse, like Tass with much thanks, here's ditto, if
he lives sameplace in the antipathies of austrasia or anywhere
with my fawngest on his hooshmoney, safe and damned, or
has hopped it or who can throw any lime on the sopjack,
my fond fosther, E. Obiit Nolan, The Workings, N.S.W.,
his condition off the Venerable Jerrybuilt, not belonging to
these parts, who, I remember ham to me, when we were like
bro and sis over our castor and porridge, with his roamin I
suppose, expecting for his clarenx negus, a teetotum abstainer.
He feels he ought to be as asamed of me as me to be ashunned of
him. We were in one class of age like to two clots of egg. I am
most beholding to him, my namesick, as we sayed it in our Am-
harican, through the Doubly Telewisher. Outpassed hearts wag
short pertimes. Worndown shoes upon his feet, to whose redress no tongue can tell! In his hands a boot! Spare me, do, a
copper or two and happy I'll hope you'll be! It will pleased
me behind with thanks from before and love to self and all I
remain here your truly friend. I am no scholar but I loved that
man who has africot lupps with the moonshane in his profile,
my shemblable! My freer! I call you my halfbrother because
you in your soberer otiumic moments remind me deeply of my
natural saywhen brothel in feed, hop and jollity, S. H. Devitt,
that benighted irismaimed, who is tearly belaboured by Sydney
and Alibany.

— As you sing it it's a study. That letter selfpenned to one's
other, that neverperfect everplanned?

— This nonday diary, this allnights newseryreel.

— My dear sir! In this wireless age any owl rooster can peck

up bostoons. But whoewaxed he so anquished? Was he vector
victored of victim vexed?

  — Mighty sure! Way way for his wehicul! A parambolator
ram into his bagsmall when he was reading alawd, with two eco-
lites and he's been failing of that kink in his arts over sense.

  — Madonagh and Chiel, idealist leading a double life! But who
for the brilliance of brothers is the Nolan as appearant nominally?

  — Mr Nolan is pronuminally Mr Gottgab.

  — I get it. By hearing his thing about a person one begins to
place him for a certain in true. You reeker, he stands pat for
you before a direct object in the feminine. I see. By maiden
sname. Now, I am earnestly asking you, and putting it as
between this yohou and that houmonymh, will just you search
through your gabgut memoirs for all of two minutes for this
impersonating pronolan, fairhead on foulshoulders. Would it be
in twofold truth an untaken mispatriate, too fullfully true and
rereally a doblinganger much about your own medium with a
sandy whiskers? Poke me nabs in the ribs and pick the erstwort
out of his mouth.

  — Treble Stauter of Holy Baggot Street, formerly Sword-
meat, who I surpassed him lately for four and six bringing home
the Christmas, as heavy as music, hand to eyes on the peer for
Noel's Arch, in blessed foster's place is doing the dirty on me
with his tantrums and all these godforgiven kilowatts I'd be
better off without. She's write to him she's levt by me, Jenny
Rediviva! Toot! Detter for you, Mr Nobru. Toot toot! Better for
you, Mr Anol! This is the way we. Of a redtettetterday morning.

  — When your contraman from Tuwarceathay is looking for
righting that is not a good sign? Not?

  — I speak truly, it's a shower sign that it's not.

  — What though it be for the sow of his heart? If even she
were a good pool Pegeen?

  — If she ate your windowsill you wouldn't say sow.

  — Would you be surprised after that my asking have you a
bull, a bosbully, with a whistle in his tail to scare other birds?

  — I would.

— Were you with Sindy and Sandy attending Goliath, a bull?

— You'd make me sag what you like to. I was intending a funeral. Simply and samply.

— They are too wise of solbing their silbings?

— And both croon to the same theme.

— Tugbag is Baggut's, when a crispin sokolist besoops juts kamps or clapperclaws an irvingite offthedocks. A luckchange, I see. Thinking young through the muddleage spread, the moral fat his mental leans on. We can cop that with our straat that is called corkscrewed. It would be the finest boulevard billy for a mile in every direction, from Lismore to Cape Brendan, Patrick's, if they took the bint out of the mittle of it. You told of a tryst too, two a tutu. I wonder now, without releasing seeklets of the alcove, turturs or raabraabs have, I heard mention of whose name anywhere? Mallowlane or Demaasch? Strike us up either end *Have You Erred off Van Homper* or *Ebell Teresa Kane.*

— *Marak! Marak! Marak!*

He drapped has draraks an Mansianhase parak

And he had ta barraw tha watarcrass shartclaths aff tha ark-bashap af Yarak!

— Braudribnob's on the bummel?

— And lillypets on the lea.

— A being again in becomings again. From the sallies to the allies through their central power?

— Pirce! Perce! Quick! Queck!

— O Tara's thrush, the sharepusher! And he said he was only taking the average grass temperature for green Thurdsday, the blutchy scaliger! Who you know the musselman, his muscle-mum and mistlemam? Maomi, Mamie, My Mo Mum! He loves a drary lane. Feel Phylliscitations to daff Mr Hairwigger who has just hadded twinned little curls! He was resting between horrockses' sheets, wailing for white warfare, prooboor welsht-breton, and unbiassed by the embarrassment of disposal but, the first woking day by Thunder, he stepped into the breach and put on his recriution trousers and riding apron in Baltic Bygrad, the old soggy, was when the bold bhuoys of Iran wouldn't join up.

— How voice you that, nice Sandy man? Not large goodman
is he, Sandy nice. Ask him this one minute upthrow inner lotus
of his burly ear womit he dropped his Bass's to P flat. And for
that he was allaughed? And then baited? The whole gammat?

— Loonacied! Marterdyed!! Madwakemiherculossed!!! Ju-
dascessed!!!! Pairaskivvymenassed!!!!! Luredogged!!!!!! And,
needatellye, faulscrescendied!!!!!!!

— Dias domnas! Dolled to dolthood? And Annie Delittle,
his daintree diva, in deltic dwilights, singing him henpecked rusish
through the bars? My Wolossay's wild as the Crasnian Sea!
Grabashag, groogy, scoop and I'll cure ye! Mother of emeralds,
ara poog neighbours!

— Capilla, Rubrilla and Melcamomilla! Dauby, dauby, without dulay! Well, I beg to traverse same above statement by saxy
luters in their back haul of Coalcutter what reflects upon my
administrants of slow poisoning as my dodear devere revered
mainhirr was confined to guardroom, I hindustand, by my pint
of his Filthered pilsens bottle due to Zenaphiah Holwell, H and
J. C. S, Which I was bringing up my quee parapotacarry's orders
in my sedown chair with my mudfacepacket from my cash
chemist and family drugger, Surager Dowling, V.S. to our aural
surgeon, Afamado Hairductor Achmed Borumborad, M.A.C.A,
Sahib, of a 1001 Ombrilla Street, Syringa padham, Alleypulley, to
see what was my watergood, my mesical wasserguss, for repairs
done by bollworm in the rere of pilch knickers, seven yerds to
his galandhar pole on perch, together with his for me unfillable
slopper, property of my deeply forfear revebereared, who is costing
us mostfortunes which I am writing in mepetition to Kavanagh
Djanaral, when he was sitting him humpbacked in dry dryfilthy-
heat to his trinidads pinslers at their orpentings, entailing a
laxative tendency to mary, especially with him being forbidden
fruit and Certified by his sexular clergy to have as badazmy
emotional volvular, with a basketful of priesters crossing the
singorgeous to aroint him with tummy moor's maladies, and
thereinafter liable to succumb when served with letters potent
below the belch, if my rupee repure riputed husbandship H.R.R.

took a brief one in his shirtsails out of the alleged given mineral,
telling me see his in Foraignghistan sambat papers Sunday feac-
tures of a welcomed aperrytiff with vallad of Erill Pearcey O
he never battered one eagle's before paying me his duty on my
annaversary to the parroteyes list in my nil ensemble, in his lazy-
chair but he hidded up my hemifaces in all my mayarannies and
he locked plum into my mirrymouth like Ysamasy morning in
the end of time, with the so light's hope on his ruddycheeks and
rawjaws and, my charmer, whom I dipped my hand in, he simply
showed me his propendiculous loadpoker, Seaserpents hisses
sissastones, which was as then is produced in his mansway by
this wisest of the Vikramadityationists, with the remere remind
remure remark, in his gulughurutty: Yran for parasites with rum
for the turkeycockeys so Lithia, M.D., as this is for Snooker,
bort.

— Which was said by whem to whom?

— It wham. But whim I can't whumember.

— Fantasy! funtasy on fantasy, amnaes fintasies! And there is
nihil nuder under the clothing moon. When Ota, weewahrwificle
of Torquells, bumpsed her dumpsydiddle down in her woolsark
she mode our heuteyleutey girlery of peerlesses to set up in all
their bombossities of feudal fiertey, fanned, flounced and frangi-
panned, while the massstab whereby Ephialtes has exceeded is the
measure, *simplex mendaciis*, by which our Outis cuts his thruth.
Arkaway now!

— Yerds and nudes say ayes and noes! Vide! Vide!

— Let Eivin bemember for Gates of Gold for their fadeless
suns berayed her. Irise, Osirises! Be thy mouth given unto thee!
For why do you lack a link of luck to poise a pont of perfect,
peace? On the vignetto is a ragingoos. The overseer of the house
of the oversire of the seas, Nu-Men, triumphant, sayeth: Fly as
the hawk, cry as the corncrake, Ani Latch of the postern is thy
name; shout!

— My heart, my mother! My heart, my coming forth of
darkness! They know not my heart, O coolun dearast! Mon
gloomerie! Mon glamourie! What a surpraise, dear Mr Preacher,

I to hear from your strawnummical modesty! Yes, there was
that skew arch of chrome sweet home, floodlit up above the
flabberghosted farmament and bump where the camel got the
needle. Talk about iridecencies! Ruby and beryl and chrysolite,
jade, sapphire, jasper and lazul.

— Orca Bellona! Heavencry at earthcall, etnat athos? Extinct
your vulcanology for the lava of Moltens!

— It's you not me's in erupting, hecklar!

— Ophiuchus being visible above thorizon, muliercula occluded by Satarn's serpent ring system the pisciolinnies Nova
Ardonis and Prisca Parthenopea, are a bonnies feature in the
northern sky. Ers, Mores and Merkery are surgents below the rim
of the Zenith Part while Arctura, Anatolia, Hesper and Mesembria
weep in their mansions over Noth, Haste, Soot and Waste.

— Apep and Uachet! Holy snakes, chase me charley, Eva's
got barley under her fluencies! The Ural Mount he's on the
move and he'll quivvy her with his strombolo! Waddlewurst,
the bag of tow, as broad above as he is below! Creeping
through the liongrass and bullsrusshius, the obesendean, before
the Emfang de Maurya's class, in Bill Shasser's Shotshrift writing
academy, camouflaged as a blancmange and maple syrop! Obeisance so their sitinins is the follicity of this Orp. Her sheik to
Slave, his dick to Dave and the fat of the land to Guygas. The
treadmill pebbledropper haha halfahead overground and she'd
only chitschats in her spanking bee bonetry, Allapolloosa! Up the
slanger! Three cheers and a heva heva for the name Dan Magraw!

The giant sun is in his emanence but which is chief of those
white dwarfees of which he ever is surabanded? And do you think
I might have being his seventh! He will kitssle me on melbaw.
What about his age? says you. What about it? says I. I will
confess to his sins and blush me further. I would misdemean to
rebuke to the libels of snots from the fleshambles the canalles.
Synamite is too good for them. Two overthirties in shore shor-
ties. She's askapot at Nile Lodge and she's citchincarry at the
left Mrs Hamazum's. Will you warn your old habasund, barking
at baggermen, his chokefull chewing his chain? Responsif you

plais. The said Sully, a barracker associated with tinkers, the blackhand, Shovellyvans, wreuter of annoyimgmost letters and skirriless ballets in Parsee Franch who is Magrath's thug and smells cheaply of Power's spirits, like a deepsea dibbler, and he is not fit enough to throw guts down to a bear. Sylphling me when is a maid nought a maid he would go to anyposs length for her! So long, Sulleyman! If they cut his nose on the stitcher they had their siven good reasons. Here's to the leglift of my snuff and trout stockangt henkerchoff, orange fin with a mosaic of dispensations and a froren black patata, from my church milliner. When Lynch Brother, Withworkers, Friends and Company with T. C. King and the Warden of Galway is prepared to stretch him sacred by the powers to the starlight, L.B.W. Hemp, hemp, hurray! says the captain in the moonlight. I could put him under my pallyass and slepp on him all nights as I would roll myself for holy poly over his borrowing places. How we will make laugh over him together, me and my Riley in the Vickar's bed! Quink! says I. He cawls to me Granny-stream-Auborne when I am hiding under my hair from him and I cool him my Finnyking he's so joyant a bounder. Plunk! said he. Inasmuch as I am delightful to be able to state, with the joy of lifing in my forty winkers, that a handsome sovereign was freely pledged in their pennis in the sluts maschine, alonging wath a cherry-wickerkishabrack of maryfruit under Shadow La Rose, to both the legintimate lady performers of display unquestionable, Elsebett and Marryetta Gunning, H 2 O, by that noblesse of leechers at his Saxontannery with motto in Wwalshe's ffrenchllatin: O'Neill saw Queen Molly's pants: and much admired engraving, meaning complet manly parts during alleged recent act of our chief mergey margey magistrades, five itches above the kneecap, as required by statues. V.I.C.5.6. If you won't release me stop to please me up the leg of me. Now you see! Respect. S.V.P. Your wife. Amn. Anm. Amm. Ann.

— You wish to take us, Frui Mria, by degrees, as *artis litterarum-que patrona* but I am afraid, my poor woman of that same name, what with your silvanes and your salvines, you are misled.

— Alas for livings' pledjures!

— Lordy Daw and Lady Don! Uncle Foozle and Aunty
Jack! Sure, that old humbugger was boycotted and girlcutted
in debt and doom, on hill and haven, even by the show-the-flag
flotilla, as I'm given now to understand, illscribed in all the
gratuitouses and conspued in the takeyourhandaways. Bumbty,
tumbty, Sot on a Wall, Mute art for the Million. There wasn't an
Archimandrite of Dane's Island and the townlands nor a minx
from the Isle of Woman nor a one of the four cantins nor any on
the whole wheel of his ecunemical conciliabulum nor nogent
ingen meid on allad the hold scurface of the jorth would come
next or nigh him, Mr Eelwhipper, seed and nursery man, or
his allgas bumgalowre, Auxilium Meum Solo A Domino (Amsad),
for rime or ration, from piles or faces, after that.

— All ears did wag, old Eire wake as Piers Aurell was flapper-
gangsted.

— Recount!

— I have it here to my fingall's ends. This liggy piggy wanted
to go to the jampot. And this leggy peggy spelt pea. And theese
lucky puckers played at pooping tooletom. Ma's da. Da's ma.
Madas. Sadam.

— *Pater patruum cum filiabus familiarum.* Or, but, now, and,
ariring out of her mirgery margery watersheads and, to change
that subjunct from the traumaturgid for once in a while and darting back to stuff if so be you may identify yourself with the him
in you, that fluctuous neck merchamtur, bloodfadder and milk-
mudder, since then our too many of her, Abha na Lifé, and getting
on to dadaddy again, as them we're ne'er free of, was he in tea
e'er he went on the bier or didn't he ontime do something seemly
heavy in sugar? He sent out Christy Columb and he came back
with a jailbird's unbespokables in his beak and then he sent out
Le Caron Crow and the peacies are still looking for him. The
seeker from the swayed, the beesabouties from the parent swarm.
Speak to the right! Rotacist ca canny! He caun ne'er be bothered
but maun e'er be waked. If there is a future in every past that is
present *Quis est qui non novit quinnigan* and *Qui quae quot at*

Quinnigan's Quake! Stump! His producers are they not his con-
sumers? Your exagmination round his factification for incamination of a warping process. Declaim!

— Arra irrara hirrara man, weren't they arriving in clansdes-
tinies for the Imbandiment of *Ad Regias Agni Dapes*, fogabawlers
and panhibernskers, after the crack and the lean years, scalpjaggers
and houthhunters, like the messicals of the great god, a scarlet
trainful, the Twoedged Petrard, totalling, leggats and prelaps, in
their aggregate ages two and thirty plus undecimmed centries
of them with insiders, extraomnes and tuttifrutties allcunct, from
Rathgar, Rathanga, Rountown and Rush, from America Avenue
and Asia Place and the Affrian Way and Europa Parade and be-
sogar the wallies of Noo Soch Wilds and from Vico, Mespil
Rock and Sorrento, for the lure of his weal and the fear of his
oppidumic, to his salon de espera in the keel of his kraal, like
lodes of ores flocking fast to Mount Maximagnetic, afeerd he was
a gunner but affaird to stay away, Merrionites, Dumstdumb-
drummers, Luccanicans, Ashtoumers, Batterysby Parkes and
Krumlin Boyards, Phillipsburgs, Cabraists and Finglossies,
Ballymunites, Raheniacs and the bettlers of Clontarf, for to con-
template in manifest and pay their firstrate duties before the both
of him, twelve stone a side, with their *Thieve le Roué!* and their
Shvr yr Thrst! and their *Uisgye ad Inferos!* and their *Usque ad
Ebbraios!* at and in the licensed boosiness primises of his del-
hightful bazar and reunited magazine hall, by the magazine wall,
Hosty's and Co, Exports, for his five hundredth and sixtysixth
borthday, the grand old Magennis Mor, Persee and Rahli, taker
of the tributes, their Rinseky Poppakork and Piowtor the Grape,
holding Dunker's durbar, boot kings and indiarubber umpires
and shawhs from paisley and muftis in muslim and sultana
reiseines and jordan almonders and a row of jam sahibs and a
odd principeza in her pettedcoat and the queen of knight's clubs
and the claddagh ringleaders and the two salaames and the Halfa
Ham and the Hanzas Khan with two fat Maharashers and the
German selver geyser and he polished up, protemptible, tintanam-
bulating to himsilf so silfrich, and there was J. B. Dunlop, the

best tyrent of ourish times, and a swanks of French wine stuarts
and Tudor keepsakes and the Cesarevitch for the current counter Leodegarius Sant Legerleger riding lapsaddlelonglegs up the
oakses staircase on muleback like Amaxodias Isteroprotos, hindquarters to the fore and kick to the lift, and he handygrabbed on
to his trulley natural anthem: *Horsibus, keep your tailyup,* and
as much as the halle of the vacant fhroneroom, Oldloafs
Buttery, could safely accomodate of the houses of Orange and
Betters M.P, permeated by Druids D.P, Brehons B.P, and
Flawhoolags F.P, and Agiapommenites A.P, and Antepum-
melites P.P, and Ulster Kong and Munster's Herald with
Athclee Ensigning and Athlone Poursuivant and his Imperial
Catchering, his fain awan, and his gemmynosed sanctsons
in epheud and ordilawn and his diamondskulled granddaucher,
Adamantaya Liubokovskva, all murdering Irish, amok and
amak, out of their boom companions in paunchjab and dogril
and pammel and gougerotty, after plenty of his fresh stout and
his good balls of malt, not to forget his oels a'mona nor his beers
o'ryely, sopped down by his pani's annagolorum, (at Kennedy's
kiln she kned her dough, back of her bake for me, buns!) social-
izing and communicanting in the deification of his members, for
to nobble or salvage their herobit of him, the poohpooher old
bolssloose, with his arthurious clayroses, Dodderick Ogonoch
Wrack, busted to the wurld at large, on the table round, with the
floodlight switched back, as true as the Vernons have Brian's
sword, and a dozen and one by one tilly tallows round in ring-
campf, circumassembled by his daughters in the foregiftness of
his sons, lying high as he lay in all dimensions, in court dress and
ludmers chain, with a hogo, fluorescent of his swathings, round
him, like the cummulium of scents in an italian warehouse, erica's
clustered on his hayir, the spectrem of his prisent mocking the
candiedights of his dadtid, bagpuddingpodded to the deafspot,
bewept of his chilidrin and serafim, poors and personalities, ven-
turous, drones and dominators, ancients and auldancients, with
his buttend up, expositoed for sale after referee's inspection,
bulgy and blowrious, bunged to ignorious, healed cured and

embalsemate, pending a rouseruction of his bogey, most highly astounded, as it turned up, after his life overlasting, at thus being reduced to nothing.

— Bappy-go-gully and gaff for us all! And all his morties calisenic, tripping a trepas, neniatwantyng: Mulo Mulelo! Homo Humilo! Dauncy a deady O! Dood dood dood! O Bawse! O Boese! O Muerther! O Mord! Mahmato! Moutmaro! O Smirtsch! O Smertz! Woh Hillill! Woe Hallall! Thou Thuoni! Thou Thaunaton! Umartir! Udamnor! Tschitt! Mergue! Eulumu! Huam Khuam! Malawinga! Malawunga! Ser Oh Ser! See ah See! Hamovs! Hemoves! Mamor! Rockquiem eternuel give donal aye in dolmeny! Bad luck's perpepperpot loosen his eyis! (Psich!).

— But there's leps of flam in Funnycoon's Wick. The keyn has passed. Lung lift the keying!

— God save you king! Muster of the Hidden Life!

— God serf yous kingly, adipose rex! I had four in the morning and a couple of the lunch and three later on, but your saouls to the dhaoul, do ye. Finnk. Fime. Fudd?

— Impassable tissue of improbable liyers! D'yu mean to sett there where y'are now, coddlin your supernumerary leg, wi'that bizar tongue in yur tolkshap, and your hindies and shindies, like a muck in a market, Sorley boy, repeating yurself, and tell me that?

— I mean to sit here on this altknoll where you are now, Surly guy, replete in myself, as long as I live, in my homespins, like a sleepingtop, with all that's buried ofsins insince insensed insidesofme. If I can't upset this pound of pressed ollaves I can sit up zounds of sounds upon him.

— Oliver! He may be an earthpresence. Was that a groan or did I hear the Dingle bagpipes Wasting war and? Watch!

— *Tris tris a ni ma mea!* Prisoner of Love! Bleating Hart! Lowlaid Herd! Aubain Hand! Wonted Foot! *Usque! Usque! Usque! Lignum in* . . .

— Rawth of Gar and Donnerbruck Fire? Is the strays world moving mound or what static babel is this, tell us?

— Whoishe whoishe whoishe whoishe linking in? Whoishe whoishe whoishe?

— The snare drum! Lay yer lug till the groun. The dead giant manalive! They're playing thimbles and bodkins. Clan of the Gael! Hop! Whu's within?

— Dovegall and finshark, they are ring to the rescune!

— Zinzin. Zinzin.

— Crum abu! Cromwell to victory!

— We'll gore them and gash them and gun them and gloat on them.

— Zinzin.

— O, widows and orphans, it's the yeomen! Redshanks for ever! Up Lancs!

— The cry of the roedeer it is! The white hind. Their slots, linklink, the hound hunthorning! Send us and peace! Title! Title!

— Christ in our irish times! Christ on the airs independence! Christ hold the freedman's chareman! Christ light the dully expressed!

— Slog. slagt and sluaghter! Rape the daughter! Choke the pope!

— Aure! Cloudy father! Unsure! Nongood!

— Zinzin.

— Sold! I am sold! Brinabride! My ersther! My sidster! Brinabride, goodbye! Brinabride! I sold!

— Pipette dear! Us! Us! Me! Me!

— Fort! Fort! Bayroyt! March!

— Me! I'm true. True! Isolde. Pipette. My precious!

— Zinzin.

— Brinabride, bet my price! Brinabride!

— My price, my precious?

— Zin.

— Brinabride, my price! When you sell get my price!

— Zin.

— Pipette! Pipette, my priceless one!

— O! Mother of my tears! Believe for me! Fold thy son!

— Zinzin. Zinzin.

— Now we're gettin it. Tune in and pick up the forain counties! Hello!

— Zinzin.

— Hello! Tittit! Tell your title?

— Abride!

— Hellohello! Ballymacarett! Am I thru' Iss? Miss? True?

— Tit! What is the ti . . ?

SILENCE.

Act drop. Stand by! Blinders! Curtain up. Juice, please! Foots!

— Hello! Are you Cigar shank and Wheat?

— I gotye. Gobble Ann's Carrot Cans.

— Parfey. Now, after that justajiff siesta, just permit me a moment. Challenger's Deep is childsplay to this but, by our soundings in the swish channels, land is due. A truce to demobbed swarwords. Clear the line, priority call! Sybil! Better that or this? Sybil Head this end! Better that way? Follow the baby spot. Yes. Very good now. We are again in the magnetic field. Do you remember on a particular lukesummer night, following a crying fair day? Moisten your lips for a lightning strike and begin again. Mind the flickers and dimmers! Better?

— Well. The isles is Thymes. The ales is Penzance. Vehement Genral. Delhi expulsed.

— Still calling of somewhave from its specific? Not more? Lesscontinuous. There were fires on every bald hill in holy Ireland that night. Better so?

— You may say they were, son of a cove!

— Were they bonfires? That clear?

— No other name would at all befit them unless that. Bonafieries! With their blue beards streaming to the heavens.

— Was it a high white night now?

— Whitest night mortal ever saw.

— Was our lord of the heights nigh our lady of the valley?

— He was hosting himself up and flosting himself around and ghosting himself to merry her murmur like an andeanupper balkan.

— Lewd's carol! Was there rain by any chance, mistandew?

— Plenty. If you wend farranoch.

— There fell some fall of littlewinter snow, holy-as-ivory, I gather, jesse?

— By snaachtha clocka. The nicest at all. In hilly-and-even zimalayars.

— Did it not blow some gales, westnass or ostscent, rather strongly to less, allin humours out of turn, jusse as they rose and sprungen?

— Out of all jokes it did. Pipep! Icecold. Brr na brr, ny prr! Lieto galumphantes!

— Stll cllng! Nmr! Peace, Pacific! Do you happen to recollect whether Muna, that highlucky nackt, was shining at all!

— Sure she was, my midday darling! And not one but a pair of pritty geallachers.

— Quando? Quonda? Go datey!

— Latearly! Latearly! Latearly! Latearly!

— That was latterlig certainly. And was there frostwork about and thick weather and hice, soon calid, soon frozen, cold on warm but moistly dry, and a boatshaped blanket of bruma airsighs and hellstohns and flammballs and vodashouts and everything to please everybody?

— Hail many fell of greats! Horey morey smother of fog! There was, so plays your ahrtides. Absolutely boiled. Obsoletely cowled. Julie and Lulie at their parkiest.

— The amenities, the amenities of the amenities with all their amenities. And the firmness of the formous of the famous of the fumous of the first fog in Maidanvale?

— Catchecatche and couchamed!

— From Miss Somer's nice dream back to Mad Winthrop's delugium stramens. One expects that kind of rimey feeling in the sire season?

— One certainly does. Desire, for hire, would tire a shire, phone, phunkel, or wire. And mares.

— Of whitecaps any?

— Foamflakes flockfuyant from Foxrock to Finglas.

— A lambskip for the marines! Paronama! The entire horizon cloth! All effects in their joints caused ways. Raindrum, windmachine, snowbox. But thundersheet?

— No here. Under the blunkets.

— This common or garden is now in stiller realithy the starey sphere of an oleotorium for broken pottery and ancient vegetables?

— Simply awful the dirt. An evernasty ashtray.

— I see. Now do you know the wellknown kikkinmidden where the illassorted first couple first met with each other? The place where Ealdermann Fanagan? The time when Junkermenn Funagin?

— Deed then I do, W.K.

— In Fingal too they met at Littlepeace aneath the bidetree, Yellowhouse of Snugsborough, Westreeve-Astagob and Sluts-end with Stockins of Winning's Folly merryfalls, all of a two, skidoo and skephumble?

— Godamedy, you're a delville of a tolkar!

— Is it a place fairly exspoused to the four last winds?

— Well, I faithly sincerely believe so indeed if all what I hope to charity is half true.

— This stow on the wolds, is it Woful Dane Bottom?

— It is woful in need whatever about anything or allselse under the grianblachk sun of gan greyne Eireann.

— A tricolour ribbon that spells a caution. The old flag, the cold flag.

— The flagstone. By tombs, deep and heavy. To the unaveiling memory of. Peacer the grave.

— And what sigeth Woodin Warneung thereof?

— Trickspissers vill be pairsecluded.

— There used to be a tree stuck up? An overlisting eshtree?

— There used, sure enough. Beside the Annar. At the ford of Slivenamond. Oakley Ashe's elm. With a snoodrift from one beerchen bough. And the grawndest crowndest consecrated may-pole in all the reignladen history of Wilds. Browne's *Thesaurus Plantarum* from Nolan's, The Prittlewell Press, has nothing alike it. For we are fed of its forest, clad in its wood, burqued by its bark and our lecture is its leave. The cram, the cram, the king of all crams. Squiremade and damesman of plantagenets, high and holy.

— Now, no hiding your wren under a bushle. What was it doing there, for instance?

— Standing foreninst us.

— In Summerian sunshine?

— And in Cimmerian shudders.

— You saw it visibly from your hidingplace?

— No. From my invisibly lyingplace.

— And you then took down in stereo what took place being tunc committed?

— I then tuk my takenplace lying down, I thunk I told you. Solve it!

— Remounting aliftle towards the ouragan of spaces. Just how grand in cardinal rounders is this preeminent giant, sir Arber? Your bard's highview, avis on valley! I would like to hear you burble to us in strict conclave, purpurando, and without too much italiote interfairance, what you know *in petto* about our sovereign beingstalk, Tonans Tomazeus. *O dite!*

— Corcor Andy, *Udi*, *Udite!* Your Ominence, Your Imminence and delicted fraternitrees! There's tuodore queensmaids and Idahore shopgirls and they woody babies growing upon her and bird flamingans sweenyswinging fuglewards on the tipmast and Orania epples playing hopptociel bommptaterre and Tyburn fenians snoring in his quickenbole and crossbones strewing its holy floor and culprines of Erasmus Smith's burstall boys with their underhand leadpencils climbing to her crotch for the origin of spices and charlotte darlings with silk blue askmes chattering in dissent to them, gibbonses and gobbenses, guelfing and ghiberring proferring praydews to their anatolies and blighting findblasts on their catastripes and the killmaimthem pensioners chucking overthrown milestones up to her to fall her cranberries and her pommes annettes for their unnatural refection and handpainted hoydens plucking husbands of him and cock robins muchmore hatching most out of his missado eggdrazzles for him, the sun and moon pegging honeysuckle and white

heather down and timtits tapping resin there and tomahawks
watching tar elsewhere, creatures of the wold approaching him,
hollow mid ivy, for to claw and rub, hermits of the desert
barking their infernal shins over her triliteral roots and his acorns
and pinecorns shooting wide all sides out of him, plantitude
outsends of plenty to thousands, after the truants of the utmost-
fear and her downslyder in that snakedst-tu-naughsy whimmering
woman't seeleib such a fashionaping sathinous dress out of that
exquisitive creation and her leaves, my darling dearest, sinsin-
sinning since the night of time and each and all of their branches
meeting and shaking twisty hands all over again in their new
world through the germination of its gemination from Ond's
outset till Odd's end. And encircle him circuly. Evovae!

— Is it so exaltated, eximious, extraoldandairy and excels-
siorising?

— Amengst menlike trees walking or trees like angels weeping nobirdy aviar soar anywing to eagle it! But rocked of agues,
cliffed for aye!

— Telleth that eke the treeth?

— Mushe, mushe of a mixness.

— A shrub of libertine, indeed! But that steyne of law indead
what stiles its neming?

— Tod, tod, too hard parted!

— I've got that now, Dr Melamanessy. Finight mens mid-
infinite true. The form masculine. The gender feminine. I see.
Now, are you derevatov of it yourself in any way? The true
tree I mean? Let's hear what science has to say, pundit-the-
next-best-king. Splanck!

— Upfellbowm.

— It reminds of the weeping of the daughters?

— And remounts to the sense arrest.

— The wittold, the frausch and the dibble! How this loose-
affair brimsts of fussforus! And was this treemanangel on his
soredbohmend because Knockout, the knickknaver, knacked
him in the knechtschaft?

— Well, he was ever himself for the presention of crudities to

animals for he had put his own nickelname on every toad, duck
and herring before the climber clomb aloft, doing the midhill of
the park, flattering his bitter hoolft with her conconundrums.
He would let us have the three barrels. Such was a bitte too thikke
for the Muster of the hoose so as he called down on the Grand
Precurser who coiled him a crawler of the dupest dye and
thundered at him to flatch down off that erection and be aslimed
of himself for the bellance of hissch leif.

— Oh Finlay's coldpalled!

— Ahday's begatem!

— Were you there, eh Hehr? Were you there when they
lagged um through the coombe?

— Wo wo! Who who! Psalmtimes it grauws on me to ramble,
ramble, ramble.

— Woe! Woe! So that was how he became the foerst of our
treefellers?

— Yesche and, in the absence of any soberiquiet, the fanest
of our truefalluses. Bapsbaps Bomslinger!

— How near do you feel to this capocapo promontory sir?

— There do be days of dry coldness between us when he does
be like a lidging house far far astray and there do be nights of wet
windwhistling when he does be making me onions woup all kinds
of ways.

— Now you are mehrer the murk, Lansdowne Road. She's
threwed her pippin's thereabouts and they've cropped up tooth
oneydge with hates to leaven this socried isle. Now, thornyborn,
follow the spotlight, please! Concerning a boy. Are you acquainted
with a pagany, vicariously known as Toucher 'Thom' who is. I
suggest Finoglam as his habitat. Consider yourself on the stand
now and watch your words, take my advice. Let your motto be:
Inter nubila numbum.

— Never you mind about my mother or her hopitout. I consider if I did, I would feel frightfully ashamed of admired vice.

— He is a man of around fifty, struck on Anna Lynsha's
Pekoe with milk and whisky, who does messuages and has more
dirt on him than an old dog has fleas, kicking stones and knocking

snow off walls. Have you ever heard of this old boy "Thom" or
"Thim" of the fishy stare who belongs to Kimmage, a crofting district, and is not all there, and is all the more himself since he is
not so, being most of his time down at the Green Man where he
steals, pawns, belches and is a curse, drinking gaily two hours after
closing time, with the coat on him skinside out against rappari-
tions, with his socks outsewed his springsides, clapping his hands
in a feeble sort of way and systematically mixing with the public
going for groceries, slapping greats and littlegets soundly with
his cattegut belts, flapping baresides and waltzywembling about
in his accountrements always in font of the tubbernuckles, like
a longarmed lugh, when he would be finished with his tea?

— Is it that fellow? As mad as the brambles he is. Touch him.
With the lawyers sticking to his trewsershins and the swatme-
notting on the basque of his beret. He has kissed me more than
once, I am sorry to say and if I did commit gladrolleries may the
loone forgive it. O wait till I tell you!

— We are not going yet.

— And look here! Here's, my dear, what he done, as snooks
as I am saying so!

— Get out, you dirt! A strangely striking part òf speech for
the hottest worked word of ur sprogue. You're not! Unhindered
and odd times? Mere thumbshow? Lately?

— How do I know? Such my billet. Buy a barrack pass. Ask
the horneys. Tell the robbers.

— You are alluding to the picking pockets in Lower O'Connell
Street?

— I am illuding to the Pekin packet but I am eluding from
Laura Connor's treat.

— Now, just wash and brush up your memoirias a little bit.
So I find, referring to the pater of the present man, an erely demented brick thrower, I am wondering to myself in my mind,
qua our arc of the covenant, was Toucher, a methodist, whose
name, as others say, is not really 'Thom', was this salt son of a
century from Boaterstown, Shivering William, the sealiest old for-
ker ever hawked crannock, who is always with him at the Big Elm

and the Arch after his teeth were shaken out of their suckets by the wrang dog, for having 5 pints 73 of none Eryen blood in him abaft the seam level, the scatterling, wearing his cowbeamer and false clothes of a brewer's grains pattern with back buckons with his motto on, *Yule Remember*, ostensibly for that occasiononly of the twelfth day Pax and Quantum wedding, I'm wondering.

— I bet you are. Well, he was wandering, you bet, whatever was his matter, in his mind too, give him his due, for I am sorry to have to tell you, hullo and evoe, they were coming down from off him.

— How culious an epiphany!

— *Hodie casus esobhrakonton?*

— It looked very like it.

— Needer knows necess and neither garments. Man is minded of the Meagher, wat? Wooly? Walty?

— Ay, another good button gone wrong.

— Blondman's blaff! Like a skib leaked lintel the arbour leidend with . . . ?

— Pamelas, peggylees, pollywollies, questuants, quaint-aquilties, quickamerries.

— Concaving now convexly to the semidemihemispheres and, from the female angle, music minnestirring, were the subligate sisters, P. and Q., Clopatrick's cherierapest, *mutatis mutandis*, in pretty much the same pickle, the peach of all piedom, the quest of all quicks?

— Peequeen ourselves, the prettiest pickles of unmatchemable mute antes I ever bopeeped at, seesaw shallshee, since the town go went gonning on Pranksome Quaine.

— Silks apeel and sulks alusty?

— Boy and giddle, gape and bore.

— I hear these two goddesses are liable to sue him?

— Well, I hope the two Collinses don't leg a bail to shoot him.

— Both were white in black arpists at cloever spilling, knickt?

— Gels bach, I, languised, liszted. Etoudies for the right hand.

— Were they now? And were they watching you as watcher as well?

— Where do you get that wash? This representation does not accord with my experience. They were watching the watched watching. Vechers all.

— Good. Hold that watching brief and keep this witching longuer. Now, retouching friend Tomsky, the enemy, did you gather much from what he let drop? We are sitting here for that.

— I was rooshian mad, no lie. About his shapeless hat.

— I suspect you must have been.

— You are making your thunderous mistake. But I was dung sorry for him too.

— O Schaum! Not really? Were you sorry you were mad with him then?

— When I tell you I was rooshiamarodnimad with myself altogether, so I was, for being sorry for him.

— So?

— Absolutely.

— Would you blame him at all stages?

— I believe in many an old stager. But what seemed sooth to a Greek summed nooth to a giantle. Who kills the cat in Cairo coaxes cocks in Gaul.

— I put it to you that this was solely in his sunflower state and that his haliodraping het was why maids all sighed for him, ventured and vied for him. Hm?

— After Putawayo, Kansas, Liburnum and New Aimstirdames, it wouldn't surprise me in the very least.

— That tare and this mole, your tear and our smile. 'Tis life that lies if woman's eyes have been our old undoing. Lid efter lid. Reform in mine size his deformation. Tiffpuff up my nostril, would you puff the earthworm outer my ear.

— He could claud boose his eyes to the birth of his garce, he could lump all his lot through the half of her play, but he jest couldn't laugh through the whole of her farce becorpse he warn't billed that way. So he outandouts his volimetangere and has a lightning consultation and he downadowns his pantoloogions and made a piece of first perpersonal puetry that staystale remains to be. Cleaned.

— Booms of bombs and heavy rethudders?

— This aim to you!

— The tail, so mastrodantic, as you tell it nearly takes your own mummouth's breath away. Your troppers are so unrelieved because his troopers were in difficulties. Still let stultitiam done in veino condone ineptias made of veritues. How many were married on that top of all strapping mornings, after the midnight turkay drive, my good watcher?

— Puppaps. That'd be telling. With a hoh frohim and heh fraher. But, as regards to Tammy Thornycraft, Idefyne the lawn mare and the laney moweress and all the prentisses of wildes to massage him.

— Now from Gunner Shotland to Guinness Scenography. Come to the ballay at the Tailors' Hall. We mean to be mellay on the Mailers' Mall. And leap, rink and make follay till the Gaelers' Gall. Awake! Come, a wake! Every old skin in the leather world, infect the whole stock company of the old house of the Leaking Barrel, was thomistically drunk, two by two, lairking o' tootlers with tombours a'beggars, the blog and turfs and the brandywine bankrompers, trou Normend fashion, I have been told, down to the bank lean clorks? Some nasty blunt clubs were being operated after the tradition of a wellesleyan bottle riot act and a few plates were being shied about and tumblers bearing traces of fresh porter rolling around, independent of that, for the ehren of Fyn's Insul, and then followed that wapping breakfast at the Heaven and Covenant, with Rodey O'echolowing how his breadcost on the voters would be a comeback for e'er a one, like the depredations of Scandalknivery, in and on usedtowobble sloops off cloasts, eh? Would that be a talltale too? This was the grandsire Orther. This was his innwhite horse. Sip?

— Well, naturally he was, louties also genderymen. Being Kerssfesstiydt. They came from all lands beyond the wave for songs of Inlshfeel. Whiskway and mortem! No puseyporcious either, invitem kappines all round. But the right reverend priest, Mr Hopsinbond, and the reverent bride eleft, Frizzy Fraufrau, were sober enough. I think they were sober.

— I think you're widdershins there about the right reverence.
Magraw for the Northwhiggern cupteam was wedding beastman,
papers before us carry. You saw him hurriedly, or did you if
thatseme's not irrelevant? With Slater's hammer perhaps? Or he
was in serge?

— I horridly did. On the stroke of the dozen. I'm sure I'm
wrong but I heard the irreverend Mr Magraw, in search of a
stammer, kuckkuck kicking the bedding out of the old sexton,
red-Fox Good-man around the sacristy, till they were bullbeadle
black and bufeteer blue, while I and Flood and the other men,
jazzlike brollies and sesuos, was gickling his missus to gackles in
the hall, the divileen, (she's a lamp in her throth) with her
cygncygn leckle and her twelve pound lach.

— A loyal wifish woman cacchinic wheepingcaugh! While
she laylylaw was all their rage. But you did establish personal
contact? In epexegesis or on a point of order?

— That perkumiary pond is beyawnd my pinnigay pre-
tonsions. I am resting on a pigs of cheesus but I've a big
suggestion it was about the pint of porter.

— You are a suckersome! But this all, as airs said to oska,
was only that childbearer might blogas well sidesplit? Where
letties hereditate a dark mien swart hairy?

— Only. 'Twas womans' too woman with mans' throw man.

— Bully burley yet hardly hurley. The saloon bulkhead, did
you say, or the tweendecks?

— Between drinks, I deeply painfully repeat it.

— Was she wearing shubladey's tiroirs in humour of her
hubbishobbis, Massa's star stellar?

— Mrs Tan-Taylour? Just a floating panel, secretairslid-
ingdraws, a budge of klees on her schalter, a siderbrass sehdass
on her anulas findring and forty crocelips in her curlingthongues.

— So this was the dope that woolied the cad that kinked the
ruck that noised the rape that tried the sap that hugged the mort?

— That legged in the hoax that joke bilked.

— The jest of junk the jungular?

— Jacked up in a jock the wrapper.

— Lollgoll! You don't soye so! All upsydown her whole
creation? So there was nothing serical between you? And Dry-
salter, father of Izod, how was he now?

— To the pink, man, like an allmanox in his shirt and stickup,
brustall to the bear, the Megalomagellan of our winevatswater-
way, squeezing the life out of the liffey.

— Crestofer Carambas! Such is zodisfaction. You punk me!
He came, he kished, he conquered. Vulturuvarnar! The must of
his glancefull coaxing the beam in her eye? That musked bell of
this masked ball! Annabella, Lovabella, Pullabella, yep?

— Yup! Titentung Tollertone in S. Sabina's. Aye aye, she
was lithe and pleasable. Wilt thou the lee? Wilt thou the hee?
Wilt thou the hussif?

— The quicker the deef the safter the sapstaff, but the main
the mightier the stricker the strait. To the vast go the game! It
is the circumconversioning of antelithual paganelles by a hugger-
knut cramwell energuman, or the caecodedition of an absque-
litteris puttagonnianne to the herreraism of a cabotinesque ex-
ploser?

— I believe you. Taiptope reelly, O reelly!

— Nautaey, nautaey, we're nowhere without ye! In steam of
kavos now arbatos above our hearths doth hum. And Malkos
crackles logs of fun while Anglys cheers our ingles. So lent she
him ear to burrow his manhood (or so it appierce) and borrow
his namas? Suilful eyes and sallowfoul hairweed and the sickly
sigh from her gingering mouth like a Dublin bar in the moarning.

— *Primus auriforasti me.*

— The park is gracer than the hole, says she, but shekleton's
my fortune?

— Eversought of being artained? You've soft a say with ye,
Flatter O'Ford, that, honey, I hurdley chew you.

— Is that answers?

— It am queery!

— The house was Toot and Come-Inn by the bridge called
Tiltass, but are you solarly salemly sure, beyond the shatter of
the canicular year? *Nascitur ordo seculi numfit.*

— Siriusly and selenely sure behind the shutter. *Securius indicat umbris tellurem.*

— Date as? Your time of immersion? We are still in drought of . . . ?

— Amnis Dominae, Marcus of Corrig. A laughin hunter and Purty Sue.

— And crazyheaded Jorn, the bulweh born?

— Fluteful as his orkan. *Ex ugola lenonem.*

— And Jambs, of Delphin's Bourne or (as olders lay) of Tophat?

— Dawncing the kniejinksky choreopiscopally like an easter sun round the colander, the vice! Taranta boontoday! You should pree him prance the polcat, you whould sniff him wops around, you should hear his piedigrotts schraying as his skimpies skirp a . . .

— Crashedafar Corumbas! A Czardanser indeed! Dervilish glad too. Ortovito semi ricordo. The pantaglionic affection through his blood like a bad influenza in a leap at bounding point?

— Out of Prisky Poppagenua, the palsied old priamite, home from Edwin Hamilton's Christmas pantaloonade, *Oropos Roxy and Pantharhea* at the Gaiety, trippudiating round the aria, with his fiftytwo heirs of age! They may reel at his likes but it's Noeh Bonum's shin do.

— And whit what was Lillabil Issabil maideve, maid at?

— Trists and thranes and trinies and traines.

— A take back to the virgin page, darm it!

— Ay, graunt ye.

— The quobus quartet were there too, if I mistake not, as a sideline but, *pace* the contempt of senate, well to the fore, in an amenessy meeting, metandmorefussed to decide whereagainwhen to meet themselves, flopsome and jerksome, lubber and deliric, drinking unsteadily through the Kerry quadrilles and Listowel lancers and mastersinging always with that consecutive fifth of theirs, eh? Like four wise elephants inandouting under a twelve-podestalled table?

— They were simple scandalmongers, that familiar, and all! Normand, Desmónd, Osmund and Kenneth. Making mejical history all over the show!

— In sum, some hum? And other marrage feats?

— All our stakes they were astumbling round the ranky roars assumbling when Big Arthur flugged the field at Annie's courting.

— Suddenly some wellfired clay was cast out through the schappsteckers of hoy's house?

— Schottenly there was a hellfire club kicked out through the wasistas of Thereswhere.

— Like Heavystost's envil catacalamitumbling. Three days three times into the Vulcuum?

— Punch!

— Or Noe et Ecclesiastes, nonne?

— Ninny, there is no hay in Eccles's hostel.

— Yet an I saw a sign of him, if you could scrape out his acquinntence? Name or redress him and we'll call it a night!

— .i..'. .o..l.

— You are sure it was not a shuler's shakeup or a plighter's palming or a winker's wake *etcaetera etcaeterorum* you were at?

— Precisely.

— Mayhap. Hora pro Nubis, Thundersday, at A Little Bit Of Heaven Howth, the wife of Deimetuus (D'amn), Earl Adam Fitz-adam, of a Tartar (Birtha) or Sackville-Lawry and Morland-West, at the Auspice for the Living Bonnybrook, by the river and A. Briggs Carlisle, guardian of the birdsmaids and deputil-iser for groom. Pontifical mess. Or (soddenly) Schott, furtivfired by the riots. No flies. Agreest?

— Mayhem. Also loans through the post. With or without security. Everywhere. Any amount. Mofsovitz, swampstakers, purely providential.

— Flood's. The pinkman, the squeeze, the pint with the kick. Gaa. And then the punch to Gaelicise it. Fox. The lady with the lamp. The boy in the barleybag. The old man on his ars. Great Scrapp! 'Tis we and you and ye and me and hymns and hurts and heels and shields. The eirest race, the ourest nation, the airest place that erestationed. He was culping for penance while you were ringing his belle. Did the kickee, goodman rued fox, say anything important? Clam or cram, spick or spat?

— No more than Richman's periwhelker.

— Nnn ttt wrd?

— Dmn ttt thg.

— A gael galled by scheme of scorn? Nock?

— Sangnifying nothing. Mock!

— *Fortitudo eius rhodammum tenuit?*

— Five maim! Or something very similar.

— I should like to euphonise that. It sounds an isochronism. Secret speech Hazelton and obviously disemvowelled. But it is good laylaw too. We may take those wellmeant kicks for free granted, though *ultra vires*, void and, in fact, unnecessarily so. Happily you were not quite so successful in the process verbal whereby you would sublimate your blepharospasmockical suppressions, it seems?

— What was that? First I heard about it.

— Were you or were you not? Ask yourself the answer, I'm not giving you a short question. Now, not to mix up, cast your eyes around Capel Court. I want you, witness of this epic struggle, as yours so mine, to reconstruct for us, as briefly as you can, inexactly the same as a mind's eye view, how these funeral games, which have been poring over us through homer's kerryer pidgeons, massacreedoed as the holiname rally round took place.

— Which? Sure I told you that afoul. I was drunk all lost life.

— Well, tell it to me befair, the whole plan of campaign, in that bamboozelem mincethrill voice of yours. Let's have it, christie! The Dublin own, the thrice familiar.

— Ah, sure, I eyewitless foggus. 'Tis all around me bebattersbid hat.

— Ah, go on now, Masta Bones, a gig for a gag, with your impendements and your perroqtriques! Blank memory of hatless darky in blued suit. You were ever the gentle poet, dove from Haywarden. Pitcher cup, patcher cap, pratey man? Be nice about it, Bones Minor! Look chairful! Come, delicacy! Go to the end,

thou slackerd! Once upon a grass and a hopping high grass it
was.

— Faith, then, Meesta Cheeryman, first he come up, a gag
as a gig, badgeler's rake to the town's major from the wesz,
MacSmashall Swingy of the Cattelaxes, got up regardless, with
a cock on the Kildare side of his Tattersull, in his riddlesneek's
ragamufflers and the horrid contrivance as seen above, whisklyng
into a bone tolerably delicately, the *Wearing of the Blue*, and taking
off his plushkwadded bugsby in his perusual flea and loisy manner, saying good mrowkas to weevilybolly and dragging his feet
in the usual course and was ever so terribly naas, really, telling
him clean his nagles and fex himself up, Miles, and so on and so
fort, and to take the coocoomb to his grizzlies and who done
that foxy freak on his bear's hairs like fire bursting out of the
Ump pyre and, half hang me, sirr, if he wasn't wanting his
calicub body back before he'd to take his life or so save his life.
Then, begor, counting as many as eleven to thritytwo seconds
with his pocket browning, like I said, wann swanns wann, this is
my awethorrorty, he kept forecursing hascupth's foul Fanden,
Cogan, for coaccoackey the key of John Dunn's field fore it was
for sent and the way Montague was robbed and wolfling to
know all what went off and who burned the hay, perchance wilt
thoult say, before he'd kill all the kanes and the price of Patsch
Purcell's faketotem, which the man, his plantagonist, up from the
bog of the depths who was raging with the thirst of the sacred
sponge and who, as a mashter of pasht, so far as him was concerned, was only standing there nonplush to the corner of Turbot
Street, perplexing about a paumpshop and pupparing to spit,
wanting to know whelp the henconvention's compuss memphis
he wanted with him new nothing about.

— A sarsencruxer, like the Nap O' Farrell Patter Tandy moor
and burgess medley? In other words, was that how in the annusual
curse of things, as complement to compliment though, after a
manner of men which I must and will say seems extraordinary,
their celicolar subtler angelic warfare or photoplay finister
started?

— Truly. That I may never!

— Did one scum then in the auradrama, the deff, after some clever play in the mud, mention to the other undesirable, a dumm, during diverse intentional instants, that upon the resume after the angerus, how for his deal he was a pigheaded Swede and to wend himself to a medicis?

— To be sore he did, the huggornut! Only it was turnip-hudded dunce, I beg your pardon, and he would jokes bowlder-blow the betholder with his black masket off the bawling green.

— Sublime was the warning!

— The author, in fact, was mardred.

— Did he, the first spikesman, do anything to him, the last spokesman, when, after heaving some more smutt and chaff between them, they rolled togutter into the ditch together? Black Pig's Dyke?

— No, he had his teeth in the back of his head.

— Did Box then try to shine his puss?

— No but Cox did to shin the punman.

— The worsted crying that if never he looked on Leaverhol-ma's again and the bester huing that he might ever save sunlife?

— Trulytruly Asbestos he ever. And sowasso I never.

— That forte carlysle touch breaking the campdens pianoback.

— Pansh!

— Are you of my meaning that would be going on to about half noon, click o'clock, pip emma, Grinwicker time, by your querqcut quadrant?

— You will be asking me and I wish to higgins you wouldn't. Would it?

— Let it be twelve thirty after a somersautch of the tardest!

— And it was eleven thirsty too befour in soandsuch, reloy on it!

— Tick up on time. Howday you doom? That rising day sinks rosing in a night of nine week's wonder.

— Amties, marcy buckup! The uneven day of the unleventh month of the unevented year. At mart in mass.

— A triduum before Our Larry's own day. By which of your chronos, my man of four watches, larboard, starboard, dog or dath?

— Dunsink, rugby, ballast and ball. You can imagine.

— Language this allsfare for the loathe of Marses ambiviolent about it. Will you swear all the same you saw their shadows a hundred foot later, struggling diabolically over this, that and the other, their virtues *pro* and his principality *con*, near the Ruins, Drogheda Street, and kicking up the devil's own dust for the Milesian wind?

— I will. I did. They were. I swear. Like the heavenly militia. So wreek me Ghyllygully. With my tongue through my toecap on the headlong stone of kismet if so 'tis the will of Whose B. Dunn.

— Weepin Lorcans! They must have put in some wonderful work, ecad, on the quiet like, during this arms' parley, meatierities forces vegateareans. Dost thou not think so?

— Ay.

— The illegallooking range or fender, alias turfing iron, a product of Hostages and Co, Engineers, changed feet several times as briars revalvered during the weaponswap? Piff?

— Puff! Excuse yourself. It was an ersatz lottheringcan.

— They did not know the war was over and were only bere-belling or bereppelling one another by chance or necessity with sham bottles, mere and woiney, as betwinst Picturshirts and Scutticules, like their caractacurs in an Irish Ruman to sorowbrate the expeltsion of the Danos? What sayest thou, scusascmerul?

— That's all. For he was heavily upright man, Limba romena in Bucclis tucsada. Farcing gutterish.

— I mean the Morgans and the Dorans, in finnish?

— I know you don't, in Feeney's.

— The mujic of the footure on the barbarihams of the bashed? Co Canniley?

— Da Donnuley.

— Yet this war has meed peace? *In voina viritas.* Ab chaos lex, neat wehr?

— O bella! O pia! O pura! Amem. Handwalled amokst us. Thanksbeer to Balbus!

— All the same you sound it twould clang houlish like Hull hopen for christmians?

— But twill cling hellish like engels opened to neuropeans, if you've sensed, whole the sum. So be vigil!

— And this pattern pootsch punnermine of concoon and proprey went on, hog and minne, a whole whake, your night after larry's night, spittinspite on Dora O'Huggins, ormonde caught butler, the artillery of the O'Hefferns answering the cavalry of the MacClouds, fortey and more fortey, a thousand and one times, according to your cock and a biddy story? Lludillongi, for years and years perhaps?

— That's ri. This is his largos life, this is me timtomtum and this is her two peekweeny ones. From the last finger on the second foot of the fourth man to the first one on the last one of the first. That's right.

— Finny. Vary vary finny!

— It may look funny but fere it is.

— This is not guid enough, Mr Brasslattin. Finging and tonging and winging and ponging! And all your rally and ramp and rant! Didget think I was asleep at the wheel? D'yu mean to tall grand jurors of thathens of tharctic on your oath, me lad, and ask us to believe you for, all you're enduring long terms, with yur last foot foremouthst, that yur moon was shining on the tors and on the cresties and winblowing night after night, for years and years perhaps, after you swearing to it a while back before your Corth examiner, Markwalther, that there was reen in planty all the teem?

— Perhaps so, as you grand duly affirm, Robman Calvinic. I never thought over it, faith. I most certainly think so about it. I hope. Unless it is actionable. It would be a charity for me to think about something which I must on no caste accounts omit, if you ask to me. It was told me as an inspired statement by a friend of myself, in reply to salute, Tarpey, after three o'clock mass, with forty ducks indulgent, that some rain was promised to Mrs Lyons, the invalid of Aunt Tarty Villa, with lots gulp and sousers and likewise he told me, the recusant, after telling mass, with two hundred genuflexions, at the split hour of blight when bars are keeping so sly, as was what's follows. He is doing a walk, says she, in the feelmick's park, says he, like a tarrable Turk, says she, letting loose on his nursery and, begalla, he meet himself with Mr Michael Clery of a Tuesday who said Father MacGregor was desperate to the bad place about thassbawls and ejaculating about all the stairrods and the catspew swashing his earwanker and thinconvenience being locked up for months, owing to being putrenised by stragglers abusing the apparatus, and for Tarpey to pull himself into his soup and fish and to push on his borrowsaloaner and to go to the tumple like greased lining and see Father MacGregor and, be Cad, sir, he was to pipe up and saluate that clergyman and to tell his holiness the whole goat's throat about the three shillings in the confusional and to say how Mrs Lyons, the cuptosser, was the infidel who prophessised to pose three shielings Peter's pelf off her tocher from paraguais and albs by the yard to Mr Martin Clery for Father Mathew to put up a midnight mask saints withins of a Thrushday for African man and to let Brown child do and to leave he Anlone and all the nuisances committed by soldats and nonbehavers and missbelovers for N.D. de l'Ecluse to send more heehaw hell's flutes, my prodder again! And I never brought my cads in togs blanket! Foueh!

— Angly as arrows, but you have right, my celtslinger! Nils, Mugn and Cannut. Should brothers be for awe then?

— So let use off be octo while oil bike the bil and wheel whang till wabblin befoul you but mere and mire trullopes will knaver mate a game on the bibby bobby burns of.

— Quatsch! What hill ar yu fluking about ye lamelookond fyats! I'll discipline ye! Will you swear or affirm the day to yur second sight noo and recant that all yu affirmed to profetised at first sight for his southerly accent was all paddyflaherty? Will ye, ay or nay?

— Ay say aye. I affirmly swear to it that it rooly and cooly boolyhooly was with my holyhagionous lips continuously poised upon the rubricated annuals of saint ulstar.

— That's very guid of ye, R.C.! Maybe yu wouldn't mind talling us, my labrose lad, how very much bright cabbage or paperming comfirts d'yu draw for all yur swearin? The spanglers, kiddy?

— Rootha prootha. There you have me! Vurry nothing, O potators, I call it for I might as well tell yous Essexelcy, and I am not swallowing my air, the Golden Bridge's truth. It amounts to nada in pounds or pence. Not a glass of Lucan nor as much as the cost price of a highlandman's trousertree or the three crowns round your draphole (isn't it dram disgusting?) for the whole dumb plodding thing!

— Come now, Johnny! We weren't born yesterday. *Pro tanto quid retribuamus?* I ask you to say on your scotty pictail you were promised fines times with some staggerjuice or deadhorse, on strip or in larges, at the Raven and Sugarloaf, either Jones's lame or Jamesy's gait, anyhow?

— Bushmillah! Do you think for a moment? Yes, by the way. How very necessarily true! Give me fair play. When?

— At the Dove and Raven tavern, no, ah? To wit your wizzend?

— Water, water, darty water! Up Jubilee sod! Beet peat wheat treat!

— What harm wants but demands it! How would you like to hear yur right name now, Ghazi Power, my tristy minstrel, if yur not freckened of frank comment?

— Not afrightened of Frank Annybody's gaspower or illconditioned ulcers neither.

— Your uncles!

— Your gullet!

— Will you repeat that to me outside, leinconnmuns?

— After you've shouted a few? I will when it suits me, hulstler.

— Guid! We make fight! Three to one! Raddy?

— But no, from exemple, Emania Raffaroo! What do you have? What mean you, august one? Fairplay for Finnians! I will have my humours. Sure, you would not do the cowardly thing and moll me roon? Tell Queen's road I am seilling. Farewell, but whenever! Buy!

— Ef I chuse to put a bullet like yu through the grill for heckling what business is that of yours, yu bullock?

— I don't know, sir. Don't ask me, your honour!

— Gently, gently Northern Ire! Love that red hand! Let me once more. There are sordidly tales within tales, you clearly understand that? Now my other point. Did you know, whether by melanodactylism or purely libationally, that one of these two Crimeans with the fender, the taller man, was accused of a certain offence or of a choice of two serious charges, as skirts were divided on the subject, if you like it better that way? You did, you rogue, you?

— You hear things. Besides (and serially now) bushes have eyes, don't forget. Hah!

— Which moral turpitude would you select of the two, for choice, if you had your way? Playing bull before shebears or the hindlegs off a clotheshorse? Did any orangepeelers or greengoaters appear periodically up your sylvan family tree?

— Buggered if I know! It all depends on how much family silver you want for a nass-and-pair. Hah!

— What do you mean, sir, behind your hah! You don't hah to do thah, you know, snapograph.

— Nothing, sir. Only a bone moving into place. Blotogaff. Hahah!

— Whahat?

— Are you to have all the pleasure quizzing on me? I didn't say it aloud, sir. I have something inside of me talking to myself.

— You're a nice third degree witness, faith! But this is no laughing matter. Do you think we are tonedeafs in our noses to boot? Can you not distinguish the sense, prain, from the sound, bray? You have homosexual catheis of empathy between narcissism of the expert and steatopygic invertedness. Get yourself psychoanolised!

— O, begor, I want no expert nursis symaphy from yours broons quadroons and I can psoakoonaloose myself any time I want (the fog follow you all!) without your interferences or any other pigeonstealer.

— Sample! Sample!

— Have you ever weflected, wepowtew, that the evil what though it was willed might nevewtheless lead somehow on to good towawd the genewality?

— A pwopwo of haster meets waster and talking of plebiscites by a show of hands, whether declaratory or effective, in all seriousness, has it become to dawn in you yet that the deponent, the man from Saint Yves, may have been (one is reluctant to use the passive voiced) may be been as much sinned against as sinning, for if we look at it verbally perhaps there is no true noun in active nature where every bally being — please read this mufto — is becoming in its owntown eyeballs. Now the long form and the strong form and reform alltogether!

— Hotchkiss Culthur's Everready, one brother to never-reached, well over countless hands, sieur of many winners and losers, groomed by S. Samson and son, bred by dilalahs, will stand at Bay (Dublin) from nun till dan and vites inversion and at Miss or Mrs's MacMannigan's Yard.

— Perhaps you can explain, sagobean? The Mod needs a rebus.

— Pro general continuation and in particular explication to your singular interrogation our asseveralation. Ladiegent, pals will smile but me and Frisky Shorty, my inmate friend, as is uncommon struck on poplar poetry, and a few fleabesides round at West Pauper Bosquet, was glad to be back again with the chaps and just arguing friendlylike at the Doddercan Easehouse having a wee chatty with our hosty in his comfy estably over the old middlesex party and his moral turps, meaning flu, pock, pox and mizzles, grip, gripe, gleet and sprue, caries, rabies, numps and dumps. What me and Frisky in our concensus and the whole double gigscrew of suscribers, notto say the burman, having successfully concluded our tour of bibel, wants to know is thisahere. Supposing, for an ethical fict, him, which the findings showed, to have taken his epscene licence before the norsect's divisional respectively as regards them male privates and or concomitantly with all common or neuter respects to them

public exess females, whereas allbeit really sweet fillies, as was
very properly held by the metropolitan in connection with this
regrettable nuisance, touching arbitrary conduct, being in strict
contravention of schedule in board of forests and works bylaws
regulationing sparkers' and succers' amusements section of our
beloved naturpark in pursuance of which police agence me and
Shorty have approached a reverend gentlman of the name of
Mr Coppinger with reference to a piece of fire fittings as was
most obliging, 'pon my sam, in this matter of his explanations
affirmative, negative and limitative, given to me and Shorty,
touching what the good book says of toooldaisymen, concerning
the merits of early bisectualism, besides him citing from approved
lectionary example given by a valued friend of the name of Mr
J. P. Cockshott, reticent of England, as owns a pretty maisonette,
Quis ut Deus, fronting on to the Soussex Bluffs as was telling us
categoric how Mr Cockshott, as he had his assignation with,
present holder by deedpoll and indenture of the swearing belt,
he tells him hypothetic, the reverend Mr Coppinger, hereckons
himself disjunctively with his windwarrd eye up to a dozen miles
of a cunifarm school of herring, passing themselves supernatently
by the Bloater Naze from twelve and them mayridinghim by the
silent hour. Butting, charging, bracing, backing, springing,
shrinking, swaying, darting, shooting, bucking and sprinkling
their dossies sodouscheock with the twinx of their taylz. And,
reverend, he says, summat problematical, by yon socialist sun,
gut me, but them errings was as gladful as Wissixy kippers could
be considering, flipping their little coppingers, pot em, the fresh
little flirties, the dirty little gillybrighteners, pickle their spratties,
the little smolty gallockers, and, reverend, says he, more asser-
titoff, zwelf me Zeus, says he, lettin olfac be the extench of the
supperfishies, lamme the curves of their scaligerance and pesk
the everurge flossity of their pectoralium, them little salty popu-
lators, says he, most apodictic, as sure as my briam eggs is on
cockshot under noose, all them little upandown dippies they was
all of a libidous pickpuckparty and raid on a wriggolo finsky
doodah in testimonials to their early bisectualism. Such, he says,

is how the reverend Coppinger, he visualises the hidebound homelies of creed crux ethics. Watsch yourself tillicately every morkning in your bracksullied twilette. The use of cold water, testificates Dr Rutty, may be warmly recommended for the sugjugation of cungunitals loosed. Tolloll, schools!

— Tallhell and Barbados wi ye and your Errian coprulation! Pelagiarist! Remonstrant Montgomeryite! Short lives to your relatives! Y'are absexed, so y'are, with mackerglosia and mickroocyphyllicks.

— Wait now, leixlip. I scent eggoarchicism. I will take you to task. I don't follow you that far in your otherwise accurate account. Was it *esox lucius* or *salmo ferax?* You are taxing us into the driven future, are you not, with this ruttymaid fishery.

— Lalia Lelia Lilia Lulia and lively lovely Lola Montez.

— Gubbernathor! That they say is a fenian on the secret. Named Parasol Irelly. Spawning ova and fry like a marrye monach all amanygoround his seven parish churches! And peopling the ribald baronies with dans, oges and conals!

— Lift it now, Hosty! Hump's your mark! For a runnymede landing! A dondhering vesh vish, *Magnam Carpam,* es hit neat zoo?

— There's an old psalmsobbing lax salmoner fogeyboren Herrin Plundehowse.
Who went floundering with his boatloads of spermin spunk about.
Leaping freck after every long tom and wet lissy between Howth and Humbermouth.
Our Human Conger Eel!

— Hep! I can see him in the fishnoo! Up wi'yer whippy. Hold that lad! Play him, Markandeyn! Bullhead!

— Pull you, sir! Olive quill does it. Longeal of Malin, he'll cry before he's flayed. And his tear make newisland. Did a rise? Way, lungfish! The great fin may cumule! Three threeth o'er the wild! Manu ware!

— He missed her mouth and stood into Dee, Romunculus Remus, plying the rape, so as now any bompriss's bound to get up her if he pool her leg and bunk on her butt. No, he skid like a skate and berthed on her byrnie and never a fear but they'll

land him yet, slitheryscales on liffeybank, times and times and
halve a time with a pillow of sand to polster him.

— Do you say they will?

— I bet you they will.

— Among the shivering sedges so? Weedy waving.

— Or tulipbeds of Rush below.

— Where you take your mugs to wash after dark?

— To my lead, Toomey lout, Tommy lad.

— Besides the bubblye waters of, babblyebubblye waters of?

— Right.

— Grenadiers. And tell me now. Were these anglers or angel-
ers coexistent and compresent with or without their *tertium quid*?

— *Three in one, one and three.*

Shem and Shaun and the shame that sunders em.
Wisdom's son, folly's brother.

— God bless your ginger, wigglewaggle! That's three slots
and no burners. You're forgetting the jinnyjos for the fayboys.
What, Walker John Referent? Play us your patmost! And un-
packyoulloups!

— Naif Cruachan! Woe on woe, says Wardeb Daly. Woman
will water the wild world over. And the maid of the folley will go
where glory. Sure I thought it was larking in the trefoll of the furry
glans with two stripping baremaids, Stilla Underwood and Moth
MacGarry, he was, hand to dagger, that time and their mother a
rawkneepudsfrowse, I was given to understand, with superflow-
vius heirs, begum. There was that one that was always mad gone
on him, her first king of cloves and the most broadcussed man
in Corrack-on-Sharon, County Rosecarmon. Sure she was near
drowned in pondest coldstreams of admiration forherself, as bad
as my Tarpeyan cousin, Vesta Tully, making faces at her bach-
spilled likeness in the brook after and cooling herself in the
element, she pleasing it, she praising it, with salices and weidow-
wehls, all tossed, as she was, the playactrix, Lough Shieling's love!

— O, add shielsome bridelittle! All of her own! Nircississies
are as the doaters of inversion. Secilas through their laughing
classes becoming poolermates in laker life.

— It seems to same with Iscappellas? Ys? Gotellus! A tickey for tie taughts!

— Listenest, meme mearest! They were harrowd, those fin-weeds! Come, rest in this bosom! So sorry you lost him, poor lamb! Of course I know you are a viry vikid girl to go in the dreemplace and at that time of the draym and it was a very wrong thing to do, even under the dark flush of night, dare all grand-passia! He's gone on his bombashaw. Through geesing and so pleasing at Strip Teasy up the stairs. The boys on the corner were talking too. And your soreful miseries first come on you. Still to forgive it, divine my lickle wiffey, and everybody knows you do look lovely in your invinsibles, Eulogia, a perfect apposition with the coldcream, Assoluta, from Boileau's I always use in the wards after I am burned a rich egg and derive the greatest benefit, sign of the cause. My, you do! Simply adorable! Could I but pass my hands some, my hands through, thine hair! So vicky-vicky veritiny! O Fronces, say howdyedo, Dotty! Chic hands. The way they curve there under nue charmeen cuffs! I am more divine like that when I've two of everything up to boyproof knicks. Winning in a way, only my arms are whiter, dear. Blanchemain, idler. Fairhair, frail one. Listen, meme sweety! O be joyfold! Mirror do justice, taper of ivory, heart of the conavent, hoops of gold! My veil will save it undyeing from his ethernal fire! It's meemly us two, meme, idoll. Of course it was downright verry wickred of him, reely meeting me disguised, Bortolo mio, peerfectly appealling, D.V., with my lovebirds, my colombinas. Their sinsitives shrinked. Even Netta and Linda our seeyu tities and they've sin sumtim, tankus! My rillies were liebeneaus, my aftscents embre. How me adores eatsother simply (Mon ishebeau! Ma reinebelle!), in his storm collar, as I leaned yestreen from his muskished labs, even my little pom got excited, when I turned his head on his same manly bust and kissed him more. Only he might speak to a person, lord so picious, taking up my worths ill wrong! May I introduce! This is my futuous, lips and looks lovelast. Still me with you, you poor chilled! Will make it up with mother Concepcion and a glorious lie between us,

sweetness, so as not a novene in all the convent loretos, not my
littlest one of all, for mercy's sake need ever know, what passed
our lips or. Yes sir, we'll will! Clothea wind! Fee o fie! Covey us
niced! Bansh the dread! Alitten's looking. Low him lovly. Make
me feel good in the moontime. It will all take bloss as oranged at
St Audiens rosan chocolate chapelry with my diamants blickfeast
after at minne owned hos for all the catclub to go cryzy and
Father Blesius Mindelsinn will be beminding hand. Kyrielle elation! Crystal elation! Kyrielle elation! Elation immanse! Sing to
us, sing to us, sing to us! Amam! So meme nearest, languished
hister, be free to me! (I'm fading!) And listen, you, you beauty,
esster, I'll be clue to who knows you, pray Magda, Marthe with
Luz and Joan, while I lie with warm lisp on the Tolka. (I'm fay!)

— Eusapia! Fais-le, tout-tait! Languishing hysteria? The clou
historique? How is this at all? Is dads the thing in such or are
tits the that? Hear we here her first poseproem of suora unto
suora? Alicious, twinstreams twinestraines, through alluring
glass or alas in jumboland? Ding dong! Where's your pal in
silks alustre? Think of a maiden, Presentacion. Double her, An-
nupciacion. Take your first thoughts away from her, Immacola-
cion. Knock and it shall appall unto you. Who shone yet shimmers will be e'er scheining. Cluse her, voil her, hild her hindly.
After liryc and themodius soft aglo iris of the vals. This young
barlady, what, euphemiasly? Is she having an ambidual act herself in apparition with herself as Consuelas to Sonias may?

— Dang! And tether, a loguy O!

— Dis and dat and dese and dose! Your crackling out of your
turn, my Moonster firefly, like always. And 2 R.N. and Long-
horns Connacht, stay off my air! You've grabbed the capital and
you've had the lion's shire since 1542 but there's all the difference
in Ireland between your borderation, my chatty cove, and me. The
leinstrel boy to the wall is gone and there's moreen astoreen for
Monn and Conn. With the tyke's named moke. Doggymens'
nimmer win! You last led the first when we last but we'll first
trump your last with a lasting. Jump the railchairs or take them,
as you please, but and, sir, my queskins first, foxyjack! Ye've as
much skullabogue cheek on you now as would boil a caldron of

kalebrose. Did the market missioners Hayden Wombwell, when
given the raspberry, fine more than sandsteen per cent of chalk
in the purity, promptitude and perfection flour of this raw
materialist and less than a seventh pro mile in his meal? We
bright young chaps of the brandnew braintrust are briefed here
and with maternal sanction compellably empanelled at quarter
sessions under the six disqualifications for the uniformication of
young persons (Nodding Neutrals) removal act by Committal-
man Number Underfifteen to know had the peeress of generals,
who have been getting nose money cheap and stirring up the
public opinion about private balls with their legs, Misses Mirtha
and Merry, the two dreeper's assistents, had they their service
books in order and duly signed J. H. North and Company when
discharged from their last situations? Will ye gup and tell the
board in the anterim how, in the name of the three tailors on
Tooley Street, did O'Bejorumsen or Mockmacmahonitch, ex of
Butt and Hocksett's, violating the bushel standard, come into
awful position of the barrel of bellywash? And why, is it any harm
to ask, was this hackney man in the coombe, a papersalor with
a whiteluke to him, Fauxfitzhuorson, collected from Manofisle,
carrying his ark, of eggshaped fuselage and made in Fredborg
into the bullgine, across his back when he might have been
setting on his jonass inside like a Glassthure cabman? Where
were the doughboys, three by nombres, won in ziel, cavehill
exers or hearts of steel, Hansen, Morfydd and O'Dyar, V.D.,
with their glenagearries directing their steps according to the
R.U.C's liaison officer, with their trench ulcers open and
their hands in their pockets, contrary to military rules, when
confronted with his lifesize obstruction? When did he live off
rooking the pooro and how did start pfuffpfaffing at his Paterson
and Hellicott's? Is it a factual fact, proved up to scabsteethshilt,
that this fancydress nordic in shaved lamb breeches, child's kilts,
bibby buntings and wellingtons, with club, torc and headdress,
preholder of the Bar Ptolomei, is coowner of a hengster's circus
near North Great Denmark Street (incidentally, it's the most
unjoyable show going the province and I'm taking the youngsters

there Saturday first when it's halfprice naturals night to see the
fallensickners aping the buckleybackers and the blind to two
worlds taking off the deffydowndummies) and the shamshem-
showman has been complaining to the police barracks and
applying for an order of *certiorari* and crying out something vile
about him being molested, after him having triplets, by offers of
vacancies from females in this city neighing after the man and his
outstanding attraction ever since they seen his X ray picture turned
out in wealthy red in the sabbath sheets? Was it him that suborned
that surdumutual son of his, a litterydistributer in Saint Patrick's
Lavatory, to turn a Roman and leave the chayr and gout in his
bare balbriggans, the sweep, and buy the usual jar of porter at
the Morgue and Cruses and set it down before the wife with her
fireman's halmet on her, bidding her mine the hoose, the strum-
pet, while him and his lagenloves were rampaging the roads in
all their paroply under the noses of the Heliopolitan constabu-
lary? Can you beat it? Prepare the way! Where's that gendarm
auxiliar, arianautic sappertillery, that reported on the whole hoodlum, relying on his morse-erse wordybook and the trunchein up
his tail? Roof Seckesign van der Deckel and get her story from
him! Recall Sickerson, the lizzyboy! Seckersen, magnon of Errick.
Sackerson! Hookup!

    — *Day shirker four vanfloats he verdants market.*
    High liquor made lust torpid dough hunt her orchid.
    — Hunt her orchid! Gob and he found it on her right enough!
With her shoes upon his shoulders, 'twas most trying to beholders when he upped their frullatullepleats with our warning.
A disgrace to the homely protestant religion! Bloody old pre-
adamite with his twohandled umberella! Trust me to spy on me
own spew.
    — Wallpurgies! And it's this's your deified city? Norganson?
And it's we's to pray for Bigmesser's conversions? Call Kitty the
Beads, the Mandame of Tipknock Castle! Let succuba succumb, the
improvable his wealth made possible! He's cookinghagar that rost
her prayer to him upon the top of the stairs. She's deep, that one.
    — A farternoiser for his tuckish armenities. Ouhr Former

who erred in having down to gibbous disdag our darling breed.
And then the confisieur for the boob's indulligence. As sunctioned
for his salmenbog by the Councillors-om-Trent. Pave Pannem
at his gaiter's bronze. Nummer half dreads Log Laughty. Master's gunne he warrs the bedst. I messaged his dilltoyds sause-
pander mussels on the kisschen table. With my ironing duck
through his rollpins of gansyfett, do dodo doughdy dough, till
he was braising red in the toastface with lovensoft eyebulbs and
his kiddledrum steeming and rattling like the roasties in my
mockamill. I awed to have scourched his Abarm's brack for him.
For the loaf of Obadiah, take your pastryart's noas out of me
flouer bouckuet. Of the strainger scene you given squeezers to
me skillet! As cream of the hearth thou reinethst alhome. His
lapper and libbers was glue goulewed as he sizzled there watching me lautterick's pitcher by Wexford-Atelier as Katty and
Lanner, the refined souprette, with my bust alla brooche and the
padbun under my matelote, showing my jigotty sleeves and all
my new toulong touloosies. Whisk! There's me shims and here's
me hams and this is me juppettes, gause be the meter. Whisk!
What's this? Whisk! And that? He never cotched finer, balay
me, at Romiolo Frullini's flea pantamine out of Griddle-the-Sink
or Shusies-with-her-Soles-Up or La Sauzerelly, the pucieboots,
when I started so hobmop ladlelike, highty tighty, to kick the
time off the cluckclock lucklock quamquam camcam potapot
panapan kickakickkack. Hairhorehounds, shake up pfortner.
Fuddling fun for Fullacan's sake.

— All halt! Sponsor programme and close down. That's
enough, genral, of finicking about Finnegan and fiddling with
his faddles. A final ballot, guvnor, to remove all doubt. By sylph
and salamander and all the trolls and tritons, I mean to top her
drive and to tip the tap of this, at last. His thoughts that wouldbe
words, his livings that havebeen deeds. And will too, by the holy
child of Coole, primapatriock of the archsee, if I have at first
to down every mask in Trancenania from Terreterry's Hole to
Stutterers' Corner to find that Yokeoff his letter, this Yokan his
dahet. Pass the jousters of the king, the Kovnor-Journal and

eirenarch's custos himself no less, the meg of megs, with the Carri-
son old gang! Off with your persians! Search ye the Finn! The
sinder's under shriving sheet. Fa Fe Fi Fo Fum! Ho, croak,
evildoer! Arise, sir ghostus! As long as you've lived there'll be no
other. Doff!

— Amtsadam, sir, to you! Eternest cittas, heil! Here we are
again. I am bubub brought up under a camel act of dynasties long
out of print, the first of Shitric Shilkanbeard (or is it Owllaugh
MacAuscullpth the Thord?), but, in pontofacts massimust, I am
known throughout the world wherever my good Allenglisches
Angleslachsen is spoken by Sall and Will from Augustanus to
Ergastulus, as this is, whether in Farnum's rath or Condra's
ridge or the meadows of Dalkin or Monkish tunshep, by saints
and sinners eyeeye alike as a cleanliving man and, as a matter of
fict, by my halfwife, I think how our public at large appreciates
it most highly from me that I am as cleanliving as could be and
that my game was a fair average since I perpetually kept my
ouija ouija wicket up. On my verawife I never was nor can afford
to be guilty of crim crig con of malfeasance trespass against parson with the person of a youthful gigirl frifrif friend chirped
Apples, acted by Miss Dashe, and with Any of my cousines in
Kissilov's Slutsgartern or Gigglotte's Hill, when I would touch
to her dot and feel most greenily of her unripe ones as it should
prove most anniece and far too bahad, nieceless to say, to my
reputation on Babbyl Malket for daughters-in-trade being lightly
clad. Yet, as my acquainters do me the complaisance of apprising
me, I should her have awristed under my duskguise of whippers
through toombs and deempeys, lagmen, was she but tinkling of
such a tink. And, as a mere matter of ficfect, I tell of myself how
I popo possess the ripest littlums wifukie around the globelettes
globes upon which she was romping off on Floss Mundai out of
haram's way round Skinner's circusalley first with her consolation prize in my serial dreams of faire women, Mannequins Passe,
with awards in figure and smile subsections, handicapped by two
breasts in operatops, a remarkable little endowment garment.
Fastened at various places. What spurt! I kickkick keenly love

such, particularly while savouring of their flavours at their most
perfect best when served with heliotrope ayelips, as this is, where
I do drench my jolly soul on the pu pure beauty of hers past.

She is my bestpreserved wholewife, sowell her as herafter, in
Evans's eye, with incompatibly the smallest shoenumber outside
chinatins. They are jolly dainty, spekin tluly. May we not recom-
mend them? It was my proofpiece from my prenticeserving.
And, alas, our private chaplain of Lambeyth and Dolekey, bishop-
regionary, an always sadfaced man, in his lutestring pewcape with
tabinet band, who has visited our various hard hearts and reins
by imposition of fufuf fingers, olso haddock's fumb, in that
Upper Room can speak loud to you some quite complimentary
things about my clean charactering, even when detected in the
dark, distressful though such recital prove to me, as this is, when
I introduced her (Frankfurters, numborines, why drive fear?) to
our fourposter tunies chantreying under Castrucci Sinior and De
Mellos, those whapping oldsteirs, with sycamode euphonium in
either notation in our altogether cagehaused duckyheim on
Goosna Greene, that cabinteeny homesweetened through affection's hoardpayns (First Murkiss, or so they sankeyed. Dodo! O
Clearly! And Gregorio at front with Johannes far in back. Aw,
aw!), gleeglom there's gnome sweepplaces like theresweep No-
whergs. By whom, as my Kerk Findlater's, ye litel chuch rond
ye coner, and K. K. Katakasm enjoineth in the Belief and, as you
all know, of a child, dear Humans, one of my life's ambitions of
my youngend from an early peepee period while still to hedje-
skool, intended for broadchurch, I, being fully alive to it, was
parruchially confirmed in Caulofat's bed by our bujibuji beloved
curate-author. Michael Engels is your man. Let Michael relay
Sutton and tell you people here who have the phoney habit (it
was remarketable) in his clairaudience, as this is, as only our own
Michael can, when reicherout at superstation, to bring ruptures
to our roars how I am amp amp amplify. Hiemlancollin. Pimpim's Ornery forninehalf. Shaun Shemsen saywhen saywhen.
Holmstock unsteaden. Livpoomark lloyrge hoggs one four tupps
noying. Big Butter Boost! Sorry! Thnkyou! Thatll beall for-

tody. Cal it off. Godnotch, vryboily. End a muddy crushmess!
Abbreciades anew York gustoms. Kyow! Tak.

— Tiktak. Tikkak.

— Awind abuzz awater falling.

— Poor a cowe his jew placator.

— It's the damp damp damp.

— Calm has entered. Big big Calm, announcer. It is most
ernst terooly a moresome intartenment. Colt's tooth! I will give
tandsel to it. I protest there is luttrelly not one teaspoonspill of
evidence at bottomlie to my babad, as you shall see, as this is.
Keemun Lapsang of first pickings. And I contango can take off
my dudud dirtynine articles of quoting here in Pynix Park before those in heaven to provost myself, by gramercy of justness,
I mean veryman and moremon, stiff and staunch for ever, and
enter under the advicies from Misrs Norris, Southby, Yates and
Weston, Inc, to their favoured client, into my preprotestant caveat
against the pupup publication of libel by any tixtim tipsyloon or
tobtomtowley of Keisserse Lean (a bloweyed lanejoymt, waring
lowbelt suit, with knockbrecky kenees and bullfist rings round
him and a fallse roude axehand (he is cunvesser to Saunter's
Nocelettres and the Poe's Toffee's Directory in his pisness), the
best begrudged man in Belgradia who doth not belease to our
paviour) to my nonesuch, that highest personage at moments
holding down the throne. So to speak of beauty scouts in elegant
pursuit of flowers, searchers for tabernacles and the celluloid art!
Happen seen sore eynes belived? The caca cad! He walked by
North Strand with his Thom's towel in hand. Snakeeye! Strangler
of soffiacated green parrots! I protest it that he is, by my
wipehalf. He was leaving out of my double inns while he was all
teppling over my single ixits. So was keshaned on for his recent
behaviour. Sherlook is lorking for him. Allare beltspanners.
Get your air curt! Shame upon Private M! Shames on his ful-
someness! Shamus on his atkinscum's lulul lying suulen for an
outcast mastiff littered in blood currish! Eristocras till Hanging
Tower! Steck a javelin through his advowtried heart! Instaun-
ton! Flap, my Larrybird! Dangle, my highflyer! Jiggety jig my

jackadandyline! Let me never see his waddphez again! And mine
it was, Barktholed von Hunarig, Soesown of Furrows (hour-
springlike his joussture, immitiate my chry! as urs now, so yous
then!), when to our lot it fell on my poplar Sexsex, my Sexen-
centaurnary, whenby Gate of Hal, before his hostel of the Wodin
Man, I hestened to freeholdit op to his Mam his Maman, Majus-
cules, His Magnus Maggerstick, first city's leasekuays of this
Nova Tara, our most noble, when hrossbucked on his pricelist
charger, Pferdinamd Allibuster (yeddonot need light oar till
Noreway for you fanned one o'er every doorway) with my all-
bum's greethims through this whole of my promises, handshakey
congrandyoulikethems, ecclesency.

Whosaw the jackery dares at handgripper thisa breast? Dose
makkers ginger. Some one we was with us all fours. Adversarian!
The spiking Duyvil! First liar in Londsend! Wulv! See you scar-
gore on that skeepsbrow! And those meisies! Sulken taarts! Man
sicker at I ere bluffet konservative? Shucks! Such ratshause bugs-
mess so I cannot barely conceive of! Lowest basemeant in hystry!
Ibscenest nansence! Noksagt! Per Peeler and Pawr! The broker-
heartened shugon! Hole affair is rotten muckswinish porcupig's
draff. Enouch!

— Is that yu, Whitehed?
— Have you headnoise now?
— Give us your mespilt reception, will yous?
— Pass the fish for Christ's sake!
— Old Whitehowth he is speaking again. Ope Eustace tube!
Pity poor whiteoath! Dear gone mummeries, goby! Tell the
woyld I have lived true thousand hells. Pity, please, lady, for
poor O.W. in this profundust snobbing I have caught. Nine dirty
years mine age, hairs hoar, mummery failend, snowdrift to my
ellpow, deff as Adder. I askt you, dear lady, to judge on my tree
by our fruits. I gave you of the tree. I gave two smells, three eats.
My freeandies, my celeberrimates: my happy bossoms, my all-
falling fruits of my boom. Pity poor Haveth Childers Everywhere with Mudder!

That was Communicator, a former colonel. A disincarnated

spirit, called Sebastion, from the Rivera in Januero, (he is not
all hear) may fernspreak shortly with messuages from my dead-
ported. Let us cheer him up a little and make an appunkment for
a future date. Hello, Commudicate! How's the buttes? Ever-
scepistic! He does not believe in our psychous of the Real Absence, neither miracle wheat nor soulsurgery of P. P. Quemby.
He has had some indiejestings, poor thing, for quite a little while,
confused by his tonguer of baubble. A way with him! Poor Felix
Culapert! Ring his mind, ye staples, (bonze!) in my ould reeke-
ries' ballyheart and in my krumlin and in aroundisements and
stremmis! Sacks eleathury! Sacks eleathury! Bam! I deplore over
him ruely. Mongrieff! O Hone! Guestermed with the nobelities,
to die bronxitic in achershous! So enjoying of old thick whiles,
in haute white toff's hoyt of our formed reflections, with stock
of eisen all his prop, so buckely hosiered from the Royal Leg,
and his puertos mugnum, he would puffout a dhymful bock.
And the how he would husband her that verikerfully, his cigare
divane! (He would redden her with his vestas, but 'tis naught.)
With us his nephos and his neberls, mest incensed and befogged
by him and his smoke thereof. But he shall have his glad stein of
our zober beerbest in Oscarshal's winetavern. *Buen retiro!* The
boyce voyce is still flautish and his mounth still wears that
soldier's scarlet though the flaxafloyeds are peppered with salse-
dine. It is bycause of what he was ascend into his prisonce on
account off. I whit it wel. Hence his deepraised words. Some day
I may tell of his second storey. Mood! Mood! It looks like someone other bearing my burdens. I cannot let it. Kanes nought.

Well, yeamen, I have bared my whole past, I flatter myself,
on both sides. Give me even two months by laxlaw in second
division and my first broadcloth is business will be to protest to
Recorder at Thing of all Things, or court of Skivinis, with mar-
chants grey, antient and credibel, Zerobubble Barrentone, Jonah
Whalley, Determined Codde or Cucumber Upright, my jurats,
if it does not occur again. O rhyme us! Haar Faagher, wild heart
in Homelan; Harrod's be the naun. Mine kinder come, mine
wohl be won. There is nothing like leuther. O Shee! And nosty

mens in gladshouses they shad not peggot stones. The elephant's house is his castle. I am here to tell you, indeed to goodness, that, allbe I discountenanced beallpersuasions, in rinunciniation of pomps of heretofore, with a wax too held in hand, I am thorgt-fulldt to do dope me of her miscisprinks and by virchow of those filthered Ovocnas presently like Browne umbracing Christina Anya, after the Irishers, to convert me into a selt (but first I must proxy babetise my old antenaughties), when, as Sigismond Stol-terforth, with Rabbin Robroost for my auspicer and Leecher Rutty for my lifearst and Lorencz Pattorn (*Ehren til viktrae!*), when I will westerneyes those poor sunuppers and outbreighten their land's eng. A man should stump up and I will pay my pretty decent trade price for my glueglue gluecose, peebles, were it even, as this is, the legal eric for infelicitous conduict (here incloths placefined my pocketanchoredcheck) and, as a matter of fact, I undertake to discontinue entyrely all practices and I deny wholeswiping *in toto* at my own request in all stoytness to have confermentated and confoederated and agreed in times prebellic, when here were waders for the trainsfolk, as it is now nuggently laid to me, with a friend from mine, Mr Billups, pulleter, my quarterbrother, who sometimes he is doing my locum for me on a grubstake and whom I have cleped constoutuent, for so it was felt by me, at goodbuy cootcoops byusucapiture a mouth-less niggeress, Blanchette Brewster from Cherna Djamja, Blaw-lawnd-via-Brigstow, or to illsell my fourth part in her, which al-though allowed of in Deuterogamy as in several places of Scrip-ture (copyright) and excluded books (they should quite rightly verbanned be), would seem eggseggs excessively haroween to my feelimbs for two punt scotch, one pollard and a crockard or three pipples on the bitch. Thou, Frick's Flame, Uden Sulfer, who strikest only on the marryd bokks, enquick me if so be I did cophetuise milady's maid, in spect of her beavers she is a womanly and sacret. Such wear a frillick for my comic strip, Mons Meg's Monthly, comes out aich Fanagan's Weck, to bray at by clownsillies in Donkeybrook Fair. It would lackin mackin Hodder's and Cocker's erithmatic. The unpurdonable preemp-

son of all of her of yourn, by Juno Moneta! If she, irished Marry-
onn Teheresiann, has been disposed of for her consideration, I,
Ledwidge Salvatorious, am tradefully unintiristid. And if she is
still further talc slopping over her cocoa contours, I hwat mick
angars, am strongly of opinion why I should not be. Inprobable!
I do not credit one word of it from such and suchess mistra-
versers. Just feathers! Nanenities! Or to have ochtroyed to
resolde or borrough by exchange same super melkkaart, means
help; best Brixton high yellow, no outings: cent for cent on
Auction's Bridge. 'Twere a honnibel crudelty wert so tente-
ment to their naktlives and scatab orgias we devour about in
the mightyevil roohms of encient cartage. Utterly improperable!
Not for old Crusos or white soul of gold! A pipple on the
panis, two claps on the cansill, or three pock pocks cassey
knocked on the postern! Not for one testey tickey culprik's
coynds ore for all ecus in cunziehowffse! So hemp me Cash.
I meanit.
    My herrings! The surdity of it! Amean to say. Her bare
idears, it is choochoo chucklesome. Absurd bargain, mum, will
call. One line with! One line, with with! Will ate everadayde sau-
mone like a boyne alive O. The tew cherripickers, with their
Catheringnettes, Lizzy and Lissy Mycock from Street Flesh-
shambles, were they moon at aube with hespermun and I their
covin guardient, I would not know to contact such gretched
youngsteys in my ways from Haddem or any suistersees or
heiresses of theirn, claiming by, through, or under them. Ous of
their freiung pfann into myne foyer. Her is one which rassembled
to mein enormally. The man what shocked his shanks at contey
Carlow's. He is Deucollion. Each habe goheerd, uptaking you
are innersence, but we sen you meet sose infance. Deucollion!
Odor. Evilling chimbes is smutsick rivulverblott but thee hard
casted thereass pigstenes upann Congan's shootsmen in Schot-
tenhof, ekeascent? Igen Deucollion! I liked his Gothamm chic!
Stuttertub! What a shrubbery trick to play! I will put my oath-
head unner my whitepot for ransom of beeves and will stand
me where I stood mine in all free heat between Pelagios and little

Chistayas by Roderick's our mostmonolith, after my both ears-
toear and brebreeches buybibles and, minhatton, testify to my
unclothed virtue by the longstone erectheion of our allfirst man-
here. I should tell you that honestly, on my honour of a Near-
wicked, I always think in a wordworth's of that primed favourite continental poet, Daunty, Gouty and Shopkeeper, A. G.,
whom the generality admoyers in this that is and that this is to
come. Like as my palmer's past policy I have had my best master's lessons, as the public he knows, and do you know, home-
sters, I honestly think, if I have failed lamentably by accident
benefits though shintoed, spitefired, perplagued and cram-
krieged, I am doing my dids bits and have made of my prudentials
good. I have been told I own stolemines or something of that
sorth in the sooth of Spainien. Hohohoho! Have I said ogso how
I abhor myself vastly (truth to tell) and do repent to my nether-
heart of suntry clothing? The amusin part is, I will say, hotel-
men, that since I, over the deep drowner Athacleeath to seek
again Irrlanding, shamed in mind, with three plunges of my
ruddertail, yet not a bottlenim, vanced imperial standard by
weaponright and platzed mine residenze, taking bourd and
burgage under starrymisty and ran and operated my brixtol selec-
tion here at thollstall, for mean straits male with evorage fimmel,
in commune soccage among strange and enemy, among these
plotlets, in Poplinstown, alore Fort Dunlip, then-on-sea, hole
of Serbonian bog, now city of magnificent distances, good-
walldabout, with talus and counterscarp and pale of palisades,
upon martiell siegewin, with Abbot Warre to blesse, on yon
slauchterday of cleantarriffs, in that year which I have called
myriabellous, and overdrave these marken (the soord on Whence-
hislaws was mine and mine the prusshing stock of Allbrecht
the Bearn), under patroonshaap of our good kingsinnturns,
T. R. H. Urban First and Champaign Chollyman and Hungry
the Loaved and Hangry the Hathed, here where my tenenure of
office and my toils of domestication first began, with weight of
woman my skat and skuld but Flukie of the Ravens as my sure
piloter, famine with Englisch sweat and oppedemics, the two-

toothed dragon worms with allsort serpents, has compolitely
seceded from this landleague of many nations and open and
notorious naughty livers are found not on our rolls. This seat of
our city it is of all sides pleasant, comfortable and wholesome.
If you would traverse hills, they are not far off. If champain land,
it lieth of all parts. If you would be delited with fresh water, the
famous river, called of Ptolemy the Libnia Labia, runneth fast
by. If you will take the view of the sea, it is at hand. Give heed!
— *Do Drumcollogher whatever you do!*
— *Visitez Drumcollogher-la-Belle!*
— *Be suke and sie so ersed Drumcollogher!*
— *Vedi Drumcollogher e poi Moonis.*
—Things are not as they were. Let me briefly survey. Pro clam
a shun! Pip! Peep! Pipitch! Ubipop jay piped, ibipep goes the
whistle. Here Tyeburn throttled, massed murmars march: where
the bus stops there shop I: here which ye see, yea reste. On me,
your sleeping giant. Estoesto! Estote sunto! From the hold of
my capt in altitude till the mortification that's my fate. The end
of aldest mosest ist the beginning of all thisorder so the last of
their hansbailis shall the first in our sheriffsby. New highs for
all! Redu Negru may be black in tawn but under them lintels
are staying my horneymen meet each his mansiemagd. For peers
and gints, quaysirs and galleyliers, fresk letties from the say and
stale headygabblers, gaingangers and dudder wagoners, pullars
off societies and pushers on rothmere's homes. Obeyance from
the townsmen spills felixity by the toun. Our bourse and politico-
ecomedy are in safe with good Jock Shepherd, our lives are on
sure in sorting with Jonathans, wild and great. Been so free!
Thank you, besters! Hattentats have mindered. Blaublaze devil-
bobs have gone from the mode and hairtrigger nicks are quite
out of time now. Thuggeries are reere as glovars' metins, lepers
lack, ignerants show beneath suspicion like the bitterhalves of
esculapuloids. In midday's mallsight let Miledd discurverself.
Me ludd in her hide park seek Minuinette. All is waldy bonums.
Blownose aerios we luft to you! Firebugs, good blazes! Lubbers,
kepp your poudies drier! Seamen, we segn your skivs and wives.

Seven ills so barely as centripunts havd I habt, seaventy seavens for circumference inkeptive are your hill prospect. Braid Blackfordrock, the Calton, the Liberton, Craig and Lockhart's, A. Costofino, R. Thursitt. The chort of Nicholas Within was my guide and I raised a dome on the wherewithouts of Michan: by awful tors my wellworth building sprang sky spearing spires, cloud cupoled campaniles: further this. By fineounce and imposts I got and grew and by grossscruple gat I grown outreachesly: murage and lestage were my mains for Ouerlord's tithing and my drains for render and prender the doles and the tribute: I was merely out of my mint with all the percussors on my braincap till I struck for myself and muched morely by token: to Sirrherr of Gambleden ruddy money, to Madame of Pitymount I loue yous. Paybads floriners moved in hugheknots against us and I matt them, pepst to papst, barthelemew: milreys (mark!) onfell, and (Luc!) I arose Daniel in Leonden. Bulafests onvied me, Corkcuttas graatched. Atabey! I braved Brien Berueme to berow him against the Loughlins, all her tolkies shraking: Fugabollags! Lusqu'au bout! If they had ire back of eyeball they got danage on front tooth: theres were revelries at ridottos, here was rivalry in redoubt: I wegschicked Duke Wellinghof to reshockle Roy Shackleton: Walhalloo, Walhalloo, Walhalloo, mourn in plein! Under law's marshall and warschouw did I thole till lead's plumbate, ping on pang, reliefed me. I made praharfeast upon acorpolous and fastbroke down in Neederthorpe. I let faireviews in on slobodens but ranked rothgardes round wrathmindsers: I bathandbaddend on mendicity and I corocured off the unoculated. Who can tell their tale whom I filled ad liptum on the plain of Soulsbury? With three hunkered peepers and twa and twas! For sleeking beauties I spinned their nightinveils, to slumbred beast I tummed the thief air. Round the musky moved a murmel but mewses whinninaird and belluas zoomed: tendulcis tunes like water parted fluted up from the westinders while from gorges in the east came the strife of ourangoontangues. All in my thicville Escuterre ofen was thorough fear but in the meckling of my burgh Belvaros was the site forbed: tuberclerosies I

reized spudfully from the murphyplantz Hawkinsonia and berri-
berries from the pletoras of the Irish shou. I heard my liberti-
lands making free through their curraghcoombs, my trueblues
hurusalaming before Wailingtone's Wall: I richmounded the
rainelag in my bathtub of roundwood and conveyed it with
cheers and cables, roaring mighty shouts, through my longer-
tubes of elm: out of fundness for the outozone I carried them
amd curried them in my Putzemdown cars to my Kommeandine
hotels: I made sprouts fontaneously from Philuppe Sobriety in
the coupe that's cheyned for noon inebriates: when they weaned
weary of that bibbing I made infusion more infused: sowerpacers
of the vinegarth, obtemperate unto me! When you think me in
my coppeecuffs look in ware would you meckamockame, as you
pay in caabman's sheltar tot the ites like you corss the tees.
Wherefore watch ye well! For, while I oplooked the first of
Janus's straight, I downsaw the last of Christmas steps: syndic
podestril and on the rates, I for indigent and intendente: in
Forum Foster I demosthrenated my folksfiendship, enmy pupuls
felt my burk was no worse than their brite: Sapphrageta and
Consciencia were undecidedly attached to me but the maugher
machrees and the auntieparthenopes my schwalby words with
litted spongelets set their soakye pokeys and botchbons afume:
Fletcher-Flemmings, elisaboth, how interquackeringly they ro-
gated me, their golden one, I inhesitant made replique: Mesde-
memdes to leursieuresponsor: and who in hillsaide, don't you
let flyfire till you see their whites of the bunkers' eyes! Mr Answers: Brimgem young, bringem young, bringem young!: in
my bethel of Solyman's I accouched their rotundaties and I turnkeyed most insultantly over raped lutetias in the lock: I gave bax
of biscums to the jacobeaters and pottage bakes to the esausted;
I dehlivered them with freakandesias by the constant droppings
from my smalls instalmonths while I titfortotalled up their
farinadays for them on my slataper's slate with my chandner's
chauk: I jaunted on my jingelbrett rapt in neckcloth and sashes,
and I beggered about the amnibushes like belly in a bowle. In
the humanity of my heart I sent out heyweywomen to refresh

the ballwearied and then, doubling megalopolitan poleetness, my great great greatest of these charities, devaleurised the base fellows for the curtailment of their lower man: with a slog to square leg I sent my boundary to Botany Bay and I ran up a score and four of mes while the Yanks were huckling the Empire: I have been reciping om omominous letters and widely-signed petitions full of pieces of pottery about my monumental-ness as a thingabolls and I have been inchanting causeries to the feshest cheoilboys so that they are allcalling on me for the song of a birtch: the more secretely bi built, the more openly palas-tered. Attent! Couch hear! I have becket my vonderbilt hutch in sunsmidnought and at morningrise was encampassed of mushroofs. Rest and bethinkful, with licence, thanks. I con-sidered the lilies on the veldt and unto Balkis did I disclothe mine glory. And this. This missy, my taughters, and these man, my son, from my fief of the villa of the Ostmanorum to Thor-stan's, *recte* Thomars Sraid, and from Huggin Pleaze to William Inglis his house, that man de Loundres, in all their barony of Saltus, bonders and foeburghers, helots and zelots, strutting oges and swaggering macks, the darsy jeamses, the drury joneses, redmaids and bleucotts, in hommage all and felony, all who have received tickets, fair home overcrowded, tidy but very little furniture, respectable, whole family attends daily mass and is dead sick of bread and butter, sometime in the militia, mentally strained from reading work on German physics, shares closet with eight other dwellings, more than respectable, getting com-fortable parish relief, wageearner freshly shaven from prison, highly respectable, planning new departure in mountgomery cyclefinishing, eldest son will not serve but peruses Big-man-up-in-the-Sky scraps, anoopanadoon lacking backway, quasi respec-table, pays ragman in bones for faded windowcurtains, staircase continually lit up with guests, particularly respectable, house lost in dirt and blocked with refuse, getting on like Roe's dis-tillery on fire, slovenly wife active with the jug, in business for himself, has a tenth illegitimate coming, partly respectable, following correspondence courses, chucked work over row, both

cheeks kissed at levee by late marquess of Zetland, sharing closet
which is profusely written over with eleven other subscribers,
once respectable, open hallway pungent of Baltic dishes, bangs
kept woman's head against wall thereby disturbing neighbours,
private chapel occupies return landing, removal every other
quarter day, case one of peculiar hopelessness, most respectable,
nightsoil has to be removed through snoring household, eccen-
tric naval officer not quite steady enjoys weekly churchwarden
and laugh while reading foreign pictorials on clumpstump before
door, known as the trap, widow rheumatic and chars, haunted,
condemned and execrated, of dubious respectability, tools too
costly pledged or uninsured, reformed philanthropist whenever
feasible takes advantage of unfortunates against dilapidating
ashpits, serious student is eating his last dinners, floor dangerous
for unaccompanied old clergymen, thoroughly respectable, many
uncut pious books in evidence, nearest watertap two hundred
yards' run away, fowl and bottled gooseberry frequently on
table, man has not had boots off for twelve months, infant being
taught to hammer flat piano, outwardly respectable, sometimes
hears from titled connection, one foot of dust between banister
and cracked wall, wife cleans stools, eminently respectable, otta-
wark and regular loafer, should be operated would she consent,
deplorable rent in roof, claret cellar cobwebbed since the ponti-
ficate of Leo, wears drill trousers and collects rare buddhas,
underages very treacly and verminous have to be separated, sits
up with fevercases for one and threepence, owns two terraces
(back to back breeze), respectable in every way, harmless im-
becile supposingly weakminded, a sausage every Sunday, has a
staff of eight servants, outlook marred by ne'er-do-wells using
the laneway, lieabed sons go out with sisters immediately after
dark, has never seen the sea, travels always with her eleven
trunks of clothing, starving cat left in disgust, the pink of respectability, resting after colonial service, labours at plant, the
despair of his many benefactresses, calories exclusively from
rowntrees and dumplings, one bar of sunlight does them all
january and half february, the V. de V's (animal diet) live in five-

storied semidetached but rarely pay tradesmen, went security
for friend who absconded, shares same closet with fourteen similar cottages and an illfamed lodginghouse, more respectable than
some, teawidow pension but held to purchase, inherited silk hat
from father-in-law, head of domestic economy never mentioned,
queery how they live, reputed to procure, last four occupants
carried out, mental companionship with mates only, respectability unsuccessfully aimed at, copious holes emitting mice, de-
coration from Uganda chief in locked ivory casket, grandmother
has advanced alcoholic amblyopia, the terror of Goodmen's
Field, and respected and respectable, as respectable as respectable can respectably be, though their orable amission were the
herrors I could have expected, all, let them all come, they are my
villeins, with chartularies I have talledged them. Wherfor I will and
firmly command, as I willed and firmly commanded, upon my
royal word and cause the great seal now to be affixed, that from
the farthest of the farther of their fathers to their children's children's children they do inhabit it and hold it for me unencum-
bered and my heirs, firmly and quietly, amply and honestly,
and with all the liberties and free customs which the men of Tolbris, a city of Tolbris, have at Tolbris, in the county of their city
and through whole my land. Hereto my vouchers, knive and
snuffbuchs. Fee for farm. Enwreak us wrecks.

Struggling forlongs I have livramentoed, milles on milles of
mancipelles. Lo, I have looked upon my pumpadears in their
easancies and my drummers have tattled tall tales of me in the land:
in morgenattics litt I hope, in seralcellars louched I bleakmealers:
on my siege of my mighty I was parciful of my subject but in street
wauks that are darkest I debelledem superb: I deemed the drugtails
in my pettycourts and domstered dustyfeets in my husinclose: at
Guy's they were swathed, at Foulke's slashed, the game for a
Gomez, the loy for a lynch: if I was magmonimoss as staidy lavgiver
I revolucanized by my eructions: the hye and bye wayseeds I
scattered em, in my graben fields sew sowage I gathered em: in
Sheridan's Circle my wits repose, in black pitts of the pestered
Lenfant he is dummed. (Hearts of Oak, may ye rooi to piece!

Rechabites obstain! Clayed sheets, pineshrouded, wake not, walk not! Sigh lento, Morgh!) *Quo warranto* has his greats my soliven and puissant lord V. king regards for me and he has given to me my necknamesh (flister it!) which is second fiddler to nomen. These be my genteelician arms. At the crest, two young frish, etoiled, flappant, devoiled of their habiliments, vested sable, withdrewers argent. For the boss a coleopter, pondant, partifesswise, blazoned sinister, at the slough, proper. In the lower field a terce of lanciers, shaking unsheathed shafts, their arms crossed in saltire, embusked, sinople. Motto, in letters portent: *Hery Crass Evohodie*. Idle were it, repassing from elserground to the elder disposition, to inquire whether I, draggedasunder, be the forced generation of group marriage, holocryptogam, of my essenes, or carried of cloud from land of locust, in ouzel galley borne, I, huddled til summone be the massproduct of teamwork, three surtouts wripped up in itchother's, two twin pritticoaxes lived as one, troubled in trine or dubildin too, for abram nude be I or roberoyed with the faineans, of Feejeean grafted ape on merfish, surrounded by obscurity, by my virtus of creation and by boon of promise, by my natural born freeman's journeymanright and my otherchurch's inher light, in so and such a manner as me it so besitteth, most surely I pretend and reclam to opt for simultaneous. Till daybowbreak and showshadows flee. Thus be hek. Verily! Verily! Time, place!

— What is your numb? Bun!

— Who gave you that numb? Poo!

— Have you put in all your sparepennies? I'm listening. Sree!

— Keep clear of propennies! Fore!

— Mr Televox, Mrs Taubiestimm and invisible friends! I maymay mean to say. Annoyin part of it was, had faithful Fulvia, following the wiening courses of this world, turned her back on her ways to gon on uphills upon search of louvers, brunette men of Earalend, Chief North Paw and Chief Goes in Black Water and Chief Brown Pool and Chief Night Cloud by the Deeps, or again had Fluvia, amber whitch she was, left her chivily crookcrook crocus bed at the bare suggestions of some prolling bywaymen from Moabit who could have abused of her, the foxrogues, there might accrue advantage to ask wher in pellmell her deceivers sinned. Yet know it was vastly otherwise which I have heard it by mmummy goods waif, as I, chiefly endmost hartyly aver, for Fulvia Fluvia, iddle woman to the plusneeborn, ever did ensue tillstead the things that pertained unto fairnesse, this wharom I am fawned on, that which was loost. Even so, for I waged love on her: and spoiled her undines. And she wept: O my lors!

— Till we meet!
— Ere we part!
— Tollollall!
— This time a hundred years!

— But I was firm with her. And I did take the reached of my delights, my jealousy, ymashkt, beyashmakt, earswathed, snout-snooded, and did raft her flumingworthily and did leftlead her overland the pace, from lacksleap up to liffsloup, tiding down, as portreeve should, whimpering by Kevin's creek and Hurdlesford and Gardener's Mall, long rivierside drive, embankment large, to Ringsend Flott and Ferry, where she began to bump a little bit, my dart to throw: and there, by wavebrink, on strond of south, with mace to masthigh, taillas Cowhowling, quailless Highjakes, did I upreized my magicianer's puntpole, the tridont sired a tritan stock, farruler, and I bade those polyfizzyboisterous seas to retire with hemselves from os (rookwards, thou seasea stamoror!) and I abridged with domfine norsemanship till I had done abate her maidan race, my baresark bride, and knew her fleshly when with all my bawdy did I her whorship, min bryllupswibe: Heaven, he hallthundered, Heydays, he flung blissforhers. And I cast my tenspan joys on her, arsched over-tupped, from bank of call to echobank, by dint of strongbow (Galata! Galata!) so streng we were in one, malestream in shegulf: and to ringstresse I thumbed her with iern of Erin and tradesmanmarked her lieflang mine for all and singular, iday, igone, imorgans, and for ervigheds: base your peak, you! you, strike your flag!: (what screech of shippings! what low of dampf-

bulls!): from Livland, hoks zivios, from Lettland, skall vives!
With Impress of Asias and Queen Columbia for her pairanymphs
and the singing sands for herbrides' music: goosegaze annoynted
uns, canailles canzoned and me to she her shyblumes lifted: and
I pudd a name and wedlock boltoned round her the which to
carry till her grave, my durdin dearly, Appia Lippia Pluviabilla,
whiles I herr lifer amstell and been: I chained her chastemate to
grippe fiuming snugglers, her chambrett I bestank so to spunish
furiosos: I was her hochsized, her cleavunto, her everest, she was
my annie, my lauralad, my pisoved: who cut her ribbons when
nought my prowess? who expoused that havenliness to beacha-
lured ankerrides when not I, freipforter?: in trinity huts they
met my dame, pick of their poke for me: when I foregather 'twas
my sumbad, if I farseeker itch my list: had I not workit in my
cattagut with dogshunds' crotts to clene and had I not gifted
of my coataways, constantonoble's aim: and, fortiffed by my
right as man of capitol, I did umgyrdle her about, my vermin-
celly vinagerette, with all loving kindness as far as in man's
might it lay and enfranchised her to liberties of fringes: and I
gave until my lilienyounger turkeythighs soft goods and hardware (catalogue, *passim*) and ladderproof hosiery lines (see
stockinger's raiment), cocquette coiffs (see Agnes' hats) and
peningsworths of the best taste of knaggs of jets and silvered
waterroses and geegaws of my pretty novelties and wispywaspy
frocks of redferns and lauralworths, trancepearances such as
women cattle bare and peltries piled, the peak of Pim's and
Slyne's and Sparrow's, loomends day lumineused luxories on
looks, *La Primamère, Pyrrha Pyrrhine, Or de Reinebeau, Sourire
d'Hiver* and a crinoline, wide a shire, and pattens for her trilibies
that know she might the tortuours of the boots and bedes of
wampun with to toy and a murcery glaze of shard to mirrow, for
all daintiness by me and theetime, the cupandnaggin hour: and
I wound around my swanchen's neckplace a school of shells of
moyles marine to swing their saysangs in her silents: and, upping
her at king's count, her aldritch cry oloss unheading, what
though exceeding bitter, I pierced her beak with order of the

Danabrog (Cunnig's great! Soll leve! Soll leve!): with mare's greese cressets at Leonard's and Dunphy's and Madonna lanthorns before quintacasas and tallonkindles spearhead syngeing nickendbookers and mhutton lightburnes dipdippingdownes in blackholes, the tapers of the topers and his buntingpall at hoist: for days there was no night for nights were days and our folk had rest from Blackheathen and the pagans from the prince of pacis: what was trembling sod quaked no more, what were frozen loins were stirred and lived: gone the septuor, dark deadly dismal doleful desolate dreadful desperate, no more the tolvmaans, bloody gloomy hideous fearful furious alarming terrible mournful sorrowful frightful appalling: peace, perfect peace: and I hung up at Yule my duindleeng lunas, helphelped of Kettil Flashnose, for the souperhore of my frigid one, *coloumba mea, frimosa mea*, in Wastewindy tarred strate and Elgin's marble halles lamping limp from black to block, through all Livania's volted ampire, from anodes to cathodes and from the topazolites of Mourne, Wykinloeflare, by Arklow's sapphire siomen's lure and Wexterford's hook and crook lights to the polders of Hy Kinsella: avenyue ceen my peurls ahumming, the crown to my estuarine munipicence?: three firths of the sea I swept with draughtness and all ennempties I bottled em up in bellomport: when I stabmarooned jack and maturin I was a bad boy's bogey but it was when I went on to sankt piotersbarq that they gave my devil his dues: what is seizer can hack in the old wold a sawyer may hew in the green: on the island of Breasil the wildth of me perished and I took my plowshure sadly, feeling pity for me sored: where bold O'Connee weds on Alta Mahar, the tawny sprawling beside that silver burn, I sate me and settled with the little crither of my hearth: her intellects I charmed with I calle them utile thoughts, her turlyhyde I plumped with potatums for amiens pease in plenty: my biblous beadells shewed her triumphs of craftygild pageantries, loftust Adam, duffed our cousterclother, Conn and Owel with cortoppled baskib, Sire Noeh Guinnass, exposant of his bargeness and Lord Joe Starr to hump the body of the camell: I screwed the Emperor down with ninepins gaelic with sixpenny-

hapennies for his hanger on: my worthies were bissed and trissed
from Joshua to Godfrey but my *processus prophetarum* they would
have plauded to perpetuation. Moral: book to besure, see press.

— He's not all buum and bully.

— But his members handly food him.

— Steving's grain for's greet collegtium.

— The S. S. Paudraic's in the harbour.

— And after these things, I fed her, my carlen, my barelean lin-
steer, upon spiceries for her garbage breath, italics of knobby
lauch and the rich morsel of the marrolebone and shains of gar-
leeks and swinespepper and gothakrauts and pinkee dillisks,
primes of meshallehs and subleties in jellywork, come the feast
of Saint Pancras, and shortcake nutrients for Paas and Pingster's
pudding, bready and nutalled and potted fleshmeats from store
dampkookin, and the drugs of Kafa and Jelupa and shallots out
of Ascalon, feeding her food convenient herfor, to pass them into
earth: and to my saffronbreathing mongoloid, the skinsyg, I gave
Biorwik's powlver and Uliv's oils, unguents of cuticure, for the
swarthy searchall's face on her, with handewers and groinscrubbers
and a carrycam to teaze her tussy out, the brown but combly,
a mopsa's broom to duist her sate, and clubmoss and wolves-
foot for her more moister wards (amazing efficiencies!): and, my
shopsoiled doveling, when weeks of kindness kinly civicised, in
our saloons esquirial, with fineglas bowbays, draped embrasures
and giltedged librariums, I did devise my telltale sports at even-
bread to wring her withers limberly, wheatears, slapbang,
drapier-cut-dean, bray, nap, spinado and ranter-go-round: we
had our lewd mayers and our lairdie meiresses kiotowing and
smuling fullface on us out of their framous latenesses, oilclothed
over for cohabitation and allpointed by Hind: Tamlane the Cus-
sacke, Dirk Wettingstone, Pieter Stuyvesant, Outlawrie O'Niell,
Mrs Currens, Mrs Reyson-Figgis, Mrs Dattery, and Mrs Pruny-
Quetch: in hym we trust, footwash and sects principles, apply to
overseer, Amos five six: she had dabblingtime for exhibiting her
grace of aljambras and duncingk the bloodanoobs in her vaux-
halls while I, dizzed and dazed by the lumpty thumpty of our

interloopings, fell clocksure off my ballast: in our windtor palast
it vampared for elenders, we lubded Sur Gudd for the sleep and
the ghoasts: she chauffed her fuesies at my Wigan's jewels while
she skalded her mermeries on my Snorryson's Sagos: in pay-
cook's thronsaale she domineered, lecking icies off the dormer
panes all admired her in camises: on Rideau Row Duanna dwells,
you merk well what you see: let wellth were I our pantocreator
would theirs be tights for the gods: in littleritt reddinghats and
cindery yellows and tinsel and glitter and bibs under hoods: I
made nusance of many well pressed champdamors and peddled
freely in the scrub: I foredreamed for thee and more than full-
maked: I prevened for thee in the haunts that joybelled frail light-
a-leaves for sturdy traemen: *pelves ad hombres sumus:* I said to
the shiftless prostitute; let me be your fodder; and to rodies and
prater brothers; Chau, Camerade!: evangel of good tidings, om-
nient as the Healer's word, for the lost, loathsome and whomsoever will: who, in regimentation through liberal donation in co-
ordination for organisation of their installation and augmenta-
tion plus some annexation and amplification without precipitation towards the culmination in latification of what was formerly
their utter privation, competence, cheerfulness, usefulness and
the meed, shall, in their second adams, all be made alive: my tow
tugs steered down canal grand, my lighters lay longside on
Regalia Water. And I built in *Urbs in Rure*, for minne elskede,
my shiny brows, under astrolobe from my upservatory, an erd-
closet with showne ejector wherewithin to be squatquit in most
covenience from her sabbath needs, when open noise should
stilled be: did not I festfix with mortarboard my unniversiries,
wholly rational and gottalike, sophister agen sorefister, life sizars
all?: was I not rosetted on two stellas of little egypt? had not I
rockcut readers, hieros, gregos and democriticos?: triscastellated,
bimedallised: and by my sevendialled changing charties Hiberns-
ka Ulitzas made not I to pass through twelve Threadneedles and
Newgade and Vicus Veneris to cooinsight?: my camels' walk,
kolossa kolossa! no porte sublimer benared my ghates: Oi polled
ye many but my fews were chousen (Voter, voter, early voter,

he was never too oft for old Sarum): terminals four my staties
were, the Geenar, the Greasouwea, the Debwickweck, the Mif-
greawis. And I sept up twinminsters, the pro and the con, my
stavekirks wove so norcely of peeled wands and attachatouchy
floodmud, now all loosebrick and stonefest, freely masoned,
arked for covennanters and shinners' rifuge: descent from above
on us, Hagiasofia of Astralia, our orisons thy nave and absedes,
our aeone tone aeones thy studvaast vault; Hams, circuitise!
Shemites, retrace!: horns, hush! no barkeys! hereround is't
holied!: all truanttrulls made I comepull, all rubbeling gnomes
I pushed, gowgow: Cassels, Redmond, Gandon, Deane, Shep-
perd, Smyth, Neville, Heaton, Stoney, Foley, Farrell, Vnost with
Thorneycroft and Hogan too: sprids serve me! gobelins guard!:
tect my tileries (O tribes! O gentes!), keep my keep, the peace
of my four great ways: oathiose infernals to Booth Salvation,
arcane celestials to Sweatenburgs Welhell! My seven wynds I
trailed to maze her and ever a wynd had saving closes and all these
closes flagged with the gust, hoops for her, hatsoff for him and
ruffles through Neeblow's garding: and that was why Blabus was
razing his wall and eltering the suzannes of his nighboors: and
thirdly, for ewigs, I did reform and restore for my smuggy
piggiesknees, my sweet coolocked, my auburn coyquailing one,
her paddypalace on the crossknoll with massgo bell, sixton
clashcloshant, duominous and muezzatinties to commind the fit-
ful: doom adimdim adoom adimadim: and the oragel of the lauds
to tellforth's glory: and added thereunto a shallow laver to slub
out her hellfire and posied windows for her oriel house: gospelly
pewmillieu, christous pewmillieu: zackbutts babazounded, ollguns
tararulled: and she sass her nach, chillybombom and forty bonnets, upon the altarstane. May all have mossyhonours!
— Hoke!
— Hoke!
— Hoke!
— Hoke!
— And wholehail, snaeffell, dreardrizzle or sleetshowers of blessing, where it froze in chalix eller swum in the vestry, with fairskin

book and ruling rod, vein of my vergin page, her chastener ever
I did learn my little ana countrymouse in alphabeater cameltem-
per, from alderbirk to tannenyou, with myraw rattan atter dun-
drum; ooah, oyir, oyir, oyir: and I did spread before my Livvy,
where Lord street lolls and ladies linger and Cammomile Pass
cuts Primrose Rise and Coney Bend bounds Mulbreys Island but
never a blid had bledded or bludded since long agore when the
whole blighty acre was bladey well pessovered, my selvage mats
of lecheworked lawn, my carpet gardens of Guerdon City, with
chopes pyramidous and mousselimes and beaconphires and colos-
sets and pensilled turisses for the busspleaches of the summira-
mies and esplanadas and statuesques and templeogues, the Par-
donell of Maynooth, Fra Teobaldo, Nielsen, rare admirable, Jean
de Porteleau, Conall Gretecloke, Guglielmus Caulis and the eiligh
ediculous Passivucant (glorietta's inexcellsiored!): for irkdays
and for folliedays till the comple anniums of calendarias, gregoro-
maios and gypsyjuliennes as such are pleased of theirs to walk:
and I planted for my own hot lisbing lass a quickset vineyard and
I fenced it about with huge Chesterfield elms and Kentish hops
and rigs of barlow and bowery nooks and greenwished villas
and pampos animos and (N.I.) necessitades iglesias and pons for
aguaducks: a hawthorndene, a feyrieglenn, the hallaw vall, the
dyrchace, Finmark's Howe, against lickybudmonth and gleaner-
month with a magicscene wall (rimrim! rimrim!) for a Queen's
garden of her phoenix: and (hush! hush!) I brewed for my alpine
plurabelle, wigwarming wench, (speakeasy!) my granvilled brand-
old Dublin lindub, the free, the froh, the frothy freshener, puss,
puss, pussyfoot, to split the spleen of her maw: and I laid down
before the trotters to my eblanite my stony battered waggon-
ways, my nordsoud circulums, my eastmoreland and westland-
more, running boullowards and syddenly parading, (hearsemen,
opslo! nuptiallers, get storting!): whereon, in mantram of true-
men like yahoomen (expect till dutc cundoctor summoneth him
all fahrts to pay, velkommen all hankinhunkn in this vongn of
Hoseyeh!), claudesdales withe arabinstreeds, Roamer Reich's
rickyshaws with Hispain's King's trompateers, madridden mus-

tangs, buckarestive bronchos, poster shays and turnintaxis, and
tall tail tilburys and nod nod noddies, others gigging gaily, some
sedated in sedans: my priccoping gents, aroger, aroger, my dam-
sells softsidesaddled, covertly, covertly, and Lawdy Dawe a perch
behind: the mule and the hinny and the jennet and the mustard
nag and piebald shjelties and skewbald awknees steppit lively
(lift ye the left and rink ye the right!) for her pleashadure: and
she lalaughed in her diddydid domino to the switcheries of the
whip. Down with them! Kick! Playup!

    Mattahah! Marahah! Luahah! Joahanahanahana!

[4]

What was thaas? Fog was whaas? Too mult sleepth. Let sleepth.

But really now whenabouts. Expatiate then how much times we live in. Yes?

So nat by night by naught by naket, in thóse good old lousy days gone by, the days, shall we say? of Whom shall we say? while kinderwardens minded their twinsbed, therenow theystood, the sycomores, all four of them, in their quartan agues, the majorchy, the minorchy, the everso and the fermentarian with their ballyhooric blowreaper, titranicht by tetranoxst, at their pussycorners, and that old time pallyollogass, playing copers fearsome, with Gus Walker, the cuddy, and his poor old dying boosy cough, esker, newcsle, saggard, crumlin, dell me, donk, the way to wumblin. Follow me beeline and you're bumblin, esker, newcsle, saggard, crumlin. And listening. So gladdied up when nicechild Kevin Mary (who was going to be commandeering chief of the choirboys' brigade the moment he grew up under all the auspices) irishsmiled in his milky way of cream dwibble and onage tustard and dessed tabbage, frighted out when badbrat Jerry Godolphing (who was hurrying to be cardinal scullion in a night refuge as bald as he was cured enough unerr all the hospitals) furrinfrowned down his wrinkly waste of methylated spirits, ick and lemoncholy lees, ick and pulversed rhubarbarorum icky.

Night by silentsailing night while infantina Isobel (who will be blushing all day to be, when she growed up one Sunday, Saint Holy and Saint Ivory, when she took the veil, the beautiful presentation nun, so barely twenty, in her pure coif, sister Isobel, and next Sunday, Mistlemas, when she looked a peach, the beautiful Samaritan, still as beautiful and still in her teens, nurse Saintette Isabelle, with stiffstarched cuffs but on Holiday, Christmas, Easter mornings when she wore a wreath, the wonderful widow of eighteen springs, Madame Isa Veuve La Belle, so sad but lucksome in her boyblue's long black with orange blossoming weeper's veil) for she was the only girl they loved, as she is the queenly pearl you prize, because of the way the night that first we met she is bound to be, methinks, and not in vain, the darling of my heart, sleeping in her april cot, within her singachamer, with her greengageflavoured candywhistle duetted to the crazyquilt, Isobel, she is so pretty, truth to tell, wildwood's eyes and primarose hair, quietly, all the woods so wild, in mauves of moss and daphnedews, how all so still she lay, neath of the whitethorn, child of tree, like some losthappy leaf, like blowing flower stilled, as fain would she anon, for soon again 'twill be, win me, woo me, wed me, ah weary me! deeply, now evencalm lay sleeping;

now upon nacht while in his tumbril Wachtman Havelook seequeerscenes, from yonsides of the choppy, punkt by his curserbog, went long the grassgross bumpinstrass that henders the pubbel to pass, stowing his bottle in a hole for at whet his whuskle to stretch ecrooksman, sequestering for lovers' lost propertied offices the leavethings from allpurgers' night, og gneiss ogas gnasty, kikkers, brillers, knappers and bands, handsboon and strumpers, sminkysticks and eddiketsflaskers;

wan fine night and the next fine night and last find night while Kothereen the Slop in her native's chambercushy, with dreamings of simmering my veal astore, was basquing to her pillasleep how she thawght a knogg came to the dowanstairs dour at that howr to peirce the yare and dowandshe went, schritt be schratt, to see was it Schweeps's mingerals or Shuhorn the posth with a tilly-

cramp for Hemself and Co, Esquara, or them four hoarsemen on
their apolkaloops, Norreys, Soothbys, Yates and Welks, and,
galorybit of the sanes in hevel, there was a crick up the stairkiss
and when she ruz the cankle to see, galohery, downand she went
on her knees to blessersef that were knogging together like milk-
juggles as if it was the wrake of the hapspurus or old Kong
Gander O'Toole of the Mountains or his googoo goosth she
seein, sliving off over the sawdust lobby out of the backroom, wan
ter, that was everywans in turruns, in his honeymoon trim, holding
up his fingerhals, with the clookey in his fisstball, tocher of davy's,
tocher of ivileagh, for her to whisht, you sowbelly, and the
whites of his pious eyebulbs swering her to silence and coort;

each and every juridical sessions night whenas goodmen
twelve and true at fox and geese in their numbered habitations
tried old wireless over boord in their juremembers, whereas by
reverendum they found him guilty of their and those imputations
of fornicolopulation with two of his albowcrural correlations on
whom he was said to have enjoyed by anticipation when schooling them in amown, mid grass, she sat, when man was, amazingly
frank, for their first conjugation whose colours at standing up
from the above were of a pretty carnation but, if really 'twere
not so, of some deretane denudation with intent to excitation,
caused by his retrogradation, among firearmed forces proper to
this nation but apart from all titillation which, he said, was under
heat pressure and a good mitigation without which in any case
he insists upon being worthy of continued alimentation for him
having displayed, he says, such grand toleration, reprobate so
noted and all, as he was, with his washleather sweeds and his
smokingstump, for denying transubstantiation nevertheless in
respect of his highpowered station, whereof more especially as
probably he was meantime suffering genteel tortures from the
best medical attestation, as he oftentimes did, having only
strength enough, by way of festination, to implore (or I believe
you have might have said better) to complore, with complete
obsecration, on everybody connected with him the curse of co-
agulation for, he tells me outside Sammon's in King Street, after

two or three hours of close confabulation, by this pewterpint of
Gilbey's goatswhey which is his prime consolation, albeit involving upon the same no uncertain amount of esophagous re-
gurgitation, he being personally unpreoccupied to the extent of
a flea's gizzard anent eructation, if he was still extremely offensive to a score and four nostrils' dilatation, still he was likewise,
on the other side of him, for some nepmen's eyes a delectation, as
he asserts without the least alienation, so prays of his faullt you
would make obliteration but for our friend behind the bars,
though like Adam Findlater, a man of estimation, summing him
up to be done, be what will of excess his exaltation, still we think
with Sully there can be no right extinuation for contravention
of common and statute legislation for which the fit remedy
resides, for Mr Sully, in corporal amputation: so three months for
Gubbs Jeroboam, the frothwhiskered pest of the park, as per
act one, section two, schedule three, clause four of the fifth of
King Jark, this sentence to be carried out tomorrowmorn by
Nolans Volans at six o'clock shark, and may the yeastwind and
the hoppinghail malt mercy on his seven honeymeads and his
hurlyburlygrowth, Amen, says the Clarke;

   niece by nice by neat by natty whilst amongst revery's happy
gardens nine with twenty Leixlip yearlings, darters all, had such a
ripping time with gleeful cries of what is nice toppingshaun made
of made for and weeping like fun, him to be gone, for they were
never happier, huhu, than when they were miserable, haha;

   in their bed of trial, on the bolster of hardship, by the glimmer
of memory, under coverlets of cowardice, Albatrus Nyanzer with
Victa Nyanza, his mace of might mortified, her beautifell hung
up on a nail, he, Mr of our fathers, she, our moddereen ru arue
rue, they, ay, by the hodypoker and blazier, they are, as sure as
dinny drops into the dyke . . .

   A cry off.

   Where are we at all? and whenabouts in the name of space?
I don't understand. I fail to say. I dearsee you too.

   House of the cederbalm of mead. Garth of Fyon. Scene and
propertyplot. Stagemanager's prompt. Interior of dwelling on out-

skirts of city. Groove two. Chamber scene. Boxed. Ordinary bedroom set. Salmonpapered walls. Back, empty Irish grate, Adam's
mantel, with wilting elopement fan, soot and tinsel, condemned.
North, wall with window practicable. Argentine in casement.
Vamp. Pelmit above. No curtains. Blind drawn. South, party wall.
Bed for two with strawberry bedspread, wickerworker clubsessel
and caneseated millikinstool. Bookshrine without, facetowel upon.
Chair for one. Woman's garments on chair. Man's trousers with
crossbelt braces, collar on bedknob. Man's corduroy surcoat with
tabrets and taces, seapan nacre buttons on nail. Woman's gown
on ditto. Over mantelpiece picture of Michael, lance, slaying
Satan, dragon with smoke. Small table near bed, front. Bed with
bedding. Spare. Flagpatch quilt. Yverdown design. Limes.
Lighted lamp without globe, scarf, gazette, tumbler, quantity
of water, julepot, ticker, side props, eventuals, man's gummy
article, pink.

A time.

Act: dumbshow.

Closeup. Leads.

Man with nightcap, in bed, fore. Woman, with curlpins, hind.
Discovered. Side point of view. First position of harmony. Say!
Eh? Ha! Check action. Matt. Male partly masking female. Man
looking round, beastly expression, fishy eyes, paralleliped
homoplatts, ghazometron pondus, exhibits rage. Business. Ruddy
blond, Armenian bole, black patch, beer wig, gross build,
episcopalian, any age. Woman, sitting, looks at ceiling, haggish
expression, peaky nose, trekant mouth, fithery wight, exhibits
fear. Welshrabbit teint, Nubian shine, nasal fossette, turfy tuft,
undersized, free kirk, no age. Closeup. Play!

Callboy. Cry off. Tabler. Her move.

Footage.

By the sinewy forequarters of the mare Pocahontas and by the
white shoulders of Finnuala you should have seen how that
smart sallowlass just hopped a nanny's gambit out of bunk like
old mother Mesopotomac and in eight and eight sixtyfour she
was off, door, knightlamp with her, billy's largelimbs prodgering

after to queen's lead. Promiscuous Omebound to Fiammelle la
Diva. Huff! His move. Blackout.

Circus. Corridor.

Shifting scene. Wall flats: sink and fly. Spotlight working wall
cloths. Spill playing rake and bridges. Room to sink: stairs to
sink behind room. Two pieces. Haying after queue. Replay.

The old humburgh looks a thing incomplete so. It is so. On its
dead. But it will pawn up a fine head of porter when it is finished.
In the quicktime. The castle arkwright put in a chequered staircase
certainly. It has only one square step, to be steady yet notwith-
stumbling are they stalemating backgammoner supstairs by skips
and trestles tiltop double corner. Whist while and game.

What scenic artist! It is ideal residence for realtar. By hims
ingang tilt tinkt a tunning bell that Limen Mr, that Boggey
Godde, be airwaked. Lingling, lingling. Be their maggies in all.
Chump, do your ephort. Shop! Please shop! Shop ado please!
O ado please shop! How hominous his house, haunt it? Yesses
indead it be! Nogen, of imperial measure is begraved beneadher.
Here are his naggins poured, his alladim lamps. Around the
bloombiered, booty with the bedst. For them whom he have
fordone make we newly thankful!

Tell me something. The Porters, so to speak, after their
shadowstealers in the newsbaggers, are very nice people, are they
not? Very, all fourlike tellt. And on this wise, Mr Porter (Bar-
tholomew, heavy man, astern, mackerel shirt, hayamatt peruke)
is an excellent forefather and Mrs Porter (leading lady, a
poopahead, gaffneysaffron nightdress, iszoppy chepelure) is a
most kindhearted messmother. A so united family pateramater
is not more existing on papel or off of it. As keymaster fits the
lock it weds so this bally builder to his streamline secret. They
care for nothing except everything that is allporterous. *Porto
da Brozzo!* Isn't that terribly nice of them? You can ken that they
come of a rarely old family by their costumance and one must
togive that one supped of it in all tonearts from awe to zest. I
think I begin to divine so much. Only snakkest me truesome! I
stone us I'm hable.

To reachy a skeer do! Still hoyhra, till venstra! Here are two
rooms on the upstairs, at forkflank and at knifekanter. Whom in
the wood are they for? Why, for little Porter babes to be saved!
The coeds, boytom thwackers and timbuy teaser. Here is one-
thing you owed two noe. This one once upon awhile was the
other but this is the other one nighadays. Ah so? The Corsicos?
They are numerable. Guest them. Major bed, minor bickhive.
Halosobuth, sov us! Who sleeps in now number one, for example? A pussy, purr esimple. Cunina, Statulina and Edulia,
but how sweet of her! Has your pussy a pessname? Yes, indeed,
you will hear it passim in all the noveletta and she is named
Buttercup. Her bare name will tellt it, a monitress. How very
sweet of her and what an excessively lovecharming missyname
to forsake, now that I come to drink of it filtred, a gracecup
fulled of bitterness. She is dadad's lottiest daughterpearl and
brooder's cissiest auntybride. Her shellback thimblecasket mirror
only can show her dearest friendeen. To speak well her grace
it would ask of Grecian language, of her goodness, that legend
golden. Biryina Saindua! Loreas with lillias flocaflake arrosas!
Here's newyearspray, the posquiflor, a windaborne and heliotrope; there miriamsweet and amaranth and marygold to crown.
Add lightest knot unto tiptition. O Charis! O Charissima!
A more intriguant bambolina could one not colour up out
of Boccucia's Enameron. Would one but to do apart a lilybit her
virginelles and, so, to breath, so, therebetween, behold, she had
instantt with her handmade as to graps the myth inmid the air.
Mother of moth! I will to show herword in flesh. Approach not for
ghost sake! It is dormition! She may think, what though little doth
she realise, as morning fresheth, it hath happened her, you know
what, as they too what two dare not utter. Silvoo plush, if scolded
she draws a face. Petticoat's asleep but in the gentlenest of her
thoughts apoo is a nursepin. To be presented, Babs for Bim-
bushi? Of courts and with enticers. Up, girls, and at him! Alone?
Alone what? I mean, our strifestirrer, does she do fleurty winkies
with herself. Pussy is never alone, as records her chambrette, for
she can always look at Biddles and talk petnames with her little

playfilly when she is sitting downy on the ploshmat. O, she talks, does she? Marry, how? Rosepetalletted sounds. Ah Biddles es ma plikplak. Ah plikplak wed ma Biddles. A nice jezebel barytinette she will gift but I much prefer her missnomer in maidenly golden lasslike gladsome wenchful flowery girlish beautycapes. So do I, much. Dulce delicatissima! Doth Dolly weeps she is hastings. Will Dally bumpsetty it is tubtime. Allaliefest, she who pities very pebbles, dare we not wish on her our thrice onsk? A lovely fear! That she seventip toe her chrysming, that she spin blue to scarlad till her temple's veil, that the Mount of Whoam it open it her to shelterer! She will blow ever so much more promisefuller, blee me, than all the other common marygales that romp round brigidschool, charming Carry Whambers or saucy Susy Maucepan of Merry Anna Patchbox or silly Polly Flinders. Platsch! A plikaplak.

And since we are talking amnessly of brukasloop crazedledaze, who doez in sleeproom number twobis? The twobirds. Holy policeman, O, I see! Of what age are your birdies? They are to come of twinning age so soon as they may be born to be eldering like those olders while they are living under chairs. They are and they seem to be so tightly tattached as two maggots to touch other, I think I notice, do I not? You do. Our bright bull babe Frank Kevin is on heartsleeveside. Do not you waken him! Our farheard bode. He is happily to sleep, limb of the Lord, with his lifted in blessing, his buchel Iosa, like the blissed angel he looks so like and his mou is semiope as though he were blowdelling on a bugigle. Whene'er I see those smiles in eyes 'tis Father Quinn again. Very shortly he will smell sweetly when he will hear a weird to wean. By gorgeous, that boy will blare some knight when he will take his dane's pledges and quit our ingletears, spite of undesirable parents, to wend him to Amorica to quest a cashy job. That keen dean with his veen nonsolance! O, I adore the profeen music! Dollarmighty! He is too audorable really, eunique! I guess to have seen somekid like him in the story book, guess I met somewhere somelam to whom he will be becoming liker. But hush! How unpardonable of me! I beg for your venials, sincerely I do.

Hush! The other, twined on codliverside, has been crying in his sleep, making sharpshape his inscissors, on some first choice sweets fished out of the muck. A stake in our mead. What a teething wretch! How his book of craven images! Here are post-humious tears on his intimelle. And he has pipettishly bespilled himself from his foundingpen as illspent from inkinghorn. He is jem job joy pip poo pat (jot um for a sobrat!) Jerry Jehu. You will know him by name in the capers but you cannot see whose heel he sheepfolds in his wrought hand because I have not told it to you. O, foetal sleep! Ah, fatal slip! the one loved, the other left, the bride of pride leased to the stranger. He will be quite within the pale when with lordbeeron brow he vows him so tosset to be of the sir Blake tribes bleak while through life's unblest he rodes backs of bannars. Are you not somewhat bulgar with your bowels? Whatever do you mean with bleak? With pale blake I write tintingface. O, you do? And with steelwhite and blackmail I ha'scint for my sweet an anemone's letter with a gold of my bridest hair betied. Donatus his mark, address as follows. So you did? From the Cat and Cage. O, I see and see. In the ink of his sweat he will find it yet. What Gipsy Devereux vowed to Lylian and why the elm and how the stone. You never may know in the preterite all perhaps that you would not believe that you ever even saw to be about to. Perhaps. But they are two very blizky little portereens after their bredscrums, Jerkoff and Eatsup, as for my part opinion indeed. They would be born so, costarred, puck and prig, the maryboy at Donnybrook Fair, the godolphing-lad in the Hoy's Court. How frilled one shall be as at taledold of Formio and Cigalette! What folly innocents! Theirs whet pep of puppyhood! Both barmhearts shall become yeastcake by their brackfest. I will to leave a my copperwise blessing between the pair of them, for rosengorge, for greenafang. Blech and tin soldies, weals in a sniffbox. Som's wholed, all's parted. Weeping shouldst not thou be when man falls but that divine scheming ever adoring be. So you be either man or mouse and you be neither fish nor flesh. Take. And take. Vellicate nyche! Be ones as wes for gives for gives now the hour of passings sembles quick with quelled. Adieu, soft adieu, for these nice presents, kerryjevin. Still tosorrow!

Jeminy, what is the view which now takes up a second position of discordance, tell it please? Mark! You notice it in that
rereway because the male entail partially eclipses the femecovert.
It is so called for its discord the meseedo. Do you ever heard the
story about Helius Croesus, that white and gold elephant in our
zoopark? You astonish me by it. Is it not that we are commanding from fullback, woman permitting, a profusely fine birdseye
view from beauhind this park? Finn his park has been much the
admiration of all the stranger ones, grekish and romanos, who
arrive to here. The straight road down the centre (see relief map)
bisexes the park which is said to be the largest of his kind in the
world. On the right prominence confronts you the handsome
vinesregent's lodge while, turning to the other supreme piece of
cheeks, exactly opposite, you are confounded by the equally handsome chief sacristary's residence. Around is a little amiably tufted
and man is cheered when he bewonders through the boskage
how the nature in all frisko is enlivened by gentlemen's seats.
Here are heavysuppers — 'tis for daddies housings for hun-
dredaires of our super thin thousand. By gum, but you have
resin! Of these tallworts are yielded out juices for jointoils and
pappasses for paynims. Listeneth! 'Tis a tree story. How olave,
that firile, was aplantad in her liveside. How tannoboom held
tonobloom. How rood in norlandes. The black and blue marks
athwart the weald, which now barely is so stripped, indicate the
presence of sylvious beltings. Therewithal shady rides lend
themselves out to rustic cavalries. In yonder valley, too,
stays mountain sprite. Any pretty dears are to be caught inside
but it is a bad pities of the plain. A scarlet pimparnell now
mules the mound where anciently first murders were wanted
to take root. By feud fionghalian. Talkingtree and sinningstone
stay on either hand. Hystorical leavesdroppings may also be garg-
nered up with sir Shamus Swiftpatrick, Archfieldchaplain of Saint
Lucan's. How familiar it is to see all these interesting advenements
with one snaked's eyes. Is all? Yet not. Hear one's. At the bodom
fundus of this royal park, which, with tvigate shyasian gardeenen,
is open to the public till night at late, so well the sissastrides so will

the pederestians, do not fail to point to yourself a depression
called Holl Hollow. It is often quite guttergloomering in our
duol and gives wankyrious thoughts to the head but the banders
of the pentapolitan poleetsfurcers bassoons into it on windy
woodensdays their wellbooming wolvertones. Ulvos! Ulvos!

Whervolk dorst ttou begin to tremble by our moving pictures
at this moment when I am to place my hand of our true friend-
shapes upon thee knee to mark well what I say? Throu shayest
who? In Amsterdam there lived a ... But how? You are trem-
blotting, you retchad, like a verry jerry! Niet? Will you a gui-
neeser? Gaij beutel of staub? To feel, you? Yes, how it trembles,
the timid! Vortigern, ah Gortigern! Overlord of Mercia! Or
doth brainskin flinchgreef? Stemming! What boyazhness! Sole
shadow shows. Tis jest jibberweek's joke. It must have stole. O,
keve silence, both! Putshameyu! I have heard her voice somewhere else's before me in these ears still that now are for mine.

Let op. Slew musies. Thunner in the eire.

You were dreamend, dear. The pawdrag? The fawthrig?
Shoe! Hear are no phanthares in the room at all, avikkeen. No
bad bold faathern, dear one. Opop opop capallo, muy malinchily
malchick! Gothgorod father godown followay tomollow the
lucky load to Lublin for make his thoroughbass grossman's big-
ness. Take that two piece big slap slap bold honty bottomsside
pap pap pappa.

— *Li ne dormis?*
— *S! Malbone dormas.*
— *Kia li krias nikte?*
— *Parolas infanetes. S!*

Sonly all in your imagination, dim. Poor little brittle magic
nation, dim of mind! Shoe to me now, dear! Shoom of me! While
elvery stream winds seling on for to keep this barrel of bounty
rolling and the nightmail afarfrom morning nears.

When you're coaching through Lucalised, on the sulphur spa
to visit, it's safer to hit than miss it, stop at his inn! The hammers
are telling the cobbles, the pickts are hacking the saxums, it's
snugger to burrow abed than ballet on broadway. Tuck in your

blank. For it's race pound race the hosties rear all roads to ruin and layers by lifetimes laid down riches from poormen. Cried unions to chip, saltpetre to strew, gallpitch to drink, stonebread to break but it's bully to gulp good blueberry pudding. Doze in your warmth. While the elves in the moonbeams, feeling why, will keep my lilygem gently gleaming.

In the sleepingchambers. The court to go into half morning. The four seneschals with their palfrey to be there now, all balaaming in their sellaboutes and sharping up their penisills. The boufeither Soakersoon at holdup tent sticker. The swabsister Katya to have duntalking and to keep shakenin dowan her droghedars. Those twelve chief barons to stand by duedesmally with their folded arums and put down all excursions and false alarums and after that to go back now to their runameat farums and recompile their magnum chartarums with the width of the road between them and all harrums. The maidbrides all, in favours gay, to strew sleety cinders on their falling hair and for wouldbe joybells to ring sadly ringless hands. The dame dowager to stay kneeled how she is, as first mutherer with cord in coil. The two princes of the tower royal, daulphin and deevlin, to lie how they are without to see. The dame dowager's duffgerent to present wappon, blade drawn to the full and about wheel without to be seen of them. The infant Isabella from her coign to do obeisance toward the duffgerent, as first futherer with drawn brand. Then the court to come in to full morning. Herein see ye fail not!

— *Vidu, porkego! Ili vi rigardas. Returnu, porkego. Maldelikato!*

Gauze off heaven. Vision. Then. O, pluxty suddly, the sight entrancing! Hummels! That crag! Those hullocks! O Sire! So be accident occur is not going to commence! What have you therefore? Fear you the donkers? Of roovers? I fear lest we have lost ours (non grant it!) respecting these wildy parts. How is hit finister! How shagsome all and beastful! What do you show on? I show because I must see before my misfortune so a stark pointing pole. Lord of ladders, what for lungitube! Can you read the verst legend hereon? I am hather of the missed. Areed! To the dunleary obelisk via the rock vhat myles knox furlongs; to the general's postoffice howsands of patience; to the Wellington memorial half a league wrongwards; to Sara's bridge good hunter and nine to meet her: to the point, one yeoman's yard. He, he, he! At that do you leer, a setting up? With a such unfettered belly? Two cascades? I leer (O my big, O my bog, O my bagbone!) because I must see a buntingcap of so a pinky on the point. It is for a true glover's greetings and many burgesses by us, greats and grosses, uses to pink it in this way at tet-at-tet. For long has it been effigy of standard royal when broken on roofstaff which to the gunnings shall cast welcome from Courtmilits' Fortress, umptydum dumptydum. Bemark you these hangovers, those streamer fields, his influx. Do you not have heard that, the queen lying abroad.from fury of the gales, (meekname mocktitles her Nan Nan Nanetta) her liege of lateenth dignisties shall come on their bay tomorrow, Michalsmas, mellems the third and fourth of the clock, there to all the king's aussies and all their king's men, knechts tramplers and cavalcaders, led of herald graycloak, Ulaf Goldarskield? Dog! Dog! Her lofts will be loosed for her and their tumblers broodcast. A progress shall be made in walk, ney? I trow it well, and uge by uge. He shall come, sidesmen accostant, by aryan jubilarian and on brigadier-general Nolan or and buccaneer-admiral Browne, with — who can doubt it? — his golden beagles and his white elkox terriers for a hunting on our littlego illcome faxes. In blue and buff of Beaufort the hunt shall make. It is poblesse noblige. Ommes will grin through collars when each riders other's ass. Me Eccls! What cats' killings overall! What popping out of guillotened widows! Quick time! Beware of waiting! Squintina plies favours on us from her rushfrail and Zosimus, the crowder, in his surcoat, sues us with souftwister. Apart we! Here are gantlets. I believe, by Plentifolks Mixymost! Yet if I durst to express the hope how I might be able to be present. All these peeplers entrammed and detrained on bikeygels and troykakyls and those puny farting little solitires! Tollacre, tollacre! Polo north will beseem Sibernian and Plein Pelouta will behowl ne yerking at lawncastrum ne ghimbelling on guelflinks.

Mauser Misma shall cease to stretch her and come abroad for what
the blinkins is to be seen. A ruber, a rancher, a fullvide, a veri-
dust and as crerdulous behind as he was before behind a damson
of a sloe cooch. Mbv! The annamation of evabusies, the livlia-
ness of her laughings, such as a plurity of bells! Have peacience,
pray you! Place to dames! Even the Lady Victoria Landauner
will leave to loll and parasol, all giddied into gushgasps with her
dickey standing. Britus and Gothius shall no more joustle for
that sonneplace but mark one autonement when, with si so silent,
Cloudia Aiduolcis, good and dewed up, shall let fall, yes, no, yet
now a rain. Muchsias grapcias! It is how sweet from her, the
wispful, and they are soon seen swopsib so a sautril as a meise.
Its ist not the tear on this movent sped. Tix sixponce! Poum!
Hool poll the bull? Fool pay the bill. Becups a can full. Peal, pull
the bell! Still sayeme of ceremonies, much much more! So please-
your! It stands in *Instopressible* how Meynhir Mayour, our
boorgomaister, thon staunch Thorsman, (our Nancy's fancy, our
own Nanny's Big Billy), his hod hoisted, in best bib and tucker,
with Woolington bottes over buckram babbishkis and his clouded
cane and necknoose aureal, surrounded of his full cooperation
with fixed baronets and meng our pueblos, restrained by chain of
hands from pinchgut, hoghill, darklane, gibbetmeade and beaux
and laddes and bumbellye, shall receive Dom King at broadstone
barrow meet a keys of goodmorrow on to his pompey cushion.
Me amble dooty to your grace's majers! Arise, sir Pompkey
Dompkey! Ear! Ear! Weakear! An allness eversides! We but
miss that horse elder yet cherchant of the wise graveleek in
cabbuchin garden. That his be foison, old Caubeenhauben!
'Twill be tropic of all days. By the splendour of Sole! Perfect
weatherest prevailing. Thisafter, swift's mightmace deposing, he
shall aidress to His Serenemost by a speechreading from his
miniated vellum, alfi byrni gamman dealter etcera zezera eacla
treacla youghta kaptor lomdom noo, who meaningwhile that
illuminatured one, Papyroy of Pepinregn, my Sire, great, big King,
(his scaffoid is there set up, as to edify, by Rex Ingram, pageantmaster) will be poking out with his canule into the arras of

what brilliant bridgecloths and joking up with his tonguespitz
to the crimosing balkonladies, here's a help undo their modest
stays with a fullbelow may the funnyfeelbelong. Oddsbones,
that may it! Carilloners will ring their gluckspeels. Rng rng!
Rng rng! S. Presbutt-in-the-North, S. Mark Underloop,
S. Lorenz-by-the-Toolechest, S. Nicholas Myre. You shall
hark to anune S. Gardener, S. George-le-Greek, S. Barclay
Moitered, S. Phibb, Iona-in-the-Fields with Paull-the-Aposteln.
And audialterand: S. Jude-at-Gate, Bruno Friars, S. Weslen-
on-the-Row, S. Molyneux Without, S. Mary Stillamaries with
Bride-and-Audeons-behind-Wardborg. How chimant in effect!
Alla tingaling pealabells! So a many of churches one cannot
pray own's prayers. 'Tis holyyear's day! Juin jully we may!
Agithetta and Tranquilla shall demure umcIaused but Marl-
borough-the-Less, Greatchrist and Holy Protector shall have
open virgilances. Beata Basilica! But will be not pontifi-
cation? Dock, dock, agame! Primatially. At wateredge. Can-
taberra and Neweryork may supprecate when, by vepers, for
towned and travalled, his goldwhite swaystick aloft ylifted,
umbrilla-parasoul, Monsigneur of Deublan shall impart to all.
Benedictus benedicat! To board! And mealsight! Unjoint him
this bittern, frust me this chicken, display yon crane, thigh her
her pigeon, unlace allay rabbit and pheasant! Sing: Old Finncoole,
he's a mellow old saoul when he swills with his fuddlers free!
Poppop array! For we're all jollygame fellhellows which no-
bottle can deny! Here be trouts culponed for ye and salmons
chined and sturgeons tranched, sanced capons, lobsters barbed:
Call halton eatwords! Mumm me moe mummers! What, no
Ithalians? How, not one Moll Pamelas? Accordingly! Play actors
by us ever have crash to their gate. Mr Messop and Mr Borry will
produce of themselves, as they're two genitalmen of Veruno,
Senior Nowno and Senior Brolano (finaly! finaly!), all for love of
a fair penitent that, a she be broughton, rhoda's a rosy she. Their
two big skins! How they strave to gat her! Such a boyplay! Their
bouchicaulture! What tyronte power! Buy our fays! My name is
novel and on the Granby in hills. Bravose! Thou traitor slave!

Mine name's Apnorval and o'er the Grandbeyond Mountains.
Bravossimost! The royal nusick their show shall shut with song-
slide to nature's solemn silence. Deep Dalchi Dolando! Might
gentle harp addurge! It will give piketurns on the tummlipplads
and forain dances and crosshurdles and dollmanovers and viceuv-
ious pyrolyphics, a snow of dawnflakes, at darkfall for Grace's
Mamnesty and our fancy ladies, all assombred. Some wholetime in
hot town tonight! You do not have heard? It stays in book
of that which is. I have heard anyone tell it jesterday (master
currier with brassard was't) how one should come on morrow
here but it is never here that one today. Well but remind to think,
you where yestoday Ys Morganas war and that it is always tomorrow in toth's tother's place. Amen.

True! True! Vouchsafe me more soundpicture! It gives furi-
ously to think. Is rich Mr Pornter, a squire, not always in his such
strong health? I thank you for the best, he is in taken deal exceedingly herculeneous. One sees how he is lot stoutlier than of
formerly. One would say him to hold whole a litteringture of
kidlings under his aproham. Has handsome Sir Pournter always
been so long married? O yes, Lord Pournterfamilias has been
marryingman ever since so long time in Hurtleforth, where he
appeer as our oily the active, and, yes indeed, he has his mic son
and his two fine mac sons and a superfine mick want they mack
metween them. She, she, she! But on what do you again leer? I am
not leering, I pink you pardons. I am highly sheshe sherious.

Do you not must want to go somewhere on the present?
Yes, O pity! At earliest moment! That prickly heat feeling! For-
think not me spill it's at always so guey. Here we shall do a
far walk (O pity) anygo khaibits till the number one of sairey's
place. Is, is. I want you to admire her sceneries illustrationing
our national first rout, one ought ought one. We shall too
downlook on that ford where Sylvanus Sanctus washed but
hurdley those tips of his anointeds. Do not show ever retrorsehim,
crookodeyled, till that you become quite crimstone in the face!
Beware! guardafew! It is Stealer of the Heart! I am anxious in
regard you should everthrown your sillarsalt. I will dui sui, tef-

nute! These brilling waveleaplights! Please say me how sing you
them. Seekhem seckhem! They arise from a clear springwell in
the near of our park which makes the daft to hear all blend. This
place of endearment! How it is clear! And how they cast their
spells upon, the fronds that thereup float, the bookstaff branchings! The druggeted stems, the leaves incut on trees! Do you
can their tantrist spellings? I can lese, skillmistress aiding. Elm,
bay, this way, cull dare, take a message, tawny runes ilex sallow,
meet me at the pine. Yes, they shall have brought us to the water
trysting, by hedjes of maiden ferm, then here in another place is
their chapelofeases, sold for song, of which you have thought
my praise too much my price. O ma ma! Yes, sad one of Ziod?
Sell me, my soul dear! Ah, my sorrowful, his cloister dreeping
of his monkshood, how it is triste to death, all his dark ivytod!
Where cold in dearth. Yet see, my blanching kissabelle, in the
under close she is allso gay, her kirtles green, her curtsies white,
her peony pears, her nistlingsloes! I, pipette, I must also quick-
lingly to tryst myself softly into this littleeasechapel. I would
rather than Ireland! But I pray, make! Do your easiness! O,
peace, this is heaven! O, Mr Prince of Pouringtoher, whatever
shall I pppease to do? Why do you so lifesighs, my precious, as
I hear from you, with limmenings lemantitions, after that swollen
one? I am not sighing, I assure, but only I am soso sorry about
all in my saarasplace. Listen, listen! I am doing it. Hear more to
those voices! Always I am hearing them. Horsehem coughs
enough. Annshee lispes privily.

— He is quieter now.

— Legalentitled. Accesstopartnuzz. Notwildebeestsch. By-
rightofoaptz. Twainbeonerfish. Haveandholdpp.

— S! Let us go. Make a noise. Slee . . .

— Qui . . . The gir . . .

— Huesofrichunfoldingmorn. Wakenupriseandprove. Pro-
videforsacrifice.

— Wait! Hist! Let us list!

For our netherworld's bosomfoes are working tooth and nail
overtime: in earthveins, toadcavites, chessganglions, saltkles-

ters, underfed: nagging firenibblers knockling aterman up out of
his hinterclutch. Tomb be their tools. When the youngdammers
will be soon heartpocking on their betters' doornoggers: and the
youngfries will be backfrisking diamondcuts over their lyingin
underlayers, spick and spat trowelling a gravetrench for their
fourinhand forebears. Vote for your club!

— Wait!
— What!
— Her door!
— Ope?
— See!
— What?
— Careful.
— Who?

Live well! Iniivdluaritzas! Tone!

Cant ear! Her dorters ofe? Whofe? Her eskmeno daughters
hope? Whope? Ellme, elmme, elskmestoon! Soon!

Let us consider.

The procurator Interrogarius Mealterum presends us this pro-
poser.

Honuphrius is a concupiscent exservicemajor who makes dis-
honest propositions to all. He is considered to have committed,
invoking *droit d'oreiller*, simple infidelities with Felicia, a virgin,
and to be practising for unnatural coits with Eugenius and Jeremias, two or three philadelphians. Honophrius, Felicia, Eugenius
and Jeremias are consanguineous to the lowest degree. Anita
the wife of Honophrius, has been told by her tirewoman, Fortissa, that Honuphrius has blasphemously confessed under voluntary chastisement that he has instructed his slave, Mauritius, to
urge Magravius, a commercial, emulous of Honuphrius, to solicit
the chastity of Anita. Anita is informed by some illegitimate
children of Fortissa with Mauritius (the supposition is Ware's)
that Gillia, the schismatical wife of Magravius, is visited clandestinely by Barnabas, the advocate of Honuphrius, an immoral
person who has been corrupted by Jeremias. Gillia, (a cooler
blend, D'Alton insists) *ex equo* with Poppea, Arancita, Clara,

Marinuzza, Indra and Iodina, has been tenderly debauched (in Halliday's view), by Honuphrius, and Magravius knows from spies that Anita has formerly committed double sacrilege with Michael, *vulgo* Cerularius, a perpetual curate, who wishes to seduce Eugenius. Magravius threatens to have Anita molested by Sulla, an orthodox savage (and leader of a band of twelve mercenaries, the Sullivani), who desires to procure Felicia for Gregorius, Leo, Vitellius and Macdugalius, four excavators, if she will not yield to him and also deceive Honuphrius by rendering conjugal duty when demanded. Anita who claims to have discovered incestuous temptations from Jeremias and Eugenius would yield to the lewdness of Honuphrius to appease the savagery of Sulla and the mercernariness of the twelve Sullivani, and (as Gilbert at first suggested), to save the virginity of Felicia for Magravius when converted by Michael after the death of Gillia, but she fears that, by allowing his marital rights she may cause reprehensible conduct between Eugenius and Jeremias. Michael, who has formerly debauched Anita, dispenses her from yielding to Honuphrius who pretends publicly to possess his conjunct in thirtynine several manners (*turpiter!* affirm *ex cathedris* Gerontes Cambronses) for carnal hygiene whenever he has rendered himself impotent to consummate by subdolence. Anita is disturbed but Michael comminates that he will reserve her case tomorrow for the ordinary Guglielmus even if she should practise a pious fraud during affrication which, from experience, she knows (according to Wadding), to be leading to nullity. Fortissa, however, is encouraged by Gregorius, Leo, Viteilius, and Magdugalius, reunitedly, to warn Anita by describing the strong chastisements of Honuphrius and the depravities (*turpissimas!*) of Canicula, the deceased wife of Mauritius, with Sulla, the simoniac, who is abnegand and repents. Has he hegemony and shall she submit?

Translate a lax, you breed a bradaun. In the goods of Cape and Chattertone, deceased.

This, lay readers and gentilemen, is perhaps the commonest of all cases arising out of umbrella history in connection with

the wood industries in our courts of litigation. D'Oyly Owens
holds (though Finn Magnusson of himself holds also) that so
long as there is a joint deposit account in the two names a
mutual obligation is posited. Owens cites Brerfuchs and Warren,
a foreign firm, since disseized, registered as Tangos, Limited,
for the sale of certain proprietary articles. The action which was
at the instance of the trustee of the heathen church emergency
fund, suing by its trustee, a resigned civil servant, for the payment of tithes due was heard by Judge Doyle and also by a common jury. No question arose as to the debt for which vouchers
spoke volumes. The defence alleged that payment had been made
effective. The fund trustee, one Jucundus Fecundus Xero Pecun-
dus Coppercheap, counterclaimed that payment was invalid
having been tendered to creditor under cover of a crossed cheque,
signed in the ordinary course, in the name of Wieldhelm, Hurls
Cross, voucher copy provided, and drawn by the senior partner
only by whom the lodgment of the species had been effected but
in their joint names. The bank particularised, the national misery
(now almost entirely in the hands of the four chief bondholders
for value in Tangos), declined to pay the draft, though there
were ample reserves to meet the liability, whereupon the trusty
Coppercheap negociated it for and on behalf of the fund of the
thing to a client of his, a notary, from whom, on consideration, he
received in exchange legal relief as between trusthee and bethrust,
with thanks. Since then the cheque, a good washable pink, em-
bossed D you D No 11 hundred and thirty 2, good for the figure
and face, had been circulating in the country for over thirtynine
years among holders of Pango stock, a rival concern, though not
one demonetised farthing had ever spun or fluctuated across the
counter in the semblance of hard coin or liquid cash. The jury (a
sour dozen of stout fellows all of whom were curiously named
after doyles) naturally disagreed jointly and severally, and the
belligerent judge, disagreeing with the allied jurors' disagree-
ment, went outside his jurisfiction altogether and ordered a gar-
nishee attachment to the neutral firm. No *mandamus* could lo-
cate the depleted whilom Breyfawkes as he had entered into an

ancient moratorium, dating back to the times of the early barters,
and only the junior partner Barren could be found, who entered an
appearance and turned up, upon a notice of motion and after service
of the motion by interlocutory injunction, among the male jurors
to be an absolete turfwoman, originally from the proletarian class,
with still a good title to her sexname of Ann Doyle, 2 Coppinger's
Cottages, the Doyle's country. Doyle (Ann), add woman in,
having regretfully left the juryboxers, protested cheerfully on the
stand in a long jurymiad *in re* corset checks, delivered in doy-
lish, that she had often, in supply to brusk demands rising almost
to bollion point, discounted Mr Brakeforth's first of all in exchange at nine months from date without issue and, to be strictly
literal, unbottled in corrubberation a current account of how
she had been made at sight for services rendered the payee-
drawee of unwashable blank assignations, sometimes pinkwilliams
(laughter) but more often of the *crème-de-citron, vair émail paon-
coque* or marshmallow series, which she, as bearer, used to endorse, adhesively, to her various payers-drawers who in most cases
were identified by the timber papers as wellknown tetigists of the
city and suburban. The witness, at her own request, asked if she
might and wrought something between the sheets of music paper
which she had accompanied herself with for the occasion and
this having been handed up for the bench to look at *in camera*,
Coppinger's doll, as she was called, (*annias*, Mack Erse's Dar,
the adopted child) then proposed to jerrykin and jureens and every
jim, jock and jarry in that little green courtinghousie for her satisfaction and as a whole act of settlement to reamalgamate herself,
tomorrow perforce, in pardonership with the permanent suing fond
trustee, Monsignore Pepigi, under the new style of Will Breakfast and Sparrem, as, when all his cognisances had been estreated,
he seemed to proffer the steadiest interest towards her, but this
prepoposal was ruled out on appeal by Judge JeremyDoyler, who,
reserving judgment in a matter of courts and reversing the findings of the lower correctional, found, beyond doubt of treuson,
fending the dissassents of the pickpackpanel, twelve as upright
judaces as ever let down their thoms, and, *occupante extremum*

scabie, handed down to the jury of the Liffey that, as a matter of
tact, the woman they gave as free was born into contractual in-
capacity (the Calif of Man *v* the Eaudelusk Company) when, how
and where mamy's mancipium act did not apply and therefore held
supremely that, as no property in law can exist in a corpse,
(Hal Kilbride *v* Una Bellina) Pepigi's pact was pure piffle (loud
laughter) and Wharrem would whistle for the rhino. Will you,
won't you, pango with Pepigi? Not for Nancy, how dare you do!
And whew whewwhew whew.
— He sighed in sleep.
— Let us go back.
— Lest he forewaken.
— Hide ourselves.
While hovering dreamwings, folding around, will hide from
fears my wee mee mannikin, keep by big wig long strong mano-
men, guard my bairn, *mon beau*.
— To bed.
Prospector projector and boomooster giant builder of all
causeways woesoever, hopping offpoint and true terminus of
straxstraightcuts and corkscrewn perambulaups, zeal whence to
goal whither, wonderlust, in sequence to which every muckle
must make its mickle, as different as York from Leeds, being the
only wise in a muck's world to look on itself from beforehand;
mirrorminded curiositease and would-to-the-large which bring
hills to molehunter, home through first husband, perils behind
swine and horsepower down to hungerford, prick this man and
tittup this woman, our forced payrents, Bogy Bobow with his
cunnyngnest couchmare, Big Maester Finnykin with Phenicia
Parkes, lame of his ear and gape of her leg, most correctingly,
we beseach of you, down their laddercase of nightwatch service
and bring them at suntime flush with the nethermost gangrung
of their stepchildren, guide them through the labyrinth of their
samilikes and the alteregoases of their pseudoselves, hedge them
bothways from all roamers whose names are ligious, from loss
of bearings deliver them; so they keep to their rights and be
ware of duty frees, neoliffic smith and magdalenian jinnyjones,

mandragon mor and weak wiffeyducky, Morionmale and Thry-
dacianmad, basilisk glorious with his weeniequeenie, tigernack
and swansgrace, he as hale as his ardouries, she as verve as her
veines; this prime white arsenic with bissemate alloyed, martial
sin with peccadilly, free to lease hold with first mortgage, dow-
ser dour and dipper douce, stop-that-war and feel-this-feather,
norsebloodheartened and landsmoolwashable, great gas with
fun-in-the-corner, grand slam with fall-of-the-trick, solomn one
and shebby, cod and coney, cash and carry, in all we dreamed
the part we dreaded, corsair coupled with his dame, royal biber
but constant lymph, boniface and bonnyfeatures, nazil hose and
river mouth, bang-the-change and batter-the-bolster, big smoke
and lickley roesthy, humanity's fahrman by society leader, voguener
and trulley, humpered and elf, Urloughmoor with Miryburrow,
leaks and awfully, basal curse yet grace abunda, Regies Producer
with screendoll Vedette, peg of his claim and pride of her heart,
cliffscaur grisly but rockdove cooing, hodinstag on fryggabet,
baron and feme: that he may dishcover her, that she may uncouple
him, that one may come and crumple them, that they may soon
recoup themselves: now and then, time on time again, as per
periodicity; from Neaves to Willses, from Bushmills to Enos; to
Goerz from Harleem, to Hearths of Oak from Skittish Widdas;
via mala, hyber pass, heckhisway per alptrack: through lands-
vague and vain, after many mandelays: in their first case, to the
next place, till their cozenkerries: the high and the by, both pent
and plain: cross cowslips yillow, yellow, yallow, past pumpkins
pinguind, purplesome: be they whacked to the wide other tied
to hustings, long sizzleroads neath arthruseat, him to the derby,
her to toun, til sengentide do coddlam; in the grounds or unter-
linnen: rue to lose and ca canny: at shipside, by convent garden:
monk and sempstress, in sackcloth silkily: curious dreamers,
curious dramas, curious deman, plagiast dayman, playajest
dearest, plaguiest dourest: for the strangfort planters are pro-
desting, and the karkery felons dryflooring it and the leperties'
laddos railing the way, blump for slogo slee.
    Stop! Did a stir? No, is fast. On to bed! So he is. It's only the

wind on the road outside for to wake all shivering shanks from
snorring.

But. Oom Godd his villen, who will he be, this mitryman, some
king of the yeast, in his chrismy greyed brunzewig, with the snow
in his mouth and the caspian asthma, so bulk of build? Relics of
pharrer and livite! Dik Gill, Tum Lung or Macfinnan's cool
Harryng? He has only his hedcosycasket on and his wollsey
shirtplisse with peascod doublet, also his feet wear doubled width
socks for he always must to insure warm sleep between a pair of
fullyfleeced bankers like a finnoc in a cauwl. Can thus be Misthra
Norkmann that keeps our hotel? Begor, Mr O'Sorgmann, you're
looking right well! Hecklar's champion ethnicist. How deft as a
fuchser schouws daft as a fish! He's the dibble's own doges for
doublin existents! But a jolly fine daysent form of one word.
He's rounding up on his family.

And who is the bodikin by him, sir? So voulzievalsshie? With
ybbs and zabs? Her trixiestrail is tripping her, vop! Luck at the
way for the lucre of smoke she's looping the lamp! Why, that's
old missness wipethemdry! Well, well, wellsowells! Donau-
watter! Ardechious me! With her halfbend as proud as a peahen,
allabalmy, and her troutbeck quiverlipe, ninya-nanya. And her
steptojazyma's culunder buzztle. Happy tea area, naughtygay
frew! Selling sunlit sopes to washtout winches and rhaincold
draughts to the props of his pubs. She tired lipping the swells at
Pont Delisle till she jumped the boom at Brounemouth. Now
she's borrid his head under Hatesbury's Hatch and loamed his
fate to old Love Lane. And she's just the same old haporth of
dripping. She's even brennt her hair.

Which route are they going? Why? Angell sitter or Amen
Corner, Norwood's Southwalk or Euston Waste? The solvent
man in his upper gambeson withnot a breth against him and the
wee wiping womanahoussy. They're coming terug their diamond wedding tour, giant's inchly elfkin's ell, vesting their characters vixendevolment, andens aller, athors err, our first day man
and your dresser and mine, that Luxuumburgher evec cettehis
Alzette, konyglik shire with his queensh countess, Stepney's

shipchild with the waif of his bosun, Dunmow's flitcher with
duck-on-the-rock, down the scales, the way they went up,
under talls and threading tormentors, shunning the startraps and
slipping in sliders, risking a runway, ruing reveals, from Elder
Arbor to La Puirée, eskipping the clockback, crystal in carbon,
sweetheartedly. Hot and cold and electrickery with attendance
and lounge and promenade free. In spite of all that science could
boot or art could eke. Bolt the grinden. Cave and can em.
Single wrecks for the weak, double axe for the mail, and quick
queck quack for the radiose. Renove that bible. You will never
have post in your pocket unless you have brasse on your plate.
Beggards outdoor. Goat to the Endth, thou slowguard! Mind
the Monks and their Grasps. Scrape your souls. Commit no
miracles. Postpone no bills. Respect the uniform. Hold the raa-
bers for the kunning his plethoron. Let leash the dooves to the
cooin her coynth. Hatenot havenots. Share the wealth and spoil
the weal. Peg the pound to tom the devil. My time is on draught.
Bottle your own. Love my label like myself. Earn before eating.
Drudge after drink. Credit tomorrow. Follow my dealing. Fetch
my price. Buy not from dives. Sell not to freund. Herenow chuck
english and learn to pray plain. Lean on your lunch. No cods
before Me. Practise preaching. Think in your stomach. Import
through the nose. By faith alone. Season's weather. Gomorrha.
Salong. Lots feed from my tidetable. Oil's wells in our lands. Let
earwigger's wivable teach you the dance.

Now their laws assist them and ease their fall!

For they met and mated and bedded and buckled and got and
gave and reared and raised and brought Thawland within Har
danger, and turned them, tarrying to the sea and planted and
plundered and pawned our souls and pillaged the pounds of the
extramurals and fought and feigned with strained relations and
bequeathed us their ills and recrutched cripples gait and under-
mined lungachers, manplanting seven sisters while wan warm-
wooed woman scrubbs, and turned out coats and removed their
origins and never learned the first day's lesson and tried to
mingle and managed to save and feathered foes' nests and fouled

their own and wayleft the arenotts and ponted vodavalls for the
zollgebordened and escaped from liquidation by the heirs of their
death and were responsible for congested districts and rolled
olled logs into Peter's sawyery and werfed new woodcuts on
Paoli's wharf and ewesed Rachel's lea and rammed Dominic's
gap and looked haggards after lazatables and rode fourscore odd-
winters and struck rock oil and forced a policeman and col-
laughsed at their phizes in Toobiassed and Zachary and left off
leaving off and kept on keeping on and roused up drink and
poured balm down and were cuffed by their customers and bit
the dust at the foot of the poll when in her deergarth he gave up
his goat after the battle of Multaferry. Pharoah with fairy, two
lie, let them! Yet they wend it back, qual his leif, himmertality,
bullseaboob and rivishy divil, light in hand, helm on high, to
peekaboo durk the thicket of slumbwhere, till their hour with
their scene be struck for ever and the book of the dates he close,
he clasp and she and she seegn her tour d'adieu, Pervinca calling,
Soloscar hears. (O Sheem! O Shaam!), and gentle Isad Ysut gag,
flispering in the nightleaves flattery, dinsiduously, to Finnegan,
to sin again and to make grim grandma grunt and grin again
while the first grey streaks steal silvering by for to mock their
quarrels in dollymount tumbling.

They near the base of the chill stair, that large incorporate
licensed vintner, such as he is, from former times, nine hosts in
himself, in his hydrocomic establishment and his ambling limfy
peepingpartner, the slave of the ring that worries the hand that
sways the lamp that shadows the walk that bends to his bane the
busynext man that came on the cop with the fenian's bark that
pickled his widow that primed the pope that passed it round on
the volunteers' plate till it croppied the ears of Purses Relle that
kneed O'Connell up out of his doss that shouldered Burke that
butted O'Hara that woke the busker that grattaned his crowd
that bucked the jiggers to rhyme the rann that flooded the routes
in Eryan's isles from Malin to Clear and Carnsore Point to Slyna-
gollow and cleaned the pockets and ransomed the ribs of all the
listeners, leud and lay, that bought the ballad that Hosty made.

Anyhow (the matter is a troublous and a peniloose) have they not called him at many's their mock indignation meeting, vehmen's vengeance vective volleying, inwader and uitlander, the notables, crashing libels in their sullivan's mounted beards about him, their right renownsable patriarch? Heinz cans everywhere and the swanee her ainsell and Eyrewaker's family sock that they smuggled to life betune them, roaring (Big Reilly was the worst): free boose for the man from the nark, sure, he never was worth a cornerwall fark, and his banishee's bedpan she's a quareold bite of a tark: as they wendelled their zingaway wivewards from his find me cool's moist opulent vinery, highjacking through the nagginneck pass, as they hauled home with their hogsheads, axpoxtelating, and claiming cowled consollation, sursumcordial, from the bluefunkfires of the dipper and the martian's frost?

Use they not, our noesmall termtraders, to abhors offrom him, the yet unregendered thunderslog, whose sbrogue cunneth none lordmade undersiding, how betwixt wifely rule and *mens conscia recti*, then hemale man all unbracing to omniwomen, but now shedropping his hitches like any maidavale oppersite orseriders in an idinhole? Ah, dearo! Dearo, dear! And her illian! And his willyum! When they were all there now, matinmarked for lookin on. At the carryfour with awlus plawshus, their happyass cloudious! And then and too the trivials! And their bivouac! And his monomyth! Ah ho! Say no more about it! I'm sorry! I saw. I'm sorry! I'm sorry to say I saw!

Gives there not too amongst us after all events (or so grunts a leading hebdromadary) some togethergush of stillandbutallyouknow that, insofarforth as, all up and down the whole concreation say, efficient first gets there finally every time, as a complex matter of pure form, for those excess and that pasphault hardhearingness from their eldfar, in grippes and rumblions, through fresh taint and old treason, another like that alter but not quite such anander and stillandbut one not all the selfsame and butstillone just the maim and encore emmerhim may always, with a little difference, till the latest up to date so early in the morning, have evertheless been allmade amenable?

Yet he begottom.

Let us wherefore, tearing ages, presently preposterose a
snatchvote of thanksalot to the huskiest coaxing experimenter
that ever gave his best hand into chancerisk, wishing him with
his famblings no end of slow poison and a mighty broad venue
for themselves between the devil's punchbowl and the deep
angleseaboard, that they may gratefully turn a deaf ear clooshed
upon the desperanto of willynully, their shareholders from Taaffe
to Auliffe, that will curse them below par and mar with their
descendants, shame, humbug and profit, to greenmould upon
mildew over jaundice as long as ever there's wagtail surtaxed to
a testcase on enver a man.

We have to had them whether we'll like it or not. They'll have
to have us now then we're here on theirspot. Scant hope theirs
or ours to escape life's high carnage of semperidentity by sub-
sisting peasemeal upon variables. Bloody certainly have we got
to see to it ere smellful demise surprends us on this concrete that
down the gullies of the eras we may catch ourselves looking
forward to what will in no time be staring you larrikins on the
postface in that multimirror megaron of returningties, whirled
without end to end. So there was a raughty . . . who in Dyfflins-
borg did . . . With his soddering iron, spadeaway, hammerlegs
and . . . Where there was a fair young . . . Who was playing her
game of . . . And said she you rockaby . . . Will you peddle in
my bog . . . And he sod her in Iarland, paved her way from
Maizenhead to Youghal. And that's how Humpfrey, champion
emir, holds his own. Shysweet, she rests.

Or show pon him now, will you! Derg rudd face should take
patrick's purge. Hokoway, in his hiphigh bearserk! Third position of concord! Excellent view from front. Sidome. Female
imperfectly masking male. Redspot his browbrand. Woman's
the prey! Thon's the dullakeykongsbyogblagroggerswagginline
(private judgers, change here for Lootherstown! Onlyromans,
keep your seats!) that drew all ladies please to our great mettroll-
ops. Leary, leary, twentytun nearly, he's plotting kings down
for his villa's extension! Gaze at him now in momentum! As his

bridges are blown to babbyrags, by the lee of his hulk upright on her orbits, and the heave of his juniper arx in action, he's naval I see. Poor little tartanelle, her dinties are chattering, the strait's she's in, the bulloge she bears! Her smirk is smeeching behind for her hills. By the queer quick twist of her mobcap and the lift of her shift at random and the rate of her gate of going the pace, two thinks at a time, her country I'm proud of. The field is down, the race is their own. The galleonman jovial on his bucky brown nightmare. Bigrob dignagging his lylyputtana. One to one bore one! The datter, io, io, sleeps in peace, in peace. And the twillingsons, ganymede, garrymore, turn in trot and trot. But old pairamere goes it a gallop, a gallop. Bossford and phospherine. One to one on!

O, O, her fairy setalite! Casting such shadows to Persia's blind! The man in the street can see the coming event. Photo-flashing it far too wide. It will be known through all Urania soon. Like jealousjoy titaning fear; like rumour rhean round the planets; like china's dragon snapping japets; like rhodagrey up the east. Satyrdaysboost besets Phoebe's nearest. Here's the flood and the flaxen flood that's to come over helpless Irryland. Is there no-one to malahide Liv and her bettyship? Or who'll buy her rosebuds, jettyblack rosebuds, ninsloes of nivia, nonpaps of nan? From the fall of the fig to doom's last post every ephemeral anniversary while the park's police peels peering by for to weight down morrals from county bubblin. That trainer's trundling! Quick, pay up!

Kickakick. She had to kick a laugh. At her old stick-in-the-block. The way he was slogging his paunch about, elbiduubled, meet oft mate on, like hale King Willow, the robberer. Cainmaker's mace and waxened capapee. But the tarrant's brand on his hottoweyt brow. At half past quick in the morning. And her lamp was all askew and a trumbly wick-in-her, ringeysingey. She had to spofforth, she had to kicker, too thick of the wick of her pixy's loomph, wide lickering jessup the smooky shiminey. And her duffed coverpoint of a wickedy batter, whenever she druv behind her stumps for a tyddlesy wink through his tunnil-clefft bagslops after the rising bounder's yorkers, as he studd and

stoddard and trutted and trumpered, to see had lordherry's
blackham's red bobby abbels, it tickled her innings to consort
pitch at kicksolock in the morm. Tipatonguing him on in her
pigeony linguish, with a flick at the bails for lubrication, to scorch
her faster, faster. Ye hek, ye hok, ye hucky hiremonger! Magrath
he's my pegger, he is, for bricking up all my old kent road.
He'll win your toss, flog your old tom's bowling and I darr ye,
barrackybuller, to break his duck! He's posh. I lob him. We're
parring all Oogster till the empsyseas run googlie. Declare to
ashes and teste his metch! Three for two will do for me and he
for thee and she for you. Goeasyosey, for the grace of the fields,
or hooley pooley, cuppy, we'll both be bye and by caught in the
slips for fear he'd tyre and burst his dunlops and waken her
bornybarnies making his boobybabies. The game old merri-
mynn, square to leg, with his lolleywide towelhat and his hobbsy
socks and his wisden's bosse and his norsery pinafore and his
gentleman's grip and his playaboy's plunge and his flannelly
feelyfooling, treading her hump and hambledown like a maiden
wellheld, ovalled over, with her crease where the pads of her
punishments ought to be by womanish rights when, keek, the hen
in the doran's shantyqueer began in a kikkery key to laugh it
off, yeigh, yeigh, neigh, neigh, the way she was wuck to doodle-
doo by her gallows bird (how's that? Noball, he carries his bat!)
nine hundred and dirty too not out, at all times long past con-
quering cock of the morgans.

How blame us?

Cocorico!

Armigerend everfasting horde. Rico! So the bill to the bowe.
As the belle to the beau. We herewith pleased returned auditors'
thanks for those and their favours since safely enjoined. Coco-
ree! Tellaman tillamie. Tubbernacul in tipherairy, sons, travellers in company and their carriageable tochters, tanks tight anne
thynne for her contractations tugowards his personeel. Echo,
choree chorecho! O I you O you me! Well, we all unite thought-
fully in rendering gratias, well, between loves repassed, begging
your honour's pardon for, well, exclusive pigtorial rights of here-

hear fond tiplady his weekreations, appearing in next eon's issue of the Neptune's Centinel and Tritonville Lightowler with well the widest circulation round the whole universe. Echolo choree choroh choree chorico! How me O my youhou my I youtou to I O? Thanks furthermore to modest Miss Glimglow and neat Master Mettresson who so kindly profiteered their serwishes as demysell of honour and, well, as strainbearer respectively. And a cordiallest brief nod of chinchin dankyshin to well patient ringasend as prevenient (by your leave), to all such occasions, detachably replaceable (thanks too! twos intact!). As well as his auricular of Malthus, the promethean paratonnerwetter which first (Pray go! pray go!) taught love's lightning the way (pity shown) to well conduct itself (mercy, good shot! only please don't mention it!). Come all ye goatfathers and groanmothers, come all ye markmakers and piledrivers, come all ye labour-saving devisers and chargeleyden dividends, firefinders, water-workers, deeply condeal with him! All that is still life with death inyeborn, all verbumsaps yet bound to be, to do and to suffer, every creature, everywhere, if you please, kindly feel for her! While the dapplegray dawn drags nearing nigh for to wake all droners that drowse in Dublin.

Humperfeldt and Anunska, wedded now evermore in annas-tomoses by a ground plan of the placehunter, whiskered beau and donahbella. Totumvir and esquimeena, who so shall sepa-rate fetters to new desire, repeals an act of union to unite in bonds of shismacy. O yes! O yes! Withdraw your member. Closure. This chamber stands abjourned. Such precedent is largely a cause to lack of collective continencies among Don-nelly's orchard as lifelong the shadyside to Fairbrother's field. Humbo, lock your kekkle up! Anny, blow your wickle out! Tuck away the tablesheet! You never wet the tea! And you may go rightoway back to your Aunty Dilluvia, Humprey, after that!

Retire to rest without first misturbing your nighboor, man-kind of baffling descriptions. Others are as tired of themselves as you are. Let each one learn to bore himself. It is strictly requested that no cobsmoking, spitting, pubchat, wrastle rounds, coarse courting, smut, etc, will take place amongst those hours so devoted to repose. Look before behind before you strip you. Disrobe clothed in the strictest secrecy which privacy can afford. Water *non* to be discharged *coram* grate or *ex* window. Never divorce in the bedding the glove that will give you away. Maid Maud ninnies nay but blabs to Omama (for your life, would you!) she to her bosom friend who does all chores (and what do you think my Madeleine saw?): this ignorant mostly sweeps it out along with all the rather old corporators (have you heard of one humbledown jungleman how he bet byrn-and-bushe playing peg and pom?): the maudlin river then gets its dues (adding a din a ding or do): thence those laundresses (O, muddle me more about the maggies! I mean bawnee Madge Ellis and brownie Mag Dillon). Attention at all! Every ditcher's dastard in Dupling will let us know about it if you have paid the mulctman by whether your rent is open to be foreclosed or aback in your arrears. This is seriously meant. Here is a homelet not a hothel.

That's right, old oldun!

All in fact is soon as all of old right as anywas ever in very old place. Were he, hwen scalded of that couverfowl, to beat the bounds by here at such a point of time as this is for at sammel up all wood's haypence and riviers argent (half back from three gangs multaplussed on a twentylot add allto a fiver with the deuce or roamer's numbers ell a fee and do little ones) with the caboosh on him opheld for thrushes' mistiles yet singing oud his parasangs in cornish token: mean fawthery eastend appullcelery, old laddy he high hole: pollysigh patrolman Seekersenn, towney's tanquam, crumlin quiet down from his hoonger, he would mac siccar of inket goodsforetombed ereshiningem of light turkling eitheranny of thuncle's windopes. More, unless we were neverso wrongtaken, if he brought his boots to pause in peace, the one beside the other one, right on the road, he would seize no sound from cache or cave beyond the flow of wand was gypsing water, telling him now, telling him all, all about ham and livery, stay and toast ham in livery, and buttermore with murmurladen, to

waker oats for him on livery. Faurore! Fearhoure! At last it
past! Loab at cod then herrin or wind thin mong them treen.

   Hiss! Which we had only our hazelight to see with, cert, in
our point of view, me and my auxy, Jimmy d'Arcy, hadn't we,
Jimmy? — Who to seen with? Kiss! No kidd, captn, which he
stood us, three jolly postboys, first a couple of Mountjoys and
nutty woodbines with his cadbully's choculars, pepped from our
Theoatre Regal's drolleries puntomine, in the snug at the Cambridge Arms of Teddy Ales while we was laying, crown jewels
to a peanut, was he stepmarm, old noseheavy, or a wouldower,
which he said, lads, a taking low his Whitby hat, lopping off the
froth and whishing, with all respectfulness to the old country,
tomorow comrades, we, his long life's strength and cuirscrween
loan to our allhallowed king, the pitchur that he's turned to
weld the wall, (Lawd lengthen him!) his standpoint was,
to belt and blucher him afore the hole pleading churchal and
submarine bar yonder but he made no class at all in port
and cemented palships between our trucers, being a refugee,
didn't he, Jimmy? — Who true to me? Sish! Honeysuckler,
that's what my young lady here, Fred Watkins, bugler Fred, all
the ways from Melmoth in Natal, she calls him, dip the colours,
pet, when he commit his certain questions vivaviz the secret
empire of the snake which it was on a point of our sutton down,
how was it, Jimmy? — Who has sinnerettes to declare? Phiss!
Touching our Phoenix Rangers' nuisance at the meeting of the
waitresses, the daintylines, Elsies from Chelsies, the two leggle-
gels in blooms, and those pest of parkies, twitch, thistle and
charlock, were they for giving up their fogging trespasses
by order which we foregathered he must be raw in cane
sugar, the party, no, Jimmy MacCawthelock? Who trespass
against me? Briss! That's him wiv his wig on, achewing of his
maple gum, that's our grainpopaw, Mister Beardall, an accom-
pliced burgomaster, a great one among the very greatest, which
he told us privates out of his own scented mouf he used to was,
my lads, afore this wineact come, what say, our Jimmy the
chapelgoer? — Who fears all masters! Hi, Jocko Nowlong, my

own sweet boosy love, which he puts his feeler to me behind
the beggar's bush, does Freda, don't you be an emugee! Carry-
one, he says, though we marooned through this woylde. We
must spy a half a hind on honeysuckler now his old face's
hardalone wiv his defences down during his wappin stillstand,
says my Fred, and Jamessime here which, pip it, she simply must,
she says, our pet, she'll do a retroussy from her point of view
(Way you fly! Like a frush!) to keep her flouncies off the
grass while paying the wetmenots a musichall visit and pair her
fiefighs fore him with just one curl after the cad came back which
we fought he wars a gunner and his corkiness lay up two bottles
of joy with a shandy had by Fred and a *fino oloroso* which he
was warming to, my right, Jimmy, my old brown freer? —
Whose dolour, O so mine!

Following idly up to seepoint, neath kingmount shadow the
ilk for eke of us, whose nathem's banned, whose hofd a-hooded,
welkim warsail, how di' you dew? Hollymerry, ivysad, whicher
and whoer, Mr Black Atkins and you tanapanny troopertwos,
were you there? Was truce of snow, moonmounded snow? Or
did wolken hang o'er earth in umber hue his fulmenbomb?
Number two coming! Full inside! Was glimpsed the mean
amount of cloud? Or did pitter rain fall in a sprinkling? If the
waters could speak as they flow! Timgle Tom, pall the bell!
Izzy's busy down the dell! Mizpah low, youyou, number
one, in deep humidity! Listen, misled peerless, please! You
are of course. You miss him so, to listleto! Of course, my
pledge between us, there's no-one Noel like him here to
hear. Esch so eschess, douls a doulse! Since Allan Rogue
loved Arrah Pogue it's all Killdoughall fair. Triss! Only trees
such as these such were those, waving there, the barketree, the
o'briertree, the rowantree, the o'corneltree, the behanshrub near
windy arbour, the magill o'dendron more. Trem! All the trees
in the wood they trembold, humbild, when they heard the stop-
press from domday's erewold.

Tiss! Two pretty mistletots, ribboned to a tree, up rose liberator and, fancy, they were free! Four witty missywives, wink-

ing under hoods, made lasses like lads love maypoleriding and dotted our green with tricksome couples, fiftyfifty, their chiltren's hundred. So childish pence took care of parents' pounds and many made money the way in the world where rushroads to riches crossed slums of lice and, the cause of it all, he forged himself ahead like a blazing urbanorb, brewing treble to drown grief, giving and taking mayom and tuam, playing milliards with his three golden balls, making party capital out of landed self-interest, light on a slavey but weighty on the bourse, our hugest commercial emporialist, with his sons booing home from afar and his daughters bridling up at his side. Finner!

How did he bank it up, swank it up, the whaler in the punt, a guinea by a groat, his index on the balance and such wealth into the bargain, with the boguey which he snatched in the baggage coach ahead? Going forth on the prowl, master jackill, under night and creeping back, dog to hide, over morning. Humbly to fall and cheaply to rise, exposition of failures. Through Duffy's blunders and MacKenna's insurance for upper ten and lower five the band played on. As one generation tells another. Ofter the fall. First for a change of a seven days license he wandered out of his farmer's health and so lost his early parishlife. Then ('twas in fenland) occidentally of a sudden six junelooking flamefaces straggled wild out of their turns through his parsonfired wicket, showing all shapes of striplings in sleepless tights. Promptly whomafter in undated times, very properly a dozen generations anterior to themselves, a main chanced to burst and misflooded his fortunes, wrothing foulplay over his fives' court and his fine poultryyard wherein were spared a just two of a feather in wading room only. Next, upon due reflotation, up started four hurrigan gales to smithereen his plateglass housewalls and the slate for accounts his keeper was cooking. Then came three boy buglehorners who counterbezzled and crossbugled him. Later on in the same evening two hussites absconded through a breach in his bylaws and left him, the infidels, to pay himself off in kind remembrances. Till, ultimatehim, fell the crowning barleystraw, when an explosium of his distilleries

deafadumped all his dry goods to his most favoured sinflute and
dropped him, what remains of a heptark, leareyed and letterish,
weeping worrybound on his bankrump.

Pepep. Pay bearer, sure and sorry, at foot of ohoho honest
policist. On never again, by Phoenis, swore on him Lloyd's,
not for beaten wheat, not after Sir Joe Meade's father, thanks!
They know him, the covenanter, by rote at least, for a chameleon
at last, in his true falseheaven colours from ultraviolent to subred
tissues. That's his last tryon to march through the grand
tryomphal arch. His reignbolt's shot. Never again! How you do
that like, Mista Chimepiece? You got nice yum plemyums. Pray-
paid my promishles.

Agreed, Wu Welsher, he was chogfulled to beacsate on earn
as in hiving, of foxold conningnesses but who, hey honey, for
all values of his latters, integer integerrimost, was the formast
of the firm? At folkmood hailed, at part farwailed, accwmwladed
concloud, Nuah-Nuah, Nebob of Nephilim! After all what followed for apprentice sake? Since the now nighs nearing as the
yetst hies hin. Jeebies, ugh, kek, ptah, that was an ill man! Jaw-
boose, puddigood, this is for true a sweetish mand! But Jum-
bluffer, bagdad, sir, yond would be for a once over our all
honoured christmastyde easteredman. Fourth position of solution. How johnny! Finest view from horizon. Tableau final.
Two me see. Male and female unmask we hem. Begum by gunne!
Who now broothes oldbrawn. Dawn! The nape of his name-
shielder's scalp. Halp! After having drummed all he dun. Hun!
Worked out to an inch of his core. More! Ring down. While
the queenbee he staggerhorned blesses her bliss for to feel her
funnyman's functions Tag. Rumbling.

Tiers, tiers and tiers. Rounds.

IV

Sandhyas! Sandhyas! Sandhyas!

Calling all downs. Calling all downs to dayne. Array! Surrection. Eireweeker to the wohld bludyn world. O rally, O rally, O rally! Phlenxty, O rally! To what lifelike thyne of the bird can be. Seek you somany matters. Haze sea east to Osseania. Here! Here! Tass, Patt, Staff, Woff, Havv, Bluvv and Rutter. The smog is lofting. And already the olduman's olduman has godden up on othertimes to litanate the bonnamours. Sonne feine, somme feehn avaunt! Guld modning, have yous viewsed Piers' aube? Thane yaars agon we have used yoors up since when we have fused now orther. Calling all daynes. Calling all daynes to dawn. The old breeding bradsted culminwillth of natures to Foyn MacHooligan. The leader, the leader! Securest jubilends albas Temoram. Clogan slogan. Quake up, dim dusky, wook doom for husky! And let Billey Feghin be baallad out of his humuluation. Confindention to churchen. We have highest gratifications in announcing to pewtewr publikumst of pratician pratyusers, genghis is ghoon for you.

A hand from the cloud emerges, holding a chart expanded.

The eversower of the seeds of light to the cowld owld sowls that are in the domnatory of Defmut after the night of the carrying of the word of Nuahs and the night of making Mehs to cuddle up in a coddlepot, Pu Nuseht, lord of risings in the yonderworld of Ntamplin, tohp triumphant, speaketh.

Vah! Suvarn Sur! Scatter brand to the reneweller of the sky,
thou who agnitest! Dah! Arcthuris comeing! Be! Verb umprin-
cipiant through the trancitive spaces! Kilt by kelt shell kithagain
with kinagain. We elect for thee, Tirtangel. Svadesia salve! We
Durbalanars, theeadjure. A way, the Margan, from our astamite,
through dimdom done till light kindling light has led we hopas
but hunt me the journeyon, iteritinerant, the kal his course,
amid the semitary of Somnionia. Even unto Heliotropolis, the
castellated, the enchanting. Now if soomone felched a twoel
and soomonelses warmet watter we could, while you was saying
Morkret Miry or Smud, Brunt and Rubbinsen, make sunlike
sylp om this warful dune's battam. Yet clarify begins at. Whither
the spot for? Whence the hour by? See but! Lever hulme! Take
in. Respassers should be pursaccoutred. Qui stabat Meins quantum qui stabat Peins. As of yours. We annew. Our shades of
minglings mengle them and help help horizons. A flasch and,
rasch, it shall come to pasch, as hearth by hearth leaps live. For
the tanderest stock with the rosinost top Ahlen Hill's, clubpub-
ber, in general stores and. Atriathroughwards, Lugh the Bra-
thwacker will be the listened after and he larruping sparks out of
his teiney ones. The spearspid of dawnfire totouches ain the
tablestoane ath the centre of the great circle of the macroliths of
Helusbelus in the boshiman brush on this our peneplain by Fan-
galuvu Bight whence the horned cairns erge, stanserstanded,
to floran frohn, idols of isthmians. Overwhere. Gaunt grey
ghostly gossips growing grubber in the glow. Past now pulls.
Cur one beast, even Dane the Great, may treadspath with
sniffer he snout impursuant to byelegs. Edar's chuckal humuristic.
But why pit the cur afore the noxe? Let shrill their duan
Gallus, han, and she, hou the Sassqueehenna, makes ducks-
runs at crooked. Once for the chantermale, twoce for the pother
and once twoce threece for the waither. So an inedible yellow-
meat turns out the invasable blackth. Kwhat serves to rob with
Alliman, saelior, a turnkeyed trot to Seapoint, pierrotettes, means
Noel's Bar and Julepunsch, by Joge, if you've tippertaps in your
head or starting kursses, tailour, you're silenced at Henge Ceol-

leges, Exmooth, Ostbys for ost, boys, each and one? Death banes
and the quick quoke. But life wends and the dombs spake!
Whake? Hill of Hafid, knock and knock, nachasach, gives relief
to the langscape as he strauches his lamusong untoupon gazelle
channel and the bride of the Bryne, shin high shake, is dotter,
than evar for a damse wed her farther. Lambel on the up! We
may plesently heal Geoglyphy's twentynine ways to say good-
bett an wassing seoosoon liv. With the forty wonks winking
please me your much as to. With her tup. It's a long long ray to
Newirgland's premier. For korps, for streamfish, for confects,
for bullyoungs, for smearsassage, for patates, for steaked pig, for
men, for limericks, for waterfowls, for wagsfools, for louts, for
cold airs, for late trams, for curries, for curlews, for leekses, for
orphalines, for tunnygulls, for clear goldways, for lungfortes, for
moonyhaunts, for fairmoneys, for coffins, for tantrums, for
armaurs, for waglugs, for rogues comings, for sly goings,
for larksmathes, for homdsmeethes, for quailsmeathes, kilalooly.
Tep! Come lead, crom lech! Top. Wisely for us Old Bruton has
withdrawn his theory. You are alpsulumply wroght! Amsu-
lummmm. But this is perporteroguing youpoorapps? Naman-
tanai. Sure it's not revieng your? Amslu! Good all so. We seem
to understand apad vellumtomes muniment, Arans Duhkha,
among hoseshoes, cheriotiers and etceterogenious bargainbout-
barrows, ofver and umnder, since, evenif or although, in double
preposition as in triple conjunction, how the mudden research in
the topaia that was Mankaylands has gone to prove from the
picalava present in the maramara melma that while a successive
generation has been in the deep deep deeps of Deepereras. Buried
hearts. Rest here.

Conk a dook he'll doo. Svap.

So let him slap, the sap! Till they take down his shatter from
his shap. He canease. Fill stap.

Thus faraclacks the friarbird. Listening, Syd!

The child, a natural child, thenown by the mnames of, (aya!
aya!), wouldbewas kidnapped at an age of recent probably,
possibly remoter; or he conjured himself from seight by slide

at hand; for which thetheatron is a lemoronage; at milch-
goat fairmesse; in full dogdhis; sod on a fall; pat; the hundering
blundering dunderfunder of plundersundered manhood; behold,
he returns; renascenent; fincarnate; still foretold around the hearth-
side; at matin a fact; hailed chimers' ersekind; foe purmanant,
fum in his mow; awike in wave risurging into chrest; *victis poenis
hesternis*; fostfath of solas; fram choicest of wiles with warmen
and sogns til Banba, burial aranging; under articles thirtynine of
the reconstitution; by the lord's order of the canon consecrand-
able; earthlost that we thought him; pesternost, the noneknown
worrier; from Tumbarumba mountain; in persence of whole
landslots; forebe all the rassias; sire of leery subs of dub; the Dig-
gins, Woodenhenge, as to hang out at; with spawnish oel full his
angalach; the sousenugh; gnomeosulphidosalamermauderman; the
big brucer, fert in fort; Gunnar, of The Gunnings, Gund; one
of the two or three forefivest fellows a bloke could in holiday
crowd encounter; benedicted be the barrel; kilderkins, lids off; a
roache, an oxmaster, a sort of heaps, a pamphilius, a vintivat
niviceny, a hygiennic contrivance socalled from the editor; the
thick of your thigh; you knox; quite; talking to the vicar's joy
and ruth; the gren, woid and glue been broking by the maybole
gards; he; when no crane in Elga is heard; upout to speak this
lay; without links, without impediments, with gygantogyres,
with freeflawforms;parasama to himself; atman as evars; whom
otherwise becauses; no puler as of old but as of young a palatin;
whitelock not lacked nor temperasoleon; though he appears a
funny colour;stoatters some; but a quite a big bug after the
dahlias; place inspectorum sarchent; also the hullow chyst ex-
cavement; astronomically fabulafigured; as Jambudvispa Vipra
foresaw of him; the last half versicle repurchasing his pawned
word; sorensplit and paddypatched; and pfor to pfinish our pfun
of a pfan coalding the keddle mickwhite; sure, straight, slim,
sturdy, serene, synthetical, swift.

By the antar of Yasas! Ruse made him worthily achieve inherited wish. The drops upon that mantle rained never around
Fingal. Goute! Loughlin's Salts, Will, make a newman if any-

IV.1   FINNEGANS WAKE   597

worn. Soe? La! Lamfadar's arm it has cocoincidences. You mean
to see we have been hadding a sound night's sleep? You may so.
It is just, it is just about to, it is just about to rolywholyover.
Svapnasvap. Of all the stranger things that ever not even in the
hundrund and badst pageans of unthowsent and wonst nice or
in eddas and oddes bokes of tomb, dyke and hollow to be have
happened! The untireties of livesliving being the one substrance
of a streamsbecoming. Totalled in toldteld and teldtold in tittle-
tell tattle. Why? Because, graced be Gad and all giddy gadgets,
in whose words were the beginnings, there are two signs to turn
to, the yest and the ist, the wright side and the wronged side,
feeling aslip and wauking up, so an, so farth. Why? On the sourd-
site we have the Moskiosk Djinpalast with its twin adjacencies,
the bathouse and the bazaar, allahallahallah, and on the sponthe-
site it is the alcovan and the rosegarden, boony noughty, all pura-
puthry. Why? One's apurr apuss a story about brid and break-
fedes and parricombating and coushcouch but others is of tholes
and oubworn buyings, dolings and chafferings in heat, contest
and enmity. Why? Every talk has his stay, vidnis Shavarsanjivana,
and all-a-dreams perhapsing under lucksloop at last are through.
Why? It is a sot of a swigswag, systomy dystomy, which evera-
body you ever anywhere at all doze. Why? Such me.

    And howpsadrowsay.

    Lok! A shaft of shivery in the act, anilancinant. Cold's sleuth!
Vayuns! Where did thots come from? It is infinitesimally fevers,
resty fever, risy fever, a coranto of aria, sleeper awakening, in
the smalls of one's back presentiment, gip, and again, geip, a
flash from a future of maybe mahamayability through the windr
of a wondr in a wildr is a weltr as a wirbl of a warbl is a world.

    Tom.

    It is perfect degrees excelsius. A jaladaew still stilleth. Cloud
lay but mackrel are. Anemone activescent the torporature is returning to mornal. Humid nature is feeling itself freely at ease
with the all fresco. The vervain is to herald as the grass adminis-
ters. They say, they say in effect, they really say. You have eaden
fruit. Say whuit. You have snakked mid a fish. Telle whish.

Every those personal place objects if nonthings where soevers and they just done been doing being in a dromo of todos withouten a bound to be your trowers. Forswundled. You hald him by the tap of the tang. Not a salutary sellable sound is since. Insteed for asteer, adrift with adraft. Nuctumbulumbumus wanderwards the Nil. Victorias neanzas. Alberths neantas. It was a long, very long, a dark, very dark, an allburt unend, scarce endurable, and we could add mostly quite various and somenwhat stumbletumbling night. Endee he sendee. Diu! The has goning at gone, the is coming to come. Greets to ghastern, hie to morgning. Dormidy, destady. Doom is the faste. Well down, good other. Now day, slow day, from delicate to divine, divases. Padma, brighter and sweetster, this flower that bells, it is our hour or risings. Tickle, tickle. Lotus spray. Till herenext. Adya.

Take thanks, thankstum, thamas. In that european end meets Ind.

There is something supernoctural about whatever you called him it. Panpan and vinvin are not alonety vanvan and pinpin in your Tamal without tares but simplysoley they are they. Thisutter followis that odder fellow. Himkim kimkim. Old yeasterloaves may be a stale as a stub and the pitcher go to aftoms on the wall. Mildew, murk, leak and yarn now want the bad that they lied on. And your last words todate in camparative accoustomology are going to tell stretch of a fancy through strength towards joyance, adyatants, where he gets up. Allay for allay, a threat for a throat.

Tim!

To them in Ysat Loka. Hearing. The urb it orbs. Then's now with now's then in tense continuant. Heard. Who having has he shall have had. Hear! Upon the thuds trokes truck, chim, it will be exactlyso fewer hours by so many minutes of the ope of the diurn of the sennight of the maaned of the yere of the age of the madamanvantora of Grossguy and Littleylady, our hugibus hugibum and our weewee mother, actaman housetruewith, and their childer and their napirs and their napirs' childers napirs and their chattels and their servance and their

cognance and their ilks and their orts and their everythings that
is be will was theirs.

Much obliged. Time-o'-Thay! But wherth, O clerk?

Whithr a clonk? Vartman! See you not soo the pfath they
pfunded, oura vatars that arred in Himmal, harruad bathar namas, the gow, the stiar, the tigara, the liofant, when even thurst
was athar vetals, mid trefoils slipped the sable rampant, hoof,
hoof, hoof, hoof, padapodopudupedding on fattafottafutt. Ere
we are! Signifying, if tungs may tolkan, that, primeval conditions having gradually receded but nevertheless the emplacement
of solid and fluid having to a great extent persisted through
intermittences of sullemn fulminance, sollemn nuptialism, sallemn
sepulture and providential divining, making possible and even
inevitable, after his a time has a tense haves and havenots hesitency,
at the place and period under consideration a socially organic
entity of a millenary military maritory monetary morphological
circumformation in a more or less settled state of equonomic
ecolube equalobe equilab equilibbrium. Gam on, Gearge! Nomo-
morphemy for me! Lessnatbe angardsmanlake! You jast gat a
tache of army on the stumuk. To the Angar at Anker. Aecquo-
tincts. Seeworthy. Lots thankyouful, polite pointsins! There's
a tavarn in the tarn.

Tip. Take Tamotimo's topical. Tip. Browne yet Noland. Tip.
Advert.

Where. Cumulonubulocirrhonimbant heaven electing, the dart
of desire has gored the heart of secret waters and the poplarest
wood in the entire district is being grown at present, eminently
adapted for the requirements of pacnincstricken humanity and,
between all the goings up and the whole of the comings down and
the fog of the cloud in which we toil and the cloud of the fog
under which we labour, bomb the thing's to be domb about it so
that, beyond indicating the locality, it is felt that one cannot with
advantage add a very great deal to the aforegoing by what, such as
it is to be, follows, just mentioning however that the old man of
the sea and the old woman in the sky if they don't say nothings
about it they don't tell us lie, the gist of the pantomime, from

cannibal king to the property horse, being slumply and slopely to remind us how, in this drury world of ours, Father Times and Mother Spacies boil their kettle with their crutch. Which every lad and lass in the lane knows. Hence.

Polycarp pool, the pool of Innalavia, Saras the saft as, of meadewy marge, atween Deltas Piscium and Sagittariastrion, whereinn once we lave 'tis alve and vale, minnyhahing here from hiarwather, a poddlebridges in a passabed, the river of lives, the regenerations of the incarnations of the emanations of the apparentations of Funn and Nin in Cleethabala, the kongdomain of the Alieni, an accorsaired race, infester of Libnud Ocean, Moylamore, let it be. Where Allbroggt Neandser tracking Viggynette Neeinsee gladsighted her, Linfian Fall and a teamdiggingharrow turned the first sod. Sluce! Caughterect! Goodspeed the blow! (Incidentally 'tis believed that his harpened before Gage's Fane for it has to be over this booty spotch, though some hours to the wester, that ex-Colonel House's preterpost heiress is to return unto the outstretcheds of Dweyr O'Michael's loinsprung the blunterbusted pikehead which his had hewn in hers prolonged laughter words). There an alomdree begins to green, soreen seen for loveseat, as we know that should she, for by essentience his law, so it make all. It is scainted to Vitalba. And her little white bloomkins, twittersky trimmed, are hobdoblins' hankypanks. Saxenslyke our anscessers thought so darely on now they're going soever to Anglesen, free of juties, dyrt chapes. There too a slab slobs, immermemorial, the only in all swamp. But so bare, so boulder, brag sagging such a brr bll bmm show that, of Barindens, the white alfred, it owed to have at leased some butchup's upperon. *Homos Circas Elochlannensis!* His showplace at Leeambye. Old Wommany Wyes. Pfif! But, while gleam with gloom swan here and there, this shame rock and that whispy planter tell Paudheen Steel the-Poghue and his perty Molly Vardant, in goodbroomirish, arrah, this place is a proper and his feist a ferial for curdnal communial, so be who would celibrate the holy mystery upon or that the pirigrim from Mainylands beatend, the calmleaved hutcaged by that look whose glaum is sure he means bisnisgels to empalmover. A naked yogpriest, clothed of sundust, his oakey doaked with frondest leoves, offrand to the ewon of her owen. Tasyam kuru salilakriyamu! Pfaf!

Bring about it to be brought about and it will be, loke, our lake lemanted, that greyt lack, the citye of Is is issuant (atlanst!), urban and orbal, through seep froms umber under wasseres of Erie.

Lough!

Hwo! Hwy, dairmaidens? Asthoreths, assay! Earthsigh to is heavened.

Hillsengals, the daughters of the cliffs, responsen. Longsome the samphire coast. From thee to thee, thoo art it thoo, that thouest there. The like the near, the liker nearer. O sosay! A family, a band, a school, a clanagirls. Fiftines andbut fortines by novanas andor vantads by octettes ayand decadendecads by a lunary with last a lone. Whose every has herdifferent from the similies with her site. *Sicut campanulae petalliferentes* they coroll in caroll round Botany Bay. A dweam of dose innocent dirly dirls. Keavn! Keavn! And they all setton voicies about singsing music was Keavn! He. Only he. Ittle he. Ah! The whole clangalied. Oh!

S. Wilhelmina's, S. Gardenia's, S. Phibia's, S. Veslandrua's, S. Clarinda's, S. Immecula's, S. Dolores Delphin's, S. Perlanthroa's, S. Errands Gay's, S. Eddaminiva's, S. Rhodamena's, S. Ruadagara's, S. Drimicumtra's, S. Una Vestity's, S. Mintargisia's, S. Misha-La-Valse's, S. Churstry's, S. Clouonaskieym's, S. Bellavistura's, S. Santamonta's, S. Ringsingsund's, S. Heddadin Drade's, S. Glacianivia's, S. Waidafrira's, S. Thomassabbess's and (trema! unloud!! pepet!!!) S. Loellisotoelles!

Prayfulness! Prayfulness!

Euh! Thaet is seu whaet shaell one naeme it!

The meidinogues have tingued togethering. Ascend out of your bed, cavern of a trunk, and shrine! Kathlins is kitchin. Soros cast, ma brone! You must exterra acquarate to interirigate all the arkypelicans. The austrologer Wallaby by Tolan, who farshook our showrs from Newer Aland, has signed the you and the now our mandate. Milenesia waits. Be smark.

One seekings. Not the lithe slender, not the broad roundish near the lithe slender, not the fairsized fullfeatured to the leeward of the broad roundish but, indeed and inneed, the curling, perfect-portioned, flowerfleckled, shapely highhued, delicate features swaying to the windward of the fairsized fullfeatured.

Was that in the air about when something is to be said for it or is it someone imparticular who will somewherise for the whole anyhow?

What does Coemghen? Tell his hidings clearly! A woodtoo-gooder. Is his moraltack still his best of weapons? How about a little more goaling goold? Rowlin's tun he gadder no must. It is the voice of Roga. His face is the face of a son. Be thine the silent hall, O Jarama! A virgin, the one, shall mourn thee. Roga's stream is solence. But Croona is in adestance. The ass of the O'Dwyer of Greyglens is abrowtobayse afeald in his terroirs of the Potter-ton's forecoroners, the reeks around the burleyhearthed. When visited by an independant reporter, "Mike" Portlund, to burrow burning the latterman's Resterant so is called the gortan in ques-ture he mikes the fallowing for the Durban Gazette, firstcoming issue. From a collispendent. Any were. Deemsday. Bosse of Upper and Lower Byggotstrade, Ciwareke, may he live for river! The Games funeral at Valleytemple. Saturnights pomps, exhabiting that corricatore of a harss, revealled by Oscur Camerad. The last of Dutch Schulds, perhumps. Pipe in Dream Cluse. Uncovers Pub History. The Outrage, at Length. Affected Mob Follows in Reli-gious Sullivence. Rinvention of vestiges by which they drugged the buddhy. Moviefigure on in scenic section. By Patathicus. And there, from out of the scuity, misty Londan, along the canavan route, that is with the years gone, mild beam of the wave his polar bearing, steerner among stars, trust touthena and you tread true turf, comes the sorter, Mr Hurr Hansen, talking allthe-ways in himself of his hopes to fall in among a merryfoule of maidens happynghome from the dance, his knyckle allaready in his knackskey fob, a passable compatriate proparly of the Grimstad galleon, old pairs frieze, feed up to the noxer with their geese and peeas and oats upon a trencher and the toyms

he'd lust in Wooming but with that smeoil like a grace of backon-
ing over his egglips of the sunsoonshine. Here's heering you in
a guessmasque, latterman! And such an improofment! As royt
as the mail and as fat as a fuddle! Schoen! Shoan! Shoon the
Puzt! A penny for your thought abouts! Tay, tibby, tanny,
tummy, tasty, tosty, tay. Batch is for Baker who baxters our
bread. O, what an ovenly odour! Butter butter! Bring us this
days our maily bag! But receive me, my frensheets, from the
emerald dark winterlong! For diss is the doss for Eilder Downes
and dass is it duss as singen sengers what the hardworking
straightwalking stoutstamping securelysealing officials who trow
to form our G.M.P.'s pass muster generally shay for shee and
sloo for slee when butting their headd to the pillow for a night-
shared nakeshift with the alter girl they tuck in for sweepsake.
Dutiful wealker for his hydes of march. Haves you the time.
Hans ahike? Heard you the crime, senny boy? The man was
giddy on letties on the dewry of the duary, be pursueded,
whethered with entrenous, midgreys, dagos, teatimes, shadows,
nocturnes or samoans, if wellstocked fillerouters plushfeverfraus
with dopy chonks, and this, that and the other pigskin or muffle
kinkles, taking a pipe course or doing an anguish, seen to his
fleece in after his foull, when Dr Chart of Greet Chorsles street
he changed his backbone at a citting. He had not the declaina-
tion, as what with the foos as whet with the fays, but so far as
hanging a goobes on the precedings, wherethen the lag allows, it
mights be anything after darks. Which the deers alones they sees
and the darkies they is snuffing of the wind up. Debbling.
Greanteavvents! Hyacinssies with heliotrollops! Not once
fullvixen freakings and but dubbledecoys! It is a lable iction on
the porte of the cuthulic church and summum most atole for it.
Where is that blinketey blanketer, that quound of a pealer, the
sunt of a hunt whant foxes good men! Where or he, our loved
among many?
    But what does Coemghem, the fostard? Tyro a tora. The
novened iconostase of his blueygreyned vitroils but begins
in feint to light his legend. Let Phosphoron proclaim! Peechy

peechy. Say he that saw him that saw! Man shall sharp run do a get him. Ask no more, Jerry mine, Roga's voice! No pice soorkabatcha. The bog which puckerooed the posy. The vinebranch of Heremonheber on Bregia's plane where Teffia lies is leaved invert and fructed proper but the cublic hatches endnot open yet for hourly rincers' mess. Read Higgins, Cairns and Egen. Malthus is yet lukked in close. Withun. How swathed thereanswer alcove makes theirinn! Besoakers loiter on. And primilibatory solicates of limon sodias will be absorbable. It is not even yet the engine of the load with haled morries full of crates, you mattinmummur, for dombell dumbs? Sure and 'tis not then. The greek Sideral Reulthway, as it havvents, will soon be starting a smooth with its first single hastencraft. Danny buzzers instead of the vialact coloured milk train on the fartykket plan run with its endless gallaxion of rotatorattlers and the smooltroon our elderens rememberem as the scream of the service, Strubry Bess. Also the waggonwobblers are still yet everdue to precipitate after night's combustion. Aspect, Shamus Rogua or! Taceate and! *Hagiographice canat Ecclesia.* Which aubrey our first shall show. Inattendance who is who is will play that's what's that to what's that, what.

Oyes! Oyeses! Oyesesyeses! The primace of the Gaulls, protonotorious, I yam as I yam, mitrogenerand in the free state on the air, is now aboil to blow a Gael warning. Inoperation Eyrlands Eyot, Meganesia, Habitant and the onebut thousand insels, Western and Osthern Approaches.

Of Kevin, of increate God the servant, of the Lord Creator a filial fearer, who given to the growing grass took to the tall timber, slippery dick the springy heeler, as we have seen, so we have heard, what we have received, that we have transmitted, thus we shall hope, this we shall pray till, in the search for love of knowledge through the comprehension of the unity in altruism through stupefaction, it may again how it may again, shearing aside the four wethers and passing over the dainty daily dairy and dropping by the way the lapful of live coals and smoothing out Nelly Nettle and her lad of mettle, full of stings, fond of stones, friend of gnewgnawns bones and leaving all the messy messy to look after our douche douche, the miracles, death and life are these.

Yad. Procreated on the ultimate ysland of Yreland in the encyclical yrish archipelago, come their feast of precreated holy whiteclad angels, whomamong the christener of his, voluntarily poor Kevin, having been graunted the praviloge of a priest's postcreated portable *altare cum balneo*, when espousing the one true cross, invented and exalted, in celibate matrimony at matin chime arose and westfrom went and came in alb of cloth of gold to our own midmost Glendalough-le-vert by archangelical guidance where amiddle of meeting waters of river Yssia and Essia river on this one of eithers lone navigable lake piously Kevin, lawding the triune trishagion, amidships of his conducible altar super bath, rafted centripetally, diaconal servent of orders hibernian, midway across the subject lake surface to its supreem epicentric lake Ysle, whereof its lake is the ventrifugal principality, whereon by prime, powerful in knowledge, Kevin came to where its centre is among the circumfluent watercourses of Yshgafiena and Yshgafiuna, an enysled lakelet yslanding a lacustrine yslet, whereupon with beached raft subdiaconal bath *propter* altar, with oil extremely anointed, accompanied by prayer, holy Kevin bided till the third morn hour but to build a rubric penitential honeybeehivehut in whose enclosure to live in fortitude, acolyte of cardinal virtues, whereof the arenary floor, most holy Kevin excavated as deep as to the depth of a seventh part of one full fathom, which excavated, venerable Kevin, anchorite, taking counsel, proceded towards the lakeside of the ysletshore whereat seven several times he, eastward genuflecting, in entire ubidience at sextnoon collected gregorian water sevenfold and with ambrosian eucharistic joy of heart as many times receded, carrying that privileged altar *unacumque* bath, which severally seven times into the cavity excavated, a lector of water levels, most venerable Kevin, then effused thereby letting there be water where was theretofore dryland, by him so concreated, who now, confirmed a strong and perfect christian, blessed Kevin, exorcised his holy sister water, perpetually chaste, so that, well understanding, she should fill to midheight his tubbathaltar, which hanbathtub, most blessed Kevin, ninthly enthroned, in the concentric centre of the translated water, whereamid, when violet vesper vailed, Saint Kevin, Hydrophilos, having girded his sable *cappa magna* as high as to his cherubical loins, at solemn compline sat in his sate of wisdom, that handbathtub, whereverafter, recreated *doctor insularis* of the universal church, keeper of the door of meditation, memory *extempore* proposing and intellect formally considering, recluse, he meditated continuously with seraphic ardour the primal sacrament of baptism or the regeneration of all man by affusion of water. Yee.

Bisships, bevel to rock's rite! Sarver buoy, extinguish! Nuotabene. The rare view from the three Benns under the bald heaven is on the other end, askan your blixom on dimmen and blastun, something to right hume about. They were erected in a purvious century, as a hen fine coops and, if you know your Bristol and have trudged the trolly ways and elventurns of that old cobbold city, you will sortofficially scribble a mental Peny-Knox-Gore. Whether they were franklings by name also has not been fully probed. Their design is a whosold word and the charming details of light in dark are freshed from the feminiairity which breathes content. *O ferax cupla*! Ah, fairypair! The first exploder to make his ablations in these parks was indeed that lucky mortal which the monster trial showed on its first day out. What will not arky paper, anticidingly inked with penmark, push, per sample prof, kuvertly falted, when style, stink and stigmataphoron are of one sum in the same person? He comes out of the soil very well after all just where Old Toffler is to come shuffling alongsoons Panniquanne starts showing of her peequuliar talonts. Awaywrong wandler surking to a rightrare rute for his plain utterrock sukes, appelled to by her fancy claddaghs. You plied that pokar, gamesy, swell as aye did, while there were flickars to the flores. He may be humpy, nay, he may be dumpy but there is always something racey about, say, a sailor on a horse. As soon as we sale him geen we gates a sprise! He brings up tofatufa and

that is how we get to Missas in Massas. The old Marino tale. We
veriters verity notefew demmed lustres priorly magistrite maxi-
mollient in ludubility learned. Facst. Teak off that wise head!
Great sinner, good sonner, is in effect the motto of the Mac-
Cowell family. The gloved fist (skrimmhandsker) was intraduced
into their socerdatal tree before the fourth of the twelfth and it
is even a little odd all four horolodgeries still gonging restage
Jakob van der Bethel, smolking behing his pipe, with Essav of
Messagepostumia, lentling out his borrowed chafingdish, before
cymbaloosing the apostles at every hours of changeover. The
first and last rittlerattle of the anniverse; when is a nam nought a
nam whenas it is a. Watch! Heroes' Highway where our fleshers
leave their bonings and every bob and joan to fill the bumper fair.
It is their segnall for old Champelysied to seek the shades of his
retirement and for young Chappielassies to tear a round and tease
their partners lovesoftfun at Finnegan's Wake.

And it's high tigh tigh. Titley hi ti ti. That my dig pressed in
your dag si. Gnug of old Gnig. Ni, gnid mig brawly! I bag your
burden. Mees is thees knees. Thi is Mi. We have caught one-
selves, Sveasmeas, in somes incontigruity coumplegs of heopon-
hurrish marrage from whose I most sublumbunate. A polog, my
engl! Excutes. Om still so sovvy. Whyle om till ti ti.

Ha!

Dayagreening gains in schlimninging. A summerwint spring-
falls, abated. Hail, regn of durknass, snowly receassing, thund
lightening thund, into the dimbelowstard departamenty whither-
out, soon hist, soon mist, to the hothehill from the hollow,
Solsking the Frist (attempted by the admirable Captive Bunting
and Loftonant-Cornel Blaire) will processingly show up above
Tumplen Bar whereupont he was much jubilated by Boerge-
mester "Dyk" ffogg of Isoles, now Eisold, looking most plussed
with (exhib 39) a clout capped sunbubble anaccanponied from
his bequined torse. Up.

Blanchardstown mewspeppers pleads coppyl. Gracest goodness, heave mensy upponnus! Grand old Manbutton, give your
bowlers a rest!

It is a mere mienerism of this vague of visibilities, mark you,
as accorded to by moisturologist of the Brehons Assorceration for
the advauncement of scayence because, my dear, mentioning of
it under the breath, as in pure (what bunkum!) essenesse, there
have been disselving forenenst you just the draeper, the two
drawpers assisters and the three droopers assessors confraterni-
tisers. Who are, of course, Uncle Arth, your two cozes from
Niece and (kunject a bit now!) our own familiars, Billyhealy, Ballyhooly and Bullyhowley, surprised in an indecorous position by
the Sigurd Sigerson Sphygmomanometer Society for bled-
prusshers.
    Knightsmore. Haventyne?
    Ha ha!
    This Mister Ireland? And a live?
    Ay, ay. Aye, aye, baas.
    The cry of Stena chills the vitals of slumbring off the motther
has been pleased into the harms of old salaciters, meassurers
soon and soon, but the voice of Alina gladdens the cockly-
hearted dreamerish for that magic moning with its ching
chang chap sugay kaow laow milkee muchee bringing becker-
brose, the brew with the foochoor in it. Sawyest? Nodt? Nyets,
I dhink I sawn to remumb or sumbsuch. A kind of a thinglike
all traylogged then pubably it resymbles a pelvic or some kvind
then props an acutebacked quadrangle with aslant off ohahn-
thenth a wenchyoumaycuddler, lying with her royalirish upper-
shoes among the theeckleaves. Signs are on of a mere by token
that wills still to be becoming upon this there once a here was
world. As the dayeleyves unfolden them. In the wake of the
blackshape, *Nattenden Sorte;* whenat, hindled firth and hundled
furth, the week of wakes is out and over; as a wick weak woking
from ennemberable Ashias unto fierce force fuming, temtem
tamtam, the Phoenican wakes.
    Passing. One. We are passing. Two. From sleep we are pass-
ing. Three. Into the wikeawades warld from sleep we are passing.
Four. Come, hours, be ours!
    But still. Ah diar, ah diar! And stay.

It was allso agreenable in our sinegear clutchless, touring the
no placelike no timelike absolent, mixing up pettyvaughan popu-
lose with the magnumoore genstries, lloydhaired mersscenary
blookers with boydskinned pigttetails and goochlipped gwendo-
lenes with duffyeyed dolores; like so many unprobables in their
poor suit of the improssable. With Mata and after please with
Matamaru and after please stop with Matamaruluka and after stop
do please with Matamarulukajoni.

And anotherum. Ah ess, dapple ass! He will be longing after
the Grogram Grays. And, Weisingchetaoli, he will levellaut
ministel Trampleasure be. Sheflower Rosina, younger Sheflower
fruit Amaryllis, youngest flowerfruityfrond Sallysill or Sillysall.
And house with heaven roof occupanters they are continuatingly
attraverse of its milletestudinous windows, ricocoursing themselves, as staneglass on stonegloss, inplayn unglish Wynn's
Hotel. Brancherds at: Bullbeck, Oldboof, Sassondale,, Jorsey
Uppygard, Mundelonde, Abbeytotte, Bracqueytuitte with Hoc-
keyvilla, Fockeyvilla, Hillewille and Wallhall. Hoojahoo mana-
gers the thingaviking. Obning shotly. When the messanger of
the risen sun, (see other oriel) shall give to every seeable a hue and
to every hearable a cry and to each spectacle liis spot and to each
happening her houram. The while we, we are waiting, we are
waiting for. Hymn.

Muta: Quodestnunc fumusiste volhvuns ex Domoyno?

Juva: It is Old Head of Kettle puffing off the top of the mornin.

Muta: He odda be thorly well ashamed of himself for smoking
before the high host.

Juva: Dies is Dorminus master and commandant illy tono-
brass.

Muta: Diminussed aster! An I could peecieve amonkst the
gatherings who ever they wolk in process?

Juva: Khubadah! It is the Chrystanthemlander with his
porters of bonzos, pompommy plonkyplonk, the ghariwallahs,
moveyovering the cabrattlefield of slaine.

Muta: Pongo da Banza! An I would uscertain in druidful
scatterings one piece tall chap he stand one piece same place?

Juva: Bulkily: and he is fundementially theosophagusted over the whorse proceedings.

Muta: Petrificationibus! O horild haraflare! Who his dickhuns now rearrexes from undernearth the memorialorum?

Juva: Beleave filmly, beleave! Fing Fing! King King!

Muta: Ulloverum? Fulgitudo ejus Rhedonum teneat!

Juva: Rolantlossly! Till the tipp of his ziff. And the ubideintia of the savium is our ervics fenicitas.

Muta: Why soly smiles the supremest with such for a leary on his rugular lips?

Juva: Bitchorbotchum! Eebrydime! He has help his crewn on the burkeley buy but he has holf his crown on the Eurasian Generalissimo.

Muta: Skulkasloot! The twyly velleid is thus then paridicynical?

Juva: Ut vivat volumen sic pereat pouradosus!

Muta: Haven money on stablecert?

Juva: Tempt to wom Outsider!

Muta: Suc? He quoffs. Wutt?

Juva: Sec! Wartar wartar! Wett.

Muta: Ad Piabelle et Purabelle?

Juva: At Winne, Woermann og Sengs.

Muta: So that when we shall have acquired unification we shall pass on to diversity and when we shall have passed on to diversity we shall have acquired the instinct to combat and when we shall have acquired the instinct of combat we shall pass back to the spirit of appeasement?

Juva: By the light of the bright reason which daysends to us from the high.

Muta: May I borrow that hordwanderbaffle from you, old rubberskin?

Juva: Here it is and I hope it's your wormingpen, Erinmonker! Shoot.

Rhythm and Colour at Park Mooting. Peredos Last in the Grand Natural. Velivision victor. Dubs newstage oldtime turftussle, recalling Winny Willy Widger. Two draws. Heliotrope

leads from Harem. Three ties. Jockey the Ropper jerks Jake the
Rape. Paddrock and bookley chat.

And here are the details.

Tunc. Bymeby, bullocky vampas tappany bobs topside joss
pidgin fella Balkelly, archdruid of islish chinchinjoss in the his
heptachromatic sevenhued septicoloured roranyellgreenlindigan
mantle finish he show along the his mister guest Patholic with
alb belongahim the whose throat hum with of sametime all the his
cassock groaner fellas of greysfriaryfamily he fast all time what
time all him monkafellas with Same Patholic, quoniam, speeching,
yeh not speeching noh man liberty is, he drink up words, scilicet,
tomorrow till recover will not, all too many much illusiones
through photoprismic velamina of hueful panepiphanal world
spectacurum of Lord Joss, the of which zoantholitic furniture,
from mineral through vegetal to animal, not appear to full up together fallen man than under but one photoreflection of the
several iridals gradationes of solar light, that one which that part
of it (furnit of heupanepi world) had shown itself (part of fur of
huepanwor) unable to absorbere, whereas for numpa one pura-
duxed seer in seventh degree of wisdom of Entis-Onton he savvy
inside true inwardness of reality, the Ding hvad in idself id est,
all objects (of panepiwor) allside showed themselves in trues
coloribus resplendent with sextuple gloria of light actually re-
tained, untisintus, inside them (obs of epiwo). Rumnant Patholic,
stareotypopticus, no catch all that preachybook, utpiam, tomorrow recover thing even is not, bymeby vampsybobsy tap-
panasbullocks topside joss pidginfella Bilkilly-Belkelly say pat-
fella, ontesantes, twotime hemhaltshealing, with other words
verbigratiagrading from murmurulentous till striduloceterious in
a hunghoranghoangoly tsinglontseng while his comprehen-
durient, with diminishing claractinism, augumentationed himself
in caloripeia to vision so throughsighty, you anxioust melancholic, High Thats Hight Uberking Leary his fiery grassbelong-
head all show colour of sorrelwood herbgreen, again, nigger-
blonker, of the his essixcoloured holmgrewnworsteds costume
the his fellow saffron pettikilt look same hue of boiled spinasses,

other thing voluntary mutismuser he not compyhandy the his
golden twobreasttorc look justsamelike curlicabbis, moreafter, to
pace negativisticists, verdant readyrainroof belongahim Exuber
High Ober King Leary very dead, what he wish to say, spit of
superexuberabundancy plenty laurel leaves, after that com-
mander bulopent eyes of Most Highest Ardreetsar King same
thing like thyme choppy upon parsley, alongsidethat, if please-
sir, nos displace tauttung, sowlofabishospastored, enamel Indian
gem in maledictive fingerfondler of High High Siresultan Emperor all same like one fellow olive lentil, onthelongsidethat, by
undesendas, kirikirikiring, violaceous warwon contusiones of
facebuts of Highup Big Cockywocky Sublissimime Autocrat, for
that with pure hueglut intensely saturated one, tinged uniformly,
allaroundside upinandoutdown, very like you seecut chowchow
of plentymuch sennacassia. Hump cumps Ebblybally! Sukkot?

Punc. Bigseer, refrects the petty padre, whackling it out, a
tumble to take, tripeness to call thing and to call if say is good
while, you pore shiroskuro blackinwhitepaddynger, by thiswis
aposterioprismically apatstrophied and paralogically periparo-
lysed, celestial from principalest of Iro's Irismans ruinboon pot
before, (for beingtime monkblinkers timeblinged completamen-
tarily murkblankered in their neutrolysis between the possible
viriditude of the sager and the probable eruberuption of the
saint), as My tappropinquish to Me wipenmeselps gnosegates a
handcaughtscheaf of synthetic shammyrag to hims hers, seeming-
such four three two agreement cause heart to be might, saving to
Balenoarch (he kneeleths), to Great Balenoarch (he kneeleths
down) to Greatest Great Balenoarch (he kneeleths down quite-
somely), the sound sense sympol in a weedwayedwold of the
firethere the sun in his halo cast. Onmen.

That was thing, bygotter, the thing, bogcotton, the very thing,
begad. Even to uptoputty Bilkilly-Belkelly-Balkally. Who was
for shouting down the shatton on the lamp of Jeeshees. Sweating
on to stonker and throw his seven. As he shuck his thumping
fore features apt the hoyhop of His Ards.

Thud.

Good safe firelamp! hailed the heliots. Goldselforelump!
Halled they. Awed. Where thereon the skyfold high, trampa-
trampatramp. Adie. Per ye comdoom doominoom noonstroom.
Yeasome priestomes. Fullyhum toowhoom.

Taawhaar?

Sants and sogs, cabs and cobs, kings and karls, tentes and
taunts.

'Tis gone infarover. So fore now, dayleash. Pour deday. To
trancefixureashone. Feist of Taborneccles, scenopegia, come!
Shamwork, be in our scheining! And let every crisscouple be so
crosscomplimentary, little eggons, youlk and meelk, in a farbiger
pancosmos. With a hottyhammyum all round. Gudstruce!

Yet is no body present here which was not there before. Only
is order othered. Nought is nulled. *Fuitfiat!*

Lo, the laud of laurens now orielising benedictively when
saint and sage have said their say.

A spathe of calyptrous glume involucrumines the perinanthean
Amenta: fungoalgàceous muscafilicial graminopalmular plan-
teon; of increasing, livivorous, feelful thinkamalinks; luxuriotia-
ting everywhencewithersoever among skullhullows and charnel-
cysts of a weedwastewoldwevild when Ralph the Retriever
ranges to jawrode his knuts knuckles and her theas thighs; one-
gugulp down of the nauseous forere brarkfarsts oboboomaround
and you're as paint and spickspan as a rainbow; wreathe the bowl
to rid the bowel; no runcure, no rank heat, sir; amess in amullium;
chlorid cup.

Health, chalce, endnessnessessity! Arrive, likkypuggers, in
a poke! The folgor of the frightfools is olympically optimo-
minous; there is bound to be a lovleg day for mirrages in the
open; Murnane and Aveling are undertoken to berry that ort-
chert: provided that. You got to make good that breachsuit,
seamer. You going to haulm port houlm, toilermaster. You yet
must get up to kill (nonparticular). You still stand by and do as
hit (private). While for yous, Jasminia Aruna and all your likers,
affinitatively must it be by you elected if Monogynes his is or
hers Diander, the tubous, limbersome and nectarial. Owned or

grazeheifer, ethel or bonding. Mopsus or Gracchus, all your
horodities will incessantlament be coming back from the Annone
wishwashwhose, Ormepierre Lodge, Doone of the Drumes,
blanches bountifully and nightsend made up, every article lathering leaving several rinsings so as each rinse results with a dap-
perent rolle, cuffs for meek and chokers for sheek and a kink in
the pacts for namby. Forbeer, forbear! For nought that is has
bane. In mournenslaund. Themes have thimes and habit reburns.
To flame in you. Ardor vigor forders order. Since ancient was
our living is in possible to be. Delivered as. Caffirs and culls and
onceagain overalls, the fittest surviya lives that blued, iorn and
storridge can make them. Whichus all claims. Clean. Whenast-
cleeps. Close. And the mannormillor clipperclappers. Noxt. Doze.

Fennsense, finnsonse, aworn! Tuck upp those wide shorts.
The pink of the busket for sheer give. Peeps. Stand up to hard
ware and step into style. If you soil may, puett, guett me prives.
For newmanmaun set a marge to the merge of unmotions. Inni-
tion wons agame.

What has gone? How it ends?

Begin to forget it. It will remember itself from every sides, with
all gestures, in each our word. Today's truth, tomorrow's trend.

Forget, remember!

Have we cherished expectations? Are we for liberty of peru-
siveness? Whyafter what forewhere? A plainplanned liffeyism
assemblements Eblania's conglomerate horde. By dim delty Deva.

Forget!

Our wholemole millwheeling vicociclometer, a tetradoma-
tional gazebocroticon (the "Mamma Lujah" known to every
schoolboy scandaller,be he Matty, Marky, Lukey or John-a-
Donk), autokinatonetically preprovided with a clappercoupling
smeltingworks exprogressive process, (for the farmer, his son and
their homely codes, known as eggburst, eggblend, eggburial and
hatch-as-hatch can) receives through a portal vein the dialytically
separated elements of precedent decomposition for the verypet-
purpose of subsequent recombination so that the heroticisms,
catastrophes and eccentricities transmitted by the ancient legacy

of the past, type by tope, letter from litter, word at ward, with
sendence of sundance, since the days of Plooney and Colum-
cellas when Giacinta, Pervenche and Margaret swayed over the
all-too-ghoulish and illyrical and innumantic in our mutter nation,
all, anastomosically assimilated and preteridentified paraidioti-
cally, in fact, the sameold gamebold adomic structure of our
Finnius the old One, as highly charged with electrons as hophaz-
ards can effective it, may be there for you, Cockalooralooraloo-
menos, when cup, platter and pot come piping hot, as sure as
herself pits hen to paper and there's scribings scrawled on eggs.

Of cause, so! And in effect, as?

Dear. And we go on to Dirtdump. Reverend. May we add
majesty? Well, we have frankly enjoyed more than anything
these secret workings of natures (thanks ever for it, we humbly
pray) and, well, was really so denighted of this lights time.
Mucksrats which bring up about uhrweckers they will come to
know good. Yon clouds will soon disappear looking forwards
at a fine day. The honourable Master Sarmon they should be
first born like he was with a twohangled warpon and it was
between Williamstown and the Mairrion Ailesbury on the top
of the longcar, as merrily we rolled along, we think of him looking
at us yet as if to pass away in a cloud. When he woke up in a
sweat besidus it was to pardon him, goldylocks, me having an
airth, but he daydreamsed we had a lovelyt face for a pulltomine.
Back we were by the jerk of a beamstark, backed in paladays last,
on the brinks of the wobblish, the man what never put a dramn
in the swags but milk from a national cowse. That was the prick
of the spindle to me that gave me the keys to dreamland. Sneakers
in the grass, keep off! If we were to tick off all that cafflers head,
whisperers for his accomodation, the me craws namely, and their
bacon what harmed butter! It's margarseen oil. Thinthin thinthin. Stringstly is it forbidden by the honorary tenth commend-
mant to shall not bare full sweetness against a nighboor's wiles.
What those slimes up the cavern door around you, keenin, (the
lies is coming out on them frecklefully) had the shames to suggest
can we ever? Never! So may the low forget him their trespasses

against Molloyd O'Reilly that hugglebeddy fann, now about to,
get up, the hartiest that Coolock ever! A nought in nought.
Eirinishmhan called Ervigsen by his first mate. May all similar
douters of our oldhame story have that fancied widming! For
a pipe of twist or a slug of Hibernia metal we could let out and,
by jings, someone would make a carpus of somebody with the
greatest of pleasure by private shootings. And in contravention to
the constancy of chemical combinations not enough of all the
slatters of him left for Peeter the Picker to make their threi sevelty
filfths of a man out of. Good wheat! How delitious for the three
Sulvans of Dulkey and what a sellpriceget the two Peris of
Monacheena! Sugars of lead for the chloras ashpots! Peace! He
possessing from a child of highest valency for our privileged
beholdings ever complete hairy of chest, hamps and eyebags in
pursuance to salesladies' affectionate company. His real devotes.
Wriggling reptiles, take notice! Whereas we exgust all such
sprinkling snigs. They are pestituting the whole time never with
standing we simply agree upon the committee of amusance! Or
could above bring under same notice for it to be able to be seen.

   About that coerogenal hun and his knowing the size of an egg-
cup. First he was a skulksman at one time and then Cloon's fired
him through guff. Be sage about sausages! Stuttutistics shows
with he's heacups of teatables the old firm fatspitters are most
eatenly appreciated by metropolonians. While we should like to
drag attentions to our Wolkmans Cumsensation Act. The magnets
of our midst being foisted upon by a plethorace of parachutes.
Did speece permit the bad example of setting before the military
to the best of our belief in the earliest wish of the one in mind was
the mitigation of the king's evils. And how he staired up the
step after it's the power of the gait. His giantstand of manun-
known. No brad wishy washy wathy wanted neither! Once you
are balladproof you are unperceable to haily, icy and missile-
throes. Order now before we reach Ruggers' Rush. As we now
must close hoping to Saint Laurans all in the best. Moral. Mrs
Stores Humphreys: So you are expecting trouble, Pondups, from
the domestic service questioned? Mr Stores Humphreys: Just as

there is a good in even, Levia, my cheek is a compleet bleenk.
Plumb. Meaning: one two four. Finckers. Up the hind hose of
hizzars. Whereapon our best again to a hundred and eleven ploose
one thousand and one other blessings will now concloose thoose
epoostles to your great kindest, well, for all at trouble to took.
We are all at home in old Fintona, thank Danis, for ourselfsake,
that direst of housebonds, whool wheel be true unto lovesend
so long as we has a pockle full of brass. Impossible to remember
persons in improbable to forget position places. Who would
pellow his head off to conjure up a, well, particularly mean stinker
like funn make called Foon MacCrawl brothers, mystery man of
the pork martyrs? Force in giddersh! Tomothy and Lorcan, the
bucket Toolers, both are Timsons now they've changed their
characticuls during their blackout. Conan Boyles will pudge the
daylives out through him, if they are correctly informed. Music, me
ouldstrow, please! We'll have a brand rehearsal. Fing! One must
simply laugh. Fing him aging! Good licks! Well, this ought to weke
him to make up. He'll want all his fury gutmurdherers to redress
him. Gilly in the gap. The big bad old sprowly all uttering foon!
Has now stuffed last podding. His fooneral will sneak pleace by
creeps o'clock toosday. Kingen will commen. Allso brewbeer.
Pens picture at Manchem House Horsegardens shown in Morning post as from Boston transcripped. Femelles will be preadam-
inant as from twentyeight to twelve. To hear that lovelade
parson, of case, of a bawl gentlemale, pour forther moracles. Don't
forget. The grand fooneral will now shortly occur. Remember.
The remains must be removed before eaght hours shorp. With
earnestly conceived hopes. So help us to witness to this day to
hand in sleep. From of Mayasdaysed most duteoused.

Well, here's lettering you erronymously anent other clerical
fands allieged herewith. I wisht I wast be that dumb tyke and he'd
wish it was me yonther heel. How about it? The sweetest song
in the world? Our shape as a juvenile being much admired from
the first with native copper locks. Referring to the Married
Woman's Improperty Act a correspondent paints out that the
Swees Auburn vogue is hanging down straith fitting to her

innocenth eyes. O, felicious coolpose! If all theMacCrawls would
only handle virgils like Armsworks, Limited! That's handsel for
gertles! Never mind Micklemans! Chat us instead! The cad
with the pope's wife, Lily Kinsella, who became the wife of
Mr Sneakers for her good name in the hands of the kissing
solicitor, will now engage in attentions. Just a prinche for tonight! Pale bellies our mild cure, back and streaky ninepace.
The thicks off Bully's Acre was got up by Sully. The Boot lane
brigade. And she had a certain medicine brought her in a
licenced victualler's bottle. Shame! Thrice shame! We are
advised the waxy is at the present in the Sweeps hospital and
that he may never come out! Only look through your leather-
box one day with P.C.Q. about 4.32 or at 8 and 22.5 with the
quart of scissions masters and clerk and the bevyhum of Marie
Reparatrices for a good allround sympowdhericks purge, full view,
to be surprised to see under the grand piano Lily on the sofa (and
a lady!) pulling a low and then he'd begin to jump a little bit to
find out what goes on when love walks in besides the solicitous
bussness by kissing and looking into a mirror.

That we were treated not very grand when the police and
everybody is all bowing to us when we go out in all directions
on Wanterlond Road with my cubarola glide? And, personally
speaking, they can make their beaux to my alce, as Hillary Allen
sang to the opennine knighters. Item, we never were chained to a
chair, and, bitem, no widower whother soever followed us about
with a fork on Yankskilling Day. Meet a great civilian (proud
lives to him!) who is gentle as a mushroom and a very affectable
when he always sits forenenst us for his wet while to all whom
it may concern Sully is a thug from all he drunk though he is a
rattling fine bootmaker in his profession. Would we were here-
earther to lodge our complaint on sergeant Laraseny in consequence
of which in such steps taken his health would be constably broken
into potter's pance which would be the change of his life by a
Nollwelshian which has been oxbelled out of crispianity.

Well, our talks are coming to be resumed by more polite conversation with a huntered persent human over the natural bestness

of pleisure after his good few mugs of humbedumb and shag. While for whoever likes that urogynal pan of cakes one apiece it is thanks, beloved, to Adam our former first Finnlatter, and our grocerest churcher, as per Grippiths' varuations, for his beautiful crossmess parzel.

Well, we simply like their demb cheeks, the Rathgarries, wagging here about around the rhythms in me amphybed and he being as bothered that he pausably could by the fallth of hampty damp. Certified reformed peoples, we may add to this stage, are proptably saying to quite agreeable deef. Here gives your answer, pigs and scuts! Hence we've lived in two worlds. He is another he what stays under the himp of holth. The herewaker of our hamefame is his real namesame who will get himself up and erect, confident and heroic when but, young as of old, for my daily comfreshenall, a wee one woos.

    Alma Luvia, Pollabella.

P.S. Soldier Rollo's sweetheart. And she's about fetted up now with nonsery reams. And rigs out in regal rooms with the ritzies. Rags! Worns out. But she's still her deckhuman amber too.

Soft morning, city! Lsp! I am leafy speafing. Lpf! Folty and folty all the nights have fallen on to long my hair. Not a sound, falling. Lispn! No wind no word. Only a leaf, just a leaf and then leaves. The woods are fond always. As were we their babes in. And robins in crews so. It is for me goolden wending. Unless? Away! Rise up, man of the hooths, you have slept so long! Or is it only so mesleems? On your pondered palm. Reclined from cape to pede. With pipe on bowl. Terce for a fiddler, sixt for makmerriers, none for a Cole. Rise up now and aruse! Norvena's over. I am leafy, your goolden, so you called me, may me life, yea your goolden, silve me solve, exsogerraider! You did so drool. I was so sharm. But there's a great poet in you too. Stout Stokes would take you offly. So has he as bored me to slump. But am good and rested. Taks to you, toddy, tan ye. Yawhawaw. Helpunto min, helpas vin. Here is your shirt, the day one, come back. The stock, your collar. Also your double brogues. A comforter as well. And here your iverol and everthelest your

umbr. And stand up tall! Straight. I want to see you looking fine
for me. With your brandnew big green belt and all. Blooming in
the very lotust and second to nill, Budd! When you're in the
buckly shuit Rosensharonals near did for you. Fiftyseven and
three, cosh, with the bulge. Proudpurse Alby with his pooraroon
Eireen, they'll. Pride, comfytousness, enevy! You make me think
of a wonderdecker I once. Or somebalt thet sailder, the man me-
gallant, with the bangled ears. Or an earl was he, at Lucan? Or,
no, it's the Iren duke's I mean. Or somebrey erse from the Dark
Countries. Come and let us. We always said we'd. And go abroad.
Rathgreany way perhaps. The childher are still fast. There is no
school today. Them boys is so contrairy. The Head does be
worrying himself. Heel trouble and heal travel. Galliver and
Gellover. Unless they changes by mistake. I seen the likes in
the twinngling of an aye. Som. So oft. Sim. Time after time.
The sehm asnuh. Two bredder as doffered as nors in soun. When
one of him sighs or one of him cries 'tis you all over. No peace
at all. Maybe it's those two old crony aunts held them out to the
water front. Queer Mrs Quickenough and odd Miss Dodd-
pebble. And when them two has had a good few there isn't much
more dirty clothes to publish. From the Laundersdale Minssions.
One chap googling the holyboy's thingabib and this lad wetting
his widdle. You were pleased as Punch, recitating war exploits
and pearse orations to them jackeen gapers. But that night after,
all you were wanton! Bidding me do this and that and the other.
And blowing off to me, hugly Judsys, what wouldn't you give
to have a girl. Your wish was mewill. And, lo, out of a sky! The
way I too. But her, you wait. Eager to choose is left to her shade.
If she had only more matcher's wit. Findlings makes runaways,
runaways a stray. She's as merry as the gricks still. 'Twould be
sore should ledden sorrow. I'll wait. And I'll wait. And then if
all goes. What will be is. Is is. But let them. Slops hospodch and
the slusky slut too. He's for thee what she's for me. Dogging you
round cove and haven and teaching me the perts of speech. If you
spun your yarns to him on the swishbarque waves I was spelling
my yearns to her over cottage cake. We'll not disturb their sleep-

ing duties. Let besoms be bosuns. It's Phoenix, dear. And the flame is, hear! Let's our joornee saintomichael make it. Since the lausafire has lost and the book of the depth is. Closed. Come! Step out of your shell. Hold up you free fing. Yes. We've light enough. I won't take our laddy's lampern. For them four old windbags of Gustsofairy to be blowing at. Nor you your rucksunck. To bring all the dannymans out after you on the hike. Send Arctur guiddus! Isma! Sft! It is the softest morning that ever I can ever remember me. But she won't rain showerly, our Ilma. Yet. Until it's the time. And me and you have made our. The sons of bursters won in the games. Still I'll take me owld Finvara for my shawlders. The trout will be so fine at brookfisht. With a taste of roly polony from Blugpuddels after. To bring out the tang of the tay. Is't you fain for a roost brood? Oaxmealturn, all out of the woolpalls! And then all the chippy young cuppinjars cluttering round us, clottering for their creams. Crying, me, grownup sister! Are me not truly? Lst! Only but, theres a but, you must buy me a fine new girdle too, nolly. When next you go to Market Norwall. They're all saying I need it since the one from Isaacsen's slooped its line. Mrknrk? Fy arthou! Come! Give me your great bearspaw, padder avilky, fol a miny tiny. Dola. Mineninecy-handsy, in the languo of flows. That's Jorgen Jargonsen. But you understood, nodst? I always know by your brights and shades. Reach down. A lil mo. So. Draw back your glave. Hot and hairy, hugon, is your hand! Here's where the falskin begins. Smoos as an infams. One time you told you'd been burnt in ice. And one time it was chemicalled after you taking a lifeness. Maybe that's why you hold your hodd as if. And people thinks you missed the scaffold. Of fell design. I'll close me eyes. So not to see. Or see only a youth in his florizel, a boy in innocence, peeling a twig, a child beside a weenywhite steed. The child we all love to place our hope in for ever. All men has done something. Be the time they've come to the weight of old fletch. We'll lave it. So. We will take our walk before in the timpul they ring the earthly bells. In the church by the hearseyard. Pax Goodmens will. Or the birds start their treestirm shindy. Look, there are yours off, high on high! And cooshes, sweet good luck they're cawing you, Coole! You see, they're as white as the riven snae. For us. Next peaters poll you will be elicted or I'm not your elicitous bribe. The Kinsella woman's man will never reduce me. A MacGarath O'Cullagh O'Muirk MacFewney sookadoodling and sweepacheeping round the lodge of Fjorn na Galla of the Trumpets! It's like potting the po to shambe on the dresser or tamming Uncle Tim's Caubeen on to the brows of a Viker Eagle. Not such big strides, huddy foddy! You'll crush me antilopes I saved so long for. They're Penisole's. And the two goodiest shoeshoes. It is hardly a Knut's mile or seven, possumbotts. It is very good for the health of a morning. With Buahbuah. A gentle motion all around. As leisure paces. And the helpyourselftoastrool cure's easy. It seems so long since, ages since. As if you had been long far away. Afartodays, afeartonights, and me as with you in thadark. You will tell me some time if I can believe its all. You know where I am bringing you? You remember? When I ran berrying after hucks and haws. With you drawing out great aims to hazel me from the hummock with your sling. Our cries. I could lead you there and I still by you in bed. Les go dutc to Danegreven, nos? Not a soul but ourselves. Time? We have loads on our hangs. Till Gilligan and Halligan call again to hooligan. And the rest of the guns. Sullygan eight, from left to right. Olobobo, ye foxy theagues! The moskors thought to ball you out. Or the Wald Unicorns Master, Bugley Captain, from the Naul, drawls up by the door with the Honourable Whilp and the Reverend Poynter and the two Lady Pagets of Tallyhaugh, Ballyhuntus, in their riddletight raiding hats for to lift a hereshealth to their robost, the Stag, evers the Carlton hart. And you needn't host out with your duck and your duty, capapole, while they reach him the glass he never starts to finish. Clap this wis on your poll and stick this in your ear, wiggly. Beauties don't answer and the rich never pays. If you were the enlarged they'd hue in cry you, Heathtown, Harbourstown, Snowtown, Four Knocks, Fleming-town, Bodingtown to the Ford of Fyne on Delvin. How they housed to house you after the Platonic garlens. And all because,

loosed in her reflexes, she seem she seen Ericoricori coricome
huntsome with his three poach dogs aleashing him. But you came
safe through. Enough of that horner corner! And old mutther-
goosip! We might call on the Old Lord, what do you say? There's
something tells me. He is a fine sport. Like the score and a moighty
went before him. And a proper old promnentory. His door
always open. For a newera's day.   Much as your own is. You
invoiced him last Eatster so he ought to give us hot cockles and
everything. Remember to take off your white hat, ech? When
we come in the presence. And say hoothoothoo, ithmuthisthy!
His is house of laws. And I'll drop my graciast kertssey too. If
the Ming Tung no go bo to me homage me hamage kow bow
tow to the Mong Tang. Ceremonialness to stand lowest place
be! Saying: What'll you take to link to light a pike on porpoise,
plaise? He might knight you an Armor elsor daub you the first
cheap magyerstrape. Remember Bomthomanew vim vam vom
Hungerig. Hoteform, chain and epolettes, botherbumbose. And
I'll be your aural eyeness. But we vain. Plain fancies. It's in the
castles air. My currant bread's full of sillymottocraft. Aloof is
anoof. We can take or leave. He's reading his ruffs. You'll know
our way from there surely. Flura's way. Where once we led so
many car couples have follied since. Clatchka! Giving Shaugh-
nessy's mare the hillymount of her life. With her strulldeburg-
ghers! Hnmn hnmn! The rollcky road adondering. We can sit
us down on the heathery benn, me on you, in quolm uncon-
sciounce. To scand the arising. Out from Drumleek. It was there
Evora told me I had best. If I ever. When the moon of mourning
is set and gone. Over Glinaduna. Lonu nula. Ourselves, oursouls
alone. At the site of salvocean. And watch would the letter you're
wanting be coming may be. And cast ashore. That I prays for
be mains of me draims. Scratching it and patching at with a
prompt from a primer. And what scrips of nutsnolleges I pecked
up me meself. Every letter is a hard but yours sure is the hardest
crux ever. Hack an axe, hook an oxe, hath an an, heth hith ences.
But once done, dealt and delivered, tattat, you're on the map.
Rased on traumscrapt from Maston, Boss. After rounding his

world of ancient days. Carried in a caddy or screwed and corked.
On his mugisstosst surface. With a bob, bob, bottledby. Blob.
When the waves give up yours the soil may for me. Sometime
then, somewhere there, I wrote me hopes and buried the page
when I heard Thy voice, ruddery dunner, so loud that none but,
and left it to lie till a kissmiss coming. So content me now. Lss.
Unbuild and be buildn our bankaloan cottage there and we'll
cohabit respectable. The Gowans, ser, for Medem, me. With
acute bubel runtoer for to pippup and gopeep where the sterres
be. Just to see would we hear how Jove and the peers talk. Amid
the soleness. Tilltop, bigmaster! Scale the summit. You're not
so giddy any more. All your graundplotting and the little it
brought! Humps, when you hised us and dumps, when you
doused us! But sarra one of me cares a brambling ram, pomp
porteryark! On limpidy marge I've made me hoom. Park and a
pub for me. Only don't start your stunts of Donachie's yeards
agoad again. I could guessp to her name who tuckt you that one, tuf-
nut! Bold bet backwords. For the loves of sinfintins! Before the
naked universe. And the bailby pleasemarm rincing his eye! One
of these fine days, lewdy culler, you must redoform again.
Blessed shield Martin! Softly so. I am so exquisitely pleased about
the loveleavest dress I have. You will always call me Leafiest,
won't you, dowling? Wordherfhull Ohldhbhoy! And you won't
urbjunk to me parafume, oiled of kolooney, with a spot of mara-
shy. Sm! It's Alpine Smile from Yesthers late Yhesters. I'm in
everywince nasturtls. Even in Houlth's nose. Medeurscodeignus!
Astale of astoun. Grand owld marauder! If I knew who you are!
When that hark from the air said it was Captain Finsen makes cum-
hulments and was mayit pressing for his suit I said are you there
here's nobody here only me. But I near fell off the pile of samples.
As if your tinger winged ting to me hear. Is that right what
your brothermilk in Bray bes telling the district you were bragged
up by Brostal because your parents would be always tumbling
into his foulplace and losing her pentacosts after drinking their
pledges? Howsomendeavour, you done me fine! The only man
was ever known could eat the crushts of lobsters. Our native

night when you twicetook me for some Marienne Sherry and
then your Jermyn cousin who signs hers with exes and the beard-
wig I found in your Clarksome bag. Pharaops you'll play you're
the king of Aeships. You certainly make the most royal of noises.
I will tell you all sorts of makeup things, strangerous. And show
you to every simple storyplace we pass. *Cadmillersfolly, Bellevenue,
Wellcrom, Quid Superabit,* villities valleties. Change the plates
for the next course of murphies. Spendlove's still there and the
canon going strong and so is Claffey's habits endurtaking and
our parish pomp's a great warrent. But you'll have to ask that
same four that named them is always snugging in your bar-
salooner, saying they're the best relicts of Conal O'Daniel and
writing *Finglas since the Flood.* That'll be some kingly work in progress. But it's by this route he'll come some morrow. And I
can signal you all flint and fern are rasstling as we go by. And
you'll sing thumb a bit and then wise your selmon on it. It is all
so often and still the same to me. Snf? Only turf, wick dear. Clane
turf. You've never forgodden batt on tarf, have you, at broin
burroow, what? Mch? Why, them's the muchrooms, come up
during the night. Look, agres of roofs in parshes. Dom on dam,
dim in dym. And a capital part for olympics to ply at. Steadyon,
Cooloosus! Mind your stride or you'll knock. While I'm dodging
the dustbins. Look what I found! A lintil pea. And look at here!
This cara weeseed. Pretty mites, my sweetthings, was they poor-
loves abandoned by wholawidey world? Neighboulotts for new-
town. The Eblanamagna you behazyheld loomening up out of the
dumblynass. But the still sama sitta. I've lapped so long. As you
said. It fair takes. If I lose my breath for a minute or two don't
speak, remember. Once it happened, so it may again. Why I'm
all these years within years in soffran, allbeleaved. To hide away
the tear, the parted. It's thinking of all. The brave that gave their.
The fair that wore. All them that's gunne. I'll begin again in a
jiffey. The nik of a nad. How glad you'll be I waked you! My!
How well you'll feel! For ever after. First we turn by the vagurin
here and then it's gooder. So side by side, turn agate, wedding-
town, laud men of Londub! I only hope whole the heavens sees

us. For I feel I could near to faint away. Into the deeps. Anna-mores leep. Let me lean, just a lea, if you le, bowldstrong big-tider. Allgearls is wea. At times. So. While you're adamant evar. Wrhps, that wind as if out of norewere! As on the night of the Apophanypes. Jumpst shootst throbbst into me mouth like a bogue and arrohs. Ludegude of the Lashlanns, how he whips me cheeks! Sea, sea! Here, weir, reach, island, bridge. Where you meet I. The day. Remember! Why there that moment and us two only? I was but teen, a tiler's dot. The swankysuits was boosting always, sure him, he was like to me fad. But the swag-gerest swell off Shackvulle Strutt. And the fiercest freaky ever followed a pining child round the sluppery table with a forkful of fat. But a king of whistlers. Scieoula! When he'd prop me atlas against his goose and light our two candles for our singers duohs on the sewingmachine. I'm sure he squirted juice in his eyes to make them flash for flightening me. Still and all he was awful fond to me. Who'll search for *Find Me Colours* now on the hilly-droops of Vikloefells? But I read in Tobecontinued's tale that while blubles blows there'll still be sealskers. There'll be others but non so for me. Yed he never knew we seen us before. Night after night. So that I longed to go to. And still with all. One time you'd stand fornenst me, fairly laughing, in your bark and tan billows of branches for to fan me coolly. And I'd lie as quiet as a moss. And one time you'd rush upon me, darkly roaring, like a great black shadow with a sheeny stare to perce me rawly. And I'd frozen up and pray for thawe. Three times in all. I was the pet of everyone then. A princeable girl. And you were the pantymammy's Vulking Corsergoth. The invision of Indelond. And, by Thorror, you looked it! My lips went livid for from the joy of fear. Like almost now. How? How you said how you'd give me the keys of me heart. And we'd be married till delth to uspart. And though dev do espart. O mine! Only, no, now it's me who's got to give. As duv herself div. Inn this linn. And can it be it's nnow fforvell? Illas! I wisht I had better glances to peer to you through this bay-light's growing. But you're changing, acoolsha, you're changing from me, I can feel. Or is it me is? I'm getting mixed. Brightening up and tightening down. Yes, you're changing, sonhusband, and you're turning, I can feel you, for a daughterwife from the hills again. Imlamaya. And she is coming. Swimming in my hindmoist. Diveltaking on me tail. Just a whisk brisk sly spry spink spank sprint of a thing theresomere, saultering. Saltarella come to her own. I pity your oldself I was used to. Now a younger's there. Try not to part. Be happy, dear ones! May I be wrong! For she'll be sweet for you as I was sweet when I came down out of me mother. My great blue bedroom, the air so quiet, scarce a cloud. In peace and silence. I could have stayed up there for always only. It's something fails us. First we feel. Then we fall. And let her rain now if she likes. Gently or strongly as she likes. Anyway let her rain for my time is come. I done me best when I was let. Thinking always if I go all goes. A hundred cares, a tithe of troubles and is there one who understands me? One in a thousand of years of the nights? All me life I have been lived among them but now they are becoming lothed to me. And I am lothing their little warm tricks. And lothing their mean cosy turns. And all the greedy gushes out through their small souls. And all the lazy leaks down over their brash bodies. How small it's all! And me letting on to meself always. And lilting on all the time. I thought you were all glittering with the noblest of carriage. You're only a bumpkin. I thought you the great in all things, in guilt and in glory. You're but a puny. Home! My people were not their sort out beyond there so far as I can. For all the bold and bad and bleary they are blamed, the seahags. No! Nor for all our wild dances in all their wild din. I can seen meself among them, allaniuvia pulchrabelled. How she was handsome, the wild Amazia, when she would seize to my other breast! And what is she weird, haughty Niluna, that she will snatch from my ownest hair! For 'tis they are the stormies. Ho hang! Hang ho! And the clash of our cries till we spring to be free. Auravoles, they says, never heed of your name! But I'm loothing them that's here and all I lothe. Loonely in me loneness. For all their faults. I am passing out. O bitter ending! I'll slip away before they're up. They'll never see. Nor know. Nor miss me. And it's old and old it's sad and old it's

sad and weary I go back to you, my cold father, my cold mad
father, my cold mad feary father, till the near sight of the mere
size of him, the moyles and moyles of it, moananoaning, makes me
seasilt saltsick and I rush, my only, into your arms. I see them
rising! Save me from those therrble prongs! Two more. Onetwo
moremens more. So. Avelaval. My leaves have drifted from me.
All. But one clings still. I'll bear it on me. To remind me of. Lff!
So soft this morning ours. Yes. Carry me along, taddy, like you
done through the toy fair. If I seen him bearing down on me now
under whitespread wings like he'd come from Arkangels, I sink
I'd die down over his feet, humbly dumbly, only to washup. Yes,
tid. There's where. First. We pass through grass behush the bush
to. Whish! A gull. Gulls. Far calls. Coming, far! End here. Us
then. Finn, again! Take. Bussoftlhee, mememormee! Till thous-
endsthee. Lps. The keys to. Given! A way a lone a last a loved a
long the

PARIS,
1922-1939.